The Half Gods

Charles G. Bell

With an excerpt from a previously unpublished novel
The Third Kingdom

Fomite
Burlington, Vermont

ISBN-13: 978-1-944388-77-5
Library of Congress Control Number: 2021947948
Fomite
58 Peru Street
Burlington, VT 05401
03/23/2024

Contents

Acknowledgments

This is a work of fiction. Neither the characters nor the places represent actual characters or places. Yet a book so aimed at history and so dependent on fact could not have been written without contributions of the kind implied in the dedication. I would like to specify some of these, while insisting that the fabric in which they appear is my own and is of the imagination. I confess to a shade of distress when even a Shakespearean or Biblical quotation stands word for word in the text. Should not everything that enters the fictional organism be subtly transformed?

For primary material generously given me in speech and writing, I thank the following:

Ann Markin and Cecil Roberts;

Abbie Houston Evans, Ramon Guthrie, Joan Bromley;

Brice Jacobson, Bill Greene, Philip Goldman, Eleanor Bontecou, James Gilbert, Gabriella de Benedictis, Rodney Baine, Stringfellow Barr;

John Beecher, William Kyle Smith, Ann Danek, Norman Berg, J. Gilman Paul, Kenneth Haxton, Leon Radolf, George Swope, Howard B. Gill, Richard Gregg, Philip Silver, Ed Leffingwell;

With others, unnamed.

For obligations more precisely literary:

John Caldwell, a Negro who lived in Greenville, Mississippi, left me poems which I have revised and woven into the fictional life of Caldwell Leflore.

To William Saunders, whom I knew when he worked and wrote in Flint, Michigan, I acknowledge the poems here attributed to Styles of the Dark Leflores. Like Styles,' his youthful genius met with a hard fate: he screwed the nuts on cars, and has been in Leavenworth for years.

Most special and poignant is my debt to William Carlos Williams and to Simone Weil. I despaired of creating equivalents for these necessary symbolic powers. So I transplanted Bill Williams as I knew and loved him (with literal passages from his poems) into the fictional setting of Patapsco and, to indicate that alteration and identity, called him Richard Ramon Richards.

As for Simone Weil, I met her at Solesmes when I was a student abroad, and (as in the novel) it was long after that I discovered the fact; but my relation to her had none of the significance I have given the relation of Daren Leflore to Heloise Frank. It would have been better to have invented a mystic and avoided this confession, but it was not in my power. However, what I could not invent I could reshape as fiction. Except for the beautiful account of the "Mansarde" which I have translated (it appears as a Prologue to her *Connaissance Surnaturelle)*, everything attributed to Heloise Frank is my own composition, however indebted to the study of Simone Weil. The genius of scholarship is accuracy, of fiction license. I have felt free to change anything I knew or recalled for the purposes of the novel. It would be wrong to search here for any kind of portait of Simone Weil, or for any insight into her writings, which happily speak for themselves, though I confess I would have wished, in an independent creation and at a distance, to honor one whose memory I revere.

I am indebted besides to many newspaper clippings and other documents abstracted and laid by over more than twenty years. But I have so far digested them, in accordance with my principles, though with the obligation of keeping them as historical as the speeches in Thucydides, that only a few need be specified. The account of the bombing of the Möhne Dam from *The Atlantic Monthly,* December, 1943, is perhaps the most literal. The Civil War Journal of Quincy Leflore is ad-libbed from that of William Pitt Chambers, in *Publications of the Mississippi Historical Society,* Vol. V, 1925, in which my mother's father happens to be mentioned. Vera Brittain's "Massacre by Bombing," *Fellowship,* March, 1944, was helpful in the revival of that terror; while the testimony of various CORE workers has been incorporated in the Civil Rights argument of Part IV.

As with *The Married Land,* I have imposed my toll on many people, sent them sketches and chapters, and used their responses to keep an unwieldy project alive through five years of troubled gestation. If I named all whose participation has helped, it would fill a page. But at least five people have fought through the manuscript from beginning to end and made editorial suggestions throughout. With their aid I have brought *The Half Gods* through several rewritings to the point at which it has been given over; for, as Valéry says: *"On ne finit pas un livre, on l'abandonne."* They are Galway Kinnell, Skip Simpson, Craig Wylie, Etta Ruth Weigl and Delia Bell.

Finally, my wife has suffered cheerfully through it all——a condition without which it would not have been realized.

PROLOGUE

Now

HAD HE made this, or was this the field where he was being made?

> *First Precipitate:* There is no containment but the fact for the life-web spun through all dimensions of the self and age…

He was writing it anyway – Daren Leflore – seated in the windowed cave of his house on the rock over the Patapsco.

Gray mist: fall, or early spring, winter, or a cloud—blotted summer-monologhi dei matti day? He had sat there through a blur of all seasons.

Outside the window was the world of sense; and within, present without his needing to turn, the place we look out from, the labyrinthine manifold. Before him, on a panel door screwed to legs ("Without surfaces," he claimed, "I cannot make volumes!"), papers—precipitate of that outward and inward—shuffled into form.

"Holy mother," his wife Anna would say, "you're not going to write again about the writer trying to write? 'Why don't you live for a change, out there, working—with the people. You'd have more to say."—Anna, glowing from some active rally: "Never such a time. A big shakedown coming, a chance for peace and justice, and you sit spinning yourself in the old dream. Not again, Daren. Not that worn-out stuff about the self groping for the self.

They had been through it so often, he was full of answers:

"Je n'ai pas faict mon libre plus que mon libre m'a faict."

"On what once was rock the forest grows in the self-engendering of its loam."

"There is nothing, fact or dream, that is not incarnate NOW."

WINTER, SUMMER, SPRING, FALL . . .

The house at least was fit and in a fit setting. The oldest mill town on the oldest stretch of railroad. A Victorian house, two stories in front, three in the rear, two of frame on a substory of stone. Its east windows backed up against the cliff over the soiled Patapsco—

Precambrian sandstone, mudstone, metaporphosed into gneiss, what deep vulcanism had seared, fused and interfolded—diorite overlaid with slaty schist, quartzite, mica—since raised, stream-cleft, shattered: a sheer drop. Suicide Rock the Indians had called it—Those Indians, who for love or other causes were always said to be jumping off somewhere (a maiden, Anna thought, sacrificed to some god), setting a pattern the palefaces, who cheated them out of the land, were going to take over maybe, not just privately but strung together, enmasse—caterpillars who follow one another, military style, so automatically that if the first should circle and nab the last, they go round and round until they die—

What was this streak of suicide through nature—the successive appearance of lethal genes? "Old stuff," Anna would announce. "It's lack of understanding, lack of plan." As if one could exercise the inscrutable: knives under the pillow, halters in the pew, ratsbane by the porridge… Stars were poised on that brink—thresholds in their burning. They exploded into novae, collapsed to dwarfs. Accident? There was a demon in the working. It was not just whales beaching themselves, not just lemmings on suicidal marches.

"But that's overpopulation." From the solitary room, the remembered bright voice of Jeffrey might chime in-always a counterpole to Anna, though Anna had not seen her since the days in England before the war, and was hardly going to now—turning it all to laughter: "They should try the ring and the loop." Well, if anybody could put contraception over on the lemmings, it would be the winning Jeffrey.

Suicide Rock. The day they moved here, the big mastiff from the Quaker house next door (Brutus, he was called, noblest Roman of them all) had charged like a tank on some stray chickens, run them across the yard and to the cliff, until they flew off squawking, and the heavy dog, heedless as if he had wings, had hurtled after them and crushed himself on the railroad track below.

Leflore stretched his hands, stiff from writing, thin-fingered, against the light. He had tried to figure it out as a boy, lounging in the hammock in the shade of Mississippi, how one could see through his own flesh—the thicker palm a bone between transparent flankings—until slowly by "winking his eyes he got it straight: not X-ray but binocular. Through the same orb, ceaselessly renewed, he stared out the window, over the cliff.

"Light dogs are best—Switzerland—not those armored dinosaurs." Except now, light and heavy, they were at the world-brink together.

And Daren Leflore—were his thoughts about suicide compulsive? His great-great-grandfather had killed himself, and his grandfather, and his mother maybe, and his father, Prentiss Leflore, had died under doubtful circumstances. But Daren did not dwell on that cliff, though he lived there, and he was not melancholy, though he might have been found brooding at that window, in what his wife called the opium dream and quietus of the West, through twelve years and in all seasons.

America had washed over that rock and left it unchanged. And Hollywood had come, drawn by a fitness even Hollywood could sense—sense and betray to a damned commercialism spoiling everything—had hired this very house, when old Sally Stovall and her arthritic husband lived upstairs and Leflore and Anna were getting settled in the ground apartment, had brought cameras and stars and starlets and made a movie, called of all things *The Goddess,* about some immigrant beauty aspiring to power—only a halfgoddess after all. The film had gravitated to the cemetery (what else from Suicide Rock?), and for days the coffin stood in the hall. "Miss Sally," said the maid, "Mr. Burt died, ain't he? I seen him in the coffin in the hall."

But it wasn't Mr. Burt that time; though within the year——Miss Sally having kept him for a decade propped like a vegetable in the wheelchair—he got the idea, and the actual coffin replaced the movie one, though for a briefer time…

The earth bare by the house, cindered, rubbed and rained. Under the horse chestnut tree moss began, where in summer the shade was too dense for grass. Then leaves tangled against the rock that heaved up from the flotsam. There the oil drum stood, rain-rusted, half filled with burned litter. "Trash," the old woman had said, "TRASH," and dumped it over the bluff … Down to where the railroad swept in a curve along the river… Boulders. Foam. White sycamores. Faint in the mist, at opposite extremes, the factory and the mill, stacks like flagpoles, flying smoke banners. Along the road between, granite workers' houses hunched their privies to the river.

"Look at that," Anna would say. "Behind those workers' shacks …"

"What do you mean, shacks? Those houses are diorite" (Egyptian Khafre, Daren's first art-love, carved of that crystalline mottling), "solidly built and beautifully proportioned, miracles of rare device."

For Anna they stayed shacks, and the outhouses behind them conspicuous poverty, a perpetual occasion to descant on capital, reviving the cellar of her childhood, the toilet out under the Chicago sidewalk, newspapers cut into strips and hung on the rusty nail…

And then, past the factory—the state park, the woods, something at this remove inviolable, surging through all seasons, summer, winter, spring, fall.

For there were redeeming features:

That horse chestnut tree growing out of the last earth of the yard, big rooted, white candles in spring, and in fall, buckeyes that fell and weathered the winter, cropping out in March through the snow, knobs of mahogany, of brown amber, to be picked up and stowed away—remembering: buckeyes, bringers of luck.

Remembering: Jeffrey Strange, first seen in the woods of Oxfordshire twenty years ago, who dared him to jump the brook, and he fell in—how was it?—wavy hair the burnished dark of a buckeye, blue eyes, a Deirdre face on a girl's body not yet grown, in her Scotch kilts like a boy (blue and green on red, and a white line—her mother's clan), and crazy kid, wearing a big regimental sporran nobody but a man is supposed to wear, symbolically or otherwise: "What do you wear that sporran for?"—"To put conkers in," she said, and opened it like an Assyrian priest bringing out the sacred pinecone. "Conkers?" It was full of horse chestnuts, buckeyes. "We conk with them." She took out one swinging on a thread. "Ibby-ibby-onker, my fine conker. Besides, they turn your luck." And later she gave him one; it must be tucked away somewhere. Well, his luck had been whirling ever since like a dervish; better it stay put awhile.

Now he had a yard full of them—conkers. Not to mention whatever else could root on the rock and grow over it: saxifrage, blackberry, honeysuckle, and woven amongst them, holding its dark green all winter, the small-leaved English ivy ... Redeeming ...

There was a stair down the cliff at the side, where the rock gave way to tulip trees on a steep slope—mayapple, trillium, bloodroot, Quaker-lady. Some steps were cut in and others were built out, following the base of the rock. One wondered what it led to: why scramble up and down the scarp to reach a railroad track by a stream too broad for leaping and almost too polluted to swim? Was it for the view looking back up, the smoky beetling cliff, the ugly house on top——but green, as in Giotto's Birth of Mary, that much small hope? No, there was more.

Under the cliff just below the house was a recess worn by water, where a spring issued, filling a rock bowl, a triangular basin with a stone lip—natural or carved, no one could say. Only that the spring had always been there, fresh with moss, watercress, grass always green in the shelter of the cliff, always the murmur of water.

Above it emptied the sewage and ground drainage of the town. Open pipes spilled into the soil or into the brook that flowed below the main road—Tiber they called that stream, a vaulted Cloaca now. As the plumber in the beer hall used to enlarge on it: "Man, when you work down there, you best keep to the middle and be ready to jump. Those pipes come in from this side and from that side, and somebody'll flush a toilet, and if you ain't lookin, you'll get it in the face." Everything went untreated into the earth, or down with an Old World smell into the Patapsco at the foot of the town. But this water, amidst so much corruption, filled the rock bowl clear, good to the taste.

For Anna it gave promise of the Great Transformation: that in some Year of Wonders all polluted waters would come out pure, like this one. What it afforded Leflore was only its small assurance, that through the crust of inveterate filth, something clean could still hold its own.

On the hill opposite, above the granite workers' houses, a Catholic church came into view through the mist. It vied with the grain elevators and stacks of the flour mill. If the church was taller (thou shalt not live by bread alone), the other bulked larger, represented more solid investment. Yet that Gothic spire was so much a feature of their landscape that even Anna, though she railed sometimes ("With what right does the parson claim the labor of the farmer?"), had come to take it in her stride.

It added, indeed, to the night scene, which was mostly dark, nature not affording much alleviation that way: the rocks, the river, the shaggy black of the wood. Under that dusty brow, the row houses were a dim sprinkling along the foreground road, leading from the wool factory to the mills, the bridge, the bar. Above them, the west window of the church glowed blue, green, heraldic gules, silhouetting a cut-out Christ on the Cross, the words above—"O VOS OMNES"—lettered at night in lights, radiating prophecy: "All you who pass by the way, behold and see, if there be any sorrow like unto my sorrow."

Being is of many dimensions, and narration strings out on one. Through seasonal windows of a present which stretched already into years, mind was reaching back for other times and places: Delta Landing, Reading in Alabama, England, Chicago; other people, to be apprehended through the self, Patapsco and now. That reality spilled over the frame, the devil and his crew in a baroque ceiling.

So he built bins along the inner wall, a spatial array, numbered across and lettered down; then he began to sift sketches into pigeonholes, shadowy categories reaching for particulars.

The goal stood before him like *Prometheus Bound,* less an action than a deathless tableau. He picked up his mother's Loeb text and stumbled through the Greek, filled with elation and despair: "The wave cries in surf, the deep laments, the springs, the ever-flowing rivers.'

Patapsco, Anna, Jeffrey—what power, what spell could turn the private landscape to such a constellation of Forms?

He faced a table heaped with years of papers:

Mythology: From earliest time he had sensed woman as the resting place, the quiet, oldest of gods, from which the small stir of day arises and into which it will subside, something larger than man has dreamed of, what a man could only worship or joke about. "And now this kind lady goanna mother that poor boy." That eternal womanly could be mastered Only in part and by a kind of yielding—in any case, to one's peril. For Leflore it was also water, the ocean from which continents have sprung, in which we float or drown.

If in myth the motherly was smiling, it had proved for him a siren smile...

Looking back through shock and tears, how could he be sure he had heard her voice (though he heard it still) deeper than love, speaking things that bore on life and death—had she invoked what was to come—there where the Blue Hole narrowed into Panther Burn? Then the car missed the bridge. He went down in her arms and she came up in his. He brought her to the surface, held her for an indeterminate time, until help arrived, but she was dead, had been dead, Doctor Paul said, before she struck the water.

"Medically certifiable, son; she did not drown. She couldn't have meant that, son; you must have imagined it. It was heart failure, An accident, a terrible accident."

And still the voice (ever soft, an excellent thing in woman) stirred in what he heard and read: "Long years ago, to me what happened, that I must seek the abyss ... my body of the rain dampened?" "We enter this overarching cave…" "Across the river of Ocean you will find Persephone's shore." "Ah, willow, willow shall be my garland." There the mystery her bardic father had brought from Wales, the strange beauty, bent over the formlessness of this water-world, their Delta.

Maybe that was why, for him, the search had been so crucial, though the women it had brought him shared in the unrest of day. Would his deepest marriage always be with the whispering night and water?

Delta Landing: When the famous old poet, Tristram Tombs, came to Delta Landing, Uncle Hazlewood had one of his cultural Sundays at Ararat, the original Hazlewood plantation outside town. It seemed more appropriate to salute the muse from an antebellum bungalow on top of an Indian mound over Panther Burn and Lotus Lake. Everybody who was supposed to know anything about the arts came. B. J. Farnham brought his great aunt, old lady Shields. Her hearing aid was on the blink, as it mostly was, so she couldn't tell if the poet was whispering or yelling. Somewhere in the longest poem, at a climactic passage about "a pinpoint in eternity," she cupped her hand to B. J.'s ear and shouted: "Why doesn't he read louder? I can't hear a word he's saying."

When the poem was done, Mr. Wilson, who had missed that sentence for the noise, leaned his blue face forward and opened his precise Presbyterian mouth: "Mr. Tombs, I didn't get that passage after 'pin· points in eternity.' I wonder if you could read those lines again?"

Tombs let out a groan like opening a coffin lid. "I never read anything out of context. I'll have to begin again from the beginning."

The old lady caught that. She leaned to B. J. "My God," she cried. ('He's not going to read the whole damned thing again?"

While Uncle Hazy, who made poetry his refuge, sat with chin raised, a mockingbird on a rosebush ready to yield to song. But if, running a slim hand through silver hair and letting his eyelids fall in languid surrender, he had spoken, it would have been to voice the Ausonian mood: "We are living out of time. I know Russians who sat as we, listening to poetry in the gardens of Krasnoye Selo. Let us retire gently from the world ..." Then the children came up laughing from the lake shore ...

The Name: He had so often blushed to acknowledge it that now he was brazed. "How did we get such a name?"

Uncle Hazy, looking as delicate a flower as that Monsieur Choquet painted by Renoir, produced the evidence:

Not from the part-Indian chief of the Choctaws, Greenwood Leflore—a sunflower if one could have claimed him. His was the Acadian line and theirs from Louisiana.

Rather see Edward Mease, traveler, 1771, who stopped with Henry Leflur at Natchez, hunter and planter, descendant of a Norman who came with a royal grant.

It was his sons who in 1806 petitioned that the new laws of Congress not deprive them of their land, to which, under French and Spanish rule, their title had been secure. But they lost it anyway.

From this disseised cmpany the first Quincy Leflore shook free and appeared by the Bayou Pierre across from Natchez among the group of resolutes heading west with Aaron Burr on nine flatboats and with such a freightage of dream as might have sunk them—to make war on Spain and alienate the western states and so hew out an empire to be ruled from the golden throne of the old Incas. And when Burr was attached by the impulsive Acting Governor at Washington (not D.C., but that Mississippi capital and seat of elegance six miles east of Natchez, now a desolate graveyard) and lived with the gentry round about until he was shipped East for his trial, it was Quincy Leflore who recouped his fortune by winning the widow Madeline McNair, in beauty and wealth the catch of the neighborhood (though some thought he caught her on the bounce from no less a lover than Burr). Anyway, the achievement didn't keep Quincy from drowning himself ten years later in his own plantation creek.

"Whatever the flower is," Daren would say, "it's not a pansy." —If only the paralyzed old poet he would thank God for knowing could have appeared when he was a boy and given him the motto he needed: "Saxifrage is my flower that splits the rock."

As for the Daren part, he had never had to justify that. It came from his Welch grandfather's birthplace, Pen-y-Daren, "Head-of-the-Cliff," and suited his mood exactly.

The Self: If the cave was his essence, his manifestation had been another thing.

To pull across the lake with Dan Byrne against mounting waves. To drift in the lull among cypress knees, To watch gar in the spaces be tween lotus pads jimmy their jaws and loll yellow tails. Bees. Dragon flies. A flower falls from a buttonbush and a bass strikes it. A row of leatherbacks slips off a log. The log rots into a slime of jellies and molds. He looks into the swamp and imagines a brontosaurus rising from the scum.

At night h e leafs the Book of Knowledge for views of volcanoes, twisters, saurians, cavemen, airplanes, bombs…

Seines fish for the aquarium. Feeds a baby gar minnows half his size until he grows too big. Scoop him in a bucket where he has to stand on his head or his tail and still he eats as he rides. Dump him in Ladybird Alexander's pool with the slobby sucker goldfish, to come back a few days later and dip up nothing but a huge gar.

Though at Oxford, when American enterprise took the caprice of swallowing goldfish alive, and he was served a flopping three inch one at a luncheon party: "A concession to your national appetite," he missed the appropriateness, having ceased to identify with the armor-plated gar of violence.

To the extent of believing himself a pacifist.

Resistance to war erupting in a delirium of protest: prison, hunger strikes, beatings, solitary confinement. Until, yanked out, he would get the chance to risk himself in disease research, The lice were nothing and the malaria he had had all his youth anyway, but the trench pneumonia almost took him off; then he proved the miracle of the new drugs, he survived, and again without warning was enlarged, pardoned by the President at the urging of Uncle Hazlewood's senatorial friends. So he was belched back into the world reclassified: "Psychologically unfit for the Army," a judgment with which nobody but Daren, at that time, was likely to quarrel…

No, the attempt to focus on self did not lead inward to any such center as Anna accused him of bending toward. The vortex of dream reversed, spiraling out into action.

Anna: He'll be wrestling with it all the time, trying to work it out, to get me pinned down. And he never can understand, because he grew up out of it, infected with class, corruption, privilege.

The poor. Slowly it took form, the communal being she bore with her always under the wondering face and wide eyes, a lovable sadness that looked out, bold, trusting, yet alarmed, a bird at once tame and afraid. She was alienated from the life of culture, England, the South, where she had moved, As if behind the veil you looked at, she was still going back the long alley street of the Chicago slum, down the stair to the cellar apartment, to watch Mom boiling clothes in the tub on the coal stove, the girl to stand silent wondering, while the mother's tears fell into the water: Why does she have to work so hard? And why are some so sad?

"It's not the present you're trying to change," Leflore told her; "you don't even look at it. It's your childhood, and you can't do it; it's fixed inside you, and you might as well get used to it."

She would only gaze at him, the gray eyes silencing (all her life she would have that dreaming distant look one sees on the faces of pregnant women): "What should you know about it, you of the upper crust and suburbs, acting as if the body of mankind didn't exist, the workers—reading from your books about maladjusted individuals and romance? What do you care about life as it is?"

(To dig down, through all levels of so-called reality: property, custom, family, love, duty, religion; to hit on some irreducible proletarian core; to hold it up triumphantly: here it is, stripped, humanity, the real.)

"Look at your kin," he told her. "They've made a killing. They live in the suburbs and maybe they've started having their psychiatrists and reading about maladjustment. At an Oxford reception, that's where I met you. I'm the poorest thing you've dealt with for years, though I come from southern aristocracy, which means pigtracks four generations removed.

No, Mom was still at the washtub, the tears falling, and in each tear, like the basement cave it mirrored, was all her past, worlds within worlds, workers, miners, the poor…

As he tried to fix on that Anna, the assumed complement to his introspection, what he caught was not the act, but the wishful child face at the porthole of the tear: "Don't you know I've always been reaching for life, always?"

Suppose one roused her up, set her in motion—there had always been urgencies—to replenish the woodbox by the potbelly stove. Saturday, when the chute came out of the second story of the Sash and Door Factory and the trucks were filled with odd-sized leftover chunks, women and children crowded from the neighboring tenement rows with baskets, sacks, homemade wagons, their arms if nothing else; for one was permitted to pick up anything that fell to the ground. If you tried to pull it out of the truck, the man above would yell at you or chunk a block of wood to clear you off; but if you sneaked right up under the chute, he couldn't see, so you could stand there picking at whatever you could reach, and sometimes it would come in a rush and you'd get half a dozen pieces—a little more and you'd have been buried under it.

Well, enough. She gets her bundle of wood and starts home. But the recall which has got her going, leading from deprivation almost to delight, proceeds by association—after wood comes coal. She meets the coal peddler plodding along with his horse-drawn wagon. The horse slips on the ice and falls, and Anna stands in her thin coat, her long black stockings sliding down skinny legs, her fingers frozen, clutching the bundle of wood; she watches while he struggles to get up and fails, his efforts weaker; she watches, as the peddler lashes him, the great thong falling: snap, crash, wham! Blame? The peddler—his money sunk in the coal, another lash driving him on? Yet something must be blamed, something deeper-society, the world...

Even in England as Jeffrey's father's saddle horses moved in the golden light, Anna was seeing through to the bony nag crumpled on the ice, shuddering. "Those horses," she told Leflore, "they are still in my head."

Jeffrey: "No, I'm no Circe; and if I were, you've less to fear than I. I saw you chewing moly that first day in the valley..."

Moly. For Leflore it would mean nothing but the mythical plant Odysseus took against Circe's charms—and mastered her: "Sheathe that sword and let us two go lie together, that we may mingle our bodies and learn to trust one another by proofs of love and intercourse." But for Jeffrey it recovered things lost until Daren plucked the random flowered herb and leaned against the oak chewing the stem. ("I leaned my back against an oak," Jeffrey sang; "I thought it was a trusty tree...")

Agnes, the old villager had grounded her in moly by the great oak that was Jeffrey's Druid God, in one of her father's pastures, when she was a child in Devon, where she would run down hill and leap and spread her coat,

"What are you doing?" Agnes asked. "Why do you run and leap so?"

"Because I want to catch the man in the wind."

And when she landed by mistake on Agnes' mushrooms, the crone yelled at her: "You'll never catch the man in the wind, but someday he'll catch you, and then" (she spat the words out, an ultimate shame) "he'll mock at you."

It was the tree where Jeffrey used to run and jump and swing on the branches, like flying. (Had she dreamed it, the peep in the bird's nest, the speckled blue eggs?) By that tree moly grew, the nondescript pithy weed with the wilted pale flowers.

"Why does it grow under the Big Tree, Agnes?"

"You see the mistletoe?" Agnes pointed to the thick bunches that spotted the crown. "That's a sacred plant. So the birds can't eat it. They know that. But sometimes if the father birds fight and one of them takes the mother bird away, the father bird that's left eats the mistletoe because he wants to die. But when he begins to hurt, maybe he changes his mind. So he sits high in the tree and tries to shit it out."

"Spit it out?"

"No. Shit it out. And if he does, he lives; but the berry goes deep in the ground, and the next year it comes up a moly plant, which is magic. 1t protects you from evil. Here, chew a piece."

Jeffrey wouldn't touch it. "It smells too bad. Worse than garlic."

Agnes knew how to hook her. "Once you've chewed moly, you can make a wish."

Jeffrey chewed, spat and wished to herself: "I want to catch the man in the wind."

When they parted at the stream, Agnes on her way back to the village, Jeffrey ahead to the Manor, "Don't use that word 'shit,' " Agnes told her. "It's a bad word."

Jeffrey tucked it away with her small cargo of bad words, execrations she could whisper to herself when the moustached peers pulled her up on their knees ("Ah, what a lovely child!") and bristled her with tobacco and whiskey kisses…

The Dark Leflores: They had leapt from Hegel's prehistory to the forefront of now, almost in a generation.

Elmonia, daughter of a Leflore slave, bearing like the rest the family name and some assumed diversion of the blood—Elmonia—more of the old than the new:

"Ah tried to staht the thing, an the cranker was broke. Well, Ah jus jack it up an spin roun the lef hin wheel. Burr, burr, burr." (Her lips like the Idiot Boy's.) "Ah kick it off the jack, an fo it could get away, Ah jump in. Ah drive to de sto fo a can o kerosene. (Elmonia,' says Mistah Verne, 'you must think you're a millionaire, crankin up that automobile to get ten cents' worth o kerosene.' Well, Ah laugh so, thinkin about me a millionaire riddin that hunk o tin, Ah got inspiahed; an Ah stop right in the road and wrote 'The Raggedy Millionaire,' or 'The Busted-Down Flivver.' "

For years Daren had tried to get a copy of that poem. "If it's so good just to hear her talk about it"—while she slapped her thigh, rolled her eyes and gurgled with laughter—"what must the poem be?"

The newspaper had published it, but Daren's schoolmate B. J. didn't know when. "Before my time." - "Whaddya think?" said Daren.

"Just because you own the paper doesn't make you a patriarch."
He went back to Elmonia: "When was it?"
"Lawd, Misser Daren, iss been a long time." (You could see old Hegel nodding his head: A-historical.) "Right smaht o years, sholy."

Uncle Caldwell, her brother, had got moving. If you asked why, of all the Negroes in the Delta, the old citizens would shake hands with him and call him Mister Caldwell, they would tell you that he was mail carrier, and besides, in his youth, he had lifted a bale of cotton single handed, and this gave him a distinction above his kind. But his poems made a better claim.

The once powerful figure, hunched in gentle old age over the banjo, chanting his lyrics to the blues melodies he gave them—that favorite of his, naive, inadequate—to sum up in gnomic economy the mystery that lined his face, the strum and wail supplying a passion the text never accomplished: "Four Words":

> *Born* is a word we use
> To tell when it all began.
> We find in *Youth* a happy life
> With few pretends.
> *Manhood* finds us as we are
> Very good or full of strife.
> *Death* is a word we use
> To tell of the end of life.

His own Annabelle Lee had died years ago, but he had helped Elmonia raise the children she conceived from a succession of worthless men, three or four siring eight, to be named fancy names: Roxie, Rooshie, Lyjah, Tabby, Lucius, Easter, Styles and Nabby. Five had trickled down into dark anonymity without giving much sign of them selves (though Rooshie, as Uncle Hazlewood's chauffeur, left a little garland of legends); but Lyjah, born about 1910, was a preacher; and Lu, just Daren's age and educated by Uncle Hazlewood at the University of Chicago, was making such headway as an organizer it wasn't politic anymore to mention him in the Delta; while Styles, the wild one, had written poetry, not of his uncle's vintage, but broken, strange and miraculous:

> I sleep in the darkness and night

> between the spaces of the stars…
> Angel, weep not, be not lonely;
> For the space of time only
> Reigns me from wild and weird into comely

Reigns? Rains? Reins? It was too late to find out, or to draw the veil of that *comely.*

But Lucius, far from ambiguity, strode at the head of his disciplined resistance army, the placard held high, the face stamped with the greatness of will and militant right. He strides; and now beside him appears the airier form of Daren—the two who played together before travel (and custom) drifted them apart, come back side by side, briefly, almost by chance, yet a chance hugely pregnant—Daren whimsically objecting:

"But you're like communists or any of the other power blocks. You issue directives and everybody falls in line. You don't think you're going to reach the happy state of freedom by manipulating men like forces, do you? Styles knew better. His directives came from inside."

"Much good it did him. To be torn apart on white laws for some poems nobody's going to read… I get things done the only way possible. And if that's the price, I pay it. I'm not a poet and I don't aim to be; I'm an organizer."

In a Now where Hegel's timelessness leaps to the future, they walk together, talking, as they advance toward the hoses and dogs.

The World: When Professor Cader Ayres at the University of Virginia stormed into the placid horizon of progress with his own fierce version of cyclical history, Daren's immediate problem was to find our place on the curve of those recurrences. Were we living in the winter of late Rome, or in the post-Alexandrian broils of successor kingdoms, or were we the Greek cities in the crisis after the Periclean rapture? If Greece, what our age called for was a Plato who would knit the strands of Western thought to glowing inwardness; if post-Hellenic, it was discipline we required, Roman law and peace, perhaps even a poem of responsible power; **if** we were already in the last stages of decline, Augustine was the aim, the City of God in the earthly ruin, or, if we lacked faith, at least John the Baptist, the warning voice: "Make straight in the desert a pathway for the Lord."

Each suggested loyalties of a different kind, contrasting styles of life and art. But the study of history, that amorphous record in which so many patterns could be guessed at and lost sight of, vague as faces in the clouds, gave no way to know which model applied. And that was only the West. Piled on these doubts was the larger of Russia and America: what was their place, and with whom did the future lie?

Then the release of power, which Henry Adams had plotted as the square of time, entered the nuclear phase——a transcendental function. How could one talk of continuing cycles when this one was preparing an explosion to end the whole shebang? The plot of history veered into a new tum.

Except nothing under the sun was new. Against time the wheel had always been time the arrow. "Such as have occurred and always will occur," said the Greek; but the Jews expected Messiah. And Christian history, from the Revelation of John to the revelation of Hegel, had continued apocalyptic; our Four Ages do not lead back on themselves, but through a crisis of spirit to utter culmination.

The bomb had returned us to that. Cyclical history was outgrown, thank God. No more room for those petty minstrel shows: cultures, empires, Trojan Wars, Leda and the Swan, the chance of new uprisings. The successor kingdoms were in the sky, a universe of lifebearing worlds, where some might blow themselves apart, while others took their turn. And even this steady-state had to yield to the cosmic arrow: if everything was expanding from a nucleus to who-knows-what, it was hardly clear the time-snake had his tail in his mouth. This earth, at any rate, faced a denouement; there was only the question: Satanic or Benign.

And yet, heads, tails, however the coin fell——the world to climax in flame, or to settle like a plant into the wreathings of its thought-enfolded biosphere—it was still only of time; and the metaphor showed how far from the consummation once dreamed of, where in Dante Paradise was fire. It was not the temporal we were after, not Anna's promise of classless plenty, much less Julian Huxley's world-park and art museum, not even a Wagnerian immolation and twilight of the half gods—no, but a passion of soul, which however out of fashion to admit it, we were, we are, we would be.

Anna's hopes, which she called material, gave no material at all, nothing but the pregnant Now. What could Spengler expect from the future of the tragic West? A daemonic flash of vision. All promised lands were glimpsed from that mountain; all wanderings in the desert opened on the same landscape, luminous, enormous, timeless as heaven and hell, the symbolic space in which we have our being.

And still that space, as if unsatisfied, was always thrusting into time, breathing great gulps of void, Brahman to Atman, gods descending to half gods—
Why should the One overflow?

Papers heaped on the board, a tumbled drama…

He had been sitting there every minute he could snatch for the last twelve years, ordering something the next years had sprung apart. It was fine to talk like Vergil about licking the monster into shape; but what if you couldn't tell the afterbirth from the bear?

So a new energy had to be generated, a solvent found, in which these elements of time and place, persons, themes could be suspended and brought into relationship—what had gathered in the Now be artfully displayed in sequences of before and after.

The self groping for the self? Always. But not that only. There was a universe at stake.

What point in the mind's wrestling if the pen did not move?

As the spinout moth in the dark corner behind the Delta house, camouflaged on the pecan tree, gray against gray, took wing and became a whir of pulsing orange arcs and waves, the pinwheel, the whirlpool of Now beats into time…

SUMMER, WINTER, FALL, SPRING.

PART I

Summer

1. Frail Clarities

June, 1949—after the first year at Patapsco City, Maryland.

The college crowned the hill over the town.

"If the place hadn't been broke, they'd never have given it to me," Professor Ayres had told Leflore when he phoned him in Chicago. "You've got to be at least as dedicated as a communist or early Christian. Because the salaries are inadequate. But the work, Daren, this Program, is real."

Daren didn't bank on reality, beyond what he was trying to put on paper in front of him, and that hadn't arrived at reality yet; but he admired Cader Ayres and he had needed a job. He came with Anna and found the house on the cliff, the ground floor rear anyway, since the old lady, Sally Stovall, was still living upstairs, looking after her paralyzed husband, Burt.

She used to invite Leflore to the dusky curtained living room with antimacassars on the old chairs and family silhouettes in mahogany frames on the wall, the tortoiseshell comb in her hair hinting at better days; she would pour herself a big whiskey and him a little one, wave him to a seat, and tell how once she had tried to paint in earnest, but the only things that sold were sickly sweet scenes on lampshades and wastepaper baskets.

"TRASH!" she accused. "I sold my soul, and they put it on trash baskets and exported it all the way to China and Africa and Australia. I had scores of women working for me, copying my stuff, doing TRASH. That's what they pay for. Sure I was an artist. In TRASH."

Leflore wanted to be an artist too, and not in trash if he could help it, though he didn't know what would save him—Ayres' Program?—where the work (you said it, Cader) was real: philosophy, languages, music, mathematics, science. Well, whoever mastered all that wasn't going to have much time left for his art.

He was like a man trying to pour a Perseus, who has got the forms ready and the metal to where it's half liquid, half lumps of cantankerous ore, and has to give it up. By the time summer gets around again, the clay molds are dried and cracked, the bronze caked in the forge. How can that Perseus be revived?

As if an artist so stymied would take up something else, start for the quarries to get marble for a new project, all his projects coming big. And again Labor Day would find him hardly begun, the mythical workshop a jumble of blocked-out stone, in which the lines of pediment or tomb could hardly be discerned.

By now he was getting desperate. His shelves were loaded with life-at-tempts: cultural history, world novel, epic poem, philosophy of nature. He had begun to go back over old projects to see what could be made of them. This summer he happened to pick up a journal he kept when he was a student abroad. He had sent it home instead of letters, and Uncle Hazlewood had gathered it up in five loose-leaf volumes.

Daren was sitting at his back window over the Patapsco, or on good days at a card table carried out under the buckeye tree, where the blackberry coiled from the rock-Thoreau's fancy in his head, how the tendrils might run a natural filigree up the table legs; he opened the first notebook, reverting from this rawboned valley to that fabulous age of escape, between the wars: romantic moods, spiry towers, the poetry he had been full of:

> We look before and after
> And sigh for what is not ...

All at once he was seeing it twice, as when the paired images of a stereoscope build a compelling perspective. Here was the record on the page, the loves and extravagances of youth, and against it what he knew of himself and the world——juxtaposed, the dream Perseus, the caked and abandoned bronze...

No wonder the Journal had let him down, years ago, when it was fresh and the fall of France gave it edge, when he revised, transcribing day to day, like a chronicle. *The Life of Dream* he had called it—a misnomer; the dream had no life.

No wonder. That story should have begun way back, in history and consciousness—wherever the infinite search spilled over into time, rooting eternities in the here and now: Gothic, Reformation, Romantic, the promise of America, all the betrayals and degradations: Civil War, World War, Depression, the rise of the great isms.

There were his family roots reaching back into those origins, a tie between that and him; there was his own soul, lifting, even from the breast, eyes of the fallen god-self to stare at the transhuman godcosmos: storm, river, flood, space-plunging planets, evolution, nitroglycerine, a world-embracing war—

That ship, after a hurricane in the Gulf, floundering, cargo loose, before a mid-Atlantic storm; that sea, lashed to its ultimate resonance of forty-foot waves, spewing phosphorescence on the wind; that mate accusing: "Damned Jonah! Talk about wantin a storm!"

As the prow dipped, overwhelmed, rose shuddering and struck the next wave, Daren clung to the rail, his face to the spray, exultant.

And the Europe they were sailing to, from which the shortwave radio below deck brought vaunts of Hitler, occupation of the Rhineland, the absurd superman screaming and the crowd's applause: "Now like a somnambulist I go the way God has chosen."

In Russia there was a national celebration and review of troops ("The working men," Marx had said, "have no country"); there was an exhibition of controlled state art, "Stalin at the Ryon Dam" ("We shall have an association," Marx had said, "in which the free development of each is the condition for the free development of all'). In France they were boasting of the Maginot Line. *Imaginaire.*

What a time of self and world to have spawned the frail clarities of those journal-bland vignettes:

Oct. 7, 1936: Up the Thames with the tide past factories, wharves, tugs, the Isle of Dogs. Into Surrey Docks on the dirty east hem. Stood the cold on deck for the sights of shore, dead battleships, mudflats of the sewerage dump, according to Baedeker, like a Dutch landscape, Greenwich observatory smothered in fog.

Customs officers came in immaculate dress, talked like Lords, examined nothing. Went ashore with Hank Brown and the Engineer in the drizzle, past seven of the girls who understroll the arclight, into a pub bursting with laughter and smoke. Tried English lager, ale, stout, bitters, each more abominable; wound up on sherry. A dingy food shop served us eels and chips. Debated whether King John died of a surfeit of eels, I, having eaten two bowls, holding the affirmative.

Whores, drunks, sailors, cockneys, in the fog of that Europe, himself there seeing it, and here, seeing himself seeing it—the old Silenus carrying the stripling Dionysus in his arms…

(And who is the self seeing Daren seeing the self? Daren at a third remove?)

He had joined Hank Brown in New Orleans before sailing.

"You grew up rich," Hank had said; "but we moved around in a truck like the Joads, all over Alabama, Tennessee, Mississippi. I remember my brother and me once in Hatchie Bottom, when we were short of food, perched in some mulberry trees like jaybirds, nothing on us but shirts that didn't cover our tails, and every now and then there'd be a noise and a purple whoosh. 'You got the diarrhea,' Pa said. 'You got the diarrhest rear in the country. You better stop eatin or you'll blow out your bow-wow-hole.' " Hank's aunt had saved him from that. She owned a little hotel in New Orleans which she had to run in the Depression as a bawdy house. She gave Hank a job as bellhop and desk clerk and sent him through college. He was a Rhodes scholar now. While they were waiting for the freighter he took Daren for a celebration at the hotel.

A curious gang, admirers of Aunt Martha. There was the sculptor who scorned anything but straight liquor: "When I was a child, I drank as a child; but now I'm a man I drink like a fish." There was the big girl from Texas who went around asking: "Have you ever been scratched by a bobcat?"

And when you said, "No," she pulled her dress up and showed you the scars, because she had been, and she was bound to prove it.

As the broad sister on the sofa kicked her shoes across the room, complaining her feet swelled when she drank, and Daren refused a second rum and coke, having to sail the next day and not wanting to waste away for three weeks (he said) like Narcissus over a bowl——a girl came in, dark-haired, melancholy, a near-divorcee; she must have ridden on the "Streetcar Named Desire."

"The tears dwell in an onion that should water this sorrow," Hank counseled the next day. They were on the prow gazing over the squall-mottled Gulf, as into a future where thunderhead beyond thunderhead converged toward whatever waited over the curved horizon. "You don't know how lucky you are." For Daren had sighed for her.

"Poetry, travel, art," she had told him. "How bored I am with these people. I want to sail with you to that lovely old country."

Oxford, October 8: Forty minutes to get out of London, smoke, damped souls. As the bus reached open land there was a moment of sun. At Henley we rushed down a hill through beech woods and crossed the Thames, here almost "silver-streaming" as Spenser claimed. Oxford by dusk, Magdalen tower gray and pinnacled.

Gloucester College: a night wanderer's impression: a castellated square, chapel to one side, hall to the other. A stone stair, steps half worn away, led me to my rooms, large, Victorian, cold.

Drew the velvet curtains and, lighting the fire, sat down to three weeks of mail, among others ten letters from the girl of New Orleans. Spent a sad time wishing her here, but got no results. So the bell sounded and I went to the college hall for dinner.

A great raftery room with a fire flickering in the midst. The unknown dons above, old friends laughing at their meal, the unknown students around, tearing into their bread and food, speaking a tongue almost unknown. Ate in silence and left, fuller, but no warmer than before.

As I walked across bleak quads, music came from a downstairs room—Brahms' *Third,* a warm, rich work. I might have listened it out, but for a fine rain, and that the soft passages, which I prefer to the loud, were lost in the intervening stone.

I went back to my room, where the tiny fire made shapes on the wall. Turned on the dim light and began to read a book of college rules: "The electric fittings must in no circumstances be tampered with. Any undergraduate who replaces the light globe fixed in his room with one of higher power will be fined one pound."

The fire was getting low. I was about to pile on coal when at the end of an alarming list of expenses I noticed the price per bag. After going to my grip and getting out Shakespeare, I laid on a single lump and huddled to the grate. The book fell open at the verse in *Lear:*

> He that has and a little tiny wit
> Must make content with his fortune fit.

The door was flung back; a big-boned fellow pushed in, cropped hair, lantern jaw opening to smiles.

"You're Leflore," he told me as positively as if I'd denied it. "From Mississippi. Christ! How d'ya stand the climate? I'm from New York, Jim Hardy. Come on down; I've got a real fire. What're ya readin? Shakespeare? That's my stuff. Thought you were in physics. Well, come on, meet the guys. Clyster's there, medic from Oregon. A riot! You shoulda been on the boat. We'll have some damned old tea."

A real fire it was, and Clyster lounged over it, hairy, pipe drooled out of one corner of a lean face, Another worthy had his feet up in the big chair. They bemoaned the climate, the snobbery of the English ("We Yanks gotta stick together"), the expenses. "Did you see the price of coal?" cried Hardy, throwing on a bucketful.

"Some chemist told em it's the same as diamonds."

"And all those taxes and fines."

"In Jesus," says Clyster, "there's a milk tax. Evans over there complained to the Head: 'Why do I have to pay this tax?'—'Well, everyone pays the milk tax, you know; it's been that way for three hundred hoary years!'—'But I don't drink milk.'—'don't worry, old chap; one pays the milk tax whether one drinks milk or not. It's what we call a tradition.'—'Maybe you call it a tradition,' says Evans, 'but we call it a damned racket.'"

"Christ," said Hardy. "You'd think we were kids; in by 10:45 or a nine pence fine. And after midnight God help you. And so much roll call and chapel!"

"You can get out of chapel," said Clyster, ' if you claim some other re1igion. Johns at Merton tried. 'And what is your religion?' the rector asked. 'Sun worshiper,' said Johns. But the scout began to wake him at dawn. 'The rector says get up, sir, it's time for worship.' A week of that and he was back in the fold."

Meals came next, how grim, and so much boiled greens. About the scholar whose father sent him a ripe watermelon, and he told the chef to bring everybody at his table a piece for dessert, but when it came it was boiled.

How the British shovel the food in left-handed, and if a poor American lays down his knife to change hands, the scouts, who are always waiting, snatch up the plate and slam down another, so while you're trying to eat your joint, there's a pudding staring you in the face.

Finally it was the women—a drab lot. Clyster told of the African lecturer who after describing the stretched ears, plastered lips, slit noses of Hottentot females, summed it up: "In fact, the standards of beauty are so low that even the girls of St. Hilda's might have a chance at husbands." Cheers from the male section, while a scattering of girls started to walk out. "Oh, ladies," the lecturer called, "I'm sorry…" They turned for the apology. "Don't go yet. There's no train for an hour and twenty minutes."

Leflore, reading, felt what he had then: a rising oppression at so much small talk, the wish to get back to his own little fire, the comfort of Shakespeare. Though the cold would settle, and as his baggage hadn't come, despite a scraping London agent who swore it would beat him to Oxford, in lieu of blankets he was fated to sleep in his clothes.

Good. He had talked a lot, those days, about the blessings of hardship. He had even written his sister June, who admired him too much already and was driving herself too hard: "Of otherwise equal choices, take the more painful, if nothing more, to exercise the will." As if the secret of life was to settle for nothing until you knew damned well you didn't want it…

A lot of stuff about the scout waking him for too much breakfast, so to save money and not get as fat as Aunt Willi Mari, he resolved to discontinue that egg, bacon, toast and tea consumption. "But you must eat somethink, sir; it won't do to 'ave nothink at all," said snowyhaired Fred.

"Some bran flakes, then, or All Bran." Fred cupped a deaf ear: to the diphthong glides of the Delta.

"I comprehend you, sir. You want *brown* bread."

"What I'm talking about is a cereal."

"A cereal? Peust Teusties, sir!"

"For constipation…"

"Constipation, sir?"

By noon a box of Post Toasties and a loaf of brown bread were in the larder…

Daren turned the pages. Silenus bored with the child Dionysus. Other people were appearing, but slowly, as in an epistolary romance of the eighteenth century. Before you found out what happened, the world might have exploded:

Horner, pleasant Dominions man, has lived all over Europe, also in South Africa, Canada, Australia, grows a brown moustache, wears brown clothes, slips along in sandals. We had come from a college meeting and he was talking to an aristocratic booby with three given names and two surnames, none of which I remember. I don't know who it was they were talking about. "With regard to his wife," Horner said, "he has found the secret of eternal youth: get a new one every five years." Then he saw me. "You're Leflore. I spent a month in New Orleans. Ah, those Southern girls."

He took Hardy and me and the booby to his room for some Tokay (a huge wicker-bound flask) and told how he smuggled it through Europe, roguering Lord knows how many ladies by the way. The wine is almost gone; maybe that was his trick with the dames.

After beer and sandwiches in the buttery, they took me out to buy a bicycle. Found me a bargain for two pounds—though the scout says I should have commissioned him; he could have done better.

The bike liberated me from the fellows. Hardy would have joined me, but his tires were flat. "You be careful," he said. "These fools all drive on the wrong side of the street. Jesus, it's terrible."

At the first stoplight I slammed for the foot brake. The pedals whirled around clicking and caught me on the shin. I swerved and hit a parked car. Before I got going again, I clutched the hand brake, aiming to remember it. When the light changed I turned right into the main street. Of course I got on the right side, which was wrong. A bus bore down on me honking. Instinctively I smashed for the foot brake, and collapsed roaring. A Bobby held up traffic while I crossed sides.

"Why don't you go to the country to learn?"

"Well, I am," I told him, "but it takes time to get there."

Evening again, Daren bundled up by the fire, in a blanket now and wool socks and a long college scarf, trying to read, but interrupted:

The first knock was brisk. A wiry fellow swung in, tried to hustle me into the cricket team. I told him I didn't even like baseball.

"Cricket's a better game, old chap."

"Then I'm afraid I might get addicted."

"But you must play something." He laid it down like trumps.

"If I get desperate, I'll let you know."

The second knock was laconic. A scornful giant with blond mustachios ambled over the threshold. "Captain of the eight."

"Eight?"

"Rowing. But you're too light for any use, except for a cox, and that takes brains. What do you weigh?"

"A hundred and twenty-eight pounds, brains and all."

"Gad, what's that in stone? Ten stone, nine stone—nine stone two. I'd have thought more."

"Wiry bones." I stretched my digits at him.

"You might make a cox after all."

"Suppose I don't want to be a cox?"

"You have to support the college. What do you propose to play?"

"I may swim. I may walk. I may ride my bike."

"See here, old chap; walking's no game."

"As much as sitting in the back of a boat bawling my lungs away."

He withdrew with a godlike shrug.

The last knock was timid. Creeping Jesus, pale, slight, dimpled chin, a trepidant wavering of the eyes. "I wonder if you would be interested in the Oxford Group? A religious organization. Inspirational. I could call for you tomorrow evening."

"Until I'm settled, I wont attend anything, thank you."

"Then I'll come later. Meanwhile, if you could read this pamphlet about our work…"

Was Leflore's face like those yearning faces in the busts of late Rome (barometers of the hunger which had drawn faith down), that Moral Rearmament in the person of Creeping Jesus kept scheming his conversion? And why couldn't he throw them off like Jim Hardy with his boxer's mug and loud ways: When the little catechumen first knocked at that door: "Oxford Group? Jesus Christ, guy! I don't even know what the fuckin organization is!" But Daren let them plague him, until finally he was seduced into one of their public confessionals. "Since I joined the Group," a plump youth confided, "and have been in constant touch with God, I've cut down my masturbation from six times to only twice a week."

"Hear! Hear!"—A new birth of religion in the Decline of the West!

"Daren!" A shout restored the yard over the Patapsco. Cader Ayres flung back the steel-gray mop of his hair. "Never try to run a college. Rewards incommensurate with the strain."

Daren brought out the spring water and another chair.

"Best water in Maryland," said Ayres. "To the state senate. Dumb oafs. Because they give a few scholarships…Just had Butler on the phone. Told him the way government is going there won't be much money outside it; and if everybody's got to latch onto the old public tit, they'd better find a way to let us suck without trying to run what they know nothing about. With those metaphors, I think he almost understood me."

Ayres had grown up on a Georgia plantation; and if he had spent his youth in the frame Gothic Negro church by the Oconee River, where in fact he did pass his Sundays, taken by his Mammy to hear the spirituals and the frenzied word of God, he couldn't have absorbed more zeal of the ministry than he did. But he had transformed it into fierce intelligence.

He was a tall man, spare, with a dusky untinted skin and when he gripped the podium and, leaning out over the lecture room, displayed the panorama of history in its waste and tenor, the rush of the dream-led masses down the dark mountain, it was as if he were cracking a whip over the class, driving them down the road where the Spengler of Unalterable Law had driven him before. He endowed cyclical history with vast tragic power, because it was his tragedy; he was wrestling with it in his own being: "Disprove it if you can; if not, 'bare your necks to the blade.' "

"This is a required course," he had told those huge classes back at the University of Virginia. "If you aren't on the dean's list, your attendance is required. That's not my doing; I don't believe in compulsory education; so you needn't listen. The exams are based on the reading list. Read if you like, but don't rustle the pages; sleep if you must, but don't snore." Then he let drive, with a force and edge that made sleep or reading equally improbable.

He liked to take a text, as a preacher would, Thucydides, Polybius, Cicero, Augustine, and by the recurrences of history bring it home, in all its universality, more immediate than the daily press:

> Words had to change their meaning and take that which was given them... The ancient simplicity into which honor so largely entered was laughed down and disappeared; and society became divided into camps in which no man trusted his fellow...

Until that freshman course, Daren had thought of himself as a scientist. The infinite ambition that can awaken pure, without an object, the desire bent and drawn, had first taken nature as its aim. Those nights when he and Dan Byrne would stretch out on the levee (after Daren had discovered his father's three-inch telescope in the attic), the great river flowing by, as the seasons brought round the constellations, Andromeda, Perseus, Orion, Cancer, Hercules, Scorpio, Sagittarius—gazing, while planets, star clusters, nebulae swam into view (and every summer malaria, old Doctor Paul sucking the blood up into a glass tube, like another big mosquito, announcing the wise word that led to quinine, ears roaring, easing chills and fevers)—that pursuit of worlds in space had seemed the ultimate road of mind.

Cader Ayres' first lecture threw everything into doubt: Man-quake. Daren had accepted progress in the terms of his mentors: Jeans' *The Universe Around Us,* where the span of civilization is compared to a postage stamp laid on the mountain of the prehistoric past, and the rational future projected, stamp on stamp, for the Lord knows how many Eiffel Towers. Though even while Jeans wrote, the death wish was lurking in the attic, kindling a torch for civilization with its discontents. And here came Cader Ayres announcing the theorem on the basis of which that was all predictable, the loss of faith, the long postponement, the romantic search and sick personality, the rise of the masses, materialism, communism—Hitler himself an item in the diagnosis, thinking by worse amputation to effect a cure: to banish modern art, Einstein, Jews, banish intelligence, the private soul, all lurking places of the disease he shared; by sheer will to be heroic again. To which Ayres: "Unnatural vices are fathered by your heroism."

"I won't go to any more history lectures," Daren had written Uncle Hazy. "The teacher is a forlorn, weak, pessimistic man."

How anyone could look at that steely archangel leaning across the podium and use the word "weak" was a problem; there was strength enough anyway to draw the unwilling Daren back to session after session and finally up to the platform, where he confronted the teacher with a protest that was almost a cry. And Ayres, who had been through the whole thing himself, smiled at the desperate pupil, sensing how far the battle was joined in his soul, a smile of barbed implication: "When you brought your troubles up here, you broke your apple cart. Don't expect me to pick the things up. They're rotten anyway."

For Daren, Chicago was the redoubt of the position he called modern.

—Sixteen and slight for his age, domed forehead, Hyperion locks, complexion of a British choirboy, he had seemed old enough that summer before college to drive used cars up for the Delta Landing dealer and bring back new ones from the factory, staying between times at the Y (fifty cents a day and food likewise), and see the Century of Progress; that old, yet young enough, entering the gate, to scrunch down, flexing at the knees a little and lifting the peach blossom face, to slip by on half fare. "How old are you, sonny?" And he, using what was left of the falsetto, "I'll be twelve this October." –"Where you come from, boy?"—"I'm from Mississippi, sir." –"By God, they sure grow em big down there"—was waved through. Such a big little boy.

The Hall of Science, the Temple of the Arts—he had glutted himself on that fair ("I understand why a vorld fair," a Viennese told him later, "but why zey hold it so far from ze vorld?"); he had thought its architecture the peer of Greek and Gothic (had not the pamphlets told him so?); he trundled it out for Ayres, evidence of a great culture.

Ayres mentioned the cardboard construction, catch-the-bumpkin show; he compared Alexandrian pavilions. Daren knew nothing of such things. He could have learned from Uncle Hazy, not to mention the family library, but he had rejected that, collecting his own books, which were of science. So the main art he could adduce was the color organ, of which much had been made at Chicago, a new form, combining music and the visual in unexplored dramas of hue and tone.

"At the moment," said Ayres, "it's a fad. But the Parthenon exists; Chartres exists; Dante, Rembrandt, Bach, exist. It's strange you'd take man for granted and think you had only to study stuff. But if you want to speculate about history, you'll have to confront its monuments."

Under the goading voice Leflore had taken culture for his province. To affirm the modern against the challenge of Spengler. Though the reproductions he pinned to his wall, the Early Kingdom Khafre, the Olympia carvings, Giotto's Death of St. Francis, Botticelli, the poetry he began to memorize, the Gregorian and Bach he went to the music room to hear, led him back toward the dawnphase of those cultures whose cyclical contour he was less and less able to deny. After three years, the modern he had started out to defend, the science, too, on which he had won this study abroad, came to him with a *Look Homeward* wail: "O lost and by the wind grieved, ghost, come back again…"

Thirteen more years had passed, and the graying Cader Ayres sat on the cliff over the Patapsco and raised his glass to the light, that spring water Daren had lugged up from the foot of the rock. "God clave a hollow place that was in the jaw, and there came out water," he said. And then:

"At our farm in Georgia, which my sainted sister runs, there was a man who used to install septic tanks so perfect he claimed he would drink what filtered out of them. It was worth buying one to call his hand. But he never failed. He stood there in the green of the old fertilizing; he raised that water against the light, and drank it down. Your spring's like that, the filtrate of this whole crappy town."

The Diaries, too, Daren thought, his eyes wandering to the type writer, were like that. For all one's filtering, there would remain some cesspool tang of the ego from which the liquor flowed. And here he was, not only drinking it himself, but planning to foist it on the world as a marketable refreshment: Stand firm, spread your feet in the lush grass, raise the beaker to the sky, and begin:

"Here's to the politicians," said Cader. "And to this Stoic rock." And drank it down.

He was still giving those lectures in which history opened out like a landscape of the Fall of the Giants: "All that they suffered was great; they were destroyed, as the saying is, with a total destruction…" If he worried sometimes about the effect on action: "Suppose some deluded ass, who bubbles with the Four Freedoms and a world of brotherly love, does the relative good more service?"—he had not yet relinquished the Medusa shield of Truth.

For graduation two days before, his text had come from the Ninth Book of the *Republic:*

When a democracy has drunk too deeply of the strong wine of freedom, anarchy ends by infecting everything. The father descends to the level of his sons; the master fears and flatters his scholars; old and young are alike; and all things are ready to burst with liberty. Such is the fair and glorious beginning out of which tyranny springs.

The people have always some protector whom they set over them and nurse into greatness, Some he kills and others he banishes, always stirring up war that the state may require a leader. Who is valiant, high-minded, wise, is the enemy. So freedom, getting out of all order, passes into the bitterest form of slavery.

When Ayres had tied that onto the hysteria already whipped up in Congress and the press: "Who are the traitors who have lost us the world?"— one awaited the envisaged protector, the Inquisitor.

'Have to get going," he said. "Dean Gheen of State College has asked me to make some more enemies tonight: a panel of administrators on the shortage of good teachers—as if they didn't squelch talent as fast as it appears. And here you sit, with your rock and spring and typewriter. What a life!"

"And where was I three clays ago?" said Daren affectionately. "Slave driver. But I sympathize."

Ayres charged up the hill. Leflore turned hack to the other water, which must be filtered from the confessional purgings of the heart.

2. Can These Bones Live?

ALONG THE PATAPSCO, under the blue beech and alder, Anna had found a place where the ground was a bed of ginger and phlox. She called Leflore from his writing. They climbed down the rock stair and walked into the park.

(Who was this woman beside him? How was he to trace her back past all disagreements and his desire for Jeffrey, restore her to the warmth and humanity in which she had appeared, after the dolls of the Delta and the New Orleans babe, a revelation of nature in the cold frame of Oxford? Should he invoke the earth, which her feet read like braille?

It was during one of the crises that have punctuated the period since the Second World War, and the morning being so clear, more jets than usual were warming up for whatever event they anticipated. They were too high to be anything but dots, almost invisible and barely heard; but their vapors laced the blue sky restlessly. Anna and Daren looked up. Then she led him under the leaf-dense weaving of the grove.

It was what life cried out for, such a roof of branches to hold it to its home, the bed of heart-shaped leaves and purple flowers, to shield us from that danger. And she too, though she thought her politics attuned to the future, was full of backward looking, glad of every hint that the Party might favor handicrafts and nature and the simple life along with mechanized production.

They walked in the shade until they came to a clearing by a sunlit bend in the stream. Then Leflore saw the shimmering. "*Gauze à Marie*" some call it, think "gossamer" derived from that, when the fine strands would settle on the fields of France, brightened with dew like a Madonna's veil.

He had been reading in a paperback about spider migrations, and here they were.

In the updraft along the river webs were gleaming and rising, as the spiders on grass blades spun them out. And when enough exhalation was launched to lift them, they would let go and soar, aim unknown, over the water, to come down to the plop of a fish, or far off on roofs or highways, impossible destinations, taking their chances, driven by the obscure urge of flight.

He looked at Anna, who was always giving her life for such a Utopian gamble; he pointed over the river but said nothing. Why rub her nose in his symbols-that they were all in it together, venturers of the sky's peril, and that the pity of it was enough to stir case-hardened eyes to tears?

Anna left him at his work and started for the bus stop—Baltimore or Washington—the life of the Cause picking up all the time. He sat down to the Journals as before:

He had actually tried in the sports deal—swimming first: the Oxford municipal pool, filled on Sunday, nothing running in or out all week except as it was swum, spat and otherwise performed in by the town fry. On Saturdays it was lent to the university team. A place sacred to the Goddess Cloaca. Daren swam, choked, almost spewed. That was the beginning of a cold that settled into a cough and plagued him all term…

And while he was in that piscina, Anna, on the *Normandie*, sailing for Europe, reaching for the last time, under an ambiguity of soul, at beauty and love—"I had worked in Chicago in the hospital and for socialism until I was sick again. I wanted to do something for the other side of me. Then Mom needed help and Chuck offered it." (Chuck Morgan, capitalist boy-husband who had jumped the gun, got her the abortion, married and lost her to the Party, won her back through Mom and was bringing her to Europe for the art she longed to see.) "We were married already. It only meant trying again. So we came abroad, and there you were…"—Anna would have gone for her dip in the first-class pool of that arty liner, Charles

Boyer and the other notables looking up curiously—where had she come from and what was she doing here, this princess in the hollow tree, this Cinder-girl at the court ball?

Except, when she hauled out of the water and put back the streaming flaxen hair, there was nothing of fairy tale; she was actual, as the barker at the World's Fair said of the real live two-headed baybee: "In the flesh, and alive."

Estranged, however, from the show in which she moved, wideeyed, the gamin in the Chaplin film. And when her kind-hearted football-Hercules Chuck gave up the punching bag and they walked to the great salon for tea with his sisters (*"Oui, madame, le décor est très chic et très moderne"*), though pleased to be approaching the carved-up continent she had dreamed about, her face had the distant look of Heidi the goat-girl; her heart was with Mom in the slums reading by the winter stove—Bellamy, say: How society is a coach which the masses drag painfully along, the rich riding in comfort on the high seats, only afraid of being pulled off by those climbing up from below. She gazed at that Babylonian splendor, wasting itself, a few more years, to pamper rich fools; she walked among them, not of them, foreseeing the burnt-out hulk rolled over, subsiding in New York Harbor.

And Jeffrey?

She had learned to swim at Torquay and Lyme Regis, where her parents went for the holidays. But near Tavistock on what had been her father's estate was a concrete pool, not unlike that of Daren's Oxford purgation, but out-of-doors. It had been left over from an army camp of the First World War, and it might as well have been a shell hole filled with seep-water, except the green mantle that would otherwise have grown on it was always being churned up by a snake-belly, frog-leg whiteness of arms, trunks, thighs, a rout of naked villagers. Or rather, when one stared, as Jeffrey did, at that eelpot of outrageous flesh, one saw those boys were indeed clothed, but in homemade cotton G-strings so brief they barely hid the essence.

The new fourth parlormaid, red-headed Maggie, had slipped Jeffrey down to watch the races. Maggie's cousin was in charge. He wore a bowler hat and genuine white woolen swimsuit. Maggie introduced him: "This is Mister Artle." All the children called him Mister, but of course Jeffrey couldn't; they knew that. Besides, the name must be Hartle, and she was doubtful which pronunciation to use. But the funny little man solved it right off, grinning: "My name's Bill, too, miss. You can call me that." Like the lizard in *Alice* in *Wonderland,* how lovely, Bill.

After the races she helped with the instruction; in fact, she went often those summers. She never saw Bill in the water. He told her secretly he couldn't swim; anyway, he taught by a device that kept him on firm turf. He had a bicycle tube tied to a long rope. They would slip a kid in there and then push him off the deep end. What a choking, while Bill dragged the novice through the water, incessantly yelling at him: "Clip them legs together! Clip them legs!"

And there stood the elegant Jeffrey, Mr. Artle's young assistant, deftly coiling the rope, or when it looked as if they had a victim who was doing more than just drowning, joining in the excited cry: "Clip them legs…"

Though, as the dripping white sacrifice was hauled out, bleeding, like as not, under the arms from the sawing of the rope and tire, she could never quite bring herself to clap the sufferer, as Bill did, on the back or buttock, though sometimes she took up the chant: "Jolly good, old chap, jolly good." Nor did she recover from the first revulsion at the pool of peeled brawn, or forget, when she went once into the women's dressing room looking for Maggie (like any well brought-up girl Jeffrey had been taught to undress, even in the private dark of the night nursery, in the Victorian way, slipping her dress off as the nightgown was slipped on, synchronized, so not the smallest gap hinted at the forked animal we are) the shock of those bulging and hanging mole-spotted hairy bodies passing a towel from one to the other, their skin-soiled damp and common rag. The plight of flesh would always fill her with compassion, but with as much reserve.

"Never touch another person unless it is necessary."

"Don't gesture; don't show your emotions; never laugh if a smile will do."

"Straight is the line of Duty,/ Curved is the line of Beauty;/ Follow the first and thou shalt see/ The latter ever followeth thee."

Daren flung back the chair and paced the Patapsco cliff. Like Saul he had raised a spirit that shook him. Everything which had come into its own last September in Wisconsin at The Door was breaking back like waves on the rocks over Green Bay, here on this rock, where the buckeye and the English ivy, Jeffrey reminders, flaunted their love and her denial. *Duty.*

He saw her moonlit whiteness and dark hair, that night under the aerie, slip from the limestone, where in the laps and hollows of the waves a score of moons were running over the water like bright apple-smellers...

The violence with which he put it from him would have thrown him necessarily from any circuit of avoidance into his own deepest involvement with water:

They could only be called blue holes because they had always received the sky, but their color shared green and brown, the earth where old floods had gouged them, the willows, cottonwoods, water oaks, gums, with which their shores were hemmed. The algal gray of the gar slides through them unnoticed, murky in the deeper murk; when the moccasin slithers off the mudbank, he goes from like into like, equally camouflaged; the leatherback sliding from a log disappears before he is out of sight. A white man hardly belongs there, not even a tanned boy; his flesh will show through corpselike. They had never called it the Blue Hole, but the Bluery Hole, Old Bleary.

Yet none of that had prevented its being for them a place of recreation—even for Daren, whose life must always revolve with a sense of something to be encountered, not around the Blue Hole itself, but where the vein of Panther Burn broke from that amoeboid spreading, fringed with towering cypress, swollen trunks and knees, a still channel, which the road to Ararat crossed on the iron trestle——that bridge the car had missed when he was a boy.

Half a mile away, on the dirt road, where the Blue Hole approached the river and the ground between was mounded from the old flood, the clay and sand shaved down steep under trees to the deepest hole. That had become a reference point of his being, not just of the old terror, but of something which, however equivocal, was a kind of floating peace.

One could say it was the same water. And perhaps treading it touched on the plowing rituals of primitive tribes, to sow seed in the devouring mother. He had swum there with his sister the summer before Oxford, and they had taken off their clothes and gone gliding through the alluvial water, so soft it made your skin slippery like the skin of a fish. They had clung to a log, facing each other, and their limbs had met, sliding together; they had stared, then laughed, drawing back, not denying—they made no decision—smilingly they drifted apart…

"I had two sisters," Horner confided as they walked to the soccer field. "No doubt I still have, though I haven't seen them for years. That was in Australia. They've had lovers since, married and made cuckolds in the usual fashion. They were the first I enjoyed. Prudes wouldn't admit that— pretend it's a sin. To fall in love with a sister, as in that poky old play, is a bore. But to sport together is the nicest thing in the world. Dear Meg called it fraternizing. She showed me the erotica in my fathers library and taught me ever so many things. 'Come on,' she said, 'I want to do some more fraternizing.' After two years I was ready to educate the younger. It worked out decently for us all."

Soccer was Daren's second attempt to play those sports everybody said he should. For two hours it was floundering in the slush under cold rain, bareheaded, barehanded, in khaki shorts, drenched and shivering, trying to boot a ball. He hadn't known there was a game where you could hit the ball with your head, shoulders, feet, elbows, knees, buttock-bone, belly-bone, but never dare touch it with your hands, and his hands were all he had a mind to touch it with; so buying spiked shoes and deepening his cough until it sounded like consumption didn't help the college; even the captain of the second team must have felt loyalty could be carried too far.

Until then Daren had looked askance at those British steeping like mackerel in the long tubs, snoozing, drunk with the heat, smoking, the ashes falling in, shaving in the same water, then crawling out unrinsed to dry on a towel as big as a blanket and shuffle over bleak quads to a fire and tea. Today he joined the decadence, though he didn't smoke, his whiskers weren't worth shaving, and, not to feel too much like Seneca opening his veins, he closed off with a cold shower.

Then he settled for cycling, as he had threatened to do—an affair of the heart: through the green valley of the Isis, over the arched bridge, past thatched cottages and under the beech wood on the hill. At Wytham he went into the inn for tea. After Galsworthy's story "The Apple Tree," he was always looking for the lonely Welch country maid. "Served," he wrote, "by a young but hideous girl. If English women have any sex, they keep it concealed."

"I want to cycle those quaint lanes with you, put up at snug old inns." The voice from New Orleans. He stamped it out like brush fire and walked to the abbey ruin, stood at a stone archway brooding over a rudely cut date that looked like 1372, and repeated the lines:

"When I have seen by time's fell hand defaced
The rich proud cost of outworn buried age…"

It was there that he decided to change his course to English.

Law had been the tradition of the family, but his father had found it sullied, and Uncle Hazlewood called it the cross he had to bear. To Daren it had seemed a trade, and what he wanted was knowledge. But as Ayres had taught him, stars and atoms weren't enough. There was a creature midway in size who inhabited a realm of powers bearing names of demons and gods. One hunted him by art-traces and reached a threshold inscribed "The Eternal Self"—not a practical pursuit; but had anybody ever called the Lefiores a practical tribe?

"Don't be faddish, Mr. Leflore," the humorless dry physics tutor warned, scheduling days of lectures, nights of calculus, vacations stuck in the lab. "A research physicist delves deeply in a narrow field."

Gloomy days, swatting at math, losing out, drifting into Shakespeare:

> To the bookstore for relief: Greek sculpture, Florentine Frescoes; bought a Nonesuch Blake. Back to calculus, looking every minute to see how time passed, or rather stood. At 7:10, chapel, the peace of old responses. Then Hall, Hardy complaining of studying Donne; I of not being able to do it for him. With Horner afterwards, to avoid math—tales of his summer conquests ("Give me libertinism, or give me death!") told for the idolizing circle.

Of the big black pill ("Creosote maybe, for worming horses") bought under the name "Preservative" as a contraceptive suppository for the French girl in the family where he was staying. "But it melted," Horner cooed, "and I left her that night scrubbing at stains which all great Neptune's oceans would not wash away."

Pitt-Beauchamp, booby-peer of the many names ("He has a job," Uncle Hazlewood wrote, "to live up to his famous ancestors"), tried to match it; but all he could fish up was falling in the Cherwell when he was punting drunk, and how he had gone on to dine at the George, dripping wet. Bravo! But it didn't measure up—much less to his great ancestors.

No, Daren decided, standing before Wytham Church, it was madness to do anything except what love fired. He cycled in a fury back to Oxford to get the warden's permission to change schools. Next morning, at matriculation, the sun broke into the Divinity School hall, lighting the mullioned panes; the fan-vaulted space became a cut-glass jewel.

Then to Leslie Cameron, English tutor, Highland Scot with tangled hair and elusive smile, books, a horn phonograph, records, Botticelli on the wall. The assignment, Chaucer, wellspring of English undefiled. Daren left whistling all the themes of *The Magic Flute;* but for the quad's sedateness he would have shouted them aloud. He cycled over country roads, up a hill, walked through orchards under the orange sun. He sprang into the air, catching at boughs; he gathered pippins to roast at his fire.

Far from that, now, grappling with the typewriter under the buckeye tree, was this a work of delight or another damned grind? And if delight—as in the configurations that are: rock oaks massive on the slope, sapling locusts down the

Servant Fred had a shape from the first, comic as a monkey-puzzle tree. But he never developed. The same old scout: baby-pink skin, white moustaches, blue starry eyes, boasting of his sixty-five years and how much better he could climb stairs than the younger set, not hearing his own breath whistle like a steam engine through his gap teeth. He would come in at eleven or twelve in the morning and find Leflore stretched out on the sofa reading, still in his dressing gown (for he used to make roll call by pulling on pants, scarf and gown over his pajamas), "What, sir! Not dressed yet!"

Always the incredulous shock. As when Daren tried to prop the kettle on the fire with a brush he thought was wire, and Fred came in as he snatched it off burning: "You've got the wrong thing there, sir. You're damaging that, don't you know? Here's what you want to stir the fire, sir. This is a pokah!" Brandishing it as if he knew an even better use for it than stirring a fire.

The dying gasp of serfdom. A man as venerable as King Lear, with silver hair, and you yelled at him, "Fred," and he puttered around with his dustrags, cleaning up after boys whom he called his gentlemen and Mr. So-and-so and Sir. Like Rastus and Uncle and Step-and-fetch-it in the South. Yet how mild beside that. How everything went satanic down in that Blue Hole swamp, where class and color tangled in an anguish it seemed nobody could ever untie:

Elmonia under the fig tree. His Mammy. Strange if he hadn't loved her. But their love lay under a curse. He swung through the branches, gathering the ripest figs. He reached far out for a wrinkled purple bag. It was too soft, sour, with a vest of mold. The devil entered him at that touch. Though if the victim had been Dan Byrne or Daren's sister June or his brother Vail, you could have called a fig from the sky slapstick. So the devil crept in by the curse that was already there. Before the fig struck, Daren was in Elmonia's place and back again in his, living the relationship history had saddled them with. Then it splapped and spread oozy over the broad upturned face, in which the look he had foreseen came, more grieved than angry, more shamed than both; and in the silence he heard how the slow heavy tones would give the event the cast he had least intended, but known, as the fig fell, it must assume: "Because I'm black—to 'little me—who love you so."

Why stir up social clouds when it was so different in England? Fred, cheery, everything bright, as in a comic play: jumping from Wally Simpson's affair to all relations between the sexes: "Speaking of that, sir, it was worse in the old days. They used to 'ave women in their rooms all night, sir."

"Why'd they give it up?"

"Well, there was diseases goin round. From the girls, sir. The gent'men was going to the 'orspital all the time, sir. *Venerable diseases*, they calls them, sir."

As if the God-search of world and man in which every American from the Puritans down had been fevered: Edwards, Jefferson, Thoreau, Hawthorne, Melville, Whitman, Twain, James were laid to rest, while one rehearsed the trvial amenities of class and dialect through a three-year cultivated withdrawal—sonnets, aristocracy and madrigals.

What else was the whole society of college effete who stalked on the stage, like a cast for *Chrome Yellow* or *Point Counter Point*: between-war sophisticates, old fossils, romantics, fools:

"M'steuh L'fleauagh, M'steuh L'fleauagh!" sung out in an accent as artificial as the gardens of Versailles. Roll call. Leflore had not even recognized his own name. It was the Snub-Rector (Sub-Rectum, Jim preferred), and before long there would be tea in his rooms: the limp hand extended, the affected bland face commiseratively smiling: "Another hour of tedium, eh?"—though what he said was: "How d'you dy-eao-uh? Very pleasant d-a-e-y-u-h," first fast and high, then sliding, grunting and straining his way through the more cherished vocables, as if he were having a bowel movement.

And the gentle old rector telling of New College in the time when he was first named don there and the great absent-minded Spooner met him at such a tea. They talked at length and seemed to get acquainted; but the next day Spooner saw him in the quad and strode over. "By the by," he said, "I'd like you to come to dinner this evening, meet a new don, named Casson."—"Sir," said the future rector, "I am Casson."—"Oh, never mind, dear chap," mooned Spooner, "Come along anyway."

The other students at the tea, like Daren, came from a distance. Besides Hardy and Horner, Wolfgang Hart, Third Reich Scholar—to whom Daren: "Then you live on my stair?" Yes, as it turned out, in the luxury suite on the ground floor. An opening, a chance to talk the language. Wolfgang was heir to the best in German culture. Dürer could have drawn him. His father, the bürgermeister on the mantle, showed a face of philosophy and progress. There were always brandies and liqueurs, fruits, nuts, great bunches of cut flowers. Wolfgang (named for Mozart) loved what he called "the finer things." But the request that they read Goethe's Faust never got off the ground. He read only the Berlin newspaper and his engineering.

"Your American press is controlled by the Jews; it never gives you the truth. Hitler is a great leader. (Try some German chocolate.) The nation stands behind him. Look at the last election. Do you think you're the only people who have elections? (It's wholesome with figs and nuts.) Picture us after Versailles: communism, inflation. Now we're strong, everybody working. It's a great age for Germany. (A little cherry brandy!) You think we wouldn't vote for the Fuhrer?"

A likable, generous chap. Who could know what to believe? "Though I would trust him more," Daren wrote, "if he claimed some other *Geist* than *Kirsch.*"

And the dreadful Boer (boar? bore? boor?) who, on the introduction of that tea, would charge into Daren's room at all times, huge, pimple-pocked, a perfect Tartuffe, crying in loud gutturals: "Lett uss go, mann!" to drag you off to some Evangelical chapel, inciting your southern blood the whole way to the praise of God and the Great White Race. Of course, he would join the Oxford Group: how could he maintain those rivers of gas but by being directly inspired (as Swift had it, blown-into) by the Holy Ghost?

Though he gave the reins as before to ambition and pride, letting morality pace along to sweeten the partnership.

> Pourpus the Boer is vexed that I shall waste my holiday bumming around Italy in cheap hotels. I should take advantage of the opportunity we are given to visit British families of the blood. He has lined up several where he can study manners and elevate himself, dreaming the while that some rich daughter, as his chuckles let out, will be thrown by his countenance, where the carbuncles are big enough to trip her.
>
> His last stay will be in Ireland, and he displays a letter he has written to the president of the Irish Free State: "The common problems facing Ireland and the Orange Free State make it to our mutual advantage to meet. My knowledge may illuminate yours and your experience could supplement my own."
>
> This man has a great future. He is ass enough to be the president of any free state in the world.

Would every thread weave back into the web? Any day now Daren might pick up the paper and read some racist proclamation out of South Africa, and before he got to the uttering minister's name, smell out the style, and looking down have his prediction half fulfilled; it would be that same Pourpus, on the make, muddying up the drinking waters of the world.

Or as the records from conquered Germany came to light, *The Rhodes Journal* would publish the vindication of a Reich Scholar, one who had given his life in the plot against Hitler; and Daren would sit marveling at the potentialities of man: what had brought illumination to creature-comfort Wolfgang? Had ideas finally broken through, some seed of Oxford, some philosophic insight from the father? Or had the actual hardening left a man of such decency no other choice?

Background, against which the characters were gathering: Jim Hardy, Hank Brown, Tutor Cameron. Let a few more be added: Jim Hardy's mother, Cameron's niece Jeffrey, peasant Anna, pacing the valley of dry bones with her promise of love and humanization—if not a plot, at least a *tableau vivant* might emerge.

3. In the Liver Vein

THE WEATHER veered round: cloud and rain. The window offered little beyond gray-green. But in the inner space of the room the chipper small reckoning of day to day bubbled up from the seething heritage of the self and the age. "Saturated with sardonic herbs, we are dying, and yet we laugh."

Like the World's Fair, the Concourse of all Nations, flags, sunlight, the blue lake breaking in waves, as airy-bright as Impressionism, and beneath it what Impressionism also sparkled in defiance of: Marx's pit of labor, Van Gogh's Potato Eaters, Courbet's Lesbians, Cezanne's first lurid Orgy and Rape, Nietzschean Rodin—deprivations of inner and outer, breaking into motion, color, plein-air. No wonder Van Gogh went mad.

So the Fair at the lake-bright edge of Chicago, and over the tracks: asphalt, bread lines, apple-polishers, bums ("Gimme a nickel for some coffee; gimme a dime for a bed"), gangsters so much in the news yon ducked every time you heard a blowout or a backfire, stockyards (a gross man rushing up as the last steer slumps down: "When they gonna slug the cattle? I gotta see em slug cattle. Doggone it! That's the third time I come and they stopped sluggin em. Now I gotta come again"), those slums where Anna grew up, her Mother Port, to which she must have returned, even then, in fever, nursing private and social wrongs—Chicago, with everything hatching under it.

Sex even. Who could make sense of that, who had, since Adam and Eve? Since Lilith? Sally Rand stripping herself down to the big bubble she balanced like the manipulated world. Miss America from some year or other exhibited in the nude. A pure, clean show, turning prurience into art.

You entered the lighted auditorium and faced velvet curtains. You saw nothing but America filing in for Miss America. Until everybody had paid the half dollar and the room was full. Then the curtain rose. And still you saw nothing but a cheesecloth hanging, which (the stage being dark and out here light) concealed everything. The trick was by illumination. As the ceiling lights dimmed, the stage lights came on. And there on a pedestal, like Giambellini's Truth but without even the mirror, completely naked but for the intervening and legalizing gauze, stood beauty itself, the perfect form. While the barker's voice, of all things, began to enumerate her measurements, height, weight, bust measure, waist measure, hip measure, thigh measure, calf measure, ankle measure. She never moved. The lights built to a climax, then began to fade, the enumeration ran its course, the audience lights came up again, obscuring; you faced a cheesecloth, "a veil of lawn, about her decent shoulders drawn"; then the velvet curtains also fell.

Yes, but as rumor had it, those who paid more, hundreds of times more, came closer… An indigent Mississippian slouched from the pavilion, ashamed to have squandered half a dollar for so brief a glimpse of nothing but beauty, took refuge, say, in the Museum of Natural History. Or if the bare-dugged cave women, the pendant ballocks and erectile parts of a labyrinth of animal males flung him back restless on the same quest, there were sideshows with hookey tonkers and belly-twitchers of all kinds. Though you did not reach the bottom at the Fair grounds. It was out where he walked one night, in Anna's neighborhood, that finally by rumor and asking you found your way past a saloon and whorehouse alley to the show of all shows, the one you had heard about as far off as the Mississippi Delta: where a greasy fat woman, like a Mexican contortionist or snake charmer, took it from a little long-eared donkey, as she was wheeled under on a pad, and he, corrupted, as she caught it in her hands and gathered it in, lunged over her, foining.

While the boy at the Fair gate next morning scrunched down: "I'll be twelve in October." Twelve? Why he was the great god of Sefar in the Sahara rock paintings, all prong and balls.

Sex. Almost right to hush it up, keep it under, as our ancestors did;

for when it appears what else gets a show? It takes over the page, the book, as Freud knew too well, civilization itself, all other search, all other meaning, gone up in holocaust, as when lightning struck the shithouse: "Foh! *Foeda est.* Give me an ounce of civet, to sweeten my imagination."

His life was not to be given to generation, and yet his body, as in the Leonardo drawing, legs spread, arms raised, formed the wheel of Vitruvian man; and for him as for all, the parts were the center, the hub into which our temporal being time and again withdraws, and from which, like a sea anemone, bodies, hearts and minds delicately unfold.

He had been in love since he was a boy—at lunchtime in the schoolyard, on the bench around the trunk of the sycamore, lifting furtive glances to the goddess, many and one, she of the honeycolored hair.

His mother had taught him to read before he could remember, and he started the first grade when he was four. "Let him try," said his father; "if it's too much he'll drop out."—"Does he know the alphabet?" asked the principal. –"Greek or English?" laughed Prentiss Leflore.

So he was always with bigger boys and older girls. With the girls he was a shy adorer. Year after year. Then came his father's death, his mother's drowning.

The vapid love life of adolescence came to focus in the big stone lion at the door of Bess Hargreaves' house, couchant, paws in front of him, a discomfited look on his face as he eyed Daren and all the other entering inadequate beaux: "OK, boy, you try; but I tried, and I got made a fool of." Dear fragile Bess, so much the eternal debutante, she would come home blubbering to Momma the night of her honeymoon—to have loved her for years and never had the gumption to tell her so: dates, drives, Cokes, junior cotillion, to cut in and say something about a nice evening, and be cut off by somebody equally piddling. Was this the mess of pottage we had taken for our phallic birthright, this dumb Presbyterian lion staring us down: "I who have bungled everything, sex, love, the moon, the flat land, the river have been made official guardian of this portal."

In high school he wrote his first poems. The young English teacher invited him to her rooms, praised his efforts, showed him a sonnet of her own. She came from a plantation by Lake Austramere, and in the poem cypress plumed the evening where long light over fields caught the rhythmic falling of the hoes, and songs of stark threnetic passion were heard down the endless furrows. Among a bunch of battered field hands chopping weeds, she stood like "Ruth amid the alien corn"; and her name was Ruth, poor dear, though he called her Miss Fairlamb; and when she caught Daren's murmured response (for there was a dream beauty in the poem), she could hardly restrain her tears.

The next week she gave him a poem she had just finished, sat while he read it, her arm trembling faintly against his. She had illuminated it like a page from Blake, southern neo-Greek, the poem in the sky-window of a watercolor scene: on the saved side an altar with the statue of Athena, on the other a comet-haired nude with the crescent coronet of Astarte. Between them stood a vestal holding a garland and a knife. This daughter of lost columns and slaves, this temple virgin, was confessing herself a weak woman—

> Keyed to strange sedition, powerless
> Against thy sister Cytherea's call.

And what she asked of Minerva was to bless the sacrifice of the filleted self, "to free this mind from body's thrall."

If the phallic blade plunging into the heart hinted at another sequel, the stone lion precluded it. Daren read, Ruth trembled. That fall she moved to another school and he went to college.

Everything opened so fast, books, science, nature—like the paths in the Ragged Mountains. Solitude was enough. One Sunday he took a run before supper. In his linen suit, he kept to the road, up Observatory Mountain. On the way down an open flivver passed.

"Hi, beautiful!" Laughter. He waved. A cry: "Let me out of here." The towhead stopped the car. A skirt sailed over the side. The car went on, still crammed, girls to spare. "Hi! I thought I'd walk with you."

"You'll have to walk fast." She trotted against his stride. See the bouncing bellibone. Soon a footpath led into the woods.

"I'm tired," she said. "Let's stretch out."

"I came for exercise."

"I'll show you an exercise." She took his arm. A strapping girl. "I'll pull you."

"Catch me then." He lit out down the hill like the Gingerbread Boy…

Summers he fell back into the vapid dance ways—denying the octopus we are, mouth, beak, eyes, brain planted in the generative center.

His last year the student magazine featured a purity test: Do you smoke, drink, have you kissed, petted, couched—increasing point losses for "once," "more than once," "habitually." Daren and his shy friend Ross hit the top, almost virginal. They agreed to run a race, who could shed most virtue in fourteen days, the prize a copy of that forbidden thriller, James Joyce's *Ulysses*.

Smoking came easy. He had only to work his mouth like a bellows to puff through a pack with no more discomfort than when he sniffed the chlorine he had made in the chemistry lab. Three times, they had allowed, would go for habitually. Daren smoked habitually and gave it up for good.

But drink required inhaling. And who would draw the line of drunkenness? They decided to face that together. Neither beer nor strong drink pleased them. Only White Virgin, a native sweet wine, the honeyed girl on the label auguring well for the rest of their Dare. They got it chilled, and one evening, under budding elms on the lawn, music drifting from a phonograph in Ross' room, they sat and sipped until their wits were in a warm muddle and they proved how drunk they were by failing to walk a line drawn on the flagstones along the colonnade.

But the crux was to get a woman, and they were no help to each other there. If Leflore had joined a fraternity, he might have nicked his innocence before. He called in two friends, Delta Pies, John Lovelady (the name urged it) and Joe Deal, who owned a car. A goat-party was to set them up with free booze, then Lynchburg, as Lovelady said, "The white-slave capital of the world," to which Joe Deal: "They got greases in the creases, them gals."

The basement, low, smoky, dark; the floor covered with paper cups, liquor, broken glass; a crowd milling around kegs and a bar. A clutch of off-key singers swayed in time, slipped and fell to the sog. What wild ecstasy. Leflore got a mason jar with whiskey, a lot of mint syrup and ice.

"Hey!" Joe pulled him into a corner. "Why drive all that way Lynchburg?" A sound question, drunk as he was. "We got a piece in the attic. Shh!" He stumbled for the stair.

It seemed they had pieces in a number of rooms, but not for the general. Under the gable, though, on a lumpy iron bed, sprawled the open etcetera. Manned; one saw only the puppets dallying. Then the deck was cleared, briefly. The girl of Observatory Mountain. He could have had her when she was fresher.

Vacated, again she sprawled. Seamy side out. Asleep? But she rose on her elbow, groping. Daren got her drink off the chair. She drained it. "Hi, beautiful." A wan little smile. The glass fell. She caught him in her arms. "Come on," she moaned, and sank back, drawing him down. Then she went limp. Passed out.

To give up or go on? He was spared a decision. Lovelady had been hunting them. "That sperm-sponge," he said. "Let's go to Lynchburg. They're inspected anyway. Come on, Joe, you drunk fool."

They drove, plugging at a mason jar Lovelady had brought along. A frame house on the edge of colored town, porches latticed and screened. Knock and it will be opened. Madam was a gypsy, her dress cut so low before and behind, you saw a deep crease between her bubs and when she turned another between her shoulder blades. You wondered how many of those fat creases the bitch had. A skipping of rabbits by moonlight; girls led into a parlor so Victorian, Daren thought of Aunt Willi Mari's in Reading. Joe grabbed his favorite. "I'm Joe Deal, honey; and this is the raw deal." He unrolled the nether proboscis, "We've brought you a lovely cherry."

Daren, however, got a girl he wouldn't have chosen, and she took him to a stuffy boudoir, where she proceeded ("Barber, barber, shave a pig") through some very professional motions. As the Swiss novitiate said in the joke: *"Die Bewegungen sind lächerlich, aber das Ganze ist unbehauptlich mässig kostspiel."*

The others were at play. Lovelady's nifty had brought him into the hall (innocent both as Adam and Eve) to display a peculiarity on which she quoted a limerick about a corkscrew and a left-handed turn, and indeed he was caudaflected, crooked as a ram's horn; but she said she could manage. "Take it baby," cried Lovelady, "and shake well while using."

Joe's door was open. His skinny was astride. "Let him alone," said Lovelady; "he's had it."

"He wants it again; don't you Joe?" she stretched him against her, for reach.

"You want it," said Lovelady. "And three dollars a throw."

"I like the feel and I like the money. No harm in that. Get it up, Joe."

Leflore dressed and went to the parlor. If he'd had any more money he wouldn't have blown it. And there, in filmy negligee, his own dream girl drifted to the sofa, oval face, sad, sweet eyes that stuck him like a pig. They looked at each other as in the silent films. "What's your name?"—"Leflore."—"You're beautiful, Leflore. I wish I'd been the one to get your cherry."

Madam bustled up like the barker in a sideshow: "Pay your money and take your girl."

"I'm out of money."

"I don't care; I love him anyway."

"No screwing without money. I don't run that kind of a joint." They kissed until the others were done.

There was still beer at the fraternity, though the juleps were gone. Leflore gagged at the taste, but swilled and swilled until he could hardly stagger home, and lost everything in the gutter in front of the house. He went to sleep dreaming of that mountain girl's eyes, her tears.

His corruption, though it won the sin race, gave no hints at any usual procedure. He went on searching in the unlikeliest places—New Orleans, England—for a Welch innocent or Rima the bird-girl.

Conceive an Oxford concert of old music, burbling pipes, a cellist wrapping her legs around a viol, abandoned face and timid tones. But the singers take the cake: spinsters leaning out stiff from the hips, hands clasped on the bosom, simpering: "There they dance, there they prance," ("If dey could shake dey tails like dey shake dey voices," Hank murmuring, in what he called the intromission, "dey be de sexiest in de universe.") From madrigals to ballads to small glees, with a romantic air on words by Mary Coleridge:

> The lake lay blue beneath its hill
> O'er it as I looked there flew,
> Across the waters, cold and still,
> A bird, whose wings were palest blue.

Some relief to scribble:

> And as he flew, he dropped a pill;
> You can deny it if you will;
> But surely it is very true,
> The pill itself was palest blue.

To stand after the concert on Carfax, looking for Jim Hardy, as the crowd surged by: high-talking horse-faced dames, schoolgirls as big as Leflore, but retarded by climate and immurement, having never dated or danced, cased to the pigtails in those gray and blue gymslips they wear from year to year, until nothing conceals their long bony legs but black stockings insufferably plain—to watch them, puzzling: "Is it the school diet of suet and spuds that makes them all shapeless as beeves?" Until the dregs of the crowd discover no Jim, and Daren starts for his college, dreaming of Tahitian nights, Dorothy Lamour, *"Luxe, calme, et volupté."*

Horner was the hopeful Don Juan. "Neu good," he protested in stage Cockney, "for a bleuke not to dip 'is wick neauw and then." He went on about a woman he knew in South Africa, who had a python called Baby, used to crawl right into the bed. "Don't mind him. He's only practicing his squeeze."

The first prey was a bearded student who lived in digs, had a Gramophone and a little mistress. Music and school tie were the bond, but the aim was to detach the mistress—naturally, for Daren's use—such was

Horner's good-natured concern. "Greater love hath no woman than this," he intoned, "that she lay down her body for her friend." But all an evening of sly glances produced was one flash in the pan: that when Horner told the host: "Your beard is becoming," the little mistress took it up, "Becoming a nuisance." Something short of a general defection.

When they got back to college it was eleven-thirty, which would have meant knocking in and paying a fine. The accepted route into Gloucester, by the Fellows' Garden, over two walls and a set of revolving spikes and into the washroom window, might have been tedious for nine pence. Daren's room was one flight above the street. He ran up a gutter, crawled on the Gothic moldings to his casement, opened it and was in. "Tomorrow," Horner sang after him, "I'll buy a rope."

The second lead was an industrialist who had known Horner's father. A daughter and her friend were spoken of, both itching for love. The Lotharios cycled one evening up Boar's Hill. The house was formal; the only access to the dates was *en famille*. The daughter was plain and silent. The visitor, indeed, was a Burne-Jones beauty with the hopeful name of Vivia Champaigne; but she had profited so much from English girls' school, she thought conversation was the art of cutting men to size. She sat in the center of a love seat, knitting, while the bolts of her wit whistled around the sex in general and Colonials and Americans in particular. Not even Horner got the impression she was amorous.

So they staked everything on the big affair, a "Sherry, ETC.," Horner was giving to pay back his friends. And now something real was on the horizon, none of that cold British meat, but an Egyptian, one Scheherazade, capable of a thousand and one nights. To prepare himself, Leflore studied the Eastern miniatures in the Bodley: a lady with a face as it were the full moon, swimming by night through a lily pond, to get to her lover on the far shore.

More cock-your-tails than sherry. Polite drinking. Nobody boasts here, as at Virginia, of getting drunk. It comes as a regrettable surprise. Like the failure of the League of Nations.

Scheherazade was looking at me and the other men of the room somewhat as Nefertiti does in the painted bust. I was sitting by her, but what could I do?

"My vegetable love should grow/Vaster than empires, and more slow."

Horner had arranged for me to take her to dinner, get the first shot. But as he came over to shake her hand, she inclined against him, smelling a flower he wore in his lapel. He clasped her as a buttonhook clasps a button and backed across the room into a closet where coats were hung. I stood on one leg and then on the other, like a crane who finds no fish but will not leave the pond.

Then I took her to dinner and afterwards to *Rhodes of Africa,* as dull a movie as I ever saw, leaving the rest to my betters.

About two, while I was leafing through Faust before going to bed, a few pebbles hit the window, and I heard the feeble voice of Horner asking to be let in. He hasn't bought that rope, and he can't climb; so I had to tie my sheets together to hoist him up.

If "Sherry, ETC.," netted so little (for Daren, anyway), what could be expected of the Rhodes reception soon after?

A dismal assemblage. One would think the devil's dam had whelped these ladies. The better to set off one, seen and lost sight of.

It was in a round robin to stimulate circulation. You pass from pillar to post and dance with what the gong catches you on.

First, one of the matrons who haunt these affairs. She served herself like a dumpling and huddled me into a waltz. By the utmost stretch of arm I was able to lodge my hand under her shoulder, where it seemed imbedded in a kind of moist putty; so that reaching so far and encompassing so little, I felt like the tenor Melchior when he plays Tristan to an equally grand Iseult, and they discover that the fiercest ardor will just enable them to touch bellies and hands.

The virtue of these dances is the gong. But what should take me next but a creature of incalculable height, legs alone the reach of my meager body. Seizing me around the neck from above, she strode backward, dragging me stumbling, a rodent to a monster's lair.

I took the third for a paradise after that—dumpy, even-paced. But she had a decayed corsage as big as a cabbage on her shoulder. Like a civet cat it fumed in my face. Before I could get clear I was almost in a swoon.

Through which a braided Gretchen appeared, smiling. She took me by the hand. Telepathy? The gong-striker should have brought down the hammer with a clang to shake the walls. But silence. I passed on to more of the old ills.

Only when the party was over and I was talking to the Warden by the stair, she came down with her coat. How is it in the Klopstock poem?

> She gazed on me; her being hung
> With this, her gaze, upon my being,
> And round us was Elysium.

The same Anna who now joined Daren at the close of the Patapsco day. He had seen her as the Gothic maiden across the dividing stream. And he would not have conceived of her bringing him anything other than the desired smile Guinevere brought Launcelot. It had taken years to learn how much more general her force was. And though that force had become a thorn in his flesh, his flesh remained what she had humanized.

Today she had marched in Washington again and had the feel of making history. "But the violence of the rulers," she said. "A big man arguing at me, shaking his fist. One bat of that and I'd be a goner. Then one of our students stepped in. 'Leave the lady alone.' While I melted into the crowd—thousands, singing for peace:

> Ban the Bomb!
> End the War!
> Hand in hand
> Around the world!"

She lifted up her voice and sang. Like the Y-girls with their crummy camp tunes; "This little light of mine; I'm gonna let it shine, let it shine." It was laugh or cringe. Daren laughed. And still she smiled.

"My poor Leflore. You're too aesthetic. And what have you done today?"

He showed her the pages.

"That tiresome sex stuff. I used to love four letter words whispered in the ear. American writers have spoiled that. They ought to have better things to think about."

He remembered a time when that gleaming hair (her mother used to liken it to milkweed down) fell on his face, and she breathed: "They call that bad, and it's the only good thing there is, the only thing good in itself alone."

"Anyway," she glowed, "I promised we'd go to a buffet on Frederick Road." Humanity, the mother-earth from which she bounced back stronger. As if that inevitable political rally were a pastoral wedding feast. "They say Laszlo Brod will be there."

Hungarian refugee scholar at Oxford, his father had fought with the Red Army under Béla Kun. Now Laszlo had been called back from State Department work in Austria. It would be good to see him again and talk about the thirties and what it was like when he went to drive an ambulance for the Loyalists in the Spanish Civil War, and whether, if history had taken a slightly different turn here or there, the torment of a world divided against itself might perhaps have been eased.

The food, however, turned out more criminal than anything even the Right Wing would have thought those agitators capable of; and despite the conspiratorial cloak-and-dagger play of whisperers at the door checking names (though it was an open meeting), the discussion was commonplace. Even Laszlo was cautious, under a cloud. "A bore," Daren told Anna, as they rode the bus home, his arm jostling against hers.

Even now, when argument had almost dried the springs between them, her touch wove a spell, as if his hand were running the contours of her body.

Her passion for him seemed to revive when he gave the least sign of going with her causes. When they got home she put on a new gown. She objected to silk on principle, thought of cotton as the fabric of the poor, though a good cotton batiste now cost twice as much as nylon. And on summer nights when the full moon (she said) roused her peasant blood, she would go out in her gown, as tonight, stand at his window and beckon him into the woods, the wind in the dark treetops, small things of the night rustling in the leaves. She would drift ahead in billowing white, a will-o'-the-wisp out of German Romantic painting, silent, or humming softly to herself. ("They say the skunk is deaf," she told him, "but I sing anyway to let him know I'm coming"), her bare feet feeling the trail until they were lost to the world (the railroad tunneling off at the bend, the night factory disappearing across the stream); then she would turn and catch him, and he would lower her to the earth bed, she pulling up her gown and spreading herself, cooing and sighing, both sighing and thrashing among the leaves…

How like those po-whites of the South, whom Uncle Hazelwood despised.

4. *The Convergence of the Twain*

Come along to tea this afternoon," said Hardy. "Meet my mother and some nice Americans."

They went by the buttery to order the food: anchovy toast, honey toast, "Crumpets?"—"What's a crumpet?" A gray pad was lifted off the table and wagged at them, like rubber: "This is a crumpet, sir. Excellent when toasted."

Mrs. Hardy was telling in the broad A of Boston how she had sold her house since her husband's death and come abroad to live more cheaply, and Jim's tutor, Cameron, had got her a place in the country with his impoverished brother-in-law, Roger Strange. "A big stone house in the Cotswolds," she said, "but he thinks of it as small.

'We couldn't keep up the Manor,' he says; 'we just had to retrench.'—'That's one thing we have in common,' I tell him; 'and if you were still down in Devon, I wouldn't have such a lovely room, or your little Jeffrey as hostess.' A beautiful child. 'Have another sweet,' she tells me. 'Thank you,' I say, 'but I'm so stout I don't dare.' She tries to comfort me: 'Don't worry. Mostly all very aged ladies are stoutish.'"

Daren was talking with somebody about how a people with no more imagination than to eat boiled greens every day (not to mention crumpets) could never have written Elizabethan literature, when the door opened and the Morgans came in, Anna's searching gaze leading them like a lamp.

It was not that she was beautiful ("Let up on that beautiful Anna stuff," she had scribbled on one of his sketches), but that the human race rode in her, its desires and aspirations. She came to the fire—the Cro-Magnan girl among the hunters in the cave. The Morgans were introduced, along with the cause of their being in Oxford: a third-year law scholar from Chicago, pontifical as a judge, engaged to Chuck's older sister, Abbie. Daren, who had taken Anna's hand at the round robin and translated a Klopstock poem in her praise, led her to the window seat to discuss these auspices. Jim threw on a bucketful of coal and turned to sister Tina—like all the Morgans, big-boned and hardy-handsome. It soon transpired that an acquaintance of some half-cousin once removed on the Morgan side had attended college at the same place and time as a friend of Hardy's brother-in-law, also that Hardy's former girl friend had studied at Northwestern and must have been seen on several occasions by either or both of the sisters—circumstances in the conviviality of which all wallowed. The room filled up, as Jim's room did at teatime. Clyster came with his stethoscope hanging around his neck, inseparable as the pipe from his mouth. He plugged it in and did his home-work, twitching those plump Morgans in the small-ribs, discovering rich anomalies of breathing and heart. While Anna in the window-bay, against velvet hangings, began to reveal the secrets of her origin.

As if, in Eliot's "Prufrock" one of those white-armed women had turned and made the opening he did not dare to make ("I... have gone at dusk through narrow streets/ And watched the smoke that rises from the pipes/Of lonely men in shirt-sleeves, leaning out of windows...") and the broached humanity had stirred the possibility of love.

While Chuck, talking across the room, perfect American specimen that he was, was out of it, peripheral to Anna's search, though the terms of her independence would not be expressed for years: "Because I wanted books, travel, art, to get out of those lower depths. And that takes money."

Was it more amazing how much, against a babble of tea-talk, she had revealed, or how much had remained unknown, for later revelation? Take socialism. It might almost have seemed to crystallize, during those years abroad, out of an ideal ambiance where it lay, with other human and artistic yearnings, as much his as hers; yet she had spent years, before that, in its service.

"My name in Lithuania is Ona." (Like Spenser's Una, Truth.)

Lips parted, soft and full. Hair, yellow flax that would fade with the years to a silky mouse-blond. "All my girls have fine hair," her mother had said. "It's because they wash it with American Family Soap. A wide-necked peasant blouse on straight shoulders, lying loose over the breasts, opening a shade as she leaned forward.

And as the curtain of the outward Anna parted for the first glimpse within?—

"You're from another world. I grew up in Chicago in a basement cave." A strange opening for the Gothic maiden: Mom at the washtub weeping, and in each tear the whole of their past: Lithuania, the mines, the slums, the life of the poor.

She asked about his courses. He overflowed. How he had pursued the science of power and now sought the arts of spirit. She understood that. She too had served power, and had come abroad for beauty, perhaps (though she did not announce it) for love.

Hank Brown arrived late. "Ah been in de Dime Sto half a hour assin de girl ef she got a little fun-hole fuh me to po wine in mah butt-hole. But Ah cain't git nowhah wid her nohow."

"Don't you come back here with any of that put-on British talk, like Fairy Davis at Tulane," his aunt had warned. Hank had hardly hit the island when he counterattacked with southern Negro. If everybody had to have an Oxford comic mask, Hank's was the systematic corruption of speech.

He would go to Mark's and Spencer's (which he called Marx and Spengler's or sometimes the Dime Sto) to buy an electrical extension (which he called an umbilical cord), though to get one under that name was strenuous (which he called strainyourass—the British with their ancient "arse" missing that pun); and suppose, more by looking than asking, he managed to find the thing, then there was the problem of paying for it; because he wouldn't call tuppence anything but a nickel (which he slurred to niuhkle), and for the other combinations, he applied the tuppence, thrippence rule all the way up, through fuppence, fippence, sippence, seppence, eppence, nippence, teppence, to 'lepence; and as if getting his pronunciation of "shiuhlin" wasn't going to be rough enough, he often called that twobits, a florin fo-bits, and a half-crown a five-bit piece; so the salesgirls had a sprightly time when he said he had given them fo-bits, and it cost only two-bits seppence, so they still owed him fippence shiuhlin. Then he would turn his head around over his new Hairy Tweed suit, that made him look like a wooly brown bear, and show his sad-eyed smile, implying: "Well, man, Ah reckon we'll get dis heah worked out in time."

And he was going to stick to his colors. After two years, at his oral exams, he would be heard (having insulted a detested examiner in his Shakespeare paper): "Massah Shipley, when Ah said in mah paper you wuz a fool, what Ah meant wuz, yo notes on *Othello* don't have de mahks uv a reasonin critter. Tha's all."

Hank squeezed into the window seat, Hairy Tweed and all. So before they broke up, Anna's rise from the coal mines and the slums of Chicago could take its place by Hank's descent from the mulberry trees.

Mrs. Hardy had promised to take the Morgans sightseeing in the Cotswolds if ever there was a clear day. Then one morning the Journal opened with Chaucer:

> My windowes weren shet echon,
> And through the glas the sunne shon
> Upon my bed with brighte bemes,
> With many glade gilden stremes…
> Ne in al the welken was no cloud.

Chuck was on business in London and Abbie's lawyer had to bone at cases. Jim and Daren worked through the morning. At noon Mrs. Hardy came with the girls. Soup and salad was a gay meal. Jim mixed the oil and vinegar with such pep, Daren suspected him of a gravitation toward Tina——a body of mass enough to gravitate the inanimate. They went out to the Chevrolet, towering like a bus over the British cars. Jim poured those sisters into the rear with him, ample people, whose combined hippage bulged the capacity. The space of front remaining from Mrs. Hardy went to Anna and Daren. "Good and friendly lady," he mused, "why were you not one foot larger in the beams, that the lightest of our company might have ridden on my knees?"

The Journal at this point turned itself into a Baedeker, giving the low-down on every mansion, church and carving—the painted hell at North Leigh, where devil scorpions lash themselves through flames, pursuing little souls like animalculae. Only the snapshots Jim had taken, which Uncle Hazelwood had tabbed to the pages, sustained the story: Daren in histrionic tears in the stocks at Great Tew, Anna inclined above him, Fidelio, smiling deliverance. These revived other moments, not told or photographed: when Anna slipped away in the state bedroom of Sulgrave Manor, ancestral house of the Washingtons. The guide droned on. Daren also wandered, pretending not to look for her. From the kitchen came a whisper. In the vast fireplace, behind the flicker of a log fire, he saw her on a chimney seat, beckoning through flame. He crept in and joined her, calling up mythologies:

Quand vous serez bien vieille, au soir à la chandelle…

Now the girls had rented cycles. "Man," Hank came to Darren, "Why'n'chew teach me how to ride de wheel? Ah never had one when Ah wuz little." Daren took him to the tow path along the Isis, thinking to get away from cars. But when Hank lost his balance he had to choose between the fence and the river. Though he always chose the fence, the other possibility damped the enterprise. By Thanksgiving he was unprepared for the planned trip to Stokeunder-Wychwood. Mrs. Hardy had got them all invited for dinner and the night.

That morning they gathered, with some curious Britishers, for the yearly football game between the North and South. Colonel Dunn from Kentucky charged in storming about the blue-bellied, yellow backed, toad-faced Federal bastards, but dropped the ball. Hank couldn't play at all, but he ran around protesting: "My grammaw could make mighty good beaten biscuits till the goddamned Yankees cut her fingers off in the Wah." Daren, who could dodge like a jackrabbit, made the only touchdown for the South; the North went through like a steamroller to an astonishing score. Horner told Scheherazade she had witnessed the Civil War.

Mrs. Hardy took Chuck and the girls, with the overnight things, in the car—Hank too, since he hadn't mastered the wheel—but Jim and Daren lit out to peddle the thirty miles: north by Woodstock, then left on winding lanes between walls and hedges, a beautiful day, the autumn light on the fields, the brown woods. As they came to the last long Cotswold hill, skirting Wychwood Forest, Daren was in the lead. He pumped like a fury, bent to the handlebars, and whistled down into the shadowy cool valley of the Evenlode, coming at an awful clip around one curve to another-almost a right-angle bend at the edge of the village. He squeezed what handbrake he had and strained to pivot, but it was too much; the bike cleared the ditch and crashed on a low stone wall (a little higher one would have turned him into a biscuit spread); he soared over and shafted to his middle in a hawthorne hedge (BOING!), his hinder parts quivering like the butt of an arrow.

Jim helped him out. The bruised shoulder was OK, and the barked shin, not to mention the facial hieroglyphics; the body could mend; but the cycle was less fortunate. The front wheel was whop sided and wouldn't turn. They found a repair shop in the village. It would take time, maybe overnight; the spoke-heads would have to be loosened with oil. Jim's map showed a path across the meadows, through a corner of Wychwood Forest, to the Grange. Daren could walk; Jim would go by road and announce the coming.

So it was in the beech, near the crossing of the stream, swinging along in his hiking stride, that Daren overtook the auburn-haired and rather mischievous-looking Jeffrey, in the plaid kilt of her mother's clan, dawdling home with her schoolbooks. If she guessed he was going to her house, she didn't let on. She loved concealment; it was never going to prey on her damasked check.

"Yon can't jump that stream, you know."

It wasn't the opening gambit, but almost; as if she sized him up right off, and knew the way to prod a Leflore into trying something was to say he couldn't.

So he jumped, and of course he made it; he wasn't such a fool as to land in the water. But the shore he lit on was a bog. And the blithe imp, who had banked on that, threw her face to the sky glimmering through bare boughs and laughed like an adjunct of the woods and stream. Daren floundered to the grass. She ran up a few yards and crossing on some stepping stones, which she might have told him about if he'd asked, joined him where he stood stamping the black mud off his shoes, England's daedal earth.

She broke a stick and kneeled in front of him. "I'll clean them for you," she said.

"An oozy island," he countered, "and tricky islanders. I'm an American, Daren Leflore."

She caught on. "You sit by Mrs. Morgan and across from me. I'm Jeffrey."

"Our hostess. That's what I call a damp reception."

"A lark, isn't it? My first Thanksgiving dinner. Mrs. Hardy has found a turkey and cranberries. And there'll be people sleeping all over the house. It's only a cottage." She jabbed at the heel and looked up. "We've lost our money, you know, and I have to go to the village school. I hate it, dull oafs. I wish *we* had Thanksgiving holiday."

She sprang up. Her walking boots were laced, one straight across, one herringbone. "That's a funny way to lace shoes."

She tossed her head. "My father says a lady should lace them straight across. I do the right one for him, to show I'm half a lady."

"And the other half?"

She leaned nearer, "Yon see this mark?"—pointing to a little dent over her left eyebrow, almost a dimple. "That's a Pixie mark. When I was little, Uncle Athol took me to the window. 'I thought you would have it,' he said. 'That's your mother's mark.'—'What does it mean?' I asked him. '*Miching Mallecho*,' he said; 'it means mischief.' When I asked my mother she only smiled: 'it means you can laugh at the world.' So I went to old Agnes, whom everyone called a witch. It was once by the Druid Oak, and she said, 'it means you can master the devil.'" Jeffrey sprang back, striking a sorcerer's pose, but lit in the mud herself.

"Sit on this log," Daren offered, "I'll fix yours."

"It's quite all right. I can do it nicely." She bent in a ballet turn that raised the small boot to the stick's jab, and flung him that pixie mask-too proud to be waited on. Then he noticed the regulation sporran—"Why do you wear that?"—and he got the lowdown on conkers...

After turkey with chestnut stuffing and cranberries, and a couple of Mrs. Hardy's unbeatable pies, after Roger Strange had brought out the ancient port and Stilton and they had put cheese maggots on the polished board for small races, and wagered salted nuts and comfits, Leslie Cameron, who had arrived late, sat at the piano to play Mozart. Jeffrey took her place to turn the pages. Daren eyed her from a wing chair. He had only seen her joking, but here was a night phase. Her face, caressed in waves of hair, sank into the brooding of music ("I am never merry," says Jessica, 'When I hear sweet music"). As a stream deepens to a pool, she deepened toward prophetic motherhood.

Daren glanced, and from across the room took the dreaming fullness of Anna's eyes. As Dante, from some innocent brightness, mere angel, might have turned to an earth-spirit that was pain, yearning, torment, hope, joy. At the same time, from another corner of the room, he saw Chuck's blunt and helpless look on Anna.

"What I felt for you," she would say to Daren long after, "doesn't belong in the New Order, but to the old world of romance and slavery."

No wonder he took her in the light of what he had read—married virgin Francesca. Though she had lived already a range of other lives; courtship, marriage, abortion, Party. As she would reveal later, when she and Daren stopped in Chicago with Mom and slept in the bed of her own childhood, her trust going out to him—even her return to Chuck had not been to bourgeois morality:

She told how she had taken a train one morning, after a night of entertaining manufacturers and their wives; how she got off at the Dunes and climbed a lonely hill over a swamp. She threw off her clothes and ran, the wind on her body. She watched a green snake slide into the grass. She put blossoms in her hair and lay in the sun. A plane droned overhead. A train stopped by the brick school out at Baileytown. What if someone should come? She was not ashamed. She was thinking of the doctor who treated

Mom, the gentleness of his hands. She drew up her knees and slept in her great loneliness.

When she got back to town, she phoned the doctor's office. Could she talk to him in his apartment before dinner? She ran in from the cab. Perspiration beaded her lip. He seated her in a chair by a tall window, curtains blowing. She didn't want a drink, but he brought her one anyway. He sat on the hassock and waited. She could hardly speak. How was it he didn't know?

"What is it?"

"I want… " Her eyes wandered.

"Yes?"

"I want you…"

He didn't understand. She caught the words like marbles and rolled them out: "to make love to me."

He turned his drink in his hand. "I can't,"

She thought he meant something else. "Oh why?"

"Your husband believes in me."

"He would never know."

"We would know."

Nestled with Daren in the bed of her childhood, Anna would confess all that. "I thought I understood," she would say, but then I lost it. He offered to drive me home. I put on my floppy straw and leaned against the door. 'You'll be sorry, someday… When you're old… Looking back on life.'

"At home he and Chuck and I sat talking like old friends.

"Maybe his way was better," she whispered, "maybe mine was. I never knew."

Embraced in the iron bed, the winter blast rattling the loose pane, Daren would try to reconcile this Anna with the one he had known: "If your bargain with Chuck was so easy, how could I have seen you as I did? I thought of you as the married virgin."

Her hand ran down his side. "Not for long. Besides, I was shy with you. You weren't just to cheer me up. I knew from the first it was like that Dante you read: you were something to tear my life apart."

Next morning, after the laughing Jeffrey had come to the loft to rout out the boys, and Hank cast an eye into the gray: "Lawd, chile, it's way befo day in de mawnin!" and they cooked breakfast on the Aga and ate in the breezeway, and Jeffrey stomped off (one boot straight and one crosswise) to the hated school; after they'd helped bring stones from the quarry for a wall, and the others had gone to see Broadway, and by something more than chance, Anna and Daren remained on the sunlit lawn—what opened through the child-port of the tear?

It was her mother's Lithuania she told him of: a clearing on a lake by a forest, a small log house overflowing with family, nothing bought, everything made, thread, clothes, candles, soap, butter; children to keep, and chickens, a cow, a garden. For a long time father Constantin out of work, and then no father. Gone neither to heaven nor hell, but as unreal, to America.

But a ticket comes in the mail; and child Dunya, Anna's Mom-to-be, by wagon, over forest roads, arriving at some port, mounts a gangplank and sails for the New World.

There it is, brooding in the tears, like the cellar cave, but worse: immigrants in father Constantin's sweat-reeking boarding house in the coal-dust mining town, rooms like noisy cells, the communal pine board heaped with rutabaga bubbling in cheap stew; and Dunya to cook and to clean.

Gregory Vaicaitis takes form, straight nose, straight back, thirtyfive, big man, a miner; he asks for Dunya's hand, she fifteen. "Yes," father Constantin says, "yes," sells Gregory the boardinghouse and flees to his family, back home.

As if Mom's tears were the little salt mill grinding at the bottom of the ocean, scene after scene: strikes, explosion, hard times. Burned out in Pennsylvania, the flames from the coal breaker lighting up the night valley, spreading to the row shacks on a driving wind: "My first memory," Anna said, "is of being snatched out of bed and carried over fire-lighted snow." For now Anna, sixth born, fourth to live, is no longer telling what she has heard but what she saw:

Illinois. Not clothes Mom is washing, but the men's backs as they come from the ground, black as the coal they have mined. Father Gregory, out of work, yawns on the porch; children and chickens root in the clay bank under the floor. A boardinghouse again, yellow rutabaga among lumps of fat in the stew, lopsided bread from an oven rusted out on the side, and those corded backs to scrub clean.

Over them, the Law: Two-hill, the detective, with his mounds of butt and belly. Father Gregory walking by the river found a lump of coal as big as your head. Two-hill sprang on him as he came home. "He had to put on his Sunday suit to go to the company's lousy jail."

And then that quiet Dunya, out of unpredictable reserves, left her husband and her home, convention, all they knew: "Keep your holy wedlock. I doubt the holiness and I break the lock." Without the help of Blake or Marx or anybody else, she had decided that religion, morality and law were walls of a prison erected for her spirit; but there were loopholes of escape, if not for her, then for her children. She bundled up the five, crated some furniture, got on a train, Anna clinging to her skirts, infant Michael sneezing and crying in her arms, and rode all night. To Chicago: the melting pot around the Church of the Sacred Heart ("Heartlessness," said Anna). You looked up through sidewalk pits and saw feet and legs pass by. Out under the sidewalk was the toilet, a two-holed wooden seat; and back in the dark, bedrooms, the floor in one rotted away, the bedlegs resting on earth.

"To be poor in the city," she said, "is worse than in the country. We left three peach trees and a garden. Now it was that basement in a slum row, where two huge factories faced each other, one boxes, one container cans. My sisters worked there, fourteen and thirteen, and I had just started school—reaching for the light. When I came home, Mom was always at the washboard, her foot rocking Michael in his cradle, while tears dropped in the suds, and problems piled up like the clothes, never ending. She had no time for me."

Then Anna told of getting wood from the factory, and of the collier, how his horse fell on the ice, the whip crashing, the lean beast laboring to rise—

Strange, in England, one of those Gulf Stream days of late November, the lawn green, the slope to the beech wood mellowed in sun, Roger

Strange's saddle horses, an extravagance he would not forego, grazing beyond the ha-ha, long-maned—

"Those horses," Anna said, covering her face, "those horses are still in my head."

That afternoon they returned to Oxford. Daren, Jim and Hank were invited to dinner with the Morgans. Daren cycled with Anna to the covered market. He had lived almost across from it for two months, but he knew nobody; Anna had been in town a week or so. "How's your bursitis?" she asked the butcher.

"It's better today, thank you, love. Pleasant trip?"

At the entrance the old flower-woman bent over her crate, choking, coughing, the crowd passing by, under the instinct of privacy, like Daren, as if deformity, drunkenness, pain were too personal for anybody but the sufferer—though a few stopped, watching, helpless, as red drops fell to the pavement, the woman leaning over, fumbling in her bag.

Anna snatched her own handkerchief and held it to the woman's face, her arm around her. "Are you all right?" The woman caught it like drowning: "Yes, thank you, ducky. It comes and goes. It's only nosebleed."

Daren reached the apartment early and left his bike by the kitchen door. He found Anna at the broiler, trying to turn the haunch. He took the fork, gave the meat a desperate stab and flopped it over. Then the fork stuck. Every time they tried to pull, the hot pan started sliding off the broiler. "Put your foot on it," Anna said. Daren plopped his tennis shoe into the saddle of the haunch while Anna drew out the fork. "I meant the pan," she said. "Keep it to yourself." So they shared their first secret, Anna's shoulders shaking from time to time through the meal, Daren looking away unconcerned—to have planted that long Leflore foot on Arum's delicious haunch.

Next day the American colony turned out to see Chuck and Anna off on the grand tour. Hank came beforehand for Daren. "Ah got to buy some aiggs. Ah softball em fuh breakfast." They dipped into the market. There were Danish eggs that came boxed under the name Crestview. "You got any dem Crestfallen aiggs?" says Hank. "Crestview, you mean, sir?"—"Yassuh. Ah wants a dozen of em. Crestfallen aiggs."—"We have Crestview eggs, sir."—"That's what Ah say," Hank groans, "Crestfallen aiggs. Gimme a dozen." He got them under that name.

Then Daren saw the old woman selling violets. "Hard to get in the winter, aren't they?"—"God will provide, sir," she said. He took a bunch and gave her half a crown. As they left the market her voice was raised behind them: "Thank you, sir. I told you He would provide."

Daren handed the flowers to Anna as she got on the train. She held them to her face, and picking one, reached it back through the window: "Remember me."

(While memory holds a seat in this distracted globe.)
Wore my violet, but it didn't help. A waiter in Hall dropped a plate against a big glass pitcher. It cracked an ellipse around the handle.

Creeping Jesus and the Boor were talking of Salvation. Fred bustled over with his wad of rags around his middle. "Easy," Jesus told him, "that pitcher is broken."—"Oh is he!" cried Fred, and grabs him by the handle. It pulled off, side and all, baptizing the holy pair.

"I'll treat you to a beer, Leflore. Drink and drown care." It was Gusty, a winking old Scholar.

"I don't care for your beer."

"Refuse a drink from an upperclassman? I can sconce you for that."

"Your sconce be damned." And now he did sconce me, for cursing at table.

The half-gallon silver tankard was brought, a napkin hung on the handle. I had made it strong cider, hating the taste of beer. If I had failed it would have gone the rounds, at my expense. But I finished without even a breath, which the rules allow. To make Gusty pay, I would have drowned myself in Malmsey.

I was admired like a potbellied god. As the great cold lump in the belly warmed, a tipsy eidolon. Wolfgang and Horner took me to a German film, weird night shots down shadowed alleys; at the close, the romantic student looks in a mirror and moons: "Sentimental Träumer," shoots the mirror and dies. *Go thou and do likewise.*

We went pub-crawling instead. Pubs have lost a lot since the days of Piers

Plowman. We were debating whether the Greek proverb, "A good wine needs no bush," applied to their women's use of depilatory, when the tapster rushed in crying: "The proctors, gentlemen."

We scattered. A big buller took after me, leather soles ringing the pavement. "Your name and college, sir!" As if he expected an answer. My sneakers gave me speed and silence. Ahead, I dodged into a lane, sprang up a gutter and into a casement recess. He pounded on.

When I got to Gloucester it was paying time. I climbed in my window and strolled down to the lodge. "I thought you were out," says the porter.

"On the contrary, I'm in. But Mr. Hart, and Mr. Horner?

There was a knocking at the gate. Wolfgang was admitted, winded. "How did you get here so fast?" He let the cat out of the bag; but the porter looked away.

Horner came later. Caught and progged. There will be a process tomorrow and he will be fined. The next time, rustication.

So he had to take it easy. Though he was like one of those crustaceans whose legs and antennae are reduced to grappling hooks for the female, or barnacles where the whole male creature has become a parasitic sex organ—he was that wrapped up, night and day, with Scheherazade. As Hank put it: "She has done caught him by de particeps crimini, which is to say, de *criminal parts.* Yassuh, she really got him in *penal suvvittude.*"

The last night of term Leflore sat thinking how memory makes a unit of a span of time. From his first Virginia year recollections rose, not in order and not confused, but blended in tone and mood. There was the observatory and the woods, those nights when he would read without going to bed, the slow coming on of dawn, the morning song of robins, filling the air like light. He was washing his hands before opening his new Shakespeare, folding back the pages and sitting down to *A Midsummer Night's Dream.* It was spring. The down comfort over his feet was too warm, but he let it lie. His old dressing gown, the "germ-trap," wrapped him in its dirty folds. At the fraternity next door Fletcher's voice rose above the others: "Drink her down, Kappa Alpha, drink her down!" A moth wheels about the lamp. Leflore catches it solicitously and throws it out. "Hey, Daren," Fletcher roars, "have a drink!" A mason jar soars up, misses the window and crashes on the wall. Daren sits and reads: "And with the juice of this I'll streak her eyes,/ And make her full of hateful fantasies." Not separate, and not of thought—an instant of moody poetic pride.

So the first English term would flow together: Chaucer, and cycling by slant sun past green fields, through beech forest, brown bracken, to Stoke-under-Wychwood, Jeffrey and Anna, the promise of love. He went to sleep musing it all into dream.

Far in the night a fellow broke into the bedchamber yelling "Quick, quick!" Daren waked ready for fire. "Horner's outside and he can't get in, He's fallen off the gutter three times. "We'll have to tie your bloody sheets together. He's been out with some bloody Egyptian, and he's too weak to climb."

Itwas Pitt-Beauchamp, competing with his great ancestors. "Next year," Daren thought, as his sheets scraped on the stone, "I'll ask for a top-story room."

Absorbing that stir and protest, the term merged back into dream.

5. Val d'Arno

ENGLISH DECEMBER. The low circling sun, lost in a sky of cloud that dripped and trailed into fog, blotted out by teatime, leaving long stretches of dark cold. It was a property of soul, that cold; it lurked in the stone buildings and the people. Under its gloom, how the volumes of colored cards from old wedding journeys, pored over in childhood, Lippi and Ghirlandaio, birds flying against a cypress sky, brightened in the mind, melodious; as if the whole landscape of the heart were the forested north, yearning for Tuscan hills, temples among vineyards, orange groves and olives: *"Kennst du das Land, wo die Zitronen blühn... Dahin, dahin, möcht ich mit dir, o mein Geliebter, ziehn.*

—Hank Brown, nine years ago, had found it an exhausted yearning:

> About the Florentine section of your diary, the less said the better. I have long dreamed of a comic guide for tourists: "Fornicating in Fiesole," "Buggering About in Little-Known Bavaria"; with remoter excursions: "In and out of Prehistoric Kunt," "Some Unusual Patterns of Incest in Upland Indonesia." I question this shadow who bears your name and is one of ten-million escapist lovers of Florence.

That was when Daren had first bundled up samples of the Journals, sending them off in a publisher's competition for big money, naming Hank as sponsor. Hank not only featured in the text, he had taken a job with the publishing house in question. A copy of his testimonial accompanied the personal letter:

> From my undercover agents, I learn that Daren Leflore has submitted his dia-

ry, The Life of Dream, in the yearly competition. If he can keep the narrative moving, despite the block of the journal form, and deal more with life and less with himself and art, he may well produce a romantic, yet modern, Wilhelm Meister's *Wanderjahre*. In any case, he deserves every consideration.

Touché. Yet what could a man do but take up his heart's heritage?

Even clown Hank had started on the southward journey—bundled in the eight-foot scarf his aunt had knitted for him: "They're wearing them long," he had instructed her. Daren had to hold one end, and Hank at the other would whirl across the room, spooling it on his neck like a cotton bale. "All de blood got to go thoo de neck, man; so keep dat warm an you can't go cold."—Daren exhorting: "Well, for the Lord's sake, take off the Hairy Tweed suit, and give the scarf a chance."

London was darker than Oxford, soapbox orators in Hyde Park stirring the dust of abdication: "Down with Baldwin, and God save our King." Hampton Court scowled the absurdity of planting Renaissance north of the fiftieth parallel. Daren's Oxford cough had reached the crisis which, before antibiotics, always hinted at the worst. "Where are you going?" a polite Londoner asked on the night crossing. And when the reply, "To Italy," was delayed by a racking seizure, "I hope it helps," commiserated—as if to the dying Keats, sleepless, pacing the deck, taking the winter spray.

At Dieppe porters grabbed the luggage, demanding tips, yelling about "Bale!" France was as cold as England, the people less reserved, but hardly of the sun. Hank remained in Paris, hunting restaurants with a cheap *prix fixe* ("Gimme de fix prick, man!") going the rounds of gray churches, each with a sign on the spring door, *"Poussez ici,"* Hank moaning: "Ah doan know what de church o God is comin to; heah's another one got dat bad *pussy heah.*"

Nose to the train window, Daren sped South from plains to hills to mountains, but still in cloud and worse cold: glimpses through falling snow of white peaks incredibly lifted over the railroad valley grimed with power. The tunnel was an interminable clacking dark under vistas lost.

The long descent began in fog; past Turin it was mountains again, but by evening they came out on the true southward slope, the Riviera, The train had filled with Italians, wine-bearing, fruit-eating, bread-chewing, friendly and noisy, like something out of Rabelais, They opened the windows. The air blew in warm, full of the rustle of palms. Daren's cough had melted with the mist. He leaned into a night of stars. From his room in Genoa he saw the moon's track over the sea of myth and Homeric song.

He waked to the glory of return to that shore the soul had been hungering for and not knowing its birthplace: streets between sunlit buildings under tile roofs, colored banners of washing, people strolling, singing, embraced arm in arm. For lunch in a cave-restaurant he could not read the scrawled menu or catch the spoken word, The potbellied host led him into the kitchen, where all the family opened ovens and uncovered pots, while he chose (and they taught him the names) his bargain banquet. Evening, he raced for sunset up the hills behind the city, and made the olive-grove summit as the harbor and the mountains took the last flare.

He did a job, of course, on the guidebook items, following the map, checking dates and names; but it was only the whole sweep of the city, land and sea that was valid. There was a separation in Genoa between the spontaneous life and the academic sights the Baedeker insisted on starring.

If that was the choice, maybe he'd have done better to have let the monuments go, and stuck to the other claim: south, where the peninsula jutted to the wave-carved Port of Dolphins, boats and nets on the strand, where one could have wine with spaghetti and fish and squid by a square full of playing children, their mothers calling from the windows above into the dusk now: "Giovanni, Paolo, Picollino, Come!"—the voice on the third call rising to a scream, until a child detaches himself from the scramble and runs home; and quiet falls, and one hears, in the almost summer air, the surf rumbling in caves of the rock headland that shuts the harbor from the sea: "O *litus vita mihi dulcius, O Mare!*"

But he had planned the trip in England with all the earnestness of his nature, so the ticket kept pulling him on, past the fleshpots of living, to the records of creative mind.

Pisa was the gateway. In that field of wonder the New Romanesque had flowered, Students stretched on the grass around the tower that bent (as the guidebook told him) like a lily in the wind. For the first time the intimation came that those poles, separated in Genoa, might coalesce, and the result would be a refining fire.

What Pisa hinted at, Florence fulfilled. He arrived in the evening. Vasari's *Lives,* some attempt to read Dante, his own heritage and the cult of love had prepared him. As the hack clattered through cobbled streets past the lighted square, the massive stones of the Old Palace, the columned Uffizi, the Loggia dei Lanzi, he foresaw the wedding of nature and art, fierce intelligence and sparkling joy.

Though nature at first was prevented. The fog was here too. Daren groped from his palace pensione along the Arno, which murmured below in a white mist, into the Uffizi, up the stately stairs to the gallery floor. He found the Botticelli Spring and Birth of Venus and camped there for the day, while the brief morning heat of the radiators died. He felt like Wells' time traveler as the sun pales and the ice descends, but warmed from another source, entering along the curved shore of orange trees over fragile waves into a realm of sad joy, the enlaced winds, the pure nude, blown bloom, the ultimate spring of art...

What if Giotto's tower was half lost in cloud? There were the doors of the Baptistry, and the lovable flesh of the paradise they opened, the marble choirboys of Luca della Robbia. What if outside it was cold or warm, when in the space of Gozzoli's windowless chapel the enclosing walls could recede and brighten to sharp Tuscan hills, castles, pinewoods full of game, and tall sentinel cypress by valley streams—a world for angels to wander, culling flowers, and Kings of three races to traverse on caparisoned horses over pebbled roads, with hounds, leopards, monkeys, falcons, and all the wingplumes, jewels, lips and eyes? Could the sun reveal such external correlatives, the cypressed hills of the actual Val d'Arno?

Those first clays, groping the fog, Daren gave himself to art, unspeakable power drawing him on, launching him on waves of force from naive joy toward the crisis of Michelangelo. While the outward scene lay hid. At dusk when he would return to his chilly pensione room to read the guidebook or do his stint of Anglo-Saxon, the solitude closed in; the nights did not keep company with the splendor of the days.

He took to hanging around the parlor after supper, listening to the other guests, a weird set of originals: the Oxford lady who talked of haunts and ectoplasm, who thought the blue figure of Boreas in Botticelli's Spring was a real astral being, and therefore preferred Botticelli to all other painters, the American ("English," she insisted, "only by marriage") hipped on politics; among these and their ilk, he sat longer each evening, hoping that when the impoverished gentlefolk who ran the pensione had finished their own meal in an adjoining room, the door would open and the daughter would come in, *"Dicendo a l'anima, sospira."* Among exploded expatriates, dowagers, art-seeking eccentrics, there she was, small, shy, demure, with Tuscan lip and brow, those pure, fragile lines.

A week ago Daren had been thinking of Anna. Now, without a break—as if he had tuned in on another wavelength, though the first was still present somewhere on the air, he had picked up this other station, a program more refined, such a strain of lutes and viols as those carved and painted angels might be weaving among the loggias and gardens of fifteen-century Florence.

Her name was Pippa. It had come into the family when a greataunt heard Browning read his poems in the 1880's to a gathering at the Villa Trollope (Mrs. Burnett coming from her room, where she was scribbling *Little Lord Fauntleroy,* to join Miss Cobb, of *Intuitive Morals,* and Mrs. Aeneas Gunn, then writing *We of the Never Never Land).* Pippa's father had found the name precious. He used to call her Pipistrella, "Little Bat"— she of the pale face hovering in a night of hair.

Pippa would be doing her homework for the university, or sometimes, being the linguist of the family, writing letters for her mother, assurances of an elegant room with a view of the Old Palace. Daren, who might be pretending to study his Anglo-Saxon, or genuinely concentrating on Dante, would wait until she looked up, catch that clear North Italian eye, intelligent, luminous, green-brown, and ask about some church or museum or the rhythm of a line, any excuse to hear her artful language, which carried over, even into English, the soul of Florence.

Tuscan is already the most nicely formed dialect of Italian, and the lisping consonant-softening of Florence adds a sweetness to that, but Pippa had found a way, from childhood, of carrying this refinement farther, so that the great-aunt used to say she did not speak Italian at all, or even Florentine, but Pippesca, and that this was the most angelic speech of all.

Five days before Christmas, Daren asked her to help him with the sonnet: *"Tanto gentile e tanto onesta."*

So they came to talk of choices and affections. She loved Baldovinetti, most fragile of their painters. "No one else," she said, "can paint the Val d'Arno." He must go to the Annunziata, and among the over-lush del Sarlos he would find one Baldovinetti Adoration, almost faded off the wall, with a landscape, a tree and a vine, the most delicate thing in Florence. Had he seen, perhaps, in London (her uncle had sent her a card) the little Apollo and Daphne (some called **it** a Pollaiuolo), she changing under his embrace into a trunk and branches? Daren promised to send her a print from England.

Meanwhile, he went to Alinari's and got a reproduction of Baldovinetti's Annunciation, one of those hand-colored photos in which the mouth spills a little over the lines. From a medium distance it looked beautiful in the tooled gold frame; he gave it to her, and invited her to go with him sometime to see the Lippis and Botticellis, its natural peers. She was moved by the disinterestedness of the gift, set it up (she told him) on her dresser where she would see it as she prepared for the day or for bed. But she did not respond to the invitation.

While the weather loured, art and the increasing life-center of Pippa supplied the place of the sun. Then one evening the mist stirred; a wind from the Mediterranean opened a long slip of clear in the west; sunset caught the tower of the Old Palace, Giotto's Campanile and Brunelleschi's dome on a burning tide. Daren was taking off for the Piazzale Michelangelo, though he wouldn't have made it in time, when Pippa called him: "To the roof garden, quick! To see the light over Florence."

They hurried up winding back stairs, out of the familiar guest corridors, through unsuspected upper quarters into which the family disappeared when they left the state rooms below: a snug living room, a glimpse of Pippa's bedroom under the eaves, the dresser, the Baldovinetti against the mirror; then she opened a door and they were on the roof, a covered area for drying clothes, a bare iron stair ascending to a last railed space where such potted plants as would take the winter upheld the name of garden.

The Arno curved beneath, surrounded and bridged by the domed and towered city of tile roofs and Gothic stone. The long rays from the sun fanned out, as if perspective had just been invented to probe and bring into luminance reaches of distance, measuring the wide valley descending between hills, Fiesole riding its twin ridge, the white crest on a wave; and beyond, past villas and hamlets and artful clumps of trees, the bare huge slopes of Monte Morello, and farther, in the clean air, wonderfully far, the snow-peaked Apennines; while Pippa, the ripest light of all falling on her Baldovinetti face, was gazing at him, like Beatrice when she lifted Dante from scale to scale, such a glad and tender pride: *"E quest' è Firenze, la mia città. Le piace?"*

The next day would be Sunday. He had planned to visit the Boboli Gardens. He asked her to go with him. As the sun sank below the hills, she looked at him and said she would.

But the next morning brought excuses. She had work to do for her mother. Uncomprehending, fretting under an arbitrary balk and stay, he went to the gardens in the warm December, ran all over the place in restless search, pitting joy against want, a strife that set him finally, on the topmost rampart, and in a light that rivaled that of the evening before, to scribble (the calligraph of almost illegible line signaling the heart's motion) a poem, in which love, for all the lets and galls of fact, rushed out in its own nature, and danced.

Was it swayed by the psychic word, or to compensate for an engagement not permitted, with one that was, that Pippa, that night, asked him to join her and her brother at a friend's house Christmas Eve, a party, and then midnight mass at a pilgrimage church in Oltrarno—to keep the festival in the old Florentine way?

A score of people were crowded in a couple of rooms, drinking spumante, eating fruit, nuts, panforte. There was practice in the language, since everyone wanted to welcome the American. But when the rugs were thrown back for dancing, Daren and Pippa could talk together. He was desperate to learn her speech, but he had not gone far enough to make it profitable. They drifted into English, without any sense of its intimacy, into French, of which Daren had learned something from Uncle Hazlewood, but that seemed cold and almost as public as Italian. So they came to German. Daren's mother had loved the German romantic above everything else but Greek. She had taught him little poems and songs when he was a boy, and communicated, despite the Leflore prejudice against Boches as World War I fiends, some feeling for that suffusion of *Geist* and *Gefühl ("Still in dämmriger Luft ertonen geläutete Glocken")*, so irreplaceably German. That was the language he had taken at Virginia, and the one he could manage now with some facility. Pippa had studied it too, much of their trade earlier having come from intellectual Germans.

As if, wandering the woods of Valombrosa thick with fallen leaves, they had followed a certain path and come into a glen arched by the Etrurian shades, the most withdrawn and secret valley of all—so drifting from language to language, they found themselves in the enfolding seclusion of German, their private speech, together.

At once, in the other tongue, it became possible for each to say things that could hardly have come out under the exposure of native speech: how she came to his heart like something from a finer time, a vision so long past that only love could remember what it was. And she: that under the proprieties and monitors of custom prying into lives, one feared to love. She could not have gone to the Boboli with him, or to the gallery, or anywhere alone, because in her circle a girl did not go out that way until she was engaged. Only at public gatherings and with her brother, as now, would they be free of gossip. Besides, she had loved not long ago, and the boy's parents (because they boasted a title) had sent him to England; he had given her up, against all his assurances. She had longed to die, was only now recovering. How could she love again? Yet no one had been so gentle with her as Daren Leflore. It must be in his country, his

South, of which she had read, that the old chivalries were more regarded—as in Dante, as in Shakespeare. She quoted: "'No longer mourn for me when I am dead.' No thought of self," she said, "only of the other." Could they not love with such nobleness of spirit, like brother and sister, but finer than her own brother, without the brutal coarse ways of Italians?

He did not tell her the sonnet she invoked was written for a fair youth, and that Shakespeare's dealings with women may not always have lived up to her ideal. There was a general stir. It was time to walk to the church for midnight mass.

They stretched out in a company, following vine-grown walls, orchards and cypress beyond, and above, a late moon among the winter stars. The warmth had lingered. For Leflore it was like fall, a heavenly air. But Pippa shivered, her face thin under the moonlight. He took off his coat and his Oxford scarf and wrapped her in them. Even in his shirtsleeves the blood went through him like wine.

The service in the plain Romanesque church was simple. Daren sat with Pippa arm to arm, and found himself kneeling out of companionship. He smiled to think how a few years back, in his iconoclastic phase, he would have called that betraying the free mind; he was ready now to participate in any worship that was beautiful—as if, not believing with faith, one could believe in believing, hold an aesthetic derivative of creed, without feeling shame at that or unrest for more.

After the service they went to the little bistro where they always had hot Christmas punch. There were toasts, well-wishes, the chaste and companionable kisses of angels meeting in Angelico's paradise. And then the descent.

Next evening, in the state parlor, the window open on the night, he leaned against the central marble column, looking back to Oltrarno. Would he always be wishing for something never to be? Pippa came quietly, and leaning against the other side of the column, her profile like that of the Poldi-Pezzoli girl, spoke:

"You are sad. Why will you be sad, my Daren? Your love, your friendship, fills me with glad peace."

Only in German could he tell her: "I am not, as you wish, noble, not strong, not eternally mild. Peace comes for me in pauses, like valleys between passionate hills."

That beauty, an aspiration as true as anything he had been touched by, still did not answer—defective—something, if it was to be no more, which the other giant-man of the soul, the wild companion, had to break with, to turn into its orbit, or destroy.

So he started out the next day for Monte Morello. As if in such a context nothing is wasted; as if leaping up mountain crags in impulsive defiance of gravity would sway her sitting below in the enclosed quiet of the pensione, rock her soul on his soul's waves.

To blaze a comet path through the high solitudes. He trotted for hours, dropping to a walk only now and then, until he vaulted the last stone rampart and took the crown: the enormous vista of the Arno, that valley where (except for Athens) the keenest motion ever to stir the human spirit had played itself, furrowing every slope and hill, olive grove, wall and vineyard, every village and church and the domed and spired spread of Dante's city (overflowing its walls now along the river), touching it all with the clarity of intellectual fire. But where Athens was a ruin, so far out of memory one could hardly trace what had occurred, this glory had lingered, nudging you at every moment with breathtaking reminders. He turned the other way, north, panting from the climb. A wind from the Apennine snowfields bore down, driving through his sweater and flesh to the bones, sending him cowering into the shelter of a sunny ledge.

He ran down, renewed; he leapt with long bounds past farms and through settlements that filled in toward Florence, while people turned from their tasks to stare at this charging apparition, hair flouncing, the long Oxford scarf snaking behind him. He entered the pensione like one of the primal powers come from mountains to the astonished eyes of householders. Opening the front door on the buzz, he ran up the four flights. Pippa met him at the head of the stair. The rush of his arrival, the bending of the bow, the psychic and physical force he had been arcing space with alone, almost swept her into his arms. "You come like a breath from Monte Morello," she said. "I have been indoors all day."

Even at that moment, lifted in the exuberance of his passing, she did not believe in the possibility of such a love.

("I learned," Anna would say in Chicago, "that if you let others make your life, you would be that Aztec girl sacrificed to the idol. You must do what they forbid you—take that clay in your hands and shape your happiness.")

Daren's ticket, in any case, had been bought before. So it was on to Rome, where lords and counselors of the earth had built desolate palaces. He paced the Seven Hills and longed for Pippa and Florence. He turned to Michelangelo, who had also come from that clarity to the heavy Roman show, drawn by historical destiny to take on the colossal Hydra Rome had always been. But even Michelangelo did not make amends. Daren, wishing in his own thought to restore the impossible morning freshness of a birth-age, was not ready to accept that involvement as his: the vortex of power and power's repudiation, world-wrinkled busts of emperors, the earthly foreclosure of Christian crypts and tombs, that giant wrestling in the will.

One day, in the Vatican, he turned from the space-buckling tensions of the Sistine vault, seeking the one room of Florentine Quattrocento, Fra Angelico's last frescoes, most of all the one of St. Lawrence distributing alms, and at its focus, the blind beggar feeling his way with his stick, the sightless face gone beyond all Roman turbulence and Stoic resignation into inner light.

It was there that he encountered Anna. He did not comprehend her yet as an emissary of the New Rome Cader Ayres conceived as rising in the East. She was still his married virgin, who had written to Oxford of the disappointments of the grand tour: showy hotels, dumb guides. The letters had been forwarded; Daren would have followed up the address, but chance took over.

During the forty minutes he spent in the Chapel of Nicholas V, and among the guided parties that squeezed halfway through the door for a hurried delivery: "Zees a chapel Fr' Angelico. Vera good painta. Eet show za life San Stephana, San Lorenzo, za firsta mar tyrs. Ere za piple stona San

Stephana; ere zey *roasta* San Lorenzo"—pointing to these only (the stoning by pupils, the roasting almost obliterated), the guides rushed on, clucking their charges behind them—in one such group, so shepherded, came the earnest Chuck and disaffected Anna.

Chuck had the glowing American belief that life can be set up, fought and won like a football game. He had come abroad to get his wife back into the fold, if it took all the Ritz hotels in all the capitals of Europe. And there was a sense in which he would succeed—if by *fold* one meant the Western world, its dreams, arts, loves. Anna was ripe for that, whatever it might cost her in the end. But she was not likely to stick to the capitalist as guide.

She came to Leflore. And Chuck, after rushing in pursuit of the party and back to the chapel, had to abandon his investment in the tour.

They went through the Vatican again, at Daren's speed, considering a few Roman things, a symptomatic bust or two, the Odysseus landscapes. They rushed through connective rooms of later display, and flung themselves into tragic involvement with Michelangelo, then wandered back to the little chapel, St. Lawrence, the blind man's face, and through the veil of the face, inalienable, our blessedness. This was travel as Anna had imagined it—to come to the sources, strip off the false, learn about life from the true.

"He showed the Court of Rome the beauty of the poor. That's wonderful."

Daren had them to lunch at his run-down pensione at the top of the Spanish Steps. A warm day. They walked onto the terrace to take the view. The Little Princess (Russian), who had lived there for years with her exiled parents, was sitting in an ancient fur reading Nietzsche in French. Daren introduced her. The box tortoises had thawed in the sun and were scraping around by the cactus pots. One crawled past the Little Princess' sandaled toes. "Ugly things," she cried, "I hate them. I would like to see them all dead."

"They live a long time," murmured Anna. "It could be the other way around."

That afternoon they went to the Forum. Chuck wanted to get the history straight. They spread out the guidebook with the plan. Urchins came up pestering them for cigarettes. "Vamoose!" Chuck said, in what he seemed to think was Italian.

"Non fumiamo," said Daren.

"How do you say 'Come along'?" Anna asked.

"Venga."

She motioned smiling, *"Venga, venga."*

The boys followed her to the corner, where a woman at a brazier was selling roasted chestnuts and that sweet-smelling chestnut bread. Daren went along to interpret: "For them all," and "How much?" She distributed her alms like Saint Lawrence.

But again destiny lashed them on—Chuck and Anna, north, to the gilded capitals, Vienna, Budapest, Prague, an interval of skiing in Tyrol. That plan had been hatched in Oxford with Jim Hardy and the boys. Daren had barely resisted it in favor of art. He might have yielded now, but the ticket ruled.

So he went all the way to Sicily, lay in the sun and swam in the Ionian Sea, ate oranges under white Etna in the garden of the Hotel Paradiso at Taormina, and on the flower slopes of Segesta saw that perfect temple renew itself daily from the Cyclopean land.

He wandered in paradise and was exquisitely lonely, both for Anna and Pippa together; he gazed at the sea and they blended in his thought like the hues of the water. But Pippa, in league with Florence, with the covered bridge and the queer smile of Flora, the thin dance of the Graces, took the ascendancy.

So he wrote love letters in Italian. And because he was memorizing great stretches of *The Divine Comedy,* the dark wood, Paolo and Francesca, dawn in Purgatory, Matilda by the stream, and refused to compromise the rush of passion by any admitted lack of language, he phrased the Blakean sentiments of his soul in all the flourishes Shakespeare might have suggested and, looking up grammar and words, hurled it over, phrase by phrase, into an Italian mediated by Dante.

"Your letters," Pippa wrote, "come to me from far off, strange and beautiful, like old language. They move me."

What fruit could her agitation bear? Like Faust, caught in what he could not avoid, Daren went on, longing to revive some lost valley of innocence—doing damage never to be repaired—

Aspiring to "the old high way of love."

6. *Love Suffers Long*

In the literal grip of winter, it was still schoolboy summer: tales of vacation—Hardy, on skiing in Tyrol:

"You should 'a seen her try the stem turn top speed, roll over, skis flying, come up like a snow doll, nothing showing but her eyes. 'Dot Anna,' said our ski teacher, Max, 'iss so reckless. But so-o sweet.'

"When she strained her leg, trust Horner to be the old masseur. But he no sooner got her limbered up than he asked her out to look at the moon. She came back double quick: 'That fool needs to cool off,' she said. Well, Max and another of those Tyroleans that look like Attila's Huns took Horner out and dumped him in a snowbank. "After that he tackled a frog-faced girl some London husband had sent away for her health. Nothing like regular doses of root-oil for that. We were wondering what they were up to, until one morning…"

Jim had worked it out like a mystery: Horner, leaving the little wife's room the night before, tying a knot in the condom and folding **it** in his handkerchief. But he forgot to throw it away. At breakfast, when he had to wipe his nose, Montaigne's abhorrence of pocket handkerchiefs was justified, especially for the little frog, who sat opposite, watching, while the laden sack swung like a pendulum, once, twice, three times—and fell in the tea.

"Cut!" Daren, 1949, scowled over the Patapsco. "Anna downstage! Sex-foil Horner bow out!" Though perhaps one should record of him four closing facts:

—That on the train coming back from Tyrol he smuggled a wad of Reichsmarks out of Germany for a Jew in their compartment, a man so jittery he was searched at the border from top to toe, though Horner breezed through, and in Holland restored the money from his underwear.

—That when he blew in from London three days late, with a doctor's excuse that he had been laid up, and with photographs of another nude in his amateur portfolio, he had to face a suit for pregnancy and breach of promise from Scheherazade, who had angled for a British passport; so it cost him a pretty penny to get that old serpent bundled off to the Nile.

—That at a second "Sherry, ETC.," a year and a half later, the Munich crisis closing in, Horner offered Daren this tipsy selfrevelation: "Sometimes when I'm drunk, my eyes magnify. I fix on somebody and they swell, bigger and bigger, like a balloon. I've done that with a woman—huge, full of pores, a Brobdingnagian mole with hairs—enough to make a man swear off. But I shut my eyes and screw myself back to normal."

—Last, that when seven more years had brought war and peace, the *Oxford Alumnus* would publish this obituary:

HORNER, H. H. C. Queensland and Gloucester, 1936. Killed in action, May, 1944, at the height of the campaign in which the British and Americans under Stilwell fought their way back into Burma. Throughout the march he set an example of efficiency, cheerfulness and devotion to duty. The most skillful jungle navigator in the column, he would lead for hours without relief, cutting a track as he went. Utterly fearless, he fell after holding an exposed position alone for half an hour, keeping off the enemy with hand grenades and calling back an accurate account of their movements.

In 1937 they were far from that. The only man who came from the holidays already caught in the crisis that was going to harrow them all was Laszlo Brod. He and Daren would grow closer later, when he had married and brought his wife to England, and Anna, discovering how much they shared, would arrange for meals in lively foursome. But Laszlo, that first January, was just coming into focus, a florid enthusiast, debating over port with Nazi Harth and Tory Pitt-Beauchamp. He had spent his vacation driving an ambulance in Spain.

American passports were stamped "not valid" for that enterprise. That hadn't stopped Laszlo from getting on a ship in Marseilles and being welcomed with cheers in Barcelona. Now he announced that the next world war had begun, that 50,000 German and Italian troops were fighting for the capture of Spain.

"Against Bolsheviks," cried Wolfgang. "To save Spain, from the Russians,"

To which Brod: "Loyalist Spain is helped by everybody who hates fascism. I was with the International Brigade."

"A communist organization," Wolfgang accused.

And Brad: "My battalion was named for Abraham Lincoln. It fought for the legal government of Spain."

The voice of righteousness—though Laszlo had been a communist for years, and his father before him.

Pitt-Beauchamp conciliated: "But His Majesty's government recognizes the Loyalists…"

"Yes. And backs the fascists, whom your capitalists admire."

A pity Anna wasn't there to take up the argument. Though polemic wasn't the phase of her which Daren would observe when she and Chuck returned from Budapest.

There were times, looking back, when he wondered if Anna the soulful innocent had been a product of his own romantic need. Then she would come in (as now) from a day of impetuous participations, greet him, for all their ups and downs, still wistfully, and the searching trust of her eyes would restore everything. She had been older than he and incalculably more experienced. But neither age nor experience was the impression she had made; and it was not an impression only, it was of the soul. There was something childlike in her, had been, was, would be—something eternally naive, hopeful, full of dreams; she was always in the act of starting life again.

After the dark return from Sicily, Daren had made work his strength.

For a month he studied all the time. Even the demon scholar Finch, to whom Leslie Cameron sent him for Anglo-Saxon, gave up staring through owlish lenses and demanding: "What is it your American universities teach you, Mistah Lefleaugh?"

Then, for a single week, love took over:

Monday: The Hardys asked me to Shaw's *Caesar and Cleopatra* by the local company. Cleopatra had just been smuggled to Caesar in a Persian carpet. Unrolled, she stood, childishly alluring, when I felt the will that turns us in a crowd, and glancing back two rows and to the side, met Anna's luminous eyes. A warmth, in Oxford winter, to find that smile.

One of those February brief pre-springs, the ultimate glory of England. Showery-bright days: the green hills swept by falling rain veils; at every burst of sun, rainbows striding the land and larks soaring for the clouds.

Tuesday: Anglo-Saxon until lunch. Then the ride arranged last night, Jim and I, with Tina, Chuck and Anna. The weather was so bright and cycling so warmed us, that at Church Handborough we flung ourselves down in the long grass of the churchyard, and did not mind the drift of sun and shade.

At Eynsham the door of the church tower was open, We filed up the narrow steps and came out over a rolling distance. Low clouds rushed across the sky, wind stirred and a little hail rattled down. Then the sun poured from the west, flooding the valley of the Thames, lighting the trees as in Rembrandt. One of those rare moments when earth is brighter than heaven.

Wednesday: A furious rain all morning. This afternoon Jim and I took Tina and Anna to the Ashmolean, the rest declining. Jim and Tina did the rounds. We chose a single picture, Uccello's Hunt by Night, sat before it, as if we could find a way into that mystery. Teatime took us by surprise. We all went to my room. The Dante was on the table; I had been memorizing it again last night. They asked to hear some. I went through the Paolo and Francesca, reading the Italian and translating word by word:

> . . . How the desired smile
> Was kissed by such a lover...

Glyster and the rest dropped in. Laughter went round. But when Jim got his umbrella and we took the girls to a cab and he put Tina in one side and

I put Anna in the other, those were no laughing eyes that held me through the glass.

How laconically, as always, the Journal went to work—destined for the weekly scrutiny of Uncle Hazy and Aunt Willi—noncommittal, until whatever was hatching below the surface grew to such life-expectancy it had to be brought into the open:

Thursday: Last night I lent Anna a notebook of Alinari reproductions. She came today, about noon, on the excuse of returning it. She stayed to lunch. Fred brought the extra plate with much hand-rubbing, winking and glee, though he commented sadly on how little we ate. I showed her the gardens afterwards, the curved walk, St. Mary's and the Camera over the wall through leafless trees. Then into the chapel, where the organist was practicing a Prelude: *"O Mensch, bewein dein Sünde gross."*

Since then Daren had lived eleven years with Anna, and she had emerged in every dimension of person, politics and passion. Yet nothing was more true or central than the child of the Prince Charming fairy tale, who lingered at the heart of the journals. To find his way back there was like searching, from this rock, through a landscape of woods and fields, the continent of her manifold being—avoiding this byroad and the next: not the Anna who in the Chicago bed murmured of courtship and marriage, abortion, free love; not the nurse volunteering in Baltimore today for a doctor she had lately met at the scene of an accident; not the Jenny Higgins who would spend tomorrow collecting for civil rights trial—turn aside from those lanes and thoroughfares, follow the old blaze marks, down the hemlock wood, under the ledge, through the rhododendron, the air cool and damp and the sound of water, until the trail ends at a pool below a fall, in the deepest valley of their merging souls—a place as dreamlike and yet as real as the Boar's Hill garden they had happened on, that February of rainbows and larks.

Friday: The day has gone to Anna. We had thought yesterday was our last. But chance solved what we could not. I went by the Morgans' early and proposed a ride. The rest weren't ready or had to pack. So Anna took off alone. A guide like Wordsworth's wandering cloud led up Boar's Hill and into a garden which puts the other gardens of the world to shame. In a sloping bowl of evergreen, laurel, rhododendron already in bloom, paths and mazes led down to an artificial lake, and in the lake an island, the ground under the trees carpeted with snowdrops. We crossed a rustic bridge and sat by the water, a glimpse of Oxford off in the valley, over the pond and through the trees.

I have kept it back until now: we love each other. Yesterday, When she returned the album of pictures, she gave me a slip of paper on which, sitting alone in the college chapel, she had written:

"Though I speak with the tongues of men and angels and have not love, I am become as sounding brass or as a tinkling cymbal… Love suffers long and is kind."

("Everything that led her to the Left," the other Anna, her childhood friend, would say, "had its beginnings in Christ. She's covered that over to build what she is now. But we used to read the Gospels together, and talk about the Kingdom on Earth. She thought faith would move mountains, and that if she could only forget self and forget doubt, and say to the blind: 'Be whole!' they would see. When she turned from that, thinking it had betrayed her, she would never have pulled through, without the other hope. But it's left her divided, always.")

The revelation that had begun on Monday in the theater closed there Friday night. Anna was at Daren's side now, between him and Chuck. Her hand in the dark touched his sleeve, and his right reaching across took it secretly, so that what each followed was not the traffic of the stage but the stir and breathing of the other. Though they were aware that in the footlighted window Eliot's *Murder in the Cathedral* was completing some historical cycle: after realism and disillusion, the renewal of mystical search, a cult (Daren thought) of increasing fervor, until the age of prophets must return. "I'd known it since I was a child," Anna would tell him later, "that world-sickness. I had even thought of joining the church with my friend the other Anne. Until I learned the church-half of the world was dying, and it was the other half that was being born."

Daren, doubtful of either, might almost have settled for Arnold: "Ah, love, let us be true…" Whatever faith in absence was supposed to mean.

Saturday: To the train. Did Tina or Abbie, who are staying, or the others leaving, or those waving good-bye, think it strange that Anna should start for America in tears?

For me, I tell over moments hidden until now: In the churchyard at Church Handborough, when we lay, all eyes skyward, the Argus sleeping, I felt a stir, and a hand touched mine with the subtlety of a wild thing. I turned to Anna, but she was looking into the clouds. And on the tower at Eynsham, as we watched the sunset, her hand fell on my knee, I almost thought by chance. And in the museum on the red sofa before The Hunt by Night, as we met in geometrical forest depths, by a swamp *so* dim you could not know if it was mist or water. And though glances had now revealed everything, there was the lunch we could hardly finish, we were so caught in what had been disclosed. And yesterday, on an island in a garden that never was and never will be the same.

I write this, Uncle Hazlewood, in the notes I always send you. You have wished to share in my experience. Do not scorn what I hold sacred.

It was an indication of the stretch required, that the account of that week had not been bound with the rest. Only after Uncle Hazlewood's death were the pages found in the innermost receptacle of the office safe—an intrusion, almost, at that stage, since Daren, in his first attempt to revise the Journals, had filled the gap from memory and imagination. But he took up the less artful record. He had been trained as a scientist; where did his loyalty lie if not to the fact?

Winter bore down again, day after day; time never tires of a tale. He fell back on Anglo-Saxon. "I keep a ledger," he wrote, "between me and the gods. On their debit side much appears." It was hard, after such a promise of love, to take up the old cleavage, the vapid search. But the hunger, unslaked as ever, stared from the eyes.

Was it time to trot out the female members of the cast, give them labels for the allegory, like the Vices in Mantegna?

Jeffrey was out of it. If one meant her abstract state—Penthesilea of British liberal charm—Daren was not ready for that; if her particular being, she was a child, and his need was for a woman, and now.

Pippa fulfilled that much; but she was in Florence, an aesthetic ultimate, fragile as the angels in Angelico. Maybe the soul was always at that embrace by the paradise pool; what it left in flesh and presence was a void, neither carnal nor mystical.

Anna was of the earth and flesh, though Daren had not fully grasped that. He needed her to become human, as she needed him for her vision of the world. But the literal Anna had gone off with Chuck, unresolved. So the other choices could take their turns.

There was the mystical. Daren had only to play the records of Gregorian Chant bought at Virginia under the impact of Cader Ayres to give direction for that, back in time, through Renaissance and Gothic, into the crypts under the Fall of Rome; as for place, those records bore the name Solesmes, the monastery where they were made. Daren was bound to go there. The mystical possibility would present itself—though that yearning, as revolutionary as Anna's, and strangely related to hers, which the woman of Solesmes, Heloise Frank, would offer, could never be clear until she was dead, and beckoning, as in a sense she always had, from out of time and space altogether. And it would be next Easter before even a hint of that would reach him at Solesmes Abbey.

So the fifth alternative, which had been the first, and which, without Pippa or Anna, without mystical Heloise in the offing, might have set up its beehive columns in his heart, the Old South, had time for a brief revival before it fizzled and rattled off, the farce of *A Streetcar Named Desire*.

Get a load of the background detailed in Cynthia's letters—the girl, or as Hank Brown called her, the bitch of New Orleans:

Grandparents: Big Momma, who ruled in the Victorian house ("Yes, Momma. Comin. What is it, Momma?"); the ghost of Big Pappa, who had fought in the Civil War and died a wasting sickness ("Tell us about Big Pappa, Momma; what happened to him?"—"Well, Pappa is in paradise; but we *do* have some pictures.") And when the itinerant painter had pieced these together to make a nondescript portrait in gray uniform: "I declare," said Big Momma, "how Big Pappa has changed, these years."

Parents: Little Momma, who married the traveling salesman (I wish you'd a been here the other night; such a carryin on of wops and niggers wroppin the razor blades round each other's throats, I'd a called the police but for the fear of wakin Momma").

And, of course, the old Negro woman, Callie, who held the place together, with itinerant help from her half-grown sons ("Lawd, Misser Toppie, Ah never been married. These chillun fum mah cowtin days").

Cynthia, growing up there, hating it ("But why didn't you look after Momma? Oh if only I hadn't gone off, it wouldn't have happened this way." For Big Momma, once, out of spite, when Little Momma went to Virginia, had rolled off the bed and broken her hip) –Cynthia, blamed and scolded, running off in the dregs of the Depression with wastrel Toppie, a romance ending in alcohol, divorce—the perfect southern setup, "The soul preyed on by woe"—and now Cynthia had telegraphed she was on the way.

"Lawd," Hank Brown said after she had appeared in Daren's room (they were working together on *The Pearl),* "that gal's mouf look like a jaybird's ass in huckleberry time."

Lipstick could not obscure the voluptuous appeal. Daren rented her a bike and they went for a ride; they climbed the tower where he had looked at the sunset with Anna. A bird under the bush is worth two in the hand. In the evening, after dinner and a silly play, they went to her room.

Daren had not written it in the Journal, and it came back with the jerky flicker of an old one-reeler:

She had rented the digs of a student rusticated for the term. They had turned off the lights and were trying to kick the clammy sheets warm, when someone reeled upstairs and banged at the door: "Dave! Dave!"

"He's not here," Cynthia cried. And in Daren's ear: "I locked the door."

But the door was yielding. "What the hell are you doing, Dave?"

"He's not here!" While the landlord came from the cellar where he and his family laired.

"You mustn't do that, sir. There's a lady in there."

"What's Dave doing with a lady?"

"Mr. Pierce has gone down, sir. He is not in Oxford." The landlord poked in his head. "I'll just lock this, miss." He took the key from inside, locked the door, led the drunk downstairs and out, bolted that door and crept back to his basement bed.

Daren went to the window. "OK. I can climb down the pipe."

Passion had almost revived, lips, breasts, thighs. The danger for Leflore was inexperience. Could he have warmed this way to any woman, wreathing, dark, sad as the French horns in *Carmen,* and not venture his soul? Good that slapstick broke in: a scraping on the gutter, a form at the window, startling him from bed.

"Sorry, Dave, it's me, Rich. Didn't know you were here. Just climbing through to my room." He groped across in the dark and was fumbling at the door. Daren pulled on his clothes. "What's up? This door's locked. Where's the key?"

Daren leaned to the pillowed dark: "Call the landlord," he said; "it's no use." And then, almost to himself: "I strove with none, for none was worth my strife." He sprang to the window and caught the drain. In his room he calmed himself with *Antony and Cleopatra:* "This dotage of our general o'er-flows the measure."

The girl took up with Rich awhile, then joined a party and continued her tour. To be so lightly freed from the Cynthias and Sibyls of this world…

Winter term ground to its close, vacation appearing as lights conglobed through fog. Letters were more real than that, Anna, over the Lake Shore, unfolding herself on the page:

> I wish we could sit together these long evenings and talk. I would tell you of my life, while you listened, tender and wise, A good life. A blend of the sad and gay.
>
> In Illinois, fishing for crawdads and no bait, our feet in the water, until we felt them nibbling at our toes.
>
> At Christmas, picking hickory nuts around the kitchen stove, gouging the meat out with hairpins and with Mom's crocheting hook.
>
> I loved it. But I was always reaching for something above. Beauty. The light.

In Chicago, my first job, I saved and bought some black velvet, made a party dress with a V-neck and puff sleeves. One night I put it on, I don't know why, went to the North Side, lonely, wishing… A house of lights, young people going in. I went in with the rest. The young men danced with me, floating, in my velvet gown. One lifted me up and stood me on a chair, admiring. It seemed the way life should be lived.

But his father approached. Where had I come from? I told him I was walking past and it looked gay. He asked me to leave. The son protested and walked out with me, said he would take me home. But I thought of the place I lived Better to part there, on Goethe Street.

Daren had seldom been more moved than by the gift of this simple confidence.

Should he spend Easter back in Florence? Why not London once and for all? He wandered Fleet Street, the Temple, the Law Courts— the Elgin Marbles like smoky casts in a railroad station; he climbed St. Paul's dome over the March cold city; but it wouldn't come to life—not even Westminster Abbey, where an intense sparrow of a lady was hopping around Dickens' tomb, picking up scraps of paper to treasure in her heart, anything; she came every day, to make her feel close to Dickens—and say, bear witness now: Was not Dickens the greatest writer who ever lived? And for once the truth seemed too grim, and Daren lied.

Hank Brown saved him. "Come on, man, 'We goin South. We doan wanta hang aroun heah."

Clacking rails. Leflore sleeping in the baggage rack, waking over the border, lively Italians poking him in the rear, the net giving way, his bottom swagging over their heads; Hank leaning out at every station to read the signs: "Lawd, we is back in *Ritirata.*"

They stopped in the gray of Milan at a hotel which Hank said in the drawl that transformed every language "warn't no palatt-so." The maid felt the freezing little radiator and affirmed *"Caldo! Si, caldo!"* Also the light, which could hardly have been rated in candle power, she magnified like the Lord: *"Si, si, brilliante!"*

It was so cold only the cats could tell it was spring. They howled all night. "Dese Dago cats is sho nuff hot. Ah spec Ah climb out dis heah fenester on dis heah roof an git some o dat pussy quick." From the W.C. he came back recklessly unbuttoned, panting: "Ah jus run into one o dem Dago cats in de hall. Dey is sho nuff hot."

Italy was not the pure retreat of south and art it had been at the first coming, not quite the same carefree people. Even the comic assumed a sinister cast. The train out of Milan was full of soldiers. Soldiers? Three yokel-madmen in the compartment, with another in spiffier uniform—their keeper? For he did not take off his stinky shoes or leap in and out of the baggage rack as much as they did, or when one, smoking up there, and given a paper cup by a lady to save her from the ashes, collected a handful and dumped them down, did he applaud as wildly as the rest. Philosopher, maybe; since he opened the window, tore papers into little strips, and let them blow away one by one, reflectively. In any case, their leader; for when the smoker had fallen asleep, he rolled a newspaper into a cone, stuck it in the open mouth and set fire to it; so they all watched it burn until it touched the sleeper's nose, and he sprang up slapping and wheezing. Their leader; for when the plumpest leaned out of the window, he took a pin from his lapel, and showed the third how to ram it to the hilt in the broad rear. Soldiers!

And in Sirmione, beautiful almost-island in the Lake of Garda, when the founding of Rome was celebrated with a parade and speeches, the mounted militia stacked their bicycles in the square, and when they came back for them, turned the place into bedlam, each scrambling for his and throwing the rest into a tangle of ripped spokes and snagged fenders. It was hard to think of that screaming melee as the Roman Legions; yet one knew that such slapstick performers were already at it in Abyssinia and Spain.

They settled in Venice to study. In the Pensione Gabbia d'Ora, which Hank called "Grab your Gold," was an Alabama expatriate who had lived there for years; a lover of Italy, she had given her wedding ring in Mussolini's currency drive. She proudly showed her citation from the Duce. It drove Hank wild. She was also a fine pianist, and Daren was ready to grant her anything for Mozart on her Steinway; but Hank had to convince her how wrong her fascist exile was. "What a dull, sleepy man," she said—for they studied in the common rooms, and by afternoon when Hank yawned off for his nap, he would have piled up the trays, cups and saucers of five or six espresso coffees—"When he stops drinking coffee he goes to sleep, and when he wakes up he calls for more coffee." But she took a fancy to Daren.

It was the corn-fed American schoolteacher, come over for a year's study, who used to waylay Hank. She had been running a temperature and thought she had glandular fever or mononucleosis: "They call that kissing sickness," she tittered. Sis Cow, they named her, as she took her place with the Dago cats in Hank's amorous takeoff. "Ah jus run into Sis Cow," he announced in the evening, "an she say, ef she git dat mononucleosis under control, she be up heah in de bullpen fo long."

And Daren's first greeting from bed to bed in the morning: "Heyo, Br'er Bull! Did Sis Cow come up fo de service endurin of de night? An how did Br'er Bull git on?"

Conditioned by Blake and in love with Florence, Daren was less carefree about Venetian art: "That Palace putting on the Dog: heifer flanked Europas raped by the bull, puffy Junos, Venice showered with gold, gold, gold." An aesthetic deflection of the moral urge.

Hank took all that in his stride. He praised the "Titsy-anos" in the "Belly Arts Museum," smacking his lips over a Tiepolo Paradise: 'When Ah git deah, Ah hope ole Peter let me bugger a baroque angel."

The Hardys and Tina Morgan wrote from Florence. And Daren had grown such a boil on the side of his neck, he thought he was going into blood poisoning. He fled with Hank to the place he loved.

Pippa used to come to his room to nurse him in his fever, between sympathy and touch, hot and cold applications, opening, bandaging, she got a little boil herself on her middle finger. As he recovered they would sit in the spring sun on the roof garden, reading poetry and talking. Daren was brotherly and shy, troubled by what seemed his duplicity. But the last and warmest afternoon, the life-force sickness had quelled rose in him. And there was the Arno, in spring flood, roaring over the rock apron into the deep hole below the bridge. He put on his bathing suit and ran down, loungers of the city gathering to stare, while he plunged and swam, surfacing like a seal in the currents and foaming whirls of milky cold mountain water.

Pippa, alarmed, looked on from the loggia. As when he had climbed Monte Morello, he returned with the rush of Boreas seizing the Southwest Wind.

That evening he took his Anglo-Saxon to the salon. He was reading those remarkable fragments called "The Later Genesis." Pippa joined him. In time they were alone in the great room.

"It was Florence you loved," she said, "what a poet calls 'its fatal beauty.' But for me Florence had become a prison. Only when you were gone, I saw how far you had broken it. I said I couldn't love again; but I loved your letters. Then you came from Venice, and you were sad. What could I tell you? But today, when you swam in the Arno against all right and reason, I made up my mind: *Dar-ren, caro, ti voglio bene.*"

When Daren got to his room, Hank was reading in bed. He saw the book Daren had in his hand. "The Later Genesis!" he cried. It was not in the mood of his Sis Cow jokes, but of his political rages. "You aren't doing her any good, you know."

He turned his face to the wall.

7. *The Incursion*

The full heat of July. In the Journal, too, Daren had reached what they called summer term, though it opened with weeping April.

The sun over Suicide Rock stood at the zenith: Zeno's paradox: the Journal becalmed on a Sargasso of art. When the day closed in stalemate, one could pay a visit—

Apart from Cader Ayres, two old codgers, not long for this world, boosted the general tone of living around Patapsco.

There was the free-verse poet, Richard Ramon Richards—Spanish blood drawn from the islands to the seaboard melting pot—trained as a doctor, though he had staked his soul on writing. Before the strokes hit him, his style was tense, hard, hermetic as Pound's. Brain damage knocked out his left side, crippled his memory, speech, eyes; he came from death barely able to peck on the typewriter his looser and more radiant poems.

That spring he had been honored in Princeton. Cader Ayres and Daren drove him up. The official committee led him stumbling and halting into the huge Gothic chapel. You couldn't tell if he would make it to the choir and the chair. They set the microphone in front of him. The pale, stricken man, never at peace with the church, craned into the academic vault, whispering an aside which the public address sent out over the sea of literati, teachers, students, the poetry festival crowd: "An awful impressive place, and not of my choosing; but if He can stand it, I guess I can."

Since the stroke, he had taught himself to read again. He took every line like a rusty pianist who can hardly trust his fingers. When he stumbled, he would shrug the shoulder that was still under command, and try again. Before he was handicapped, in the old days, he used to read as from a tower of alienation. When he had finished, he would cough and people would file out—as another poet recorded it: "A professor in enormous tweeds, drained spittle from his pipe, then scrammed." Now it seemed he could feed thousands from his basket of broken loaves and fishes.

In the last poem he tripped on the final line. He smiled like old Lear, went back to the beginning, hit the same hurdle, missed. He craned into the vault: "By God, I'll try again." He started, built up speed, approached, he soared up, up—and over. He bowed his head, while the crowd of occasion-hunters, caught in a sacred enactment—what they had never known poetry was, the leap beyond words, all scratches and grunts of sound, gestures of the marketplace falling off like a charred wick from the spaceless flame—stood in total applause. "To reconcile the people and the stones."

—One could visit Richard Ramon Richards.

Or there was the Chicago painter, A. B. Conway ("As simple," he used to say, "as ABC."). Anna had known him in the old days when he was back from Europe out of work, painting for the W.P.A. To come to Patapsco City and find him teaching in Cader Ayres' program was like a reunion for her; but she was soon troubled by the visionary impracticality of his art. His studio lean-to backed over the slope and woods a bit farther up the hill. He had outlived his cares and connections, wife, family, everything but the creative plight, which was that of the soul in time.

He would spend a day in the studio, puttering around, messing up old pictures, waiting for Light. And it was sure to come at dusk, as the actual light was fading, the landscape out the window looming into somber power. He would begin to paint. "The owl of Minerva," he would say, "flies only in the deepening dusk." Of Minerva, maybe; but a dim rule for painting. Daren and Anna would find him squinnying through his fist at darkness, rushing up, scratching off paint, daubing on more. "Gloom it up, Dad, gloom it up!" his son, now teaching abroad, used to say.

From time to time, in spite of himself, he might finish a great picture, fail to destroy it. Then his task became to hide it, belittle it, run it down. Last fall, when Daren and Anna were first invited to his house, his wife was still alive and they needed money. Daren had been staggered by the beauty of an unfinished picture on the wall. "It's a sketch, a failure," A.B.C. groaned, took it down, and stuffed it into a closet. The phone rang. He had been nagged into putting another picture in a Baltimore show, where some manufacturer had taken a fancy to it. The fellow could have bought it directly from the gallery, but in an evil hour, he thought he'd like to talk with the painter. A.B.C. was heard at the phone, while his troubled wife held her head: "It's only a sketch, not finished. Oh no. I'd rather not. A failure. What size room? Twenty feet? It should be seen from twenty yards. How do the windows face? South? It needs a north light. Why don't you give it up?… What color scheme?… Wouldn't do. You're making a big mistake. Forget it. That's the best thing… Good-bye."

Tonight, as he *scowled o'er the darkened landskip*, A. B. C. was grieving about having to teach all the time when he wanted to paint.

Daren remembered that other evening. "Why don't you sell some of those paintings rolled up in the attic, old man?"

"Paintings? Nobody would buy my paintings."

"You've set your heart on that. You've tried to stay obscure."

A. B. C. flung up his arms. "I've succeeded beyond my wildest dreams.

Before these shadowy landscapes, the problem was, as always, to open out that middle ground of Oxford, between foreground Patapsco and a backdrop of youth, forebears, history, to plot the incursion of past and to-come into the facile interlude which was the Journal Now.

Daren had begun to write Pippa as the train between tunnels gave flashes of the Riviera, a swell rolling in on a shore where oranges ripened in the sun, perfect swimming weather. He had posted the letter at a station somewhere far in the Alps, fir forests stretching up to white peaks under a moon. Back on the train, he found a compartment empty but for a goateed Frenchman, who for the dignity of the goatee, sat upright. Daren stretched out opposite. While the letter of his inadequacy ("Pipistrella, I am torn") made its way back to Florence.

A tangle of lives, each looping over and giving direction to the rest: Tina Morgan, pleased with the Pippa revival in Florence, writes brother Chuck to have hope for his marriage; Anna, getting wind of this, thrusts back like a gyroscope at right angles to the impressed force, heightening her exchange with Daren.

As in *The Magic Flute,* a first triple clarion opened the term: *spring, love, absence.* But whose absence? And love for whom? Daren had thought of summer vacation in southern Germany and Austria. He had written Pippa and asked her to join him—however out of touch with her nature that might seem. Suppose she had? He would have been loyal. So there was a sense in which he was ready to give up Anna. But how could a vague readiness hold out against the pressed Bleeding Heart that arrived in the mail, or the lock of hair, or the little French calendar in which the regular festivals had been replaced with a series of "Our Days," from the Rhodes House meeting to the last Oxford week, decorated like Easter in a sacred missal? Daren was sure to interrupt his study and even his thoughts of Florence to dream over such reminders.

By this time the Morgan girls were back in Oxford; and of course they would have heard of Anna's correspondence. Like bushbeaters or tireless bawds, they began to run in dames for Daren. *Love* in *absence* yielded to the affability of spring, as Tina and her subject Jim scheduled picnics, cycle rides, puntings on the Isis and the Cherwell: with the lean girl from St. Hilda's (British as they come), the jolly tomboy from California, the sunny-haired great Dane. Competent appearances, they did not give the feel of having wagered life itself as Anna had done—were not, as she (strange, that softness in a woman of such force), vulnerable.

To spotlight the Dane, Tina told snowy-haired Fred that Daren had been married in secret and his wife was going to come to tea. "I'll clean," Fred cried, "I'll clean. They're particular that way."

For the first time he brought out a beat-up vacuum cleaner. Daren was on the sofa, translating from the Chronicle:

> Then they rode thither and they met the prince in the town where the king lay slain, and they had shut the gate to, and they hurried thereto. Then they

offered them their choice of money and land if they would grant him the kingdom, and they told them their kinsmen were with them and that they would not go from them…

The air was getting darker than the Anglo-Saxon. The roar went on, back and forth through the mounting gloom. "This a'n't doing any good, sir," Fred cried. But he kept at it, until Daren got up coughing: "What're you trying to do?" Fred shut off the machine, "His bag's busted," He pointed. The whole top was ripped out. "That's the way. Whenever I wants to use'im, 'e's out o fix.

The Danish girl canceled; so the nearest thing to a wife was child Jeffrey, whom Mrs. Hardy brought along. Jeffrey had heard about Daren's messy room, the floor so littered with books he would trip on them and spill his tea. As it happened, he had just bought a shelf of old leather-bound plays, and they were heaped everywhere. Jeffrey couldn't have been more pleased—especially with the dust; she rubbed her fingers on tables and shelves and went into stitches of glee.

That evening a letter broke into the spring. It trumpeted the second triple theme: *Mississippi, self-slaughter, pain.*

My dear Daren: I have stayed in the office alone to write you tlhe hardest letter I have ever had to write. We have been worried about your brother Vail at college. His grades had fallen off; it seemed he could not concentrate. Yesterday we were phoned. He had shot himself playing Russian roulette. He would have been killed if a friend had not knocked the revolver. The wound is superficial, but he has had to leave school.

Also your sister has been working too hard, and now with Vail's attempt, we are frightened for her. Her poetry, which was always strange, is brooding and irrational.

You have planned to spend your summer on the Continent, and I hate to upset that; but with your steadiness and maturity, you might be able to help June and Vail if you were here.

We send our love.

Uncle Hazlewood

Hard to convey to those not born in the South the weight of family past: at Ararat, where evenings and Sundays would be spent less reading books about strangers than poring over memoirs, letters, albums of lost Leflores—or of the rest whose names, Quincy, Prentiss, Hazlewood, his of Daren and his brother's of Vail, worn like matronymics, tied the living to the dead. In Rome, those gloomy statues of Immolators of the Republic toting their ancestors in solemn procession had presented Daren with his own likeness.

This ill-defined, slight mask was of Great-great-grandfather Quincy Leflore, who adventured with Aaron Burr, took his amorous leavings, and jumped in his own plantation bayou ten years later, for causes unknown. And this one, filled in by his war journals in such bitter detail, was his grandson of the same name, a captain in the Army of the Confederacy. And there was Daren's father, and his mother, both darkly veiled. And all these heads bore on the present crisis.

Choose one. Captain Quincy, at Vicksburg:

> I was with the battery on the hill. The whole surface of the river was lighted from burning buildings on the other shore, revealing six steamers and two gunboats firing as rapidly as their guns could be worked, while our batteries poured out shot and shell.
>
> One of the boats took fire. A volcano of sulfurous flame went up into smoke rosy as a sunset cloud. Through the bursting of bombs and screaming of shot came the cries of the burning and the wild hurrahs of our men.
>
> To walk eye-deep in the death-work of hell.

Rain in torrents. Men slithering through mud under bombardment in the perpetual presence of wounds, gangrene, death; dwindling rations: horse, mule, peas, dog, grass, rat; polluted water; and that great serpent of a gunboat river spilling in overflow all the infections of bog and fen: measles, mumps, malaria, yellow fever, bloody flux, dropsy, quinsy, pleurisy, jaundice; and no medicine but a bitter tea of dogwood and willow bark.

Two forays they made from there before they were bottled up in the last siege: one a mere wandering, into the flooded swamp of the Delta. Grant was up there, and they groped for him, steamed up the Yazoo and the Sunflower and Cypress Bayou, which the flood waters were backing into. They wound north and west, brushing the stacks on overhanging trees, almost to the river again, the bank of Lotus Lake cropping out of the universal brown flood, a plantation cleared in oak forest, a brick house with verandas on a sawed-off Indian mound, slave quarters stretching back along the shore of Panther Burn—Colonel Hazlewood's Ararat ("Arry-rat? Narry-rat All of em drownded"). But Delta Landing had been fired and Grant had moved on. When Quincy's company was returned to Vicksburg, he carried in his breast pocket a little embroidered Confederate flag: "An ever-watchful eye be over thee. Gracia Hazlewood."

And then that starved pitiful army struck south across the Bayou Pierre, almost to Leflore's native country, the gentle ladies of Port Gibson lining the streets, cheering through their tears:

> The deep thunder of artillery was almost drowned in the roar of muskets which enveloped the whole front in folds of smoke. Laggards met their flying squadrons, cut to pieces by a force five times our own. We had barely formed a new line when the enemy opened a withering fire of grape, canister and musket shot. Utterly exhausted, my friend Pitt had thrown himself down against a tree. When the bullets began to whistle around us, he caught his gun by the muzzle to draw it to him. The hammer struck the tree, the cap exploded and the whole charge fired into his arm, tearing it to shreds from the wrist to above the elbow. "Oh Quincy," he cried, "I have destroyed my arm." He was placed on a litter and borne fainting to the rear. I never saw him again.

Speak of Russian roulette! What was the Civil War but a gesture of suicidal despair? Vicksburg fallen, the Confederacy split, Mississippi abandoned, deserters stealing home everywhere—Quincy and his like fought on, two more years, hopeless; they were shot down and left on the field, they staggered from the grave; a rabble at last, barefoot, black with lice, skulking in the swamps, they would creep out to pillage and loot, living off their own routed people, as much a plague as Sherman's foragers. Surrender belched them up. Step by step, as Quincy trudged west, not to his burned-out Natchez farm, but to the floodplain of the Delta, a tiny spot of light in the great night swamp, his mind ground it over, bitterness lashing him on:

Whipped. North and South, Black and White. Betrayed. Thirty millions of the same race under the same Hag, to tear themselves and their country apart, only to demonstrate that republican governments are a failure, have always been a failure, and always will be. The worst waste in history. I have learned things of man I could wish never to have known, and things of God that are no comfort to the race of mortals.

"Imagine men in chains, all condemned to death, some killed every day in the sight of the others, the rest to wait their turn, seeing their fate in their fellows, looking around without hope. An *image of the condition of man.*"

Quincy had closed the journal with that quotation from Pascal. Though the Delta, when he arrived, was crisp with fall, the clearings white with cotton, good hunting weather. By canoe at last, he came to Lotus Lake and found Ararat unchanged, the low sun stretching out the oak trees. He mounted the piazza and heard Gracia singing at the piano: "When this cruel war is over."

Next day she took him to church, though he was not a believer. That would have been in the brick Episcopal chapel, since burned. Miss Gracia had ridden over the neighborhood before the war, collecting for the reed organ, which she played afterwards on Sundays. But it had broken down and there was no one to repair it. The bishop, who was visiting that day, called on the white members to raise the tune, but Miss Gracia had to carry it almost alone. He called to the gallery, where the colored brethren raised it with such fervor he hardly knew how to turn it off. He did not want the sober Word swept away by that Pentecostal cry from the gallery.

You would have thought a man who had suffered through so much, when he came at last to Ararat, would have planted his vineyard for life. And he did, on the surface. His thought, however, once he had closed his war journal with Pascal, went underground. What one heard afterwards were public encomiums: "The Leader of his People," "The Lone Hawk of the Delta." It was thirty years later, when the shot was fired and he was found slumped at his desk, another passage from the same book copied on the page before him: "The struggle alone pleases; the victory is death"—that he spoke from the same depths.

Why else, after four years of war, after marriage, and settling in the Delta, watching three children grow a little and then (as if the fen he had moved to was not for human continuance) be cut down by yellow fever, which he and his wife burned through but did not die of; after taking up life again and fighting through slimy bogs of Reconstruction, tackling the physical habitat as well, establishing a levee system and opening huge tracts of woodland to agriculture, bringing in railroads that threaded the low country and turned what was waste into wealth; after draining, and providing clean water, screening houses and paving roads, slowly consolidating that malarial half-jungle into a polity; and then, like old Job, starting a new family, fathering two sons who lived, and begetting a daughter soon to be borne by the wife he must still have loved; after so emerging from the dark that is supposed to try the soul, coming out at an almost peaceful shore, family, fortune, respect, the honor of a term in the U.S. Senate, though he wearied of that and came home—why else, just then, should he have bowed out, with no account given but the copied charge: "The struggle alone pleases; the victory is death"?

It would be easy for Anna later (any Anna) to sound the hollowness of that success: white supremacy raised on the Klan and sharecropping of bamboozled Negroes—not a pretty struggle Quincy had led: to impeach Governor Ames and throw the carpetbaggers out of power, use the freed slaves who had followed him from Natchez and shared his name, and those others whose singing had stirred him when he came to Ararat, turn their trust against the Yankees who, lifting them up, had made a grab bag of the state, maneuver them to vote themselves out of power, a chicanery which only the assumption of moral right could have rendered palatable—and how hard to maintain that in the face of the po-white deserters he had scorned during the war and had to side with now—not a pretty fight, though it opened with burlesque, the funeral he planned and announced mouth to mouth: under cloud and rain a long line of mourners to follow a coffin on a wagon from the courthouse, the pallbearers Confederate officers, the wagon black with crepe, wails of grief and rolling drums, until the box was lowered into a grave and the rebel yell broke for the last official time over the Delta, and dirt fell on the despised old carpetbag they had buried in lieu of a corpse-under the statesman's mask, the falseness of all those values: the show (Anna would say) of bourgeois marriage, which everybody had to keep smiling over pretending it was true-surely all that (she would claim) might sour on a Lone Hawk, without the need of Pascal's pessimism.

But Daren labored at a deeper mystery, bottomless as the Pascalian text—the death call to which every refined nature is attuned, without which our nobilities would be unthinkable: (as Homer said) "And now battle became sweeter to them than to go back to the pleasant land of their fathers." He wrestled with a longing as winged and arrowed as the word "expire." If it had struck like lightning from generation to generation through his family and through the family of man, was anybody to know where it might strike again?

The contrast of that Blue Hole heritage—he, brooding in Gloucester College over the letter of his brother's self-hate and his sister's derangement, the old nemesis so deeply laired in time (grandfather, father, mother, brother) miasmal around him (like the time Uncle Hazlewood, taking up the stem role of father, offered Daren a dollar if he would read Bulwer-Lytton's "Haunter and the Haunted" late one night and walk out and wait in the cemetery until the town clock struck midnight, and he did, though the malice that had mesmerized everything in the fictional London house crept from the white tombstones and lurked in every pit of shade) –the gulf between that heritage and Oxford had never caught him with such force as when the door opened and Cyril Mercer walked in.

Uncle Hazlewood had been after Daren to make some English friends, but he hadn't found any that seemed enough alive. Not until Cyril Mercer came along—a sort of holdover from another century: money to burn and shockingly in debt, housed in the best room in the college, from which he had banished the furniture to install antiques; he dined like a character in Dickens and had his own space in the college wine cellar. He read French novels, drank his port, laid on flesh, hated drafts, eschewed every exercise but fencing, bought eighteenth-century drawings at what Daren considered scandalous prices. "You know, sir," he said one evening, as he surveyed himself in Daren's room, Piranesi architectural engravings he had just bought spread before him, "I look every day more and more like a splendid baroque church."

The figure loomed in the Journal like Dr. Johnson—though the snapshots Uncle Hazlewood had mounted there showed a bad little fat boy, Tweedledum or Tweedledee, just opening his mouth to say "Nohow" or "Contrariwise"—anyway, Daren had an English friend at last, though Mercer's exuberance didn't come from nowhere; his father was an old-time money-lending Jew.

"Monstrous evening," he cried. "Sir, I am drunk. When I am drunk no woman can resist me, for then I am very passionate." (Mussing his hair over his face.) "But she was a guest, sir, a married woman. My girl friend brought her along, out of pity; little hubby gone abroad. But to eat my food and drink my wine and talk of married happiness: 'I love every little inch of him.' Sir, I resolved to take her home. Smuggled a claret as we left. Rather a bill. She wanted me to see their little love nest. Feel how happy they were. I ditched the bien aimé. At eleven-fifteen she caved in. Then she wept. Had to see me again. Monstrous evening. If she hadn't thrown it in my face. Love nest indeed."

Steadiness? Maturity?

True, he decided to drop Europe and go to Mississippi for the summer; but he couldn't do it without slashing out like sick Hamlet, as if his brother's and his sister's disorder could purge itself through him in wild and whirling words.

When Cyril had gone, Daren wrote Pippa a letter calculated to detach her from one so congenitally unfit: "Fall in love with an Italian, marry and be happy, for my sake… Remember me as an incident, a threat you have outlived."

Though he would go on writing her from that heavy summer at Ararat and in Delta Landing:

> My sister has gone to the sanatorium and my brother has tried to take his life again. I live much in the past, and from all years choose chiefly the time in Florence to inhabit. Every day I swim a mile for my exercise. Then I study and write. I have gone over my sister's poems and designs, trying to understand what has happened to her, and a mood has settled on me like a spirit from another world. I find myself tracing shapes in paneled wood or sketching illustrations for poetic lines. I hope to see you Christmas, but cannot tell what I will feel. No doubt what I always did. Love…

Blowing hot and cold.

It was not in Pippa's nature, so discouraged, to press on. Though Anna, to whom Daren wrote the same night in the same vein ("…for virtue cannot so inoculate our old stock but we shall relish of it… Get thee to a nunnery…"), would be harder to dissuade. Had she not sealed her bond already? *"Love suffers long…"*

Leflore gave warning. Then he launched into the third of the triple chords, closing the term. It was *Jeffrey, Wales, the sea.*

8. *Thy Father's Spirit*

The cycles were to be left for the summer at Stoke-under-Wychwood. Clear evening after rain, mist rising from the valleys, drifting over the road, bringing smells of the earth, pine, new-mown hay, the clay banks of streams. Jim and Daren rode into the sun that circled toward the north, imperceptibly setting. As they plunged through the shadow of Wychwood, they took the whiff of flowers; and now they saw them, diapering the ground, kingcups, wood hyacinths, anemones. They picked a bunch and went on to the Grange. Jeffrey was at the gate.

"We have a little sister, and she hath no breasts. What shall we do for her in the day she shall be spoken for?"

Fill her arms with flowers…

Mornings they would help cut the grass, weed, clean the saddles and bridles, groom the horses or walk with Jeffrey in the meadows. Daren bought her a kite and put it up under racing clouds, skylarks fountaining around it in the sun; but the kite went wild, plunged and immolated itself in the high-tension wires that went striding over the Cotswolds behind the farm.

Afternoons or evenings they would go to Stratford for the plays—the bard as always at the mercy of anybody's bad taste. The Russian director made a hash of *Lear,* put steps all over the stage to give the old gasper the right eminence for the first scene; so all the rest of the play people had to be stumbling up and down those steps. Hamlet had gone Freudulent-mother-loving manic-depressive with homosexual leanings. Hank, with them for the day, upheld a Dutch version he saw over Christmas, where the Ghost bawls: *"Ik bin der Spook deins Papa."* When Jim tried to get serious, Hank would break in: "Ah know Hamlet poked him tho' de arras; what Ah wants to know is—what's his *arras?*"

Only the matinee of *As You Like It,* to which they took Jeffrey, was unspoiled. And there was the picnic before in Ann Hathaway's orchard, when Daren ran up an old apple tree, and leaning far out, picked South African pippins from his sleeve by sleight of hand and tossed them down to Jeffrey.

Then Wales. And then the sea…

The blue diesel of the Baltimore and Ohio throbbing under the Patapsco rock, stopping, backing, belching fumes, and again the roar and geyser of oil exhaust, the couplings groaning as the line of empty coal cars picks up speed, Lackawanna Valley, Pittsburgh and Shawmut, Coast Line— strange how our westward valleys all lead northerly, up into the mine fields, Anna's father's mine fields, Daren's grandfather's mine fields—as the present opens to a background stretching out forever, ramifications never to be told…

> If Reading, Alabama and Delta Landing, Mississippi, had not been one so large and the other so small, you could almost have called them twin cities through that time.

He wrote it and scratched the words. Opposites: Reading crass and new, Delta Landing creped in antebellum. And yet, as the old families would have told you, this was the third Delta Landing. The first, behind Lotus Lake, had been silted up and abandoned. The second had been fired by Grant and caved in the river, "a town" (as a local historian wrote) "of whose earlier avatars" (that grand old Mississippi word) "no vestige remains to show where people lived and loved, knew human hopes and fears."

So it happened that when the coal and iron of the Reading hills began to be exploited, the present Delta Landing was also taking shape. Soon they were joined by a railroad, in which the Leflores had a family interest, and the industrial giant and the cotton-broking river town became poles of a common axis. Delta girls would go to Reading for the cotillion dance and the opera; Reading men would come to the Delta lakes and forests to fish or to hunt deer, bear, alligator. And, of course, there were business connections:

Theodore Freeman, heir to certain coal mines, was on the board of the Delta-Reading Railroad.

Among the old pictures at Ararat was one made on a shooting platform by Lotus Lake. Teddy was laughing in one corner, while Willi Mari, in a long classic gown, and slim as a blossoming spray, swung from the waist, leveling a gun over the windblown wide water. It had always been a puzzle for Daren and Vail: could that be their straitlaced, plump and religious Aunt Willi, so deeply widowed she seemed the archetypal old maid—she who would rather have handled a rattlesnake than a gun?

And there was the flood picture of 1914 in Delta Landing: couples with parasols strolling the levee between the swollen river and the flooded town. A steamboat was coming into the wharf; and Teddy and Willi Mari were skipping along laughing, as if the whole show had been put on for their benefit, a precious lark.

The First World War broke into that, blighted it maybe; though if so, the damage did not at first appear. Since no time promised more in the records than the years after the Armistice, when Theodore came back to marry Willi Mari, and Ararat and cotton were booming, and Uncle Hazlewood went to write poetry abroad, and Daren's father Prentiss, though the younger son, began to take the Lone Hawk's place as political leader of the Delta, and Judge Byrne was building a columned mansion and dreaming of politics, and even the dregs of the town, Bull Slaughter and the rest, who would side later with violence and the Klan, were war heroes, come like the sun from the East in a morning phase.

Here were the central four: Teddy and the still girlish Willi, Prentiss with Daren's slight and mysterious mother, Iris; the women seated, the men standing in a single small skiff sunk to the gunwales among cypress knees, where Panther Burn flowed out of the Blue Hole, hauling up huge strings of saddle-blanket white perch, so the whole setup looked ridiculously like Raphael's tapestry of The Miraculous Draught of Fishes.

Or there was the hunting camp deep in swampwoods between the lake and the river. That was already beginning to take on a sinister cast, the men too huge, the whiskey jug too conspicuous. Dan Byrne, the old photographer, had taken it, caught Captain Poindexter, the enormous Major Shields and the rest, as they lounged in front of the tents one fall day after the hunt and a meal (Dan Byrne, the outsider, who didn't drink their whiskey and didn't share their tales), the guns stacked against the water oaks as at the bivouac of an army. Dogs were lazing around, hounds and pointers and some big tough curs. On a board shelf nailed between trees were the whiskey and the molasses and the cornmeal.

A little more and one of those dynamic beefy men could have been Teddy Roosevelt, and it would have been that hunt when the President had come to these same big woods and for two days missed even seeing a bear, and that night around the fire Colonel Alexander told him: "Mr. President, you'll see a bear tomorrow if Hoke Collier has to lasso one and tie it to this tree." And sure enough, that Indian-Negro wonder-worker Hoke trapped one somehow, and there it was tied and roaring when the President came back from another fruitless day.

But the time the picture was made they had done better. From a jutting limb hung the carcass of a mammoth bear, and beside it, with all the pride of ownership, looking as if he had not shot but wrestled it to death, was the even grosser form of southern aristocracy, dressed in the padded coverall he called his hunting suit. It was Willi Mari's Teddy, thickening toward the mass in which, not long after, his liver dragged him to the grave.

Yet even from those years there was one picture of joy, the only companion to the shooting scene by the lake. In a morning room in Reading, gauzy curtains blew from an Art Nouveau French window, and from the window and the curtains came a light that made everything translucent, and in that light, by a pot of Christmas fern, stood Willi Mari in a thin mull strawberry-printed gown, loose hanging, caught under the paps with the turn of a velvet sash, swelling below to a Burgundian belly...

Fine photographs are swan songs, pearly reminders —that the sexless aunt, Willi Mari, in this particular fleeting room, had been that girlish bearer of a son as brief as her own marriage, youth, happiness, as elusive as the light recorded there.

Theodore drank, chased women, piled up debts. No wonder in Daren's youth Willi Mari had been in all things the voice of prohibition. What did they expect, those gowned dreamers—Aunt Willi, engaged—how long was it?—six years, and through a war, to a bourbon-swilling piece of flesh like Teddy Freeman? Poor Aunt Willi—a few years playing at lady in the big house (under what revelation? something more than husband-sot and the child's death to veer her from gay southern ways, to make her the corseted Calvinist foe of every indulgence); and then to be left with a mine and the house and other properties, all mortgaged into ruin.

That was when Daren's father, though he had enough to do, with his practice and politics in Delta Landing, besides the plantation (Uncle Hazy sending back fragile evocations in the Parnassian and Symbolist vein from Athens, Olympia and the isles of Greece), had often to be in Reading, staying with Willi Mari, or when he had taken her back to Delta Landing, going it alone in the big place, salvaging what he could from the shipwreck of her affairs—

Enough to do, with the revived Ku Klux Klan fanning out from Reading, Colonel Stump come over to take the Delta by storm, Bull Slaughter and the other Gyves men (backbiting Governor Gyves, who died later—fit scourge—of cancer of the mouth) gathering their forces—until Prentiss Leflore met them and their Colonel in a courthouse debate and so wrapped the facts and fancies around Stump, with all his local backers, that he looked like a webbed-up fly—while the Delta aristocrats rallied, campaigned like old times and won the sheriffs race for Major Shields, who was too fat to function, but whose heart was in the right place; so the Klan was knocked out of Delta politics once and for all—

And as if that wasn't enough to keep a man busy, Prentiss had to be commuting over, staying and working in that house haunted by the splurge and debts of Teddy Freeman's past…

> Daren, my dear: The news of your brother fills me with terror. There are things
> I must talk with you about. They cannot be written. I have always loved your

family. Stop with me in Reading on your way home this summer. Before you see your people. It is a matter of life and death.

Your father's friend. And yours,

Isabella Wynne

Among other things, Daren was assigned Restoration Comedy for the summer. Heretofore his love-search had been in terms of Gothic Romance; but what it was leading him into was more like fierce Wycherley, *The Country Wife*—and he did mean cuntry matters.

Daren got on the S.S. *Deutschland* and behold! another desperate woman whose husband had sought her gratitude by sending her abroad stood with him over the moonlit sea, after they had left the third-class crowded dance floor, and as Daren weighed possibilities, pressed against him, raising her lips, her hand at the same time descending, as she whispered something about a cause of thanks and a countervailing curse, that the blessing of a single cabin was annulled by the phase of the moon. And he was so inept that it took him several minutes of contemplating the heavenly orb to realize it was not that she was talking about, though like that it would change...

Then it was Bella Wynne meeting the train in Reading, and Restoration Comedy mingled with his father's tragic end.

She must have been almost forty, but you would not have believed it, she was so kittenish and full of southern charm, bubbly as a girl—telling his fortune (and caressing his palm) almost before she could get him off the train:

"This last year has been a critical one for you. You have done a lot of thinking about yourself. Don't carry it too far. I see danger." Perceptive— if she had not already known his family affairs. Or been overheard that night at a party in his honor, voicing the same fortune for a young broker of Reading, while she paddled his plumper paw.

That was in the living room of her Reading house, her third house, she said, a bungalow, where she was camping out until her ship came in and she could build the place of her dreams. She was standing beside one of her

123

own paintings, a parasoled voluptuous self-study, à la Renoir, in a garden.

She had pursued art in college and for a time in New York and had developed an Impressionistic skill. Certainly she had the most extraordinary model right there under her clothes, and she could strip it down whenever she wanted to, and with a couple of mirrors get it displayed in any posture she pleased, and she loved it—like Whitman—every little inch, it was all so luscious.

The house was full of her. If you ate, over the sideboard, displayed like a milk-white sea, was the beautiful Isabella. Retire to the small study for a tête-à-tête, those pneumatic blisses lure you from the wall. In the guest room we dream under the sultry languor of Isabella reclined. Even in the tub one was hailed by the buttock and lifted breast (as in the Munich Boucher) of Bella laved in sun. And always those arms stretched over that head, inviting reckless necks to swing in love's halter.

A husband had been tangled there—now a traveling man; he had engendered a son—not in evidence (all males turning to specters under Bella's emanation). There was a daughter also, studying dance in New York. Daren and Bella enjoyed lunch alone.

"We have to face it now," she said, "together." And looked at him, the blue of her eyes swimming a little onto the lids. She took his hand, led him to the car and drove to the house he already knew too well, gray stucco and oak, "half-timbered" Teddy had called it, though it looked like a dirt-dauber's nest, where Daren had stayed off and on with Aunt Willi and his father before the Flood, and being lonely and thinking of Uncle Teddy's run-down coal mine, had dug as far as he could into the clay bluff behind the sumac bushes, until one day as he wormed out to dinner the bank caved in on his legs with such a weight, he felt how barely he had been spared—that house he had never liked, even before his father's death there—she drove to it and parked under the frowning front, the bees still buzzing from the crossbeam where they used to swarm out in the spring and pepper anybody they didn't take to:

"Daren," she laid her ringed Titian hand on his thigh, "brace yourself. Because I have to tell you. You know I bought this house and tried to live here. I loved your father, your whole family. I loved this house too. You believe in the power of the spirit? Your father's spirit, Oh it was so powerful.

"That day I walked up to the screen porch, just there, I heard a shot that rang through the walls. There was a scream and the sound of a body threshing. The world of vision opened. I saw into the house like a stage. It was the attic. The body of a man was lying with one shoe off, far back under the eaves. And I knew it was Prince. (I never called him Prentiss, I didn't like the name; I called him my Prince.)

"Until then I didn't know how your father died, only what was in the papers—though they called it suicide. I went to one of his dear friends. 'Where did Leflore kill himself?' I asked.

"'I don't think I should tell you all that.'

"'I know already,' I said. 'I saw it yesterday. I saw him dead way back under the eaves.'

"'1 wish you'd never moved to that place,' he told me. 'But now you know. He crawled under the roof in the attic; he took off his shoe. He put the shotgun in his mouth and pulled the trigger with his toe.'

"'I'm not afraid,' I told him. 'Prince wouldn't hurt me. I loved him.'

"But it's hard," her hand tightened on Daren's thigh, "to love the dead. Such a strong spirit. So many visions. One day I came back to the house (I could never call it home) and there had been so much pounding on the doors and shaking of walls and shots and cries from the attic (I was used to it, but we had to get new servants all the time) that the cook had phoned the police. A policeman was on each side of the attic door (I kept it locked) and another was standing back from it, ready to shoot through the panel, while the door and the whole wall shook with the crashing of some great force on the other side. Oh, he was a fierce spirit, your father.

"'Don't shoot, you fool,' I told the policeman. 'All of you, put up your guns and go away.'

"'No, Mrs. Wynne,' they said. 'We're goin to protect you.'

"'Go away,' I said. 'I know who it is and I loved him. I'm not afraid. Go away.'

"The bishop had given me a Latin prayer and a candle to burn. (In France I had joined the Church, though it's not known around here; the Klan makes it hard for Catholics.) When I did that, the pounding would ease off. But I never knew when it would break out again.

"One night Mr. Wynne was away, and a friend was coming to call. I was changing. My dress was half over my head, my arms raised, and that hubbub began. 'OK, Prince,' I said, 'I'm busy now. Give it up.' For a minute everything was quiet. Then there was a rap, like this, in a rhythm… "

Bella Wynne reached out and tapped the windshield of the car: *tap-tap-tap, tap-tap-tap, tap-tap-tap, tap-tap.* As the sound signaled around them, it drew from her lips an accompanying chant, "Go-to hell, go-to-hell, go-to-hell, sweet-heart."

How she could tell, only from the rhythm, that it was "sweetheart" rather than "old bitch" or "hot babe," Daren never asked; for she looked at him with tears brimming her eyes and said: "I knew I had to move. If Prince could be that scornful, it showed how terribly he had changed, and that my powers were not equal to the need."

She turned toward him, her head thrown back, waist curled, breasts, as in the Scopas Nereid, raised. Almost as she appeared in the bedroom painting.

"When I heard what your brother did this spring, I knew I had to see you. Your father, Daren, had no reasons. None. He had money, intelligence, health, a fine family, a future. And so much love; everybody loved him. It was that old curse. His father too. And now Vail. I can tell you something else I heard in a rumor. That Vail came over here, one weekend from college, and found your father's gun in a secondhand shop. And he bought it, or had a friend buy it, I don't know. Anyway, he has it now. I wish it had been pounded up and melted down and thrown in the river, because metal, most of all things, attracts and carries the evil.

"Also, I've heard what they say about your mother and that car. Dear Daren, I don't think she would have meant that. And if you think so, you ought to look out, because it may be the curse working out in you, drawing you on."

That was the last time he had been through Reading. Twenty years, like one of those metal objects carrying the curse—steel town, coal town, town of hate and ignorance—he avoided it. The Delta-Reading railroad, into which so much family fortune had been poured, failed the next year anyway. Uncle Hazy had wanted to get out earlier, but the stockholders put it to him as an affair of honor, "If the Leflores pull out, who were the founders, the whole thing goes down, and we lose what we have put in; but if you stick with us, we can still make a go. It depends on you." So he stuck, while the small investors, one by one, recovered what they could and left him holding the bag. Not a sharp businessman, Uncle Hazy, but the soul of honor. Anyway, the trains stopped running, and one took the other route to Delta Landing, with the five-hour layover in Memphis.

There were opportunities enough during the summer for Daren to ask his brother about the gun—but how to interpret the denials of a person as secretive as Vail? "I tell you I've never heard of the gun. Bella Wynne! For God's sake don't keep on about it."

When the next attempt came, it was with sleeping pills anyway. Uncle Hazlewood and Aunt Willi had gone to Memphis to visit June in the sanatorium, and when Daren came from his swim across the river, he found Vail unconscious. When he shook him up, Vail lost some of the dose, so after that it was just staying with him through the night, slapping his face and making him drink water, keeping him stirring.

By morning they came to a settlement: that Daren would say nothing to Uncle Hazy, if Vail, on his honor, would forswear escape—in this harsh world draw his breath in pain. To this, Vail stipulated that he was not going to return to that impossible seminary of Swalee. Daren agreed, though he couldn't blame Swalee for everything: even as a child Vail had eaten a lot of castor beans, left a suicide note and been pumped out by Doctor Paul, who pretended it was an accident. Daren suggested instead that Vail be given a year abroad, to spend wandering about as he pleased.

So before the month was out, a freighter was going to shunt him to the Mediterranean; and after that what they had from him would be little notes mailed from far back in the mountains of Greece, where he traveled around on a donkey, living with peasants and falling in love, as if the Age of Gold had come again.

But if Vail's denial of the gun was true, what remained of Bella's account of her Prince in the attic? Not even Uncle Hazlewood could come to terms with that question. He would rise from his chair and pace in grieved agitation: "I never should have gone away. The Klan had threatened before. 'When I got back, what could I learn but what had been in the papers? I had to put it out of mind, like the other terrors of life. ·

"As for Bella Wynne, she's a fraud. I wouldn't credit anything she says. Did you go in the house?"

Daren had wanted to. Under the stucco front, that cloud of bees humming from the central beam, "I've got to see the attic," he told her.

"We can't," she said. "The Lathrops live there now. And they've remodeled everything."

"So what about the ghost?"

"The Lathrops," she said, "have no spirituality. They couldn't see a ghost if they tried."

Bella took him back to the party she gave in his honor that night: the smart new-rich of Reading, with her own overheard efforts at palmistry, enacted under the glow of those genial (though already somewhat historical) nudes which regaled the visitor from every wall.

Next morning Daren took the train across the rolling Alabama and Mississippi hills, down the Yazoo slopes, onto the dark, flat spread of the Delta: cotton rows bounded by swampwoods, trestles over cypress-bordered bayous, the pink morning mallows they used to call buttercups blooming along the embankment and spilling out into the fields.

9. Fact of Crystal

Between one generation and another lie gulls of reserve and silence. Had Uncle Hazlewood made any romantic commitments? He had the air of one who has loved and lost, but long ago and far away, a man sorrowing in black under a huge oak tree. Yet one tiring was clear, whatever that might mean, he had loved Daren's mother, Iris Vail.

Her room at Ararat had been kept as she had left it, a windowed porch, enclosed during her second pregnancy. The light, as Daren entered it now, had a leafy cast; it filtered through window plants (while the sun sank over the river, the Delta land), a bronze mingling of hues, the orange and the green.

The chintz chair was still by the window and before it the footstool where Daren had sat the first time she took up her morocco-bound Plato, ever so tentatively, like tackling a mystery too great for their powers, and began the myth of the cave:

> Behold! Human beings in an underground cave, chained, facing away from the fire and from the light. Figures bearing images pass behind them; before them is a wall where the shadows are thrown. They have lived there since childhood, prisoners, as we all are.
>
> For them there will be nothing but shadows of images cast on the wall of a cave.

It was among her other Loeb volumes in the bookshelves under the window. On the table, beside the iridescent blue shimmer of a tropical butterfly tray, lay an illustrated Bible, a last gift from her father. Its tooled leather clasps opened on a black-letter text with woodcuts in the manner of Burne-Janes, long-robed ladies with wistful faces and a glory of tumbling hair—the soul's longing for Florence. On the parchment pages in front she had gathered a few signatures, then qnotations, touchstones of her pilgrimage: from Euripides, "Could I take me to some cavern for my hiding"; a memory from Yeats,"… having no part with the lonely majestical multitude"; and Chaucer, "Flee fro the press and dwell with soothfastnesse."

Daren stood at the window and looked down at the rocks: rose quartz, tourmaline, banded amethyst, huge chunks like carvings, displayed on the window shelf, shaded over and grown around with potted plants: staghorn fern, shamrock, grape ivy, philodendron, poinsettia and the crown of thorns, its blossoms like blood in the sun. It was a luminous sunset room, filled with books, rocks, fronds, transient leaves growing over the eternized fact of crystal.

He had come from the lust of the boat, the affairs of Oxford. Bella Wynne in Reading had displayed as clearly as her torso, that his father, his mother, must have pitched their marriage in the same sullied field. Yet here, in this room, the swirl of sex became sacramental, a watery bow, in which smiled the always wonder-working image, the transfigured womanly: *Marah* raised to *Mary.*

By the Bible was a photograph of Daren's grandfather, the tutelage under which the mother had been formed. Owen Vail sat at his desk, his long fine hair brushed back, the Book open before him. But for some spare strength of the coal miner—as if that head had been quarried too out of the rectangular stone of the Black Hills—you would have thought him the aristocrat of them all; not those Leflores on gilded showboats, relaxing after slogging through bogs of white supremacy, but this blend of Celtic warrior, priest and bard. No wonder Iris had despised Reading of all places, crass and loud, full of bigotry and pose, had gone there as little as she could, a rigor for which she must have accused herself in the end—this man could have looked through the well-born Teddy Freeman and out the other side without ever taking the meditative hauteur off his laureate face.

It was in search of Owen Vail's origins that Daren had gone to Wales, driven by Jim and Mrs. Hardy, after Stoke-under-Wychwood.

The last afternoon at the Grange had been clear and warm. They went down the back pasture where the brook that flowed among pollarded willows to the Evenlode had been damned to make a little lake with a waterfall. They all swam and showered under the spray. Almost Daren's last memory of Jeffrey was of the child shape, one of those Renaissance angels of either sex, standing on the dam over the rainbowed falling water, her wet hair like seaweed on her shoulders. Though the very last was that evening, when she brought him one of her buckeye conkers—and would not explain—wrapped in a green leaf and tied with a dandelion.

They left the Cotswolds early, the journey from Broadway Hill spread timeless before them: the fruit-flowering Vale of Evesham, the Severn, the Malvern Hills—they would climb the Happy Valley (Mrs. Hardy in the town comforting herself with elevenscs), Jim and Daren hunting the stream where Langland "slumbered in a sleeping," up the path to the summit, where beyond the green farms, woods and orchards of the Wye, they would take nearer the same dark tilt they had glimpsed from Broadway—the Black Mountains of Wales closing the landscape to the west.

At Ludlow they stopped for the castle ruin where Milton's *Comus* was first played. Daren scaled the ivy to the highest tower and recited: "To the heavens now I fly…" Mrs. Hardy screamed; but he didn't take off for "the broad fields of the sky." When he made it down, they found lodgings in a half-timbered pub and played darts until bedtime, the quaint speech of the locals flowing around them: "'Er'd 'ad three childer a'ready; but beggin me, 'er slipped it on the last and now 'e's a widower."

Next day they followed the river Teme into the highlands, Celtic names beginning: Rhos-y-meirch and Cwm Aran and all the Llans and Bryns and Fawrs. South, they crossed the gorge of the river Wye and sloped up again to the headwaters, the dark spread of hills. Moor ponies wandered a tundra of heather and bracken dotted with pools. Ahead, in the sun, like the mist of many waterfalls, a great smoke appearing, darkened and spread, volcanic; and now the highlands fell away, slag-heaped and scarred, where a scurf of slate houses clings to the drop under the Brecons; and below, Sodom and Gomorrah fume in the steep valleys that go down like fingers to the sea.

And was Jerusalem builded here...

Daren saw himself on the crown of Pen-y-Fan, bending the burning arc.

"Have you heard of Pen-y-Daren?" they asked, as they neared Merthyr Tidfil, capital of what was still called the Principality of Wales.

"I was born there," said a lounger.

"How do we find it?"

"Make room. "

He guided them over Dowlais Heights where grave slabs of slate leaned from the grass, carved with Welsh characters and sometimes English. "If yer mother was a Vail, ye'll find enough of yer kin here." He pointed. "That's Pen-y-Daren."

A narrow double row of houses, the same bleak stone as the tombs; it would return, a *déjà vu,* thirteen years later, when Daren first came to Patapsco City.

"Cardiff is off yonder." The sun from behind slanted into the smoking cleft of the old glacier. "And there below are the pits."

The scene had come down in legends Daren's mother had told them in the room of rocks and fronds. Down there Owen Vail, a lad of four or five, had waited for his father at the shaft; and one day, walking him home, swinging on the grimy middle finger: "When I grow up," he announced, "I'm going to America, and study, and be a minister." The father looked down and smiled.

At seven, the boy went underground, sat all day in a side corridor, with a light on his cap, a stranger to the sun. When he heard the donkey carts coming from the gas-reeking central shaft, he had to jump up and open the safety door.

"And that's the school." Their guide motioned to a prison of the same dark stone. Owen had gone there, off-days, with chalk and a hunk of slate picked from the heaps; and that pedant used to come for him, ferrule raised—to break him for his social role. Until he was doing a man's work in the mine:

"I lifted the slate. 'One more step!'" (The first person narration flamed from father to daughter and daughter *to* son.) "He made that step. I hurled the slab end over end, with all my strength, and I had plenty. He raised his shoulder. It struck the thick pad of his winter coat. He went white and turned away. After that, he never tried to touch me again."

Voices, journeys, places, persons, threaded up by memory—as by the rays of the sun, setting over the Delta, the same sun that ten days before stretched out the valley of Wales, the same that earlier still (twelve years it was, when Daren's father and mother were alive, and the family made a summer trip to the stations of her childhood) had lengthened the shadows of the oak and tulip woods in the new forested Wales of Pennsylvania; her voice, like the rays of that sun, threaded the scenes on a strand of Celtic wonder: "How under the shining stars…"

—While the Pierce Arrow touring car, day after day, headed north and east from Mississippi, over all the hairpin mountain curves and ferries and river bridges—winding down a sun-sloped valley toward a rocky wide water (was it the Susquehanna?), straight for the drop, but the road dodged, right, along the stream, then left, onto a rattling covered bridge that ran for the cliff on the other side, but dodged again, hugging the bluff, until a side valley opened, and they wound into the hills beyond the river, always north and east—

Her voice told of Owen Vail. How until he was twenty he had worked in Wales, underground, saving every penny he could keep from the family till—thirteen years to buy a passage, one-way steerage, a bunk on sacking in a hold. So he came to the New World, but plunged back underground, digging anthracite from the Mammoth Vein. In nine more years (at American pay) he had dug enough coal to send back tickets for his father and mother, brother, sister, his sister's fiancé, besides making the down payment on a house where they could live.

And now she voiced the miracle of it all: "How under the shining stars, slaving in the dark, twenty years there and here, could he have found time to learn and master all the Welsh-bound meters, a prosody as hard as any, and have made poems to satisfy a jury of the college of bards and be crowned with laurel and enrolled among their number, 'The Man from Daren'—as they told me later, 'the rarest singer in the New World'—and how could he sacrifice it, when that beauty" (think: the prisoner in the dark seam, glancing up for the Platonic sun) –"must have been his life?"

He had put it all behind him. He no sooner got the family over and the men working then he left that New Wales and his bardic fame and started on foot for Western Reserve, where he enrolled in lectures in history, philosophy, Bible, Latin, Greek, Hebrew, sat through three years of them, though they flowed over him in English, a language he had yet to learn. Then a Welsh minister he met his first year wrote from New Hampshire: "Come and join us; live in our house; we'll get you a scholarship at the seminary here." Owen had no choice; though he would always regret the appearance of having lowered his aim. In New Hampshire he worked three more years at the same studies. The night he got his diploma, he gathered all his Celtic poems, his pride and consolation for so long, and flung them on the fire.

"But why?" Daren's mother's voice shook as with the original imploration: "O why? And how could you?"

He had looked up, as he looked in the picture at Ararat, the Book opened before him: "I couldn't manage both. I knew it. And from childhood I had chosen the other, the sacred muse."

His ministry began in New Hampshire.

—The account here taken over by the grandmother, whom Daren and his family had visited that same summer, continuing north and east from Pennsylvania, she rheumatic and failing, though what she told had a weathered pastoral smile—

How she and her aunt had hitched up the buggy and gone to Fellow's Church to hear the new preacher. They were sitting in the old Allen pew, just under the eagle beak of the pulpit, looking up at Owen Vail. There was fire from his eyes like sparks from coal; he was a preacher of the old order, when men fought wars of faith and prophets shared in the energy of Satan, not one of those obsequious scribes and pharisees who slouch round the churches today calling themselves men of God. But he was not sure of himself. In the rush of riding by horseback to preach in three churches, he had forgotten to practice the set scripture. Glancing ahead at the unfamiliar verses: "Know ye not that ye stand in jeopardy every hour," he wrestled with that grim-looking word, pulling it apart: "J-e-o, JO: p-a-r-d-y, PARDY." And now he took its "Know ye not that ye stand in jo-PAR-dy every hour?"

A titter from the front pew called him to a bonneted girlish face disappearing behind a lace handkerchief. The preacher took a grip on himself. At least he had lavished on the sermon his midnight and morning devotions. As he read, his force and passion returned.

But the prayer was another crux. It had to be improvised. He closed his eyes. From the darkness before the Lord's altar his voice was raised. Slowly the fear of the language, the remembered tittering, fell off. How natural when the soul, alone with godhead, flowed like a spring under a rock, pouring prayer. And the titters did not arise... Spellbound? Only as he reached the "Amen" did Owen Vail realize he had sloughed off English with the husks of self, and was praying to his God in Welsh.

As he stood at the door to shake hands with his parishioners, he looked for the face he had seen. (All those years, from childhood to that day, he had sacrificed everything, even the poetry he loved, to mount this pulpit and preach. He had done it now, like crossing the ridge into an April valley, and all the other stirrings, life, love, were conceivable, beckoning, like flowers,) Abbie and her aunt introduced themselves.

"Ah, Miss Allen," he took her hand. "I saw you... or heard..."

She leaned over and whispered in his ear: "Jeopardy."

"Thank you, my dear."

"But it was a beautiful prayer," she said. And she repeated that, for them all, as she rocked by the fire, forty-five years later, in the New Hampshire farmhouse: "Beautiful."

The marriage took them back to the Pennsylvania outpost of Wales. It was losing its character, like all heirlooms in the melting pot; but in Iris' youth there were still the Eisteddfods, with Celtic poetry and choral singing.

You would see the known bards standing in the central green, humbler aspirants crowding around; a man in mining clothes would come up, deferential, dig in his pocket for a slip of paper with his own attempt at an Englyn. It was here that Iris learned of her father's other name. For the older people he was still Darenydd, who in his boyhood had conquered the bound meters and written those beautiful lost poems.

"And it was here," she told them, as the car coasted down into her childhood valley, "when money was scarce and I was thinking of college, that he went back to the mine, digging coal all week and preaching on Sunday. Until the great disaster—days of waiting—then bodies only-victims of the cave."

They planted flowers on his grave, and she took them to places where the Eisteddfods had been held and told them again of the old customs and how their grandfather had been a laureate bard. But what Daren wanted to see was the mine. She looked at him with wide dark eyes; but his father took him down into the infernal din, lights along low passages haloed in dusty air. Though the lonely mystery of the true cave—furrowed limestone and the water-drip—did not have the leisure to settle...

Journeys, weaving and interbranching: there had been an earlier one, unconnected really, and Daren could not have remembered it at all, if it had not been retold as an example of his ambitious abuse of language: at Coney Island, when he begged to ride the roller coaster, and his father, hating it, agreed, and they climbed, poised and plunged, almost free fall, to a concavity that drove the neck into the chest, and flung you up a weightless summit, your guts beating in your throat, then a dizzy curve, another drop, a rise—on the third hump Daren had leaned and shouted to his father, who was suffering this only for him: "If I had *knewn* it was this way, I would not have *came.*"

They repeated that in the mine, laughed off the gloom of a labyrinth where men gnawing at the carbon rock suggested Owen Vail, whose life, around an interval of day, had begun and ended in those dens.

They stayed a day or two, but the region was changed, ugly, no roots but the sinister ones of the mine. Even Daren's mother found little to revive, gave up, as the grandmother had done before. They drove on, north and east—to the modest white farmhouse by a stream rushing down from Chocorua, and orchard valley under crystal rocks (as the collection in the Delta room witnessed: beryl and agate, garnet, quartz), nineteenth-century wallpaper tidy on the walls, coal-oil lamps and the hand pump in the sink, china pitchers and washbasins and wood fires, the bottle of Lydia E. Pinkham's Vegetable Compound half-used on the medicine shelf. It seemed the long ride in the Pierce Arrow had translated them in time as in space, back to this remnant of long ago—not, as in the South, rundown, but with the quiet gentility of country custom, as ancient and pleasing as the lilac at the door…

Daren had remembered these things at Dowlais Heights among the Vail graves, the sun almost at his back pouring down headlands and valleys of the scarred land into the far-off sea, a castle ruin on a pyramidal hill throwing a shadow as long as if Sir Gawain had stopped there when he wandered through the icy woods and mountains of the old magic Wales.

In the shadow of the valley, steam jetted up and a whistle blew. "They're letting out at the pit." That anthill under the derrick belched a grimy stream—workers off to their families or to the pub, a child maybe swinging to his father's finger as he looked up and announced extravagant dreams. "There they go," said the guide, "like the old Owens and the Vails."

The next day Daren had caught his boat; and the landscape from which Freud took off the lid bared itself again. So many discontented wives: that one, in her last freedom, snatching at something thicker than a straw. But before her moon had changed, they had spent so many hours in that cabin beating around the bush, the steward suborned to spy on them might as well have fed Daren saltpeter; when the all-clear was sounded—cloyed under those swagging breasts—he abysmally and irrecoverably failed.

He had come home from that. The first night, in the town house at Delta Landing, Uncle Hazlewood had invited friends to greet the scholar and to talk of Europe. They were warming up when the phone rang. It was long distance for Daren, Anna, in fact, begging him to visit them in Chicago.

(An urgency that would be heightened through the summer, until he took that route of return, stayed in the showy flat high over the curving lake and the city. But the closest he would come to abusing Chuck's hospitality was the last morning, when Anna slipped into his room to wake him, and sitting on the bed like the lady in *Sir Gawain and the Green Knight,* talked of her marriage: "Chuck has a good heart. He tries. There's something he'd like to make up for, some thing he did years ago. But it's too late. The whole thing is wrong." They kissed each other good-bye— Anna, socialist woman, claiming to manage her destiny, caught in a force she couldn't handle.)

The passionate natnre of that first call to Delta Landing was bound to trickle through to Uncle Hazlewood, Aunt Willi and the guests. When Daren rejoined the party, the conversation was palsied. It had hardly begun to rally when there was another of those insistent rings they used to call long distance just by the sound. It was the boat woman's husband this time. He had the steward's schedule of the nights Daren had spent in that cabin. "She says she's innocent. I've got to know what happened. I love the bitch, and if I could be sure of the truth, I'd forgive and forget."

(Fat chance. That would be tested, too, at the end of the summer, when Daren reached New York after stopping with Anna in Chicago, and found he'd lost a day somehow, and the S.S. *Deutschland* had sailed. He rushed to the office. "Where have you been?" the agent insisted, as he transferred the value of the ticket to the Normandie—they were cavalier about missing boats in those days—"there's been a man phoning all the time. Said you were bound to be in New York, and where were you staying? Be sure you catch that boat tomorrow. And don't get in touch with anybody. You know what I mean? It might be dangerous.")

Forgive and forget. By the time Daren had finished protesting that, despite appearances, nothing really adulterous had occurred, Uncle Hazlewood's sallies at chat were past reviving.

The following day they drove to Ararat. Mississippi plantations were laid out to imitate the tidewater estates of the Chesapeake and the lower James, as those had tried, in a new world, to suggest the parks and mansions of the old. Since each attempt was made in an increasingly backward and malarial swamp, it was amazing how much had been achieved. The vantage at Ararat had been the mound, that and the slightly raised bank of red clay that meant so much to prelevee floods.

Where had that clay come from? Uncle Hazlewood had brought the geologists from Ole Miss to look at it, and one said it was deposited by the Arkansas River when the Mississippi was off east in the channel of the Yazoo; and the other said, no, it was from before the Ice Age, when the Ohio came that way with the eastern streams, and the Mississippi ran far to the west, beyond Crawley's Ridge in Arkansas.

Nobody knew, in so liquid a land, what that saving red bank had been the bank of; lately it was Lotus Lake, detached from the river before the white settlers came. The Blue Hole had been gouged about the same time, with Panther Burn, by which it drained into the lake. When it issued again lower down for its windings across the Delta, south and east to the Yazoo, it had changed its name to Cypress Bayou. It was up this waterway that Captain Quincy Leflore had steamed to a mansion in a flooded land.

That separation of lake and river had saved the house from the gunboats. A lawn groved with pecans and bordered by forest had stretched more than a mile to the bend at Hazlewood Landing. So an English estate might open to the Severn or the Thames. But how strange to build with such peaceful civility to that demon of mud and flood which had already in its westward lashing silted up the first Delta Landing down behind Lotus Lake, and now in its eastward backlash, where the current from the new bend to the north set in against the clay bluff, had chewed off most of the grove and lawn and was ultimately, for all the arts of matting and revetment, going to swallow the house.

They crossed the Burn bridge and came past outhouses and old slave quarters to the dress facade, facing south to the gentle cypressed vista of Lotns Lake. The legendary formal garden with its rose window of radiating flower beds had staged a slow retreat, until it was mostly a lawn, dominated by a

Swamp Spanish oak, perhaps the largest in the Delta. And even that, after flood and depression and Uncle Hazlewood's management, the river worse than the boll weevil gnawing at the best land, wore an air of desuetude, the tree half dying, a few cows from the pasture staked out on the lawn. The place had the melancholy glory of a ruin.

The sun was setting. Daren walked into his mother's room. After the Oxford year and the salt crossing, Reading and the phone calls of the night before, he stood by the chair looking at the plants and rocks, the shimmering blue butterfly tray, the Bible, the picture of his Grandfather Vail. He did not sink to his knees, or even shed tears; but he was not unaware of the strangeness of that sanctum in the sullied field.

10. Despair of Summer

A HINT OF FALL in the air. The Journal, begun as a summer project, stood stalemated. Of three Oxford years, only one was done.

"O the merry go-round broke down."

With a sound as dismal as any conked-out carousel, Daren got up and paced the yard. The old woman came from her door with a load of garbage and cans.

"How are you, Mrs. Stovall?"

"Damn these new teeth. Chinese pagoda in my month." She champed like an unruly horse.

Anna, who had been watching for a break, joined them. "Hello, Mrs. Stovall."

"Trash," she accused. "Trash." And dumped it down. Anna looked far away. "Let's go for a walk, Daren."

Above the factory dam the water backed into the woods. You could find a deserted place—past where the railroad tunneled off at the bend— strip and swim between walls of trees, a resonance which brought up all those other scenes of earthy and algal water, going back and back almost to the birth of time:

That first Oxford summer, when he went home, and the Blue Hole and lake and the brown river became his lairs, into which his being withdrew, nursing ancestral wounds. And the deep bend in the Natchez bayou, where the first Quincy Leflore had tied a grindstone around his neck and gone under. And the slough in East Mississippi where his grandson, Captain Quincy, after he was wounded, returning from furlough to a hopeless war, stared into the guns of four deserters as he crossed a ford, and though one of them, from his own company, called him by name, he rode on and did not reply. And always Panther Burn, where it flowed out of the Blue Hole, just above where it was spanned by the trestle bridge.

There he was floating in that legendary water, and he had to get up and make for Oxford, work through two whole years of life and study, and he had only the closing paltry days before the big cracked bell (are all institutional bells cracked?) in the cupola of Patapsco College called to another year at quite another labor.

The *Normandie* was flashy, loud with Legionnaires going back to see their battlefields. The shops, however, were good. Daren bought a silk scarf for Jeffrey. He went from Oxford to Stoke-under-Wychwood to get his bike, thinking of a playful presentation. But Jeffrey had been liberated from the school she hated and sent to France by Uncle Athol. The scarf had to go by mail.

A new year in a new room, fourth floor corner, the cheapest in the college. An iron gutter mounted to the bedroom dormer. All fall it bore no traffic. Daren studied as if Milton and the rest were his grip on life. Whatever had settled on him in that summer of Blue Hole meditation, whether from his sister's strange poems and sketches, or his own small progress toward Experience, filled him with notions: "Chaucerian laughter and the grace of original sin." "The affirmation of tragedy," "the Metaphysical theology of rape."

"That's a first-rate paper," Cameron said of his last, on Milton's soul and Milton's God. "Let's drink a sherry, and I'll call you Daren and you call me Leslie."

Xmas vacation. As usual a bunch of scholars had come as far as Paris. At the Hôtel de Ia Gare Madame checked the passports. "Le Flore," she cooed, and stroked his peach-down cheek. He bowed like Don Quixote: "High born damsel…"

The others were going to The Sphinx, famous nightclub of almost naked waitresses. Why pay so much to be teased? Daren took up Johnson on the vanity of human wishes. He read an hour then dropped it and went for a walk.

Past windows of the Bastille slum, blue arcs on mascaraed woman, glimpses through dingy doorways: tipped glasses, laughter wrapped in penury and gray hairs. At Montmartre the style changed, white gloved fingers, soldiers with feathered caps. *Vive le sport.* A penny arcade: *Le Déshabillé de Madame.* For fifty centimes a chorus girl of the nineties, in twelve faded photos removes her dress, all her peticoats and undersilks for the public joy. Daren bent to these antiquarian studies. *"Voyez! Voyez!"* a soldier was crying, outraged, before him a peepshow: *"La Passion, spectacle extraordinaire."* He had dropped a coin and was calling the world to witness. Passion indeed. Daren peeked: Christ on the Cross, the Passion of our Lord. He reached the hotel hungry, stopped at the restaurant for some onion soup and wine. And there at the table in front of him was a ravishing girl eating and drinking with an ugly fat sugar daddy. Through the whole meal, she and Daren caressed and petted with their eyes. She went out lugged by her beau, almost walking backward.

From the Sphinx the scholars returned, bare-bubbled of their money. But Daren? It was his heart that was continually bubbled.

Next morning in the cold of Notre Dame he sat sketching. He left in the high mood of Gothic, only to encounter the postcard vendor. *"Non capisco,"* he shrugged. The pitch was repeated in Italian *"Bin Deutsch, kann nicht Italienisch."* The vendor pursued in demotic German. "Sorry, I don't understand."—"M'sier, m'sier, you are Eenglish. You want to buy ze postcard?"—To be chased through three languages to the terminus of "No!"—"Ah, but m'sier want zc feelthy peecture?" He crept close, uncovering a shot of flesh in a pose of possibility. What was left but buskinned rage?—"Do you pimp for these dead shapes, necrophiliac false seducer?"

Daren had overdone it. Flinging out his arms, he had pulled the last button off his raincoat. He went into a drugstore to get a safety pin. Not knowing the name, he drew a perfectly clear picture of what he wanted. The druggist, grinning and winking, brought out a condom.

That night he took the train.

Again Florence was cloudly. But this time torrential rains fell; the Arno rose overnight almost to the hanging houses of the Ponte Vecchio. The next evening, as he sat with Pippa and the rest in the salon, there was an earth tremor that swayed the whole building. Should he run to the terrace to see if his return to his heart's home had been greeted also by a comet flaming in the sky? Useless; he couldn't have seen it for the rain.

He had written Pippa not to believe in his love; but he was unprepared for the mode of her estrangement. She was, as always, dear, eager to talk, sisterly, hoping for his approval. She had found a friend: he must not think it strange.

"You remember the poem I loved: 'No longer morn for me…?

Shakespeare didn't write it for a woman. You knew that? Why didn't you tell me? That's why it's so selfless. But the ones for the Dark Lady have all the fury of sex. My friend comes tomorrow night. We'll have a group upstairs for you to meet her. She's been in Rome with the opera; she's the first soprano. Australian. I want you to be fond of her."

Daren imagined it all: some Lesbian out of Courbet, big and hard, Wagnerian metallic voice—everything about her metallic, one of those scaled dragons of romance, copper hair, a sheen of flesh, a glint of eye, innocent Pippa fluttering like the bird hypnotized by the snake, trying to believe in the Platonic myth, which the serpentining coils denied. And there was nothing he could interpose but the discredited cry of heterosexual love.

The party was in the family living room. Brunhilde had introduced the cognoscenti of Florence: a critic, a poet, her pianist-teacher, as refined and soulful an epicene as ever wore long hair. Was it inadequacy or strength that in such a nest of Jamesian Europe Daren began to wish he was in a third-class carriage going somewhere else, or back on the Miississippi rounding Choctaw Bend on a floating log?

Yet Pippa's friend was richer, subtler, more beautiful than Daren had conceived. She had studied in London, Paris, Vienna; the Australian twang he had looked for was pure English; she spoke German, Italian, French, everything. She deployed herself as if the opera had come to life and she was acting the lead, advancing as across a stage, with a ripple of sensuous command. Her very speech was recitative. Her profession was charm; maybe she could have charmed Daren if she had pleased; but that was not her inclination.

She had felt him out, had known before he entered the room, before he came to Florence, that he was the antagonist, not just hers, but of her cult, the thing she had to overthrow in the accomplishment of whatever her strange beauty aimed to accomplish.

She came to the crisis slowly. To the fairy tinkling of her idolatrous maestro, she began with Spanish lute songs, arias by Caccini, Monteverdi; she opened low registers almost contralto, in love broodings of a baroque somnolence Daren had hardly encountered before. She advanced through Gluck and Mozart *("Deh, vienni non tardar")* to the turning point of *Fidelia*. The voice swelled and rose on itself, drawing endlessly from its coils the swaying lights of its coloratura. And now the pianist was tossing his hair and crashing the keys in forlorn accompaniment; as in flamenco dance some lesser claimant is brushed aside by one of those magnificent, tragic women, his frail effort was towered over and thrown down by the voice, which for the first time proudly displayed the copper glint of its scales, as it shook the carved rafters and the tile floor in the power display of Wagner.

And now Pippa, too, assumed the mask of her envisaged role: she sat in the corner, looking at Brunhilde like an alarmed and fascinated bird.

Inordinate woman. She hadn't needed to unroll the dynamics of that enormous voice to threaten the walls of Pippa's small loneliness. It was at Daren that it was launched, a battering ram, and what it broke down was his quiet, his confidence. Unmanned.

In the self-accusation of having brought this on, he spent days trying to see Pippa, to win her, warn her. She was friendly, distant, dear, sad that he was sad, full of ideal assurances, ignorant of implication, yet beyond his call, carried on the other tide. He felt the helplessness that would claim him again and again through life: that we do not make the world, we suffer it, that our freedom is not to choose, but to ride out the storm.

Christmas Eve, the singer in Rome, Daren and Pippa went with the others to the midnight mass. But when the bells of the city broke into last year's Hallelujah, they sat shivering in a cold church, Pipistrella sad, Daren sullen: Christmas morning he filled his pockets with lire and tried to find comfort giving to beggars; but his heart knew the pretense of the charity, his mind how little it relieved the poor.

That afternoon Anna wired that she was coming. It was almost at the risk of a total break with Chuck that she was accompanying his sister, Tina, abroad; and now Tina was on the ski slopes and Anna was off to study the art of Florence.

Art was the program she had promised to maintain. Though as the carriage took them through the cobbled streets past the Duomo, the cyclopean back of the Old Palace and along the Arno, it was clear her love for Florence and her love for Daren would be hard to disengage. The pensione became her defense. She settled in a little room opening off the public sala, which now, at Christmas, was almost a colony of Oxford.

Sightseeing got humanized. They went to the Uffizi with apples, tangerines, nuts and figs. By one, when the radiators had died away, not even hanging over a charcoal brazier, which no lack of language prevented Anna from sharing, with all kinds of welcome, with the guards, could keep the art urge thawed. So it was a cozy little den with spaghetti and wine; and as neither had drunk often enough to be inured, a glow which brought their hands and knees and finally their lips together, and made the clear images of Florence swim like late Turners.

The next day was hideously cold, the Arno floating such hunks of ice you could have played *Uncle Tom's Cabin* on it. Two hours in Santa Croce left them so frozen they had to warm up in a wineshop in order to tackle the Bargello, where Michelangelo's Bacchus seemed tipsier and more lecherous than ever; and before his Brutus could recall them to sterner stuff, they were hanging with the guards, laughing, over another charcoal fire. At one, in the favorite restaurant, the host hailed them as his honeymooners, gave them a table half behind a screen where they could sit wrapped in themselves. Only pale Pippa, working at the desk as they came and went, gave a pang. But Anna took a fondness also for Pippa.

New Year's Eve was warmer. The Alpini convened from the north, parading in pickled crowds, climbing the equestrian statues, trying to direct traffic—such warm country bumpkins, one forgot they were legionnaires. After dinner the lovers walked to the Piazzale Michelangelo to view the lighted city. Hank searched all over and found them embraced at the last verge. He had been sent to fetch them to a party in Pippa's rooms. The singer had returned. But tonight she was jolly and led them in folk songs.

"When I was a girl," Anna whispered, "I sang with my sisters in harmony, though we couldn't read a note. If the movie scout had come, there we'd have bee things happened that made me stop singing. But now it seems right for me to sing again."

As the bells pealed, they drank resolutions in spumante. Hank began with the usual "thou shalt not." "No, no," cried Pippa. "In Florence we say 'I shall!' And for something nice." Daren and Anna clicked glasses.

His resolution would have broken the assurance she gave Tina in Tyrol. When Daren learned of that, he teased for what Andreas Capellanus had permitted in the old chivalric code: to lie stripped, not even a sword between them, and remain chaste. As if her concern had been with formal chastity.

With what loving patience she submitted to the medieval test. He stole to her one afternoon at siesta when Hank and the others were away. If he had urged that pure bundling as a leverage for going beyond, it was not the place or time. Motions in the hall made them uneasy. Only when he confessed the woman of the boat, his failure, his secret fear—"Don't be foolish," Anna said; and to dispel his doubt or her own, forgot what had been resolved, and with the simplest undulation showed him for an instant how whole, and how easily, they could be man and woman. "I'll go with you to some other town tomorrow, and coming back we'll miss the train."

San Gimignano of the beautiful towers was the scene of their consummation. They saw the town, the church, the frescoed hell, where adulterers of his kind were hauled by the tarsus and the wives raped by the tails of devil-baboons. But it did not trouble them, that night in the hotel over the square; nor to look out in the morning on the petrified Gothic city, hardly changed since Dante was ambassador there—the court of the podestà, where blown leaves revived horses, ladies, robes, trumpets, banners, knights, and as the wind died, settled into the corners of an empty square: "The dead are dancing with the dead."

They returned to Florence on the Feast of the Madonna. The Palazzo Vecchio was wildly beautiful, all the battlements and the tower lighted with flaming torches. Daren stood with Anna at the pensione window looking across toward it, one of his rhapsodic bunglings of Italian rumbling his inner spaces:

> *Come mi sento ritornando felice*
> *A le braccie tue amate, bella Firenze.*

A momentous change, by which Anna had taken Pippa's place on the dream balcony over Florence.

Daren did not know until that spring how deep a life-rift it had opened, not until they went to the movie called *Ninotchka* and saw Greta Garbo (she reminded him of Anna anyway) play the Bolshevik come to Paris on official business only to be seduced by western pleasures, the boulevards, the Eiffel Tower, gaudy nights, oysters and champagne, jewelry, silks and, of course, love. In the film the heroine's defection was treated as commendable, an awakening to life. But whoever made it must have suspected the smallness of giving up a birthright of world-vision for a spicy mess of private porridge. Even Daren felt the letdown; and Anna couldn't have been more distempered had she been Claudius, when the play-within-the play shows his treachery—It was what Laszlo Brod, at the same time, would taunt her with: "A hell of a communist you are. Why don't you do something for the party? You've done plenty for that other side of you. And what about your aesthete Daren Leflore? Any plans for him?"

Yes, she had plans: to get him out of that capitalist circus where he could only play Harlequin the lonely clown, and into the struggle for the common man.

She had opened for Daren like a cluster of Byzantine dolls, one inside the other and each with a different form. In San Gimignano, she had put off the guise of Married Virgin; on the shed robes of her innocence, she lay, a naked Venus smiling human love. It would be months before that second image would yield to the third, a stern devotion to cause.

But the days in Florence were ended; she had to join Tina Morgan in Austria. Daren left the station as the fog closed in. He sat in the Novella square where they had fed the pigeons. It began to rain. He walked to the little den where they ate spaghetti. The host flung up his arms: *"Dov'è la Signora?"*—*"E partito, e sono desolato."* The next day he started for England with the gang.

Again it was study which gave amorphous life a form—until another February of showers and larks, when he got the call from London, and heard Tina's voice: "We're coming to Oxford, can you and Jim find us a room?"

And he shouted into the phone: "If I can't, I'll build one."

Secret and precious, the memories that welled up now, not recorded in the Journal: the night Jim Hardy lured Tina to Cambridge for a hockey match, and Daren and Anna were alone in the cold little digs by the flickering fire—

Les soirs illuminés par l'ardeur du charbon.

It was not the Freudian inversion of sitting with her feet cuddled in his fraternal hands, while the little tongue of fire flickered at the oval hearth, but simply of having a love, a human love, of warming her against the physical cold, of resting there, between peaks of abandon—still so high they felt awe stir across them in the dark like wings. He left before dawn and climbed the gutter four stories to his room.

Now spring began, and everything pepped up. Cyril Mercer had a fling at Anna; invited them for "a little lunch" in his rooms, oysters and guinea fowl, peas and salad, dessert and cheese, and with three wines. By the time the young lady who was painting Cyril's miniature arrived, he was propped up in the wing chair with such a bloated smile on his face that she messed up what she had done before. Daren and Anna walked him to his fencing, and then took a cycle ride. They were thinking of a bowl of soup for supper, but Cyril hunted them down, said he was still lonely and they would have to dine with him.

"What about the *Snatch* Bar?" said Daren.

"The Snack Bar, sir," Mercer said, "is a place to go after the theater for a cup of cold coffee or a bad sandwich, but to dine, sir, on a Saturday evening—to dine! Besides, it is drafty in the Snack Bar. You will come with me to the George and we will dine."

So they had it heavier than at midday, Cyril shaking his hair over his face and ogling Anna. He complained of a pain in the stomach which he got fencing—"Lunging," he said, enacting the thrust. "Lunching, more likely," said Anna. While Daren quoted the Greedy Glutton from the *Ancren Rule:*

His heart is in the dishes, his thought is in the cup, his life is in the barrel, his soul is in the crock. He comes with a dish in one hand and a bowl in the other; he slobbers his words and holds his great belly, and the fiend laughs as if he would burst.

Next day they asked Tina to join them in a walk to Boar's Hill. Cyril started out skipping like a kid, rolling his barrel form down the banks. As they looked back at a gate, they discovered they had been in a quarantine pasture for hoof-and-mouth disease. Cyril fagged. His feet, he said, were like horn. Would Anna look in his mouth? His tongue felt coated. At the top of the hill he groaned that he was undone, shuffled to a teahouse, ordered tea for the bunch, and a taxi from Oxford to take them home.

In his room, he soaked his feet and drank rum toddies, bragging about his gout. After dinner, while Daren was studying, he took his port to the girls' place, got Anna aside and offered her a Schiaparelli outfit if she would come to Paris with him.

When he got the notion she was always going to treat him like a naughty boy, he decided to encamp his baroque siege around Tina. A good thing. She had been guarding so closely over the fold that the only way Daren and Anna could meet was to cycle out by Nuneham Courtney and crawl into the fragrant room of a haystack eaten into by the sheep, the mews crying above like lost kittens.

Cyril invited Tina to tea, and at the crucial moment threw himself down on his 1800 priest's chair, like some lover of the age of romantic sentiment (you hurled yourself in facing the back, as at an altar rail, but astride, to save your knees), and poured out such a rigmarole of impetuous passion that she was amazed.

Cyril could never keep a thing like that hidden. He read Daren a French note he had written, apologizing for his *gaucherie*. Daren was going to the Morgans' anyway. He watched Tina. Every time Cyril was mentioned she looked queer. But she didn't speak until the note was delivered, with an armload of yellow roses. Then she broke down: "What can I do? Are all Englishmen like that?" Daren dictated a reply:

> Sir: My pleasure in the flowers has almost compensated for the vexation you afforded me. If you ingratiate yourself by a few other kindnesses, you will have reached with me the plane of neutrality and will be entitled to resume your annoyance.

Cyril brought it up that night to Daren, to discuss by what miracle a plain American girl could have mastered the mock-heroic vein.

Oxford was settling into its usual state, a paradise of mannered devices—when Chuck Morgan sailed in, determined to break it up, though all he could do was launch it forward.

He had rented a little car. It was spring vacation. Somehow Anna got Daren invited to join them on a trip to the Wye:

> These waters rolling from their mountain springs
> With a soft inland murmur...

The front seat was crowded. After lunch Anna said there would he more room if she rode in back, a kind of half-seat, jammed against the other. The triangle was complete: Chuck concentrating on the road, Daren talking, Anna leaning forward to hear, her elbows on the back of the seat, drawstring blouse loose, lips parted, eyes shining, taking him in. He turned, facing Chuck as it were, his arm over the seat, as the car swerved, brushing her knee.

Beyond that, and in such a context, he would hardly have gone. It was she whose arm left the seat, whose hand, taking his, led it along her thigh. Herculean Chuck drove, putting in a word now and then. The woman Daren had thought of as incapable of concealment sat with her elbow on the back of the seat again, touching her husband's shoulder, while her lover's hand… The silk, mounded and warm, yielded as in immersions of the Delta to a liquid stir…

They rode, bouncing, while Daren talked on and on, of Mississippi, art, poetry, quoting old lyrics:

> In arms he hent
> That lady gent
> In voiding care and moan;
> That day they spent
> To their intent
> In wilderness, alone.

Anna's face had the look of child-wonder; her low voice answered in coos, not his speech but the other contact, deeper than words.

At Tintern the trip was canceled. They had hardly climbed at sunset to the churchyard on the western hill, where children played over the graves, as in the Wordsworth poem, and one girl in a blithe voice called over each mound "'O's in 'ere?"; they had hardly taken the view and returned to the guesthouse when Tina reached them by phone: the elder Morgans had been drowned.

Lake Michigan, one of those whirlwinds so rare it was called by its Swiss name, "Seiche" (a rising of the waters), when the cold lake air shifts at the close of a warm day, and the two winds meet on a tangent so that twenty-foot waves rear up; they had been sailing, when at the heart of a perfect calm that sea bear had heaved and fallen.

For Tina and Chuck it meant going home, for Anna a decision. She could stick with a husband who now had money of his own; or be stranded in Europe with Daren and love. Daren could not conceive of her choosing anything but him. She did, however. He went back to his lonely high room in the spring-deserted college, daily hoping for a telegram announcing her return.

One night, in the frustration of that dependence, he took a block of wood which had served as a doorstop and hacked it with his pocketknife to the leering face of a devil, his hands devilish raw. The next night, no wood offering, he spat out sonnets of such bitter scolding ("How can the watery flame of your faint love/Wrap me about in such hard-bellowed fire?") that the college magazine caught them up as nuggets of modern love. The third night the muse and all deserted him; he stared out of the window; he beat his head against the wall. Then he gave up and packed for the Riviera, where Jim Hardy and his mother had taken an apartment and invited him to come.

By Easter week, friends, swimming and sun had almost brought him round. He was memorizing reams of mystical poetry and writing a verse play on Dalilah's betraying Sampson in the service of her God. It was time to explore the ultimate arts of spirit.

From the warmth of Juan-les-Pins, he came, in a fine northern rain under the leaning prophets of Chartres, the yearning, eternal faces. The rack of divine war, Nietzsche's stretching of the bow, was still drawn in us. But what it aimed at now was the rebirth of faith in the Western fall, not the medieval synthesis but beyond it and before, when the honey of Gregorian Chant poured out of the crushing of Rome.

Easter weekend, in the Solesmes Abbey church, that martyr-grace was before him in its culminant form, though how nearly it was offered in the person of the Girl of Solesmes (she who had run a course the reverse of Anna's, who had been a socialist formally, and was now waiting for God—"Other music," she said, "breaks us up on the forms of earth, air and water, plant, beast, bird; only Gregorian, by its single line, opens a silence, a void in the soul"), how could he know, who had not recorded her name, and had still to learn that she was Heloise Frank, whose writings and sacrifice would mean so much to him during the war?

He returned to Oxford absorbed in his play, which the Girl of Solesmes had taken for a work of genius; he listened to the organum of Leonin and Perotin, read the Bible and Augustine; he was ready, like a monk, to cut Anna once and for all from his life.

For her, too, it had been a time of decision. "I swear to God, Anna, if you go, I'll divorce you without a penny." In the face of that, she sailed; though Chuck in the sequel took his lawyer's advice and set up some alimony—until remarriage. Daren met the boat train. He had not chosen it this time, but he embraced his fate.

> London. The station dark and cold. I paced the platform reciting the close of Marlowe's *Faust:* "Ah, half the hour is past, 'Twill all be past anon." Husbands waiting for their wives, swinging gold-headed canes, betraying a touch of the Moor. "For Christ's sake, whose blood hath ransomed me, Impose some end to my incessant pain."—"She docked at five."—"Adders and serpents, let me breathe a while."—"The boat train left at seven."—"Come not, Lucifer, I'll burn my books."—"They're late, very late."—"Ah, Mephitophlis!" In she came with a thunder and roar, bags flying, people running, hugging, kissing, then quiet, the moon in a dark sky, and Anna, like the vision of Pearl across the stream…

That night in the little London room: "I could never have left you for long. I've felt you since the first time in Florence." And then a sigh, made of all the vowels: "O U A E I."

Typing in the Patapsco yard, Daren had thrown it into high, leaping ahead—as he used to knock out the original Journals on his travels, in the third-class car, the portable on his lap, he, looking out the window, and that Gatling gun going off, raising scowls from the other passengers; or in Paris, back from the Riviera, when he had to wait from dawn until after breakfast for a train to Chartres, and he set up press in the cafe, to the shock of the proprietor, and typed at his Dalilah, a man at daybreak in an estaminet, pounding as if the world were coming to an end and he had to set it all down before the imminent doom—so now he was rolling in page after page, knocking through and ramming in the next; but Maryland time was gaining on Oxford time; the inexorable countdown of his summer was almost at the null hour, and he had only got himself squared away with Anna; Labor Day, the Perseus was unpoured, the tomb a jumble of blocked-out stone; even if it could be completed it would not arrive.

> Should Solesmes and the mystical road be heightened? If so—earlier, after the news of the brother? Should the brother's suicide succeed? Remove Anna from Florence? Let the Tintern trip initiate the sexual phase? Play up the despair of Pippa's loss, and let the fall to Anna be in consequence?

NO, NOTHING WORKS EXCEPT WHAT IN FACT OCCURRED. ACCLAIM IT THEN.

But what was the point, if so much poring over the past led to the acclamation of what might better have been blamed, the folly whose consequences, private and public, were going off like land mines all around him—war and postwar, collaborations of the Right and Left, the hardening of love and of the will? Tomorrow he would read in the papers that Laszlo Brad was on trial for concealing his communism in the State Department; a day or so after, there would be a letter asking Daren to serve as witness; and it would not be long before his own time would come to be investigated. If that had been the Mad Flight, in which every flagrance and irresponsibility focused in the holocaust of values, maybe the conservative return would be wiser than the continued splurge.

As when he had bundled the Journal up before and sent it off and nothing came of it, no prize, no honorable mention, not even a hint "could we see this when it's done?"—nothing but the alienation of Hank and a sinkhole into which so much work had been poured.

But whatever the project had kindled went beyond the private lesson. Suppose—shaking the head of wisdom after the event—he could frame some gray little book out of the confrontation of past and now? Suppose in the tide of reversal, pumpkin scares and scorn of globaloney, it could even have been successful, have pushed him up with the Foursquares? What if he should gain the whole world, and lose his own cave?

He jettisoned the diaries, turned his back on fulfillment of any kind, held to whatever course he was bent on, while, as in *Moby Dick*, the electric storm candled the yardarms around him.

The cracked bell rang over Patapsco. Cader Ayres welcomed the new class with a vitriolic condemnation of them and their age: "In the Classical cycle Carthage was abortive. Is that the fate of America in the West—to be rotten before it is ripe?" Daren turned in to teach—of all things—mathematics and Greek. The halcyon summer was ended.

Ended Part One.

PART II
Winter

1. Alarms of War

I T WAS the winter of 1954-55. Daren had been fired, after the first O'Malley Investigation (and in the sick leave of Cader Ayres), so teaching no longer hindered what he had to do; he could hack at that through all seasons. The problem—what he brought from his mine being less profitable than coal—was to maintain life and spirit in a world so geared to commerce and against the imputation of an idle toil. There was America hustling around him, getting rich, spoiling and wasting, and all he could fetch up was a scritch-scratch nobody cared for anyway, not even Anna, though she wasn't urging him to get on the gravy train.

What he had pitched on now to bring to light seemed even less promising than the Oxford Journal. It could only have been called philosophy, though it grew like the other from self-search. He had no journals of the war years, only meditations as fragmentary as the Leonardo and Pascal they were modeled on:

> The life of the world is a mansion so large that all parts of it can never be kept in repair. Who patches one wall draws from the ruin of another. So creation destroys and destruction builds, and every action admits of opposite views, where both are just and sound. The gauge of truth is the loyalty of the heart.

> The arguments of faith and question pass me by; for each resolves to this: that our being is infinite and nothing, the world a shambles and a glory, the self, multitudinous and one, incomprehensibly defiled and fine. So I give thanks for whatever in me and beyond me, bodied and disembodied, rides eternal afflictions of joy. For these words do not flow from this flesh or hand or pencil, which they stir to life and which sink to death behind them.

The problem was not only to order years of such fragments, but to validate the voice; to explore the sanction of a brooding consciousness holed-up in landscape of crusading war.

Ineradicable, the sense of mission—like the toothless old janitor in the toilet room that last grim trip to Washington: "Smell anything?"

"What should I smell?"

"Acid." He pointed to a bottle on the floor. "Cleaning off the yellow."

Not a job a man would like, Daren thought. "Waste of time, isn't it?"

"Have to keep it clean. Over and over they come to me. 'You work here?'—'Sure,' I say, 'Anything wrong?'—'No,' they say. 'Cleanest damned place I ever did see.' The boss, he leaves me alone—do as I please. He knows I'll keep it clean."

He spat tobacco juice through pink gums into that cleanest of all urinals, picked up the bottle and went to scrubbing at the next piss yellowed bowl.

Daren sat at the basement window and looked through unwashed panes. The snow gray with use, a sheet long past changing.

Dan Byrne must have told the story, and his Aunt Betsy had fetched it out with solemn amazement whenever the local citizens, the Impeccable, Aunt Willi Mari and the rest, were offered a sight of the book Einstein had autographed for her—how Danny lived across the street from the sage, and little Octavia used to play there and come back rather confused about a man with a woman's hair; "Mr. Einstein, *she...*" she would say, and "Mrs. Einstein, *he...*" always splitting the sexes; and how Daniel had to go over there once to get a sweater Octavia had left, and was told to look upstairs, so he wandered around and came to Einstein's room, where the bed was unmade, the pillow pressed and printed—months that profound head must have rested there—"Can yon imagine?" Betsy Byrne would insist (and perhaps it comforted her as her own dirt accumulated around her), "Such a great man, and his pillow was greasy gray."

You picked up the pen and looked over grimy snow, past the winter-dried brambles by the bluff, out and down, steep as the Tarpeian Rock, where the mucked-up Patapsco fell from the factory dam, boiling its detergents into a yellow foam. On these trash-littered slopes, the held-over December snow dingy as Einstein's pillow, surely one could cushion something, rest the confrontation of some earnest thought. "For the containment of summer," he wrote, "was pride; but the containment of winter is thought."

From the ultimate post of the war years, the solitude of prison, how silly the motions that had led to it seemed; those involvements in the world that weren't involvements, that were trivial and unreal; those detachments from the world that had not yet paid the price of detachment—Oxford halcyon summer spilling over into a time of troubles.

When had it occurred, as in the maze of tracks in a switchyard, that forking of the ways that would cut him off from the stream of talent sensibly employed, on which most of those all-round Rhodes boys were heading for success and power? Did the deflection go far back in his birth and blood? If so, he had kept it out of sight, playing the old college game, until he had won that award.

At Oxford it began to emerge. The futures were cropping out in the faces: this boy was a University Chancellor, that other, a Chief Justice; here a Secretary of State, there, of the Army; and as for that bright-eyes who on the second day of the official crossing (the one Hank and Daren had missed, sailing from New Orleans) presented the only girl on board to the contingent, calling every blessed one of them by name—if he didn't die as a hero first, he ought to be President some day. In such a company, what could Leflore's face reveal but the vain pursuit of inwardness? When they met, those others guessed his future as he guessed theirs, and both began to act as was appropriate to their divided ways.

For Schools, at the end of the second year, he had crossed out the questions set for him, and written his exams on English literature in the light of cyclical history with all its cultural parallels, He passed with a grudging Third. Hank Brown, who had insulted Massah Shipley, did the same. They were granted the graduate year on petition. It was thesis time.

Hank warmed up with a limerick:

A Rhodes scholar once wrote a thesis
On the nature and forms of faeces,
It was only four words:
"All faeces is turds."
The examiners tore it to pieces.

They were working all day among the chained leather books of the old Duke Humphrey Library. Daren was comparing Chaucer's *Knight's Tale* with Boccaccio's *Teseida*, translating, bringing in other romances, music and the arts—deep in the Middle Ages all the time. For his digs Anna had found him part of a fifteenth-century cottage where the gardener of Gloucester College lived. She used to walk in Gloucester gardens the spring before, while Daren was boning for his exams, and had taken a fancy to Broome, a Cotswold man, with rugged peasant ways that reminded her of Mom. She liked to talk with him about the class struggle in England and the abuse of power; and he told stories that matched exactly her view of the rich. In the country he had managed the shoot for the beermagnate Rosen. "Broome," said Rosen one morning after a dismal show, "I'm sorry I missed that last bird, but I was took short. You poke in the covert where I ducked out and you'll find something for your trouble." - "Some o his smut, I thought," said Broome; "but cripes if the blighter 'adn't wiped 'is arse on a five pound note." Broome gave Daren a special rate on the digs (though his wife made it up by borrowing sheets and clothes). There couldn't have been a better place to live: heavy walls, low ceilings, a good fireplace. Anna rented a drafty cheap room across the way, but spent most of her time at Daren's. There was a Gramophone and a beat-up piano. Daren was collecting all the records of early music, *Anthologie Sonore* and the rest; they took up the recorders, and used to blow duets until the discords almost drove them mad. With such a place and Anna to fix lunches, Daren was bound to be popular; Hank and Jim and the rest would come around for music and soup and salad, and sometimes take Anna to the movies, which Daren in his retreat from the world had forsworn.

Anna had come into his life more than he had gone into hers. Though she and Laszlo had taken him to meetings in North Oxford, and he had helped with a petition about alliance with Russia to stop Hitler, words seemed ineffectual as everywhere else. The addlepates and the madmen stayed in the saddle. If the mark of the age was escape (and Hitler the silliest escapist of them all), if that was why war was inevitable, because there was no center, every motion peripheral, Daren preferred the eccentricities of art. And Anna shared that love, with an energy that must have compensated for her political frustration.

She got big rolls of paper and heel-ball and cycled to nearby churches rubbing brasses for examples of all styles. The fifteenth century appealed to her, as to Daren, that simple realism, with its pious plain discovery of the world and man. In music she was trying to learn to read by picking out old tunes: *"Ave Maria, Virgo pia"*, and "Sweet was the song the Virgin sang." She got into the Bach choir and practiced the B Minor Mass all winter in the floreated iron Gothic hall of Ruskin's University Museum, where Daren used to pick her up afterwards—like the night the moon was in eclipse, and he went in as the dark bite seized on the disk and paced among mammoth and dinosaur bones, fantastic steam-pipe arcades reaching to raftery skylights, while the chromatic Crucifixus grieved around him, until they met as always by the saber-toothed tiger, and walked out under the moon, which was now blood red. How dull after that spell of nature and music the next bout of revolutionary politics seemed.

On the surface Oxford remained the never-never land it had been. Cyril went romping through, throwing coppers in slum streets to watch the kids scramble. He bought his landlady a little turtle in the market, with some special food he said would make it grow; then from time to time he bought a bit larger turtle and substituted for it. She was in ecstasies, talked of nothing else, "Marvelous food…already as big as your palm!"—until Cyril threw it into reverse, and the turtle began to shrink. He had to tell her finally, to ease her nerves, though it didn't help their relationship.

The trick Daren played on his landlady was less whimsical. He ransacked the house Sundays when they were gone, to steal back his clothes, hiding them at Anna's, and still groaning about their loss. The more puzzled Mrs. Broome got, the more she went on about how the other college servants stole: "Woi, the last man to come 'ere 'ad no sheets. Oi went to 'is scout, Oi did: 'Looky 'ere, Mr. Pearse tells me 'e got no sheets.'—'Oi reckon 'e ain't; Oi 'ad them.' They was laid out warmin at the fire, 'is naime on 'em, and all. 'Orrible ain't it?"

At Hank's digs the maid fainted away and had to quit. Jim and Daren accused him of the worst. Next day he put on the hang-dog look. "Ah got to go home, Ah'm so tiahud. Been tryin out new maids all mawnin,"

That was the surface, but underneath, the world-storm was brewing. To revive it the Oxford Journals, even if he had wanted to revert to them, would not have been enough.

Since he had lost his job Daren did not hang around the college; but the town library had a basement full of old news magazines, and the librarian said he could borrow them any time if he would only put them in order. Hours, days, months wasted away, while he pursued, week to week, the events that began when he was a boy in the Great Depression, the Japanese gnawing at China, a sequence that reached ahead through Hitler's rise and the occupation of the Rhineland (Daren's freighter wallowing toward England); Mussolini's go at Abyssinia, with all the British pretense of sanctions (the dinner with Cyril at the George when the waiter protested: "I'm sorry, sir, no Bel Paese. Remember the sanctions."—"Well," said Cyril, "bring the Gorgonzola."—to Daren's amazement: "But what about the sanctions?"—"Shh!" Cyril hissed, "The English have always eaten Gorgonzola." And it was the same with selling oil); then Spain, Austria, Czechoslovakia; to the march on Poland—from Hybris into Ate.

But who would have believed that the drama to which history aspires—Thucyclides' Greece, Caesar's Rome, but vaster, the tragic sequence of all time—could lurk in the pages of a slick magazine?

Daren had shut himself off from that; he had hardly read a paper the whole three years, mindful of Thoreau: fit for busybodies and old wives over their tea. So there would have been nothing for the Journal to record but the trivia of detachment. Well, even that had a relevance: he had not played the ostrich alone:

The Rhodes banquet. It had been the custom to toast the three governments represented. But the year before, raw Americans had refused to stand in honor of Hitler. The first toast this year was as usual: "To his Majesty the King of England." But the second left the Americans little choice: "To the President of the United States *and* the Fuhrer of the German Reich."

Daren drank to the deserts of the Thebaid.

He would not even have known of the occupation of Austria, but for a sherry party, where he encountered, of all people, the horse-faced spiritualist last heard in Florence affirming that the green complexion in early painting was the genuine astral hue. Daren was concerned that there should be three angels in Botticini's Tobias, where in the Apocrypha there was only one. The subject had almost become general, when the voice of Laszlo Brad broke in, haranguing a moustached imperialist: "You know they've taken Austria today. I was in Spain last Christmas. They've got Spain. It'll be Czechoslovakia next, or Poland. You think they'll stop there? You've got to join with Russia, and the longer you wait the worse."

The moustache bristled: "That's alarmist talk. I don't care for Hitler any more than you. But there were injustices. Nobody wants war, least of all the Germans. We need a strong force between us and the East."

"You'll get your head bit off," snapped Laszlo, "by your pet lion."

While the lady of seances restored the conversation: "And you know, of course, the figure of Boreas the North Wind in Botticelli's Spring coming in from the right, a green-blue puffy creature, utterly gave me chills when I first saw it, for I knew then and have since confirmed it is simply an astral being. I much prefer Botticelli to all the other painters; for no one else had been able to paint a really and truly astral being."

As Daren testified afterwards, Laszlo Brad had not concealed his views at Oxford; he would talk socialism through anything—as when his wife trimmed his beard one afternoon in Daren's room, and Daren put on music and she trimmed in time, and he stepped it up to the fieriest presto he had and the flying scissors almost finished the beard, through all of which, music and snipping, Laszlo preached Marx. Anybody, Daren testified, could have known he was a communist, so how was he to be indicted on the grounds of concealment? Yes, but the State Department loyalty oath was there, signed with Laszlo's name, and in small print, a disavowal of the membership he had made no bones of with his friends.

That sherry party and the beard clipping had occurred while Anna was home for the last time with Chuck. When she returned, she entered the political discussion:

Jim Hardy produced a girl who had fled from Spain and who tried to tell them about the government. She had bought stewed cat for a dollar a plate in Madrid. "It's horrible: peasants with cars who can't drive, imbeciles with guns on every roof popping away at what they call snipers. They come in the middle of the night and lug off anybody who says peep-turkey. As for the finances, every soldier can peel off a bank note, fill in whatever amount he likes and confiscate your goods. They took my friend's house for a barrack, broke the mirrors, smeared the precious carpets, threw knives at the Goyas."

"If your friends have palaces," said Anna, "with paintings by Goya, you aren't likely to sympathize with revolution."

Somebody had picked up one of those news magazines Daren was now poring over. "Listen to this. Here's what a loyalist police officer invited this reporter to witness: 'Our prisoners are gagged. When they come for execution we walk behind them, as if to loosen the gag. Then we shoot them through the back of the head. The dumdum bullet mushrooms as it goes through, and blows off the face from behind. That way none of the victims can be recognized.'"

"But those aren't communists," Anna cried. "Read the Soviet Bill of Rights: 'No capital punishment.' People who blindfold you and shoot you from behind and brag about it are fascists slipped in to discredit the Cause."

"Bravo!" Her appeal made anybody want to agree. And when German planes had bombed and fired Guernica and machinegunned Basque families fleeing over the fields, a passion for the Left did not seem the least noble stand.

That summer Daren's sister came to England after a year in the sanatorium. She was remote and unsure, but Anna brought her out. It was good, eating steak and kidney pies on the top deck of the bus riding over southern England, to hear the two of them joke and tease: talking about Bristol, where Daren had told them to look at some esteemed pre-Norman carving.

June said to Anna, "I thought he meant that nice carved screen."

"That screen," said Anna, "is nineteenth century."

"No wonder I said we had one like it in Memphis."

"But he thought you meant the pre-Norman carving. And we had warned him not to correct us all the time, to let us think what we pleased— remember? So he clapped his jaw shut and walked away."

"You mean I never saw the pre-Norman carving at all?"

"Well, you didn't miss much."

They tittered on about how the stiffer and darker and older a thing was, the better Daren liked it. While he gave his superior smile to the undulating Downs.

Vail joined them in Italy on his way from Greece. They had a talk in Florence one night over a flask of wine. 'I'm still here—as you see. That's what I went to Greece for, to get life enough to keep on as I pledged. And now I'm going to study Greek philosophy. But sometimes this way stretches out so far, and the other is so easy. He looked into the candle on the table of the cellar bar. He was the handsome one, had an easy way with drink and women which Daren had never managed—like one of the gang. But he looked at that flame, and his face drained to a mocking stony mask. The next day he had migraine. He had suffered from it since he was ten, since Aunt Willi took him to church, a sermon of old fire and brimstone (she had only insisted on Sunday school before that) : "I won't see these children grow up in the godless despair that has ruined this family and would have broken me if I hadn't learned that my Redeemer liveth and will come in the latter day." Migraine had followed the sermon. Uncle Hazlewood's answer was an aside, years later: "The Calvinist commitment has always been a headache."

Vail sat on the loggia over the Arno in an ennui that was pain.

While the mad roulette that was to give him release quickened around them. Hitler came through on his famous visit, yoked with Mussolini. Pippa joined the Americans in the double room at the front. Peering through windows they were forbidden to open more than five centimeters, they saw the long black touring car pass between ranks of soldiers, the supermen saluting—one, operatically for the crowd, the other for himself to himself. That was Anna's account; Daren wouldn't look; he sat and read Isaiah—he, too, playing a part, but for whom? Though he heard the loudspeakers below, in the absence of pro-German cries, roar "Heil Hitler, Heil Hitler." To which the Corporal waved. They drove on; the "Mussolini" shouts died down. "Heil Hitler, Heil Hitler, Heil Hitler" dinned the record-playing megaphones. Machiavellian cleverness. Even Pippa gave the quizzical Italian shrug, in which the whole future seemed to lie; shells whistling over Florence, the bridge in front of the pensione "made-to-leap." *"Che cosa vuoi?"*

Hitler's visit was the prelude to Czechoslovakia, of which they were unaware. Anna had made Party contacts in Rome, but hers was the party out of power.

They couldn't have started for France at a jumpier time. They had piled their heaviest bags in the middle of a crowded train and gone to the rear to find seats. At the border there was a hue and cry for the owner of those bags. A cocky rooster flung back the door and began to fuss about their English money, for which they had lost the papers. He came into the compartment. A cold wind was blowing from the snow peaks. Anna reached across and slammed the door. The officer jumped as if she had shot him and screamed they must descend at the border. Daren had learned some Italian. Nonsense, he said, they would not descend at all. So that order was put aside. But customs men piled in and went through everything, piece by piece, leafing the books and manuscripts, while Daren chattered like an ape taunting jackals: "Take it easy! That may be a bomb. Toothpaste! Try another bag. Ink! Ha! For writing secret papers. All those scratchy notes. About fortifications. And photographs! The devil! Art, nothing but art. Keep looking! What about that powder? Dope, that's what it is. Dope!…" That shrill mockery was Leflore's farewell to the peninsula he had loved.

They rode to Paris, laughing about Italy: Naples, where they ate ripe figs and threw the skins out of the window, and the traffic cop stormed into the room pointing and screaming, his beautiful white uniform splotched with gummy stains. Or June and Anna would giggle some more about Daren's taste in art, how he would rush them through a gallery closing his eyes to the "works of decadence," then stand hours before some venerable smear.

"What was that Gothic palace in Florence?—rooms like a shoebox on end, a little window way up each wall, and that marriage frieze a foot high, thirty feet from the floor, in cheerful browns and grays? How many hours did we worship at that one? And that smell of antiquity, privies and all."

The French had called up the reserves and Paris was full of soldiers. June and Vail caught the boat train, They went off waving at the window, Vail's handsome face a tanned, inscrutable mask. Daren and Anna met Hank and headed for the Channel.

There was a storm that flung the boat up, her screw out of water, shaking, then sucked her down in a dive, and up again like an elevator, screw racing. Daren had bolted most of a Camembert cheese and had gone to a third-class bunk to sleep out the voyage. Lying in the wooden bin, he got the first hint of some nightmare relation to the time. He went through a series of crises increasing toward the dread event. By willing it away, he almost fell into a troubled sleep. It was the attendant who roused him, slapping down a pot by each bed (Be Prepared!). He glanced into his and saw a crusting of the last sufferer's malodorous gorge. Reluctance heightened the pangs. He gave up and slid down a black incline into the irreversible spasm.

Wells' *The Shape of Things to Come* in London confirmed the familiar dream, the Apocalyptic last war so many were expecting that one to be: rubble fields cratered with holes, the sun rising over the waste where green fog blows in the withered hollows.

The first night in Oxford they listened to Hitler's ultimatum, the radio voice building violence like a Wagnerian prelude, from lonely weariness to brass and percussive strength. And then the cheers of thousands.

A Canadian Catholic who had joined them said the jig was up unless the Pope could bring moral influence to bear. And next morning the reliable *Times* bore the regular full-page autumn ad for the hunting elite: "There is still time to reach Czechoslovakia before the shooting season begins." Ostriches all.

Chamberlain took the hint. "It is peace for our time," he said. Even Daren, with some coaching from Anna and from Laszlo was able to predict: "If we live no longer than next spring, he may be right; and by that time Romania will be a German satellite…"

"We thank you, we thank you," the English greeted Chamberlain at the airport, breaking into maudlin tears. As if a new Christ had been found. Then they gave up, and faced what they had yearned to avoid.

Daren and Anna went with the rest to a distribution center for their gas masks. A trivial circumstance; but when every Englishman got one of those worthless little respirators and walked home with it, it seemed he turned a corner and faced the war.

The pot had been clapped down at the bed's head.

The slide down the black incline took almost a year. And of course there were evasive regressions, even behind the Maginot Line. A fact, that at the last Glyndebourne performance, when everybody knew it was just a matter of days, the entrepreneur, who had been a master at Eton, got up during the intermission: "I"m afraid I have a very grave announcement to make"; and everybody hushed, thinking, "This is it"; and he went on in his dapper voice: "Harrow beat Eton today by six wickets." Weakness, or strength? Under every British officer would be that schoolboy playing the game.

Anna, too, wanted to live while there was time. For the last Christmas she invited her favorite brother, Michael, to join them, the one she had looked after when they were small. He had some of her starry-eyed hopes, but American, wanting to get to the top in something; at the moment it was the car business. Anna laughed at his politics, his aesthetics too; gave up on both, and tried to give him a good time. They went through

Holland and Germany up the Rhine, heading for the ski slopes under the Matterhorn. Hank accompanied them as far as Frankfurt. In Cologne, Daren was reading the Apocalypse and writing a dream-vision of the world destroyed by war. Later, when he was in prison, and the fire fell on that city, he saw the winding streets they walked those nights as leading to such a judgment: gutted synagogues, storm troopers chasing Jews, stoning houses, the crash of glass, cries—a tragic waste of wrong and retribution. The German he had learned from poetry turned to polemic. Everywhere, in hotels and shops, on hams and trains, he questioned, harangued, accused, only to be shrugged off: cocky American, what could he know of urgency, he had no ground.

In Freiburg he wanted to cross the Rhine to see the Isenheim Altar piece. Michael was fed up with art, Daren took off alone. But his French visa had expired. He had to get off at the border village of Breisach and wait hours for a returning train. From the Romanesque church on a hill, he looked over the frosty wide valley. As in panoramas of the seventeenth century, the battleground spread before him: a pontoon bridge for cars, the railroad trestle so turreted that either end could blow up the other, then forts and barbed wire entanglements stretching on both banks back from the Rhine.

The urge that took him sprang in a curious way from Anna. She and Laszlo had produced the Czechoslovakian refugee who had stolen through Germany and across into France with underground secrets, and was writing a book about it; he had made an Oxford tea party memorable with his adventures. Now Daren had a chance to find out for himself.

A lane led through fields boarded off with high palings: "Forbidden— Keep out"; he ignored the signs. Knotholes framed a view: a hill half excavated, cement pouring, burrows, such as they made when he was a boy in the Mississippi orchard, but running from pillboxes to the main emplacement—cancer, the crab. At the railroad bridge a guard sprang from a shelter and covered him with a pistol.

If the problem was to pass the time, it was taken care of: a day's workout in German, escorted from post to post at gunpoint for more and more frenzied questionings. Though it was almost cut short at the first hut when the guard bent over the passport filling out a form, and Daren reached in his pocket, and the man spun on him with the pistol, screaming: *"Was ist das?"* But it was not a gun: "A book, poetry. *Ich lese gern.*" To be frisked for arms and taken to the next authority.

"If you run, I shoot."

"Why should I run? There's no train."

"Have you made the military?"

"I would refuse to kill and destroy."

He wound up with the Gestapo, a bull-neck out of the spy story, leafing the passport and wheeling with a snarl: "False! This seal doesn't go through the photograph."

Daren laughed like the idiot child: "Three years I've traveled with it, and never known."

"When did you enter Germany? And why no stamp?"

Daren had not left the train. "I must have been reading." He shrugged.

"When?"

"Five or six days ago. I can't remember."

"Where was that? And where have you been?"

"Up the Rhine. We were in Cologne. Terrible, the Jewish pogrom there."

"How old are you?"

"Twenty one.'

"When were you born?"

"October thirty-first, nineteen-sixteen,"

"That makes twenty-two."

"I mix it up; it changes every year."

"When were you in Germany last?"

"About nineteen-thirty-six. I would have to count back."

"Do so!"

Daren began subtracting from 1939.

"But this is nineteen-thirty-eight!"

"Oh."

"Why were you trying to get into France?"

"To see the Isenheim Altar."

"The what?"

"A painting by Grünewald. You've heard of that. It's the pride of German art."

"Where are you staying in Freiburg?"

"I know how to find the hotel; I don't remember the name."

A baffled stare. "In God's name, where are you now?"

"This town? I hardly know. Zweiback? Tie-rack? I didn't mean to come here."

There was a man swatting all this on the typewriter and getting nowhere. But they had to have the Freiburg hotel. Daren tried the list in his Baedeker, reading each name, and each sounded right: "Hospitz!" "Yes!" While the cannon hands pounded at the keys. But that was wrong. "No… It's not the Hosspiss." The cross outs went down, a curse on everyone. "Stuttgarter Hof, that's it." The barrage again. "No… It's not the Sruttgarter Hof… Schwartzwald…" He exhausted the list, the police surging forward, the machine rattling, then everybody falling back under the curse and canceling X,s, "I don't know which it is."

They put him on the night train—heel-clicking and Heil Hitiering, Daren shaking hands and saying *"Grüss Gott."* The armed conductor would guard him; a deputation was to meet him in Freiburg, take him to the hotel and check his story. He got off the train at the end of the platform. No deputation; snow was falling. He sprang off the platform, over some tracks and a fence, and went to his room, not bothering with the station.

Michael and Anna had bought some Kaiserstuhl wine. He told them everything. Michael burned the wine cork and daubed himself with a little moustache. They were all clicking heels and Heiling, when the door was flung open, and the black-banded party men burst in. They had got the hotel from the records.

But the leader was a Rhinelander, who knew of Grünewald, music and wine. He even had a sense of humor. He saw that moustache and saluting, and laughed at the whole thing, checked their papers, and left them with assurance of the friendship of the German people for the people of the United States of America.

While the concentration camps were filling with Jews and the gas chambers were being prepared. Leflore went through as in a dream, out of contact, reading St. John the Divine, acting the Revelation of St. Daren the Absurd. Though a time was coming when his protest would have to pay the price and be real:

(*The first incarceration:* Cook County Jail: electrically locked cells eight-feet-by-five, three steel walls and a fourth of bars, a straw tick crawling with life, a basin charged with offal; twelve hours in the stale stench, and then to the bullpen, nodding to the others in the half light from windows too high and too opaque to see through ("I be damned, they got me cause I killed a man, and they got you cause you won't"); eleven paces the long way, eighteen men to pace it, all but the Pole who sits staring at the wall; and you pace all clay, counting the one-to-eleven thousands of times, anything to get tired, to fight for sleep against the bedbugs at night, the man in the next pen vomiting his grub ("Ya can't eat it. Ya pour it down the head when he ain't lookin, or ya puke it up later"); the Pole, far in the dark, going stir crazy, beating the walls and screaming until he falls exhausted.)

Greece and Egypt, that final spring, afforded the final escape. On the cruise ship at Easter, standing off Olympia, the paschal lamb was served whole, stuffed with dainties in high Roman fashion and draped again in its skin. A few miles north, Albania was dished up to a rougher palate.

But if art was the escape, it had led round to the central search: to document the cycles of spirit. Like the yearning Ikhnaton Daren stood, the temporal kingdoms behind him, reaching ahead for the devouring one. In Athens, where the monuments epitomized Classical culture, from the first seventh-century stirrings, through Pericles and the rule of Rome, to the other world of Byzantine, he was determined once and for all to spell out the historical parallels: out of the fall of Mycenae and Troy, to trace the coming of keen Hellenic joy, to see it fulfill itself, soften and go down; to try each point against some Western cognate, Gothic, Renaissance, Baroque, Romantic; to extrapolate all toward an imagined future where faith would surge back in the ruins of our luxury, stripped of mean egoism, flawless, sure.

For Anna it was the regeneration she and her party had already made. As they climbed the summit of Delos over the cave of Apollo's birth, where Daren looked east toward Patmos, her search went north, beyond the horizon of water, to the great Russian plain.

They came back to the old dispensation, Oxford, Cyril Mercer, sherry parties, music of the Romantic salon: Chopin, Delius, Brahms. Daren wrote:

> When these walls, ivy-covered, stand in ruins,
> Gray to the night of slowly altered stars,
> And men in wonder strike the savage harp
> And sing the work of heroes, giants of old—
> They will not know that in this crusted hall,
> Where music wails the specter of a rose,
> A man of peace leagued with an age of wars,
> Welcomed destruction, darkness, hunger, Death,
> To find again strength without compromise.

From the concert he went to Christ Church for evensong—to store in the heart the power of Norman columns, the Lamentations of Tallis weaving like the fan vault of the choir, rich to the point of tears. Specter of another rose.

By summer his thesis was in. He and Anna took a farewell tandem ride over England, a garner of Gothic cathedrals and parish churches; and everything they saw they caught at, as if for the last time, under that cloudy threat billowing up the sky.

They sailed for Daren's job in the bare corn West, the northern prairie winter, the fact—no longer the dream—of war. And with it, protest and imprisonment. In Daren's private cycle the Dark Age he had called for was settling in.

That was the motion he set himself to revive in Patapsco as summers yielded to winters, and now the seventh winter was on him, of exile again, and of war with the state. From the gilded forehall of Oxford, he had moved into the vault it framed—not of the personal, not of politics even, but of mind, the why of inwardness.

> Each man embodies in infinitesimals all the depraved desires and all the noble aspirations. There is a continuity in nature. The most devoted pacifist in some suppressed corner of his being loves and glories in war. It is the fluctuation of this denominator which hurls millions periodically to do what (with their other mind) they despise. For every latency peaks to creative act, continuously in a few, and from time to time in the many, as the distributions of energy in space-time require.

The briefcase Anna had given him, already stretched out of shape by the Journals, cast its untimely fruit. The halcyon summer was past. Winter spread the soiled gray of snow hills, the stripped hieroglyphic of trees. It was the Augustinian withdrawal Cader Ayres had heralded long ago, and which, dying of multiple myeloma, he confronted now with new urgency.

Those evenings, when the slaty coppice of cloud gave way to a cold distance hardly tinged with the spent sun, a receding space where the winter stars showed a frosty sign, the whole world of flesh and temporality seemed yielding to a quest as intangible as those stars. It was with this nucleus that the briefcase began again to swell, and as the organizing germ-plasm gathers around itself a sustaining texture, weaving the miraculous net where awareness rides, so the search for meaning wove into a circulation the events and scenes of those middle years:

> And wynter wyndes agayn, as the worlde askes,
> No fage...

2. *Vigilante*

A far cry for Anna: to come to Delta Landing in the steam of August; to enter, for the second time, the bourgeois state of marriage, not only with the son of a planter family, but (in deference to Aunt Willi Mati) under Presbyterian sanction; to receive the Uncle Tom devotion of the old-time black serfs on whose labor the family past had been reared; to honeymoon at Ararat; to go out to the garden, in blouse and apron, trim as a Dutch girl from De Hooch or Vermeer, gathering fruits and vegetables; afternoons, to swim in the Blue Hole; and at night... but they were loving all the time.

As a wild element is bound by affinities, she was tugged by generation. The child-face, always ready to start life afresh, wore the dream of wife and mother. If the announcing miracle at that moment could have offered— as to old Joachim's Anna, to Elizabeth, to Mary—fruitfulness, would the fate that was driving to absolutes have eased, have left her smilingly planted in the maternal cycle? That possibility had already been burned out of her. And without issue, what can love do but build its own sacrament or risk dwindling to a pastime? Daren had accepted that. Why else, after his brother's attempt, had he written those Hamlet letters? But they were both exposed to the violence of compensating urges.

Yet Anna was carefree; she sang. Only *The Daily Worker*, which reached her by mail, was a reminder: "Listen to this; it's what I've been telling you:

> "Man's spiritual desires are breaking loose and cutting new channels. Those who cling to the church dry up and atrophy. Those who preach faith-healing, food fads, mystery cults of all kinds, offer no relief. The sickness of soul turns on itself and festers, antisocial. Only to the vanguard of the people's struggle can we look for a new manifestation of the religious spirit."

And, of course, the morning paper would touch off little discussions:

"But how can you swallow it? For Stalin, against all his claims, to make a pact with Hitler?"

"I'm here; the Premier's over there. I have every faith in the new policy."

"As you had in the old. I'm asking for reasons; and you claim faith, like a Dark Age peasant."

"That's another kind of faith. To have political power, you have to keep political contact, and that means follow the Party. You can't decide whatever you please for yourself; that's idealism."

But it was not a time to argue. It was their honeymoon.

The morning after their return to town, Daren was waked by a street cry. He walked onto the upstairs balcony, and saw the newsboy with his sack of papers, strolling along the oak-lined avenue shouting: "WAR EXTRA WAR! Read all about it! March on Poland. France and England WAR EXTRA WAR!" Daren went in and waked Anna. Fresh from Europe, they were struck with awe: the ruin of what they had loved.

Pacifism and communism had never more ardently embraced.

Uncle Hazlewood had been lured into the Rotary Club years before on grounds Daren never understood; now he invited the European traveler to give a talk on the state of the world. Daren had been a famous orator in Delta Landing since he wore knee britches.

Those plush little corduroy suits his father had the old Negro tailor make, one for Daren and one for Vail, wonderfully stout and regal, but they must have been modeled on an illustration from *Little Lord Fauntleroy*, because they didn't look like anything anybody else wore. Little Vail got teased and hated his and cried until he was let off of wearing it; but Daren took to his: "There's not another boy in town with a suit like mine."

He had got up in front of the assembled classes of the elementary school, those corduroy britches shaking at the knees, and delivered, in the teeth of southern convention, Lincoln's "Fourscore and seven years ago." The next year it was "Liberty or Death," and so he continued, getting more florid in his choices, until in his junior year in high school he took the silver palm in the state—a prize appropriate to Bryan's warhorse: "You shall not crucify mankind upon a cross of gold."

The last year he wrote his own speech: "The Forgotten Man." The Great Depression, that ferment of radicals everywhere, had inspired him with a vision he thought his own, as original as Einstein's discovery of curved space: if the state would take over production and technocracy would produce, that old radish of all evil, MONEY, could be bypassed; no more starving in a land of plenty; Utopia would be at hand.

Luckily, he had cloaked his message under more eagles of freedom and plumes of oratory than all his models had managed. Fierce socialism assaulted the auditorium at Jackson, waving purple patches of style, and was not only cheered but given first place, the golden palm. Though by that time, with a raw throat and a shade of fever, after days of preliminary heats, Daren couldn't have delivered at all, if Uncle Hazlewood hadn't gone backstage and swabbed his throat before each competition, half bringing up his gorge with some gagging opiate that numbed everything and pulled the frayed chords almost to their right timbre—as you would tuck a little dope under the tail of a sick horse you were grooming for the steeplechase. Uncle Hazy had never seemed more fatherly than in priming Daren for that exhibition in the manner of their fathers.

Now the florid style was outgrown, everything put aside but the stripped utterance of the world-plight, in which these free-enterprise American chamber-of-commerce Christians—settling back for the normal platitudes after a fried chicken dinner—were unwittingly involved. Daren fetched out the Spenglerian Medusa, with all its snaky coils:

Talking of history as if it were subject to physical law: of the rising and expanding motion of a culture, when freedom cracks the inherited molds; talking of the falling or constricting motion, when freedom has gone too far, and the drive for unity fevers the warring parts—a time like ours, when even revolution, under the terminology of liberation (Napoleon, Hitler, Stalin), builds always stricter regimens, reaching out to consolidate the world.

What nation (he asked) is likely to supply the binding form? Not those which have sustained the rising motion. Though they make the attempt (Alcibiades, Dionysus of Syracuse, Alexander, Pyrrhus) they do it (as in the Third Reich) by driving backward from laxity and disillusion, under temporary and unnatural strain. "Leadership falls instead to a new people, *born in discipline,* which can slowly loose itself as it binds the world."

(He had improvised the talk, but the core of it he set down that night while it was fresh, and it used to give him, even when he should have outgrown it, the almost chilling sense of destiny he got from a Bach fugue. But when he showed it to Cader Ayres years later, thinking a teacher might be proud of what he had so obviously inspired, Ayres, already failing, though he did not know it yet, and with only two years to live, had fallen out with those 'Wave of the Future" manipulations. "I suppose you know," he said, "that Spengler was almost writing Nazi propaganda before he died. There is an idiotic little book called *Hour of Decision,* in which he totally misrepresents the military potentials. The wish in him was always father to the thought. 'Bare your necks to the blade.'" Ayres winced under a bodily twinge. "Whatever you learn from the past, the future is to be shaped by vision and prayer.")

But Daren was facing the Rotary Club: and now he came to the particular woes of democracy, which had not much changed since the days of "The Forgotten Man." No wonder he puzzled that audience. When he spoke of unemployment, he let Wolfgang Harth give his version of what Hitler had accomplished. When he examined the pressures that would drive us into war, he sided with Anna and Laszlo. When he touched on the scandal of race, he might have been born and reared one of the Dark Leflores.

—Though that insight too had been mediated by Anna. Theoretically, Daren had it before. His father had been an old-time southern liberal *(noblesse oblige);* his mother (which was more) had grieved for the Negro lot; in England, Africans and Indians had been his fellows and equals. But homecoming was to the old acceptance:

Those Freeman cousins of Aunt Willi's lost Teddy, who dropped in after the wedding. When Cousin George had eaten all he could, he flung himself back in the oak chair and began his nigger tales, which nobody had objected to in the memory of man:

"Nigger name Rastus, up Tutwily way, got drafted in the las wah; stead o goin to France, wound up fightin the Huns in Africa. One day he got los in the jungle and come on some monkeys, brainiest monkeys you ever did see. He up an tame one, and when the wah was over he brought it home. Well, suh, he taught that monkey to pick cotton, and fo long it could outpick Rastus and his whole fambly. So he went to the boss man. 'Marse Percy, Ah got a proposition. You back me up, and we be rich.'—'Whuchyou mean, Rastus?'—'Ah got a cotton-pickin monkey...'—'Rastus, you know there never was any cotton-pickin monkey, and there never will be.'—'Marse Percy, you come long to de fiel. You bleege to b'lieve whuchyou see.' Ol Percy went. When he saw that monkey draggin the long sack down the row, strippin the bolls like a cotton-pickin machine, he was staggered: 'Ah reckon you got him, Rastus. What's your proposition?'—'You finance me back to Africa,' says Rastus; 'Ah get enough o these cotton-pickin monkeys to breed, an we cawnuh the market.'

"'Lemme think about it,' says Marse Percy, scratchin his head. –'Whuchyou want to think for, Marse Percy? We make a fawchun.'—'Ah doan know. You see me tomorrow.'

"Nex day ol Percy was in the dumps: "No, Rastus, you cain't have em.'—'Fuh the Lawd's sake, Marse Percy! Iss easy money.'—'That's the trouble, Rastus. You breed youah monkeys and pick youah cotton. Fo long some other nigger'll get a greedy white man to send him to Africa; an for you know it, this whole cotton country, all the way from Virginy down through Georgia an Alabama an over to Texas, be nothin but cotton-pickin monkeys, fiels an fiels of em; and then, suah as God's white, some goddam Yankee'll come down heah an make us set em free an give em an ejjication.'"

The Southerners laughed; Anna froze. Cousin George went on—a true story for a change: about an uppity nigger who fought in France and came home thinking he had earned his freedom, so he went in the white barber shop and stretched out in the chair and said, "Gimme a shave,"—"OK," said the barber, and lathered him up. He stropped the razor sharp and started on his chin. "He gave him two or three little clean strokes," says Cousin George, "and then he split him fum ear to ear. 'Oops,' he says, 'my han slipped.' An eveybody agreed he had done jus right."

"You ought to be ashamed to tell a story like that," said Anna. "I don't believe it happened, and if it did, it only proves the filth of the South."

Cousin George was a southern gentleman. He stared unblinking, an alligator from a swamp, at this girl whose wedding into the old clan of Leflores he had come to celebrate, and when he spoke again, it was of crops and the weather.

The next day, Anna contacted the first of the Negro leaders whose names she had received through her Chicago cell…

"I always think," Daren told the Rotarians, "of that Bosch Paradise where black and white enjoy the fruits of the world together. How long will the South fight its human calling—talking of states' rights? There are no states' rights to do wrong."

He closed with five possibilities for individual action.

One: to muddle along, talking of free enterprise and of saving the world for democracy, and drifting toward depression, fascism, imperialist war. This popular old program he dated 1890.

Two: to work for democratic socialism, equality, world peace and union. This beautiful ideal, which he dated about 1905, was unfortunately subject to disillusionment.

Three: to join the Party and work for communist revolution. This required some dogmatic closure of mind. He dated it 1916.

Four: nationalism, a deliberate totalitarian choice. This way of the passionate and headstrong, rabble-rousers and hate-mongers was not outmoded and would have to bear a recent date.

The fifth, his own preference, brought him to The City of God: the Gospels, not meant for Rome, not for businessmen protecting their investments, not for militarists pushing war: "Resist not evil, turn the other cheek, love your enemies"—a pacifist leap of despair for those who had found the state irremediable.

"And who can say if the modern world, even this spangled democracy we are so proud of, has already become the horned dragon John saw, from which the souls of the righteous, refusing its wars, will fly into the wilderness, seeking the waters of life?"

He had turned to oratory without intending it. But where seven years before it had won him a prize, now it stirred the barber shops, poolrooms, cotton exchanges, against him.

"Bank three in the corner pocket." *(These sayings are reported by Calypso, who had them from Hermes, the guide:)* "Turns out young Leflore is a *Nazzi*" (sound of *nasty)*. "Been over there three years and took it hook, line and sinker. Get your elbow off there, will ya? Whoopin it up for Hitler."

And the Italian barber Prentiss Leflore had helped into the country long ago: "Tell me young Leflore pacifist. Not fight for country. His pappa have yellow streak. Sell out to Yankees. When publish—BOOM." He aimed the right forefinger at his head.

Barbers weren't among the Rotariana yet; but the lathered customer sold autos and had been there: "Pacifist, hell; I'm not for the foreign wars myself. But we can't have commies telling us how to run things. And that's what he is—a dyed-in-the-wool commie."

Across the street in the rival establishment. "Bible maniac? Who cares? Bubble-talk. But in the South, at a time like this, to come out with that nigger-lovin incitement to riot. If anybody but a Laflore did it, they'd lynch him." Until the hot towel muffled the witness.

Daren got a call the next morning from Bull Slaughter: "Daren? About to say good to have you back home, feller. But that speech of yours has made a lot of talk. I wonder if you'd come into the office? I didn't hear it, and I'd like to find out what you said."

Slaughter's grandfather had been a captain of barges and flatboats trading in pork, lumber, cotton and flour along the Ohio and Mississippi; he had settled in the Delta and served in the Civil War, so even old Bull could have claimed to the "First Families"—except whatever dignities that ancestor conferred, he also boozed away; in fact, he drank so much the family hadn't sobered up for two generations.

Picture the Mississippi, the ferry search-beam over swirling water, catching moths and Junebugs, fingering the bank of willow for a secret door, the chute to the high-water landing. A jangle of bells. The wheel slows, plashing, then pounds on the back pull. She comes to, sidling the channel, Bells signal forward. Plash, plash, plash. With a jar the mud takes her. From the open windows of the pilothouse spills a volley of cursing.

Somebody on deck: "Damned drunk. Sink us yet."

"Not Bull. He's goin in the army."

"What they gonna do, make a tank of him?"

"Sure. Get him tanked up and sick him on the Boches."

The door to the pilot's cabin was flung back. "Bull Slaughter, there are ladies aboard this ferry."

"Who in hell…" Slaughter whirled.

Now the jaw advances in the dynamic, plump, moustached face: "Judge Byrne. I warn you, Slaughter. You are drunk and endangering this ferry. We can't change that now. But you can keep a decent tongue in your head."

"Sorry, Judge. Forgot about the ladies."

The little judge marches back where his wife, Octavia, gazes over the dark water. Oblivious, she had not asked to be protected.

The boat came off the bar, angled upstream, plunged for the chute again, made it. Coasting through the willows, it moored with a final crash. Hazlewood Leflore went down with Judge Byrne and the rest for his car. He had been to Lake Village to say good-bye to a friend. He, too, had volunteered, and for him as for Bull Slaughter it might have seemed the last run.

Then Bull turned a corner and got on the upward course that had led him to success, influence, some attainments even, of a self-made and pigheaded kind.

Piece it out—from stories heard when the veterans of the town would get together, Uncle Hazlewood among them, trying to maintain, through other differences, what had been a common cause (once a year, the only time he wore the uniform and decorations which did not make his soldier role any more conceivable to Daren)—conjure it from the talk: on the wide fields of the Marne, the breakthrough near Chateau-Thierry.

Did the action wear for the participants the surreality in which rumor and imagination had invested it: Daren's father in his flying machine hovering somewhere over the same fields where Uncle Hazlewood strolled nonchalant, and William Slaughter, nicknamed not Bill but Bull, slodging from the mud (the rum- and river-soaked squalor of his past) and tearing through barbed wire, made his famous charge?

Catch it there—one of the dream moments: by the Forêt de Fer, that sunken road of corpses behind, and before, a wide hostile space rising toward summer clouds, the soldiers flung down under the bank, chummy with dead Krauts, waiting for artillery, planes, tanks, anything; and then the order comes to take the ridge. See them straggle out, after days of advance, like sleepwalkers, dirty, unshaved, preternaturally tall against the sky, rifles slung forward, moving toward the entanglements. They cut their way through, falling under shrapnel bursts and the crossfire from machine guns above; but each goes on, no bullet meant for him; while the Germans on the heights, not asking how they got into four years of this, or if they are ever likely to get out, pump cartridges into crashing engines, toward which the Americans, caught up and thrust forward by an incalculable pressure, leap, scrambling over the fallen.

And then their captain stops, snuffing the air. As Uncle Hazlewood was to put it in one of his anniversary addresses: "We have all seen strength and courage break and go mad." The company wavering, world-pressure driving them on, their appointed leader with a cry making for the rear—a shock-haired hulk of a man (Horatio Alger charging up the hill of success), rifle advanced from the hip, meets the captain head-on. There were too many slugs flying around for anybody ever to have investigated that captain's death.

"Follow me," Slaughter roared. As men sloughed off around him, it purified his force. He never tired afterwards of marveling at the transformation of that moment. So he must have seen it all, the future against the past, as he tore a grenade from his belt.

At the same time he glimpsed a figure strolling up from the road, dapper—as if one could keep on right through the war in the sporting spirit with which the French and British had begun: "Fine shooting, today. Your bird, sir"—elegant, the slim face raised (was he reciting a poem?), familiar somehow, but out of place, serving only to stir by association Judge Byrne, the ferry, the Delta shame. ("Wince, Bull, here wince, as you hurl the grenade.)

In the nest. If the one German still alive kept up the habit of firing, and managed (as Bull claimed) to nick the flesh of his arm, what could one expect when that quiet little man, who had done what he must have heard called his duty, held up his hands in mild surrender, but that Slaughter, planting the bayonet in the uplifted vacant face and lunging with it downward into the throat, neck and spine, should twist it there with the spasmodic force of his shoulders, then draw it out, spurning the corpse with his foot.

"Nasty, eh—Slaughter?" It was the incongruous saunterer over the smoking field, and at such range that Bull could not fail to recognize Hazlewood Leflore—Colonel Hazlewood he noticed, the first with whom he must take a surer tone.

"Lucky I beat him to the draw."

Hazlewood had observed the encounter. "Your charge," he said, "was courageous. I am aide-de-camp to Major General Hynes. It will not go unreported. At the moment I was sent to your officer. But I assume he fell?"

"In the charge."

"Good you took over."

The rockets went up from the heights. "Let's shoot off this machine gun at anything, heat it up and have tea."

It was hot already. They chummed up in a rather elegant dugout which now faced the wrong way. "There are contingencies," said Hazlewood, "for which even the German engineers do not plan."

They had tried, through a lifetime of divergent ways, to keep the spirit of that ironic truce.

Looked back on from the dark solstice of '54, when Daren's real Washington investigation had lost him his job, Bull Slaughter's little attempt in Delta Landing dwindled to a forehall—small potatoes. But what if a girl's first love gets stranded in the home pond? That doesn't change the fact of his primacy. Bull had made the first impact of dumb, ruthless power on Daren's virginal soul.

It meant something that in Florence Daren had read the Bible when he should have been looking out of the window at Hitler and Mussolini. He was still wrapped in a distance which they and the furies of their Europe didn't penetrate. That was where his pacifism took root, sheltered and hedged around with all the dalliance of privilege and escape.

Now he had come to earth, in his own country, his hometown, almost in the shadow of his father's house, and Bull's vigilant, muddled, self-righteousness had reached out and swatted him, pacifist hopes and all, as a girl walking the streets in a rosy love-dream might be swatted by a boorish accusing cop.

Of course, martyrdom had been part of the Christian vision. What else had one meant by "going to the deserts of the Thebaid" and "withering to a bag of bones"? But that was all literary. It didn't have the feel of this humiliating, jarring blow. 'When Daren came up (spitting figurative teeth and blood) he found himself not a saint at all, not looking out of the picture with Christ's olive eyes: "You have spoken"; but in there sweating and swatting, blaming, arrogating, scorning.

He didn't abandon his pacifism on the spot. How could he? He clung to it the harder. But he watched what was going on. He had been trained as a scientist, and this was an experiment in falling bodies. It was not Christian theory he had to come to terms with, but the inner and outer events. Until that tussle with brute fact, he had undervalued Machiavelli.

A dark back office in Bull's cotton brokerage, rigged up like a court-room of the underground, a seat against the wall for Daren, Bull standing before him under an American flag, and on either side of Bull, seated, his joke-fellows of justice, a couple of loafers he had called in, so whatever account he made would be corroborated by witnesses.

"Daren, I hate to say this to one whose father and uncle I've always admired…"

(An admiration that must have been strained when Colonel Stump of the Klan made his foray from Reading into the Delta and Slaughter was on that side, and Daren's father led the other and a little bit more and they'd have shot it out in the courthouse.)

"But it's reported that you said some dangerous and un-American things: communism, fascism, pacifism, mongrelizin the races.

"As you know, we have no laws in this country to keep you from thinkin what you please, however, subversive your thoughts may be. We have no laws to stop you from sayin to the Rotarians or anybody else things that betray the principles on which this government is founded. But we need such laws for our own security; and in time we're goin to have them. And already some of us who sense the danger are tryin to save this country from its internal destroyers. The first job is investigation. That's why I've summoned you today."

(Amazing, how this man, in some jerky southern way, had anticipated the vocabulary of Senator O'Malley's Era of Investigation, all the distorting techniques, the very style and rhythm.)

"I wonder first if you will raise your right hand with me and swear allegiance to the flag and to the nation for which it stands."

Like testing a witch by fire or a Christian with the oath to the gods. And now Leflore was as passionate as Bull; he had taken the bait, was roused to talk in this hostile company about the things nearest and dearest: pacifism, socialism, mysticism, the rights of man and the course of history:

"Why not play soft music and fall on your knees and worship together according to your rights? Un-American! What you've said is more subversive than a thousand refusals to fall into an attitude and take some oath with you. Allegiance to what? To the Constitution you've undermined, the flag of the liberties you aim to take away?"

"We record that you refuse the oath of allegiance. Will you now tell me…"

Half an hour later Daren broke it off: "Look, Mr. Slaughter. Each one of us thinks the other's opinions are dangerous. That's what democracy admits of. You're not my keeper any more than I'm yours. And if neither is going to convince the other in the slightest, why should we try?"

Daren left, certain he had won the debate, and that even Bull Slaughter or those scribbling coadjutors might have learned something. But the rest of the day and all that night, fevered rumblings rose in him, forensic, as if he were forever answering some dense accuser.

Bull did not reveal his next move; but the town couldn't keep its purposes hid. There was a revivalist who had been holding forth in his sweat-vapored tent for a week of Sundays. He came from the sharecropper hills and hated those Delta aristocrats and liberals whose politics and religion he was always trying to show up as Satan's spawn. He devoted most of a terminal hour to degenerates of good family, bred in the seats of luxury and ease, witness that young Leflore, who was spreading the poison of his *isms* against God and country, wherever he could find an audience to listen to him.

Daren and Anna had been fishing that afternoon in the willows across the river and it had come on to rain. She was catching cold and had gone to bed. Uncle Hazlewood was upstairs in the study searching out the law for a case he had to try. Daren was reading *The City of God*. There was an almost inaudible knock at the door. It was the Baptist preacher, their neighbor, come to say he had gone that night to see how the revivalist managed to steal away so many of his congregation; it had distressed him to hear Daren brought in like Antichrist; he was afraid to say anything publicly, though he sympathized; they could see how he was circumstanced, his church members feeling as they did; they must not even reveal that he had come tonight, but he had to tell them for old friendship's sake—terrible how the town was divided—that the revivalist had got the crowd simply wild telling them to storm out of that tent and get red and black paint and paint swastikas and sickles all over that antebellum mansion (it was only a Reconstruction bungalow); and that he figured the family should clear out the back way and go to some friend's house (he didn't offer his), because there was no telling what a mob like that might do.

They thanked Brother Sheperdson for what he considered a signal act of courage, beyond the line of duty; then they let him hustle home.

"All right," said Uncle Hazlewood, "what do you propose?" Though he had been debating enough with Daren these last days to infer what the answer was going to be—to stick by the Sermon on the Mount through the envisaged sacrifice.

"I'll turn on the lights," said Daren, "and wait in the yard."

"You can do as you please," said Uncle Hazlewood. "But I'll be on the balcony, like Colonel Sherburn in *Huck Finn.* As long as I'm alive, they're not going to paint swastikas or crosses or anything else on this house. If I begin to shoot, don't get in the way."

He got his pistol and the double-barreled shotgun that was always loaded with buckshot, and set the automatic rifle by the front study window where it opened like a French door on the railed balcony over the veranda—Daren pleading with him in a voice more and more aware of its own vacancies, to attempt passive resistance.

When the cars began to gather in front of the house, beyond the great oaks, and the loud-talking devotees moved forward—even while Daren was still pleading—Uncle Hazlewood turned on the floodlight and stepped out, bringing the shotgun to his shoulder.

He didn't have to make a speech as in Mark Twain. There was hardly time for Daren to come out beside him and continue his remonstrance (what would he have done, invite them in for juleps? It was all ideal) when the crowd began to drift away. They weren't a lynch mob, but a bunch of idlers coming from a prayer meeting, and they idled right along. They'd never had any notion of painting anything on any house anyway—certainly not if they had to do it under fire.

The illumination for Daren was greater than that of the floodlight.

The day he and Anna had reached Delta Landing, Uncle Hazlewood had driven them to the cemetery to see the monument to Daren's father, completed while Daren was abroad. It was the more than life-size bronze of an armored knight, not at all a Quixotic figure, but Arthurian—out of Tennyson—bowed head, crossed sword (was it the spirit of Prentiss Leflore, or of Hazlewood grieving for him?), a responsible chivalric champion, ideal defender of the right.

But if Prentiss Leflore had in fact eliminated himself at the upshot of a rumored affair with Bella Wynne, it was hard to see the relevance. Maybe, like the ghost of Hamlet's father, it was to remind Uncle Hazlewood that the world's account must be a lie. To remind him too, that whatever abyss the embattled Prentiss had been dragged into, it was his own obligation to carry on in the warrior role his birth and fate had assigned him.

Yet until this moment Daren had not known how far Uncle Hazlewood could assume that face and mien. He had even wondered if the statue might be some sort of sentimental wish-fulfillment.

But when he saw that slim aesthete, the last poetic refinement of the Old South, raise the gun, his face, too, raised into heroism—the girl in the Goya etching who leaps onto the cannon—then the patriot knight, with Uncle Hazlewood's uniform and war medals and the stories that had accompanied them, incomprehensible before, came into focus.

The jolt threw Daren for a moment outside his pacifism and outside himself. (How deceptively our virtues are rooted in world-vices, the very word "virtue" meaning of the male and power.) He saw the two of them as from above, a floodlighted pair: the violent boy crying "Peace," the peaceful old man armed for war.

3. *Prairie College*

BULL AND DAREN had discovered each other's dangerous folly. But where Daren's knowledge of Bull stayed quietly at home, Bull's of Daren was communicated through channels (which were Legion) over several states and wound up filed in Washington.

The first sign came from Prairie College, where Daren, before he left Oxford, had been hired to teach. The alerted veterans there phoned the governor, the governor the college president, the president the dean; in a few days Daren received a letter in the evasive style of all those administrators who (except for the dying Cader Ayres and maybe a few more) seemed to be taking over American colleges, announcing with chagrin, but without explanation (for what could be explained?) that the position in the English department which the college had thought to offer Mr. Leflore for the school year just about to begin, did not in fact exist—signed—the dean.

The gray autumn rains beginning—the Delta stretched out bleak, already passive to winter—in Leflore's consciousness, which was to labor years under that gloom, the trap and shame of the future stood baited and laid; the blindness of the many, the ineffectuality of the few, time servers Whitman visited always gaping before us: races, riches, poverty, corruption, unemployment, the dearth of true leaders. Against the bloodbaths that would drown the South, what road remained but this of martyrdom, on which he was already embarked?

And then the sacrifice was interrupted; and what came to the rescue wasn't the saint of the vision, flying through storm to the imperiled vessel, but the remnant of political and humanist power, the ally Daren made believe he had cut loose from. As if St. Catherine, threatened by the wheel, should have been saved not by the angel but by the Roman prefect in his tour of the provinces.

Uncle Hazlewood took him to Jackson for a lunch with an old Federal judge (his father's friend), a younger adviser to the governor, and the ranking Legionnaire, a man of some refinement. Daren was able to express his position with the subtlety required for bringing it into the rather amplified democratic fold. But whatever he had said or however little could have been clarified, the result would have been the same, because what was at work was not doctrine but influence, laid down generations before, when the Lone Hawk buried the carpetbag and helped establish the order Daren used and defied. So the saint boggled, fighting fire with fire.

A more urgent call went from that region to the affiliated prairie one: earlier directives were countermanded. In a few days a cautious note came from the dean; the difficulties experienced with regard to the appointment seemed to be clearing up; Leflore could therefore come according to plan, on condition that he remain within his competence, giving no public speeches on matters of general concern.

Daren answered that he could make no such binding engagement on his tongue, but the contract was only for a year, and they could see how dangerous he was. The dean showed no inclination to reply. So Daren and Anna proceeded over Chicago to the windy wide corn lands with the great elms and oaks in the valleys incised by streams.

There he found that the head of his department, who by political infighting was slowly working up to be dean (whenever the present incumbent got motioned to loftier seats), and his confidant, who would take his place in the department (unless in the meantime he saw some way to cut his clear friend out and be dean himself—which by the head's death almost occurred), were both (as might have emerged without Anna's insights) Party men.

"We teach Lincoln Steffens two-thirds of the first year," the head told Daren. He was a likable enthusiast, though his human intentions were always knuckling under to his place and his aims. "It hits these kids where they live. Wakes them up to corruption and revolution; makes them write about it, too."

"Here I come from all that fuss in Mississippi," Daren looked up from grading his hundred-a-week illiterate papers, while Anna brought in the pot roast from the kitchen, "old Bull Slaughter determined to keep me from teaching communism, fascism, pacifism, abolitionism to the youth of Prairie College; and they put me in a department where they teach revolution all the time. And nobody minds. And you know why? Because English teachers can teach every treason and subversion, year in and year out, and never stir up a soul."

Though the book that was supposed to prepare for the take-over, Steffens' *Autobiography*, was a product, if ever there was one, of free inquiry; so that not only those true-blue farm students, but even Leflore (who thought he wanted to teach old masterpieces) stood to gain by it. 'I'm an aesthete of the old school," he told himself as he finished the section on Lenin, "and I'm married to an immigrant revolutionary, and maybe that combination remains the hope of America. Lords knows what favor they do us, these schemers."

That was hard to remember, looking at the corny sly face of Joe Jones, those absolutely round, black-rimmed, light-reflecting glasses distorting red, sleepy eyes. "But my God," Daren told Anna when she defended him as a social visionary, "he's a crummy, lecherous, climbing little man, like Governor Gyves of Mississippi; why he even looks like Gyves, only he says he's on the Left. Who gives a damn? A creep's a creep, whichever side he's on."

"He's had to work up from the bottom. Just because he looks seedy... "

"That's what worries me about your Revolution: all these Joe Joneses in power. No wonder Russian bureaucracy has been depressing."

Yet, charitably considered, poor old Joe was God's most pitiful citizen, growing up in the Dust Bowl, a tow-headed, long-necked, big-Adam's-appled, gawking farm boy, robbed of everything by the crisis that debouched in the Great Depression, going as a raw and bitter adolescent to the prairie city, and coming, as who wouldn't in a country so careless of his welfare, to hope the present misorganization had spent itself and that something more responsible was on the way. He had worked in a packing plant heaving boxes, had joined the union and got political training, gone to night school, and finally, scraping and saving, to teacher's college, where he met people of more hope and vision, who helped him get a fellowship and pull himself out of that slavery; one had been a communist, so Joe had been steered toward an action which was supposed to put an end to the deprivations he had suffered under all those years.

But what a pimpled poor pitiable scab. How destitution had queered him and made him ready to climb by any means or betray anything, maybe even the Party, if doing it would nudge him ahead. But so far nothing had promised that much; so he remained secret agent of the Comintern in that drabbest of English departments, pushing Lincoln Steffens to soften up the youth, and doing free government a favor without meaning to.

As it turned out, drink was his besetting sin, drink and dames. It was at a New Year's Eve party, swayed by toasts and Anna's charms, that he began to unravel his history. That was the first year, when Daren was still regarded with hope; for both Joe and the department head theoretically admired energy, and Daren's energy would have been hard to hide. Besides, the world-famous anthologist (who by including himself in his collections had almost got a reputation as a poet) had lately been on the campus for the visiting writer's stint, and Daren had come across in the panel with a brilliance that might have offended his peers, if Oscarmeyer, with nothing to lose but the tedium, hadn't talked up "that young fellow" as a genius, considerably boosting his stock with the head; he insisted on an evening with the big shots at Daren's house, where the conversation ranged over everything and far into the night; finally, he had his protégé to his hotel room for breakfast the morning he left, and in a fit of royal favor shipped off a four-leaf-clover necktie he was wearing and gave it to Daren for luck; so at New Year's Eve, and cinched in that lucky tie, there was still a glow of promise on the young man. The head had just told him of his embarrassment at the administrative fuss of the summer and how personally he had sympathized with Daren's position.

That stirred old Joe Jones, that and the cocktails and the always dynamic Anna; he sat half hidden in a green lampshade that was mounted on his head (for it was a charades party and everybody had to represent some title or poetic line and Joe had dwindled to "a green thought in a green shade"); he told them of his past, the suffering of the dust years and of his political faith, and it was rather touching, especially for Anna, who tried to take up for him after that. Still, drink and dames were his besetting flaw.

He'd been too poor and harried when he should have been building up a tolerance, and here they were, drink at every faculty get-together and girls in every class, strapping, corn-fed girls. Even a person with a wife like Anna was jolted (it was a time when skirts had gone up above the knee) to see them sitting with their legs cocked in the front row, and if you grabbed the roll call to get your mind on other matters, there were those immigrant midwestern names: Fielerfelt, Hurlbutt and (what did the girl's parents mean, sending her to college with a name like that?) Patricia Mae Rassul. In the old days Joe hadn't attracted a creature but his plain pill of a wife who had got him early and stuck to him until they were fed up with it, each reminding the other of all they had suffered through; but they wouldn't admit it, especially dear Agnes, because she couldn't have got anybody else, not another scabby soul. But Joe had risen to a position of sway; he could really stir up a class: pitching on a question more related to the social need than to the text, then whirling and pointing like the angel of the Annunciation when a bold hand was raised, conjuring another notion from across the room, throwing them together and demanding a reconciliation, or if neither served his turn, puncturing them with a barbed jest; like other subtle vendors of the fruit of knowledge, he had a following, especially those girls…

What a pity for the Party, what an overthrow for the cause of the Left at Prairie College. For when the student got pregnant and sued Joe as father, and he was found drunk in the gutter escaping from his plight, he was cashiered, that was all, and just as the department head had conked out and the dean was retiring and Joe had every chance of being next in line. But that was after Daren had left Prairie College and gone on to even wintrier pastures.

The first years it seemed to them both that they were banished to the bottom of the round world. Anna stacked away the brass rubbings she had meant to mount and frame. There was no Bach Choir, and the church choirs would have discouraged faith itself. She relinquished all that, and switched to her other phase, working as Party_representative among church groups and intellectuals. At the meetings of the college cell, she appeared as the superior of Daren's superiors.

But Daren's pursuit of culture dug in to keep alive. He got a camera and began photographing from art books in the library; he took up old instruments and organized a madrigal group; and to make sure of reading his Dante, Goethe, Augustine and the rest, he enticed refugees and others, who like him felt their exile, into reading groups in five languages. For exercise that fall, and again when the blizzards let up in the spring, he cycled over the corn prairie he could not yet recognize as his own. Though sometimes pedaling through the cold gray along a road that crossed the river and bore left on a low ridge paralleling the town, it seemed he was at Oxford again, riding from Wytham village skirting the hill. He would look across the valley (here it was the Sioux) half expecting the stacks of Centerville to fuse into spiry towers.

Or there was the ride to Turkey Creek, with the long coast into the wooded valley. It was like Wychwood Forest down the steep hill that led to the village and the Grange. Daren might almost have missed a corner, plunged over the handlebars and waked with child Jeffrey looking down at him in her kilts, holding out those lucky conkers; and as the war advanced and the shadow deepened over Europe he used to wonder: Where is she now?

Though events at first lurched slowly: Poland, Finland, Norway—the United States veering around ponderously from its neutrality. Then, as the school year was ending, came the famous lightning war, the fall of France. That was the theater in which the soul was engaged. But right here in Prairie College the war of the English department had begun—the Rape of a Bucket, the parish battle in *Tom Jones.*

What was it, at such a juncture of history, that this revolutionary faculty, under its radical whipster Joe Jones, espoused as its aim? To standardize the grading of English themes!

Who first seduced them to that foul revolt?

Immortal Fame. Let Oxford sift old texts and notions, cobwebs of bourgeois idealism, let Patapsco wrangle over the Great Books, and atheist professors at Chicago teach Catholicism to Jews, let Appalachian Art School debauch itself on the creative, and Swalee Seminary refine the English of its own hermetic *Review;* they were all sweeping the sand in the wind and the wind was blowing it back again, but Prairie College of the Practical Arts, under the aegis of Joe Jones, would make one sure and concrete advance: reduce the hocus-pocus of composition once and for all to the rule of science.

"The first problem," as Joe said, "is to schematize the problem"—to apprehend excellence of composition under six and only six heads: Purpose, Subject, Material, Arrangement, Expression, Mechanics. It did not take long to get theme paper printed with a six-by-six graph at the top, and to replace the grade with a plot of checks from superlative to unsatisfactory in each category. All that remained was to set criteria of performance in Purpose, Subject, Material and the rest; and since Mechanics was normative, that was the place to begin. Nothing could be easier—Joe said—than to define a group of Serious Errors which everybody could mark with a special star. Then all they had to do (in that category) was to count the words in a paper, count the Serious Errors, strike a ratio and arrive at a check. The rest of the time Daren was at Prairie College was spent trying to tie down Serious Errors.

The second year a pasty fat chestnut worm from Chicago Teacher's College was invited, on a consultant's fee, to assess their progress. Joe had to produce. The faculty sat all one afternoon, marking Serious Errors in mimeographed themes. But to weigh the divergence among all those asterisks was a problem in statistics, and Joe's mathematics had halted at converting a fraction into a decimal. The day arrived; the chestnut worm, the faculty, even the dean met for the victory. Joe referred to his analysis, already distributed, and proclaimed, with the sly smile, that Mechanics had been objectified and that they could proceed to Expression.

Daren had spent the night with a slide rule on the figures. (He hadn't won a scholarship in physics for nothing.) He went to the board and graphed their situation: almost nobody was calling the same thing Serious Errors; subjectivity could hardly have had a wider field for its operation, unless in Joe Jones' statistics, where lack of knowledge had bestowed freedom from the facts. The dean looked as if he had been trepanned. Wasn't this making utterances on matters of general concern?

That second New Year the head told Daren rather sadly that while he liked him and would give him another year to shop around, the college wasn't going to require his permanent services.

Shopping was dismal. "See here," Daren told the head that spring. "You misled me when I came. You said you wanted new ideas and frank criticism. But you want somebody to help standardize theme grading. I don't believe in it; but I can try. Why not let me run some tests?"

Feats of endurance: the faculty hunched like guinea pigs, grading lot after lot of mimeographed themes, Daren making Bell Curves and calculating deviations, cracking the whip over aberrants, until like rats they began to run the maze, slapping down little asterisks in the same places, the group coefficient rising, the chestnut worm rushing back to applaud, the dean himself nervously smiling, and grateful Joe Jones all aglow—to get such a boost where he expected to be kicked in the pants. "I guess we're on the right track now." He'd sidle into the office with his head on one side and his crooked grin, to talk about writing it all up for the *Education Journal.* "We'll show em, huh, Daren?"

The next spring Daren was advanced, with tenure and a title of his own: "Adviser on Statistics to the English Department." There were people who would hardly turn in a grade without asking him what it would do to the probability curve.

For the academic burlesque to have been mounted in such ridiculous form at such a time—destruction fanning out over continents and seas— was staggering; but for Anna's world-changing Party to have been at the heart of it, Daren and sleepy-eyed Joe Jones pulling the wires together, swept even her at times (though she didn't like jokes about serious matters) with catspaws of laughter. Which would die out in the doldrums of Centerville.

"You know what you're doing to me in the Party?" she looked at Daren through a dreamy distance. She had sacrificed the love of art, but not of him. "'What are your plans about your husband, Anna?' they ask. 'Wait,' I say. 'He understands. He's going to be a writer.' And even Joe Jones puts the smug look on his face. Because at least he brings Agnes in to type and cut stencils. But you have Dante on Tuesdays, when you should come with me."

Why remind her that in Chicago that summer, when she got him to the open meeting, she went up to welcome the strangers: «some of you are not communists. We are glad to have you with us, of course. 'We are brothers to all. But we urge you to think about joining us in a deeper sense." As at a revival, gazing soulfully at Daren.

He was always disappointing hopes. The day he got his tenure, he struck out for putting Shakespeare into freshman English. When it was hooted down, he did it in his own sections, without permission. The head staggered under the first attack of the fatal high blood. Well, between his nature and his place he had always labored under a strain.

As for the Shakespeare, Daren pretended it went across, though not everybody claimed to like it—that fat boy who insisted: "Can you prove *Hamlet* is better than *Popeye?* Because I like *Popeye,* and I don't like *Hamlet.*" Daren staring, as through the Whistler monocle: "If anybody can be such a fool as to ask the question, no proof on earth can touch him."

"I hate poetry," said another of *The Tempest.* "Why do we have to read it?"

"Oh come on now, just do this speech aloud, and you'll see." The boob stumbling into Prospero's valedictory ("We are such stuff as hash is made of"), Leflore suffering awhile, then cutting in: "Christ! I wouldn't like it either if I read it that way. Why don't you practice, and learn?"

And could one forget, the year before, the engineer who tried to read from "The Eve of St. Agnes" ("What's eating on Keats?" he had asked), and when he got to the twenty-fifth line, about the beadsman: "...and soon among rough ashes sat he for his soul's reprieve," and it was a college two-column text with the line-numbers scrunched up against the print, he droned right on: "And soon among twenty-five rough ashes sat he for his soul's reprieve," and never felt the jar? So maybe Joe Jones was right and they weren't quite ready for Shakespeare.

Amazing they kept on good terms, Daren and those students. But the department was ready to ride him out on a rail. Then draftees began to pour in, and he was called over to teach physics to the Navy. Saved. Ironical, since he had declared himself a pacifist.

•

These Patapsco walls narrowing, setting to bare cement, the window shoved into a grate far up, which, even if you climbed, would offer nothing but a snow-drifted prison court, and above, one precious framed sector of sky. And yet that absolute of the solitary cell was better than all the compromise and slippery temporality by which his pacifism had cooperated with the world.

The arrogation of judgment. To treat one's fate in a time of public seizure as if it stemmed from the private will. Day and night a cry of moral alternates to be decided and redecided; Peacetime Conscription, October, 1940:

Heart: If the rape begins with registration, break there. Protest the draft. Go to jail.

Mind: Registration is signing a card. Taxes are worse, and you pay them all the time. You can register as a pacifist; the law allows you that…

The basement of a school. Light from old bulbs mingling with clay, spreading, aging, falling yellow with age on the floor, peeled and overpainted, battleship gray. "Next man." Feet pass, crushing the butts of cigarettes, and one cigar.

(Mating bodies, of course he and Anna had mated souls: Christian and socialist making the same appeal: "Keep out of war and a plague on both your houses, and how do we trust the news that filters through the warmongering press?" Who could avoid being that word not invented yet—brainwashed a little?)

201

He looked at a mechanic sitting by him, grease-smeared, holding the smoked end of a fag. Daren's eyes only speaking: "What have you come for?" And the other's eyes: "China maybe." And from the desk: "Next man." Feet pass on the floor. Daren's soul, mated with Anna's, conjecturing: What if all those cigarettes were from workers, like this man, and that one cigar from some Steffens' plutocrat ridiculously caught in his own machine?

Recess. The children break from school. You can see the wind in their clothes. The game turns to a fight. A teacher wades in: "Bad boys."

"Your name, your father's name." *You could have tossed in the grandfather too, and all of them would have fought* in *the wars.*

At Ararat on the sofa with Dan Byrne, leafing a diary browned with all that was recorded there. How Captain Quincy, late in the war, stormed an entrenched hill north of Atlanta. A friend, who had found Christ, mounted the railroad and crashed back, a Minié ball ranging from throat to spine. "Lay me down. Want to live. Poor family." They left him and charged against a curtain of fire.

At the crest Leflore turned, waving his company on. A handful scrambled to him and were mowed down. His other Christian friend, who had hoped for Quincy's conversation, staggered: "Brother, I am gone."

"Have hope."

"My hope is with God."

A shot shattered Quincy's gun and took the tip of his finger, another tore into his shoulder; he fell. "Pray for me," said Chambers. (The ledger darkly recording the reality of that pain, the hollowness of the prayer.) "'Oh brother, I have received my third wound." The hand closed on Leflore's. A fourth ball had entered the brain.

Quincy lay, feeling the thud of balls as they struck the shielding body of his friend. An officer sprang from the trenches and waved a sword. The fire lulled off. Quincy got to his feet and ran.

Weeks of retreat, in rain, in fever; and now the bullet was cut out in an Army hospital in Alabama, he seated on a bench, another wounded officer gripping him from the side. "A kind gentleman," he wrote, "Captain Charles Clayborne, of Mississippi."

"That was my mother's father," said Dan Byrne—they too arm to arm, gripping the smudged record of war.

The bell clanged. Recess was over. "One, two, one, two." The children marched back into school. Leflore registered, the will boiling, the scribble taking it out on the card: "I object to the draft and to all participation in the war."

But we had not yet entered the war. Having registered, he took deferments as they came. First a respite for the married man. When that was done, he went to the city armory for his physical, after another crisis in the will: "Why not refuse?" But the law on which one had compromised enough to register was clear: "If you are to be rejected by the army anyway, establishment of pacifism does not arise."

In filling out the forms, when he got to the question: Which of the services do you prefer: Army, Navy, Air Force or Marines, scratched the lot and wrote: "All equally undesirable." A soldier, overseeing the forms, nabbed him: "What's this?"

'I'm a conscientious objector."

"A communist objector? Are ya yeller?"

Leflore had debated that point with himself enough to be primed *(you call yourself a teacher, teach him);* so they had it out, long and bitter. When the doctor got to him Daren's blood pressure was way up and his false murmur was going strong. They put him in 4-F, a physical wreck. He argued that, too; but they sent him back to grade themes, at least for another year and a half, until the cards were reshuffled. By that time he was in physics.

How could the Bible-maniac of the Rotary talk teach Navy engineers?

It had seemed easy in Oxford, reading the Gospels, to affirm an absolute and think you had mastered life, when all you had done was to precipitate a timeless pole. But we do not live on the timeless. The problem, flux as we are, was to maneuver by trial and error in the field between that pole and the world—to slack off, go with the tide, though in imminent danger of losing a qualified ideal. Feel it out. There is a certain point at which nothing will serve but a counterswing. He would have to risk everything for an absolute in which he no longer absolutely believed, but must follow into the deepest dens, a gratuitous gesture of redeeming play. And when that martyr's fling, like his brother's Russian roulette, had offered only death (for there is no answer but to weather—continual reciprocity), could he ease off then in the loves of life, Jeffrey and the world—temporizing? Though ready, at the least senatorial thunder or the night cry of a bird, to junk it all and come from the grave for judgment?

So far he was on the first course. He neared the solstice, slipping from the absolute, as deferment after deferment led to more and more doubtful roles: while reason accused, vacillated, backlashed in self-scorn:

> Crouched in this, at the best, inglorious
> Corner, what have we borne?

Not long after the draft, a Friends' Service camp appeared on the wooded slopes past the golf course, where Turkey Creek flowed into the Sioux, Daren and Anna used to go for Quaker meetings and talks about peace. These boys, too, were on the rack; they had registered, were doing busy-work in the camp, dependent on relatives, charity, their wives.

Even the testament they had made was compromised: isolationism and America First homing in from the Right, Peace Mobilization and the communists from the Left. Who could tell what cause he might be ghost-dancing for?—as the cartoons every week in *The Peaceful Objector* divulged: there would be a carnival tent placarded "The World in Flames," bony Death lifting a curtain to a big top of bombers, superdreadnoughts, trench-warfare, the barker no other than the top-hatted, gold-plated stereotype of Uncle Sam Capitalism, almighty dollars bulging from his pockets, summoning to their fate the workers and the poor; the artist, it would turn out, was someone Anna had known.

That complicity and doubt troubled every discussion: thus the young preacher Floyd, who was going to walk out of camp soon, preferring jail:

"The militarists have a plan and an action; the communists have a plan and never lose sight of it." (Anna from her seat in the circle smiling into the Celtic brown eyes.) "We have a few meetings and these wishy-washy work camps the government allows us, to keep us out of the way. But we have no plan and no real action. Gandhi said: Nonviolence is the weapon of the strong. How do we know we're strong? Maybe all these retreats should be abolished, and each of us resist to the limit of his power."

There was no toehold on the absolute for a relative distinction: that hunger strike Daren shared with the camp. How was it ever moral to eat again where eating sustained a world of wrong? So the plea for life became a death urge. One had to give in somewhere. Then everything began to waver. Without the sign Floyd waited for, Christ bowed out and left Erasmus, saint of the relative.

For some years Daren had attended the mathematics club and the physics seminar. The head of physics, Wilson, another Rhodes scholar, had asked if he would help with their cloud chamber experiments in atomic structure. Like Leonardo, to know the whole of it. As the English department turned on him, Daren crossed the campus, taught Navy engineers in the winter-gray room off the long corridor, then ducked into the basement to tend events of the cloud chamber. In the lulls which research seemed full of, he would scribble his meditations:

> The whole of nature seeks the ultimate resolution and therefore moves. Since the ultimate resolution is beyond, only the partial is found.
> When the partial is found, it is taken for the ultimate; this is the fact of inertia,
> Yet suspension remains: activity and desire, decay and fresh birth toward decay,
> So, in finite being, all things are paradox, believing and disbelieving in themselves, each bearing the flaw of the real; that death does not kill life, but life dies; or in science: energy runs downhill.

Or he would write a letter to Hank Brown, whose last brief word (the affair of the Journals having come between them) was of accepting the draft "to suffer with the world":

> Not to have suffered has been to me also a cause of self-reproach:

Caught in a festered calm, we shall go down,
Old rotted hulls of ships that never sailed.

Sometimes I think I am like one of Dante's trimmers, neither rebel nor faithful to God, but thrown by scruple out of action into thought. Then I comfort myself, that a time of proof will come, however little we seek it. Yet the army is not my proof; though I have so far relativized my faith, that if I could believe in a future to be won by violence, I might almost go along.

As I cycle through winter between this campus and my house, the alternatives seem as clear as the road behind me and the road before; and who can go at once in both directions? Behind me is responsible humanism, where a controlled force led to a possible good; before me is the world we have increasingly faced since Nietzsche where the forces are out of control, so that attempts at mastery lead through unnatural vices to worse ruin.

We did indeed witness, a while ago, an unseasonable thaw, like a false promise of spring. But the weather has turned, and as I look back at the road you have chosen, I see nothing but a windswept waste of snow. What more can I hope for than a night-clearing, and to search, as from a prison, for the winter stars?

To have seen the terror he and Hank witnessed on the night streets of Cologne seize the world; to watch the Europe they had loved go under, occupied and blockaded, one great concentration camp, crammed with the sick and undernourished; to envisage no way of remedy which did not plow through worse; to try to hold a personal pacifism against that tide, where everything you heard and saw pushed the crusade of force: Dick Tracy chasing fifth columnists, Joe Palooka drafted, grinning over the *Defense Manual* (that same pamphlet of instruction Bull Slaughter took the trouble to send Daren: "The point of the bayonet should be directed against the opponent's throat, especially in hand-to-hand flighting. Other vulnerable and frequently exposed parts are the face, chest, lower abdomen, thighs, and, when the back is turned, the kidneys. The armpit, which may be reached with a jab if the throat is protected, is vulnerable because it contains large blood vessels and a nerve center..."), even children's books gone wild with it: Burgess' syndicated nature stories praising little Jimmy

Skunk who always goes armed and lets his enemies know it, and how "some folks and some nations could follow his example to advantage, yes sir, they could"—as if the kiddies were to carry a gas bomb next time they went to play, and not take any nonsense from the little bastards, either—to be swept along on all that, trying to resist and yielding, was enough to make one write of prisons and of winter stars.

Though Daren's actions were not yet of that order. He went on from day to day, teaching, watching with mounting excitement the vapor curls that betrayed atomic surprises in the cloud chamber. His thought groped toward an understanding of all structure as strung between the poles of energy itself, entropy and anti-entropy—hardly a mystical insight, but a proud formulation of this world. With his German group he began Hegel and Hölderlin. South of town, where the river valley cut down through the productive vast spread of the plain, oaks and maples purpled with unopened buds; jn the library, he photographed a Bohemian landscape by the romantic painter Friedrich, in which such river hills beckoned to pantheistic spring.

Russia was fighting for its life. Anna shed pacifism like last year's skin. She threw herself into practical work as never before, bundling for Britain and food for Russia, war bonds; it was a new birth; she had always felt estranged under the German alliance. "Russia and socialism," she said, "are one. I know that. And I know all about the destiny of fascism." She bought a big folio of communist art: There was old Joe grinning with workers at the opening of the Ryon Dam. Through the billboard blatancy Daren searched for what billboards did not have, the vital conviction of the common man. One read Sholokhov and listened to Shostakovich. It was not just in Daren's soul that the revolutionary hope came out of hiding, the whole Allied world stirred to the battle of the freedom-loving peoples. As in everything, Daren was split down the middle. He wrote Uncle Hazlewood:

> The purposelessness of the between-wars begins to wane; one feels the organic force of the whole man groping toward a new resolution, in Russia and the East, if not here; and though the new age will have its drawbacks, the vulgarity of which our own mass-media have given us more than a taste,

a driving purpose, which these have not, might almost redeem all, and at least give us more to write of than Babbitts and the ghost of desire, or an age noble, but past five-hundred years.

Trying to ride the wave; to affirm, in "Smiling Joe" and blatant Shostakovich the "organic force of the whole man"; while his own winter cave of martyrs opened into the basement of science hall with its consequences of public power. Yet neither that, nor the world alliance with Anna, nor the day to day postponement of his pacifist claim, taught him how much he was part of Hank Brown's heroic war. He learned that, as he learned so many things, in a kind of vision, where objects assumed symbolic sway:

When you wake in the night not knowing where or why, not remembering anything but a dream of the old confinement, and you roll over and catch the sound of an open throttle way off, as a motor comes toward you, and it rises to a shrill hum, piercing the room, drops a fifth and goes by, somebody making all hell to get somewhere; and as it dies the other roar begins, and grows and grows until the house shakes with it, drive-wheels pounding on rails, steam, pistons, the thud of loaded cars (as if, whatever energies had been loosed or harnessed since, the great locomotives of our childhood were the ultimate vaunt of power); and as that too slams by, you think: where am I? in what house by road and rail? until it comes back over you: the green house on the rock, the Patapsco below with the B&O and the west bypass beyond, those sounds mounting in the night, suggesting another place and time, the frame-built house between rail and highway, those war years at Prairie College:

They lived more than a mile from the college in an ugly place rented from an oil dealer, who had bought it for the lot and filled the backyard with gas-storage tanks. A block from the house in front, one of the great highways went by, and half a block behind, the trunk railroad between Chicago and the West. Daren could cycle to early class in the winter dawn through subzero air, where snow drifted with a waste whine across the flats, and loaded trailer trucks plowed past, whipping up stinging ice, against which he lowered his face and pedaled on; or in better weather, Anna would walk with him along the railroad to pick dry stalks of goldenrod, Queen Anne's lace, spiked grasses for a decoration, and they would duck down the embankment when the great transcontinental freights drove by.

It was a busy line. Trains came through at all hours, shaking the rented shanty through and through. As the nation lashed itself up for war, the throttle was advanced: fuel, scrap iron, timber, girders, flatcars heaped with armor, plane parts, guns, rows of boxcars labeled: "Care, Explosives." Through dusk and dawn Daren watched them go. He was a man of peace. Yet that blood beating in the veins of the nation quickened a pulse in his.

The night after he wrote Hank Brown his Augustinian letter, he walked out sleepless, late, and saw the headlight sliding around the bend on polished rails. He stood, as the sledgehammer blows of the locomotives fell, doubleheader, firegates swinging for coal, white hot, fanged with steel, then the crash of car after car—it was not outside him; it was a fury loud in the darkness of his own being. For all his conscious protest, he too was entrained, pounding at the smithies that would send bombers over Europe sowing phosphorous and detonation, until the white sands of New Mexico would fuse in a blaze as ultimate as the sun.

Then Wilson called him to Chicago, and for a brief time, he was literally caught in that chthonic unbinding.

4. Chicago, Mother Port

Agalnst Prairie College, through those years, the other center had been asserting itself, heightening, even more than the productive expanse of cornland, the opposition between Dark Age theory and dynamic fact.

When he had come as a boy to the Century of Progress, Daren had shared in the Utopian myth: but now, having put that behind him, a gray precursor crying in the wilderness, "Prepare the Way—and mark it with our bones"—it was strange to be caught in the rush and amplitude of the wind city of towers.

Heading for Prairie College that first fall after Oxford, they had checked the heavy things at the I.C. station and, carrying only a rucksack and a canvas bag, had mounted their English bikes, Anna leading the way, threading traffic, holding out her hand for the turns, looking back at her burdened Daren with a smile gayer than on any of their Cotswold rides under a sky of singing larks. She guided him into the gaunt slums of the West Side, to her Mother Port, where they stayed a week with Mom and slept in the iron bed of Anna's childhood.

As she stood with him at the back bedroom window that evening and looked into the alley, the twilight and the moon on cinder yards, broken steps, the factory rising dark across the way, clotheslines strung crisscross from windows of all the poor tenement earth, she sighed that she had never seen anything so beautiful before.

Daren was not the only one who labored under an antithesis.

That slum she hated and had chosen her politics to wipe away remained what she most deeply loved.

It couldn't be accident; as Uncle Hazlewood had said, some deep search had made Daren give half his life to Anna. Whatever it was, he never felt more on the track of it than that autumn of 1939, as the melting pot of Chicago folded around them.

How much the swineherd's daughter in the fairy tale could have taught the king's son. An abiding present she led him into, an initiation from day to day: along factory row, past the old cave under the sidewalk, the organ-grinder still playing on the corner by the penny candy store, the skinny girl hanging at the showcase, wistful childsoul of earthy Anna, her eyes on the glittering candies, like Keats, wanting them all, until the corseted square Czech widow dressed in black, stiff to the ankles, bellowed, "Don't stand all day!" and you put a finger on the glass: "No, no, not that; that one there," and went down the street clutching it—

Under the window where the little seamstress (the seal-stoled lady driving off in a polished car) leans out: "Anna!" and she runs, pigtails flying, a nickel an errand; and is that the old milk woman who gave change for five instead of one, and Anna in secret joy took it to Mom, but was guided back, schooled, "She's as poor as we are, and what's worse, she can't see." Yes, and the butcher shop Pigeon Joe acquired and lost; and the window where Mrs. Gundrun would be calling her dopey son, he stomping flat feet like shovels: "I won't come in, old woman, hell no!" until she lowers a sandwich on a string—

But was it revealed in hate or love? The marvel lived, or the shame of democracy, the wrong of capital?

In Maxwell Street market—love: the Indian woman with the sleepy boa constrictor: "I don't fear no snake crawlin, only the twolegged kind goin around in the nighttime knockin you on the head"; the pawnbroker Jew hawking watches: "A hundred jewels—three dollars"—the movement lying open, shiny—"a hundred jewels"; far off the little old balloon man, balloons bubbling above him on the wind. Love.

As they passed the movie house on Halstead: "Old Stinky Foot," Anna said. "My brother Paul used to take me. We doubled, for a nickel, two in a seat. In summer the boys would pull off their sneakers to air their dogs; and between shows they'd stand up and yell and throw wrappers and orange peels; but when it went dark and the reel whirred, everybody settled down." (The screen a magic window, like her memories now, her eyes: no more Stinky Foot, no more slums; floated out on wonder.)

Even that cave underground would yield to the Gardinases upstairs, Christmas, and a tree with colored candles: "Ahh!" Anna drew her breath with the original catch of that climb to light. "And New Year's Eve, how long we had to wait, playing, telling stories, until the factory whistles would blow, almost in your ear, and we would scream into the street, bitter cold, hugging each other, laughing and dancing in a ring."

But the *Zillgaro* had disappeared, their one-man summer-Sunday band—drum on his back, cymbal on his head, accordion in his hands, mouth organ swung from the cymbal; he would stamp, stamp, stamp, and the clapper would come down "Crash, Bang!"

Zinga-rata, zinga-rata, zinga-rata, Ra.

The kids crowding after him like he was the Pied Piper. Gone. And the blind fiddler couldn't replace him—a sad man: he would hardly play a strain before the clink of a coin from a window would set him groping after the sound. "Where is the zinga-rata man?" Anna queried; and blamed Spring Foot de Wulf and Blotchin of the Newberry gang. "They would sneak behind him and grab the clapper and give the drum a swat, to make him whirl around and put him in a rage."

Her brother Paul was in the liquor business; he was part owner of a tavern now. Anna took Daren to meet him the first day. They sat at the glass front looking into Canal and Port Avenue:

"See that humped woman over there," Paul said, "comin out with the kids? That's right, Stella, lived across the passage from us. Only one of all those Hummel girls who didn't die of consumption. Her husband's left them so they can get dependent aid. But I can see him when he comes home at night. Somebody said I should report it. Hell, it's the system that's wrong, not the little fellows down here."

They still agreed. Though Anna detached such sentiments from the profession of selling booze. Blame that on the system, too.

Old Kiss-Kiss Karkas came in; he had been pawing the girls since Anna was a child. He hobbled over on his cane to appraise her with a moist eye: "Little Anna Vaicitis. Gimme a kiss." At the bar, he got the usual, then joined the boys at the back table, drinking and drooling spit from the corner of his mouth, boasting of his prowess with the dames, how he could have a woman every day, lay her all night and come two times.

"And there's Pigeon Joe's fat woman that lives in his flat and pockets his Social Security. Let em alone, I say."

Pigeon Joe was an old man now. He had been the butcher in Anna's youth, worked his way up until he owned the shop, bought tenements, was almost rich. Then he began to let go. He liked to visit Mom, talk in his broken English about the origin of species, religion and the state—the only woman, he said, who knew anything but gossip. He raised pigeons on his roof. At first he would bring the Vaicitises squabs for Sunday dinner; then he said he couldn't kill the pigeons anymore. He took Anna up to see them. They fluttered in a cloud around him, while he fed them and called them his loves. When he put a bit of grain between his lips, a bird would beat the air in front of him, catching it out with creamy bill. Anna looked away, ashamed. People began to call him Pigeon Joe and whisper as he went by: "Birdbrain."

He lost all concern for money. "You can't take it with you," he said, as if he had invented that notion. He began to go to the tavern, not to drink, but to treat women and bums. That was the time when a child found a check for six hundred dollars, the quarterly rent on a tenement, in Joe's garbage can. The child's parents took it to him, but he waved it away. Now he was cleaned out of his property, except for one condemned house with no water or electricity. Anybody could bum there. Joe slept in a filthy room, let his beard grow, went around grubbing from garbage cans.

Some of his squatters thought about his Social Security. They took him to the office. As he came out with a hundred dollars' back accumulation, they snatched it and ran. Joe shrugged and went home. "She left her husband and kids on a farm and came to the city," Paul said, "had a big time until she was too baggy for anything but a room at Pigeon Joe's. She's comin in here to cash his check; she does it every month."

Next day Daren and Anna met Pigeon Joe on the street. He seemed glad to see her at first, but drifted into distance. "Why do you grow that beard?" "I don't," he protested. "That's nature, it grows by itself." So Anna realized he was a philosopher, one who had seen through the falseness of material values. "Like Diogenes."

"He looks the part," Daren agreed.

They stopped again at the liquor store. Dopey Gundrun had come to work. When he was half sober, Paul paid him for moving boxes and stacking liquor on the shelves. "Anna!" Friendly as a wet dog. But worried about his looks. A lump like a horn growing on his forehead. "Like I'd a been swatted by the Newberry gang—remember, in the old days…" They talked of Halloweens when mean Blotchin and the rest would range the streets, their faces slashed with red and black, and whack down on you with a stocking filled with ashes and soot.

Dopey pretended to work awhile. But he hadn't been at it long when he got jumpy. "I got to run home," he said, and skedaddled off.

"What's he after?" said Anna. "Liquor?"

Paul shook his head. "His wife. He can't work an hour without having to run home, see what she's up to. Only person he ever loved, he says. Well, she can't say that about him."

"That's what the system does, generation after generation," Anna mused. They were on the train west of Chicago, crossing the River, heading for Prairie College. "His Dad only got drunk on weekends. Every Saturday night he would fall up the stairs and lie pissing all over himself. And Mrs. Gundrun would drag him up and put him to bed. 'As long as the man works,' she would say… And sure enough, Monday, he was back at the grind. But when Dopey went to work, he began to drink all the time; and then he met Fanny in the saloon, and she's a stewpot and sleeps with all the men."

("Where's Dopey?" Anna had asked Paul that morning. I'd like to tell him good-bye."—"Charlie? He's in jail. Beat up Fanny again.")

"What a waste. 'We used to play together when we were little. It's because the Gundruns are down that the others are up."

Daren put his hand on hers. It was still their honeymoon. "He's not exploited; he's a drunk. Not even the Russians could prevent that. And it doesn't make the stock market boom."

She shrugged. "Paul would understand. We've lived there. We know."

Then it was Joe Jones, trying to revolutionize English grading. Then Chicago again, New Year's, after Christmas in the Delta; and then summer, and another winter:

Kiss-Kiss Karkas in jail now: "Poor guy. Broke a building code he never heard of. And didn't answer the summons. When the cops came he ran over the roofs from building to building, yelling, 'Don't shoot!' But the real crooks are in city hall, at the top."

And Pigeon Joe wandering out of his head. "At least he gets a shave in the county hospital. But you know that fat woman still cashes his checks? Signs them herself. Why blame her? She'd be a rich movie star if she could."

And Dopey Gundrun in the charity ward, to have the lump cut off his forehead. And Fanny strangled in her bed, nobody knew how, or, except for Dopey, much cared. "Caught herself in the covers," said Paul, with his round-shouldered shrug.

Yet none of the timeless trajectories stood out in such starry relief as the one Anna spun of herself as she lay snuggled in the childhood bed, a blizzard from the lake beating at the window of the old Mother Port, she and Daren wrapped in cotton quilts, her voice murmuring through the blast, on and on (a tale so slow gathering, it was harsh to break in, picking up a phrase) :

"…Birth. People used to pray for birth. But not here. Not these women:

"Mrs. Kelly upstairs, a Czech, pretty, but with too many kids; and he was Irish, a shrimp with bandy legs; worked for a motor company and stole tires; big shot; got himself a blonde and moved in with her; so there were all those mouths, and no support. That was when Dopey used to sing under her window: 'Has anybody here seen Kelly?' She called in the law and Kelly went to jail. But he wrote her a letter like poetry. She brought it to Mom: 'You see, he does love me.' And flew to the judge. Kelly came home for a night and got her pregnant again. Then off with the blonde. She bore that child. She starved for love. One Sunday at church she found a boy friend. Sweet life! He bought her a hat with a flower sticking up, perky. And bang, she was pregnant. She drank paregoric, almost killed herself, vomiting everything, but couldn't lose the baby.

"To be stoked into so much pain, and another mouth to feed...

"And Mrs. Hummel across the passage, her daughters dying of consumption. And then she was rushed to the hospital, the whisper going round: 'Bleeding. A loop of wire. She stuck it up inside her."

•

Mom had removed herself from that. You felt it in the clean order of her being. Daren and Anna would come in to tell her good night, those stopovers in Chicago, she sitting up in bed reading Mark Twain, a dictionary beside her (she had taught herself to read), her flannel nightgown buttoned tight at the throat, her hair in curlers; she would look up and ask the time. Her Big Ben had stopped after fifteen years, and the repair men were no good anymore; she had listened for the cuckoo downstairs, but he went so fast in the high numbers she lost count, and was it eleven or twelve?

"Eleven or twelve?" She might ask the same question now, years after, the same neat person, only a little grayer, looking up from Dickens as she sat in bed upstairs at Patapsco City—for the whole house had been left to Daren, and Mom had come to live with them, Anna as delighted as a child: "You feel bones in flesh when you hug her, not those corsets and brassieres, just Mom; you feel the beating of her."

That small quiet peasant woman had made the revolt against birth: no more the breeder flat on her back mounted by the crowing male, but the new Amazon, providing, cooking, washing, sewing, keeping track of everything, soling the shoes even, bending over the iron foot she had bought at the junkyard, cutting the leather, spitting nails from her lips and banging them in. She was the center of everything, the manager.

"It's a knife edge," Anna said. "When you're at the bottom, so little coming in, everything depends on the woman. One slip, the girls are prostitutes, the boys thieves."

As soon as Paul could leave school, she found him a job. They rose from the cave under the sidewalk to the first floor front—this Mother Port: electric lights, inside toilet, a bathtub with lion's paws on a raised dais, a tub so big yon had to heat buckets and buckets of water on the kitchen stove to get a bath. "Such a change," Anna murmured. "Up into the light. You could climb for a lifetime, but never such a change."

Mom had made lacy white curtains to screen them from the street—middle-class reminders—curtains that had to be washed every Saturday and stretched to dry on wooden frames with little nails all round.

Sunday morning they would peep through the gauze and see how the brawls began. A woman would come from a house screaming, her husband, back from a night of drinking, after her; he would knock her down, beat her, until the paddy wagon came for him, drove off, left her sobbing, the children clinging to her skirts. Church bells rang. People coming in their Sunday best from mass filled the street, men and boys kneeled at the corner, rolling dice: coins bouncing on the pavement, dollar bills piling up; and then the squad car, whining, everybody trying to get his money and run, the cops pocketing the balance.

Behind the lace curtains they played games, worked and sang; Mom read to them, taught them fables of the old country, charms come down from pagan times: to the new moon, to the Earth Mother, to little Gabeja, the fire, to stay on the stone, not to wander in the house. And Mom, too, was working a charm, to keep the circle closed—no more sex, no more woeful engendering.

"But we were growing up," Anna sighed; "and how beautiful **it** was. In the summer, families would hire a truck for a hayride to the Dunes. Celia wore a pair of velvet knee britches she had made, oh so daring, and a hat to match. She stretched out in a grassy place, like Maid Marion, propped on one elbow, and smiled under the floppy brim at the boys sitting around. While I went off with the other Anne to explore the woods.

Sometimes we talked about God, and sometimes about how babies are made, and how it was wicked, but they said it felt good.

"I began to read. I read the Bible and I read love stories. I didn't know whether to love God or boys. But I gave up on the other Anne's church, those fat priests in all their finery. I felt closer to heaven lying in a field. I talked with Mom about religion. I said God Was everywhere, like a song. But she was sick with gallstones. 'If there was a God,' she said, 'he wouldn't have made life so hard.' And I thought about that, too.

"Everything was changing. We played Hide-and-Seek and Run-Sheepie-Run, but when you hid in the dark hall, you remembered how Dopey's sister stood there at night with the boys, bumping against the wall, while Celia and I in bed in the front room hugged each other, giggling; and when the boy found you, he would grab you, and you would break and run, and you could hardly wait for the next night to play that game again.

"When I was fourteen I had ice skates and went to the park rink with the boys. When I fell they picked me up, holding me under the arms. 'Holy Mary!' I wanted to cry, 'Holy Mary!' That night I began to bleed and had cramps, so I had to soak in the big tub in steaming water with a handful of dry mustard. 'Everything in life, you pay for,' Mom said.

"Soon Marie and Celia began to take me to their parties. I didn't dance yet. At fifteen I was small and slim. But my eyes were older. A law student came over and talked with me. Next day I got my first love letter: 'I see your eyes. I can't work. All I think of is you, you, you.'

"Sunday evening he came in an open roadster and drove me to the lake, a little moon in the twilight, the evening star. I began to wonder why, in our slums, we had to see everything through tears.

"Dangers. Mom was always warning me: Nellie Chodl, who used to climb into boxcars on the railroad track with boys. So she wound up with a baby, on relief, in that cave we came from, and one cold winter the baby froze in the cradle.

"But I was lucky. I had brothers and sisters. I thought of them as ships, beautiful Celia a schooner, Paul and Michael strong freighters, but all ships, sailing out for cargoes of experience, bringing them home to the Mother Port to share with me. And when it was my turn, I went out like a white clipper, launched and tended by the rest. As long as they were with me I was safe."

(Daren touching her face, feeling her lips sometimes, as she talked on, like Conrad's Marlow, but breath to breath, not even the glowing point of a cigar between them in the dark.)

"I wanted to take science in school. But I needed a job. I hated the shorthand and typing. In the spring I would play hookey, take my lunch to the end of the carline and lie among wild flowers looking at the clouds. I saw how each little fleece was melting away while the whole cloud went on growing. That meant more to me than all they tried to teach me in school.

"I began to take men for my teachers, people standing above me, gentle, ready to help me up. Some were artists. One was a graduate student at the university. Once I was snowed in at his place. He offered me his bed. 'We'll share it,' I told him. We took off a few things. I kissed him once, then I said 'No,' and we went to sleep. He wanted to marry me later; but I had seen too much of that.

"They weren't all so easy. An artist I modeled for caught my hand and pressed it against him. 'See what you do to me. And then you say no.' I didn't go back there.

"Once Babe Kling the wrestler took me to a dance. In the gangway at the back entrance of the house he kissed me hard. It wasn't the moon, but the death-sound of Liz Hummel's cough, a rasp dying in a rumble that left me weak. All at once his finger came out of me covered with blood. I screamed and ran in the house.

"And there was my first boss, wanted me to go to a show. 'What kind of a show?'—'Nice show…Girls.' I stalled. He began promising me all kinds of things, a bracelet, a riding habit, a little car. I changed jobs.

"I was reading all the time and asking questions: Why was the world the way it was? I had just found Ibsen. One Sunday in Lincoln Park I was reading *A Doll's House.* A long black car passed several times, then stopped. I saw the chauffeur first. Then a fine-looking man with iron gray hair got out of the back, came over and talked with me, what was I reading and where did I live? 'Come for a drive,' he said. 'I'll show you my place.'

"It was high in an apartment hotel, like the one Chuck took me to later, a view over the lake. And he was an opera singer. Even I had heard of his name. When he took me home, he invited me to the opera. Friday night all the neighbors ran out to see the shiny car with the chauffeur. Mom was ironing. The singer came in, bowed, gave her a box of candy. Then he took me to dinner and afterwards to Carmen."

(She had dreamed of being a barefoot Carmelite and Sister of the Poor, but Daren always observed how the cultured and rich took to her, and how well—if she let herself go—she made out with them.)

"He was a nice man, sad; I thought of him as wise. I began to ask him about life: about the little boy who had drowned in the canal while his mother was at the rag shop working for a bit of food, low pay, and as she told Mom, they had to lay with the boss or lose the job. Newsmen came; police dragged for the body; excitement; a big show; but until he was drowned, nobody cared.

"And about Adanassoff ('Orrible One-Bum' the kids called him); he walked the streets with a dog the size of a pony, his long overcoat and black whiskers blowing on the wind. He ran the newspaper *Novi Mir* and offered himself, a widower, man of property, seeking a wife. Widows would answer from farms, small towns. He got them to the city and put them in his tenement. He had five at one time, each in a flat, and he slept with whichever he chose. When they found out, it was too late. One tried to get away. He locked her in. Later she came hurtling from the window, her long hair flowing around her. 'He killed her,' Mrs. Kelly told Mom.

"'In a world so beautiful,' I asked, 'why is everything bled dry?' My singer looked over the lake, weary. Then he led me to the study. He pulled out books from opposite sides of the room. 'Two answers,' he said. 'Take your choice.'

"I knew the Bible already. I couldn't change the Fall. The other was Shaw's *Intelligent Woman's Guide to Socialism*. I opened and read: how production would never be for the group until it was taken over by the group; socialism didn't depend on the heart, but on power... 'I'll borrow this,' I told him.

"'Take it,' he said. 'I prefer the other.' He drew me to him for the first time. 'Good luck.' And kissed my forehead. The chauffeur drove me home. I knew I wouldn't see him again."

(Should one remind her of the close of the book? "Marxism is not only useless but disastrous as a guide to the practice of government." No, let her talk.)

"And now the Depression had begun: Mom sick, Liz Hummel dying, Paul married and out of work, Marie and Celia gone away. I met Chuck at the university. He was good to me. Life began to break into two parts: the grimness at home, and with Chuck, riding, dinners, plays, sailing over the lake on a smooth swell under first stars, the city lighting up, and off south by the dunes, the furnaces reddening the twilight.

"His father owned those—a self-made man. He took to me. 'Give Chuck a year,' he said, 'to finish engineering. And then, why don't you two get married?' And Chuck was urging every night, and Mom in the morning: 'Save yourself. We can't do anything for you. He's a good man.' One day in the Art Institute I told him all right. So we were engaged.

"It was summer now and we would drive to the dunes. I hated to go back to that cough. I heard it all the time in my room. The lake was sighing on the sand. 'We're going to be married,' he said, 'married, married, married . . . Shhhh.'

"For months I was afraid to tell Mom. I lay in bed watching the moon. When it came back, new, I said the charm she had taught us when we were young: 'You must grow round, I too; watch over me.'

"At last Mom noticed. It wrecked everything she had worked for."

"Curtains and all," said Daren.

"Curtains and all. I stood before her like the woman taken in adultery. She called me a common whore, a worthless common whore. Who'll marry you now?' I bowed my head."

("Et inclinato capite... ")

"I said Chuck would. I told her to call him if she didn't think so; and she said, 'Call him yourself.' He came in the morning. 'We can marry right away.' That should have warned me; Mom had been wrong. But I was nineteen and she was twice as old; I thought she was wise; I didn't see she was lost, out of her depth, as we were, swept along. 'We can marry,' said Chuck. 'But I can't tell Dad.'

"Mom groaned. 'A secret marriage. And even then six months is too few. They'll never believe in Anna again. Why did you do it? Oh why?'

"Chuck had been worrying all that time, and with nobody but students to talk to. 'I know a doctor,' he said, 'who can fix it. We'll be married in secret, and later be married again; and then we can have another child.'"

Daren's tone shook the midnight spell. "You mean you married to legalize what you had a criminal abortion to undo?"

"Until then, I thought they were wise. Like the Aztec girl sacrificed to the god."

"What happened?"

And now she caught him to the rocking of her breast. She was a strong person and did not easily give way to shudderings and fears. But he felt her body and voice seized by an old passion savagely reborn. As if their flesh had indeed fused, hurling him too into the pit where the revolt against birth turned on her with goring horn—childbirth fever without benefit of any child—a delirium of the cruel and mean, sharp abortionist, sharp nose, face, eyes, voice, sharp tools, flaming in scorn for the illegality of his trade, when all she wanted was bit of help, of sympathy.

Daren calmed his voice, in the need of calming hers: "If Chuck was rich, why did you go to a quack anyway?" She answering his quiet: "He didn't have money. He had an allowance which was overdrawn"—only to slip out again in the recall of riding a taxi home in a pool of blood.

She had seen it all many times, it was established now: the infection that succeeded the hemorrhage had begun long before, had its roots far back in that Mother Port, in the first cave, Mom's weeping over the clothes, the Hummels coughing away their lives, Dopey Gundrun, Pigeon Joe, her opera singer with his costly flat and sweetness and his weary gaze, in all the scorched laws and sanctities and stale submissions. That germ had been waiting through generations to break out and riot in the melting pot of the slums, the breeding place of her lions, a fire that would consume her childhood, her belief in the world and in others, in

Mom even, though she loved Mom still, poor outraged Mom—that had vaporized morality and convention and religion, had pared her of pretenses body and soul, and left her stripped for the love of what, hereafter, she would call the Truth. *(And you shall be as gods are, knowing good from evil.)*

It was from the resurgence of that crisis that her voice burned in his ear: "I knew it from the first. I heard that sickness working in my blood. Not physical, but the poison of entering a world those grownups had made what it was, had laid under ban. I had read Shakespeare that year, and I heard it in my fever: 'Dry up in her the organs of increase.'

"For the last time I fell back on the Bible I used to read. I knew the curse of the world had sealed up my womb, that like old Sarah I might become the mother of a race,"

Through those Chicago stopovers, when the world lay under the eclipse of war, and Daren, thinking to revive in his own soul devotions fit for an age of darkness, was copying Medieval music in the Newberry Library, he would cycle from Anna's out to the lake and take the outer drive past breakwater stones painted with names, initials, hearts, past beaches where swimmers, white and black, running up from the waves, flung themselves in the sand, the old fallen shame shed with their clothes— bodies, legs and arms fused in an energy that cried its Blakean delight: "For everything that lives is holy."

How incongruous against the twilight of the proposed retreat from the world was this rapture: to cycle at breakneck speed in and out of traffic, to slide into the wake and suction of a huge truck and be whirled along past rocks and sand and water, swimmers, lovers, past the museum, aquarium, planetarium, out into the park, where fountains, towers, the whole glass and steel city, broke in waves of wind, the joy of light—a sheer antinomy.

And how juxtaposed against either was Anna's loved and hated slum.

Stymied in opposition, where is progress?

Salus ad victimam procedis,

Domine.

5. *Workers of the World*

THE FIRST SUMMONS also had come in the winter, preceded, as the last brown leaves yielded to a dusky wind, by an inquiry, which in fact never reached Daren. He was at Patapsco College; Anna was in the front room reading. She was always sampling the literature of the world for signs of new life, although this paperback by a postwar smart Englishman was bound to confirm her wan hope about the West. She had only reached the telltale page 69, and already she was bored. She glanced up and saw two plain-clothesmen coming into the yard.

"I can always spot a cop," she used to say, "by those stool-pigeon shoes." They showed their credentials. She blocked the door.

"Think you're big boys, don't you? Playing cops and robbers on the taxpayers' money. Government is to serve people, not to spy on them. Get off my property" (that bourgeois prerogative she disclaimed) "and don't come back without a warrant. Scram."

She raised the paperback. They humped off. It sailed after them, its clever trivial pages whipped out on the gray wind that bore down like the prelude of another cold entanglement for Daren:

—Cader Ayers off with his sister to die in Georgia, the college lost to reaction, a blessing to have A.B.C. up the hill defiantly glooming his canvases; and down in the town the doctor-poet Richards (between the fourth stroke and the fatal fifth), sitting on the bedside trying to put on his shirt—one the day when he would dance naked at the mirror in front of yellow blinds, waving the shirt over his head and chanting: "I am lonely, lonely, lonely; I am best so"—mumbling now, as his arm missed the sleeve: "Can't write, can't talk, can't read, hardly can get around. Still shit, shit, shit!" Though he waved help away—the indomitable genius of his household.

Back to the winter task, stomping off mud or snow at the basement door where the kitchen drain stuck out, wrapped with a sack to keep it from freezing at the bend; Daren would go into the study and settle down in his old sheepskin and fleece slippers to the war musings:

The great peace-loving nations have always arrived at empire more successfully than the hasty tyrants of nature—as if the ideal and ethic in which they believe, but cannot manage to follow, gave them the strength to move slowly and surely toward its antithesis, exploitation and world-rule.

Until fresh snow would fall on the gray December coat, and Anna, stirred as at every display of nature, would call him to tromp the woods, she running, wading ahead, until she hits the deepest drift, where she throws herself, laughing.

The winter stations stretch out one behind another in recessive array: Patapsco, Prairie College, Europe, Anna's Chicago, Daren's South—caught now, superimposed:

The time he had wanted to go to Egypt and wound up with Anna and her brother after the trip up the Rhine on the ski slopes under the Matterhorn, and she had the notion of assaulting the pass, and they went up with rough wax on their skis to keep them from sliding, but before they could reach the border hut to get it melted off and start back, a snow blew in from the ice and rock pyramid hanging above, and day failed, so they went down, skirting cliffs and falls in the gloom, the snow sifting and whining as over bleached bones; and when Anna fell through the old crust and strained her ankle, Daren lashed her skis between his and tobogganed with her, down, sheer plunge, hurling himself sideways for a brake: Oh she had trusted nature like a romantic those days, materialist as she claimed to be...

And bleak December in the dirt-dauber house in Reading when Daren's father's body was found; and on the winter mountain at Swalee when his brother first put the pistol to his head with the one shell and five empty chambers and made a bet of pulling, and pulled; though he didn't hit the jackpot that time.

And the opening winter at Patapsco, when Daren was pining for Jeffrey, after the autumn at The Door, and Sally Stoval began to invite him up to have a drink while she told him of her troubles: "I took old Burt down to Florida three times," motioning to the vegetable propped by the window in the wheelchair, that cold light falling over withered flesh, suspended animation. "Doc Richards said it might help, and every time it snowed. 'We can freeze in Maryland,' I said; so we came back, and we been here ever since."

In a year Burt had died, and then for two winters it was watching Miss Sally drink up the dregs of her days and ways: "Trash. I made fifty-thousand in one year selling TRASH. That's gross. I had expenses, of course, those women painting for me. After I bought this place I began to lay it up. 'Put it in government bonds,' a fellow told me; 'that's safe.'—'Hell,' I said, 'the government's there to waste money not to make it.' So I bought a building stock and the man ran off with the kitty. 'I told you so,' said the fellow; 'they were makin money too fast.' Then I thought about telephones goin in new houses all over the country. I bought Tel. and Tel. 'Too conservative,' my lawyer said. 'You want growth stocks.'—'Phones will grow,' I said. And they did. I been drinking off them ever since." She drained her glass.

By the next winter she was in bad shape. Leflore used to do her shopping and take her a cooked meal from time to time. "I won't die with much," she told him, 'but I'll leave this house, and it might as well be yours. You're my kind. I'm not sure about that Anna; but that's your problem."

One more winter, Miss Sally half-blind, her memory drowned, she sleeping, waking to a perpetual morning, every meal a breakfast: "Good morning. Is it time for breakfast yet?" At night, fumbling through the dark house: "Don't know where the bathroom is. As soon be dead and buried as so lost I can't tell where I am." Then the hospital. When it was over, Daren got a letter from the lawyer: the house his, though entailed away from Anna. "Who cares? Capitalist trash." Yet she thought of it as hers. And the fall of

'54 she brought Mom from Chicago; so after a cycle of seven winters there was a second old woman, waiting in the house.

Winter too in the slums long ago when Anna renounced her abortive marriage and spent those crucial months, after the fever abated, by the chunk-stove, reading.

It was the same year Dan Byrne taught Daren a trick with the telephone: to phone a number and if a woman answered, say you were making a check on the volume level, and, "Would you please step back five feet and count five in a normal voice?" And when she got back on the line: "That's a little weak, ma'am. Could you help us with a simple adjustment? Have you got a screwdriver handy? Well fetch one. Now ma'am, there's a screw right under the phone." (It was the bolt that held everything together.) "Put the screwdriver in it and turn counterclockwise. That's right, ma'am, just the way you would unscrew a jar. Now just keep turning until it won't turn any further…" Waiting for the crash, the cry swallowed in darkness. Saboteurs they were, obstructors of production.—

While Anna opened the chunk-stove to put on a wood slab or a lump of coal, seeing in the smoky whirl of fire the vortex of history rushing and crowding into the sooty round dark of the chimney; then sat down, copying pages from borrowed books:

> We have mastered nature. A child produces more than a hundred adults once did. And what is the result? Increasing overwork and misery for the masses, and every ten years a Great Depression. Darwin did not know what a satire he wrote on mankind when he showed that the struggle for existence, which economists praise as free competition, is the normal state of the merely *animal* kingdom.

Bread lines in a land of plenty, slums, injustice, economic fevers. She had hardly risen from the bed of her own crash, the Great Abortion; Mom freezing water outside the window, chopping it fine to go in the hot water bottle, to be laid on the swimming belly, the sight of which set off recurrent moans of, "How could you?"

The demand that had dropped long ago with Mom's tears into the washtub: "Why do some have to work so hard?" merged with another: "Why can't love be a paradise of equals?"

Mom couldn't help—her mind rooted in marriage like the Chinese state: "Go back to him; it's a woman's bargain. He wants you back." (Chuck writing apologetic notes, sending flowers.) "But you left our father."

"That's another thing. Chuck is a good man."

When what did she mean but *sufficient,* Shylock's *sufficient? You're in the market to sell.*

"I can't, Mom; I can't."

An intern tended her, loved her a time, got her a job in the hospital, brought her the books which gave her for both questions the same breathtaking answer: "Your mother was overworked because she was economically exploited; and the same exploitation has turned love into bondage."

(Anna nestled close to Daren under the sleet-tattling blast):

"When I pulled myself up from where I lay dying in a pool of blood, I stood outside morality, society, everything—no, not outside life, not nature; I was in them and they were in me. But I saw the lies that had been spread over things in stories, movies, songs. I saw that not even sex could go right in an age of sale."

For Daren, those years, she had been the locus of sex. "You mean we have to tear society up and put it back together the other way round so you and I can do this better?"

"Oh, you! Talking as if sex was everything…"

As she curled on his body in the trough between waves, she would tell him of those free times; it seemed she could tell him anything:

Of Carlo, who had also come from the mine country, but lately, an organizer. One night they went to give out handbills at a factory west of the city. They waited in the zero cold an hour, each at a gate. Then the joyful part began: closing time. "I loved it," Anna said. "As the cars drove out, to see the men's faces, to wave and cheer and hand them leaflets, left, right, until they were all gone. And I stood half frozen, stamping and clapping my sheepskin gloves.

"Carlo came back gloomy. It hadn't gone right with him. His clothes were thin. He looked like a motherless child. And our ride didn't come. I opened my coat and wrapped it around him and rubbed my cheek on his.

He had been stiff and shy, but he melted and clung to me. We hugged and jumped, until headlights came through the dark. Our friend had had trouble with his car. I took them to a restaurant. I was working in the hospital, and Chuck sent me money besides. When we had eaten, I went with Carlo to his place. If only there had been a fire; but there was nothing but the tub. I filled it with hot water—let somebody else run short. I took off his clothes and pushed him in. Then I slid down beside him. The wave almost overflowed the tub.

"We worked together a lot after that. A real Jenny Higgins, he called me. When he said even the police had to smile.

"That summer we were chosen for a Marxist camp-school up in the Michigan woods, the theory of revolution. I had never been in a real forest, like Mom told us about in Lithuania. I would walk out in the moonlight among great pale trilliums, and Carlo would follow…

"People talk about how the Left draws you in like a conspiracy. It's not that way at all. It's your heart draws you in. You go looking for somebody who sees suffering as you do and who thinks you can do something about it; you all look for each other; and when you come together in that hope, there's joy and love."

For Anna it had been a legendary time. Daren saw it through the other end of the glass:

Those first Chicago summers, when Anna and the communists joined the War Resisters in Roosevelt Park, haranguing crowds of loafers, workers off for lunch, businessmen, hecklers, it was as if a great actress, with all her powers and dreams, had been promised a part in a play and cast in a puppet show:

A Jehovah's Witness reading from the Army manual on hand-to-hand fighting: "Gouge the thumbs into his eyes, forcing his head back, follow up by driving the knee into his crotch. If the opponent is down, attack with the usual type kick to his vulnerable parts. Sportsmanship and consideration have no place in the practical application of this work." It was the time when Bummy Loomis had just been suspended by the N. Y. State Boxing Commission for kicking in the groin, but he had been welcomed in the services.

"Birds of a feather," the Witness yelled in a shrill voice. While a beefy man in shirtsleeves pushed up in the crowd: "What's that guy sellin, anyway?"

The next speaker was a college type: "The people of India have almost won their freedom from Great Britain without firing a shot. If we were as ready to sacrifice, we could find a better way than war to defend ourselves."

"What's India got," yelled a loafer, "that America ain't?"

"Loincloths," laughed a businessman.

When Anna got the rostrum, she said the best way to keep peace was to build social democracy at home, improve the lot of labor, eliminate poverty and discrimination. "Why let big business lead us into war and fascism on the claim of resisting war and fascism?"

"How ya gonna stop Hitler?" an old man asked.

Anna pointed to the last speaker. "Like the young man said; we ought to learn from the Indians."

"Are the Indians all Hindus?" the old man earnestly inquired.

Anna refused to recognize the question as relevant, though several in the audience had taken it up; so one of the cops detailed to keep order told them to go to the public library and find out.

"You pacifists are full of theory," the businessman told her, 'but it won't work. We're all Americans, but you have to have the police on your side to keep order."

"Give the lady a chance!"

"Not if she talks nonsense,"

"It's still a free country .. ."

Cycling home from that absurdity, Anna, face aglow, would be telling of old heroic days in the Party—a romance, an initiation—and who could gainsay what had come under such auspices?

To climb the dark stairs over the speakeasy to the big garret at the top, a dirty view over slums, and at night dim bulbs burning among the rafters, like those seven or eight gathered together in Marx's name.

Or the afternoon youth parties they gave, she, among card tables covered with red-checkered cloth, passing out punch and cookies, smiles and pamphlets to the boys and girls of the neighborhood, black and white, rich—no, no rich—only poor.

Or the Saturday night dance to raise funds, Drummer Mick hunched over, rumbling the sticks, the saxophone and trumpet blaring, Anna whirling into the waltz with comrade workers, or in the pauses improvising games, a floor show, laughing through folk tales she had learned from Mom.

Then the regional meeting in the downtown hotel under some camouflaging Christian name, invitation by the grapevine, and monitors at the door to let in only those who belonged, Anna moving into the higher conclaves, looking around her: "Here are the hundred best, the cream of the city, chosen from millions to fight for truth and justice, and—Mother of God—I am among them."

There she stood, as rapt in holy zeal as the Dark Age believers Daren had been so far from, when he had thought he was so near. It pulled him up short. To ask how such a frenzy was compatible with the warmth and humanity he had found in Anna year after year was to question the possibility of her existence (as the Kantians say) *überhaupt*. Simpler to start at the other end; to inquire what sinister giant wills, working through history and the world, had turned human hopes to rancor and class war—

Carlo, at that '33 regional, reporting on certain executives of Ford, Harvester and the rest, said to be traveling by chartered bus through midwestern cities to study unemployment and see what could be done to alleviate these terrible conditions: "Imagine that gang of money-grubbers shedding crocodile tears as they roll between cocktails from city to city, tryin to figger out a way to make a fast buck."—Carlo, pegging those home-loving burghers down as liars and crooks, as they would have brushed him aside as a devilish conspirator.

Anna listened, glanced around, embracing the hard-bitten comrades in the bravery of her smile.

A smile that would flicker up through the war years, the joy of recollection hovering like hope over narrations even of hell: in the poorest tenements one Sunday morning, as she circulated a petition for better housing laws, a mother, cooking at the stove, kept warning as Anna talked: "Don't come out, George. Don't come out, George." Anna thought George must be the dog. But a curtain was flung back, and from the bedroom came the local ward boss, red-faced, crusted white around a bristled mouth, buttoning his pants, and behind him the daughter of the house, a girl of fifteen maybe, wearing nothing but a thin wrapper open at the front, her nakedness showing through. She was carrying a tray of half-eaten eggs and spilled coffee. George glared at Anna: "Whaddyuh want?" as he threw three dollars on the table. The mother didn't sign, though Anna told her how much the cause was hers.

Under the elms of Roosevelt Park, as that cheerleader smile beckoned from the girlhood of the old days, it seemed something Daren himself had known/from his own past, when he was staying at the Chicago Y and crossed the footbridge over the Illinois Central tracks one morning on his way to the Fair, and such a vision of a girl placed in his hand a propaganda page, which he read, over his cream cheese lunch in the Dairy Building, and discovered to his surprise that the schemes of his speech on the Forgotten Man were not his sole invention—"But maybe I saw you in '33. Did you distribute pamphlets outside the World's Fair?"

"I distributed pamphlets all over—at the Fair, in the parks. I paraded. Once I was in a street fight. A woman egged on some men to beat up Carlo. I grabbed her by the hair, and she ripped my blouse across. When the police came, I hid in the crowd, holding the torn pieces together. And one May Day I carried the Red Flag and had my picture in the Sunday News, the flag blowing on the wind."

That smile, taking every disillusion in its stride, even the jolt—one of those war resisters' harangues—of running into Carlo again. "He was so slim and beautiful," she told Daren, "and now he's thick and plump, like a pizza cook. How did that ever happen?"

"Could it have any bearing, saintly Anna, on the way labor and materialism have sold out the soul?"

She, playful, over the rift that was always there: "It's good you've kept your shape; and no doubt you cultivate your soul; but you don't know a thing about labor or socialism, and you never will."

And she started another adventure, of picketing some fascist film.

"How did you know it was fascist? In Mississippi, Bull said I was."

"Bull's not a comrade," she said. "We knew. Comrades don't try to deceive each other."

And she told of carrying placards around the theater with some other ringleader who was sweet on her then.

"How many affairs did you have?" Daren asked, with a shade of bourgeois astonishment.

"Affairs?" she echoed. "That's how upper-class people pass their leisure time. I never had one. If I loved somebody it was for serious reasons.

"Take Sam Ham. Somebody will write about him when the climate is different. He was trained for a priest, but he saw through it; saw through a lot of things; so he went to the Left. He published books, labor books and books by real poets. I met Clarence Darrow there and Carl Sandburg; and Sam used to tell me about Dreiser and Crane. I was with him the last time he talked to Sandburg. 'How come, Carl?' he said, how come you leaving the working-class movement?' He was a lonely old man and I loved him. He came to my house for dinner on Sundays until he couldn't walk anymore. And then he died.

"I used to work with a theater group. We went to ritzy left-wing houses to see previews of Russian films. Men liked my sad face; I don't know… The Shakespearean actor Burke used to act for me, on his knees sometimes, while I listened. He died later in Spain, when I was in Austria, and I cried. And there was Vance, the newspaper man, who nsed to call me Carmen. He went to Spain too, and died. And then that bourgeois idealist Daren Leflore… But affairs? I never had time for affairs."

"When I got you," said Daren, "I got two jigsaw puzzles in one: Here's Chicago. There's Oxford, Florence and me. How did you get from here, to there?"

"I've told you long ago. I was tired, working in the hospital at night and

233

in the day for the Party. Yon wouldn't believe how thin I was, and such a cough. I thought of Liz Hummel. Sometimes I would go the Art Institute— searching—that other part of me. I loved those little Flemish pictures with bright backgrounds, rivers and hills and angels, trees glistening with real gold. Even when I was a girl and wrote my life-wishes, about Mom and the rest, my last wish was to travel and learn.

"Then Mom's gallstones came back bad. They began long before, in that cave under the sidewalk. 'We were sick a lot there. She had typhoid fever and it left the stones in her. She would moan when the pain came, and swallow. I would see that swallow go down her throat while I stood at the stove heating water for the bag. They told her to drink a lot of liquids. We used to save and get canned grapefruit juice, and for years the attacks eased off. But now they came on worse than ever. Old Doc Murphy in Halstead said: 'She's got to have an operation.' Paul was sitting with me. I saw him clench his hands, and he sobbed for the first time since he was a boy: 'She may die, and I'm in debt already and can't help her.' His round shoulders shaking. So I made up with Chuck, Mom had worked all her life for me, and people don't do things for me and not get paid.

"That fall I went to Europe. But I never dreamed how it would change my life."

What might have been answered—"You mean draw out your ambivalence?"—wasn't. Maybe Daren hadn't formulated it then, though it should have been clear since Oxford. One had only to ask why she had taken to him, to uncover (as cracks in a metal start from flaws in the crystal overlap) the aesthetic claim, that last infirmity of communist mind.

She had thought even then to make it an argument between him and her. When Laszlo and his wife took them to the exhibition of contemporary North Chinese art - Daren looking for monks in a solitude of lotus and waterfalls; and when he protested: "But they've thrown away everything refined in old China, and all they've got for it arc these war posters, so blatant, so bad"—Anna, though fresh from Florence, rallied to the Party line: "The old art was an opium dream. This is true, and it has power."

"Suppose I grant the cause." (It was one of their first debates on politics.) "I grew up in the Depression." (Daren remembering Mr. Cloone, whose bank had failed, so he used to mangle "My 'Wild Irish Rose" on the radio, and everybody had to write letters saying how good he was so they'd keep him on and his kids wouldn't starve or go on relief.) "That doesn't make it art."

They argued. But he had only to look in Anna's eyes to know that she, too, was divided. And when they went to his digs, and she put away the scrapbook where she was pasting photos and prints from Florence, it wasn't to pick up Marx or go out with a bomb after some earl of the realm, but to come where he was translating Boccaccio, push his book aside and slip into his arms. If she had sacrificed the aesthetic at the art show, she embraced it more deeply in him.

And she was going to keep on. The same smile with which she had told him of old days in the Party would win through the bars into the murk of Cook County Jail: "They keep saying at the meeting I've got to break it up. Sometimes I wish I could. And then I think of you down here and I have to see how you are. If only the fascists had put you in jail. But to drag your feet, when Russia and America are fighting together for the people's cause." She sighed, and reaching through the bars rubbed his cheek.

As Uncle Hazlewood told him later: "She's loyal. I like that. I used to wonder why you married, and I invented psychological solutions, as that you had no mother and she no child; but I guess it was more than a private matter. As well ask why we are allies with that 'Great Peace-loving People' I am so doubtful of. There's a destiny in it, deep in history. Though God knows how it will end."

The wind blowing down the Patapsco from the north, roaring in gusts and pulses, snow driving past the window, flat with the earth; you couldn't believe any would fall, but there it was, gathering on the ground.

Leflore had thought of winter out there on the prairie as the historical season; and as he walked or cycled past stubble fields coming to classes or going home, he had watched the smoke from the great college stack drift with the wind. One day it would be from the damp south, settling down in mist or fine rain; then it would stir and turn, swing the great circle, the prairie wind building up, freezing the drizzle into snow, huge sticky flakes lashed on the wind, the smoke torn back ragged veering a cold compass, until it set due south, and the blizzard from the Dakotas, like armored war, seized on the world. But by sunset the wind would dissolve the clouds, a luminous long slip would appear in the west; at cold midnight the stars were glinting in the vault, Pleiades, Hyades, Orion, with Jupiter over the dog star.

That was the sequence he had tried to reenact: in the hardening of winter and through the cyclical blizzard of war, to search for the constellations of faith. It was what he had set himself, here in Patapsco, ten years after, and in a time of reaction ("Your old men shall dream dreams," no longer), to recover on the page.

"What is it you're writing?" Anna would ask. "Once it was your own life and now you call it philosophy: poles and fields and forms flowing into each other. I don't get it; and if it's for professionals, I don't see them asking for it. If you've got a philosophy, you ought to give up all that concealment and speak out, so it can be understood. You owe that much to yourself, if not to the people. You're sealing yourself up in your narrow cave because you don't know how to give. I could help you, lead you up to the light, give you something to write about. But you don't go for criticism. You'd rather have your little students and admirers. You're missing your chance at greatness when you don't follow me."

His soul sometimes would be a swamp of drowsiness; as in lowlands he had to dig ditches of sleep to run it off, separate water from dry land. When he began to nod at his writing, he used to stretch on the floor for a nap. He preferred the floor; it kept sleep thin and brief. A moment the dream would rest on him, and he would get up renewed. Today the room became the cave. He was wandering far in it with a torch, and he entered a part which was all crystal. He raised the torch and the ceiling shone with glints of light; he lifted it higher; the roof melted back. Those glints resolved into the known shapes; he had learned them as a boy: the Bear, the Cross, the Lyre. He was on a rock outcrop under the sky. Aie! the high wind of ether through those spaces! He waked, and returning to the table scratched off something, and laid it down among the other jumbled pages. If the cave of subjectivity became the universe, Daren had the sign he was after. He picked up the sketch again and wrote across the top: THE TRANSFORMATION OF THE CAVE. It went down in a convection like the stir and coupling of thoughts in the sleepworking brain.

He had started that winter of exile to gather up and sift the meditations of his Prairie and Chicago and prison years. The papers were before him; but this which had now been delivered was less thought than action, requiring for its origin some maker outside Daren, or if Daren, *Daren at a third remove*—when the former projects would come to life, the Journals and Meditations and Politics, caught in the fictional containment of the last; when the pigeonholes he had built along the back wall of the room— his two-dimensional manifold—would begin to percolate like the brain he made it the analogy of, drawing into order not that gray little volume of winter communings:

> (On Shostakovich): Open your ears to the clamor of this crescendo. If we thought Europe Was enough, wait, we have witnessed nothing yet. All the heaven-stormers from Babel down pale to shadows as the drum-pounding pride of this rising people breaks across us. And if one should answer: That triumph is not of Russia but for all men—it is this that will lead more swiftly to the envisaged end. Always the dream betrayed gives the force to move toward its opposite. We push the gyroscope in one plane, and it advances in another…

—not such broodings, but the life that had environed and deposited them, the sick oyster of war and imprisonment, in which thought had secreted those rather dusky pearls.

6. *Solitary Confinement*

Daren's winter concern had been with meaning. He had not tried to tell a story, but to frame his thoughts. Yet the thoughts stirred associations. The very paper on which they were written (Prairie College, Chicago lab, scraps from the Ashram and from prison) pointed to the event; or where the event had faded—months of confinement toned into even gray—it was still the wash of the experience that swept him like a wave.

To revive it he had no journals. That was the stump of another amputation. When he had tried to write Uncle Hazlewood or Anna any details of his situation, the letters never reached them, or arrived so censored that almost nothing remained between the salutation and the close. So he began to make notes in a little memorandum book he carried in his pocket, to give particularity to an otherwise dogged sameness of protest and penalty. That record would have triggered something—a match to light up the dungeons of memory; but it had flamed too early.

A brave line he had talked when stripped of that, as of everything else, the third time he went into solitary, when the smoke of those jottings rose with the daily incineration of prison waste. Bunyan, he told them, had been free to write in his cell; but the new tyrants put their ban most of all on the word, to suppress the record of what they were and of what had occurred. But they had not yet set their foot on what was seared and graved in the sutures of the brain… A brave line.

Now that boast had turned out not to be true. He needed those traces to recover what without them had gone under, suppressed not merely by the prison authorities but by a sentience which had conspired with them, refusing to be saddled forever with unregenerate fact—the anguish that everywhere stifles awareness: Jews in concentration camps, that girl-child crucified on a tree, families bombed night after night in London and Warsaw and Berlin, soldiers in the tunnels of Corregidor under the flaming rock or starved after the capture of Bataan, Japanese dying of radiation sickness—even what daily in hospitals and peacetime homes the human creature suffers: schizophrenics moaning in sleep, addicts stabbing burnt-out veins, cancer victims thirsting and swelling—let it all go down with the river; the psyche too burdened already, without preserving the moment by moment tally of its wrongs.

Why else would he, always preoccupied with writing, have delayed the reconstruction of that journal; why not have set it down, as he threatened to do, while the recollection was fresh? But he had put it off from year to year, until it lay behind him like far-off mountains, huge and misty forms. He had stumbled through those slopes and crevices, had known the cleft rocks and firescars and windfalls; and now it was vague as the map of a city left years ago—the stone alley-windings of Florence; there was no going back and almost no will to. The energy had discharged itself. The original scribblings, though confiscated, had done what the soul had to do, spit it out now and forever, like Goya's Execution, how man could be brute to man; like anything once accomplished, it no longer pressed for birth, Lost or preserved, what matter? It had burned space with its cry.

When Professor Wilson took his research project from Prairie College to Chicago, he invited Daren to go along. Anna soared into one of her high raptures: "To be working together for victory, for peace! Mother of Joy!" While Daren shrank back: "What a rhapsode! By God, what bulldookey!"

She even got herself a job in a munitions factory, though she didn't hold it long. She was supposed to sit at a table with a bunch of women inspecting and packing rifle cartridges; and as an incentive each woman had a tally card displayed on the wall. Before long, Anna, who thought herself as motivated against fascism as anybody, appeared at the bottom of the heap.

She narrowed her eyes and began to look around. "All down the table," she told Daren, "those women were talking and laughing, not looking at all, just shoveling those bullets off the chute and into the boxes.

"That could kill somebody. I went to the boss's office. A big-bellied man at a shiny big desk. 'I don't want a tally card,' I said. 'You can't win a war by sloppy work.'

"I told him what was going on; but he knew it already. All he wanted was the contract. So I was in the wrong, because I had squealed."

Whenever she looked up from her work after that, she saw the floor manager watching her. Then they stuck her in a windowless office where she did nothing but check tallies. She got fed up and quit.

Daren quit too, but for different reasons.

From newspapers boasting every day of stepped-up bombings, he should have known that what he was participating in was destruction. But scruple had taught him that breath itself is a participation. He mooned along, a sleepwalking Leonardo, counting scintillations in a cloud chamber, disturbed more by the pettiness of that puttering in the electronic undetparts of nature than by any fear of world consequences, until it was revealed to him that he was part of a project aimed at incinerating cities in flashes of atomic fire.

"We would set up distinctions," says Pascal, "and nature will not allow them." In that continuum Leflore had drifted, until fact threw him back like a pendulum.

One day, in the basement of the university lab, where he was working literally in the dark, he got a call from Wilson: would he bring some results over to Stagg Field? He went, and the atomic pile, in one siren exposure, bared itself and lay before him, pointing to the future, Hiroshima, Nagasaki—who could assign an end to that pointing? And Wilson and the rest were so hypnotized by the unclear purr with which it announced its chain reaction, they could think of nothing else, talk of nothing else—their talk too a chain reaction, though it could go on only in the lab; they must not even take it home to their wives.

That night Daren went to Wilson and told him he had to quit.

"Nonsense. You can't change the project. It takes the war as an excuse. Like destiny."

Daren had not seen the light or been washed in the blood of the Lamb; there was no certainty, either of faith or knowledge: "In peacetime, I might venture, even with that fire. I've read *Prometheus* and *Faust*. But right now, I can't. It's not a question of *should*. It's an incapacity."

"You support it with your taxes," said Wilson, "if no other way."

"When I walk out of here," Leflore took his hand, "I'll be in jail; and it's your taxes will support me."

As a matter of fact, it was not so fast. The draft board had to get word he was a deserter from essential employment. They shifted his classification to 1-A, and he was called for another physical. Only when he had refused and been found a suspected delinquent, and notified of that, was the local sheriff in a position to act. There was plenty of time for a visit to Mississippi.

Never to such estrangement, not even after the Rotary talk. "Hello, Daren," friends would greet him on the street. "What're you doin home?"

Was he to pass it off with a trivial half-truth: "Been workin at war research in Chicago and come back to see the folks"; or blurt out what their embarrassment seemed half to anticipate: "Got a few days before I go to jail as a draft dodger"; and watch them draw back, horrified less by the fact than the flagrance of its proclamation?

Mostly he stayed at Ararat and walked the levee. By this time it was clear that in a world of such losses, the Old South, father, mother, all the bombed cities of the Oxford years *(sonnets, democracy and madrigals)*—the plantation and home of his boyhood, their deepest earth-tie, was going to be cut off from them. Not even Uncle Hazlewood was to blame, though he was no businessman; too many things had happened beyond his control: Freeman's waste in Reading and Prentiss' death, and flood and crash and the long Depression—besides that river moving in all the time as if it owned the place.

The levee built after the 'twenty-seven Flood was only two hundred yards from the house. And now, in the last months, the channel had shifted from the outer side of Catfish Island a mile away and was running right under the levee, so as Daren and Anna sat at breakfast (the end of the June rise) they saw big rugs and scows booming above them almost in the yard.

"Makes me feel like a rabbit's run over my grave," said Aunt "Willi Mari.

Nobody had known quite where the first Delta Landing stood until that channel shifted and a sandbank sloughed off south of the old Hazlewood landing; it bubbled into the liquid brown, exposing, like a natural bridge, an arch and abutment of brick and masonry, foundation corner of the silted up courthouse, built before anybody remembered, when the whole Delta was still swampwoods. Despite a local historian, one of those ancient "avatars" had put in its melancholy appearance.

Daren and Anna walked there on the levee. It was their last day. Crowds of sightseers had come up from the town; so Daren had to run a final gauntlet of being asked what he was doing, and telling what he could, though with the premonition that the news had already been whispered around. And above them the ruined arch, already toppling back into the river, and in a world where every day beloved towns sank into such rubble, assumed the mood of Luxor and Persepolis.

It was evening when they returned to Ararat. The low light, as on another occasion, flooded the flat land and water. Daren entered his mother's room in a present that was already of the past: a dead mother, dead father, lost land, a self committed to the void. "We live by relics; a bronze knight on a grave, presences caught in the orbit of their change—*per loco eterno.*"

They came from the Delta broke. Daren went to the Ashram, a settlement house named for Gandhi's community in India. He and Anna had discovered it earlier; but she was off pacifism now. She stayed mainly with Mom.

It was a big stone house in a dismal block of saloons and crime. Some CO's and their wives had bought it, and the wives kept it going while the men were in jail. There was always a flow of draft breakers coming from camps or prisons, staying at the Ashram, and being siphoned off again as fast as the courts could process them.

Daren had been invited by Alan Gill, English-born Quaker he had known at Prairie College. Gill had refused to register when the draft first went through. The temper of the country then had been more or less opposed to war. (It was when Pepper first suggested lend-lease and got himself burned in effigy; though a year later, when he announced: "Call it war or call it what you please, America is not going to let England fall to Hitler," he was cheered.) Gill's judge, that first trial, might almost have been a pacifist himself; even his sentence was an apology: "America isn't normal today. You must be charitable to us. There are people all over the country who share your ideals. I feel like Pontius Pilate, but I am here to enforce the law. I sentence you to a year in jail." But Gill had come back from that term and been given·another, and was now to be summoned a third time for what would prove a bitterer trial and longer imprisonment.

It was Alan Gill who met Leflore when he arrived at the Ashram. A bespectacled dreamer, he opened the door to a living room he was papering in cheerful tints of pink and green. Upstairs, loud thumpings came from the arts and crafts workshop where underprivileged children of various races were modeling clay and doing carpentry. In the kitchen a couple of wives were preparing the charity lunch and getting ready for the afternoon open house.

Those weeks at the Ashram were a revelation in radical religion, how the fervor of the absolute could reach through life, taking every cause and protest for its own. It was the height of the war, the summer of '43—democracy big with neglected causes:

"It's cold here," a cousin wrote Lee Sung, Japanese-American of the Ashram. (They had been evacuated from California, driven to sell at bottom prices to profiteers, bundled off to barbed-wire stockades.) 'We have no privacy. Long rows of toilets face each other without partitions between. Floodlights are turned on us at night. There is no place for the children. We hear them crying night and day…"

Or a Negro student of Gill's who had gone into the Army wrote from Arkansas. He was training with a regiment of Negro engineers (the military, like everything else in America, had remained segregated through generations of laws and wars). Near Little Rock, on a routine march, they had been arrested by state troopers and vigilantes: "No niggers have a right to be paradin on our roads." By the time the letter reached Gill, the regiment had been quietly transferred to Michigan.

Encroachments on races, classes, alienation of rights: teachers fired for not conforming, children who wouldn't salute the flag, strikers, Mexican migrants, Puerto Ricans, sharecroppers, the destitute, and insane—all the outrages and neglects which, under banner headlines of destruction, scarcely rippled the press, were caught up, prayed and agitated over, in the slum-surrounded sessions at the Ashram.

It was not religious sentiment only. That room was a germ plasm of defiances that would come to birth in twenty years. Night after night pacifists, students, teachers gathered to read the texts and discuss the techniques of civil disobedience. During the time Daren lived there it was *The Sword of Peace* by Micah Glenn, who had worked with Gandhi in India:

> Pacifists have thought the techniques would appear when men were ready for peace. They have put the cart before the horse. It is the techniques that are ready and must be learned and applied. Only by disciplined nonviolence, hunger strikes, picket lines, mass obstruction, by flooding the jails with people who refuse to cooperate, are we able to cut through discrimination, injustice and war. We cannot wait for an impulse of the heart. We must train thousands in sacrificial nonviolence.

Daren read with the group, unaware that this man had been his father's friend, or how significantly their paths later would cross.

The Ashram revealed what faith could do. At the same time it reminded Leflore how far his own system of antinomies had dislodged him from that ground.

Maybe Germany was on the skids, plunging toward barbarism as fast as the devil could drive. Maybe there was no road of war that did not lead to the same precipice. What else did indiscriminate bombing mean?

> Human life is God's. It is the duty and calling of believers to do the work of

God in the world. In this we have the presence of the living Christ.

War wastes life. War distorts and destroys the human mind and body, temple of God's spirit. Shall we who know a better way kill the brother for whose sake Christ died?

No state has the right to wage war or to conscript men for war, nor can I as a Christian cooperate any longer with conscription by such a state.

The preacher, Floyd, who joined them briefly on bond, as sure now as he was doubtful in the Prairie Civil Service Camp, voiced that pacifist absolute.

But for Daren, in a world of ambivalence, there must be a spectrum of relatives. Switzerland had managed the draft for a long time. Were there not heroic wars? What was Homer about, if our virtues had not been formed in such a school? Must one despise Nietzsche and Yeats because they heralded that complicity in the soul?

When Alan Gill rose in the Ashram Meeting, he closed his eyes and spoke as the Spirit moved: "We bring love into the silence that it may know itself, standing at the silent center of Love"—oblivious, though a baby broke out in a yawp of assertive flesh. But all that the spirit could move Daren to explore were the tensions of his field-philosophy, however much he couched them still in terms he had learned from theology:

By creation in time, each will is displaced from the center and appears under a gravity of its own, pursuing impulses at once evil and good. Union with the One to which every part aspires, is not possible in a field where each act implies its opposite and the drive of the self toward God becomes idolatry or the negation of life.

When this absolute war is over, we must find a way to live at peace with what we are, to make an art of the possible.

He was seeking the humanistic resolution, which he had told Hank Brown was of the past.

For his own capricious protest he had no general validation. Society he pictured as a web of thrusts and movements, in which, by some gratuitous prompting, nonviolence was his role. Its sanction was private:

One day after he had asked in a discussion: "What is this Void that is greater than all, and how can we trust it not to swallow the world?"—"You're welcome here with us, of course," Gill told him kindly; "but you aren't a pacifist, you know; you're a philosopher, a sort of God-inebriated Lucretian,"

Strange, when he had wrestled for years with the fact of compromise, and come up with a kind of permissive and sliding scale (on which he had slid and slid): do what you can decently get away with, that he saw, with Sophoclean irony, that what he had been getting away with was murder, and that if he was to be anything but a Creeping Jesus, some absolute act was required of him, not because it was right, but because in the suspension of his fate and the moral fabric that cleansing testimony was in the cards.

Sow the wind and reap the whirlwind. There were times in the months that followed, when all Western history seemed to have suffered under the martyred and uncompromising bent of that absolute God-Son. If He had come with subtlety to palliate, adjust and compromise, to tickle the devil on the mountain, and nurture His kingdom on the terraces of time, would the hundred- and thousandfold harvest of intolerance reaching down to this here-and-now, this cell of dark in which soul brooded, sealed up from things, have been allayed, have been avoided? Some had preserved the sanctities in a balancing role. Why did others find no way to champion earthly good but with the consuming spiritual sword?

Judge Musco may never have been a calm man; lately he was outraged by "that bunch of draft dodgers on Halstead who think they're greater than the laws of the United States." At Floyd's trial he saw Lee Sung (who was on bail) sitting in the court with a couple of wives from the Ashram. "You there," he bellowed, "you foreigner, you half-Jap, get out of here. I don't want you in my courtroom. The worst offender I know. I wish I could revoke your bail." Then he sentenced Floyd: "A slacker of the worst type. Getting misled by that alien. I hope this term will teach you smart alecs a lesson." Finally he called up the girls, especially the one who had given bail for Sung: "You ought to be ashamed the way you're misleading these men, ruining their lives. Traitors to your country. I wish there was a law empowering me to punish you, too, every one of you."

The sheriff came for Daren at dawn. He brought nine FBI men with him. They barged in with flashlights and ordered everybody out of bed. As they frisked the men for guns, one of the women said: "These people are pacifists, officer."

"Lady, it don't make a damned bit o diffunce to us."

They turned the place upside down searching. When Gill suggested a warrant, the sheriff said it wasn't needed where criminal acts were involved. While they were being questioned in one room, cupboards, drawers, books were ransacked; all mail was read. A dossier was drawn up on each of them: draft classification, membership in what organizations, how long resident at the house, jail record, what was the purpose and work of the group and what other people belonged.

Daren was taken to the medieval dog pound of Cook County Jail. He spent the first night in a heap with drunks and bedbugs: sleepless hours: bite, scratch. With no money to post bond, he expected a month before trial.

Next morning he was put in a four-bunk cell. The car thief spotted him for a pacifist: "I'll kill you, yellow bastard. Not fight for your country?"

But the dope pusher broke it up: "What the hell? Where ya get that patriot stuff? Everybody's screwin everybody else, so who gives a damn? A hell of a lot we owe the country."

At mess he found Floyd, and in a couple of days Lee Sung joined them, sentenced to five years—both waiting for transfer. Sung didn't waste a day before he organized a protest.

(A curious activity for a philosopher, almost as alien as war. Back in his early teens, when he played at Tarzan with Dan Byrne and was stirred by outward danger, Daren might have made a soldier; or at Oxford, when he thought he could seat himself in the Apocalypse, a pacifist maybe. He had outgrown them both. Still, he had chosen. There was nothing for it but to lash the tiller and ride out the storm. When in jail, do as the Christians do.)

Negro and white were supposed to sit on different sides of the mess. Sung got up at dinner and led them to the Negro section. The guards dragged them out, along the corridor, bashed them against the wall, flung them into their cells. After that food was poked in to them as to beasts. (Poetic justice—having arrogated to a will above one's kind, to be turned into a brute, a thing, knocked down and hurled into a cage.)

But he didn't have to stick it that time. Alan Gill brought a wad of hundred dollar bills. They had mortgaged the Fellowship House to bail their Lucretian. Alan counted out twenty bills and stuffed the rest into his pockets. You'd have thought it was play money.

At the trial Daren pled as objectors did, neither guilty nor not guilty—*nolo contendere*. It didn't soothe Judge Musco. "It's people like you who cause war, appeasers who don't know enough to stand up against a take-over." Daren launched into a vindication of pacifism on dynamic principles. Judge Musco listened awhile: "You better persuade the Germans before you persuade me. You think the world's out of step, but you are. First offense: three years."

Daren lost fifteen pounds the next fifteen days walking that bullpen and fighting bugs at night, waiting for transfer. Anna came to see him every day.

She tried not to nag him about his pacifism, though now and then she would groan: "If only you could have done this in Germany where it would make sense, it wouldn't tear me apart." Then she would touch his cheek and talk of something else: the old neighborhood, her family. How she was worried about brother Paul. The liquor store was bad, and his wife was a mess. Paul was drinking too much and taking it out on his son. When the boy came to them, she and Mom had to hide him. And Paul would come after him with the leather strap. Anna sighed, and read a letter from her best-loved brother, Michael, who was with the Marines in the Pacific.

The placement of CO's was left to the Federal Bureau. They acted sometimes with an understanding which Judge Musco would have thought soft. Daren was delivered from his dungeon and sent to the Alleghenies, a minimum security prison, more like a camp, intended for people who weren't trying to escape.

Except for the CO's, they were mostly mountain bootleggers, not crooks, really, but family men, always talking about their wives and children and their little tobacco farms. The government would give them new teeth and the doctors would look them over and they would go back to bootlegging, a little better off for the food and care. The old ones had been there time and again. They were full of laughs and stories, weren't interested in the war, didn't blame the CO's a bit. A relaxed lot. Only one was gloomy, a young fellow, tall and skinny, who had just been married. He sank into the dumps and one morning tried to cut his wrists. Though even that had its comic side. The psychiatrist had to be brought in, and one of the old fellows they called Pap was curious: "Wha'd he say, Bud?"—"Well," Bud drawled, "he said I wasn't crazy, but I was so near bein crazy it wasn't even funny."

The conversation occurred in the stockade where they worked with sledgehammers making little rocks out of big ones. It looked like busy work—there must have been plenty of little rocks in nature; yet when they had built up a pile, gravel trucks came and hauled it off for roads.

After the city jail and the crooks and bedbugs, it was fine out in the mountains that bright fall: fresh air, exercise, all you could eat. You began to feel you had made your protest, cleared the moral air, that everything was taken care of and outside your will, as when you've bought a ticket somewhere and settle down on a bus or train.

Certainly the Jehovah's Witnesses took it that way, and they accounted for more than half the COs in America. They weren't total pacifists anyway, were ready to fight in the Army of Jehovah whenever it came along. Once they had denied the secular draft, they were good prisoners, did as they were told, sat out the war in safety. If you asked them, "Why work just because you're in jail?" they would give you a Biblical quotation: "Render unto Caesar the things that are Caesar's," or, "For the hope of Israel I am bound with this chain."

The rest found it harder. Whatever had stirred the original rebellion went on prodding them, as if the madness of war had set seed in them, and was bound to bring up a glorious harvest of tribulation. Even breaking rocks began to look like a compromise. While the Witnesses plugged away at it, the COs leaned on their mallets arguing about the morality. The mountaineers loafed along, swatting a rock now and then, and seeing who could fart the loudest to vex the guards. The guards had come from stricter prisons; they didn't like treating convicts like boy scouts; they looked on, getting more and more fed up with the show.

The first trouble came when three Negro objectors were transferred to the prison. One had been at Sing-Sing since the beginning of the war. The FBI records showed him to be fifty-six, but when he joined Father Divine's heaven, he was reborn under the name of Moses Israel. "If I'd a been fifty-six," he said, "I'd a registered, but bein as I was only six now, I didn't think it wuz time." The other two gave less colorful accounts, but their skins were as dark; the head warden tried to institute segregation.

Daren went to his office. "I want to tell you in advance I may not go along with your notions about black and white."

"I'm from Georgia," said the captain, "and I know all about niggers. I believe in segregation and I always will."

"And I'm from Mississippi," Daren grinned, "so maybe I know as much as you do. But I didn't come to argue. I just want to tell you I disapprove."

If he had been alone they might have sent him off at once; but that afternoon all the COs went on strike. They refused to eat, work or cooperate with any routines. They were stowed in the bins for "inciting to riot." It was a row of dark solitary cells, nothing but a low toilet seat to sit on, a thin mattress pushed in at night for sleeping, But they weren't too solitary, because you could yell back and forth through the walls.

Some fasted and some didn't. When they were let out and reappeared in the dining hall, the mountaineers rose as a body and cheered them. But as the Negroes had already been sent to another prison, the protest hadn't helped, and a further hunger strike petered out without achievement.

It was deep winter now, snow drifts everywhere; no more rock breaking. They were cooped up a lot, Daren in a dormitory with five others.

There was the big-jawed Jehovah's Witness asleep with the Bible open on his stomach. And the socialist who had torn up his registration card and mailed it to the Secretary of War, Stimpson. He had ranted so at his trial about conscription for war and capitalist imperialism, calling for a government again "of the people, by the people and for the people," that the judge had leaped up, crying him down: "You have committed a blasphemy on the great American who spoke those words. I sentence you to five years, the longest term it is in my power to impose." He was playing checkers with the "rabbi," as they called their Polish-American Jew, Sol Kaplan. The "mystic," Don Clare, was looking out of the window for cosmic rays, which he said anybody could see if he stared hard enough. Daren, for lack of something better to do, was sweeping the catwalk, while the absolutely intransigent Germantown Quaker, Pendle, paced the floor, hatching ways and means to bring God's will, which he had been bred to by his fathers and forefathers, into the fiercest confrontation with a nation at war and with all its official prison Myrmidons.

They didn't have long to wait. The government, in preparation for the winter, had been equipping a shop adjacent to the prison, and now the men were ordered to get to work stitching parachutes in lieu of breaking rocks.

The COs gave notice. They had not come to prison to boost the war effort. They even seduced a few Witnesses and about half of those relaxed mountaineers to go on strike with them.

Pendle and Leflore were declared the mischief makers and bundled off in different directions. Daren was held awhile in a county jail back in the mountains. The sheriff was a local fellow, would bring coffee and sit down and talk things over, how you felt about the war and why you felt that way: "Well, that's intrustin. I don't go much for war myself." But before the end of the winter, the U.S. marshals came and drove Daren in a car, handcuffed, all the way to Indiana, to a maximum security prison there.

He was elated by the long drive, the air, the motion, even by the meal in the diner, handcuffed to the deputy, the girl staring at them from behind the counter; so his smile as he lined up for reception meant nothing more rebellious than that, believe it or not, he was gay. But to the guard who singled him out and hung on like a bulldog, hating his guts as long as he was there, that smile must have flaunted the mocking superiority to which the transfer was sure to have referred.

"Wipe that smile off your face."

"Isn't it better," Leflore asked, "to he more or less happy with our earthly lot?"

The guard didn't answer; he didn't even admit a question had been asked; but the florid face, sunk on heavy shoulders, flushed pimento, like a heated potbelly stove.

Daren was put in isolation immediately. Good. He was ready; fed up with cooperating. There was no company around he much coveted. They led him down a long corridor to a stone bin with one high barred window, four walls, not a stick of furniture, a cement floor, a flushing drain in one corner. He was stripped to cotton overalls; it was winter and there was no sign of heat in the room. The damp and cold sank into the body and stayed there. (Funny how he had complained that first night in Oxford when his baggage hadn't come and he had to sleep in his clothes.) Cold grits, cold milk, cold water were brought three times a day. The guard came every day to search him for paper, pencil, anything. Daren offered no resistance, tried to be indifferent, to look out of the window, always practicing the expression of Giotto's Christ before Pilate: "Thou sayest"; he gazed, as if through that window he could fix on the winter stars.

The man must have taken it for his bounden duty to break Daren's will. Sometimes he brought a rubber hose and used that; sometimes he threw him against the wall, knocked him down and kicked him, as he said: "Have you wiped that grin off your face yet, you yellow bastard?" It was a strain to put it on; the face didn't feel like smiling. But how else was one to strike back, where the tempted will had always to remind itself: if you wanted to fight you needn't have come here? Daren managed to raise it a little, like the flag of his hope.

All that was long past, and the original notes destroyed; the dragged-out heaviness of cold nights and days shrank to an empty blank, like sleep. That was the paradox of time: the torpor that stretched it around you let it collapse when you had gone through, and left nothing, endless weeks reduced to timelessness; where a time rich in action goes by, too quick to savor, yet looms in the memory, stuffed with the transiencies of duration. There was nothing to recall, except looking through that high window for a glimpse of Orion over a roof of late-winter snow; or in the afternoon, when a spot of sun struck it briefly, to squint the eyes, making rays and arcs, spectra—lonely light contriving in its loneliness a society of colors.

After three weeks he was loosed into the common prison—from the self-made suffering of solitary to a world torment, against which his pain had been hurled in protest, though beside that agony it dwindled to insignificance, a pimple on a planet of mortal eruption. In the commons room radio and newspapers were almost thrust upon them, reminders of what they were walled off from, of the strangeness of this jail skulking, dragging the feet through what everyone was calling the noblest undertaking of man.

It had been hard enough as Nazi planes fanned out over Europe bombing and strafing, putting loved countries under the reign of violence. But when the tide changed, and it was our own people, the liberal democracies, who at first had denounced the crime of indiscriminate bombing, but took it now for their official aim; when the power of which even the imprisoned were a part turned its magnified reprisal on central Europe, allied leaders boasting daily of the destruction of German cities and the death and demoralization of civilians—it was a worse trial and nightmare for the attesting spirit.

The technique of saturation bombing on a scale which the Germans had lacked the force to perfect was increasingly used and proclaimed (how many growing up who would say with Anna, "My first memory is of fire"?)—those thousand and two thousand plane raids; to ring the city with green guider flares, then plow and sow the inhabited space with blockbusters, fire bombs and phosphorous, building to a delivery rate above a hundred tons a minute, a hundred times the intensity of Hitler"s worst; until the whole residential complex of those old wooden towns became one sea of flame which nothing could oppose, a mile·wide fire tornado that sucked air from all directions, suburbs, streets, shelters, evacuating the center, blowing down and burning and reducing every structure, charring and suffocating all life: 20,000 killed in Cologne in one night, under a destruction vaunted as seventeen Coventries; 30,000 killed in the great Hamburg fire raid; Berlin's 5,000,000 cut to half by death and evacuation; Düsseldorf blotted out after 58 raids, of its 600,000 persons, 26,000 killed and 400,000 homeless; the juggernaut swept on as city after city received in a single cascade the weight that had fallen on London during the whole of the blitz; one followed, as populated areas larger than England were "softened up," "neutralized," withdrawn from civilized life. The blanket of ruin spread up and down the Ruhr, the Rhine, the Main, the Neckar, east from Prussia to Bavaria: Aachen, Münster, Mainz, Stuttgart, Nuremberg, Augsburg, Munich—search rather for the towns one could not name. Before the atomic bomb had entered the race, technique had aspired to match it, advancing toward a climax night when a hundred thousand would be killed in a final, and needless, raid on Dresden.

The newspaper accounts were cloudy; but the reading room boasted a few monthlies, semi-slicks, which, drawing on the European press, sometimes put things in focus. From these came the worst shock—that such facts could occasion such exultation. Of Hamburg:

> The most striking bombing event in history. Makes London look like child's play. A city of 1,800,000 inhabitants lies in ruins. A Swiss observer reports that corpses are all over the streets and even in the treetops. Charred adult bodies have shrunk to the size of children… When the typhoon of fire sucked the oxygen from the cellars, wome and children were the first to panic, running into the streets where they were turned into blazing torches. People went mad in the shelters and threw themselves screaming against the locked doors, biting and clawing. At least 20,000 are said to have perished there alone. When some shelters were opened later bodies were found in ashes, the bones more reduced than in the chambers of a crematorium… Air war in this new form can turn an entire city to a fiery grave from which no one can escape who has not had the courage and strength to flee in the early stages through the rain of phosphorous and high explosives and incendiary bombs… This is the fate to be meted out to the whole of Germany from end to end.

Jail sometimes, more than any other place, seemed to afford the perspective from which the historical explosion could be viewed in the insoluble reach of its ambiguities. Action ranged you on one side. How crass that could be, struck like a physical blow, when old Bull Slaughter sent Daren a clipping from the Memphis paper——it came through, of course, with no trouble, though pacifist and Christian journals were intercepted and even the Shakespeare Uncle Hazlewood tried to send bounced back with a bundle of "subversive material."

MISSISSIPPIAN EAGER FOR NEW BLOW

With the Eighth Army Bomber Command in England. "Listen, brother, there's not a damned thing left in Frankfurt." Bud Slaughter of Delta Landing, Miss., was speaking. And Bud ought to know. He had just come back from the 1500 plane raid which left the German city in smouldering ruins.

"You had to line up, just like for a movie," he said. "We wheeled in, and when the boys really got swinging you couldn't see the bombs exploding because the fire down there was so big. I never knew a town could burn like that. Ask Honeychurch here; he was one of the first in line." He pointed to his buddy. "This is Jock Honeychurch from Brooklyn. He's nuts about the Dodgers."

Honeychurch was an engineer before the war; he spoke with enthusiam. "We blew those Krauts to frankfurters. The fighters and the flak were all firing wild. Nothing could take what we gave them."

"You tell the folks at home to keep the real stuff rolling," Texan Beezley put in, "and we'll end this war sooner than you think."

"That'll please Honeychurch," said Slaughter. "Then he can get home to Brooklyn for the World Series."

Maybe, as Yeats said, everything was changed and a terrible beauty born (as ducks far off on the dammed-up stretch of the Patapsco stirred ripples, which caught the low winter light, so that each, in his ignorance, aimed a bright spear); but it was hard to think that Bud Slaughter, like his father before him, was a newspaper hero with Lord knows how many decorations, and that Daren Leflore, unlike any ancestor he had been told about, was in this jail—not even sure what he was advancing or defending by moping here. Was it to maintain the antithesis Bud neglected—to bind what was done and suffered into the tensile fabric of mind?

You would have thought that was the least imagination could afford, to offer the other slant, to put a man down there, walking those streets that were about to he exploded, let him go in one of those houses, join the family for the mutilation which pulling this lever was to precipitate on their heads. And as the bombs fall and the press-acclaimed "uncontrollable fires" break out, it could hardly have taken much to have been the sufferer, to have heard one's children, pinned under wreckage, scream as the flames closed in.

No, that was exactly what imagination out there was schooled not to indulge in. As the returning bombardier answered the questioner: "Crews have no time to dwell on the terror of the attack; they are too intent on carrying out their mission and preserving themselves."

And if the world process had placed a man aloft in the avenging skies, maybe it was better, as in the *Blwgavad-Gita,* to abnegate the will altogether (or try to), becoming part of a cosmic retribution, inhuman as it was vast As the wing commander wrote of the bombing of the Möhne Dam:

> It was a sight such as no man will ever see again. Down in the valley we saw cars speeding along the roads in front of this great wave of water. I saw their headlights burning and I saw the water overtake them one by one, and then the color of the headlights changed from light blue to green, from green to dark purple, until quietly and rather quickly there was no longer anything except the water.
>
> I felt a little remote and unreal sitting up there in the warm cockpit of my Lancaster, watching this mighty power we had unleashed; and then I felt glad because I knew that this was the heart of Germany and the heart of her industries, the place which itself had unleashed so much misery upon the world.

Seventy-thousand people were drowned in that flood, families sleeping in the shelter of home. And it was only the insistence on retributive justice that saved the account from the inhuman delight which, in the Abyssinian affair, had roused the world against the stupid son-in-law of Mussolini.

What was Daren defending? Was it the thought that contained all this? Yes. And also the outcry: that there was not and never would be excuse or palliation for such agony mounted by gods or men against the random and helplessly opposed. But that was the cry sent up—without him—from those unquenchable fires; and in what somber grip of thought could it ever be contained?

Only in participation. The prison was built in the country by a railroad line. He would wake far in the night to the earth-shaking of the trains—as at Prairie College when he came from the basement of the physics lab and walked home, those winter nights, along the tracks, and the locomotives plunged by, and his heart quickened at that unleashing and harnessing of power.

Rooted in tragic process, flood and storm, how could one not respond to what had been voiced everywhere: from Queen Tomyris, "You asked for blood, now drink it," to the daily press: "Germany, the originator of war by air terror, is now finding that terror recoiling on herself with an intensity that even Hitler in his most sadistic dreams never thought possible."

It was Churchill most of all who rose from the newspaper print and came with the force and rant of Miltonic vision into the cell of brooding. It was easy to answer Hitler—call him a Wagnerian madman; but this potbellied old god of righteous indignation, demanding "The systematic destruction of the war production, the life and economy of that whole guilty organization"—he was the antagonist.

If the between-war questioning (Cader Ayres and Oxford, the modern arts) had taught a man anything, it was that this blatancy of battle, which had spearheaded human virtue and violence since the wrath of Achilles, was out of date, that the world couldn't afford it anymore. Yet now, in its worst need, England had to wheel out the grandiloquent old warhorse and put him in the traces, with all his rhetoric of "blood, sweat and tears," as old-fashioned as the position it enforced. And not only the free world, but Leflore's imprisoned heart responded.

Even now, in Patapsco, long after the event, those pompous histories, spread by book club or picture magazine, revived the fatigue suit, set jaw, cigar and V-sign that had bolstered the flagging West—was it going to turn out, willy-nilly, that we still lived in a world like that, where the only way to dignity was the Roman and Star-Spangled-Banner one of embattlement: to fight on the beaches, fight in the air, fight on the high seas, until, if necessary, the whole damned earth was exploded; and if that was required of us, what was the status of the protest Leflore had raised?

Flamethrowers reaching into jungles, touching pillboxes from which men issue in fire, to fall blackened, writhing. And arching over it all, the great voice rants on, invoking the Anglo-Saxon race, striding over islands, glorying in the patriotic virtues bought so dear: "Long may the tale be told in the glorious republic."

As if from the dry rot of jail, fusting in idleness and floundering in thought, Leflore could look out on soldiers plodding through the steam of jungles, sleepy, muddy, lugging the wounded, the civilized arts laid aside, poetry, benevolence, wisdom; stripped down, poor white trash of the soul: "Take to the foxholes and fight to the death."—"Hey, Burt, got a weed? Gimme one." And yet, under the camouflaged helmet, as the cigarette is offered, breaks the irrepressible bravery of… Of what for God's sake? Smoke? A belch? "Gee, thanks, guy." (Guy?) The incongruous flicker of a smile.

Not that the larger operation was noble, striding over the world, and the details crummy and crass. The ambivalence vexed the particular as the whole: the global war outmoded, wasteful, mad, and in the same measure illustrious, grand; that foxhole instant, bestial, scurvy, heroic, true. Daren looked from prison to that and from that back to the bootlessness of prison. He believed in his calling and he utterly doubted it; he despised the Churchill claptrap, yet echoed with its epic tones.

He was building up material, as it were, stocking his mind with arguments, characters, scenes, all he needed for the nightmare dramas of his third and worst plunge into the solitary bins.

If Anna was the immediate cause of that interment, she also turned out to be the saving messenger.

For a month after Daren was taken to the maximum security prison she had heard nothing, no answer to inquiries: clothes and books and all sent back with a printed card: "Returned by Prison Authority." At last came a letter from Daren, but so canceled and excerpted that she could only tell something was wrong. She wrote the warden and requested a visit. After another month of dickering, it was conceded that she might ride down all the way from Chicago for about ten minutes of monitored conversation across the screened and barred table by which prisoners communicated with those of the outer world. When that interview was over (and it was shorter than they had promised) Anna didn't ride back to· Chicago as she had planned. She kept right on south, pounding her ear on the "Great Houndbus," as she called it, until she was closeted with Uncle Hazlewood (and Aunt Willi Mari) in Delta Landing. "He looks like a corpse," she said, like a mummy. What they've been doing to him shouldn't be done to a living creature. You've got to get him out of there." She told her story:

She had gone from the bus station in a taxi shared with another prisoner's wife. As the outer wall loomed over the rolling corn country, topped with barbed wire and with armed turrets at the corners, and as the gate opened to a cement court around the gray granite Romanesque central pile, those high barred windows reaching up through three cage levels of floor, what they were up against settled on her as never in the theatric murk and dinginess of the Chicago jail. She, who had spent her life, as she thought, outside society, and scheming its overthrow, felt for the first time the weight and cost of being hunted by the clan; and as she was challenged and OK'd, and entered the central space, and took in the whole cross-sectional partition that walled the reception and interview hall, it was as if the mass of that concrete, and girder-steel, with all its tiers and bars, rested on Daren and her.

She stood in line behind the meal-sack woman she had come in the taxi with, and heard her ask for Joe Bridgman. "When did he come in?" gaped the guard; and when that was answered he turned around, puzzled. "What's his number?" He searched through file after file. Such a huge store bin, so many walled up and stowed away. Would Daren Leflore be such a nonentity?

That was not the case. Anna did not have to repeat the name or give any dates or numbers, and the guard did not need to search in any file. "I want to see Daren Leflore." The man at the desk looked back at the other attendants, a glance of knowledge and maybe of consternation. ("Get a load of this.")

"You take seat number thirteen, lady," he said, "right over there, and wait."

It was a plain bench facing a long table down the middle of which ran an iron screen. Through this Anna saw Daren brought in, gripped by a heavy-set guard. That guard she recognized at once: "The counterrevolutionary thug in the Russian picture of the trial of a young Bolshevik." He showed Daren his place and stood like the satanic prompter, leaning to catch every word.

The first were hardly worth catching. But it was not in Anna's power, nor in Daren's, to maintain the front of polite exchange.

"Why didn't you write all that time?" she asked of the Late-Roman mask his face had become.

"I was in solitary." The guard jerked forward. "What?" she asked, "All that time?"

"Three weeks. Then I couldn't write for a while. I was sick. It was cold in there. And this friend rubber-hosed me every day."

There should have been a soundproof portcullis to let fall, or a censoring key as on the radio. But the guard could only interpose the pimento face. "I told you it's against prison regulations to talk about the discipline. If you go on this way..."

Anna was quick on the draw: "What do you mean, you fat bully? Why shouldn't he talk? He's a citizen of the United States. And a thousand times better one than you are."

Despite the death mask, Daren managed a wink. "He threatens me with the bins if I talk. That's solitary. Well, why not? I didn't come here to be good, but to oppose as long as I can," He faced the guard and raised a skeletal grin. "They want me to wipe off that smile." For Anna—cracking a ghostly defiance in the ashen face—it seemed irrecoverably razed.

"All right, fellow, you asked for it. That's your last visit in this prison," He motioned two other guards. They led Daren out. "That's all, ma'am. You go that way."

"What right have you…"

"Subversive talk. It's my duty to stop it."

"Why don't you say your sacred duty?" Anna wheeled and headed for the warden's office.

He was a fatherly old man, gray haired, and when he heard that Mrs. Leflore wanted to see him, he left his lunch and came running out, chewing his food like the cud of his troubles.

"You remind me of my daughter," he said as he led Anna into the office and gave her a chair. "She's just your age. And that boy you're married to—I guess he's a fine boy. But I don't understand these pacifists. They won't work and sometimes they won't eat, they won't take orders, and they're always stirring things up. We had one wouldn't wear any shoes made out of slaughtered cows; and not long ago one killed himself right here in this office. Broke down in solitary, so we took him out; but he didn't want that. Left a note that he had failed and lost his faith. The truth is, jail's for crooks; it's not set up for people who thinks they're saints and martyrs. I tell you, they drive me crazy…"

He didn't have to teach Anna that COs were a problem—the Legion screaming to put them in the Army: "If they don't want to kill, they should be out there on those atolls with the soldiers, moving up ammunition and food, helping the wounded, burying the dead, yes digging latrines, the nastier the job the better for men who have refused to fight for the principles on which this government is founded." Judges like Musco were for prison terms and stiff ones and give them another when they finish the first; but the Bureau of Prisons was begging to transfer them all back into Civil Service Camps. As for the COs, that was what they had broken with in the first place, the camps and the army—Anna knew: why, not even the socialists could make headway with them.

"I tell you," said the warden, "they got me sometimes where I'm ready to beat my head on this desk. But what can I do?"

"Not what you've done to Daren. Look at his face. You might as well have killed him."

The old man broke into tears. They were making a mockery of prison law every day, trying to deal with impossible jerks like Daren. The warden loved rules, and here he was breaking them himself; he liked to be decent, and what kind of guards could he get in wartime but dodgers and sadists? "You're like my own daughter," he mumbled again. "I wish I could do something. But I can't see what it would be."

The pious wish didn't prevent Daren's going back into solitary; and if Uncle Hazlewood, alarmed by Anna, hadn't roused a senator to send the inspector of prisons, there's no knowing when, or in what condition, Daren would have come out of there.

He was in darkness this time; there was no window at all. He was on bread and water. The adversary did not come as before to tangle with him, and that, incredibly, did not seem better but worse. You have rebelled against society and been sent to prison; you rebel against prison and are sent to solitary; and now in solitary the guard who gave you a last external focus withdraws; and what is there to keep you from rebelling against yourself? You do crazy things, jump, shake the bars, shout, sing—in German even—partly to pass the time, to push back the cold, but mainly to vex somebody, somewhere, outside you, to keep thought from hounding itself down into that snake pit at Springfield, where they're so eager to send troublesome cases anyway.

As the outer life is stripped off the inner swells and takes over, tyrannous. He never knew if he was thinking or soliloquizing: "You fight to be yourself and the fight changes you into void. You hold to what you are, and the harder you hold the more it slips away." He had seen the pencil-smudged account thumbed through and called contraband; his eye had followed it into the trash bin and his thought to the incinerator behind the prison. The flame had smoked the air with the recorded Daren Leflore. The vaunt and defiance he had flung out fell again and again on silence.

"Who stares into a void long enough," said Nietzsche, "the void stares back at him."

Now mind as never before became a labyrinth. That self-immersion was the ultimate trial; and yet, as he looked back, he saw it was what had sheltered him, what kept him whole. All his life he had been practicing for that descent into earth and water:

The fall of '26, when he honeycombed the orchard with trenches wandering from a central room out to little hutching places, and covered them with boards and threw back dirt. He would light a candle and crawl in and thread the maze to the last secret den. Who could comprehend, that winter, after his father's death, the mood of crouching in the stillness and earth-smell while the candle burned and guttered and left dark? Until the spring rains and rising river flushed him out with seep-water and the flood came and washed up the boards, and he went with his family to Arkansas. It was after they returned in the fall that his mother drove the car off the bridge. And Aunt Willi Mari had Uncle Caldwell fill in the soggy holes, which reminded her of graves.

Then Daren almost died. He had a fever they called pleurisy, or sometimes pneumonia; but he never waked, gasping for air, the night whispering words of endearment, he wrestling with the car door to heave into breathing what weighed him down, but to the touch of a hand, and voice, as low as his mother's, but calling to the comfortable, clownish shore: "Now honey, take it easy. You goan he all right from now on." It was Elmonia. And when Doctor Paul had decided on the tonsils and had them out, Daren floated from under ether to find her still there, a gulf of darkness rippled with luminous slow waves: "Doctor says you goan be nausurated a whole nother hour; so jus make up yo min not to min."

•

The first days in solitary he could not sleep. An overflow of the conscious will. Somewhere in the second night he began to doze. He entered a room with a big chunk-stove, like Anna's at the Mother Port. It was filled with smouldering coal. He opened the draft and sat down in an overstuffed chair. Air sucked through the coals. The iron began to glow cherry red. And now, at all the cracks of the draft and lid and door, gas flames played lambent, carbon monoxide, blue. It had been seeping out before from the damped combustion. The room was charged with it, odorless. No wonder he had slipped into the chair, lethargic, sliding into a stupor, which would be the last. He must spring up, clear out of there. He struggled and broke free—a snapping wire; he came to, sitting in wakefulness on the floor of his cell. That had not been death, but the sleep he craved.

By what seemed the third night he had sore throat and fever. All the dreams of life returned:

Under amber-green water, a gun-shot body, a tent-pole preacher, Slaughterers, Error Jones, pimento guards—grains in a dust-devil—whirl. Lord Prince demons in, poking hot darts in Poor Tom's head. Blaspheming blood, sweat and tears, he banishes him, Asmodeus the fiend…who had collapsed into dry sticks and branches. But they stir, climbing bony fingers from the soil. And he would flee. But the clockwork of night booms with the passing trains.

He wakes in chills and dark. But it was no longer dark, not emptiness. The nightmare in which the eternal man had lived through all the generations of his fall, his vegetative body stretches through sad shires: vaults of Tiberius' Rome, a crown prince's dugout city, the London tube. Giants under rocks, bulging eyes.

Werc every space opens to sound, bass viol, tuba, shawm, creation's scalded ants gnaw themselves in the Dies Irae of time. Will the sunken music lilt, lull? Pippa, Jeffrey, Heloise… tender? Naked… crouched… Before drums!

To enforce what, read, must be seen! From the bombed Tiergarten beasts stalk, a pride of lions, Loved screams. Who with the dead child runs a pavement where the asphalt burns? Under the fireball beat of the bell? The crash of trains?

Timeless. Sleeping and waking merge. He could not tell thought from the world, so repeatedly had the Muskostrom of breathing sucked sense into its pool and spewed thought up again in the semblances of sense.

What came to focus, standing in a physical glare, Daren took at first to be the ghost of his father, wasted from world-sickness: "Dost thou weep, old man?"

But it was Uncle Hazlewood, and behind him the inspector of prisons, who had come earlier, talked to the warden, and then stopped in Delta Landing on his tour of the South:

"I didn't want to stir up a fuss," he had told Uncle Hazlewood, "until you'd secured his release. But anything could happen. The psychiatrist thinks he should go to Springfield. 'Sexual psychopath,' he told me. The warden's at a loss. 'Must be crazy,' he said. 'Fiendishly clever at thinking up annoyances. Why he wouldn't even keep his things straight in his room.'"

"But why wouldn't Daren keep his things straight if he knew they wanted him to?" It was Aunt Willi Mari.

Hazlewood looked at her. "Well, well"; and to the inspector, "What can we do?"

"I can get him paroled to civilian service if you can persuade him to accept it. As soon as I'm in Washington, I'll fix it up. Then I'll wire, and you meet me at the prison.

The cataclysm of first light pierces the chaos, calling up Lazarus again and again:

"How long do you think you can go on this way and not lose your mind?"

Light. And the darkness comprehended it not. Daren surfaced, beating the heavy murk, clutching whatever drowned identity he had gone down to save. "Longer than they've given me the chance." As he clung to the burden, which had more the feel of being dead than alive.

"Mr. McGraw, of the Federal Bureau of Prisons. He has arranged for your transfer. It's your turn to help now—by accepting…" Uncle Hazlewood had meant to advance Anna's claim, how she had kept them in touch ("She's loyal…"); but what was more imperative broke in: "You're the last… Your brother Vail is dead." Daren rose, swaying, as from long sickness.

In the warden's office, the fatherly old bungler smiling (to get that menace off his hands!), "Just have some coffee, Mr. Leflore. And Inspector McGraw, make yourself at home. I'll leave you to talk it over with this young man. I'm sure he'll see the light."

WITH THE FIRST INFANTRY DIVISION: The heroism of Captain Vail
    Leflore of Delta Landing, Miss., who died while directing American artillery

fire to allow the safe withdrawal of his company of sharpshooters was lauded July 18 in a division citation.

His company had been almost surrounded and was under heavy fire. Leflore, according to the citation, walked forward with a radio in the open field in full view of enemy artillery and machine guns to direct Allied fire. Shot several times he stood at his post, until mortally wounded by the direct hit of an enemy shell When the squad leader went out to bring him in, "Leave me," Leflore told him, "and save yourself." When he had been returned to the command post, he refused medical aid and ordered that he be placed in a position from which he could supervise the safe withdrawal of his unit.

"In full sight," Uncle Hazlewood said. "He walked right up."

And now the last letter. It was dated July 6, a month after D Day, when Vail, with 150,000 others had been landed on the Normandy beaches. That was when Hitler had charged every soldier to resist to the death, and it took fifty days and a hundred thousand of our casualties to make the breakthrough. Vail had described how they crept forward, foot by foot, over rolling hills, flushing Germans everywhere from walls and ditches, farmhouses, woods; how Frenchmen with hunting guns joined our forces, crouching in the hedgerows to pick off snipers; and how the Germans held on, even when tanks and antitank guns were rolled up at point-blank range.

"I have felt it out," Vail wrote, "and will throw myself like dice. It's not one chamber loaded, but four, or maybe five. But where one was called cowardice, five is called glory."

"It was against his promise," said Daren.

Uncle Hazy looked at his hands: "To be a hero? I've seen it on the Marne. Don't think he was the only one. You've gambled, too. With less cause."

Daren decided for alternate service, in a research hospital, orderly first; when he was built up a bit—medical guinea pig.

The lice experiment was a farce. He sprang around the fields of the sanatorium catching grasshoppers, crickets, beetles, anything, putting them on those lice-infested shorts: his lost lice he called them—and in the words of Simon Stylites: "Take the food God has given you"—a legend to the soberer volunteers.

By fall it was the hunger experiment. A semi-starvation diet, with work on metered treadmills, shrunk their bodies, left even the spirits not as perky as ascetics had claimed; though Daren made some progress reading philosophy and writing his meditations. Rations of dried milk, yeast and soy were tried for rehabilitation.

Last, they advanced to vaccines: flu, malaria. The trench pneumonia almost did the job. Again Uncle Hazlewood intervened. The senators jogged the President; Daren was loosed, scot-free. He joined Anna in Chicago as the Russians, like avenging nature, spilled over the eastern borders and the mechanized Americans rolled under clouds of planes from the west and south. "Vengeance is mine; I will repay, saith the Lord."

"Strange," Daren wrote, "that by the arrogation of judgment men build the universal against which they offend."

Anna was living in a dream where peace-loving workers joined hands around the globe. What she felt, Wordsworth had recorded of the French Revolution:

> ...a glorious time,
> A happy time that was...
> As if awaked from sleep, the Nations hailed
> Their great expectancy.

Though the world-hope had cost her dear. Her favorite, Michael, had fallen in the capture of the Philippines—a colonial cause. If only he could have clasped hands with the Russians at Torgau.

Daren saw ominous signs: Patton's blast at Russia, Churchill's coup in Greece—the rift his own "Studies in the Future" had forecast long ago. But the vision of the peace-loving peoples rallied, even in the American press. Staggering, how far that alliance had led:

> Here are the fundamentals of the Greek problem. On one hand are the British. On the other the great mass of the Greek people, enrolled in an enormous popular movement, the E.A.M. In between are Greek fascists, collaborators and monarchists, who have joined with the British to save their skins and to build a dictatorship under the aegis of British imperialism...

Daren had kept it among the clippings: 1945: "The Fate of Greece Hangs on World Sentiment"—*Daily Worker* stuff; though it wasn't from the leftist press; it was one of a series of articles from the stodgiest Chicago paper: how from Mussolini and Metaxas and Franco down, the old imperialist stooges had stamped out popular reforms to proceed with their established fleecing of the world.

No wonder Senator O'Malley, ten years after, was insisting, 'Who were the traitors who sold us to this hope?"—forgetting how deeply it was a shared crime.

What would make O'Malley storm renewed Anna's faith. For her the time was ripe. If only like-minded people would give the crucial push, could not the whole tyranny of the privileged past topple—in Yugoslavia, Greece, Italy, Central Europe, the Orient, India, Africa—until the United Nations became the organ of socialist man, and even the United States and Britain, between pressure and conversion, would be brought into line?

Chicago was a center of fervor. Anna—always ready to work and never insisting on money, gave her days and half the nights to *Justice, A Journal of One World.* Among retired New Dealers, liberal professors, atomic scientists and the wise old Jews who had fled from Nazi Europe, she tried to actualize the common future.

But Daren, after the last swing of the pendulum had virtually cut loose from causes.

It was hard, fresh from prison, to get a job. For years he barely made a living teaching adults at City College. He and Anna settled back into the slums, a dark flat on the third floor, looking out over cinder blocks to a mirror likeness of their own rickety wooden stair. When they opened the window at night they could never tell what smell it was going to be: southeast, the biting sulfur fumes of Gary and the steel mills, west by north, the dried blood and death of the stockyards, south by west, the burned garbage of Calumet (the Indian name prescient—"of the big stink"); how one wished for the northwest, the keen air from the lake, though they were too far to hear the crash of waves.

As for the teaching—to lead those little businessmen, those immigrants and housewives (his adulterators, he called them) who hardly knew the language sometimes, into a program of Great Books, with philosophy and science—and by means of seminar discussion—it was a triumph of the divine and the ridiculous.

One night when Anna was away, reading proof for an issue that was late, Daren stuck to Kant until his eyes closed, though it was too early for bed. He remembered that the Marx Brothers, at the neighborhood theater, were making Duck Soup out of war—a picture from the halcyon days of Oxford. He went, and it was worth it; but he stayed for the newsreel: a shot of Americans moving in on a Jap island. One saw the regal fleet covering the high sea, lobbed around with random spouts from shore batteries. One watched as the whole island, at the focus of our fire, burst into smoke and flame. The commander on the bridge checked the time and pushed the button of a vaster clockwork. The great ship disgorged amphibious craft which made for the land. When a beachhead was won, the camera went ashore, climbed a hill littered with the enemy, closed up on a shelled face, twisted limbs—the theater responding with an involuntary gasp. Now smoky Yanks turned a flamethrower on an embankment. Japs ran out burning. One dashed toward the camera, tearing at fiery clothes and skin, collapsed in a twisted pile not ten yards away. There were actual moans from the audience this time, and one or two cries, almost of protest, which the announcer, as if they had been anticipated, met with spruce words about "the little yellow boys getting their medicine." And suddenly, with a flash of color and a jukebox roar (a chuckle spreading from ear to ear), Popeye the Sailor stepped forward, to a thunder of applause, in a cartoon where Japs were also chewed and beat and blown to smithereens, but under the escapist irreality of slapstick farce.

Daren got up to leave that spectacle of America at war. As he came under the lighted canopy to the box office at the street, a commotion formed in the ticket line. A brown-skinned man had been knocked down and was being kicked to cries of "Jap, Jap!" while he gasped, "I'm from Puerto Rico, from Puerto Rico."

Daren opened his mouth. But the expected clarion came choked under the grip of the time, frail as the plea of a child: "Let him alone."

In the knot of tormenters one wheeled: "Keep out of this. What are you? A Jap lover?" Self-righteous—as if the Kantian Imperative those adults had to discuss the next day were nothing but the stamp men put on willful action.

Not fear, but the powerlessness that falls on the soul, adrift, beyond its range. Daren's voice could hardly have attempted another word. But the little brown man, in the infinitesimal pause, had slipped through the ring into the dark. Daren too stole home, alien and outlaw to the loud rectitude the crowd throws around its beastliness.

Next day the long and secretly expected bomb fell on Hiroshima. The genie was out of the bottle. The war was at an end.

Winter too had passed, that literal Patapsco winter in which Daren Leflore, suspended from his job, had worked to revive the other, its prototype. The Patapsco winter was over, and the next spring and summer; and the book of meditations, like the Oxford Journal, remained in fragments, irreducible, a lost cause.

The leaves began to turn. One morning Richard Ramon Richards was found dead. On his typewriter, which his doctor had ordered him to leave alone, a yellow sheet had been rolled in, crumply, some time in the night. Through a scramble of letters picked out with one finger and that almost out of control, skipping and hitting wrong, crossing and and trying again, one deciphered (as through stammering) his last words:

> The rose fades
> and is renewed again
> by its seed, naturally
> but where
>
> save in the poem
> shall it go
> to suffer no diminution
> of its splendor.

For ten years he had been snuffing death like glue, as vessels broke and flooded the memory; and each time he had come up, bearing those less and less shadowed poems.

Daren found himself again in solitude, Anna gone abroad, maybe forever. The fall crisis bore down, another fierce encounter with power.

PART III
Fall

1. *The Door*

Fall, 1955: Virginia creeper scarlet on the rock and up the bandy ailanthus, red in their summer green. In the green state park gum and dogwood going crimson. Gold leaves mottling the tulip trees; the ash and hickories tawny. Swamp maples, sassafras, buttonwood lighting an arch over the water, drawing the eye on and on. And now the fall slopes, from the rock, rolling off like standing waves of fire.

It was Daren's birth season.

He had grown up looking west over water, across the mile-brown Mississippi, where the enormous Delta sky towered from willow flats—clouds like Prospera's gorgeous palaces, that broke the sunset on rose domes and flung the shattered remnants in shafts and fingers up that sky.

But here in this green house chance had given him, one looked over the Patapsco east—the reversal Anna had always talked about (though she had no patience with those symbols): that where the old advance was westward, and the East the closure of an ingrown past, the poles for us had interchanged; the pioneer wave reflecting from the Pacific was eddying eastward to a still center of contemplation; while the East (like Gogol's troika) was rushing forward, Pan-Slavic Prometheus, flaming the walls of our world, *vis inertiae* become *vivida vis*.

But if Daren's moving to Patapsco should have meant his facing east, as to a Mecca of timeless faith, it had come at the wrong time. The war had been his turning point in that, and his search since was more for the temporal radiance that had lingered on the spires of Oxford and the river of his childhood, or back, through the door of his birth, on the promise of America: "God himself culminates in the present moment, and will never be more divine in the lapse of all the ages."

Even Ayres' program was a move in that direction. The Bible and theology could not hold their own against the proud Greeks and Renaissance darers and Faustians of a later age; while *The City of God,* once central, had staged a slow retreat until, under the strain of teaching so crabbed a text, it had disappeared from the seminars.

That metaphorical shift from winter to fall had declared itself most clearly almost seven years ago, when Daren escaped Chicago and rode in the bus hour after hour, along Lake Michigan, north, through the crisper air and cleaner country, dairy farms, apple orchards, cherries, to the cliffs of Niagara limestone, evergreens, goldenrod blooming in the fields along the cut edge of the blue flat expanse of glacial water.

At The Door, where he was to teach, a camp at the end of the peninsula, one faced west again, over Green Bay, and as he stood looking at the sunset ("What!" Anna would have groaned: "Not another of those symbolic sunsets?"), the stages of that September day rehearsed themselves in his mind, the cycle of such a civilization as he had assumed the West to be.

The night of mystical stars had yielded, as on the shore of Dante's Purgatory, to a Gothic morning of dew. The birth phases of confidence and warmth had succeeded, until the monarch of the sun stood in his pride at noon. The succeeding Rococo languor had been broken about three by the Revolution of thunder. The day had sweetened then through post-Romantic successions, ebbing like the slow movements of Schubert or late Beethoven, to this present, when the sun, lighting the lower clouds from gold to crimson, sank, withdrawn to other times and races. Leflore stood in what seemed already to be twilight, the moment of history in which he had so long assumed himself to be living. When one great cumulus cloud, the last heir of thunder, boiling up from the horizon like steam, broke into the tangent rays, to hang exalted, pouring into the dusk the richest light of all; then faded—and the world to darkness.

Like Augustine, he had opened the book in the garden, but had received the opposite message: not to strip off flesh for spirit, but to climb for the actual light.

(The tinsel of actuality? After the world-search of winter, the merely personal again? Where the war-meditations had recorded: "The crisis of the individual has become a laughter to the gods. Only one tragedy is left: the historical tragedy of man.")

He turned. A car drove up, the last—adults for the week of seminars he was to teach. A man in uniform, a woman, beautiful. When the man had put her bags in the women's dorm, he gave her a husband's kiss and drove away.

Daren did not think of Jeffrey, and if he had, he would have doubted the coincidence. Though the only coincidence was her being married to an Air Force officer at the Glencoe base. The seminar had been advertised in the paper with Daren's name.

Even while the war raged, it had lost its suggestion of world winter. Only Daren's commitment to prison had delayed the change of seasons which was already prepared for in him. And that too had been mediated by a sunset.

He had come up one day from the science basement at Prairie College and walked out for a breath of air where a stream went through a little valley.

The stream, the clouds, winds and light were all borne down, swept in the current of nature, like the energies he studied in the lab. But as he looked, a flight of grackles beat up from an elm, winging with plaintive cries against the downward field.

Was the universe of living and nonliving to be fused only by miracle, that special creation faith-mongers called in? But the world was one and actual: the elm rose from the earth, building light into leaves, birds fountained from the elm, heightening desire into song. What was he but the sensory organ of nature?

He felt himself carried along on the old Emersonian rapture. It was not enough. 'What he needed was a base in physics. And then he caught the clue, as simple as inertia, the paradox with which he had wrestled in teaching the Newtonian laws: that mass resists motion only by moving, the acceleration and inertial back-thrust being counterfaces of the same stress. He took out his papers, leaned his back to the elm and wrote:

Two marvelous observations: All matter, systems, worlds and living things express the need of energy to buttress against its own decay; and, in this sense cosmic history is a heightening and unfolding of the perceptive ambivalence of energy, that its activity is the fall by which it dies, its life in time a transcendence using and used by the destructive urge.

That validation of the earthly had turned his heart from winter to fall.

The first year in Patapsco (fresh from Chicago and The Door) it had seemed a costly turning. Even in waking hours Jeffrey would come to him, so clearly, he knew the witch-mark in her forehead was not there for nothing. He would begin a letter, as if it made sense to write:

> The time is past when I thought to free you from commitments to which you hold as if sustaining what is dead were a virtue. But even friends can talk together. At the pool under the rock today, I saw dragonflies over the water, reflected, dazzled, caught between light and light...

Or it would be the dream of her. He would wake far in the night and reach in a half doze for the lamp, pen and paper, the will to commune shaking the conscious pool:

> Tonight your image, in truth or teasing, has told me to put the best construction on your silence: that you have not forgotten. But uncraven souls are so bare of outward sign. How can you tell indifference from control? Did your mentors give hints of that?

He would fall back, knowing he had no address for her, and would not use it if he had.

He had stuck it out with Anna.

"Putting everything aside," she would cry, "to work with you." (Those geysers of enthusiasm when she thought she might lead him across some watershed into the basin of her panacea. That they might run and aspire together.) "Joy dancing in me. Mother of Love!"

But he turned away, seeking the solitude: "You expect the impossible. One doesn't have that kind of communion even with God. Besides, you want it on your own terms. A take-over."

"You teach me, then," she would say. "Set me some reading I should do—to understand."

And suppose he did—Blake, or Yeats, or Thoreau—either she would come back in the rapture of having converted it to her own vision, or throwing it off, exclaim (as at Daren's paradoxes and polarities): "Fan me with a brick! There's a philosophy for you."

Poor Anna—to have pitched her love on something so remote from possibility. Moments of clarity, when he asked himself: "Why stick with her then? Is it doing her any good? Or you either?" The only answer he could find: "It's not my choice." For she remained a plant reaching for the light, a search in which he was supposed to play a part—the best of him even, the poet and dreamer she espoused, though remade in the image of her wish—as when the Marxists champion Don Quixote—idealist fired by a peasant girl. To get those loved powers over into the camp of the creed!

Ironic it should have happened at The Door, that nature retreat Anna had learned about through fellow workers at A *Journal of One World,* which she had attended for political seminars, had promoted and tried to guide like a creation of her own. It was she who had got Daren the place; and she would have been there too, seated across from him in the stone council ring, her head tilted to the left, listening to those lectures on the philosophy of nature, questioning, trying to let in a little light, and the whole Jeffrey business would have been overshadowed—if she hadn't been called to Washington in connection with one of the spy trials that were to consume her time and stir her passions for so long—she was needed for the picketing, the congressional sit-ins, the radio argument before the nation, the whole protest marathon which was to draw the attention of the world to that unfortunate verdict.

"Imagine—it will be me—'Pigtail Annie,' legs like broomsticks, people poking me, poor starved child, to make sure I was alive—it'll be me, pigtails flying - off to Washington, with the professors and the bigwigs, to fight for justice, love of mankind, a better life for all."

So the discussion of science and nature opened like the forest clearing where they took place—breakers on glacial boulders, red granite under the limestone, the sun setting over the water, the amber light refracted through green-cresting waves—that pure and unexpected, a last promontory of natural good.

Lars Larson had bought the wooded site thirty years before. He was an immigrant nature lover and self-taught landscape architect who took Thoreau's *Walden* as his guide. The Door was to be what its name implied, a portal for all into a world of natural relationships. Larson had searched ten years for his land, knowing what he had to have: that symbolic view from wooded rocks west over water. And in the Midwest, the heartland of America, where he had risen by love and work from stirring soap vats in a Chicago factory ("I had to quit," he used to say, "or be an anarchist") to supervisor of parks, fighting for lake front and a forest preserve, scheming ways to bring nature into the life of the city. He had tramped all the bluffs along the Mississippi, but that was already too civilized. Then he heard of the peninsula of Door County, where there wasn't even a railroad—not only the right place, but the right name, The Door.

He had designed the buildings and put them up of native materials, pine logs and limestone, with the help of his students, followers and visiting friends. One might have looked for signs of Rousseauian pose—and indeed, there was something of the romantic feel of Marie Antoinette's village - but here everything worked, the lodge, the dorms, the craft-school; quiet planes of limestone and wood blended incredibly into the cliff, the lawn, the trees. It was simple, honest, real.

Though for Daren it had been a setting only. Could mind win back to the center?—mind, always shunted in arcs and peripheries; mind, busy to describe The Door as a background, do a research paper if need be on Lars Larson and the whole back-to-nature movement—anything to avoid what, framed by that, beckoned (even at the moment of its actualness) untellable—Jeffrey.

If the Patapsco room could serve as a metaphor of consciousness, that file Daren had built on the back wall must be memory, and this window, sight; but when he walked to the window, what he saw was not the cedared nook in white limestone over Green Bay, not Arethusan Jeffrey coming from the night swim to the cliff aerie to warm herself naked at the fire: it was only his own black rock heaving from fallen leaves, the English ivy green among the red Virginia creeper; and all memory could return were hints of a communion irrecoverable as the touch of their bodies. It was the third possibility of the room that gave a road, however circuitous (projections into others always creaking with the uncertainty of an amateur play); neither the window of sense nor the files of recollection, but the table spread with papers—among the rest, a bradded bundle put together through lonely nights of the first Patapsco fall. That account he still had; but all it could capture was what Jeffrey had been able to tell—hardly a comfort— how the marriage had been formed, to which, in the cold light of dawn, she had decided to return.

In that typed and bradded form not even Jeffrey's talk retained its tone. What she had told him through the week (at meals together in the raftered hall, strolls to the council ring for seminars, sunset under the pine on the rock, evenings with the others by a log fire, or afterwards, the two of them walking the trails as the moon waxed from crescent toward full)—talk that had begun with the larks and rainbows over the Evenlode, and deepened to the last night's whisperings—all that had regrouped itself, taking a new point of view, which was significantly that of the antagonist, the husband, of whom Daren could only demand again and again: How did you filch the treasure, and how do you manage to swing on? And get no answer but the specter-smile of the uniformed and knowing airman.

Ask history then. By what trick of Boone and Buffalo Bill, Deerslayer, Melville, Twain had merely clean-shaven and athletic American boys, freed from towns to which they would return, country clubs, white supremacy, business as usual, seemed for a time, liberating Europe, so liberated, a phenomenon of humorous passion, Gargantuan Kilroy?

Lawless was one of those heroes for whom London had transformed itself into a night carnival of marketable pleasures. In the daytime maybe it was the moral city of blood, sweat and tears which had stood up to years of Hitler's drubbing. At night even, if you kept responsible company, you might catch the fiber of that resistance. But if you came on furlough from an airbase northward on the fens for a few drinks and a grind, what you encountered was the Mr. Hyde of the divided being:

Servicemen of all nations, milling about among teenagers, working girls, widows, wives, innocents, whores—assimilated by dark and the style to a hot denominator, short skirts, sweater hubs, searching eyes: a bedmate, a kindred soul: "Love me today, for tomorrow you die."

Taxi drivers never had it so good: a pound a throw, the cab swaying like Madame Bovary's hack. It was cheaper than a room, and the pros could push on from job to job. If a girl insisted on a festive seduction, there were the hotels gone American: The Texan, The Montana, The Broadway—dinner, cocktails with the magic names; Sidecar, Stinger, Pink Lady, Virgin's Delight.

You could see the hard ones playing their hand: a Cockney tart, dressed in tawdry elegance and trying (without any Pygmalion) to talk like a duchess, putting on airs at the Ritz for a Yankee oaf who happened to be a colonel, setting her cap not just for the cash and PX nylons but the big stakes in the New World, while the few British at the other tables, in the know, winked. Lawless didn't aim to be taken in like that. He knew Alabama "quality" if he didn't know the British. Virgin's Delight. Passport to heaven à la Hollywood. For anybody as handsome and adept as Tom Lawless, the whole thing was a grab bag to get what you wanted and get off unhooked.

He had got it from the mixed-up girls in the hotels, the weeping nymphette who had run away from home and stole his watch in the end. He had tried the clubs which sprang up off Piccadilly faster than the bobbies could raid them, where touts hung around hawking devices and it was one big lay in the doorways, rooms, alleys.

Once in an air raid he had gone down the long escalator into the surreal tube. "God, man," a Canadian had told him, "they go down there with nothing on but an overcoat. You just walk along the platform until you see a likely piece." But Lawless couldn't see anything but muffled forms. The air was too cold for exposure and too dense with breath and sweat to abet passion. You might chance to lie down between husband and wife: "Wot's the big oidea? This 'ere spaice is reserved. You're not gain to crowd me out. Oi live 'ere." As for listening to the sirens as the Canadian had claimed and merging in escape, it was too deep to hear anything, even the bomb-blast. Let the British lads hail their girls: "See you in the Underground." It wasn't for Tom Lawless.

But above ground he knew the ropes, he had played the field. The professionals, he decided, were the best. As somebody had said, honest: that's what they came to the market to sell. And the best place was in the taxis, or on dry nights when you didn't have to take it standing, in Hyde Park, where the mates lined up like dogs, voyeurs, until their turn came for those "five-shilling-play-around, one pound-the-real-thing" girls, littering the ground with souvenirs the sober citizens shook their heads over as they walked to work next day.

This was the off-duty habitat of Lawless. Love didn't enter. He didn't believe in the existence of an estimable lady in all that night-fevered bowl the Thames flowed through. Until he met Jeffrey. And still he wouldn't have trusted it without Uncle Athol. But nobody who valued surfaces could have faced that glossy-moustached empire builder at his desk in the War Ministry and not have esteemed the connection.

It was Uncle Athol who had winked at Jeffrey's age (knowing she always had her way), tricked her out in uniform, and got her a job in the Ground Ops Room, that secret Hole which was the nerve center in the defense of London. He even managed to billet her on her beloved Aunt Ev who had lived fifty years in solitary and eccentric retirement (the sort of artistic retreat only a city can afford) in a mew off Kensington Gardens.

The house was of the Peter Pan era, three stories, plain outside, modest inside, but with as many treasures as a museum. Aunt Ev had dabbled in various arts, but in weaving she was supreme. Despite two operations for a slowly spreading cancer, she still sat through the day, chipper as a bird, at the great loom which filled the living room, producing unique fabrics, which she gave her friends, and received in loving return Chinese scrolls, pottery, carving, watercolors; for she was not only a saintly person, who regularly gave away most of her settled income, she also had a flawless taste, and the friends she had made early were now among the connoisseurs and artists of England.

Jeffrey had a dormer room which, thanks to the bombing, looked through a shell of walls across to the park. The antiaircraft were out there. During the raids you could see them pounding away, and the windows would cavort and rattle, while the flak fell back from the sky in a rattling rain on the roof, and bomb fragments now and then pitted the soft Portland stone. Mostly they closed the shutters, but neither Jeffrey nor her aunt made a practice of going to the shelters.

Once when Ev was on the way to the Home for Bombed-out Old People (she went there regularly and read them poetry for their entertainment), she was waiting for a bus when the alarm sounded. The queue scattered; Ev raised her umbrella. "There's a raid on, ma'am; you better go to the shelter," a man told her. "Thank you," she said. "I have an appointment and I'll wait for the bus."—"There won't likely be any until after the raid."—"It's no matter," she assured him. "I'll wait for the first that comes,"—"Well, ma'am," he said, "let me hold your umbrella." And he stood there, holding it over her—in case a bomb fell.

She even refused to evacuate the house when a huge black land mine appeared one morning hanging by a parachute from the plane tree. She took no interest in the proceedings, except once when the workmen brought a dray horse clopping by she ducked out as always with the coal scuttle and shovel to scrape up a precious dropping for her garden. The men had just deactivated the mine and were at ease. Ev popped in again and brought out an orange a daughter of one of the bombed-out ladies had given her—a rare commodity. "Which one of you has children?" she asked. "I'll give him this." No answer. "Come on, men, speak up. Which one?" Not the claimant, but the other, pointed: "He has."—"Here then." She gave the orange a toss; he grabbed it; and she went into the house.

Jeffrey, too, though less picturesque, was cavalier about the raids. She thought if Hitler had marked one for her, there was nothing she could do about it.

Her shifts were the worst thing about the job: first day 8:00 to 1:00 and 5:00 to 11:00 at night; next day from 1:00 to 5:00 and from 11:00 to 8:00 in the morning; third day off for sleep; then back to the beginning again. Tonight she was off at eleven. The stars were out; the first raid had aborted. It was too lovely to hit the sack. One would almost have defied bombers, like that crazy lady in *Heartbreak House:* "It's like music; it's like Beethoven. I hope they come again tomorrow. Oh I hope so."

Lyons Corner House off Piccadilly was too dreary, a few old women pouring sloppy tea or handing you a ham sandwich. She turned into a smaller street, saw an Italian restaurant, cavelike in a massive stone building. She went in.

Flight Lieutenant Lawless had been ordered out on a regular bombing raid over north Germany, and as they closed in on the target antiaircraft caught them. It was before there were enough Flying Fortresses to go around, so they were in one of the big Wellington four engines. They were supposed to have kept formation and held the course for the bomb run, but the flak broke it up; there was a burst near the plane; one of the engines went dead. "For Christ's sake," said Lawless, "let's drop this stuff and get out of here." They veered off, laying in the bombs, expecting any moment to go up in flames. A German fighter drove by; their own rear gun was silent. It was touch and go if they would make England. Lawless did it on that much-invoked wing and a prayer. A long breath he took as they roared for the field, hit short, in the rough, bounced, settled, but taxied to the stand. He banged the navigator on the head. "Welcome home, Jake," he grinned. But the gunner had got it from below, up through the belly; the blood had congealed and they had to hose him out.

It took the grin off the return. A Blue Ridge mountaineer, he had said his pap was a moonshiner. His sister, anyway, worked in a canning plant in Asheville, and she used to go in at night and seal up mountain dew in fruit juice cans and send them to him. A big time in the Quonset hut when Clem would open one of those terrific quarts of fruit and pass it around: "Best damned fruit juice I ever tasted,"… Turn down an empty can. The wing commander gave Lawless the night off. To break the gloom.

London seemed quiet. The serious sleepers had gone down to the Underground or into the block shelters with their palliasses. (What a word! You could hear the prim Girl Guide leaders urging their campers on: "Come on now, girls, spread out your pally-asses.") Tom checked his billet at the hotel and went to the Armed Service Club for a drink. Then he walked around. The hectic crowds thronging the black-out dark of Leicester Square, Piccadilly, the Mall, the Strand. Beyond that center the city was silent, asleep. Maybe he would pick up something in a restaurant. The Italians had run most of the places before the war. They had been yanked out and sent to camps on the Isle of Wight. But Lawless knew an English woman, still running her husband's business… He stopped in.

Daren had not recognized Jeffrey as she got out of the car that first night at The Door. And her new name wouldn't have helped, even if he had made a practice of noticing names. But as he walked along the bluff next morning toward the council ring for the first seminar, he became aware of her on a point of rock. She turned. What that passing glance opened between them was so compelling that when he reached the ring, he took out his notes, and while the others were gathering, tried to peg it down, like a metaphysical problem:

> You are out for a walk. Suppose you reach a point at which a girl is standing looking over the water. You do not know her. Since she was standing there before you came along, her looking cannot have any particular reference to you. But if her gaze implies search, you begin to read yourself into the context of that search, Suppose then she looks at you, as if you had become the object of her gaze. And suppose you find her beautiful and are moved. What is the relation between you?

> Before you came along the relation was nonexistent; so what you see as personal in the meeting must be illusion. Her gaze was the general form of an appearance in which you as well as another might have played a role.

But that account does not answer the intuition of what you feel. For you also were not expecting to meet her; yet as soon as you have done so, you cannot believe that a general form of appearance has been temporarily met by one object where another would have served. You discover the relationship to be personal, particular, burning and destinate.

An eternal possibility has become real in exactly the flesh it had to wear. You stand in the tragicomic mystery of the Incarnate, which is the birth of love.

Daren's conclusion was right; though his premise, "You do not know the girl," was wrong.

Something should have told him that when she drifted into the leafy circle humming an air he had heard her sing long ago in Wychwood Forest. But the phantom he had invoked on paper stood between him and the living power.

> O the summer time is comin
> And the trees are sweetly bloomin
> And the wild mountain thyme
> Grows round the bloomin heather
> Will ye go, Lassie, go?

Jeffrey's mother had been named Letitia. But Roger Strange, when he joined the other aspirants on the untrodden ways to her father's Argyll tower, wanted something gayer than the Latin Joy. He called her Lassie; and while it wasn't an original designation for a Scotch girl, it stated the case. Jeffrey grew up calling her that; and in time the name had gathered around itself the Highland song, whose runs and lingering delays brought up the heath wind and flowers:

> I will build my love a tower
> Near yon pure crystal fountain
> And on it I will build
> All the flowers of the mountain;
> And we'll all go together
> Where the wild mountain thyme
> Grows round the bloomin heather
> Will ye go, Lassie, go?

She had died of meningitis in what seemed the beauty of youth, one of those rare women age perfects, heightening even sexual charm under silvering hair. It was known that Jeffrey and her father were to leave Childe Manor; they had only delayed for Lassie. So when the pipers came to the funeral and played that song, it became Jeffrey's farewell, not just to her mother but to her home, most of all the last verse, strange, like Adam and Eve leaving paradise (the world all before them, where to choose):

> If my true love she were gone
> I would surely find another
> Where the wild mountain thyme
> Grows round the bloomin heather
> Will ye go, Lassie, go?

Jeffrey hummed it now, drifting through sun and shade. But Daren had forgotten, or had never known.

That afternoon warm summer flooded back. Campers trooped down the rock stair where the sun reflecting from the bay rippled under the limestone overhang, and focusing direct and mirrored turned the shingle to a tropical resort lapped round with clean brisk waves. Bathers stretched like seals, in the Kipling story, on the rocks. As Daren leapt down the path in his shorts, Jeffrey slid into the water and swam out over wavering ledges that shelved off into blue. She shook back her streaming hair and, as he approached, she waved.

Water, the world-solvent, where mating began. "When I was a tadpole and you were a fish."

And now he saw her, the girl who had dared him to jump the brook and he had landed like a tadpole in the mud, but she had cleaned his shoes and they walked through the beech wood, he not knowing that his destination was hers; he saw her on the little dam of the brook, her damp hair falling to her shoulders and the water falling...

"What is your name?"

"Jeffrey Lawless."

"Strange. And your maiden name?"

"Strange. That's the best part of it. Strange and Lawless." They had been sitting at separate tables until the air-raid siren went off, whooping up and down like something concealed in the room. The windows were boarded and the low ones sandbagged outside but there might be cracks. The proprietress went around checking the curtains. A warden poked his head in and winked. "Better get to a shelter while you can. Looks like a noisy one." The place began to empty out.

Tom looked around and spoke in general: "When I come back in a shot-up plane from Hamburg, I don't want to crawl down a London tube."

Jeffrey sipped her coffee. "The small deed" (her father used to say), "masters the big word."

When a wind blows in the woods you hear it far off stirring the leaves. A space opens in the dimension of sound, in which you mark the force coming toward you like a flight of birds. But what they heard coming was bigger than any wind.

"You're a mighty brave lady, ma'am," Tom said. "Join you?"

She nodded. Indians and pioneers. She had always liked Americans.

That was when she learned his name, and her child-delight almost betrayed her *age:* "Why it's out of the wild West."

"No ma'am, the wilds of Allah-bahama. And may I be so Lawless as to ask yours?"

And it was then she told him: "Jeffrey Strange…But Strange and Lawless. I don't know which I like best." Tom hadn't thought of giving her the choice.

It was when radar was coming in, replacing the old audio·spotters. "Surprised you aren't eating carrots," Jeffrey gave him a knowing glance, "I hear you people eat them all the time. They say that's why you have such luck now with the night fighting."

Old Tom Lawless wasn't going to give anything away. Even a beautiful Britisher might he a spy. "I had a big bunch on the train," he said. "If I eat too many, the light hurts my eyes."

"Same as my Aunt Ev," Jeffrey confided. "She hates anything but candles or an oil lamp."

There was a crash that made you swing to the table and wonder if it was a chandelier. Chunks clobbered the front wall. "Big hardware" Jeffrey remarked.

The explosion tapered off in an ongoing roar. The proprietress peeped through the curtains. Flames. A groan: "The pigs have hit the gas."

The warden again: "Sorry. We're evacuating this area. Proceed to the shelter or to your billets, please."

(That war, which in prison nightmares had coiled Daren so indisputably in the real, had glints of tinsel in accounts of those who had witnessed what he had only dreamed—the sort of D Day Churchill might have seen from the bridge of H.M.S. *Belfast.*)

"There's a blackout, of course," Jeffrey would say, trying to put it all before him, ("But don't think you're walking in total darkness, when those things are popping all around. And the noise…")

Roar of planes, bombs, falling walls, incendiaries burning magnesium white sputtering down the street like ball-lightning, showing a double line of people drawing back on either side, stretching up weird in the acrid smoke and glare.

"This is nothing," Jeffrey told Tom gaily. "We've got them on the run now. You hear that engine? That throb? That's one of theirs. If our number's on it, there's nothing we can do. But knock on wood." She tapped her forehead as if she had invented that little joke.

"Seems peppy enough to me," Lawless said.

"There was a time—when I first came back from France—top secret, now!—when for ten hours we didn't have a plane to put up or a crew to have flown it."

The voice pattered on, how she was studying in Paris the first year, the phony war, they called it, behind that silly Line, and how an officer she knew had to report for orders. "It'll be pith helmets," he told her. "Egypt is next." But when he got his posting, it was skis. Norway. "That's how much they knew. And then Belgium."

She had made for the Channel with an English officer's family in a lorry, black paint smeared on the chrome, not to glitter. "That night I tried to clean my teeth over the tailgate and there wasn't any place to spit. It was Poles, Belgians, British, Jews, French, soldiers and refugees, tanks, cars, wagons, wheelbarrows. "When you have to swallow the toothpaste," she said, it's a rum go."

They had made it across the channel, zigzag, in a tug heaped with wounded soldiers bandaged in brown. "Not to show the blood," Jeffrey speculated. "Then the Blitz. Some say they even tried to land, but we set off oil slicks and burned them as they came to shore." The bright voice went dark. Her father had died about that time. "Anyway," she said, "they had us by the throat. This is *naethin' ava'*."

As they came out by St. James's Park, the throb-throb-throb bore down. Knocking wood didn't help. Explosions converged. They ducked under the shrubbery. Something went off near, the ground squirming like a snake. In the silence that ensued they heard a ticking beyond the bushes, like a big clock. "Lord," Jeffrey giggled, "I bet it's a time bomb. Let's get out of here."

They caught a number nine bus. It rumbled along, keeping its schedule, spent flak rattling down on the roof, the headlights masked but for a tiny gold slit where a thread of dimness crept through. "Talk about eating carrots," Tom said, "that driver must live on them. I can't even see the road."

They got off at Albert Hall, ducked down a side street and into an old-fashioned narrow row of façades squeezed together side by side. "So that's where she lives," Lawless thought, setting it against his father's big place in Alabama. As a matter of fact, his house was on the skids, the whole suburb endangered by Negroes moving in from both sides; but he forgot that for the contrast. For him hers was any old middle-class row.

To strip back the smoky wall, draw it away like a stage drop, and discover what Lawless' had never yet encountered and had small chance of glimpsing but through Jeffrey, though she too relied on glimpses, guessing at an essence by outward signs: the curtained lamplit room, prints and sketches on the walls, wonderful old books, the Blakean mystery of the loom and, beyond the visible, merging into spirit, streams of devotion that flowed toward Ev and out, as from a source and renewal.

Lawless took the surface of the house as a measure of what one might accomplish with Jeffrey. Even a practiced guy can get confused, especially in foreign parts, as now, when she turned to thank him, he jumped at the mere gamble—anything to break her serene possession of an unchallenged hand—and caught her to him (what else had he come to London for?), though he didn't usually offer so much without a sign of its being desired. And he was more lost than ever when, with the elevation of one always brushing off advances, but hardly to be offended by the follies of the world, she gave him a cool sweet peck and said: "We are grateful to you Americans; but we can't reward you with everything. Good night."

It was his panic then that surprised him: "Jeffrey Strange! Wait! How can I see you again?"

"I would note down the address," she said, "and write." She waved, and clicked the gate.

He wrote; he phoned; they had various meetings.

The time he came in talking about how he couldn't be any worse off if a bomb had hit him—feel there, on his head, that lump, one helluva lump. He had to take a shower, of course, to see his girl, but what a shower. First you fix those faucets hoping for a mixture that wouldn't freeze or scald you. Then you pull the chain. You only get water while you hold the chain. And if you need your hands to wash your feet, what do you do but tie a brick to it? All right. You finish your feet; you straighten up in a hurry; and there's that crazy brick.

The next time he wouldn't have been able to joke about conking heads. The plane after his had come in with the bomb release jammed and a bomb still aboard. When they struck it blew the whole thing to hits. Everybody was dead hut the pilot, and the propeller had taken the top right off his head, laid the skull hack, so you saw the brain like a jelly, working. "He was conscious,', Tom said, "still talking. You wanted to clap that skull hack on; thought he'd be OK, hut nobody dared touch him, and before the doctor came, he died."

They went to the flick, something as far from war as possible, a hitchhiking romance: *It Happened One Night*—Tom's pride heightened by GIs' passing remarks: "Hey, buddy, where'd you get her? Has she got a sister, maybe, or a girl friend?" And Jeffrey's queenly acceptance of subject homage.

A lovely movie for escape. Until the raid came with the old sirens and people clearing out. "I'm not thinking about going," said Tom. But there was a hit somewhere; a big plate glass decoration crashed down all over the place; the picture went off, and there was nothing to do but give it up.

They came out to quite a little bonfire. "You better get down, miss," a Cockney soldier cautioned, and dragged Jeffrey into the gutter on the rough cobbles. Tom didn't know whether to thank the guy or tell him to go to hell. When the fireworks eased off, they made their getaway.

"Damn, damn, more than damn!" said Jeffrey. "I'd like to use some of my really had words."

"What's the matter, honey?" Tom asked her.

"That dear boy," she said. "I hate those thick cotton stockings, and silk is so hard to get. I'd almost as soon have been bombed."

After that Tom sent her three pair of PX nylons, expecting nothing now but the general grace of her smile.

When he found out she worked in the famous Ground Ops Hole, where reports from everywhere were telephoned in and written up on blackboards all around, and counters were moved with sticks over the table map, and decisions made which coordinated the entire defense effort, he was mighty impressed. Next time he could get in, he met her as she came from work. The Hole had got a direct hit while Jeffrey was helping out at the switchboard, She was flung to the floor and every light on the board went red, then blacked out. She had hardly picked herself up and begun to grope for something when the engineers with flashlights came pouring through the room, buttoning up their britches as they went; they'd been having a nap. They replaced the circuit in a jiffy and the defense of London was mounted again.

It was the same night Jeffrey was to take Tom Lawless to meet her aunt. They got on the bus as usual, but around Hyde Park Corner an oncoming bus had been hit by a bomb, soared into the air and lit in a tremendous hole. Their driver managed to stop. They got out at the edge of the crater, groans coming up, a sizzling and smell of benzene… Policemen and wardens were running over with flashlights. Tom Lawless was the first into the pit, helping the injured out and plunging back for more, the native crisis hero.

He was less at home seated in the candlelight before the mysterious bird form of Ev, who could receive at any time of night or day with equal earthlessness. But he covered his bafflement with the charm of southern manners.

As Jeffrey had opened the iron spiked gate (it was beautiful moonlight, English March, the days always cloudy but the nights coming clear) and led him under a trellis covered with vines, down steps like a leafy burrow, through a tiny sunken garden, a fish pool among rocks and fronds, and into the basement, which was hall and entrance now; as the cramped eighteenth-century front opened into artfully planned and subtle spaces, where Aunt Ev offered them China tea in thin porcelain with curious bone spoons (she used to take in women just released from prison, give them a place to live while they were getting a start, and one went off with all her antique silver; she wouldn't report it, of course, or replace it either, ashamed of having had anything that posed such a temptation; after that she never would put up with any service but bone).

As they sipped she quietly soliloquized, as if to the spirit of the hearth: "I have such a happy life. It seems I float on happiness. I have just finished a bedspread for a friend. It took me five months; weaving when I'm able. For someone who has done more for me than even I can realize. Now I have started on scarves for those who have helped me in my illness. Their love is like a nimbus; it keeps the bad from getting at me. There's a poem I wanted you to read, Jeffrey. I laid it out. By Gascoigne, such a joyful one. I have realized, these days, a lovely truth about our Elizabethan writers. It was the nearness of death that made them so lightsome, so childlike and gay." What Jeffrey picked up from the table was not an ordinary book at all, but a portfolio of poems and quotations gathered over years, mystical fragments from Blake, Traherne, Clare, pieces Ev's poet friends had copied for her: translations by Waley, an autograph from Masefield: "Death opens unknown doors; it is most grand to die"; a letter from Wilfred Owen with a first sketch of the great "sad shires" poem: humble voices mingled with the known (they were all humble when they wrote to Ev): there was Rose Sidgewick's "New Decalogue," Fiona McCleod's "Deep Peace" and a rich poem by Gibson, "The Golden Room." As Jeffrey read Gascoigne's quaint "Garden" and Aunt Ev responded, Tom Lawless was aware that his first diagnosis of ordinary middle class was off the beam. But what the beam was, or whether this old girl was sane or crazy, he couldn't have known less. He was in his element at the bus crater, but his heroism wasn't spiritual.

The next entertainment was more to his taste. A quiet night, they went to the Mecca Ballroom. Tom had met with bad luck at dances at the Officers' Club. The better he danced the less the English motions seemed to match his. But Jeffrey not only looked perfect, she could follow every step he made. Up to now (as he told himself) even what was fascinating in her had too much of the Strange. But this put him right back in the Old Colonial Ballroom (of the new country club) at Reading, dancing with the Cotton Queen of Alabama; in fact he was there in thought, showing Jeffrey off for just such an occasion.

Not long after, they had dinner with Uncle Athol, who took them to his club and put on the dog. Jeffrey was his favorite niece, and he could see that Tom Lawless was pretty fair provincial material, though he hadn't thought of him yet as an aspirant to Jeffrey's hand. But why not? Her impractical father had left no inheritance, and Athol Strange had children of his own.

In any case, the mere existence of Uncle Athol clenched the matter. As soon as Tom could get in on Jeffrey's free day they went out to Hampstead Heath, bought fish and chips and a bottle of cider, walked around Highgate Ponds (the peak of hawthorne-powdered May), ate in the twilight, then sank into the beauty of spring, their own youth, the world, its force and rapture. On the hill where Cromwell had his guns, they lounged under a chestnut tree and saw, over the night bowl of London, planes, searchlights reaching, dogfights, tracers, and below, fountains of fire—as in old pictures Lot and his daughters embrace over the destruction of Sodom. At the climax of the raid, Tom disentangled enough to focus on eyes remotely luminous under dark hair, and murmur—still perhaps to his surprise—a proposal of marriage to this now established virgin.

The question hung on the night. To keep it there; to stretch out the silence, as Zeus assays the foreknown fate of Troy in the scales; as if a narrator's deliberation could make Jeffrey decide again: why buy an America whose movie image was not instinctively her goal—Reading most of all, that knot of Kilroy contradiction, up-and-coming steel giant of the South, at the same time a cesspool of backward taboos?

Call the lucky name Lawless an open wedge, stirring under British propriety and in war-fired London a force so burning it could only lance outward. Picture Jeffrey as peculiarly exposed, cloven by her father's quixotic losses, her mother's death, the parting from Childe Manor, that upheaval in the picture-book life of the well-born lady. Allow for something else that had struck her at Stoke-underWychwood: "I used to ask Uncle Leslie about you. I heard that you had gone home and were married." What is to be her future? Discount the radiance behind her maiden aunt's gray facade (compensation for another loss in another war); Jeffrey's claim was not to inwardness. What it was or where **it** was leading, she did not know. Why not westward? Why not with Lawless? He was handsome, he was well-bred, he was brave.

And still Daren detained the question on the night: *I'll have grounds more relative than this.*

"Well," Jeffrey said, as if it explained everything, "there was that dog."

"Dog?"

—A whining under a bombed house. Lawless, tearing at brick and stone, enlarged a crumbling space through which he crawled, until she heard from under the heap a muffled "Here, good boy," and again the whine, and she saw the dark flickered by a match. "A big one. I'll lift the beam." Then a heaving, and another match. Silence. Another flickering flame. "What's the matter?" Jeffrey whispered. For she seemed to be living backward, as in the Looking Glass House, toward a known wrong and terror, which culminated in a shot.

"He didn't go armed, for God's sake?"

"He wore a pearl-handled pistol under his jacket; his grandfather brought it from Wales when he opened the mine in Alabama. The rubble started falling; I thought it was all going to come down on him, but he squeezed out. 'Broken back,' he said. We walked away. It's easy to love animals. But not everybody knows when to do a thing like that. My father did…When my horse broke his leg."

Self-confidence was so much a part of Tom's appeal, he hardly wondered when Jeffrey looked out over the flaming town, and drawing him down again by his shock of blond hair, sighed his name, Tom Lawless, and said, "I will, yes; I will."

The leave of their honeymoon took them to north Wales, the lonely hills and flowered headlands over a polished expanse of sea.

> Where the wild mountain thyme
> Grows round the bloomin heather.
> Will ye go, Lassie, go?

The day after the recognition scene at The Door, Daren took Jeffrey rowing across Green Bay. A thunderstorm came up, silvering the water. They raced back like sailing, but at the slip the wind and waves caught the boat and the oars fouled; they were crested toward the rock jetty. He sprang over the bow, clothes, wallet, watch and all, interposed himself, an anchor, a drag, slowing the motion and taking up the shock, then with all his strength heaved the boat back into open water, as he spluttered with Homer: "Hold the ship out from that surf and spray!"

A love that arises in nature seems to consist in activity, as if bodies in their muscular exuberance had been sporting with each other. Though in retrospect all that had settled into quiet: Lars Larson's aerie on the cedared ledge under the brow of the cliff, invisible from above, a window looking over the bay, evening, moonlight, stars, a log and stone hut of silence, where, bodies asleep, it is souls that are communing.

As the moon advanced he had left the teacher's lodge and spent the nights on the bunk there by the fire. The last night of all he and Jeffrey had walked away from the others along the washed layerings of dolomite under the cliff, until they came to a faulted chimney between cedars, and she saw it above, stone and logs, blending into the cliff like a growing thing. He had not taken her there before.

He helped her up the rock ladder, unlocked the door; they entered, stooping for the lintel. The day's fire had died to coals; through the window the last light rocked on the waves. The moon just showed in the south, between half and full. He had a bit of sherry he had brought and hardly used. He poured hers in the glass and raised the bottle. "Cheers."

"As our gardener used to say: 'Ere's to tomorrow." It had meant a lot to her, that toast, and she would always keep the gaudy crystal goblet the old man had given her when they drank his homemade wine her last clay at Childe Manor, and his voice had failed. Again tomorrow was foreclosed. But she smiled. "'Ere's to now."

The waves on the rock, the wind murmuring a little in the pines, the fire flickering on the hearth. Bats flying back and forth across the moon. Sighs, lappings, wordless as water on stone.

Later they climbed down the chimney for a swim. Anna could run naked in the fields as she pleased; she had posed in the nude for artist friends. But for Jeffrey life was a dance of seven veils, and only at the climax and for one person would the last veil be lowered and flesh and motives stand lovingly revealed. Not for Lawless. In deep pensiveness, she looked at Daren and put off the plaid skirt and cardigan which up to now she had worn. He saw her figure under the dark mass of hair whiter than the Niagara limestone, lowering its loops of beauty down the ledges into the moonlit sheen.

He swam beside her. "Why didn't you tell me that first night in the dining hall you were you?"

"That was for you to remember." Upending like a forked mermaid, the patch of dark between Nereid limbs, she surface-dived into the clear cold. His eyes open, he followed her down, Mars in the Scorpion sluicing the waves with red.

They went back shivering, heaped the fire, embraced in the glow. She combed out her hair. If this had only happened years before. At Stoke-under-Wychwood. But how was that to be? "There you were," he murmured, "a little girl. You didn't even have any wychwood to stoke under." They slept fitfully and waked in the deeper dark. The moon had set. Argument was behind them:

"You call it morality. I call it cowardice. You say it's strength, and I say it's weakness. Because I don't believe in denying what nature tells us is good. I take this retreat called The Door seriously."

She took it seriously too, but as a retreat. She had known before she came that she would go back to her bargain and bring up her two sons.

There would be times, those Patapsco nights, when he might have accused her of treating him as a diversion, already resolved that she would let him go. But the accusation, like the love, must be voiceless. As old Uncle Caldwell used to sing to a blues tune:

> So many things never to be told
> Buried between your heart and your soul.

Theoretically, Anna favored free love; but she would have regarded Daren's as a symptom of the sick bourgeoisie.

And it was Anna who would rejoin him for the move to Patapsco—gloomy after the fulfillment of the verdict she had fought so hard to change—fought, until her life seemed tied up in the lives of that convicted pair.

"Anybody born of the people could tell there was something wrong: a housewife and a poor engineer made out to be master spies. And the machine only stayed execution to let the protest spend itself. Oh, they know, they know. Picketing, picketing, no time to eat or sleep. Saturday and Sunday we were thousands marching at the White House. By Monday down to a few hundred, and crowds pressing in, calling us Jews, spies, whores, every filth they could imagine. Our petition was barred at the gate. And then on the radio they asked me if I thought they would be executed that evening. And I said no, there couldn't be such injustice in America. The radio men looked sad. I think in secret they were on our side. As the time drew near, the mob gathered against us with signs: 'Death to spies' and 'Traitors die.' Cars, too, and all in fierce silence, waiting. Until a policeman dropped his hands: the signal. It was all over; they were dead. And the horns went off and the people screamed like New Year, like Fourth of July. We laid our signs down, weeping, and made our way to a park, guarded by policemen from that mob, threatening to lynch us. We were led to buses and taken out of town. Since then, whenever I lie down to sleep, I hear the sound of feet, marching—as if we were cut off in a world of our own, all the other noises of the street and the crowd thinned out, and just that tramp of feet, our pickets, or maybe those innocent people waiting for the chair, pacing. I still hear those feet in my head."

Daren would return to Anna, and Jeffrey to Tom; Tom, who had gone home looking for a house—no longer war pilot, no longer instructor at Glencoe, but mustered out, manager in his father's bank. For behind this paradise of The Door lay the other and prior paradise of north Wales, dominant, leaving this one merely recessive. There Tom Lawless athlete, soldier, waked the eighteen-year-old Jeffrey to the radiance of flesh: on the burnished hills of Caernarvon, a youth and girl climb through heather hand in hand, the moss between the bracken a springing deep mattress on the ground. Wind blows the clothes tight to the limbed creatures; their heads thrown back, sunlight takes their hair.

At the peak of that flame, Jeffrey had realized…

But being of a happy nature, she remained in partial content. It would be years before—looking at Tom—another of those clean American boys become businessmen, like all the rest at conventions and class reunions all over the prosperous land, the war vitality she had linked with his name seeming now the brief rejuvenation of those who have drunk radium salts—she would laugh with amazement that mere recklessness had brought her to such a port of proprietary ease:

"Tom Lawless, indeed! Why don't you change your name, and not deceive poor girls? Lawful, you should make it, or Lawson, righteous child of the law."

When Daren waked the last time it was the gray beginning, as in old romances, the separating dawn. He thought Jeffrey was asleep. His arm was around her and her head was on his shoulder. Then he felt tears wet her cheek where it lay on the muscles of his chest. She did not sob. Reluctant, voiceless tears. The time for persuasion was past, but at least she could weep. "Jeffrey," he said, "why don't you go on and cry? It can't do any harm."

But she could no more yield to that than she could break her word, and the refusal beat up from the silence like a father's spirit, choking back her tears: "Cowards cry!" Daren had still not learned the circumstances of that reproach, though he was familiar with the quotation that followed: "No coward soul is mine…"

That was the memory he had waked to again and again the first year at Patapsco. Seven years had passed and it had not let up altogether. Perhaps it had harmed his love for Anna—though he did not doubt the plurality of loves. Besides, their separation was bound to come, predictable as the courses of the stars—her eastward return, the perihelion from which she was now signing off in ardent letters:

Moscow, October 1, 1955

Dear Daren:

I send you glowing news of a new development in man. The Russians are far ahead of us, a serious people. Beside them we are corrupt, spoilers and wasters, trivial We have been lied to for so many years. We make all the wrong assumptions. In Cuba, Berlin, China, everywhere we are going wrong. And we will have to pay.

A fly lights on my paper. I watch it, I do not crush it. Even that fly, so tiny, wishes to live. Every living thing lives under fear. For man it is to be burned by bombs.

The Russians will never make war; they are beyond all that, a people of peace. But if attacked they will fight as we cannot dream of. Our economy rests on war (62% this year); all over the world we have to meddle and fight wherever the old false ways are collapsing. And then blame it on the others. Is that what you call being free?

301

Men have no right to destroy the world because they have missed their chances in it. If you could feel the human purpose of this people, then you would believe. But you are like the rest, sealed in self-deception. But for that I would have been

Your own,

Anna.

Present or absent, she was planted in him, a warning and exhorting voice. His thoughts would come round to her again with something of the old tenderness—her very blatancies, her dedications. In them, as in a tarnished mirror, he caught glimpses of the high thing he had seemed in her admiring. Suppose he no longer loved her——he could at least be loyal.

While the sun set at his back, shafting long rays out east over thePatapsco, striking fire in the summits of the fall wood.

And to reach Jeffrey there was no door.

302

2. *The Mansard Window*

Daren waked early these mornings to have time at his desk before going to the college. He saw the sun rise over the Patapsco. What did it mean to be so oriented? Anna had sailed to the new East; as for the old, Daren had toyed with it long ago. His life could never be plotted until someone had established a mystical center. Yet until that morning he did not know who it would be.

"The Vyne," Boar's Hill, Oxford, 1 October, '55

Dear Sir,

I have been translating and editing the letters of Heloise Frank for the Sheldonian Press.

If you never knew or corresponded with her, forgive me for troubling you. But I have been told by her friend Denise Pierrefont that the name of an undergraduate she met at Solesmes in 1938 "may have been Daren Leflore." And since I find from a university list that you were at Gloucester College at that time, I thought you might know something about a series of letters apparently to the "young Englishman" of whom she has written in what she called her "Spiritual Autobiography."

They are drafts of letters to a correspondent addressed only under the salutation "Silex Scintillans." If you did in fact know her, I would appreciate your telling me anything you can about the circumstances of these letters.

Sincerely yours,

(Sir) Francis Pearce

The fifth possibility of Oxford loves thus came to light, not as a feature of halcyon summer (when the meeting had occurred), nor of Augustinian winter (to which its history belonged), but of this poignant earth-affirming fall.

The letters Daren had never received. He had not even known who the woman was, identified in his Journals as "the Girl of Solesmes."

True, in the Prairie years, when he happened on an essay of startling insights: "Greece, the Tragic Myth," the cover blurb set him wondering if the woman he had known might have been that Heloise Frank, if the hours she spent in her hotel room between migraine and the writing she kept as secret could have gone to the production of a work by which he was now so deeply moved.

And later, at the Chicago Ashram, when one of her mystical pieces was discussed, and he learned of the fasting which was her protest and participation in the Jewish plight, he wondered even more, but gave it up as a fruit of the romantic wish.

Silex Scintillans. That dog-eared volume of poems by Henry Vaughan was the first thing he had shown her when she came up to his furniture-heaped attic room. "Certaine Divine Raies breake out of the soul in adversity, like sparks of fire out of the afflicted flint." More a description of her condition than of his. He had given it to her that day, and later the poems of Herbert in The Muses Library. That was when Anna had gone home for the last time with Chuck, and the Hardys saved Daren from solitude with a fortnight of food, sea and sun on the Riviera, where he lounged on the beach memorizing Gothic lyrics, Milton and the metaphysicals, "smit with the love of sacred song." But whatever was driving lashed him on, from the wine of Provence north.

After a crowded all-night train ride and the brief impact of Chartres looming through cold fog, stone prophets leaning out, staring, as through a maudlin rain of regrets—the stern alienation of the soul from time—he was dumped with his bags at the monastery gate in the village of Solesmes, world-center for the Dark Age mystery of Gregorian.

There was no room in the inn, not in the cheap bar or even in the expensive hotel; there was no room in either of the boarding houses; a crowd of aesthetic faith-seekers had gathered for Holy Week. There was no chant until vespers, and how could he hang around for that with no place to stay? He sat on his bags under the projecting church roof while the gray rain fell. The monastery door opened and a visitor came out talking with a priest. Daren leapt to shake her hand and (as she recognized him) to kiss the proffered cheek. It was the expatriate pianist of the Old South, the Signora as she loved to be called, who lived in the Pensione Grabbia d'Oro in Venice. Daren explained his case. "Don't think about it a minute," the Signora said.

She was living in a guesthouse that served as an overflow for the hotel, and it had its overflow too, high up under the roof, an attic into which all kinds of broken and outmoded furniture had been relegated through the years. There was no electricity and no water, but plenty of what might have been called beds. The Signora arranged it with the management, told them to set the lowest possible terms and get Daren some candles up there, as he was a student; then she invited him for dinner in the hotel.

As they walked into the lobby, he saw a girl slumped in a leather chair, absorbed in a copy of Marlowe's *Doctor Faustus*. Something in the intensity of her being related her to Anna from the first, but she was a severe Jewish Anna, thin, unkempt, in mannish clothes. It was not the woman he hailed, but the book; he began to quote the great soliloquy:

"Ah Faustus, Now hast thou but one bare hour to live..." She looked up. She had suppressed whatever beauty she had, so that it had retreated into the solemn depths of her eyes. Those eyes were beautiful; but Daren was fresh enough from the Magnolia State to wish charms more externalized. The defiant plainness of Heloise Frank would have handicapped any amount of spirit.

The Signora moved in with an introduction; so if it had been Daren's custom to pay attention when names were called, he wouldn't have had to speculate all those years about the identity of the Girl of Solesmes. In an accent which pinpointed her problem, she asked Daren to proceed with those true sounds; that he recited like a Greek rhapsode.

For five years he had been memorizing poetry, until he knew anthologies by heart, hundreds of pages; there was no chance of his running dry. So the Signora, who paid for the dinner, got little profit of the conversation; Heloise and her companion joined the party and kept the rhapsode employed.

Until he left for vespers. It was the most moving of the services, but as it involved entry into the cloisters at night, it was forbidden to women.

When Daren reached the gate it was closed. There was no outward light or sign of any performance. He thought he must have got the time mixed up, and walked back to the hotel to inquire. No, they assured him, he was already late. He ran again to the dark portal and knocked. With the click of a magnetic latch it swung open, and he was in a dim court, a great redwood tree towering over the monastic buildings. But he didn't know where to go; there were no lights and nobody to ask—only an eerie sense of having stolen into a dead place for a ceremony that had happened years before. Then the humblest of brothers came by, dumping a trash bin into the box at the gate. *"Que cherchz-vous?"* "The service of Vespers." He pointed: *"Ouvrez la-porte, monsieur, et entrez.'*

A deeper night, vaulted, in which there came to the eye a single candle flickering far off on the high altar, barely lighting a shadowy choir, a containment of dim air liquid with incense, where the black-robed brothers, a darker crystallite of dark, had already taken their places. But before sight could focus on that, or accommodate itself to anything, in blindness and the negation of phenomena, the plain-song had dilated its single line—as if the dimensionless star of the candle had been a point of entry—spinning the spaceless ritual of the soul's rendition. Leflore sank to the rail, the pulsing void become an ether of invisible holy light.

Was not that the reason they had come to Solesmes, all of them, seeking such surrender, but aesthetically, not prepared to pay the other price, which was more than joining the Church—a total abnegation, the fall of the earthly kingdom, the beast-shape in the desert, world-darkness, the plague?—A sacrifice the pseudo-mystic meant to avoid:

The veritable Madame de Tornquist the Signora would introduce him to at breakfast—a romantic pantheist in her youth, Thomist now, who saw Nietzsche as Antichrist tearing her world apart, a world of amenities she repudiated in theory but clung to in fact, as the velvet dress clung to her body, the same evening when she found her way up to his candle-lighted storeroom ("Perfect for a seance") and running her hand up the curve of belly and breasts, spoke of Gregorian: "It stirs me in the secrets of my being"—Daren over the flickering candle where he had risen from his writing, facing the swooning eyes of that antiromantic Thomist: "Isn't it lovely," she cried. "We have all eternity to know God in?"

As Flaubert said: "Some will seek it in the flesh, some in ancient religions, some in art; humanity, like the Jewish tribes in the desert, will adore all kinds of idols." Yet from that Carthage of yearnings the true sacrifice (Ikhnaton from the bed of Nefertiti) might arise; and why let the false obscure the real; why make it an excuse for missing the phenomenon of Heloise?

She had set herself more ruthlessly than Daren could ever manage, even in prison, against all those lilacs out of the dead land.

("What lilacs?" the ghost of Anna impatiently demands; and he: "Mystery pandering to the itch of flesh, the mingling of memory and desire.")

From girlhood she had tried to strip off the amiable person, friendships, chatter, flirting, marriage; in some Joan of Arc deflection of love emptying self for service. The first discipline had been the study of Greek, which would bear fruit in the essay on the Tragic Myth. Socialism was next. Like Daren, like Anna, she took that vision early. But unlike Daren she had given herself to it entirely; and unlike Anna she had been disillusioned and had advanced to a lonelier outpost.

Daren had learned these things since. At Solesmes he knew nothing of her, used her only as the foil for his own rendition—as he must answer Sir Francis Pearce:

> She discovered that I was trying to write, and she was the first to whom I read anything of my own; the first also who attributed a kind of power to me, and such was my creative need that this became for me the central thing about her.

I could describe the scene in my furniture-heaped little garret where I wrote late at night on a verse play called *Justice to Delilah,* the candles the Signora had got me propped all around; I could tell how Heloise Frank came up the next morning, and we sat for a bread and cheese lunch in the mansard window in the sun, looking over the town and the river, and I read her a speech of mystical longing I had just written for Delilah; but it would tell nothing of Heloise Frank, only of my own preoccupation. And all I could remark would be the pity of having been so self-enclosed, of finding no way to such a person—to have had no means of advancing anything but one's own *folle volo.*

Unless a packet of letters addressed (though not for mailing) to the Silex Scintillans who had bestowed the little Herbert and Vaughan implied *communication.* He closed his reply to Sir Francis: "What are the letters I am supposed to explain?"

He flung himself into a leather chair in the faculty mail room. To reconstruct Solesmes in the light of Heloise Frank. It was after her worker phase, when she had gone to live and teach among the miners of Depression France, writing for a Party she refused to join. It was after the Civil War in Spain had called her into the Ambulance Corps of the International Brigade (Daren then in Florence and Anna on the grand tour)—until the brutality she had hoped to blame on privilege broke out like a Yahoo fever in all parties: "The future" (she wrote), "a bait the unscrupulous promise the dissatisfied. Leaders? They are focal points of a violence they could not master if they tried. In the gravity of power they have fallen to the top." It was the experience of Spain that had led her to Solesmes.

There, in the afternoon, walking by the river—how the scene revived, changed by new awareness, a potentiality from some Adonis garden of what might have been; for they had walked, indeed, a minimal brief space, and the suggestions of Daisy, Chaucer bending to a daisied field, marguerite, The Pearl, "dayes eyes in this dales, notes suete of nychtigales," brought up that passage from Blake of infinity opening at the heart of a flower, the throat of a bird, "how from so small a center such sweets come"—but where the actual Girl of Solesmes had shown nothing but a reserved pleasure, a desire to note the source, that bare shell opened now like the gates Og and Arnak fiercely guard: Heloise Frank would face him with the smile of the blind-folded deep-seeing Synagogue in the Strasbourg carving and voice what in fact he would read in her book at the Ashram:

It is always and only through the smallest point, the contraction of here and now, that an existence infinitely removed from the spatial effects its entrance into time: A grain of mustard seed.

As they stood by a curve in the river and the wind blew, grass rippling and cat's-paws running over the water, Daren had puzzled, in the context of freedom, over our pleasure in natural law, a deterministic bondage. The Girl of Solesmes said nothing, the Word within the word, unable to speak a word; though in the garden where the true walk was made, Heloise Frank beckoned now like the Leonardo girl over the water, and spoke what, again, she had only written:

The geological mountains furrowed by streams, shelving limestone, the weight and gravity by which waves break and fall, the solemn order of the world—it was Leonardo who first made that natural bondage the object of our love. It is for us to be as docile to a love which operates under the form of absence, to fall upward into the void, submissive, as clods of a plowed furrow fall. Christianity, the religion of slaves.

In the mail room where he had received the letter, Daren could no longer sit in the chair. He was driven to express the wonder by which the Girl of Solesmes, least real appearance of the shadow-world of Oxford, had, by the systematic estrangement and self-abnegation which were her way, arrived at a reality she could hardly have come to by living—a presence like that in Augustine's *Confessions:* "We two alone, leaning in a certain window."

But to whom could he confess? To answer Pearce with the truth (and there he saw no choice) seemed already in bad taste, to boast of something one ought to be ashamed of. But to tell it around, priding himself on her regard, apologizing for his neglect—it would make him exactly that hound who crawls up, flops on his back, lays out his yard and wags his tail. He did not want to play that hound for everybody. But there was Cader Ayres, poor old dying Cader, with whom he had talked before of modern mystics and the writings of Heloise Frank.

He went upstairs and into the office. Cader was at the desk in his wheelchair. He looked up; Daren gave him the letter; Cader read.—"What are the facts?"—Daren told him.—"It seems hardly fair you should be that 'young Englishman' who has puzzled Heloise Frank's biographers. Are you prepared to play such a role in her life? Have you read the so-called 'Autobiography'?"

Daren had not.

"Reach me that book up there, fourth shelf down, in the corner, just beyond, the green and white paper one," He leaned forward and took it in a bony claw. It's not very detailed, but here's what she says: 'At Solesmes there was an English student who first gave me a sense of the saving power of ritual. He used to come from the service literally glowing with angelic light!'" [1] Cader looked at Daren and twisted his mouth.

The hound wagged his tail…

The hypnotic pulse of the responses, which the seeker had intoned under his breath with the monks, the swinging of a spiritual censer on which the life-blood of heaven and earth depended, the choirs left and right, *"Sancia Maria," "te rogamus audi nos,"* inducing a trance state, negative containment for the soar and melisma that rose in long flights from the alternate ground. Then silence, the little tinkle as the Word again is made flesh, to be answered from beyond the vault, as if the sky itself had broken into pealing, with the three high, three mean, three low of the bells, a triple trinity, then all together, crossing in clamorous changes, while the worshipers file out, as past kingdoms of the dead, mysteriously into light.

Maybe he did shine a bit. Maybe it would have taken a saint to be more transfigured. Oblivious anyway to the small traffic of the temple, over which the Signora would laugh afterwards: glances, contention about seats and prerogatives, the obsequious monk creeping by to check on whether

---

1   *Though obviously suggested by a letter from Simone ·Weil to Father Perrin, these details are freely altered and have no bearing on anything outside *The Half Gods*. See general acknowledgment (p. viii).

the student guests of the monastery were in their right places and that no goat of the outer world had stolen among the hopefully saved sheep. "And did you hear the young man's stomach," the Signora asked, "growling like a bear through the silence of Transubstantiation?" Daren had been praying for a ritual to outlast the fall of the world. So maybe some rays did focus on him, however much it was a flash in the pan.

"That Englishman," Cader went on, "introduced her to the mystical poetry of the English writers. She says she learned the pieces by heart and used to recite them as he had. Here it is: "They gave me the first sense of the life of spirit not as tragedy but as joy. I used to repeat them when I had attacks of asthma or migraine, and it was once, as I reached the last line of Herbert's 'Love,' where God invites the soul: 'So I did sit and eat,' that the Christ came in a visible form and took me in his love."[2]

Daren had sat down, but he got up in a commotion of pride and shame—a satanic office, this, of mystical correspondent. "But I didn't even belong to the Church," he blurted out, as if that cleared the air.

"Both of you," Ayres observed, "might as well have been of different planets. For her you were *un jeune anglais,'* and you never took the trouble to ask her name. Yet somehow she served your ego; and you were a Messenger to her. I find that typical, under such figments to exert such sway."

Cader turned to the back of the volume. "There's something else it's almost a pity to read—from the posthumous papers. I always thought it the most beautiful thing she had done. I don't inquire what bearing it has; even for me it seemed a reminder of something I had lost; though the only upper chamber in my experience was scriptural:

He came into my room and said: "Miserable creature, who know nothing, understand nothing. Come. I will teach you things you never dreamed of."

He led me to a church. It was new and ugly. He brought me to the altar and said: "Kneel down."

"I have not been baptized," I told him.

---

2   The previous note also applies here

He said: "Fall on your knees with love, as if this were indeed the place where truth existed." I obeyed.

He took me away and we climbed to a garret under a mansard from which through an open window I saw the whole town. There were scaffolds of wood and a river where boats were discharging their cargo. He had me sit down.

We were alone. It was no longer winter. It was not yet spring. The branches of the trees were bare, without buds, in an air that was cold and full of sun. He spoke. The light mounted, blazed, diminished, then the stars and moon came through the window, and again the dawn mounted.

Sometimes he was silent. He brought bread from a cupboard and we ate. That bread had the very taste of bread. I have never found that taste again.

He poured wine for me and for himself. It had the taste of sun and of the earth where that city was built.

Sometimes we stretched on the floor, and the sweetness of sleep came over me. Then I awoke and drank the light of the sun.

He had promised me a teaching, but he taught me nothing. We talked of things at random, all sorts of things, as old friends do.

One day he told me: "You must go now." I embraced his knees; I begged him not to send me away. But he thrust me to the stair. I went down without knowing anything, as if my heart were in pieces. I walked the street. It came to me I had no notion how to find that house again.

I have never tried to find it. I understand that he searched me out in error. My place is not under that mansard.

I cannot help repeating sometimes, with dread and remorse, a little of what he said. How can I know if I remember it as it was? I do not have him to tell me.

I know very well he does not love me. How could it be that he would love me? And yet in the depths of my being, something, some part of me, cannot keep from thinking, and trembling with fear, that perhaps, in spite of everything, he loves me. [3]

Cadcr Ayres' voice was so weak he could hardly read. A long time had passed since he had leaned in dusky, dynamic youth over the podium at

---

[3] Translated from Simone Weil, the Prologue to *La Conaissance Surnaturelle*.

Virginia and transformed the life of Daren Leflore. A long time since Oxford when he came on a Guggenheim heading for Athens and Rome (the summer term after Solesmes it was) and had the conversation in Daren's room with Leslie Cameron—the former teacher pitted against the new:

"You'll think me a moron," Cameron leaned his head sideways and struck like a tired cobra; "but I lose track of conversations that go in terms of Faustian, Oceanic, Promethian, Dionysian, Apollonian, Uncle-Tom-Cobleyan-and-all symbolisms. I recognize such fabulous creatures in their stories, but I can't take them as categories. What is a Dionysian culture, or how painful is a Faustian pain? I should have read Hegel and Nietzsche and Spengler, but I shudder away from mystagogs from Germany. And when chaps like Knight start up, I have to clutch the handrail."

"Maybe it's as with calculus," said Cader, "not a question of your liking it, but whether you want to master certain aspects of reality."

"Pshaw!" said Cameron. "Art is a matter of taste, and Symbolism is the fad. Part of the damage Yeats has done."

"If it weren't appropriate to something," said Cader, "Yeats couldn't have swung the trick. Even fads have causes."

"There were partners in the crime, of course. You Americans above all—Hawthorne, Melville. I think *Billy Budd* is fine; but I can't read *Moby Dick* at all. That ridiculous, inescapable whale. I prefer 'The Hunting of the Snark.' I'm a medievalist; I like my devils funny. And Melville's not funny, however he tries. Even with *Billy Budd* it's the story. That absolute Good and Evil leaves me cold. I'm not a Romantic; I refuse to he. I'm a post-Romantic."

"Nice you use those mystago-Germanic terms," said Ayres. "I suppose you do it because they have no meaning…"

A long time since the founding of the program at Patapsco, when Daren and Anna moved into the house on the rock. The College had been so keen and high-souled then; but these last years, in Cader Ayres' sickness and withdrawal, it had slumped like Prairie College to a nadir of bickering and fear, the opportunism which seemed everywhere the educational norm.

As Heloise said, "the gravity of power." The bigger a leader is or the more he tries to transform things, the more he has to come to terms with bright-eyed followers, those ambitious boys who come wriggling in, enthusiastic for just his envisaged reforms. Daren admired Cader Ayres as much as possible (this side of idolatry), but he couldn't agree with him for the sake of agreeing; in fact, he was a damned nuisance at everything that didn't stem from his own creative vision. The dangers on the other side were considerable, as Daren used to communicate in terms that seemed both prejudiced and personal: "Zach Taylor and Starry Wagoner are creeps; you can't trust creeps, Cader, as you're damned well going to learn." What could Ayres do? He had the lethargic body of an old college to revolutionize and he needed committeemen. That was the talent these brainy young fellows had; though it's true what started as a bold and manly enterprise, as it began to flow from their subadministration, orders going out and questions returning for rubber-stamp approval, got verbalized and prissied up, set into a yes-man mold (what are we doing all the time but creating in our image?)—they talking about how organon is related to *ergon,* because what defines an *organ* is its *work;* and how *hyle,* which means *wood,* becomes the *matter* and is equated with *dynamis* as potentiality for an actualizing *Form*—Daren interrupting now and then to their astonishment: "What was least intelligible to the Greeks, 'the blankness of matter, the execration of the gods,' has been made the cornerstone of understanding; that Platonic cave, where men sat watching shadows, has been expanded and exploded to a universe where flesh climbs to godhead by creative toil."

By the time Cader Ayres took sick, Patapsco College was a shell, eaten out from within, dependent on his power. Meanwhile the upheaval of liberal education, breaking with all tradition, had triggered radical discussion and jerky students, sex vaunters, Left-wingers, long hair, bare feet, beards. It would have distressed anybody to feel on what freaks of personality a daring and ambitious program had to base itself. Certainly it distressed the town and state. They were always in a turmoil of reaction against that nest of un-American eggheads. Only Cader Ayres, as if waving Aaron's rod, kept back the sea, caulked the seams, got even that

gang of academic timeservers to man (and woman) the pumps. But when
he himself turned out to be no less threatened, the hulk of a body
dissolving with bone cancer, Wagoner and Taylor were the first to begin
whispering tluough the portholes, looking for somebody they could surrender the ship to, and in return, get themselves hoisted a little nearer the
helm ("Better to rule in hell than serve in heaven").

That was in the spring of '54, when Daren had gone under the cloud
of the first Washington investigation. Ayres began to lose weight and suffer
such aches and cramps that by summer the diagnosis was complete—
myelomatosis, a cancer of the marrow, from which there was no recovery.
The next year he Was on leave, tended by his sister in Georgia. At once
Daren lost his job, public pressure (after the show he made in Washington)
urging exactly what Taylor and Wagoner would have wanted anyway. So
he had that winter to give to his thoughts and his papers, pursuing the
war years, the break of conscience with society. Not that the congressional
investigation had anything to do with the old imprisonment. The inquiry
was into left-wing subversion in science, which in Daren's case meant his
brief period of atomic research, the one "patriotic" thing he ever did. That
was what O'Malley chose to blame him for—convinced that anybody with
a marriage like his and such a trail of fellow-traveling, could throw light
on how the Russians, handicapped by communism, had managed to crack
the secret of the bomb.

Now Ayres had come back, fighting for life. Daren was on the staff
again. He had just received the letter from Sir Francis Pearce and had
run upstairs to share it. Cader, in the wheelchair, held the posthumous
volume of Heloise Frank in the distressing talon of his hand. How could
anyone, face to face with that skeleton in its last human glory (another
holy martyr if there ever was one), not interrupt whatever fabric was on the
looms, Heloise Frank or the crucified Christ himself, strip it off and thread
up for a more urgent weaving:

The central problem throughout had been the relation of soul to
body, of mind to the body politic.

When Ayres had left the Church in the thirties, and then, with the

Patapsco experiment, had undertaken the secular and philosophic reform, he knew he was breaking with whatever cloistered search the Decline of the West might have made imperative. He could still quote from the *Republic,* how the philosopher in a violent time, "seeing the madness of the multitude, and that no politician is honest and there is no champion of justice, is like one who in the storm of dust and sleet which the driving wind hurries along, retires under the shelter of a wall, content if he can live his life pure and depart in peace…" But he had not resigned himself to that; he was acting as if virtue could be legislated in the world. And what threw him back from that militant humanism was not the discouraging turn in the Battle of Patapsco itself, but the deeper foreclosure. When the temporal context on which we most of all rely—body—gave such short notice of eviction, no wonder if he had reverted a time to the faith of his origin.

It was after the first onset, when the bone marrow seemed consumed by wildfire, and the red blood cells fell away, with tissue and nourishment and all. The doctors had given him over. His sister Miriam came and took him back to Georgia; he lay in the upstairs bedroom of the old plantation house (where Daren visited later, on his way to Mississippi). By August Ayres had sunk into the coma that was supposed to mean death; he had gone down into the shadow; then he had rallied strangely and returned with a mystical new shine on his face; it was hard to fix on reasons for the recovery. The Atlanta doctors credited the blood transfusions, along with experiments in radiation therapy, not to mention the fluctuations referred to in clinical accounts of the sickness. But Cader's sister, who had trusted more to prayer than to medicine, attributed the upsurge to the power of faith, and in this reliance she seemed to have taken Cader along.

Miriam Ayres had been stricken by rheumatoid arthritis in youth, and the struggle to come to terms with a twisted and half-invalid frame (and always under the threat of total paralysis) had shifted her from any usual course of southern fashion (to which she had every birthright) into a kind of saintly fervor, compassionate, tender, yearning, but fanatical. Her beauty, like that of Heloise Frank, had withdrawn into her eyes, brown like those of Cader Ayres, but with sudden shadows and lights. What those eyes witnessed was something wilder than the mystical search of Heloise Frank; it was a watchtower of prayer. Miriiam Ayres believed, or as she would have said, knew, ("knowledge of things unseen") that her physical continuance, her very living and moving, was a perpetual victory of faith, an ongoing miracle.

About twenty years ago she had read in Ezekiel: "Make a chain; for the land is full of bloody crimes, and the city is full of violence." She began in her quiet but unfaltering way to put herself in touch with mystical healers in all parts of the world, organizing them into a society called "The Wave of Prayer." She had hit on the notion that all release of energy occurs in resonances of consent, as when cells of the body and especially of the nerve tissue join together in the pulses of will, motion, thought or healing, forming a channel for powers beyond their own; and her aim was to build through the whole social fabric a nerve fiber of communing believers, who by simultaneous vigils of prayer could release such energies as Christ and his disciples must have tapped in the age of faith.

"All summer," Ayres had said on Daren's visit in December of '54, "I lay here dying. I kept my eyes on that maple tree outside the window. There were two clumps of leaves I used to call my boxers, because they seemed to be sparring in the wind. In all that pain I fixed my life there, as the Mariner did on the water snakes. I watched them, while I went down into coma; when I came out on the other side, the rest of the leaves had turned red and were falling. One by one they fell from every tree; but from October into November my boxers hung on, sparring in the winds. I think they were kept green by my love."

They were gone now; the tree was bare. But Cader Ayres had rallied. He had come with Miriam to meet Daren's train—she struggling along with her shrunken legs and elbow braces, neck awry, the intense face raised, Cader, holding her arm and leaning on a cane, each impossibly supporting the other—he lean as Mahatma Gandhi after a long fast, but moving; he had actually persuaded himself that the destruction was stayed, the bone, under a flux of spirit beginning to regenerate. Mornings, he had started to teach in a nearby Negro college—determined through service to justify his healing.

That night there was a prayer meeting around the bedside. Cader formed the center of a spiritual pile. He lay, as Miriam had instructed, in trusting meditation, emptying the conscious self, creating a void into which the healing spirit would be drawn. It was at once an act of will and the will's abnegation. Every egoistic awareness must surrender to the life-tide pouring through the cells, rebuilding the reef-work of the bones. In the room, local devotees had already gathered. What counted in this religion was not birth, education, or manners, but faith. They were led tonight by a Blue Ridge healer who might have got her start in a cult of snake-handlers. She was the first, Miriam said, through whose touch Cader had put off doubt, back in the crisis of August, and yielded to the psychic vibrations. And beyond the walls of the room, unseen but present, spread the soul-net of the society; they were all concentrating, at the same pre-arranged time on the same suggestion, the group in the sick room praying in fellowship with another at the town church, and with nucleus after nucleus over the state and the country—to whom Miriam would write reports of progress:

"Thank you, dear friends in Christ, for the special waves of Prayer on Friday the 19th. Surely *when two or three are gathered together…* It was an unforgettable tryst as we kneeled here to feel the force of your faith converging upon us. The operation of the power was so evident I refuse to be discouraged because the disease has not cleared up all at once. Who are we to set times and seasons for the Lord?"

When the session was over and Cader Ayres had gone to sleep, Miriam talked a long time with Daren about his condition. Faith, in her own case, had cost less. But with this older brother whom she had loved and admired above their parents, she was haunted by doubt. She did not want to betray him to her own enthusiasms.

As she rocked her way across from the stove with the hot chocolate, gesturing to Daren not to move, it was her task; as she took her place at the table and leaned forward, detailing the history of the sickness; as he listened to the soft voice and looked in those searching eyes—he felt the strain between the refined sensible woman and the mystic believer. It was a rack of impossibility.

She wanted proof of what prayer was accomplishing. But medical science offered only its mocking material mask. The doctors refused to share her hopes; the X-rays showed no regression of the malignancy. She admitted to Daren, in a kind of reluctant whisper, that fluctuation was said to characterize the disease.

But she had seen Cader sink into a coma where the doctors had renounced hope. She had called in her own spiritual allies; they had tented in the doubtful field, keeping the vigils by which she herself had been given life and activity all these years. She had felt the breath of prayer pour into Cader's abandoned frame, had seen him revive. She had won him over to believe in his own recovery. She had nursed him through setbacks of influenza, pneumonia, the shingles which right now were blistering the skin off his back. She could not afford to doubt. That would be the last sabotage, simply to doubt. Though in the face of the X-rays, she saw how far faith must ignore other evidence, how utterly the mind in that venture was at sea.

Daren surfaced from her eyes. "But what does Cader think? How can he go on believing, and those X-rays in front of him?"

Her face opened to a deeper trouble. "I haven't shown him the X rays. Whatever else, I saw one thing clearly. His faith was all we had."

"Faith or illusion?"

The eyes flared up with their sad wild light. "Faith! It's working. God saved him once. He will save him again."

Breakfast next morning was a hushed affair. Cader came to the kitchen in his dressing gown and sat by the window, his anemic face in a shaft of winter sun—the blind beggar in Angelico, such peace out of pain. It was a face as deserving the sun's halo as that of any saint painted in art. But what could one say? Daren did not share the faith, and he would not raise questions. He could not even speak honestly of Patapsco. Cader was curious what was going on, how about the investigation, and why was Daren traveling around without a job? Cader's calm seemed already to depend on withdrawal from life, though under the fable of renewing its ties. In grief and brooding Daren took the train.

Thinking how Cader Ayres, one of the keenest critical minds, was caught up and responding to a kind of voodoo—a Blue Ridge Mountain healer backed by a fantastic circle of prayer, people out of touch with his whole humanistic discipline. To look at those women, to hear their voices as they put on their wraps in the vestibule, was to read their thoughts, their style:

"Not a doubt in the world, sister, it's God's hand. All that sloughin off of the bones His judgment on a man who left his preachin and left the church and gave his soul to atheism, riotin in the tents of Sodom and disbelief of the Lord; and now he comes broken for the savin grace of prayer. Well, the Lord has always loved the sinner who repents."

Or the one from whose hand he had taken the first vibrations—off to her mountain mission—who knows?—distributing Bible tracts for the red-headed preacher:

> Immoral garb…indecent exposure… If a woman is not selling her body on the altar of lust, let her get it off the display counter. And now preachers' wives strip off and gad to the beaches in the naked craze. I know whereof I speak. If a preacher dares open his mouth about the bondage of sex and shame, a drunken cursing father, a cigarette smoking, beer-guzzling naked mother, a couple of lost children taught with radio and comic books, they call him an old fogy. But God has commanded him to cry aloud, to chastise the demon of lewdness out of a generation of vipers!

Cader Ayres hadn't been a preacher for nothing. Or conceived the Western world as tearing itself apart, desperate for a new birth of faith, without being in quest of that power. A part of his wisdom had been his freedom from mechanical reductionism. He regarded the laws of nature as fixed habits of a matter which was itself the crystallite of inwardness. If those laws had come into focus in the same way that we feel ourselves coming into awareness in the flow of time, why shouldn't faith—if only one knew where to lay hold of it—move mountains? Maybe his malingering on the plains of Sodom had been too much the historical observer's standing outside creative passion, into which the crisis of body had hurled him, reason and all.

Daren journeyed on to Mississippi to attend the death of Aunt Willi and back to Patapsco to an account of the death of Mom; and all the while the Wave of Healing continued its wakes and marathons of prayer. But the symptoms did not abate, nor the rift between medicine and dream. When cramping spasms of neck and chest came in defiance of the prayer trysts, Cader was taken to Atlanta, where massive X-ray treatment was recommended hy someone who was supposed to know. The radiation, it was claimed, eased the spasms, but immediately hip cramps developed and had to be Xrayed in turn. At this point, almost unbearable pain fixed itself in the head and would not yield to any opiate or drug. The doctor decided on a measure he had never tried; he X-rayed the head, assuming myeloma lesions of the skull were causing the pain. The result was brain swelling, encephalitis; for a couple of weeks Ayres was wildly irrational. To Miriam it was a diabolic seizure for which she had made way by giving those faithless doctors so irresponsible a hand. She fell back almost wholly on prayer.

And again Ayres rallied. He went to his Negro school to deliver the graduation address. He tried to rise from the wheelchair, but fell back. It was impossible. He spoke from where he sat. And now diagnostic X-rays showed spontaneous fractures of the pelvis. Miriam wrote Daren: "I do not know what to do. If I show him the Xrays he will lose hope. But not being able to walk, having to be lifted from wheelchair to bed, has already done the harm. Write him; try to cheer him up. He speaks of you."

Dearest Cader,

We know from what we feel how these setbacks must weigh on you. What can I say? If faith is of the essence for healing, I am a poor healer. I can only sit like old Jerome with the death's head, repeating what you taught me long ago, that we cannot hold God to earthly performance. If I were in your place, I would want to see the X-rays. Then I would read the Devotions of Donne. He looked on death in peace and recovered and lived. Maybe such a wise peace always lengthens the life it has agreed to resign.

Love,

Daren

Dear Daren:

Thank you. I have seen the X-rays. What has kept me going is will, and I can will in the face of knowledge. For whatever time I've got, I might as well be where I can do the most good, and that's at Patapsco College. I'm writing Wagoner and Taylor that my voluntary leave is over. Miriam will come to look after me, with a couple of old retainers to lift the wheelchair. I expect you to teach next year, whatever protests may be made in the college, town, state or nation. "If we are dying," says Thoreau, "let us hear the death rattle. If we are alive, let us be up and about our business."

Yours,

Cader

Easter Sunday, at Solesmes, when the Gregorian service ended and the Bach postlude broke out on the bellowing organ donated by the rich American, it was revealing, in a composer one had thought to admire above the rest, how the soul shrank from that assertive moiling of ego, the tension and resolution of conscious will. That was what Leflore had come to Solesmes to repudiate — to enter the selfless anonymity of plainsong.

How far he had ranged since - he who had spent the last ten years, without even Anna's approval, trying to hammer the links of selfhood into knowledge. Anonymity! He had found the *alpha* pre fix merely privative, not in itself a good, but as absorbed, void in the greater void. And to be so absorbed was not in his election, however much he might have wished to think so.

Like it or not, he was heir to Michelangelo and Milton and Beethoven, to all from Dante to Yeats who had forged Promethean personality. The frothy abuses ("lost and by the wind grieved, ghost . . .") were failures in a high calling. They did not cancel the obligation; and when Yeats wrote, "We were the last romantics," maybe he hadn't foreseen the outbreak of an art from the floodplain of the Mississippi and the Yazoo.

Leflore had waded so deep in blood, he had as soon go over. For others he couldn't say, but for him there was no issue from the petty cult of self, but to make it not petty. When the romantic ego, caught and participating in the energy of its source, should be indistinguishable from the universe of power which it was always trying to comprehend and utter - then it would be cleaned up, proper; one could say it had arrived.

But when would that be? Would it be when all should rise, though all would not be changed?

In life, as in narration, he had strayed from Heloise Frank. Had she found the road of selflessness he had missed; and had it turned out to be, not a cistern of the past, but a birth and resurrection? It had always been birth she was seeking. That had sent her to the Left in her youth, and shied her away when she felt it harden around her, like death. It had led her to religion and kept her out of the Church, aloof, searching. That was the meaning of anti-entropy, not to flow out and set in any of the massive responses and traps which appear everywhere as Success, Progress, the Plalanx, Maginot Line, Nuclear, Defense, Bureaucracy, the Totalitarian State — to heighten desire, avoiding the downstream which is force, yet not drying up; to remain negatively alive.

Yet what if the road sign of life, in an age like ours, should lead into literal death -an immolation? Daren left Cader's office strangely troubled, waiting a reply from Sir Francis Pearce.

Dear Mr. Leflore: I cannot answer in detail; the deadline is before me. I thank you for the information, and trust I may use it. You ask about the letters. I enclose a copy of the last, which I have just translated. As you know, Heloise Frank sailed for England intending to be sent to France for work in the Underground. She died, however, not long after landing, of consumption exacerbated by a semi-starvation diet. This letter, the longest, was found with the rest among her effects.

Silex Scintillans: I have sailed through the gates of Hercules, convoyed toward your island, and it comes to me that I am going, as Gregory said, not among Angli but Angeli, such Messengers as you.

What I am seeking in your Albion, however, is not an actual person any more than in these desert wanderings I have tried to find a road back to the window where we stood. Our meeting is to be of another kind. I am not even in search of the brightness in which you seemed to move, but the darkest of all centers, which our Father, who comprehends the light and the dark, penetrated to change death itself. I am seeking a cross. And already, on the Hill of the Skull which Europe has become, I feel the point of the Nail at the focus of my soul.

Do you know the significance of the Nail? To you of the Light, the world of vision is a pyramid rooted in the dark spread of creation's gravity from God; but it rises to radiance, and at its apex (as in Dante) is the flesh-enfolding point of infinite joy. On the other side is the universe of our alienation, in which we of Darkness have waited since the eternal fall. And it has the same shape, the same pyramid or cone, which is the Nail of our affliction, down which, from the infinitely spread head of God's withdrawal and surrender (the whole created universe groaning and travailing on itself), the blow and pressure of death is funneled and shafted to a point. At that point the Nail is being driven into the soul.

And shall I reveal a mystery which you already know - since, in the upper chamber, the Messenger gave it to me in the mediation of your flesh? Those two points, though seen from opposite sides of the universe, are the same point, one and the same. That is the meaning of the Crucifixion and Resurrection. At that center we are to meet again, as (in the Blakean vision to which you introduced me) Spectre and Emenation clasp in the flame of love.

As I approach that point from my side, I feel you approaching it from yours. May your way be as much of peace as mine is of pain. For surely the death of Christ has liberated some to reach him not by degradation but by joy and light. Therefore I do not follow the scripture to wish for you what I wish for myself. If that be imputed against my charity, I answer with the vision I have seen: Mine is the pyramid of the nail; but yours is the other, for which I have only borrowed names: the lily of Los and Enitharmon, the spire of the rose.

On this ship, where weakness of body grows on me, I am reading the Gospels. And it is strange that the always increasing worship of the Christ who is there prefigured should take in my heart the form of mortal sin - the envy of his Cross.

For her to have placed him among the saved and herself among the lost, when if anything is clear this was, that she was of the elect and he of the damned. Or did the motions, as she pictured them, converge? Were those ultimate points of separation impossibly the same?

3. Conspiracy

Leflore's new bout of teaching did not last long. The second investigation broke out that same October, and Cader gave him leave to answer it. Fall had brought Daren back into the world; right he should deal with the demons of the world.

He had been through the wringer before, but he had not written about it. His mind and briefcase had been full of the other tangle with authority, the wartime one, of which the consequences had been prison. O'Malley kept threatening more of the same, but the grand jury didn't follow through. When Daren had been eased out of his job, the investigation had shot its bolt. He had accepted the winter exile—a note from a timid colleague: "Someday when things are better, let us resume our former relationship"; he had mulled along over the meditations Anna called a waste of time.

Now all that had died in the womb, like the Oxford Journals. He cleaned house and started again; and this session he not only went to Washington and argued, he wrote it down.

He was tempted to begin way back—with the inevitable Critique of Freedom and Tyranny; but before the woods between Patapsco and Washington had shed the last leaves, passion had caught him up and brought him, as never before, to the service of immediate fact.

Though even the immediate had its opening phase, almost two years earlier, with the feint and gambit that preceded the first hearing: "Next time you're in Washington" (the chipper note from someone claiming the Oxford connection), "drop in… A matter of concern."

"Fussing and Bitching Investigators," said Anna. "Don't go."

He went anyway, talked as always, freely, left thinking he had made some palpable hits on the boys; though they boomeranged later, quoted out of context from the tape. By that time he realized he was not among friends.

How could he fail to, when the subpoena came, and he rode down on the bus with Anna, and as they approached the hearing chamber, they saw a Negro woman in hysterical tears, talking to her lawyer and her friends. All Senator O'Malley or lawyer Gold needed to do was to poke their heads out of the hearing room to be convinced of her innocence; but they were done with her. Some prolific informer had recalled her name from an old communist roll, had supplied her an alias and a whole undercover career, and the committee had browbeat her at such a rate she'd hardly sandwiched in a word.

"But it's all wrong," she wailed, "They've got it mixed up somehow. Sure I lived in that apartment house and worked in the signal corps like they said, but I never did any of those other things. It's like I was somebody else. I don't know what the Communist Party is. I never go to any meetings but church meetings. I sing in the choir and try to help my neighbors. And now I've lost my job and I don't know what to do. I never see that woman who says she's in a cell with me. I never been in no cell. I got up from chills and fever to come here, and they scream at me, and I'm so scared, it's like a bad dream."

Daren and Anna were let into the room. But Daren wasn't called up that day. O'Malley was polishing off small fry who had worked on contracts for the signal corps. A woman was on the stand:

"I inspected some kind of finders. Whether they're radar I don't know."

"Of course they're radar. You had to know that to inspect them. What else did you do?"

"I checked coils, I counted nuts and bolts, I worked on personnel, getting people to buy war bonds and give blood, keeping absenteeism to a minimum; I did all kinds of jobs."

"Then why did you put on an application of that date that you were a radar tester?

"How should I know what name to call all that, years ago when nobody expected to be pulled apart for every word and phrase. I don't even remember what I wrote, and I don't think it's important."

"It may be more important than you let on, Miss Kretchmar. You have taken the Fifth Amendment when asked if you were a communist sympathizer in those years. That means a truthful answer would incriminate you, which is a cowardly way of saying yes, you were a part of a conspiracy working to destroy this nation; and you were employed in one of the most crucial and secret areas of American defense…"

The next case was a man who had worked in the same plant, but had finished his doctorate since and was now teaching at Yale. The southern senator, who was always trying to put in an oar, took up that doctor's degree, as if it might be the clue to everything. "Could you tell us, sir, the subject of your thesis?" (Looking around like Dogberry—"Here's that will drive him to a noncom.")

"The title, Senator, was 'The History of Existence and Uniqueness of Theorems in Ordinary Differential Equations.'"

"And it deals with what?" ·

"Well, it's rather technical."

"I see. You would say you wrote a history of the difference in existence and the uniqueness in existence today, and you probably went back to Euclid to bring it up to date."

"Beg pardon, Senator?"

"It's not material." Senator Bourbon looked at the cameras like a comedian waiting for the laugh.

The witness made a serious statement. He had been a communist in college, until he had discovered such rigid formulations didn't fit his world. He would speak of his own political misjudgments, but he would not involve others by mentioning names. None of his associates had broken any law that he knew of; he was not trying to hide the guilty, but to protect the innocent. In this he hoped the committee would respect his conscience.

"Fine sentiments for a communist, mister. But it is not up to you to decide; it is up to us to decide. You will not be allowed to protect conspirators because they share in your crime."

O'Malley set himself to worm out the names of others who had been in the cell: "Are they in war work?"—"No, sir."—"Are any teaching?"—"One, yes, sir."—"At Yale?" No, sir."—"At Harvard?"—"No, sir."—"At MIT?"—"I cannot answer through a checklist of American colleges. That is only aimed at identification."—"In other words, you yourself will decide what to reveal?"— "Who else would, Senator, on a moral issue, but the man who has to act?"

"Very well! Every time you refuse you will be cited for contempt, like all the rest - much as I hate to decimate your university staff."

Lawyer Gold took over: "Did you collect funds for the defense of Mr. Platt when he was accused of being a communist spy?"

"I did. He is a relative by marriage, and he has been my friend. Besides, he was acquitted."

The senator could not contain himself. "It is suspected that funds contributed by communists were used to buy off witnesses. What do you say to that?"

"I refuse to believe it."

Gold again: "You know Platt traveled under the assumed name of Ham?"

"I know that was an allegation which was never sustained. Mr. Platt told me it was ridiculous, and I believed him."

"Who else contributed to this cause?"

"I refuse to give you further names to pursue in such a matter.

The senator: "Are you refusing on the grounds of the Fifth?"

"No, I am refusing on the grounds of conscience."

"Good, mister. Just keep on. Pile up the counts. If you were loyal you'd cooperate one hundred percent with this committee. Why did you yourself knowingly go to the aid of this accused spy?"

"You mean as soon as a man is accused, his friends and relatives have to drop him as if he were guilty? That's a fine doctrine for a courageous democracy, Senator. At that rate there wouldn't have to be any trial at all."

O'Malley: "You may step down. As a courtesy to counsel I may say this case will obviously be submitted to the Senate for contempt, and to the grand jury. Indeed, in the opinion of the chair, this is one of the most aggravated cases of contempt which has come before us. To me it is inconceivable that any university or college would keep this kind of a creature on the payroll, teaching our children. The sooner we get a law to take citizenship away from his kind, the better—claiming conscience to destroy this nation…"

"I would like to make a final statement."

O'Malley and Gold were consulting over their papers. The gentleman from the South wavered: "Make it brief then."

"First, I don't work in a defense plant; second, I don't do any classified work at all; third, I'm not a communist and haven't been for years; fourth, I've never had any sympathy with spying or sabotage. I have always been a lawful citizen. But I am opposed to the spirit of this investigation. Nothing can alter that. I have just come from a lecture tour in Canada, where I was continually asked: How is it possible for a country like ours, an honored country, to give O'Malley such power? I was ashamed."

"You can leave the country if you feel ashamed," It was a statesman later admired who spoke, one of the young aspirants caught in the wave— sure to regret it later.

"What right have you to say that to me? I was born here. I love my country. It's not treason, I hope, to be ashamed of Senator O'Malley."

The senator came up from his notes. "I told that man to step down. What do you mean, Senator Bourbon, letting him speak? Mr. Marshal, remove the gentleman."

He was followed by the mere clerk in an airplane factory, who had been on the outskirts of the radar operation during the war, and whose intense Jewish lawyer got so upset he kept interrupting and being roared down by O'Malley: "We will not have communist lawyers filibuster the proceedings."

The witness categorically denied he had ever been a member of the Communist Party; but maybe he had attended meetings the senator might call "communistic" or "Left Wing."

"List all communist meetings you have attended," Gold demanded in his hard precise way, "giving places and dates and the names of your associates."

"I didn't say I had been to communist meetings. I said I didn't know what you would call communistic or Left Wing. Would it include public meetings? A meeting say at Symphony Hall?"

Senator: "I don't know where you communists hold your meetings. Did you have one in Symphony Hall?"

For the Defense: "He is talking about public meetings, Senator. Lectures."

"Mr. Counsel, you will observe the rule of silence or I will have you removed. I don't want to do that. I don't want to deprive even a communist of legal counsel."

Defense: "He has just sworn he is not a communist."

"Mr. Counsel, this is the last warning."

The lawyer glared and subsided. The senator turned to the witness: "You say you're not a communist. If you aren't paying dues to the Communist Party, mister, you are cheating them out of those dues. You belong to them lock, stock and barrel. I order you to give the names of all who attended Communist Party meetings with you."

The lawyer sprang up: "Senator, I am a member of the American Bar. I cannot sit here and watch this travesty."

"Then you can clear out. Mr. Marshal!" The senator grabbed the mike as the lawyer was expelled. "I will not have this room used as a transmission belt for the Communist Party." And to the witness: "Mr. Arpp, is your lawyer known to you to be a member of the Communist Party? Has he ever discussed communism with you? How long have you known him?"

"I only employed him for this hearing."

"Then you do not deny he is a communist?"

"I know nothing about it."

"Birds of a feather. You may step down. Consider yourself under continuing subpoena."

Just when Daren had built pressure enough to long for his own hearing as a chance to explode, the marshal was advised to clear the room for executive session; the open session would continue at 10:30 next morning.

Daren and Anna went to lunch—everything around the Senate office building boiling with investigation. At their table sat a plump researcher who didn't look as if he could have betrayed anything but a partridge. "Didn't I see you coming out of the hearing?" They began to talk cases:

"A pyrrhic victory. Four years I've fought for clearance, and now I've changed my job. My wife went to a school in Connecticut with that girl who defected to China: 'The Atom Spy who got away,' the papers claimed. 'Does your wife make a practice of wearing overalls?' they asked me. And, 'Is **it** true she sleeps on a board to keep in touch with the common man?' Hammering it home with all those subpoenaed witnesses: 'Have you been in his house? Notice any thing queer about the beds there?' Hell! She slept on a board because she had a herniated disk…"

And from a table across the aisle: "The best man in our plant is only cleared halfway. 'Anything I write down,' he says, 'gets too secret for me to look at.' Investigators!—Paid spies to give aid and comfort to the enemy."

Days of waiting, Daren haunting the chamber, obsessed, watching that gavel grind down on big boys and little boys, clerks, professors, workers:

Union men with foreign names who had already been threatened in closed session and were now to be pilloried:

The little guy who began refusing so fast on grounds of self-incrimination he refused before the question.—"What are you refusing now? I haven't put the question"—"The previous question."

—"You refused that already. Just step down. And send a transcript to his plant. Let him be stricken from the rolls."

When the fellow tried to protest: "No speeches from Fifth Amendment cases."

Lawyer: "May a statement be put into the record, Senator?"

"Counsel is not allowed to speak. If he has guts enough to say 'Yes, I'm a communist,' let him make his statement."

Lawyer: "Are you ruling that he cannot put a statement in the record unless that statement is the confession you desire?"

"Next witness!"

A man like Michelangelo's gray-haired prophet Joel, Bulgarian born machinist: "I'm sixty-five. I've worked thirty years **in** the plant, and I'm put here today to turn political informer or lose my job."

"We aren't interested in your politics, man!" said O'Malley.

"We're talking about conspiracy. Why shouldn't you tell us what you know about that? You don't seem a typical communist. You don't appear an evil man."

"Nobody ever considered me an evil man; but they might, if I squealed on buddies because of what they believe."

"Looky here! You've been mentioned as a member of the Party. You have valuable information. Will you give it to us?"

"I never touched no classified information."

"Mister, nobody's accusing you of being an espionage agent; I don't think the Party would pick you. But if you refuse to give us the names of your fellow communists, you've tangled with trouble."

Someone in the audience jumped up and screamed: "Senator O'Malley, I accuse you of conspiring with the company to take away the jobs of union workers fighting for better pay."

Gaveling. Cries: "Order! Order!" Then the thick voice into the microphone: "Let the record show that the man who made that outburst is L. J. Griffin, who is not here today on subpoena. He has been identified as a communist. He has been given the chance to deny it and has invoked the Fifth Amendment. He has been fired from his job. I guess that disposes of him."

Then the dumbest laborer of all: "I said I ain't no member of no Communist Party."

Senator: "You said you aren't now. I'm asking you how you go about getting out of the Party."

Worker: "What this committee is doin, it looks to me, is not to find subversives, but havin fellows with twenty years' service, like in my shop, thrown out of a job—askin about how to do this and that, and as far as sabotage is concerned—"

Senator: "I'm not asking you about sabotage. I'm asking you how you get out of the Communist Party."

'I don't know nothin about no Communist Party."

"Then say so! That's all I'm after."

Worker: "You don't have to yell."

"I want you to hear. You say you don't know about this and that, and that you want to help this committee, and then you say what you think this committee is doing—trying to throw people out of jobs. I think you are trying to conceal communists."

"I ain't trying to conceal nuthin."

"Not even when you say an answer will incriminate you?"

Scratching his head: "Tryin to say what will incriminate me?"

Senator: "You said nothing you could say would incriminate you. You said it under oath,"

"I didn't say no such of a thing."

"And I still ask how you would go about getting out of the Communist Party."

Bamboozled: "I insert the privilege of the Fifth."

The shaky old Southerner tried to ease things off: "Have you ever thought of going to the FBI and giving them information about the Party?"

"I refuse to incriminate…"

O'Malley roared him off the stand. "Incriminate you to think of the FBI! Let this man step down, and send a transcript of the record to his employer. What kind of cooperation are we getting from that firm? If they fail to cooperate, notify the government contracting agency. Take care of that, Sam."

He faced the press: "At this time I'd like to thank the following laboratories. It may be embarrassing to them to have it publicly announced that they have laid off all the men we have mentioned as security risks or as uncooperative with this committee, but they have cooperated to the hilt, and I want to commend them for their patriotic concern. In the past one got the impression that the high barbed wire around those laboratories was to keep the communists from being disturbed in their work of obtaining secrets; but since we got to work there's been a changeover and at least a beginning of the job of housecleaning… Next witness!"

A man was called who had taken the Fifth in secret session and been reminded that he had a wife and kids, and that he shouldn't separate himself from employment and the whole body of good Americans. Now he was ready to squeal - the chair buttering him up: "Freely admits he was duped; confesses it all; wants to cooperate in every way." When he had spilled out names, suspicions, allegations: "Are you willing to help the FBI with this information or anything else you may know?"—"Yes, sir!"—"What are you doing now?"—"I am unemployed, sir."

"There's a career opening up for you," muttered Leflore, "in the kind of government we're aiming to build."

He was followed by another who had raised similar hopes, but who fell from grace, arguing that a communist had a right to a job as much as another man. That invited the usual question: "If the Communist Party were to give you orders to sabotage, would you follow those orders?"

The fellow met it square: "The answer is no."

"You would use your own judgment rather than follow the line?"

"I would use my own judgment on any order, any item, anything."

"I'm reluctant to praise a communist," said O'Malley, "but that sounds straight. I wish you'd think it over and come in here and be a good American."

The man faced him. "You mean squeal."

The senator banged the table. "When you've shown a spark of independence, I hate to see you backslide…Send in his transcript!"

After the vigilante ingression of the Deep South, Daren had faced such a dread in his dreams. To see it now, seated in the nerve center of the nation, televising itself outward, fascism twenty years after: "It Can't Happen Here"; but "It will," said the Marxists, and it seemed to have come; to see that creeping in from the Right, and to have lived a decade under the zeal of the Left, to have watched it harden the mind of one he was contracted to love—to be so harried from either side shrank life to a margin that seemed hardly more than the rock and cave of private retreat…

The Patapsco, charged from the wool factory with the new detergents, churning the gray water under the dam to balloons of yellow foam, big as cotton bales, which the wind would lift up among the trees, sun struck—the shine of a drowned swimmer, of gangrened limbs, fox-fire, the glow of Sodom from the hills.

There was America, radio, movies, newspapers—a sellout:

Today's beauties are created with bottles, sticks and cakes of color. The trick is Springtime's "Natural Contour." Keep the foundation light for a fragile, more feminine look. Apply Peach-Skin Silk-Tone Powder lavishly over the face and throat patting it into the cheeks, blending out toward the temples, a half-moon at the top of the chin to block out aging shadows. For a rosy blush of lipstick, use our color chart. For glamorous eyes, line the lids with blue pencil. Brush waterproof mascara on the lashes with a light upward stroke; etch the brows in soft feathery arcs, a touch of Platinum or Gold over the tinted eye shadow. One of our matching washes will give a seductive tint to the hair. Avoid hard colors and unnatural lines. The secret of beauty is to be as *natural* as spring, with Springtime.

The movie house around the corner:

Lost Women. Have you ever been kissed by a woman like this? Tenfoot gorgeous Amazon girls. Beautiful, kissable, but deadlier than a black widow spider. Also: Extra Horror Show at midnight: The Hidden Corpse with five cartoons and FREE CANDY FOR THE KIDDIES.

The Federated Church of Laurel County pitching the woo in the same style, the same column: "DRIVE-IN CHURCH SERVICES— For the Modern-Minded. Harvest Moon Drive-In on Columbia Road, Sundays at 9:00 P.M All denominations. Worship in casual clothes if you wish. Rev. K. Fearing Price, with his free *Travelogue of the Holy Land.*

Local politics: Up-and-coming Joe, with the suction-cup mouth and the national aim, running for sheriff and everybody asking why, until a deed comes to light, the owner of the newspaper (the most reactionary in the state) and the crookedest and richest real estate man around, conveying joint ownership in the biggest stretch of undeveloped land in the county, heretofore blocked by zoning laws and the lack of an entrance on the throughway, to accommodating Joe, who as sheriff would appoint both the zoning board and highway commission - a corny job, sheriff, but what does a poor boy planning to run for Congress need so much as a cool half million; or how can he get it if a deal like that (with all the other permits for wrecking and exploiting the land) won't bring it in? Hopes of that caliber to egg him on, and on the other side, if he should lose, political washout, those dear supporters on his tail—you could just imagine how high-toned that campaign was going to be.

Economics: A boom based on prodigality, squandering resources, cold war, a scurf of shoddy housing: that loan service down the hill named for the truest American president, Lincoln, sending out stamped certificates, numbered and signed, with a covering letter: "Come on in. It's time to rid yourself of financial problems. Mail or bring your CAREFREE Loan Certificate immediately, and get money for all your needs." Sending that broadside out to teachers even; so that one hurled it with a curse into the wastebasket, then took the trouble to get up, pull it out, write on it and mail it back (though one had better things to do) : "Solve money problems by borrowing money? Teach your granny to suck eggs."

The cold-war nation pumping lies through all its departments: "Spy plane shot down…"—"No! Routine flight. Unarmed. Communist aggression."—"What? Pilot confesses overflights! Well tell another lie." As **if** the Big Lie had become the tactic of that government of, by and for somebody called the People—of whom Hitler: "Repeat a lie often enough and they'll believe it." And every day, as in wartime, crappy double-talk poured out like hog swill: "Army's authority on germ warfare says: act of barbarism to deny American troops use of biological weapons, since the new germs and gases make earlier war child's play."

What was to stand against it? Ayres in Georgia out of the race.

The college, with Zach Taylor and Chuck Wagoner, hotfooting around the brazen calf; even the good old philosophic pursuits gone dry; Aristotelian Zach briefing them on the *Ethics:* "In the realm of morals the end will be action. You proceed by stating what the end of moral action is, and then you inquire the means. And the means too will be an activity, just as the end won't be a terminal point separable from action. Only then, when you've talked about goals and circumstances (ends and means) can you begin to do more than demarcate an area…" And Chuck chiming in: "You mean in the nonconnotative, the cognitive sense: that you derive from the right rule which is involved in the moral virtue, but isn't manifest until it's drawn out in action and applied by the prudent man…"

And God save us, here comes a Foundation with more cash to spend than would have maintained the whole of Renaissance art, and it pours a fortune into something called the Advancement of Education; so climbing Zach invites one of the chief projectors to give them the dope, and first he distributes a report in colored type on fine paper soon to be broadcast to college mailboxes all over the country, seventy-five costly pages, and proceeds to read aloud a half-hour of its most essential jargon (education hanging on this poor language of ours, so easily whored and corrupted):

> By programmed instruction I mean the kind of learning experience in which a "program" takes the place of a tutor for the student, and leads him through a set of specified behavior patterns designed and sequenced to make it more probable that he will behave in a given desired way in the future—in other words that he will learn what the program is designed to teach him...

Education for democracy. With a vengeance.

The students, of course, still made a core of rebellion—volcanic life. They burned Zach Taylor in effigy when he was appointed dean and were always moaning for Cader Ayres and the good old days. The New Left, or Beatnik Protest, or whatever else it should be called, was stirring among them. They would persuade Daren to join them in a trip to the research lab for chemical and biological warfare out at Frederick, where they would stand all day protesting for peace. But at what a cost of internal and psychic disruption the salutary flurry was maintained. One had thought of baroque palaces, the whole courtly manner, as requiring a lot of misery to keep up its gilt and sarabands; but in terms of human dislocation, soul after soul beat up and thrown on the dump derelict from the strain, surely no civilization was ever so costly as ours.

Being confessor-favorite to whom students came for disburdening, Daren had caught hell-glints enough rising from those depths.

Suppose the ostensible modern Knack was more or less that of Restoration drama, easy sex, to sail those tragic seas lightly and without any keel. "Look, Mom, no hands!" They would fling them up carelessly; and the next moment crash into some ancient crippling wall.

There was the comic surface, of course, the slapstick of Daren's student days, but looser and wilder, hinting at the overthrow of old values and the new unformed. "Victorian virtue," Ayres had said, "rested on class. Whores took up the pressure. It's equality now and coeducation. Which means free love. Let the students deal with it. I can't make mores for the world." Student law was instituted, student police, student court, a little Robespierre Republic of Virtue, on paper; but in the flesh, the dance went on.

Case in point: student model in A.B.C.'s life class—got the notion he was in artwork. One day, drinking and sporting in the girls' common room, he decided he needed a shower, and instead of adjourning to the men's dorm, he walked upstairs, stripped the body-beautiful and began squeezing into the showers where the girls already were. They were squealing and having a gay good time, until one fat spoilsport who had been teased downstairs as belonging in Plato's hog state, came into the bathroom. If only she'd notified the proper student authorities, it would have gone down the drain like everything else, but she boiled over to the dean. The boy was expelled, and enforcement for a while reverted to the faculty. It got so tight the boys could hardly visit in the girls' rooms without permission; and when the little daughter of a teacher came for her guitar lesson (she studied with a coed on the third floor) she had to send her name up and wait for clearance. Her name, though, was Sandy, which was the name of that shower-loving model-boy. "Lord," the head resident thought when she got the message, "that Sandy guy is back for another bath." So Sandy girl had to cool her guitar a spell until her identity could get straightened out.

The comic mask was on—comedy, since Balzac, being *La Comedie Humaine* and bitter.

Eve Gwynne and Cyril Page, lovable pair from that most romantic of all freshman classes two years before, totally enamored, who came to the poetry group one night with the older students, were served a little glass of *"Est Est Est."* The cut-rate liquor store had got some at a bargain and Daren had laid down a couple of cases. He told the story as they sipped, how Barbarossa's courier used to go before as he headed for Rome and Naples, to test the wines and mark the best inns with chalk on the door: *"Est"*—"This is it." Until he came to Montepulciano and drank so much and got so emphatic he scrawled on the door: "*Est, Est, Es*t"—which they've called the wine ever since.

Next day Eve and Cyril came along, wondering if they could take Leflore's path into the park for a picnic. They had their little sack of brown bread, bologna and cheese, but as for wine, they had tried Abe's Liquor for that *Est Est,* and Abe said Mr. Leflore had bought it all. "I didn't mean to get a monopoly," Daren said. "I'm sorry. I'll give you a bottle."—"Oh, we couldn't take it that way. But let us buy one." So the dollar and the wicker flask changed hands. The picnic passed sweetly; the kids knocked on the way back. "Thanks. It was lovely." They strolled on, arm in arm, barefoot, carrying their shoes and socks and the flask, which was still half full.

Near the courthouse, they met some student friends. "What you got there?" They told the story. A husky, loud lad raised the flask for a try. Cops rushed in from all sides; the kids were minors. Daren had never thought of the law. "Where did you get the booze?"—"our tutor sold it to us," cried honest Cyril Page.

When Daren heard they were in jail, he went to Cader. "Here's my resignation. And now I'm going down there and tell the judge what happened."

"For God's sake," said Cader, "take it easy. I've talked to the judge. He'll give them a suspended sentence. It'll he hushed up. Don't rock the boat."

They sailed on lightly, and with no keel at all. But the shores were mounded with hulls and drowned swimmers. Eve and Cyril, before long, were bound to hit it worse, to capsize with others, the pick of that dreamy class: "I have been faithful to thee, Cynara! in my fashion"—the *fin-de-siecle* cult of decadence willfully revived. Go down! Down, into those twittering depths.

Of a score to withdraw, bust out, be expelled (pregnancies, drink, dope, nervous breakdowns), fix on those two: Cyril, bubbling with mystical urges, always ready to join the peace line at Fort Dietrich, standing in bare sandals through the first snow, so he came down with fever and hysterical paralysis and couldn't do his work for weeks; dark-eyed Eve, as flown with love of man and equality of races as if she had just come from Brook Farm—using all that soulful power to lure and deny, or more destructively grant—until Cyril took the sleeping tablets, and, barely saved, was sent to subdue his psyche in narrower confines; Eve, during the intervals of going over to walk with him in the sanatorium woods, becoming a focus of other ardors; so that when she ran off with Bill Rudge, orphan, with a Van Gogh cast of head (and of passion too), who had surmounted the slums and every satanic handicap to get to college and now threw it away—who could tell if in fact it was his child which had precipitated the marriage?

Go down into that circle of revolt, ideal self-wasters, *"Piangendo là dove' esser de' giocondo."*

Daren had received a letter from Cyril, enclosing one from Eve:

[Cyril to Daren] There was a guy in high school she was supposed to love but got physically sick if he touched her. He came over to college once and raped her. Afterwards she blamed herself. Thought she had some disease of soul that lured and infected. She took men and despised them. Rudge used to get drunk and come to her in violence, then break down, a strong man who weeps. She told me everything the day I tried to kill myself. I think that closed a door for her, one of many doors. She has written me from Washington. Here is the letter. You have been good to us and we trust you. She needs help.

•

[Eve to Cyril] I told Bill about you in June. He has not been alive since, And I too died with him. I was the only person he ever trusted.

The guilt of you and him. For I have killed you too. When he comes home tonight I will have to tell him of this letter and it will all start again. He used to hit me, throw me down, burn me and then try to kill himself to see if I would stop him. "Why don't you go to Cyril?" he would say. "He'll take care of you."

The baby is called Absalom. I will take Absalom down the street and mail this, and then Bill will come home and I will tell him. I killed him. Have I killed you too? Sometimes I cry and scream and hit my head because it hurts with the guilt. Would I hurt Absalom more alive or dead? I have a curse on me. Everything I touch dies. How is it possible that so early in life I should have begun to hurt and hurt?

I am slowly losing my mind. I go to work every day, come home, feed Absalom, clean house, sleep, go to work again. Though I do not believe in God, I pray to be washed of my sins. Then I wish you and Bill would meet and kill me. Would insanity bring me ease?

And now my quivering fear is all at the surface. Do you hate me? Your letter makes me feel that you do. And yet the times I don't feel old and worn out, I feel so terribly young, and in a way, innocent. Destroy this. Love, Eve

Maybe that maelstrom of the student soul was the same Daren had circled twenty years before: but it had changed in style, like the shift from Greece to Rome, like his own life—the relation to Anna—darker and fiercer. America too had suffered a style change, from Roosevelt and the New Deal to O'Malley and now. A Fall of Man.

Daren and Anna were standing in the bar of Hall's old waterfront restaurant in Washington, the copper spit-trough underfoot, more like a urinal than a proper fixture. The place was a relic of the Gilded Age, Steamboat Gothic, when politics was more primitively clawed, chawed and swilled over than now. There was a floor show in those days and gambling, as in wild West movies, and upstairs a bawdy house. Many a backwoodsman come to town or country politician must have waked up there with a mammoth headache and a charge of guilt, bewailing what he had lost and more what he might have picked up. So the painting that filled the wall where the stair had given access to the whores was appropriate—a huge oil of the Expulsion, or rather the moment of realization after completion of the Miltonic sin. That original Eve was stretched on the grass in the most voluptuously "had" position; Adam, risen above her, had clutched and was beating his head with knotted, penitent hands.

Daren stared at the picture, thinking of his own commitments, the headlong self-deception of the Oxford years, gorging the fruits of a garden of love and appeasement. As he downed his sherry he seemed to be clenching his own threatened brow: "What a headache! My God!"

Though if O'Malley had put squarely what he often seemed to be hinting at: "Why haven't you left the woman?" Daren would have justified his sticking, not just on personal but on political grounds; he would have vindicated Anna's troublesome causes: "Something's going on in the world whether you recognize it or not. To call it conspiracy doesn't reveal why all those people want to *conspire,* which in Latin means 'breathe together.' I don't want to hedge my understanding any more than birth and loyalty have already hedged it."

Like Milton, he would uphold the Fall.

Besides, Anna had just come from her own hearing, her first and only summons. It was when Daren had been at it for weeks and must face it again. He didn't know how Anna would stand up or what foibles of a dedication he had never much inquired into might come to light. But she had carried it off so much like a lark—as always at her best in action—that he had brought her to Hall's afterwards to celebrate with a drink and clam pie. How much better her disciplined collective stood up under fire than the eruptive members of that amorphous unrest to be called (God knows why) the New Left.

Though Anna had been lucky. O'Malley was out of town. The lesser senator had tried to take over, but she had snatched the reins from his doddering hands and run the show, dodging questions and blurting out what she had to say, so knowledgeable and lively she soon had the audience laughing on her side:

"Don't tell me how to answer. I don't even like your questions, and I certainly won't adopt your answers. If you subpoena me, you aren't going to get an echo."

"You have been asked if you are a member of the Communist Party. Do you intend to answer?"

"I answer in the words of Bernard deVoto: 'It's none of your damned business what I think, with whom I associate, or with whom I have love-feasts. You aren't elected to tell the people what to think. It's for the people to tell Congress what to think.'"

"You refuse to answer?"

"Yes, and I'll give you my reasons, apart from the First, Fifth, Ninth and Tenth Amendments: I won't become a stool pigeon to further your political purposes."

Anna's voice was drowned under the pounding gavel. She gave the chair her look of total innocence: "Are you afraid to hear my reasons?"

"I'm getting tired of your contemptuous attitude."

"You'd better get used to it. I have nothing but contempt for this committee."

"Madam, we are carrying out our painful duty to investigate, to know the facts before we make the laws."

"The biggest hoax ever put over on the American people. You aren't interested in facts. You're here to accuse and punish. Go ahead. I scorn you. You aren't even a duly constituted committee. Two of you are from states where a considerable portion of the electorate is denied the right to vote, in defiance of the Fourteenth Amendment. You're not even legally elected congressmen."

The southern jaw dropped. "That's a deliberate untruth, and you know it."

"Then cite me for perjury. I'm under oath. You're not legally elected. No wonder you want to deny me my right of opinion and association. If my opinion was in, you'd be out."

"You've not been called to question the legality of this committee."

"Is this a hearing? All right. Is it my hearing or yours? Then I'd like to be heard."

"You can be heard answering what you're asked."

"Stop interrupting me. I'll answer my own way."

"If this is what you call answering, I withdraw the question."

"Why don't you withdraw the subpoena and I wouldn't have to answer at all."

In the heat of the argument, Anna had overreached herself. Why should she have cut off what she was evidently enjoying?

•

As for Daren, he had imagined his hearing in a more earnest vein: he, and O'Malley standing at the bar of justice where ultimate issues are weighed, O'Malley forever spotlighted there, the bogy and ranter he was, Daren in the true armor of the knight on his father's tomb:

"Very well, Senator" (thinking he could meet that cat-and-mouse game by speaking honestly as far as he would, and stopping when it seemed improper to go on), "I'll give it to you straight, though you have no right to ask. I never joined anything at all, not even the Church, much less a totalitarian party. I'm not the joining kind. But if it were a question of choosing between you and the communist friends whose sincerity I have admired, I would rather be sacrificed to their vision than to your deceit."

By the time Daren took the stand, he had been so sucked down, whirled and beat in the crisis of the eternal hearing, there was little likelihood the actuality would be as forceful as the dream. And then one day, after the most ridiculous exchange in weeks of waiting, his call came.

"Mr. Klein," committee lawyer Gold had been saying, "I want to be frank with you. We have an allegation here made to one of our investigators. We cannot reveal our sources, of course. It states that your mother-in-law, Mrs. Fried, and I quote: 'has been lying low as a communist for some time, and is now getting into the peace movement. I wonder if you could comment on that."

"What are you talking about?" the man blurted out. "My mother-in-law is dead. She died eight years back. Before I ever met my wife. Is that what you call the peace movement? Is that what you call lying low?"

"Witness dismissed," O'Malley roared. And to Gold: "Don't waste time with these petty cases. Get to the real thing. The atomic conspiracy."

"Daren Leflore . . ."

4. *The Rift*

In the solitude Anna had left by her withdrawal, the arguments that had filled their years went on sounding:

"When you argue with me, you don't understand I'm not just myself. Behind me are the masses everywhere, in Russia and China, Africa and Burma, all those struggling people this government you call a democracy keeps down. Their power is in me; so I'll be right in the end."

Before the threshold of her Oxford appearance she had begun to vibrate in him, and she would go on, a damped wave, spreading and reflecting through space and time:

"How can anybody be happy in America today, with all the lies and corruption? Deterioration is going on at all levels, and fast. This sick old ruling class trying to hold their seats on the coach."

She was like one of those dreams you have before you wake, so compelling you want to set it down, but it melts as you cross the room, and by the time you get to your desk and have pen and paper, there's nothing to record.

Yet she was in him still, an amorphous power.

"There you are planted in the ground of my soul, and why can't I bring you to life?" He got up and called into the hollow room: "Anna, you are a dead thing."

And always, as in *The Duchess of Malfi,* the echo would come back altered: *"You* are a dead thing."

"If you could understand myth," Leflore told her, "It might help. I mean the Garden." (They had been talking about the roots of war.) "'Throw out the kings,' said the Age of Reason. They couldn't believe ordinary middle-class folks would perpetuate such a madness. So they got rid of the Old Regime, and the wars got bigger. 'Throw out the bourgeoisie,' said the workers. And you still believe it—that those people's democracies won't fight. With the Russians armed to the teeth and the Chinese out to catch them. Why they'd be at it now, if they didn't have us to growl at."

"They'd better be armed: the revolution isn't over yet. That's why there are wars."

He shuffled, and came up with his old "Studies in the Future":

> War is not, as socialists have taught, a thing forced on the many by the unscrupulous few. It is the integral of all particular drives and prejudices, a release for pressures that in the primitive world set every family against its hillside foe.

"Talk about the Garden! You call that an explanation?"

By explanation she meant cure, something to stand between her and the bomb. Suppose Daren turned it to a joke: "Make a little sun of us: unto us a sun is born. And his name shall be Wonderful" No Seventh-Day Adventist could have been more shocked, "Why not?" he would say. "World-spirit is plugging in and out of us like a telephone operator plugging into phones. BOOM! Old Rocky Face pulls those connections: PLOP—the whole damned earth—and starts plugging in some more. Plenty of sockets. 'Try the dwarf companion of Sirius; try the Hercules Cluster; try the galaxy in Andromeda.'"

Nothing shook her like a joke in the wrong place:

"Money brings problems, doesn't it?" the Quaker neighbor laughed, figuring his income tax. Anna could hardly get home to go off like gunpowder: "Nobody in the world ever said such a thing but somebody rich, who doesn't know what a problem is. If it's so painful to him, he can give it up, can't he?"

Daren: "For the Lord's sake. Suppose he'd said, 'Dogs bring problems'—that brute of theirs does. Would that mean he'd got to get rid of him? Be human."

"You mean, be upper crust."

Yet a joke—or even a symbol—could be admitted on her side. "In the doctor's office," she said (for she had been troubled with insomnia), "I read about an experiment on rats. They put them in a pen of numbered squares. A normal rat runs around, crossing all numbers. But the disturbed rat creeps into a corner, cowers and craps. Only the magazine said defecates.

"You're that emotionally disturbed rat. You crouch here all the time spinning some spidery stuff from your own bowels."

He faced her unblinking gray-blue. "And Marx spent his life crapping in the British Museum. That's what distinguishes a man from a rat—progenitive craps. You know what A.B.C. told me? Once in Spain a little brown boy about as big as a fishing worm was watching him paint. *'Cago en la cara de Dios,'* he said, 'I shit in the face of God.'"

"I don't get the point," said Anna. Daren smiled: "And in Delta Landing, when the circus elephant broke loose, and Uncle Caldwell next morning was in front of his cabin staring at an enormous pile of elephant do: 'What's the matter?' said Uncle Hazlewood. 'Don't you know what that is?' — 'I know what it is,' says Uncle Caldwell; 'but I don't know what to do about it. I was studyin whether it'd be better to move that, or move the house.' Now with a real creative crap in the face of God," Daren concluded, "you'd as soon move the world."

It was from that same doctor's waiting room that she came, excited about the spread of resistant venereal disease among teenagers. "They want to vaccinate everybody. Prepare them to be promiscuous. A society of horrors."

"I thought you believed in free love. Why take risks?"

It shunted her onto the old track. "'Better change society than have a vaccine. The reason for venereal disease is the position of woman."

"You catch it in any position."

"Be funny. You know what I mean. Give women an equal place. You end prostitution, and that takes care of venereal disease."

Centuries off the beam, back with Blake: "How the youthful Harlot's curse… blights with plagues the Marriage hearse." To lead her down to the Indian Spring and wash her lids: "Teenagers don't do it for money; they do it for joy, Blakean joy. As Cader says: equal, classless, no prostitutes to take up the strain. This venereal disease comes from what you want, the liberation of women."

Sick of those interminable discussions: art, freedom, life:

"Good-bye to all those Faulkners, Eliots, Williams, Salingers, Capotes, Millers. They sold out to violence, novelty, sex. Ash-can books. But the question is survival. That's creative—to be turned toward life—hopeful—growing." She stretched up her lovesome arms.

And where had she come from but a book club harangue by the author of *Disarmament Now:* how all the energy going into weapons should be turned to making a better life for everybody. She sat in the wicker chair and began to read from her autographed copy: "Listen to this…"—truisms she had been telling herself for the last twenty years.

Daren more and more confined himself to the handful of books for a lifetime: the Bible, Homer, Plato, Dante, Shakespeare, Goethe—Trust not every new unfledged companion. Anna, browsing over everything, fastened on a hard core of limited editions from the Vanguard or Masses in Motion Press, jackets in red and black, with a clenched fist maybe, and blurbs sporting foreign names in ecstatic praise: "Throbbing with life," "The vision of a better world," "Laughter and tears of a people," "A poetry and strength rare in America"—how a child of old Poland, or China, or Czechoslovakia woke up to exploitation and class war.

And you opened it and found:

His back is bare. Someone is lashing him. A swine's head with little evil eyes and a broad snout.

The blood of a people, erupting even into neo-Shelleyan verse:

> Imprison us, you tyrants,
> Lash and mow us down;
> New fighters spring untiring
> From the blood that sows the ground…

Blood! The blood of every wound. Greben's blood. They are lifting him in a robe of red, a robe of blood, lifting and singing, all over the world: Long live the Revolution!

"Let freedom reign, Amen." Leflore invoked the satiric antithesis, e e cummings, "a small violet-colored nuisance"—less costly to the world.

Once he reminded her of Hank Brown, shinnying from his mulberry tree to take Mickey Finns to the customers in his aunt's bawdy house. Anna was beating the tom-tom for some *Pages from a Worker's Life* (torn by the White vultures from his liver), where Fuchik tortured never broke: "Farewell, friends; be on guard! And O what a crop will rise from this frightful seeding!"—

"What did Hank Brown have on all these Grebens and Fuchiks who hardened into hate? A sense of humor? Some grace?"

"That grace," she said, "is opportunism—to sell out to the society that perched him in that mulberry tree, crapping like a jaybird."

"Hurrah for opportunism," said Leflore; "and down with consistency that turns a man into a beast."

But where was Hank Brown anyway? Out of range.

Sometimes Daren wondered how naive she thought he was, or rather he despaired of getting any answer to such a question—whether she was trying to pull the wool over his eyes, or was herself that rhapsodically out of touch.

When he saw no other way of communicating, he used to leave her a note on the kitchen table (for it seemed the question in black and white might stand more chance of getting across than in the volatile evanescence of voice), as when she shared in a Quaker drive for world peace:

> Do you feel the ambiguity of working for peace with those who don't know of your political alignment? You use their religious sacrifice to advance a formulation which would be repugnant to them. Isn't this what the capitalist press rather aptly calls "subversion"? Every time you link their peace with your regime, you narrow the ground between the cliff and the wall.

For a week she was writing answers and laying them on his desk, but they didn't meet the problem. Either they were for the comfort of her own soul, or they banked too much on the simplicity of his. She could have silenced him by saying she had gone beyond good and evil, that the old dispensation must fend for itself; but her materialism had lost resilience, no longer dialectic but sentimental:

> You have been taken in by the capitalist myth that communists "use" people. The capitalists have done that so long they conceive life that way. Whereas we meet at the level of love, for the good of man. If we disagree at other levels, it is not important. Socialism is a process. The many must want it before it can come about. It cannot "take over." It never forces itself. That is the capitalist myth.

When they had both lived through revolution and class war and the Dictatorship of the Proletariat—terms not invented by the capitalists at all, but by Marx! After the Russian purges and the Spanish war and the betrayal of Warsaw and the Czech massacre did she think that "working with Love for all mankind and for the Beauty of Life" was going to mean much? "Read the *Manifesto*," he answered. "What is all that hate doing in there?"

For the wisdom of her heart and the truth of her body to be so moiled by high-mindedness—the woman question and the scandal of capitalist sex:

"Writers now have a myth about man and woman: some mystical business about light and dark and the elements of fire and water. As if good women were passive and bad women active. That comes from the bourgeois structure of the family—all those parasite wives, selling themselves night after night to a man they don't love…"

(Making a living out of a pretty indifferent product—Mrs. Schultz, the plumber's wife, who gave crummy Joe Jones a room for tending the furnace when he was working his way through college; and as he crept down from his garret one morning, he heard her twang from the bedroom: "You want to use me, Mr. Schultz, before I put my drawers on?")

"So they pay. Pains, discharge, always going to the doctor. Then he gets corrupt: a thousand bucks for an exploratory…"

(They were back in the Garden; all the ills of life from the tree of money.)

"Well," her face took a pensive look, "it's a tremendous job to arrange a society where men and women can live in harmony."

"A tremendous job for any man and any woman to do it in any society; and when they do, 'a joy to their friends and a grief to their foes' (for it's as old as Homer: *malista de t' ekluon autoi)*, the strategy should be studied. But you would discount it as a product of bourgeois morality and old religion and corrupt investments."

"Sleepy old donkeys who help each other scratch. That's your stable marriage. And you can't see how worn out it is, because you shut yourself in this little cage of false society."

(Slide out under the parenthesis: "This cabinet is formed of gold/ And pearl and crystal shining bright,/ And within it opens to a world/ And a little lovely moony night."—Beulah)

"If you want to write, you ought to get straight on the woman issue. Feminism's got no right to be out of date just because it's in Shaw. But weaklings gave up. It took energy, same as socialism. And America got tired. Then advertising and the mass media took over, Luce, television, Hollywood, pushing glamor, hair, fingernails, foam rubber breasts for ten year olds, get them a man. And the novelists, afraid of politics, hawked sex and more sex. Woman got shoved back into the house—all those machines and the same old cooking and washing, and to be mother, and bedmate, man's luring little bedmate.

"Fluffy mannequins. My mom was a heroine beside them. Since Madame Bovary, woman has been cut to size. If I were a man, I wouldn't want a passive woman, but someone who could take hold of life with a knowledge of the forces... A socialist woman. Anything else would be too little for me."

"Look Anna. You talk about the female, and to get straight on the woman issue. And then you go for a little bustling ideology, the last assertion of the strutting male. It's cut off from the all-mother, from everything of the night and water. What if its human aims are just? The Eternal Female was never so betrayed."

She bent her head. "People talk too much. The world is a huge talking machine—words, and ninety-nine percent confused, useless. I'm not interested in occult notions. I mean the place of woman in society…"

The dry mills of talk, grinding. Where was the smile of Francesca, the pool of Undine?

She would prop her elbows on the kitchen table, wreathe her fingers in her hair and gaze at him with the mystery of a sphinx; but the questions that came out made Pilate not want to stay for an answer:

"It seems all life is art, forever changing, shaped according to our freedom; but freedom, what is that?

"I have to be careful now, because you're my teacher and I want to get it right; I'm thinking slowly, carefully …

"All this talk about freedom—our critics—saying the Soviet artists aren't free; how can I put it?—they're half-men, those critics; they don't understand society has bought them with that empty freedom they talk about."

A tragic mask. To see that wishful wonder self-betrayed and time-perverted. A phrase from Yeats began to stir under the surface: "because of her opinionated mind."

"Here in America there is only one freedom, to keep the ruling class in power."

She leans, her butt billowing over the kitchen stool. No desire is worth the price of silence:

"I get tired of theories of America that don't take account of you and me. You oughtn't to go on year after year with the same old formulas. Not even smart Marxists believe them that way."

And now she burns: "Of course, I should shut up, be the wagewife. Well, what about my freedom? I've got stuff in me, might be philosophy, poetry ﹍ ﹍ Oh, I could tell a thing or two… About the unsatisfied dreams, nameless impositions, curses, brutalities, hungers, beaten resignations… Make a book way above this middle class stuff, maladjusted women, boring bed business… But I grew up to be exploited for your freedom, your art."

If this was the fruit of poverty, she was her own best argument. Doubly deprived.

"What do you want to do with that freedom you think you'd lose under communism? Write your private dreams? Have private tantrums? Outside life. Afraid of life."

And now the Yeats which had been laboring toward the surface broke through and undermined even the theory of poverty. It was "Out of the mouth of Plenty's horn," that Yeats' lovely woman bartered every good, "For an old bellows full of angry wind." Deeper than deprivation. What were the seeds of that pain?

It was hate, the river of hate. She was dipped in it from earliest time. The salamander that lives in fire. "You talk about love. All right. No doubt you feel a fierce kind of love. But it carries hate as its shadow, like bodies in the light. Like that Black and White violence where I grew up.

"You and the other Anne split apart, Left and anti-Left, each accusing the other. You think I want to spend my life on that kind of a rack? You think the world does?

"There has to be a peace and a decorum. And I'll find it if it means pulling my horns into my own skull…

"If you want to peddle that stuff, do it in your part of the house, and leave me this table down here."

On the table, papers, where thrusts and counterthrusts jockeyed, seeking an abstract array:

The other Anne: What she shared with Anna.

Origin: Lithuanian father, Bohemian mother, immigrants.

Poverty: Father asked on forms how his father died, didn't know; asked a relative: froze to death.

(A fate that was almost theirs those winters out of a job on the barge-boat tied up off the lake, the wind stretching the waves into ice; until he got work and the barge docked in the river not far from Anna's…)

Dreams: Reading the Bible, talking of being nuns. ("In the end;, the other Anne would say, "we both took vows. But knowing her, and reading Marx, I expected her to pull apart, like a wishbone."

Where they diverged:

The other Anne: "I had a father and I grew up by the lake. Maybe that made the difference. We were ragged, too, and short of food; my mom wept peeling potatoes, and they called me a slob and a Bohunk in school. But we didn't keep stewing about why somebody else had more. I remember walking with my father on the winter lake shore getting driftwood for the fire. Maybe I had big sad eyes and bare legs, and my hands were cold, and we needed fuel. But I loved those times together by the icy lake."

She had entered the Church when Anna veered to the Party, had become a teaching sister, joined a mission to Europe after the war, until a perennial mysticism related to Bergson, Hinduism and Tao had weaned her from dogma; she followed a married sister to Baltimore, heard news of Anna, and used to come over to Patapsco to see them.

She had been in touch with relatives in Lithuania and Bohemia. Her mother's people were being squeezed off their land, old people over seventy working in communal fields, children sent to munitions factories. They got word to her in Germany by a priest: "Don't send any more packages. It makes trouble. If you must write, keep it to the weather. Don't ask how we are." And then her uncle ("When a good Bohemian can't take it anymore," the proverb said, "he'll go out by hanging.") was found swinging from his last pear tree.

As at Oxford, Anna rose, not in callousness but desperation: "Propaganda!"

"It's what my relatives saw with their own eyes—poor farmers. The leaders can't farm, know nothing, don't care, cover up for each other, steal, bungle…"

And of Lithuania: "How can you swallow it? There was oppression under the czars, of course. My uncle was caught in a plot. But he had a fair trial, a lawyer from Saint Petersburg. He didn't want to be saved; he denounced the tyranny. So he went to Siberia. But even from there he could appeal. These new rulers come at night, like the Nazis. No legal process. And if there were, you couldn't find a witness—everybody afraid the same thing would happen to him.

"You've been in this country where you have the freedom to dream, and you've dreamed yourself into a bubble. But in East Berlin I've heard those guns. And it was always in my mind: Why stand you against a wall; you're going to fall; the wall won't hold you up…"

For three years Anna had argued, sent letters, peace appeals, played on their old dreams, tried to win the other Anne over. But suppose she could have ignored what she called the facts, the mythological bareness remained. There was nothing in communism to match the pagan birth, death and rebirth, the Christian Crucifixion, Burial, Resurrection. No Baptism, no Redemption, "For religion," she said, "there has to be a water of life."

"I'm not going to talk any more about your philosophy," Anna broke it off at last. "I used to think you couldn't express yourself clearly, but now I see your thought's confused and it comes out in your expression.

"That confusion, which you call freedom, is death. Be a nun, live in a cave, eat berries, go naked. While warmongers blow the world to pieces. Our roads are separate, from now on."

To Daren she sighed: "I can't see any more of Anne. I've loved that woman. But her life is so ugly. Pulling back from the world, frustrated, hating the people she comes from, blaming them somehow for her plight.

"'There will always be war and theft and murder,' she says, 'because men's minds are evil.' If I thought that I'd give up and die. I tried to pull her back, but it's no use. Something's happening to her mind. She's drawing into a shell. Like you. I think she loves you, and that helps destroy her."

And now the other Anne would call him over, driven to hysterical alarm: "I'm afraid, Daren. She has terrible power. And they hold such grudges. 'You'll have to pay, pay!' Here's a book she gave me years ago. She's always saying: 'Everything in life has to be paid for… America is going to pay for that.' And look at the book. When she gave it to me she said it was for amusement—by a countryman of my mother's:

That was the aim: to cut down the number of nuisances who flourish on the earth without paying too much in tolls on the way.

This is about a preacher:

Could he change his tune and march in line with us? Kick out the teeth of all the bosses he's been buttering right along? No. He's got to pay. Maybe he thinks it's easy to change sides. Let him. And when he dies trying, we'll be the first to cheer.

And look at this one, about a banker:

Bring the water in the cistern to boil and dip that moneylender in and hold him there. Then in addition to our other valuable experiences, we'd know what it was like to drink tea flavored with black reaction.

"I read that last night and my hair stood on end. I have relatives behind the curtain, and she could take it out on them. I picked up the phone and started to call the FBI. I had my finger on the dial, but I couldn't What am I going to do?"

"Both of you," said Daren, "live in a world of terror. I won't, I can't,"— Though his refusal did not solve Korea, Berlin, or even America, Washington, Mississippi, let alone his Anna and this other Anne.—"You think of her as a schemer. For a long time the truth to me has seemed simpler. You know the horror story about the man hypnotized to believe nothing could hurt him, how he got his throat cut with a razor, but it closed up and he went on, until the hypnotist died, and he fell down slashed to the windpipe and choking in blood? You threaten the voodoo she's lived by ever since the abortion cut her down. If she's dropped you, it's because she can't afford not to."

"You make her sound soft; but she's hard, she plots. All her friendship has been a trap, to get me in."

"To the Party? You? All that work? The devil couldn't afford it for an immortal soul. I've lived through it for twenty years, and it's been worse on her than me. I can't stop her. If history doesn't know where it's going, at least it's bigger than my will."

Poor Anne, turned in on herself, a nun out of cloister, afraid on all sides. Teaching in a slum school and afraid of the boys. Afraid of her sister's husband, working class, brawny, drinking his beer in his undershirt in front of the TV show (liquid bread and circuses), grumbling when the news, between commercial sells, interrupted the game: "Blast those commies, blast them off the earth."

Anna almost with him there, more afraid of communists than of him, materialism settling in like the ice of a polar winter, the threat ened takeover.

Afraid of the Right, ranting about the historic liberties of this nation, when what was to be found but the steel rails of the past leading to the overwhelming future?

Afraid of the Church she had left, that smothers the God in our hearts under creeds and sterile authority; and had Christianity ever stopped Christians from killing Christians?

Afraid of progressives, random adventurers pushing an iconoclasm already pushed too far, avant-garde immoralists, the suicide of liberation, playing into totalitarian hands.

Afraid of the machine, technical specialization, a blind skill fixed on the part without a sense of the whole.

Afraid of militarism, the planet girdled with rocket bases, atomic warheads, missiles enough at any moment to blow it all to nothing and more in the making, and always the chance of malfunction, madness, error.

Down every road of the future horror and explosion, and nothing to oppose it but a dream-hope, the new individual, some divine Omega—save the heart and the world is saved—but not this old individual, bought, sold and corrupted:

Not sister's potbelly growling at the TV show.

Peace, yes, but not the peace movement, undermined, suborned and penetrated by perverters of all kinds.

Science, yes, Teilhard de Chardin; but not this science of university teams working high-pressure under government contract...

Nightmares increasing on her: "If Anna wins we are lost, all of us. And if anybody else wins..." What remained but the fragile film, to skate on the mystical Now. At the craft shop she took up weaving. "She wants to go off to some corner away from the world," Anna said, "and do her weaving."

Daren (counterthrust or containment?): "You're always talking about what a sense of justice you have, that worker's compassion and feeling for others. How do you square it with throwing off a friend? And it's not the first time. You gave old Lovinsky the boot at The Door when he announced the lectures you said were anti, though you'd strung him along before; and by some power I don't understand, you got a lot of people to blackball him, so he had almost no students."

And she: "That course was going to flop without me. You're like the rest who think the facts of history come from dark conspiracies. But there are roads that are played out, like Chiang; and if you insist on taking them, you don't get anywhere. Blame nature; don't blame poor Anna."

"And there are worse things than that, too..." Daren broke off. Hal Corshin, the last fearless liberal dumped from the State Department, had been a Chicago socialist years before. He had fought Stalinism in Washington and Europe, and his skill at telling independent partisans from undercover members made him more dangerous to infiltration than any number of O'Malleys. For Daren, the future of American diplomacy hung on those Corshins, men who could steer Left without capsizing; and when O'Malley caught the tiller and in a ranting confusion of everything left of center with communism, jerked to the Right, he set us on a course which could only mean our loss and maybe world disaster. But the Party must have noticed, in secret deliberation, that O'Malley could be used to expose embarrassing liberals. So stool-pigeon members came forward with sheepish confessions about Hal Corshin: "He supported American Peace mobilization"; "He showed me his communist card at a meeting"; "I saw a big banner of the hammer and sickle on his wall." Anna had known Corshin and sparred with him of old. But Daren did not accuse her. He had nothing but hunches, unsure. He reverted to familiar ground:

"A wonder you haven't thrown me off years ago. I guess you keep hoping I'll see the light. Well, sometimes I see too much. More than my eyes can stand."

"If you want to work in the world, you can't be blinded by the light."

"The devil said the same thing to Faust: 'You make a pact with us –you want to fly—and your head swims?' But it's not the pact I aspired to."

More and more they were a laceration to each other.

But whatever had drawn her to him in Europe, the dream of stretching to the light, had meant too much. She stayed by him, though his openness was a Damoclean sword. To root him up and transplant him into the closed ground of her system.

She had a place for him there. He was the romantic idealist, hostage to the old order, sealing himself in lonely dreams. That phenomenon her ideology could accommodate. But the accommodation did not explain her continuing love; and it was love that caused her pain.

As for Daren, he too had a frame of the world, and in it a place for her, and she knew what it was (he had been her teacher, after all): she was the romantic seeker, who had broken under the strain and in a gamble of compensation hardened into creed.

Her vulnerability was her love. It threatened to draw her into the houselessness from which she had fled in desperation twenty-five years ago. She had to get him in her containment or be dissolved in his.

("Don't talk to me about Freudian motivation and that I'm a socialist because of frustrated desires. I've known from the first that I was right, that my impulses were good, and that society was wrong. I've always served the true, nothing but the true…")

Through the honeymoon of the war, her confidence had been strong. Even in Patapsco, these last years, it would be renewed, but as a fever that could only be labeled: *The Possessive Phase.*

Their beds had been under separate windows at opposite sides of the bedroom. She moved them together now, so they could talk of old times before sleeping. It might be England, Italy, her childhood, Mom; but always it would lead back to the vision and cause, the Human Hope.

If they went to a party where the couples were seated apart, she would work it so as to move over by him, clinging to his talk as she had in Jim Hardy's Oxford room. She got out her old rubbings of church brasses, glued them on monk's gray cloth and hung them around the walls; she took up the Florentine scrapbooks to pore over Lippi and Botticelli.

Leflore, in his windowed cave, felt, with increasing dread, Anna's attempts to worm her way in, to take the stronghold he had hardly been ready to yield, even to God. As if, from the porthole of the bathysphere in which we plumb the depths (the bifocal eyes opening on the single Cyclopean view), one should see an octopus approach the glass, see it curling, probing, embracing, flattening suction cups against the spirit's panes.

His most private comfort had been reciting poetry. He would repeat it to himself when walking, driving, sometimes just sitting in his room—those anthologies, in whatever languages he knew, which he had begun to exhibit at Solesmes, but kept now for his silences, almost like prayer, that much a part of himself. In her need to encompass him, Anna began to reach out for that. Sitting in the dark, mumbling something he loved, he would feel her enter the room; or as they rode the bus to Washington for the hearings, and he took the motor noise as a cover for "Lycidas," stirring his lips and voice only enough to fill his own reverberances, she would lean against him, curling her ear up like a beggar's hand, cupped for the last worn coin of his soul.

"I can't hear. What are you saying?" Though she must have known it was poetry and grudged him the preoccupation; but because it was his, wanting to suck it up, to make it her own.

"My life is a success," she would say. "Everything I want has come to pass. But only by reaching. Happiness must be worked for. It doesn't grow; it doesn't shape itself."

And then, like a faith-confirming ritual: "One thing I know, whatever else, I'm true; my life is true. Whatever I have done has been true and good."

While she had whored and plotted and coveted and lied—self deceived—an honor. Yet the heart of the impulse she expressed, after all these years, had never left her face—incorruptibly naive, a gaze like the sky. "Who acts from love," says Nietzsche, "acts beyond good and evil." Did one dare quote Hitler again, remind her of that? "And now like a somnambulist, I go the way God has chosen."

What brought it to a crisis was the death of Mom. As long as that old earth-goddess of Anna's childhood could be turned to—most of all when she had come to Patapsco City, bringing in her train Mother Port with all its associations—Anna had something of her own to wait on and talk to, the strength of significant service.

When Mom died, Patapsco died with her. Anna's old life-wound opened. The rift poured with blood.

5. Earth Mother

WHEN OLD MISS SALLY had given up wandering the night reaches of the house and died, it was Mom's turn to supply the widowed place that complement of its dark.

Anna had wanted her to come at once, but as long as she could she clung to the home port. When she got pneumonia (looking after Paul's house while his wife gadded to Florida), it was Anna who went to her, put her in bed near the back window with a view of the sky and the moon, and for five days and nights, as she said, breathed her own life into Mom.

"If you won't come to us, you'll have to stay with Paul." She had tried that: Paul's wife, a loud silly woman who kept them in debt, though the liquor store made money now; the kids brought up on radio and television, whining for whatever they saw in the commercials; Mom turning it off and Madge screaming: "Let them turn on the television if they want to; that's what I bought it for"; Paul shrugging his fat shoulders: "I'm sorry, Mom, but what can I do?"

The oldest boy was always in trouble, pampered by his mother and strapped by his father. In his teens he took the car for a joyride and smashed a loaded taxi. During the Korean War he busted out of college and went into the Army. His girl also left school and followed him around from camp to camp. The war ended; he was mustered out; they married. That was where her wants began, like the ladder Blake drew reaching for the moon: "I want, I want, I want." She wanted a baby, though they had no money; she got the baby. Wanted a new house; got the house. One morning, wanting God knows what, she climbed a trunk in the attic and hanged herself from a rafter. The parents had to take the baby, already, as

Mom put it, "the Devil's young un." Little Paul hit the bottle harder than his dad. No place for Mom there.

Even Anna's loyalty was troubled by brother Paul. "How hard to formulate a person," she told Daren. "My brother, lovable, plain, of the people; but he drinks, and that makes him hateful; and it's taking him over, changing what he is. Suppose I were a writer and could make that real. There'd still be no point unless I showed the society the poisons that made him go that way—like Zola, Dreiser—unless I brought home the blame."

Marie, the oldest sister, had cleared out and gone to California. As for lovely Celia, she had married a Polack in North Chicago; but her family was worse than Paul's; and now the sixteen-year-old daughter had run off in the Volkswagen with a little Mexican man-boy. A phone call had come from Arizona: she had married him, she didn't know why, and he had stolen the car, wrecked it, and now he was in jail.

"So goes our society," Anna grieved; "decay and monstrosities on all sides. But it can't go on, no matter how much money they pour into telling lies to the people."

Mom held out in the old apartment, until that whole slum area was condemned by the city for clearance, a park, high-rise apartments, a branch of the university.

"University," Anna snorted. "That place was my university. People would sit on the steps and talk to each other. Those bribing old commissioners don't even ask the people. They bring in bulldozers and knock down the buildings where I grew up. Those were homes, where people learned how to live."

"But I thought you wanted planning; I thought you hated slums."

"Planning! What's planning to them? To get federal funds and make a killing and call it progress—more roads, more autos. I'm going out there for Mom, and I'll go to the city hall and tell those loafers it makes me sick to see the people go to the polls; they know as much about politics as a billy goat does about astronomy."

The destiny of offended spirits, to haunt forever the house, the scenes of their outrage. And when all that would be lugged off, brick by brick and stone by stone, until there was no recognizable trace, where could the ghost go then for its rituals of love and pain?

Anna had one shrine left, that faltering and failing Mom. She bundled her up with a trunk of her treasures, Paul's first shoes and Celia's bit of lace, and brought them to Patapsco City. They arrived one fall evening in the rain, Anna helping Mom from the taxi to the door, a small woman, in a short coat, hood thrown over her head, which she put back as she reached the porch, and showed her face, tired, delicate, strong.

Next day Anna phoned her Jewish doctor from Baltimore. She had met him the first Patapsco summer when she was walking past a building site and a steel beam swung loose, battering a young workman, crushing the pelvis and penetrating the body cavity. The doctor, who also happened to be passing by, took over; Anna phoned the ambulance for him, helped keep off photographers and the rest who rushed forward, all that apparatus of press, lawyers, insurance closing in (as she put it) for the kill. She had worked as a nurse for years; she went with the doctor to the hospital and helped him far into the night. Next morning she was there again. The blood pressure plummeted. The doctor came back and laid on hands. The third day gas gangrene developed. "Always fatal," she heard another doctor say. Her Doctor Levin opened the belly across the groin and put on an oxygen tent. In two weeks the patient was beginning to mend. "There was a beauty," Anna said, "in the way he worked. He took all his time and gave it to this young worker." She used to go as a volunteer to help in his clinic, and had only slacked off when she found he represented insurance companies and was paid to protect them from exaggerated claims. "Corruption all over," she grieved. "Wherever big money comes in, men do anything—doctors on each side saying opposite things." But she went on admiring Jed Levin. He came over now to look after Mom.

She had a series of small troubles, bronchitis, pains in the chest, insomnia, a cyst to be removed. "The body," she said, "old, grows wrong things on it, lumps, warts, moles, like the old stump of a tree." Daren was often trotting down to Fat Holden's for medicines.

Fat had just put a display of jockey straps, supporters and hernia belts in his window. Years ago, when he was married, he'd displayed douche bags and syringes. When the first baby came, it was diapers and bottle warmers, and nipples in floral patterns. When his mother-in-law arrived from Memphis, he responded with bedpans, enemas, everything for the household invalid. Now hernia belts. "Stretched a gut," thought Daren, "heaving his belly."

Fat's blondined wife was at the cash register and Fat was back in the glass cage where he made up prescriptions. "Have you got anything better for a cold than Myraculin?" Daren asked.

"He's putting it up for you." She leaned over confidentially. "He can hear a dollar bill fall from the other end of the store."

In a minute Fat came from his booth with a brown bottle. "Here it is," he said.

"How much?" asked Leflore.

"A dollar," said Fat.

"Any discount for hypochondriacs?"

Fat roared. "They're the life of the trade."

"I hope it's good." Leflore looked dubious. "'Will it do the job?"

"Do the job! Who's it for? Both of em? Well, let em take one at bedtime and every hour after, up to three pills; but don't let em take more than four, whatever you do."

When Daren got home he read the label: "Warning. Contains opium. Habit forming. Keep out of the reach of children. Do not give to elderly people unless prescribed. Consult physician."

Mom was a good patient, and easy to get along with. She had been through experiences as alien as anything in Gorki, but she told them with the offhand air of every day, Anna listening as to an oracle.

How her brother Michael invited her on a trip to southern Illinois to meet their half-brother, Joe Golub.

A gay start, Mom dressed up, hair in a little bird's nest on top, Uncle Michael carrying the battered gray cardboard suitcase tied with cords. It was her first ride in a sleeper.

But nobody met them next morning. They set out on foot, trudging the dusty, hot road, asking the way, until about noon they came to a picket stockade, a shack inside, a big hungry cur tied to a stake. He struggled up, growling. Joe heard the noise and came out, led them into a grubby room. Right off, he asked for money, to get beer. Michael gave him five dollars and he went away.

By two he hadn't come hack. Michael wanted to go for food, but the stockade was locked and the dog came over, snarling. They made out with scraps of bread and fatback, flinging what was left into the yard.

By night Golub came home, drunk. He had picked up his rifle from somewhere and stacked it in a corner. Mom came forward. But before anybody had said so much as a "Howdy" or "Where have you been all day?" or "all these years?" Golub began screaming about communists, traitors, Russians.

He ordered Mom into the bedroom and locked the door. She never protested. Just smoothed her coat over the filthy straw tick black as coal, and lay down. While the voices rose from the other room, Joe cursing about the Reds and how somebody had stolen his money, and he'd shoot whoever it was, Michael talking slowly, calm, calm.

In the morning Golub unlocked the door. Didn't say a word. Mom and Michael packed their things, told brother Joe good-bye, walked out past the starving dog, to the station, took the next train home.

It was from brother Michael that Mom inherited the only money she ever had. He also took to drink in time and died in a flophouse. But there was an insurance policy by which Mom and mad Golub shared three thousand dollars. She would never touch hers, for sickness or anything, left it with the company, to cover her funeral. Said she'd depended on people all her life, but she wouldn't depend on anybody once she was dead.

The end came suddenly, at Christmastime. Daren had been called to Mississippi for Aunt Willi Mari; so what he knew of Mom's death reached him on his return, and from Anna:

"What I remember above all, as she lay dying, was one beautiful tear that trickled down the side of her nose. Why did it fall? Loneliness? She was already so far on the road. Or was it for me, standing there by the bed? A farewell to the world. She knew.

"And when she was forty and I was twenty, coming from the Stinky Foot Movie House, she would race me to the Sacred Heart, and she always won. She would be breathing a little deeper, hardly winded, while I was gasping for air.

"You remember the three wishes I made when I was a girl?

"That Father might die before Mother, because she loved us more;

"That her death might not be too hard;

"That I might grow up to travel and learn.

"They've all been granted now, so I should count my life a success. But I never felt so lost, so sad."

In the corner of Anna's eye one of those maternal tears grew, welled out and trickled down her nose.

With the stopover in Georgia to see Cader Ayres, Daren had spent three days getting to Mississippi, and when he arrived there was a telegram from Anna begging him to return: Mom had been stricken. But he had to stay for what he had come for.

Anna's prayer had been granted, but Daren must have neglected to pray, and here was Aunt Willi Mari, after two colostomies, dying of a cancer that had spread all through her body and erupted in her face. At the first operation the doctor had given her six weeks. Nine months had passed, the last merely on liquids, the stomach rejecting solid food, craving only water; and still a being which thirty years before had lost the joy of youth, setting into the laced stays of such an old-maid widowhood that Daren had hardly considered it life at all, clung to these dreg-ends as if they were a good, stretching out the final pain.

"Ay me! I don't know how I can keep on going," she had sobbed to herself in the adjacent room the night she came back from Reading after Thea's death, Daren hearing from his own bed, through the transomed door, awed at an outbreak too personal for other ears, as disjoined a moment as the snapshot by Lotus Lake (its opposite), a last cry of betrayal as the nymph of that picture hardened to the woodenness of Aunt Willi Mari: "How can I stand it, day after day?" Then the creaking of the solitary bed.

Song lingered from her girlhood, but devoted to the church choir; and if her voice had ever been enjoyable, it had lost that. When she sat down to the piano every day at the ordained time to go through a hammered sequence of "Do-ray-mi-fa-so-la-ti-screech/" it was all the windowpanes could stand, let alone the human ear. Old Mr. Grimm, jack-of-all-trades for the Leflores, had raised his ladders and boards once in the central galleried hall, and was trying to slap some paper on the ceiling, when she broke loose. The paper began to go crooked and to strip down off that high awkward ceiling, bottling the old man up like a cocoon. "Do-ray-mi-fa-so-la-ti-screech/" He shook his head, got down off the scaffold, rolled up the paper, stacked the ladders in the corner and went home. Uncle Hazlewood had to make him a schedule before he would come back, with the hours of song-attack blacked out and the all-clear indicated with a sufficient margin of safety.

The Church was the only institution that could have absorbed these offerings without a kickback. As the preacher used to rant in the Presbyterian barn where they went on Sundays (for the male Leflores, though they had long been unbelievers, yielded, with other good families of the South, to the chore of Communion), raising his arms toward the rafters: "We are the sheep of thy pasture and the flocks of thy hand; 0 Lord, make us meet for thy joys!" mumbling the phrase through his false teeth, so Daren grew up under a vision of a great feast of barbecued lambs, flinging themselves into the divine grinders with a cry of "Holy, holy, hal-leluyah! Make us meat for thy jaws!" As for Aunt Willi, when she took over the child-rearing and stepped up the church attendance, giving her life (and song) to that praise, she inverted the metaphor of feeding: "If Christ the Redeemer hadn't fed me on the blood of the Lamb, I don't know how I'd have lived through this time." To lap it up like a brown gravy. If only it had given her less corseted fat and more fine frenzy.

She had scarcely entered their lives. Elmonia took a mother's place—mammy's anyway, as the boy in the southern story answers the visitor: "And what do you love best?" "Mah Mammy, suh, and old dawg Tray." Aunt Willi Mari was too redeemed to matter.

The time Daren and Dan Byrne and B. J. Farnham, all three, went with the double-barreled shotgun as big as a cannon in the tippy canoe, paddled up the bayou until they saw a moccasin like a boa constrictor sunning himself on a log. "I'll stand up and shoot," Dan said, "and you lean the other way when it goes off, so the kick won't tip us over," He aimed point-blank. "Now," he said, and pulled both triggers. The others lurched forward and swamped the boat. He had forgotten to reload. Dan plunged with the gun almost in the moccasin's face. They sloshed out slimy wet, the gun a mess. "Let's build a fire," B.J. said, "and dry off." They soon had it roaring with straw from the field, but the wind took it and headed for the hay barn. "Beat it out with your clothes!" Quite a homecoming for the snake-conquering heroes, not just drenched and muddy, but their jackets and britches charred where the damp had been conquered by the fire. What had Aunt Willi been on such occasions but a straitlaced reminder in black of the magnitude of their fall?

Into the needs of Daren's sister, June, she had entered as little. One would have thought the Reading photo of the married and pregnant Willi a mere forgery (as O"Malley could fix pictures of his enemies hobnobbing with whom he pleased), to saddle her falsely with the experiences of womanhood. June's inner life would have been hard enough to penetrate in any case; Aunt Willi Mari never guessed there was a mystery to be explored.

Only long after, when the crisis was past and June had mastered her depression less by psychiatric help than by teaching spastic children ("You have to have been sick," she said, "to feel for the sick. Isn't that why God had to become a man?") and wanted to be quietly married to an older and quieter teacher, did Aunt Willi get steamed up, thinking to bring off a wedding in the old Leflore style. But the cards were stacked against her. Not only June and Orville, determined to keep it humble (his very name insurmountable, Orville Lomax, corrupted from childhood to Awful Lummox, though, except in the ways of the world, he was not dumb); fate had a trick up its sleeve. That was before B.J. jacked up the town paper; and it would have been bad enough for the *Herald* to have done the usual job on the marriage: "Miss Leflore reveals nuptial plans" (as if the poor girl had squealed under the thumbscrews); but they had a surprise for Aunt Willi this time: the normal vacuities of Mr. Lomax facing the altar with June Leflore were enlivened by picking up two lines from the feature printed below it, about old Shorty Eubank's pet goats and what a special breed they were and how intelligent; so that the wedding account rose through names, decor, dress and corsage to a rather sudden conclusion: "We are ready to credit the special qualities of the breed, but both of them smelled like goats."

Aunt Willi Mari was so incensed, she tore right down to the office, and by the time she finished, Editor Collins was ready to run a whole series of retractions. But what could you do? As Uncle Hazlewood said (in the words of Don Quixote when Sancho fouled his britches), "Stirring will only make it worse."

And now Aunt Willi Mari, after false alarms and night ambulance rides to the hospital, recoveries and returns, was installed in the room she liked best, the front bedroom of the house in Delta Landing, with Elmonia and a nurse to attend her dying.

For three weeks the ocean we carry with us, in which the old garfish of the soul swims, had been deserting her by every available opening, mouth, nose, colostomy, in streams of blood. Elmonia waked them far in the night of Daren's arrival, to another expected dying. The others had faced it before, but for Daren it was a new shock, to see such fountains from a living creature; and as he bent to take her hand, Elmonia on the other side swabbing the blood, he saw what he almost doubted—a Dantean deceit—her eyes too were oozing not tears but blood.

Christmas was approaching. Each morning Aunt Willi Mari asked: "'What day is today?'—"Christmas Eve," Daren told her. The Birth, with all its wept-over memories of joy: lighted tree, stockings, church bells, reading from the Gospel of Luke in the family circle around the fire: "It is accomplished," she said. Over a sterile waste of gray—love and death, the twin realities.

She died in a last hemorrhage, fell back stiffening in Elmonia's arms—or rather she died twice; for as Doctor Fisher, called when the seizure began, rushed from across the road with his black bag and into the room, Aunt Willi began to stir and moan, Drusiana from the bier, asking to sit up. The nurse, who had been waked and come from the back room, helped Elmonia raise her. "Hello, Doctor Al," she said with a girlish little smile, and slumped forward. Before he could cross the room she was dead.

"Displaced," Anna's sister Celia (now she had moved into the middle class and been psychoanalyzed) used to call Anna's love for Mom: because you don't have any children of your own." Anna wouldn't hear of it: "I'd have loved Mom if I'd had a dozen children. I've got oceans of love in me." She preferred Pigeon Joe's account in the old neighborhood, that she was the "best" of Mom's daughters.

"We were working on the Christmas things, talking and laughing about old times. She went downstairs to iron some clothes. As she climbed back up, something took hold of me. I looked at her, but she didn't say anything until she had put the things away. Then she sighed, 'I got such a pain. Such a pain.' She lay down on the sofa, quiet at first. Then a soft moaning. I undid her dress and ran for her nightgown. I phoned Jed Levin. But long before he came that whimpering little cry, like a hurt bird, told me.

"It was dark. I was looking out of the window. 'Nobody yet?' she asked. Then the headlights.

"'Where does it hurt?' Jed asked her.

"'All over,' Mom said. 'Give me a pill. I want to die.'

"When they lifted her into the ambulance, even under the drug, she pulled her gown around her knees and the shawl over her shoulders. 'A fine face,' the assistant said. I watched the lights along the road. All my life I'd seen ambulances go by, and been the person by the stretcher grieving.

"Next morning Paul and Celia came and I went home to rest. But the phone rang. It was the blood pressure. When I got there they were bathing her. 'Why now?' I whispered. She dug her heels into the bed and tried to lift, but she couldn't. Then her breathing changed.

"'She's dying,' Celia heard me whisper, and ran to the office. Down the hall came a clatter. Oxygen. 'Not that,' I told them. But they came in. I bent over Mom and kissed away the last tear. Then I went into the hall. I couldn't even say good-bye.

"When they called me back, they had tidied her up, lips apart, eyes open, like dead Juliet. When I was little she never had time for me. Now she was gone. I leaned on Celia's shoulder. No use. I leaned on Paul's. I straightened up and went home.

"The print of her head was on the pillow. 'Mom,' I said, 'I've got things to tell you yet.'

"At the funeral the police had to stop the traffic for her. She would have liked that. But not that sound of the clods. She used to bend over when she combed her hair. Swept **it** out until it touched the ground. Like the willow tree where they buried her. Enough to make you mad."

Anna had more trouble sleeping now, as Mom had done. She read somewhere about relaxing, to concentrate, first on the toes, slack them off, then the ankles, calves, knees—by the time you reached the head you would be asleep. But she concentrated too hard; it left her tingling all over. She would read far into the night, turning the pages, nothing sleepy but her eyes. Sometimes when Daren was awake she would talk, mostly of Mom: "She doesn't like being dead; she had things to say to me, like milk in a breast when it wants to come out and it hurts." Other times it was old days in Chicago. It wasn't that she was sad all the time, but that memories, even of joy, took on a nervous fluorescence. He would hear her laugh in the dark. "Yes?" And it would be something about Pigeon Joe, or how the organ-grinder would come Sunday afternoon, and the children would crow and dance, and how once she gave the skinny little monkey perched on the organ in his brocade jacket and top hat a penny, and he pulled a folded fortune from a box tied to the organ and handed it to her, such a wonderful fortune: "You will change the world for the better."

"All my life," she murmured, "we worked to make that fortune come true."

Mom had left a big bottle of Syrup of Phenergan, along with some pills the doctor had given her for sleeping. Three or four times a night, Anna would get the syrup and have a lick, and when she fell asleep, she always gave the credit to Mom's medicines. "It's only for children," she said, when Daren found the bottle nearly empty. By that time she had advanced to the pills.

She had always fostered baby birds, orphaned field mice, a bat once. Now she wanted to save everything. The house was overrun with mice, but she would only put up with a live-trap, and whatever was caught she would take out and turn loose in the park: "Turn those town mice back to nature." Like the progressive *Little Red Riding Hood* the Quaker child Debbie had next door, where not only the Grandmother and Little Red Riding Hood had to be saved from the wolf, but the wolf had to be reformed—poor crud, he'd been hungry all his life: "All right," the woodsman said, "we'll feed you, and you'll be a good dog after all."

Though even Chaucer's Prioress, "all gentleness and tender heart," told a story of hatred about Jews. For Anna, the sleek cat from the rich house across the road was the scapegoat. "If a cat's domesticated," she said, "it can't be wild too. It's got to choose." One day she rushed out scolding and saved a robin it had grabbed. But the bird pined and died. "If that's a cat's nature," she said, "he's going to have to pay for that."

It distressed her to see birds fighting at the feeding station. "Hey, you chickadees," she would yell, "don't try to be capitalists. Share with your brothers." As the nesting season came around: "I begin to hate those mockingbirds," she grieved. "Oh, maybe they know how to sing. But they're too selfish by half. Someday they'll pay for that."

In April she had bad luck with a hawk knocked out of the nest by a storm. She gave him a box of straw and all kinds of food, but he was too small; the spark ebbed. When he was almost gone she took him into the woods and put him under a tree. "He stood up," she reported to Daren, "all wobbly. The wind blew and birds whistled. He let out one little peep and then another: 'I'm here.' Then he fell over and died. Like Mom—breathing hard, restless."

In a few days she had better luck with a sparrow. But when she wanted to loose him, thinking he was old enough, a bunch of other birds came down to peck him. "That's society," she said—though it was nature. She phoned the Baltimore zoo. "I have a bird," she said. "He's been brought up tame and he's no good for the woods, so maybe you should take him."

"What kind of bird?" the woman asked.

("What difference does that make, she thought.) "A little one. He has yellow all round his mouth." But she told: "He's a sparrow."

"I'll call you back," said the woman. But she never did.

"Looking for some bird of paradise," Anna grumbled. "If you're a sparrow, nobody wants you."

She kept him a few days more, and then he got out of the cage and flew away. "See; he didn't need any zoo keeper anyway. Another hit of life gone back to nature."

(Like Mom.)

It was a slow spring. There were snows in March. Then dark. Anna would walk out under baggy clouds, the ivy leaves heavy on the rock, like cups holding water; she would climb down the stairs and follow the Patapsco into the woods. The great drops from the branches over the stream fell slow, spinning like tops on the water. There was a deep propriety in the laws of gravity and liquids, the weight thrusting down and cohesion drawing hack, stretching the sphere until surface tension pinched if off and it pulsed in silvery fall, to merge rippling with its own, the stream, the ocean, water to water—"the army of unalterable law." But it was not her law. A universe of dead things. She was waiting for spring as for life renewal.

Now the buds had appeared; bloodroot on the slope had put up folded leaves through fall debris and opened to eight-pointed stars; birds had nested and hatched; trees had changed from the first yellow green to clumps of dark against the lighter grass; and still what Anna waited for did not come.

In grief as in pleasure she let herself go, with primitive trustingness, as if instinctive feeling would lead her home. But what feeling told her now after the snows and tears of winter was the impossibility of the unassuaged continuance; that Mom had been dead long enough; that it was time for her to come up again. She stood at Daren's window one mist-veiled evening in May (the climax of the possessive phase, when, fighting or loving, she was with him much of the time), and he heard her voice, as from the child waiting at the lace curtains for Mom to bring home some of those broken chocolates she used to buy cheap at the candy factory: "Come on, Mom; come on. You've been gone long enough."

The half-wild invocation startled him. Next day he came up behind her as she stood looking out into the same cool mist through which the lost spring was working. "Would you like to visit your mother's country?" he asked.

One cannot always be turning over stones of self-motive looking for centipedes. It had come to him that it would be worth digging up the cash for such a gift—call it a gesture of love.

Life generally didn't have to knock twice for her; but Daren had time to say it again: "I'll buy the ticket, if you want to visit the old country."

She kept her eyes down, her head bowed in ambiguous humility; he had to speak again: "Would you like to go?"

"Yes," she said quietly, "I would. Yes. Yes. I would."

When the doubt was driven home at the second investigation (the letters, books and propaganda from Anna then pouring in), what was the purpose of that trip, and why had Daren Leflore been ready to use his small Mississippi inheritance to subsidize it, he could only fall back on what Anna herself had stated in the application for a Russian visa: ·· "My mother was Lithuanian, and now she has died. I want to go back where she came from, to feel myself in touch with her." Though the letters were not of discovering maternal roots, but of being shown utopian Moscow and the vacation villas on the Black Sea. Daren did not know how far her going had played into other hands—the upheaval of de-Stalinization then threatening to split the party she had served.

She sailed on a Russian freighter from New York through the Mediterranean past Athens and Constantinople. She had turned her back again on the art-search of their early days. The American battleships in the harbor of Piraeus blotted out the Periclean call from the Acropolis. "If they were the school of Hellas, it was a long time ago."

Then Istanbul:

The first thing we saw as we steamed in was a dilapidated building swarming with people, men in rags hanging out of the windows. "What is that?" A madhouse. Like the city. A poverty different from any in America, old, with none of the shine. Children running out of caves where they live, green snot hanging from their noses, begging, their brown eyes old with grief. Grown men standing around on dung-flecked cobble streets, patch on patch, nothing to do. Animals like the people, caught in some unnatural decay: a sick buffalo, lean cats with pus from their eyes. A few big American autos honking the crowds out of the way. And over it all, those great domes and spires going up into the sky—mosaic churches with beggars down on all fours, in despair of man, begging from God.

She fled to the clean Soviet steamer, where the sailors listened, how kindly, to her tale of the sorrows of the people of Istanbul—"the land," as American ads had promised her, "where the sun always smiles."

For Daren, whose pilgrimage to Byzantium would have paraphrased that of Yeats, she brought the matter home:

"The Artifice of Eternity." You can have it. But the poor aren't interested. And they won't go on generation after generation putting up with it, for some old saint in the gold mosaic of a wall.

That night, at the prow, wind whipping her clothes, she searched north over the Black Sea. And Daren, reading the letters, was searching too—how to trust the evidence of what she had seen:

First signs count: of Istanbul, the insane asylum; of Odessa, a yellow warbler, who came to our rail, and was greeted by a woman worker with a cry of delight. Then green hills enclosing a clean town, factory chimneys tall above, and in the harbor boats with colored sails, like butterflies. Work and play. I had come from the old world and this was the new.

The tone of conviction Daren had heard since he was a boy from absolutists of all colors, indiscriminately applied to communist Russia and fascist Italy and Nazi Germany and agrarian China; and where were the external correlatives? Had he not written in his own meditations: "The gauge of truth is the loyalty of the heart"? All her faith and Jesuitry, guile and foolish devotion poured over the Atlantic in those letters that built, as in love, toward a final flood tide.

As she made new friends—comrade Ossorgin, about her age, of quiet assurance and reserve, who boarded at Piraeus, who stood with her as they steamed into Odessa, and turning, revealed of all wonders, that he too was Lithuanian…

Letters as naïve as if she had never traveled before, never seen the palaces of Italy and France—amazed at the pleasure gardens of Yalta, sanatoriums now, seven hundred housed where seven had lived in luxury. She wrote of the love of flowers and song, concerts, study groups for the language; of bookstalls everywhere, people lining up for books as for baseball in America; of how they honor poets and artists, composers; of the house of Chekhov, a national shrine. Most of all, how they want peace: "You ask about war and they clasp your hand. They know it too well. They say they are fed up to here."

Only the food troubled her, so much butter and black bread, spices, red peppers, with vodka to drink and champagne. She got upset. But longing drove her on: by jet over the snowy Caucasus to the Ukraine, cities, factories, rivers and farms, farms—a land like a jewel stretching endlessly, she flying over it, elated in soul, guts in a turmoil.

> How is it possible here (in what the West calls a slave state) that I feel a freedom I've never felt before? It is the freedom to be human, to be caught up in something great with others who care.
>
> American freedom is loneliness and insecurity. How does it help to be told, "Do what you please," if what that means is shift for yourself, buy your own bomb shelter, drink yourself silly, watch your children take to dope, pay for your own neuroses?

The alone before the Alone—the price of soul in the West. How clearly she saw it. But she could never understand how for some that was life itself— the vigil on the headland of rock.

In Moscow her indigestion focused in the gall. She wrote from the hospital:

Sick. Sick. But they look after you. Not for gain, but because you're a human being. Because they care for life. You sense a higher relation than is produced by competitive society.

I have been reading through things I read long ago, that became part of me, to be reread now in their own language. Dostoyevsky's Notes from the House of the Dead. Of prisoners who have to run the gauntlet, and one who invents a dream to save him from fear. But what happened to his dream when the first lashes fell? No accident the Russian people revolted from that past.

I lie in bed thinking of the future, My eyes burn. But what I feel is happiness. There is one bright star up there in the sky, and it is our Mother. Every night she forms herself into a star and watches. To hold me in the love of life.

Slowly his answers reached her over gulfs of distance and travel:

If your protest is against the world as it is, it's valid and should be made. If it's against those battleships off Piraeus threatening the peace-loving East, it's special pleading. Bombs are being tested there through this very time, and you don't mention it. I hear it is never mentioned in the Soviet press. If that's your flower-happy people, they can eat their damned daisies. The power to know, write and speak (said Milton) is the greatest power. Condemn politicians, police, false promises, double-talk, lies, the littleness and deceit everywhere; but don't think it's an affair of East against West. The habit of finding scapegoats undermines thought.

Mistrust easy solutions, of the Left, Right or Middle. Nature has not presented us with easy answers. And mistrust anything believed in year after year without revision. "The man who never alters his opinion is like standing water and breeds reptiles of the mind," says Blake; and "I must create a system or be enslaved by another man's."

Wake up, Keep your eyes open. Try to learn.

Advice that enflamed her answers:

I am here on the spot seeing what you need to find out about. You don't listen or credit my experience; you go on preaching, trying to tell me what the facts are. Telling me to learn. It's you who's got to learn.

Anybody who thinks the Russians are dying for a chance to live as the Americans do is crazy. They live in a world they have made for themselves, and they're going to keep it that way. They know their history better than we know ours; and their history has led them through common sacrifices toward a common goal. When anybody achieves anything, they don't say "Good for him," but "good for us." They live in the family of man.

As for you, you're as set in your ways, as blind as the rest. Why should I come back to it? They need people here to help build the future, not to argue about the past. Thirty years I've had to wrangle about the simple facts of life. It's time for a change.

That was launched across the airways, while Daren was still answering from weeks before:

To get your letter about freedom during the latest trial of dissenting authors is ironic.

The struggle to reconcile public and private good goes on forever. But if you can't see it's being fought right here and now in this America (like the ninety year-old Titian painting his greatest picture), and that this will remain for all time a memorable radiance, then you've got blinders on.

If you could only understand how complex the motions of history are, and give up those stereotypes you lay down on it like a child cutting out mudpies.

We don't need the New Left to tell us the vulgarity of slogan capitalism (Cummings did it better) or that the world requires a society based not on mine but thine (Christianity taught it before Marx was heard of). There has to be a radical break through for the whole; but to tie all that to the revolutionary violence of a dumb labor class is outmoded. We want a new manifesto: "Thinkers of the world, unite!" Why don't you join?

Love, Daren

Her last letter was postmarked Vilnius. There was no return address:

I am staying. There is no difficulty. "We need hands," they say. "And hearts." It is my world. I would rather give of myself than scratch for gains.

I won't write anymore. It keeps me on edge. Otherwise this is happiness. The greatest happiness, struggling for your fellow men. I know, because I have it. Happiness, It is an assurance that the best you could ever hope for will inevitably come true. I keep saying to myself: the future that is bound to come. I've had luck all my life, but never as now. Never so bright. My last word to you is happiness. Here. Now. If you, if that world of yours, could only know…

O light… O happiness…

The mother of a race…Sincerity (and how rare it was) had brought her, as in old tragedies, to this pass. He folded the letter with the rest, marveling.

And when the honeymoon was over, when she had settled in and begun to work with others in a state as controlled as that, she—but for the one surrender—so uncontrollable? Had anybody ever gone from here to there, not just as a tourist, but to settle down, who hadn't in the end repented and longed to return?

He saw that landscape neither of them had ever seen, which her mother had left as a girl, so that only memories had reached them, filtered down as through tribal dreams: the log cabin by the forest, the lake shore bending off in a misty curve. He summoned it up with a kind of wistfulness, an imagined setting for an Anna he had known and never known.

Would she flow in there, find something she had always been denied—if nature, not our nature; if soil, no Western soil? Or are there souls who in this world and the next will always be stewing like the demons in hell?

Whatever had kept her restless, fighting, let it ease off there; let the lot be better; let the mother and father be married in peace.

But when would that come? Would it be when all should rise, though all should not be changed?

6. *Continuing Subpoena*

IN EACH of the earlier sittings there had been a separation (against a back-drop of woven family lines) of foreground and middle ground: a time of observation, a time observed: Oxford from Patapsco summer, from exiled winter the war and prison years; but here, at the height of this sunset fall, and lashed to a fury like its own forest blaze, what Daren was snatching moments in anterooms and on commuting buses to write about, was the investigation itself, the second O'Malley hearing, as it crackled around him in the scrub-growth of the American soul.

"Mr. Leflore… or should I say Professor Leflore?"

(The investigation this time was of infiltration into colleges and universities, and O'Malley had begun by buttering up the learned witnesses: Did the photographers' lights disturb them? They had only to speak up, and that would be eliminated.)

Daren cut through the polite opening game: "At my college we don't use titles. We have nothing to profess." (It wasn't this man's fault, after all, that the grand jury had dropped the earlier citation for contempt.)

"Very well, *Mister* Leflore. This committee is concerned with the extraordinary way education in America has undercut our values and played into the hands of subversion. We don't see this great un-American drift as the result merely of incompetence and stupidity. We suspect (on a disturbing body of evidence) that the mismanagement has been deliberate. We are trying to follow the clues, to ferret out the precise individuals responsible. Maybe you're naïve. But it's time to wake up and come clean—to give us the facts, my friend."

(Trust Cader's old claim that in ages of decline "honorable punishment" must be risked again and again. But it was no light matter. Evidence Laszlo Brad, lately ganged and murdered in prison.)

"Senator, when I was here two years ago, I didn't find you a friend; so why don't we drop that term?"

"Thank you, Mr. Leflore, for your reminder. I don't like to thank a communist, but I thank you. No, I certainly am not a friend to anyone who plays along with the most villainous of conspiracies. I am not a friend to any promoter or dupe, whichever it may transpire, of world communism. Your campus, however, in this regard, has the most sinister reputation of any place outside Harvard. Your president, Professor Ayres, has said that he will not dismiss Fifth Amendment cases, or others who defy this committee. He will be friendly to you, I am sure, as long as he is tolerated." (Poor old Cader, running his wheelchair into the grave, still formidable to this mudhead.) "It is exactly friendships of this kind that we must inquire into."

Before the other hearing Daren had thought to meet questions as openly as among students in the political forum at Patapsco. But he had learned, listening to others and being trounced himself, the menace of O'Malley's hairsplitting "Doctrine of Areas," by which almost anybody could be flushed into contempt.

"Have you engaged in espionage?" That would be one of the questions, with the qualification: "If to answer would incriminate you, you have the right to claim the Fifth—which is an evasive way of admitting, Yes, I've been a spy."

Suppose the witness protests that the Amendment doesn't say that; it says no man can be compelled to testify against himself, that it leaves undecided the question of guilt, and that to assume otherwise is to rob the innocent of protection.

"If we get a few innocent commies· behind bars, it's tough, isn't it, mister? Answer the question. And I would advise you, unless you want to spend some time in jail, that you accept my understanding of the Constitution rather than yours."

At that point, and under the fact of having the Amendment so twisted, assume the victim confesses—though the senator has no right to ask—that he has nothing to do with espionage. Imagine, in the heat of the moment he adds that he has broken no law, committed no crime, that he is as innocent, he hopes, as O'Malley; when the questions now are pressed home—who joined you in signing such-and-such an appeal; or was so-and-so a participant in a certain peace march?—the witness discovers he has no longer any ground for refusing to answer anything.

"When you stated that you never engaged in espionage, you waived the Fifth Amendment insofar as espionage is concerned; and when you volunteered in addition that you have committed no crime, you waived all ground to the Fifth, whatsoever. If you are guilty of no crime, nothing can incriminate you, and you have no right to conceal anything at all. You are ordered to answer."

"I refuse on moral grounds," you say—invoking those higher justicers. At that moment you are in contempt.

"May the record show," says O'Malley, "…repeated opportunities… still refuses. Build up the counts, mister. Keep on dodging. As good a way as another to get some of you protected spies out of your colleges and into jail."

"You make your purposes too plain. I've said I have nothing to do with spying. You only want citations for contempt."

"Mr. Marshal, remove the gentleman."

"Let the record show the senator is afraid to have the truth declared."

The gentleman, for all that, is removed.

There was no compromise. You had to take the Fifth throughout, face the imputation of every crime, and likely loss of your job; or become O'Malley's informer on whatever count he raised. Anything between was turned to contempt, which was no safer for your job, and might mean prosecution as well.

By the second hearing Daren knew all this. But he could not bring the muscles of his mouth to form the sheltering sounds. He was called on three separate occasions. The first two, he tried to answer questions as before.

"Do you think a man who belongs to the communist conspiracy should be allowed to teach? Before you answer, you understand you have the right to counsel."

"I don't have the money or the inclination. I try to counsel myself."

"Should a communist be allowed to teach?"

"Half the world is communist. If the mind cuts off from that, how can it comprehend political reality?"

Senator: "Let the record show he hedges and does not answer the question."

"I phrase my own utterance. If you can't understand, it's not my fault."

"Here is a man, teaching the sons and daughters of this great country. And when asked whether a teacher who conspires to destroy this nation should go on teaching, he hedges and almost says 'yes.'"

"Universities have better things to do than play cop against robber."

O'Malley: "How can anything be better than defending the country on which everything else depends? I'll ask you a simple question. Come on, mister, let's see if you're fit to teach."

"Luckily you're not the judge of that."

"If you interrupt the questions, you are in danger of contempt. Is murder right or wrong?"

"Must I tell you that, Senator, at your age? We aren't here to establish the bases of morality."

"If a student were to ask that, would you answer; or would youdodge and tell him there wasn't an answer?"

"I would tell him to get better prepared for college. Then I might give him some books to read: *Crime and Punishment*, the Bible, *Oedipus*, *Julius Caesar* — though they wouldn't give the yes or no you ask for."

"Murder is wrong," said O'Malley, "whatever you say. Now answer me this: Is murder a worse crime than conspiracy to destroy a whole nation?"

"There are revolutionaries, Senator, who have been called great men. We can't deny that. Even the communist conspiracy you make so much noise about has never been punished as confidently as murder. So the law has answered your question—our law—anticommunist law. You may go down in history as a villain, for all your high claims; while Sacco and Vanzetti, who were executed as murderers, have already been called heroes."

(Anna, out there, sending back letters, pamphlets, books, proclaiming the reverse of this man's creed—two worlds, matter and antimatter.)

Senator: "So this is what you teach the young of the nation?"

"I try to teach them to think. If you were young, I'd even try to teach you…"

When O'Malley began to slug wild and miss the blows, lawyer Gold would be there tapping him on the sleeve with the annoyed look of a man who knows just how to open an armadillo, if somebody would give him a chance.

"Oh yes, Mr. Gold. You may proceed."

The leveled gun of his finger would plunge them from high generality to the circumstantial and hard, though Gold could he as misinformed as anybody:

"Did you attend a communist meeting last year at one hundred and ten Western Lane, Patapsco City?"

"That's the wrong address."

"You admit the meeting!" cried Gold. "Where was it?"

"Meeting? I only know Western Lane runs out to the park. It stops in the fifties somewhere."

Gold slumped back into his papers. The senator returned to the great issues: "Have you taught the overthrow of the United States by violence?"

"I have taught Jefferson: 'An occasional revolution is salutary.' I have taught Thoreau 'On Civil Disobedience.' I have taught Whitman: 'The perpetual need of thunderstorms, births, deaths, new invigorations of ideas and men.' I would teach the blessings of overthrow right here in this committee."

Gold came from his desk with a smile of reconciliation. "Mr. Leflore, you could help us if you would. We have enough evidence to know that. Is there anything you care to tell us about communist influence in colleges where you have taught—about the relation of President Ayres, for example, to the Left?"

"Mr. Gold, if I had anything to communicate, it wouldn't be to this committee. There is an inscription—I've been told—on the FBI building, 'Framed through Mutual Confidence.' Something of that kind. I mistrust your use of confidence."

Too much for O'Malley: "I order you to answer the question. Every commie who comes here wants to hide his background in communism."

"If I had a background in communism…"

"Will you be quiet while I'm talking? I don't know why some of you commies don't have the guts to say: 'Sure I'm a commie; I believe in it. And here's why.' But you're afraid and ashamed and stand on the Fifth Amendment."

"I haven't mentioned the Fifth. As for guts, which takes more: for me to stand here, or for you to sit up there?"

"Well, you may step down. If the state board follows the rule we have formulated, and I imagine they will, in spite of your president, you might apply for a job over at Harvard. Until we can do something about it, that's going to be a hotbed of conspiracy. The public session is adjourned. Mr. Marshal, clear the room for the closed session. Mr. Leflore, consider yourself under continuing subpoena. You will be notified when to return."

When Daren was called for the second round of that second hearing, O'Malley knew more about him.

"Mr. Leflore, when I look at your record, I am impressed and amazed. You have had every advantage of origin and training. One of your ancestors sat in this House; that name, Leflore, is recorded in the distinguished annals of this body. You have been educated at one of the great universities of England, and have taught in colleges and universities here. Now when you stand up and tell me that you were taken in by the communist conspiracy—don't interrupt, Mr. Leflore; you have said you are not a communist, but your own statements, not to mention your refusal to help this patriotic committee, make it clear where your loyalties lie-you have been taken in, a man of your background and seeming intelligence—now when this has happened, how can you fail to see that somebody has betrayed you and led you to betray others, that there are powers subtler than you are, villains behind the scenes who have entangled you and are destroying what you should believe in; that they are hidden in government, schools, industrial plants, these traitors, Hisses, Brods, Rosenbergs, Peresses; that it is your duty to hate them, hound them, uncover them, make sure they get the punishment they deserve—these criminals, who, but for our opposing, but for this committee and those we have helped to see the light, would have sabotaged the nation and seized the world…"

(The folly of misplaced causality, cloak-and-dagger boys, thinking fate hung on their shenanigans—communist or anticommunist—spying on each other and Washington, microfilming trivia, shifting sides, turning the hallucination of power into the accusation of betrayal—a crazier case of Tolstoi's Napoleon-child, sitting in the carriage pulling the strap, thinking he's running the team. Cocksure—when as a matter of fact who could have known at any moment of history, even with hindsight, how to have moved? In the old world of fossil misery, democracy not enough, or there wouldn't have been socialism, socialism not enough, or why the Bolsheviki? And once a revolutionary extreme was precipitated, what could its action be but violent? Yet without that radical thrust, the world-catenaries of Fabianism, Sun Yat-sen, New Deal, on which progress so much depended, would have gone slack.)

"How can you go on," O'Malley asked, "joining in the treachery of those who have betrayed you?"

"Senator, the argument might almost begin to get interesting. But if so many have been betrayed, leaders, thinkers, the masses who wanted freedom and equality—you must be on the wrong track to blame secret villains. Maybe the history of the modern world is a history of betrayal; maybe we have all been betrayed by our dearest hopes. And for you, of all people, not to understand that…

"Mr. Leflore," said the senator with an equivocal smile, "I would like to know who it is you are covering up for."

"And I would like to know, Senator, if you never read anything but detective literature. It seems you can only be satisfied when you haul out some villain who has schemed the destruction of man. But sometimes nobody is to blame. That's what I meant just now. We live in a world where our highest ambitions end in betrayal—as yours of saving democracy betrays both democracy and you."

O'Malley shrugged and turned to Gold, who had also filled his quiver with facts.

"Did you attend an integration march in Washington, January, nineteen-fifty-two? And did you join the peace agitations at Frederick through the last fall and winter? And did you sign such-and-such petition? And did you know that all these were organized by communists, that the Party was exploiting such unrests all over the country?"

Not likely he wouldn't have suspected something, living the whole time with Anna, or have debated it with himself, long before Gold, thrusting the lean jaw home in the delight of his strategy, voiced the external demand.

And twenty years earlier, at Virginia, in Cader Ayres' Christian Fellowship, the same forces had been leagued: Bill Norris, devout believer, canvassing money for the defense of the seven Negro boys in the Scottsboro Case, and being called a communist by outraged whites, for whom the flower of southern womanhood (those train hopping girls in the boxcar with the Negroes) had suffered a fate worse than death (and suffered it so many times); the tensions had all been displayed at the meeting of the Integrated Church Council to which Cader took Daren as secretary of the University Fellowship, where the Fundamentalists deplored the "substitution of politics for spiritual concerns," and the old southern moderator advised the colored brethren to calm their congregations—"avert this unfortunate flirtation with agitators and communists."

"Gentlemen," Deacon Moses St. John, opening the great pale mouth in a black prophet's face, boomed over the washed-out contenders: "We know we got our head in the lion's mouth; but we aim to tickle that lion.

"When Lazarus wuz layin there at the rich man's table eatin the crumbs, the dogs come and licked his wounds. We been layin a long time at the rich man's table, and now these communists come along, and they're like them dogs, lickin our wounds. You got to know we gwyne to pet them dogs.

"The Gospel of our Lord is a doin Gospel. The Lord didn't set up there wonderin what wuz gwyne on with his people. He sent his Son. Now I ast you: what you folks gwyne do, and who is it you gwyne to send?"

And fewer months ago than that was years, the other Anne, talking about Anna's role in CORE, had stirred the same argument: "So the commies have got their dirty snoopy noses in our race riots."

"If the communists take over the race fight," Daren comforted her, "it's because we let it slide. Better blame ourselves and get on with it."

Though he hadn't seen the South, or even himself, headed that way.

So many things unrecorded, for all his scribblings and bins of papers: the visit Anna made to Mississippi when Daren was in jail. Those southern liberals had been sitting on their principles for years and hatching nothing. They weren't even aware of the case of the two Negroes accused of rape by a girl whom northern investigation had shown to be a soliciting nymphomaniac of staggering promiscuity. It took the communist hothead Anna, with her underground connections, to get the facts from Chicago, local interviews and all:

Pearl's reputation for chastity around Meridian was bad. The first time I met her, I thought she was a nice girl. I bought her a sweater for Christmas. "Now I've got a present for you," she said. "I'm going to let you have some." She took off her slacks and we had sex. She said she couldn't get pregnant anyway.

The day before she said she was raped by the Negroes, four of us left the poolroom and went to Pearl's house. We took her out in the car to the gravel pit and had it several times. Steve's little brother, who had been swimming came over. He was thirteen. "Come on," she said, and looked sick afterwards. She bragged he was the sixteenth that week.

About what happened that night, Steve told me they had gone for a nude swim and a gang bang. He said he did yell at the niggers and call them black motherfuckers and cocksucking sons of bitches. He said the police told him to say he didn't swear, and how to answer the questions he would be asked.

The night after all that, Pearl called me over. "I got raped last night by two niggers," she said. She got in the car and we had it. "Niggers are good," she told me, and that they were bigger and better than white boys.

A lawyer was being sent down to try to save the Negroes from the chair. Before the Delta people knew what was going on, Anna had caught the bus to Meridian. That night in the hotel, when the lawyer staggered into her room bludgeoned by somebody, she got an ambulance and went along to the hospital, though the police warned her off, stayed by his side and got him to the trial; though as far as saving the Negroes it did no good; they were unanimously convicted by a white jury which sat the briefest time, and were executed before the gang that would have preferred to lynch them could get on the job. "A victory for law and order in Mississippi," Anna said ...

"If we cut off from good causes," Daren answered Gold, "because the Left backs them, we'd long ago have been driven to the suicide you Rightists are trying to push us into. Something has to be risked if anything is to be saved."

When the exchange with Gold had spent itself, O'Malley resurged for a final bash and fury: "What are you hedging about? Why don't you answer straight?"

"Because weighing and suspension before judgment is the method of the open mind. It's called de*liber*ation, the teetering of the scale."

"Open mind! You want to question everything. Think the country should support you for that. Put you in a professor's chair. Can't you see these are the times that try men's souls? That every American has to get behind this committee or into that other camp of subversion and conspiracy?"

"The moderate part of the citizens perished between extremes."

"What are you saying?"

"Thucydides observed as much in the dark days of Greece."

O'Malley dragged out the booby trap he sprang on everybody: "If the Communist Party were to order you to commit espionage or sabotage, would you obey those orders?" A sly look. "Your answer could get you in trouble with your friends, but that's not my worry."

"Senator, you presuppose what I have denied under oath. Either you are ridiculous or you are a menace; and it may be you are both."

"Officer, remove this man! Take him out! I want no further speeches from a man who refuses to tell whether he is trying to destroy this nation."

The continuing subpoena might not have brought Daren back to the stand but for the volume of Russian mail pouring in from Anna, postcards of bronze Lenins plopped down in whatever landscape, from steely Siberia to silken Samarkand, and they were sprawled with Anna's greeting, large, to spread the good word all the way to Washington:

> There is a full-length mirror in my room before which I waltz, arms raised. The air is without tension, of love for man. From my window I see the river, where boats and barges pass slowly. Moscow, a great city, center of hope for the world.

And another:

> Visiting the free schools. Meetings at night where the young discuss "What is happiness?" and "What economic structure is best for man?"

The sealed mail had leaked too; and the packages. "Don't say you have freedom there and we have censorship here," Anna wrote, when the book, her favorite, on freedom and the individual, disappeared from the bundle— to be produced later—"You may be the committee," Daren would say, "but you haven't got a license to steal from the mails."

Yes, the Anna business would come up again, all those unseemly questions about a man's rambling wife. To which Daren could only answer out of Homer: "Do you know what the Shade told Penelope in the Fourth Book of the *Odyssey?* 'Of that I will not tell you at all. It would be a bad thing to speak lightly of that.'"

Nor was Anna his only charge: "Was the late Mrs. Stovall a communist sympathizer, or why did she leave you her house?"

—Imagine! cashing in on trash baskets and hoarding Tel. and Tel.— "She was independent enough to defy anybody who tried to tell her what to do; and maybe for this committee that's suspicion enough."

And there were bigger surprises: the report that he had spread communist propaganda over the town by means of the children—boxes of letters

Anna had received over the years: greetings from worker friends, as a card of the new hammer and sickle building, France, 1944, the tragic year for eastern Europe, with a gay note: "I know you will agree that this is the most beautiful building in all France"—when stumbling over that stuff had become unsufferable, Daren had piled it in the yard for the trash collectors—though kids, it seemed, had canvassed it for the stamps.

"Why didn't you turn all that material over to the FBI?"

"I would have thought a tax-supported institution had better things to do with our time."

Such answers were startled out of him. Although, in general, he had meant, this last encounter, not to cooperate at all. A talk with Cader Ayres had changed his mind about the Fifth. He had known it all along, that O'Malley's worst threat was to turn that shelter into a confession of guilt and means of punishment. The last hearing Daren had attended, there was a teacher, the spit and image of poor old Joe Jones, who, under application of the Doctrine of Areas, had broken down and, afraid of losing his job, had coughed up names of associates, other teachers, people who had signed this or that—good citizens, he protested; but as the Romans used to say, he pricked them down. Daren had known, but had kept on his own way, high-minded, ineffectual; it seemed he always needed something to jog him into a change.

"You're making a fine personal show, I'm sure." Cader said one night, as Daren at the bedside read from his notes on the last hearing. "You can afford to. You know the court won't push contempt, and while I'm here you've got your job. Besides you travel light. But there are plenty who can't risk it, and they're being robbed of the Constitution, which means their chance to be human. Maybe it's time you came off your height and joined the threatened human race and took the Fifth and helped make it honorable again. Don't stand up so much as Daren Leflore, but as a citizen claiming the Bill of Rights."

"I have never taken the Fifth before," Daren told O'Malley. "I tried to answer questions. I was wrong. The Amendment was made to protect men from blacklisting. You know that, so you strike at the Fifth: 'Either you're lying,' you tell a man, 'because if you're innocent you have no such privilege, or else you're a criminal and avoid confessing it this way.' But there's not a court decision which doesn't say the amendment is for the innocent even more than for the guilty.

"So I refuse to answer on the ground of the Fifth, and I refuse to admit there is any shame in it." (However much, he felt the shame, betraying his old dignity—call it a "salutary stooping.") "With pride I take up the slandered badge."

"Against so much high talk, Gentlemen of the Press," boomed O'Malley, "I would like to have the record show that the witnesses called today have been identified by one or more people as sometime members of the Communist Party. That may put a new light on Mr. Leflore's refusal to answer."

He should have known it was a cross he was taking up; but as his Quaker friend Gill had said, Daren wasn't a Christian yet. He sprang back against the shouting and the gavel, goaded almost into the old righteousness, to have his cake and eat it too:

"I have testified in the past that I have never been a communist. If I lied, let them cite me for perjury. They've had plenty of time. But today I take the Fifth, for better reasons. If any witness can identify me as a communist, bring him forward and let me question him. But to have accusations put in the record, and ten months later produced as proof of guilt… Let the newsmen hear the testimony."

"No communist will cross-examine our witnesses. If you want to start answering questions honestly, we'll hear from you: Are you now, or have you ever been…"

"I answer from Suetonius: 'The word of no informer was doubted.' From Tacitus: 'None could trust each other, not relatives, not friends; the very walls were suspect.' That is not a reference to wiretapping and bugging; that is Rome, first century A.D."

"About wiretapping," the senator seized the microphone, "this witness is not alone in pointing up the absolute necessity of making it legal here and now to use wiretap evidence in cases of espionage and sabotage. Why should a traitor to his country, a man like this, suspected of being in the pay of communist military intelligence, be protected by the laws he seeks to destroy, by this ruling about wiretapping? Why should a man like you, Mr. Leflore, dedicated to the destruction of our Constitution, come before a committee like this and take advantage of that Constitution to sabotage it and protect themselves?"

Under the flood of talk Daren subsided, shrugging, invoking the Fifth, while O'Malley trundled out the stock in trade of questions faced in former hearings, to chalk up, on each, the witness' incriminating refusal.

And yet, in a curious way, the Constitution served its purpose. When Leflore took that defense instituted by the Fathers, he found himself liberated from the dens of the private struggle. He had been in there slugging like a hot-headed fool, giving his mind to it, pretending there was an adversary susceptible to words, with whom he could debate world issues, and Cader was right; all it deserved was a formal shrug, like this the Amendment afforded. For the first time he had space and perspective.

He began to sec what was in front of him. O'Malley, a man, like others—self-righteous, self-doubting, self-sold. The embittered Bromion, jealous, at the heart of every Leflore. As if he too had rifted from an Anna he once loved, had hardened his diatribe against her. What else had aborted her dreams, hounded her from Western opportunity back to the Mother East of peasant toil? Study the features of that specter seated in the late-cycle soul, pommeling the hostile air:

Disenchantment marred the ultimate thunder. How had Daren missed it before? The pocket flask, those retreats to the inner chamber, under the knowing smirks of the aides. O'Malley was drunk and bored. From the Olympus of his fury he flung a glance at Gold—impervious to argument, shame, rage, everything but the half-despised and opportunistic sport of humbling people, escape from ennui, a poor pep pill, already beginning to pall.

Since Cader Ayres first stirred him up at Virginia, Daren had been asking of history: Where do we stand? Greece, Carthage, Rome? Can it be late Rome, the laceration, the vicious malaise? In those hearings he had quoted both Thucydides and Tacitus, wondering which applied. But when O'Malley flung Gold that look, it brought reality into the theorizing mind.

If this was Rome, there was no Pantheon, no Stoic vault—it was the corniest bloated Rome of Hollywood. "What the hell," the look said; "I've had enough of the public circus today."

To enter O'Malley in the way of fiction, to penetrate that soul, lacked probability. Daren couldn't have done it and didn't want to try. But a certain sick pathos began to open through the dumb, tough, clever, patriotic, malign façade. Façade after façade. And behind them? Was even the pathos a show?

As well go back to the cave and carry on the dialogue of the mind, trying to open solitude into something more than the reflected self. But action had ranged Daren here, at the bar. From the florid puppet master sated with the show, the bronze knight averted his eyes. Whatever else, he was going to charge the windmill.

"Senator, don't you know the men you're pitted against? Marx, Lenin, Mao. Those are tragic heroes, Senator. We need a leader as prophetic as any America ever produced: Jefferson, Lincoln, Thoreau, Whitman. And you're a clown. You belong in Opera Buffa.

We can't contend against world communism this way. You ought to step down."

But the void went on sounding with the abuse and contempt it had turned on the shakiest claimant to the sanctuary of the Fifth.

> Down, down I come like glistering Phaeton,
> Wanting the manage of unruly jades.

Daren had not known how close the senator was to that demise.

Looking for the confirmation of theory, the shore of freedom and human good overmastered by a violence rising like monsters from the sea, he had missed the basic recuperative signs:

The day O'Malley pounced on the lawyer who vexed him: "You're not the typical type communist lawyer that appears before this committee, so why should you oppose… "

And the new senator on the committee broke in: "I don't like that statement. It assumes guilt where no guilt is known."—To be swatted by O'Malley: "Go ahead, Senator; take up for the communist attorneys who appear before this committee. If you'd served as I have, month after month—let me finish—watching members of the communist conspiracy squirm and hedge and lie, you wouldn't butt in as you do."—The other senator piping down, biding his time…

O'Malley was not just tired of himself. The country was growing tired of the crusading wild man with the corny criminal ways. "Have you no shame, sir?"

Politicians everywhere were getting up spluttering, keelhauled by a wave they had thought they could ride like another. "This isn't the good old high jinks," they grumbled; "this is a disaster."

Already counter-committees were inquiring into the hysterical abuse of freedom. There was the congressional hearing on local laws, when the director of the Delaware police was asked about the Un-American Registration Law, by which anybody who had joined any of the hundreds of organizations on the attorney general's communist-front list was required to register immediately on entering Delaware, under penalty of two to ten years imprisonment:

"What is the name of that bridge… ?"

"The Delaware Memorial."

"You come off it, and go through a corner of Delaware to hit the Jersey Pike, right?"

"Right."

"And this law would include everybody going over that bridge?"

"It would."

"How many cars do you have going over there?"

"Anywhere from twelve thousand a day to seventy-five thousand on weekends."

"And the law aims at everybody in those vehicles, travelers, transients, whatever? That would be quite a job of enforcement, wouldn't it?"

"It is a job of enforcement."

"And how many communists have you caught in this net, Captain, in the two and a half years it has been in effect?"

"I don't think we caught any."

"That net must be full of holes. Ten million possible violators on one bridge, and you haven't nabbed a one?"

The perennial mayor of Patapseo City was called to defend his 1950 act requiring the registration of all communists and communist sympathizers:

"Well, I was worried. I got the feeling there were undercover communists in every city in the country plotting to overthrow us, and I wanted to smoke them out into the open."

"And how many have you smoked out in these five years?"

"That's the sad part of the ordinance. If we had the FBI working for us… But with our police force, there wasn't any way we could force the commies to register. We never registered a one."

"But did you ever question anybody to try to find out if he was a communist?"

"We didn't want a lawsuit on our hands."

"You mean you passed a law with no intention of trying to enforce it?"

"Well, we thought at the time the communists would come to the city hall and register."

"Why didn't you pass a law that thieves would have to give you notice before committing a robbery?"

The maligned Cader Ayres was accorded a respectful hearing when he addressed the Judiciary Committee from his wheelchair, on the threat to constitutional freedom:

> Civilization is a course of creative daring, to lift ourselves from the past by our spiritual bootstraps. Creative daring is always a source of danger.
>
> The fire-bearer, Prometheus, was tied to the rock and punished. But the way of Oceanus, who cautioned him to submit, is no less hazardous in a world requiring progress.
>
> The tradition of an open society, our constitutional freedom, is a technique for assuring that the risk-takings of the human spirit, at once fiery and containable, will not be prevented; and at the same time lessening the odds that they will destroy us.
>
> Our Constitution is strung between these poles. But it is less endangered, as De Tocqueville said, by rebels than by those who demand conformity.

For the way of Oceanus is easier.

And that other liberal, Micah Glenn, whose book Daren had read in the Chicago Ashram, without suspecting the ultimate convergence of their lifelines, was fighting the passport rulings of the State Department and had just won a crucial decision.

He had been denied a passport on the ground of communist sympathies, after he had led the public protest for a sane nuclear policy. Or rather he had been kept two years under investigation, submitting noncommunist affidavits without a decision, and with no power to appeal until a decision was made. Only when he sued for a mandatory injunction was the passport, in fact, denied. Then he appealed and spent another year defending himself against charges never stated. Finally he filed a complaint in the district court that the State Department was depriving him of liberty without due process. Thirty minutes before the case was to be tried, and when it had gained national publicity, he was handed a passport by the government attorneys.

Micah Glenn was not the man to let it go at that, and unlike Daren, he knew something about politics. So MacLean, the State Department hatchet man, whose preparatory experience was a low pass in a business college, then a poor success as want-ad salesman for a newspaper, then small-time reporter, until the threat of draft inclined him (1942) to dedicate himself to the FBI, as an agent for which he went around the country and even into the Caribbean chasing draft dodgers, and would have made it through the war unscathed, but for an irony of fortune, by which one night in a San Juan cabaret, as he was trying to get a line on some AWOL and to pick up at the same time a tan dancer, whom he was plying with drink, a brawl broke out over the girl, flared through the nightclub, with chairs and bottles flying, and MacLean got swiped in the right eye with a broken Coke bottle, eliminating that vile jelly, so ever after his gaze was more asquint than before, though the accident put him out of all danger of Pacific beaches, and landed him, by one shortcut or another, in the Washington passport office as overseer of so-called security aspects of the operation—that MacLean was now to be had over the coals:

Does it occur to you that for the Department to deny a citizen and former American soldier, a wearer of the Purple Heart and the Cross of the Legion of Honor, a passport on the charge that he is a concealed communist, and to hold to that denial until he brings suit, and then, without any additional evidence of his alleged communism, to issue the passport, implying that he is no longer a concealed communist—doesn't it seem to you that such a procedure is unfair, and not in accord with the constitutional guarantees to which a citizen is entitled?

MacLean's answer bared the death's head of security:

A judiciary system is meant to punish overt acts of disloyalty. The burden of proof is on the state, and as long as there is a reasonable doubt, a man is to be considered innocent. But a security system is intended to prevent such acts. No guilt is needed, no proof can be adduced; future acts are not susceptible of proof. A security system proceeds against all who are alleged doubtful, all who might constitute a risk.

The decision, however, took it out of the province of the State Department to deny a passport without giving reasonable grounds.

It would be years before that context of resurgence would come to light, revealing the inevitability of O'Malley's overthrow; and when it did, one could not take it for an unmixed assurance—since it could also be construed in the terms Ayres had quoted from De Tocqueville: that no such eccentric and egoistic jerk, whether of Left, Right or Middle, genius or charlatan, serving God or the devil, would long be tolerated by the conservative establishment of shopkeeping America. That what would send Leflore back to brood in his study would also squelch his antagonist O'Malley.

As he worked late nights on his account of the investigation, Daren had not foreseen all that. But in the last minutes of the hearing, he had caught the essential glimpse: vacancy, a jaded scorn. He ended his book, *The Hostile Witness,* which he had been writing all fall and into the spring:

What have we been doing? We have been at the old pastime of making devils out of cardboard masks.

7. The Unmarried Land

Woodruff Farm, Sept. 28, 1958

Dear Daren:

I don't know why we haven't kept in touch. Climbing trees and looking at stars might have bridged the family gap. But you're a public figure now, and can expect fan mail. Hurrah for the Hostile Witness, and down with the Committee of Ill Fame!

My own negligible success has been in painting, but I have an unpublished book I'd like to show you. It springs from a trip I made summer before last to look after Aunt Betsy in Delta Landing. It'll take a Mississippian to get the drift. The rest of the county regards fiction as a chicanery for keeping serious people focused on trivial concerns.

My second wife is a gentle Quaker, and I have two half-Quaker daughters who, for a blessing, partake more of the Woodruffs than of the Byrnes. That's a theme for the novel; but the immediate tie is that all these Quakers are related, and that Lucy turns out to be second cousin to your next-door neighbors the Tysons.

We are planning to drive down Sunday week to see them and that Patapsco City of yours, which we hear is a spectacle, and I hoped we could take you in as one of the natural curiosities of the place. Cousin Barbara is impressed not only by your stand, but by your anchoritic solitude; but I'm hoping you can be lured across the yard for Sunday dinner.

We were born, I think, in the same year, went to the same high school, both studied abroad before the war. I have even heard that you worked at Chicago, where I did my last teaching; and now we find ourselves in the blessed state of Maryland. If your Hearing means you're also as reckless as I have the reputation of being, we could practically pass for alter egos.

Lucy is arranging with her cousins, and they'll be in touch with you. Join us. It's about time.

If I didn't think it might scare you off, I'd say I'll bring the MS.

Yours,

Dan Byrne

A letter to be glossed:

Gloss 1) *Climbing trees:* The title of Tarzan in the Ape Club to be defended by leaps and swings in the Byrnes' great rope-rigged oaks. Leflore, the rangier, was better at the wide leaps and stretches; but the muscular compact Dan Byrne could have swung onto a cannonball. Daren challenged the title once, dropped the knotted rope as he stood on a high limb, and as it swung back leapt far out for it, letting go at the end to sail for another rope hanging from the neighbor's tree. Dan Byrne tried, stood on the same branch and dropped the rope again and again, watched it come back far out, but couldn't bring himself to leap, until finally, with beating his chest and giving the bull-ape cry, he got steamed up, hurtled into the air, almost missed, held by his finger tips through the arc, then let go or slipped off, aiming for the other rope, but off balance, so he soared over Ladybird Alexander's bushes and came down in her flower bed with a thud that brought her from the porch screaming: "Are you hurt? Where are you hurt?" while Dan lay groaning about his back, his back. "Which back?" she cried. "My lower back," groaned Dan. Because he had lit in her rose bush on his tail.

To get even, Dan invented what he called a catamaran. He tied the longest rope to the end of a short one that hung from near the crotch, and then rode it down. It was like the monkey who lugged the rope up to the limb where it was tied and jumped off with it. When the slack took up in the short rope, there was a jerk that sent ropes, knot, Dan and all whiplashing in a loop-de-loop. He came down still on the knot, though it almost robbed him of his boyhood. By sheer dumbness he had hit on the killingest challenge of all. Daren had to risk it or lose his place.

He swung. When the jerk came, his lankier frame couldn't take it. His hands tore loose and he went on down, spinning, hitting on his back on the sidewalk, not his lower back, but that whole upper and middle back from shoulder blades to loins, and if his head hadn't been off the concrete (or as Judge Byrne would always speculate in such cases, made of concrete anyway) he might have cracked that too. He sank into a blackness he thought was death, his last reflection being how nonsensical to go out like a candle for such a foolish cause. But his breath came back, though for a while he was afraid to move, and had to challenge Dan Byrne from the ground to try it that way, flying through the air with the greatest of ease.

For weeks he hobbled around in cramps and stitches. What a bonanza! If the old nose doctor who drilled everybody's sinuses and made them slaves for life, always coming back to be drained, had been a bone surgeon and known about disks, he'd have strapped Daren down and grafted his shinbone in his back and kept him half a year in a cast; but nobody in the Delta was up to those tricks yet; so all the interference he suffered was from Aunt Willi Mari's osteopath, a colossal woman, who twisted his arms around his neck at odd angles and popped every joint in his spine, until the damage of the fall disappeared under the dislocation she was supplying. Aunt Willi kept sending him every few days for a month, but he got well anyway. It didn't even stop his climbing (into colleges, or elsewhere); all the harm it did was to give him aches between the shoulder blades in damp weather for the rest of his life—but everybody needs fallen reminders.

Gloss 2) *Looking at stars:* Leflore leafed through the flle and found it, set down years ago; Oxford, romance of science; accounted for.

Gloss 3) *The family gap:* Hard to specify.

Since the house Judge Byrne built of solid brick with its walls two feet thick and its great library and law study was grander than anything else in town; and there was a lonely eminence about the judge, rather embittered by life, sitting in his lighted study under the great columns, reading his history and Dickens and Shakespeare, far into the night. To yokels driving by, he must have seemed as nobly remote as Milton's solitary Platonist. They could not feel the strain with which that antebellum imitation pushed into the Old South, as the midwestern and middle-class Byrnes thrust into a planter aristocracy the Leflore's had led since before the Civil War. That was the rift of origin, and it had come to a focus once, before Daren or Dan Byrne was born, when Judge Byrne supported the demagogue Vandamar against the Leflore interest, and Vandamar's follower Gyves snaked up from below, accusing and backbiting, and came to power through the rift in what should have been the well-bred. ("What can you expect," the old-timer had said, "when a retiring Yankee photographer and a climbing Kentucky demon of a wife set out to rear a talented but naive son?")

Gloss 4) you... *a public figure now.*

Yes, one of the seasonal sittings had at last borne demonstrable fruit. Cader Ayres had read *The Hostile Witness* and sent it to his own publisher. A month before he sank into the final coma ("Of course, I back my friends; all I ask of them is to be worth backing"), he heard of its acceptance.

Almost a year had been given to the writing; another went by in revising, waiting, reading proof; the best part of a third produced minimal sales and desultory reviews; then suddenly, out of the clear blue, the book took a national award, everybody began talking about it, Daren became an authority on investigation. As O'Malley went out of favor, magazines began to ask for articles on that topic of national concern. It bid fair to become the business of Daren's life, when in fact there was nothing he was more determined to put behind him. Every review of his book vexed him, though he went on reading them, looking for them, and that vexed him more. He kept thumbing through his copy, making marks in it, as if it were in his power to do something about it, when in fact it was gone from him and should have been banished from his mind. Whether people praised it or damned it tied him equally to a past he needed to avoid. After the splurge of that fierce action, no new work, outer or inner, caught him in the compulsion of its charge. He picked up the old books, read them and missed the rapture. It seemed Anna was right and that without her all he called spirit would wither to a dream of idleness. Mere mummy. What was the flaw of the self-contained?

Though both philosophy and religion have conceived of the divine as too perfect for want, and have described the highest human activities (contemplation, charity, beatitude) as self-rewarding—yet caught as we are in process (as God perhaps is), a withering attends the circular, the blight of a Second Law: that every isolated system comes to rest. The pure pursuit of soul has shriveled time and again to a circle of recurrence, boredom, the rat's maze of pastime. Staring from the same window on the same course of the seasons—was it possible that success should have brought him the dreariest interregnum of his life?

Gloss 5) *Your anchoritic solitude:* As well the Quakers didn't know all the facts.

The physics of Daren's youth had tried to crack atoms with charged particles, speeding them up for the crash landing, hoping to give them force enough to penetrate atomic fields. Then neutrons appeared, uncharged, sliding over the thresholds, free to enter and leave the sanctums. With regard to the heart, he discovered he had become a neutron.

He verified what Aunt Willi's tutelage and the spell of the stone lion had obscured in his youth; how instinctive, common, easy and plentiful "that boring bed-business" is—and not so boring either—one could almost say with Faulkner's Old Man ("Did you get it, and was it good?") "It's always good." What it lacked was life-significance.

Without exactly pining for Anna, or even for another marriage—like the widower in the minstrel show, he had tried that:

> Wuz a man, named Misser Poe,
> Had a raven, jus a plain ol crow
> Wuz always a croakin of "Nevermo,"
> Weil, sub, if dat old crow had knowed what Ah know,
> He would a said "Nevermo," an *den* some mo—

Daren recognized that the sequence of modern loves didn't accomplish much.

Not the wife of Zach Taylor, bored with her Aristotelian, who used to pop in on her way to town, to see if Daren needed anything—and he did for a while, until she moved on to the freer exchanges of the student body.

Not the Italian girl from the vineyards of Lake Canandaigua, who had gazed at him darkly over the walls of his teacher-fortress until she graduated, and returning for Homecoming, surmised at the cocktail party that the portcullis was withdrawn, Joseph Andrews no longer struggling for his virtue, and she came to the house, and they met in the twilight sleep of the new mores, a passion like wind on water, that blows and leaves no sign: "You men," she moaned through a dark curtain of hair, ·we invented you for our amusement, to fill our vacancy." Mother-void, giving birth to the brief stir of day.

Not the wife of the Baltimore lawyer, who had always come over to his lectures, and brought him her rather confessional stories from time to time. ("Let him marry a woman, good Isis, who cannot go.")

To resist the luxurious slopes on which he was already descending, he thought of *la pauvre mère*, Minkowsky space, the labor theory of value, anything to distract him from that longing face and willowing frame, to slow him down. And now he had skirted the maelstrom, arrived at his second wind, so why shouldn't there he hope, even for her?

> My man is a deep sea diver
> with a stroke that can't go wrong:
> He dive way down to the bottom,
> and he hold his breaf so long…

Depth was not enough. He changed positions, bringing the hand also into play. Slowly she warmed, quickened into thrashing, he, hoping every tamp would do it. On and on, in desperation. Furtively her own hand slipped under his; the yearning face hardened, "To tear our pleasures with rough strife," the hand too going wild. She was manipulating herself, he the supplement only, almost an interference. And still there was no abandonment. How could there be? The soulful beauty, which had weathered lust and frenzy without fulfillment climaxed into grief. She was lying, deeply stroked, stroking herself and weeping. Forty minutes of satyr play had come to nothing but autoerotic tears. "There, there," he kissed them away, subdued. The power to yield, to spend become a weakness rather than a strength. The electrodden rat, jumping on the treadle for the pleasure-prod. If God would take flesh again and again it would become a titillation.

Gloss 6) *Reckless:* Dan Byrne? It seemed to have landed him in a bed of ease.

Gloss 7) *The MS.:* 'Well, why not? But there was no need to write him; he was bound to bring it anyway.

Anna had shared the Quaker stand on peace. Pacifism, she thought, was fine for noncommunist nations. But the tidy alliance with wealth and propriety put her off. The Tysons had invited them the first year at Patapsco to a tea party. But when Howard Tyson told of his admired Germantown Uncle Steward, how he was out in his pony cart once and saw a cop chasing a slum kid, who was about to get away, when Steward Cope (he was a young man then) sprang from his seat, leaped over the road and, with a flying tackle, brought the culprit to the ground, gave him to the officer and went back to his cart, brushing the dust off his jacket—Anna couldn't contain herself: "I think the slum kid must have appealed more to Christ than Horatio Alger, the conquering Quaker."

They had lived on decent terms with the Tysons all these years; but it was another thing for Daren to sit down in a Quaker circle broken only by himself and Dan Byrne—and more conspicuously by the flamboyant Byrne, though he had married into it. The Quakers seemed to have a way of being as queer as all get out without the flaming egoism of southern revolt. Dan Byrne stood out like a sore toe, talking in a big voice about his three categories of people: "the people who eat a lot and get fat; it's clear what's gone with the food, there're *fat-producers.* And the people who eat almost nothing; they don't get fat, but they're full of pep: they're the *energy-producers.* Now the're these other people who eat all the time, but they don't get fat, and they don't stir around much. What have they done with all that food? There's only one answer: they're the *dung-producers...*" While everybody around the table, fat and lean, was gobbling as much as he could—

But when Cousin Howard, getting ready to serve the dessert, came across a chipped bowl, and without a word hurled it back over his head at the radiator, smashing it to flinders, except for a regretful small start from

Cousin Barbara and a squeal (of delight) from the six-year-old daughter and the ringing for the maid to bring another, nobody paid it any mind at all, and that very successful Quaker broker, Howard Tyson, didn't so much as ripple the retiring tenor of his talk; for he had been breaking the flawed china that way, and even the pieces that didn't take his aesthetic fancy, in the dining room, or washing up in the kitchen, for years. Daren was the most stirred, because suddenly he realized what those crashes were he had heard off and on coming from the house, and could never account for. A pity Anna wasn't there to hold a disquisition on conspicuous consumption.

Which Daren (or better still, Dan Byrne) could have matched with another on the contained antithesis of violence in Quakerdom. With the Tysons it showed also in the dog. They had owned that original armor-tank mastiff who chased the chickens off the cliff and smashed his carcass on the railroad track below. He had been replaced with another, harmless, they said, as he roared up to the guests; but nobody liked to cross him, so the whole house hung on his whims. You'd have thought they liked to live, as in a police state, under a power they couldn't quite control. They had to put all the food out of his reach. Of course Lucy forgot and set the fruitcake on the coffee table, and that brindled big son of a bitch grabbed it (you could have put your head in his mouth) and went to wolfing it on the floor. There wasn't a soul who wanted to take it away from him, though the teen-age boy had a cache of mousetraps laid by for these occasions. He cocked them up one after another and flung them at old Brawn's backside, thinking the metal snap and maybe a pinch or two would teach him, and it did make him jump a little and growl as his jaws crunched down. When he had pretty well had his fill, Mrs. Tyson used moral persuasion: "Now, Brawn, aren't you ashamed? A big dog like you to be so naughty." And Brawn, who was foolishly fond of her, when he didn't have other concerns, wagged his rump and put his great drooly mug in her lap, looked sheepish, then stalked across the room and flopped by the hearth. While the liberal Quaker Tyson went on talking of other matters.

It was a foretaste of Dan Byrne's book. Daren had known the Mississippi characters all his life; and now he got introduced to the Quaker ones: Lucy's clear voice came from across the table, telling of her grandfather, how he used to drive from Germantown in his shiny black Buick. He was her idea of the perfect Quaker gentleman, tall, slim, quiet, in his gray striped suit and starched collar, as if he had just come from a board meeting at the Germantown Trust. And how her father had tried to make some dandelion wine, and brought out a bottle for a treat, bragging about how clear it was, "Look at the color of that," opened it and poured Grandfather a glass. They were standing in the yard, and that smiling Quaker gentleman, one shiny black boot on the running board of his shiny black car, took a big mouthful, and all at once, with a noise like blowing his nose, spewed it out on the ground. "Damn," he said. Lucy couldn't have been more surprised if he'd opened his mouth and a bat had flown out.

Dan Byrne had already written his book and brought the first form along, but he was still ready to plaster it over with enriching matter, so whenever Lucy or the Tysons would open up, he would grab for his pen and his pocket papers and try to scribble it all down:

About the stuffy old English teacher at the Friends School, who told the town girl if she wanted to write a paper on Frost's "Birches," she'd have to get the feel of the thing, find her a birch and ride it down—could hardly fathom the poem until she'd plumbed the fact. She never asked the dope how he could go on teaching it year after year when he couldn't tell a birch from a cottonwood; no, she located a birch in the Arboretum, went up and sprang out, only it must have been a sick birch, because it broke, and she crashed to the ground with a compound fracture of the leg. "Well, it was a good theory," the old dodo told the class. "After all, poetry is emotion recollected in tranquility." And he tranquilly folded his hands on a belly that would have staggered the birch of all birches.

Dan would interrupt sometimes, seeing everything in terms of his fiction, but even Leflore, hearing the stories of Nathaniel Pendle, mystic and eccentric of Germantown, had already thought of Dan's aunt, Betsy Byrne.

"Oh, he was a careful driver; never went more than thirty; and when he had to turn right, he'd pull way over to the left against traffic, slow down almost to a stop, and then make this wide, careful turn; only once he miscalculated and ran into a car coming out of the same side road. He dropped the wheel and clasped his hands. He'd done everything he could, and he didn't want to blame the other fellow, so he sat in silent prayer.

"One night," Tyson said, "coming back from Haverford, he got on the wrong side of the four-lane speedway and drove miles with all the cars honking and swerving. But he didn't get flurried or speed up at all. Always cautious, always steady. He didn't even notice the cop with his light and siren. We'd been going the same direction on the right side of the highway and saw him turn into a gas station, so we stopped to find out what the cop would do. But he never had a chance. All you could hear was Cousin Nathaniel's shrill voice: 'So good of you to stop to help me, officer. I don't know what's wrong with the car. It never burned oil before. But it's burning oil now.' And steam spouting out the front like a geyser. That was the only reason he'd got off the road. He hadn't heard the siren at all."

"Doggone it," said Dan Byrne, "I can't put that in. It's too much like Aunt Bets. Unless I could make it part of the bridge. You see," he said to Daren, "there are these family oppositions. And I don't want to blur them too much."

He led him to the window—Daren remembering now how tired Dan Byrne used to make him feel, one of those supercharged vitalities. If people claimed fatigue, he would say he'd never experienced the sensation. And his damned nerves so easy he could drop off to sleep anywhere and wake whenever he wanted to. Why during the Great Flood when the two families were stranded on the levee in the cold rain waiting for a barge to get them out of there, Dan Byrne had curled up in a little packing box hardly big enough for a dog and snoozed away, then jumped up peppy when everybody else was worn to a frazzle.

They sat in the window seat, and Dan talked so much about *The Married Land* and the "reconstructive novel"—"If a thing exists, I say it's possible. And generation exists. We don't live in fragmentation only. Look how society has put itself together since the last war. I study my own marriage as the type of that"—he was so wrapped up in it, he missed Lucy's quiet, bright voice talking with Cousin Howard across the room:

"When the Susquehanna was frozen over Daddy used to take us down skating. He had a big sail he'd lift into the wind. We'd swing to his belt, and when the train came along the shore, 'Here we go,' he'd say, and spread the sail, and we'd race the train. And when the wind was good, we'd beat it, too."

By the end of the day, Daren was so deep in the family he started to call Barbara Tyson cousin. He knew about her childhood and what a trouble she was to her mother, always pretending to be something she wasn't. Her mother caught her once chewing a dead mouse, and when she tried to get it away; "Mother," Barbie cut her off sternly, 'I'm an owl." He knew about her child Debbie, whom he'd wondered about before. "Maybe Quaker independence has gone too far," said Cousin Barbara.

"It started before she could talk. She loved things that were round. Her first words weren't 'Daddy' and 'Momma,' but 'lid' and 'wheel.' When she was three she began to call everything a lid. Then she said she was a lid herself. By the time she went to kindergarten, I couldn't tell her to climb up and wash her hands. 'You don't climb up,' she'd say; 'and you don't have hands. You roll up and you have wheels.' The same with her nose; we had to wipe her button. And she kept changing her name. I never could remember which name she wanted, and if I called her Debbie she had a fit.' You're not a Debbie!' (She always called herself 'you.') 'You're not a Shasta Daisy and you're not a Tinkle Bell and you're not a Singing Pipe. You put all those in a room and lock the door and they're crying. You're a Spinning Wheel.'

"I still can't read her a story the way it's written. In *Alice* whenever it says 'the poor girl' she grabs the book. 'Not poor. She's not poor.' And I have to skip all that about tears or change it so it doesn't make sense."

"I took her to the zoo this summer and a mother came along with a child bigger than Debbie. The child came up and gave her a shove. 'Don't hurt the poor little girl,' the mother said. Well, Debbie trailed that woman ail over the place poking her head up at her and saying: 'Dearie, I'm not poor. I'm not poor, dearie.'

"Where are those children, anyway?"

"They came in the back. I heard them going upstairs," said Lucy. "I'll see."

There was a giggle from Hester and Mardie. Lucy found them in the dark closet with Debbie and the boys from across the street. "What are you up to?" They were standing pressed back amongst the clothes, their arms straight to their sides.

"Shut the door," said Debbie "This is an elevator."

But Cousin Barbara wanted to tidy her up before her great-great aunt arrived. It had been arranged by letter, but the phone call came all the way from Germantown. "Yes, dear," said Howard; "when is thee coming? I'll meet the train,"

'I'm phoning about the timetable," said Aunt Hester. "It says the train leaves Philadelphia at two-thirty. But with this queer time, tell me, please, docs that mean one-thirty or three-thirty? Cousin Barbie flung back the door. "Come on out now, Debbie."

"I'm not Debbie. I'm a record, honey." "Well, let me comb your hair."

"Not hair, honey. Grooves."

"Don't be silly. All children have hair."

"But honey, I'm not a child."

"Of course you're a child. And you'll know it too, when you get older."

"But honey, I *am* older. I'm sixteen…"

Looking up at her mother with long-suffering, six-year-old impudence.

Daren took the manuscript of *The Married Land,* along with an invitation for the next weekend to Woodruff Farm.

The novel—he thought at first—was a soggy mass. Then, like a baroque painting, it began to stretch into form. His playmate, crazy Dan Byrne, had done that, and it was almost there, almost alive. "He's brought it off—the egoism and family pose, that interminable *Sound and Fury* style, the arrogation and slime-mold of the South; he's put it all on his Tarzan shoulders, and he's walking off with it. Toward Lucy, his Holy Light. Well, she's a sweet person. God help her."

Byrne met the train at Aberdeen and drove Leflore back over Deer Creek, up the river hills, down the lane through the tulip wood, pointing, as if to famous sights: "That's the spring—at the beginning, where they kneel"—the visit for him another means of projecting the book. Daren had visualized it already. Most of the week, in his own Patapsco cave, he had been with Dan Byrne in Betsy's Delta dens, reaching for this dream of calm.

Hester and Mardie came from the house with Corny, the yellow bitch cur, all in full cry. Lucy had committed Daren to a game of Hare and Hounds that afternoon. "Naw," Byrne had said, "let him run. I got fallen arches on my phallic feet." And Lucy to the kids: "Well, he's a jackrabbit, I'll bet." While they ripped up newspapers until they had a shopping bag full of tiny bits.

With a fifteen-minute lead, Daren lit out across rolling fields, through fall woods, over streams, sifting shreds of paper all along those beautiful river hills, making false trails, doubling back where he had started and veering off another way. In the next valley, where a stream gullied down to Broad Creek and the Susquehanna, he dodged through the honeysuckle and briar, hearing far behind the first yelps of Dan Byrne and Lucy, Hester, Mardie, the cousins and neighborhood kids. He ran upstream to a bridge, started a trail up the steep bank on the other side, flinging paper into the brush—over the hills and far away—then ducked back across the stream and down, his loops and crossings more frenzied, a hare catching the cry of the hounds. Where to hide? He seized clairvoyant impulse, better than maps or knowledge, slid over the clay bank, where a flatrooted beech had been undermined by floods. Curled in the earthcave, he looked through trailing roots and vines across eddying water to the slopes on the other side. His trail ran right above him, but he was pocketed, underground.

The chase neared and passed, baying, feet pounded, loosening dirt in his hair. They crossed the stream and came back; they went up the hill on both sides, beating in the bushes, scouting for a lost trail. The sounds of pursuit faded. He might as well be dead. The next time they closed in, not baying now but debating, "He must be around here somewhere." Daren gave a moan. From the grave. But what they heard was the echo. "On the other side," said Hester, "across the stream." They appeared with Lucy in the gossamer and sun motes there, Mardie in her red sweater, bright as flame. Daren gave another moan. They couldn't see him for the curtain of vines. He moaned again. And Hester, with her quick eyes, caught the paleness of his skin through the veil. "I see him, I see him there." Lucy lifted up her sweet muzzle and bayed. After such a long wait, it was a pleasure to be found.

"There's one little point in your novel," said Daren that night, "which isn't quite clear to me. You were out there in the pinewoods at the beginning, pulling that poison ivy as if the farm depended on you. But when you got the call from Mississippi, all you had to do was postpone some lectures in Baltimore, and rush off to look after your aunt. And even your farm-wife Lucy, who's so strong on the hussifly chores" (he flung Lucy a glance as she sat by the fire knitting) "could pick up and go to her uncle in Germantown. Now I've never run a farm, but I thought: It must be haymaking time, and how are they going to throw it up and disappear in opposite directions?"

Daren had inferred the answer. He had gone out with Dan Byrne a little before to talk with an impoverished hired man about painting the barn. "You've got that bad allegation condition," the fellow said, peeling off the flakes. "It ought to be all burnt off of there and redid."—"Well, don't let your boys burn it off," said Dan, "or there won't be any barn left to paint. They got to keep cutting corn anyway, haven't they?"

"I couldn't go into the whole economics of the farm," Dan told Leflore. "But we're going to take you for a picnic tomorrow over to Dudleyville, and you can meet Ma and the rest of the Dudleys. They're the ones who farm the place. (That was her husband to day, though he's a Mullen.) And we invited Tilman Page from Baltimore. He knew your father long ago. And your mother. Says they met at his house."

Tilman Page arrived early—a Jamesian bachelor, stately, impressive. He was a man of family, wealth, intelligence, refinement, everything but the knack of getting ahead in the crass world of power. In youth, under Wilson, he had done the state some service, but had been jostled out, to join those Americans aware of themselves since Henry Adams as the disqualified best. Had not Uncle Hazlewood been of the southern branch?

"Your father had a client, Comelia Ireys, I believe, who broke her hip in Baltimore when the trolley started as she was stepping off. He came up to try the case, and stayed with us (through some Virginia connection); and your mother, who was teaching Greek at Goucher College, was invited that evening."

Woodruffi Farm had been Tilman's defense against the betrayals of the world; and while Quaker families might have seemed large enough already, he had always been a loved addition to their country junketings, the more perhaps for his being so quaintly of the town—as when he stretched out once in a steaming tub, trying to shut off the leaky tap with his great toe, until it came loose and the hot water spurted out, and he sprang up yelling for help.

"The Dudleys are the first land-grant settlers," he told Daren, "and we're the parvenu. If you could have seen them at family reunion boil out of the barn like shrapnel from a trench mortar, the boys flinging themselves on steers and bulls, the beautiful fifteen-year old Irene (she's run off now) on a bony mule, lashing it with a loop of wire, and her red hair flying. It was only the missus who kept things together."

They were walking in on the old coach lane, rutted and grown up in trees, a footpath now where coaches and phaetons had clattered by. They had crossed the stream on stepping stones where a Dudley of twelve, maybe, was sucking on a corncob pipe, leaning against an oak tree older than the farm. He answered their greeting with a grunt not so much surly as dumb.

Lucy, in the lead, walked with a gangling grace, a motion she had picked up as a child, slipping barefoot through the weeds. You would have thought the world was the snakepit through which she danced her way.

As they came out on top, the land went rolling off in all directions, fields with zigzag rail the fences, then woods, dropping to the Susquehanna, a blue lake stretching to the dam. On what had once been a terraced lawn stood the ruins of a stone mansion, burned down a hundred years ago, below it the gaunt, unpainted box in which the family lived, like those two-story bare houses built in the South after the Civil War. The old barn was an enormous skeleton of hand-hewn and mortised timbers, built like the keel of a ship. It had lost its roof in a storm and never been repaired, and most of the silvery pine sheathing had gone for the other barn, pretty large, though not up to the ruin, and already leaning and weather warped.

They walked to the house. Uncle Abe was on the porch with a broken leg; he had fallen off the roof shingling; a grandchild sat by him with his false teeth in her mouth. A boy came up from the river with a pole and sack. "Any luck?"

"Just enough to make the skillet stink."

"Where's the missus?"

She was in the barn.

A big woman. More muscle than fat, but plenty of both. She wore a faded blue-green dress with a blue-green old-fashioned bonnet tied over her head. A large face looked out, sunburned, but still showing signs of the clear milk-and-cream complexion of English settlers, and sparkled through with the most luminous blue eyes. She was standing by a great black cow, struggling to get a calf to take the tit. It was a wall-eyed calf, blind, misshapen, a hung-down chest and a square lumpish head, feet cloven way up the shank; it would break loose and go in circles, butting her as it staggered around. She would grab it, practically lift it up, turn it around and aim it back under the cow. "Mooncalf," she muttered, "you got to shit or get off the pot."

Then she saw them: "That ornery old black cow don't like this blind calf, no siree. It's not hern, and she don't want to feed it. T'other day she backed up against me with her rear all messy, and took me just here," patting the floursack bosom. "She knocked me against the mooncalf and he butted me back against her. Looked like they had ganged up to pass me back and forth betwixt em."

"Do you mind, Miss Dudley" (Tilman Page never called her Mullen), "if we have a picnic out on your beautiful point?"

"You know you're welcome, Mr. Page, and all the Woodruffs, always."

"And won't you join us?"

"Maybe I'll come later to pass the time of day. But I can't eat. Thank you."

They walked out past the burying ground, where the marble monuments of the eighteenth century yielded to planks and unmarked mounds. The old box bushes were charred skeletons, fired by one of the boys, trying to burn off the weeds.

They were washing down broiled chicken, dark Virginia ham and Lucy's brown bread with the Pouilly Fuissé Tilman had brought in a plastic ice bag, and he was telling about how he used to come to buy hens when the Dudley kids were little, and they would sail out of the house, and throw themselves on the chickens as they dashed clucking around the yard. "You were lucky to get one that had a cluck left in it." And how all nine of them would line up at milking time, even little Elsie, the baby, like Br'er Rabbit's chillun, their heads leaning against the sides of the cows, milking away.

"Well how do they find time to farm for you Byrnes," said Daren, "if they got a farm of their own?"

"They lost most of the land," said Tilman. "And it never pays. They have to hire themselves out like sharecroppers to keep up with the debts."

He looked across the field and saw Mrs. Mullen coming from the house. She was not alone.

"Oh no," he said, "No. But it is. That's her baby brother. The only reliable, hard-working, energetic male Dudley. The pick of the litter, and he's made good; he's a well-driller, has his own rig, the oldest kind of a rig, but he can feel his way through the rock. And he's honest and ambitious. And you know, he's gone absolutely mad over communism and Negroes and Jews. He argues all the time. The rabid Right. And I can see already he's got one of those pamphlets he's always trying to educate me on. You think I can crawl into that groundhog hole?"

"Mighty lucky to find you here, Mr. Page." Bo Dudley wrinkled the skin between his honest crow-foot eyes. "I've got the proof on that plot we were talking about. You remember, by the Jews. To take over the world. Published by Christian Common Sense Press. It's a translation from the Russian."

So they had to submit, as if to a new thing, to the 1905 likely forgery of Sergei Nilus, Pan-Slavic fanatic, which when first translated in 1921 had stirred up Henry Ford and others, and was now to be resurrected and exploited by the new defenders of Constitutional America:

THE MOST DIABOLICAL PLOT IN WORLD HISTORY. PROOF THAT COMMUNISM IS A JEWISH WORLD PLOT TO ENSLAVE THE GENTILES BY CREATING WARS AND REVOLUTIONS, AND TO SEIZE POWER DURING THE RESULTING CHAOS AND RULE AS THE CHOSEN PEOPLE.

How so-called Liberals, Socialists, Atheists, Professors have become blind agents to carry the banners of Jewish anti-Americanism.

"Why do you carry that pistol?" Daren asked, pointing to the six-shooter swelling the holster at Dudley's belt. "Why, mister, we got to be armed to defend our freedom any minute—with all the niggers, Jews, communists and hoodlums around, and every president for twenty years in secret cahoots with em. I wouldn't go out of the house without a weapon."

He had dug a well at Woodruff Farm for the cattle; for with the water table always falling and the droughts, those deeper irreplaceable stores were everywhere being tapped. "For five days," said Dan as they walked to the car, "his drill and his tongue kept a-pounding. There's no reasoning with him. It's paranoia; all your arguments serve his proof. He brought his little girls one day, and Hester was talking about a Dracula who sucks your blood. 'Well that must be a Jew or a nigger,' said his five-year-old, 'because white people don't do that.'"

They drove back along the Susquehanna past the dam. There were dead fish everywhere, and an appalling smell.

"They shut off the flow," said Page, "to put in more dynamos. First thing anybody knew, ninety tons of fish had died in the pools under the dam. So they opened the floodgates and washed all those rotten shad and rock down the river..."

"It'll smell worse," Dan groaned, "if the Pennsylvanians flush their sulfur-polluted mines down here."

"Who can stop them?" said Page with the helplessness of one deeply invested in all the companies he deplores…

"So here you are living on this beautiful Susquehanna farm," Daren told Daniel that night, "as if you were a farmer, though you can't farm and you don't farm, and you're dependent on a broken down family of original settlers vested centuries ago by royal grant in the entire county out of which your claim and the other claims have been carved, so all the Dudleys have left is some rocky slopes over a crossroad that still bears their name, a remnant so unproductive that the whole family have to hire out like serfs on their own lost acres, scratching for money that doesn't come from the land anyway, but gets piped in from cartel investments somebody has left you happier few endowed withal—"

Laying it on in high Mississippi style, though with a more collective message (the voice, the voice of Anna), and at the same time ironically aware that the one scrap of possession he could pull over his own threatened head was the fruit of an export trade in painted trash baskets—

"Talk about a symbolic fiction. You're writing of the Married Land and you've left out the Mooncalf and Bo Dudley's gun-happy freedom-fascism spreading like wildfire in the grassroots of Amer1ica…"

"Don't be hard on Bo Dudley," said Lucy (like her father, when a conversation got abstract, disarmingly out of it). "They've had troubles since before I can remember. His pa was our hired man in the Depression. We laid him off time and again, thought he was shiftless and no good, but he'd come back begging for the job, and finally he went to coughing in the hay barn and had a terrible hemorrhage and died not long after. It was TB that had been getting him down. We were hard up, too, even with the money from England: I don't know how we'd have made it that year, if my sister hadn't found a stamp in the attic with the picture of Washington upside down…"

"No," said Leflore. "That's impossible. Say that again."

"It was in a trunk of old letters, and Dad sent it to a dealer, who offered a couple of hundred. 'Just hold on,' said Mother. So the dealers snooped around to make sure it was real. Then they began to bid, first two thousand, then four, then five. That was what we took, though we found out later the dealer already had a buyer for eight.

"For years after that, anybody in the neighborhood who happened on an old stamp would run to Mother: 'What about this one? You think I ought to send it to Scotts?'"

"All right," Daren said, getting up and pacing the room, "I knuckle under. Your whole life is symbolic; it falls into a fiction; and maybe you're right it's just the bridge between you and Lucy's order—certainly nobody but a fairy godmother could have Washington—and the Republic—topsy-turvy working on their side. So your novel is a celebration of structure, harmony out of discord, *The Married Land.* You've got it. But I haven't, And in a world of what you call fragmentation, I'm naturally doubtful of easy settlements."

"Easy?" said Byrne. "You have to reckon the cost."

"The cost is negligible as long as it's a little less than everything."

Dan Byrne turned to Lucy and nodded his head. He got that.

"Very well," said Leflore. But my life suggests a novel, too, the opposite of yours. *The Half Gods pine for your abode.* Someday I'll write it. There's Anna shaking the world with her communism, and me on my rock, mining within."

It was not Dan Byrne who put the question, though it required him to be framed. It vibrated in the space between them, where Leflore's fiction, first outwardly exhibited, could be inwardly tried.

"You mean communism is the active, and is of the East and your introspection is the only Western way?"

No. The plot was open-ended, not yet performed. As with Daniel's Sybil and Lucy, there had to be another woman in the case—someone as active as Anna but her contrary. The requirements hovered in the air: charming, British, well-born—a temporal glitter of deeds,and under it silence, mystery, perhaps love. Daren knew very well who it was, but he did not know where. Or how far the vanished Jeffrey could have prepared herself for her fictional role.

He waked early the last morning and went to the window to watch the dawn, the mist rising from the pond, the pine woods dark across the field. From overhead somewhere came a far-off haunting cry. Daren looked up. In the blue sector between the roof and maple there was nothing.

The house door flung open and Lucy ran out, her shoulder-length hair and pale gown billowing around her. It seemed her father and mother had always sprung out of bed to welcome that migratory honking. "The geese, the wild geese," she cried.

She looked at Daren and waved. He saw it as Dan Byrne had in *The Married Land*, Gluck's Dance of Blessed Spirits among the Elysian Fields. No wonder the book was so desperate to reshape that from within.

"It's the first flock of the fall."

And now, across Daren's range, the long straggling V cut south-ward, pulsing wings:

Facendo in aere di sè lunga riga.

Their eyes met in a momentary contagion of tears. But there was nothing Lucy could have done for the lonely alter ego of her own Dan Byrne but to have loved him, and that was not in the cards. If the whole show could be run again, a fresh pull from the grab bag, maybe this very generative fortune might be his. But once the shock-haired Daniel was planted there, like the rhinoceros in the watering hole, there was not much chance of anybody else coming in for a drink. Leave her to her destiny, which must have been partly diverting, if partly a perpetual trial. A craw-dad's motion is caudad. Leflore's move was the retreat he was accustomed to.

As the train left the river hills, skirting the lowlands and the Bay, he felt in his pocket for the nucleus of notes he had made, a germ of hope against the solitude, to hatch in that shell of darkness his own Unmarried Land.

He entered the low light of the basement room. There is a danger in objects proportional to their power: the incommunicable wash of feeling association triggers, an ultimate Ulro of titillation without meaning. Yet how else to reach incarnate actuality, where things glow like sacraments?

What took his eye, gathering the half light in its own iridescence was the butterfly tray his father had brought his mother from New York when she was near her time with his brother Vail. A tropical blue swallowtail was in the act of lighting on a cluster of dried field flowers: yarrow, daisy, sweet millet and clover—so gleamingly nostalgic, it seemed less Iris Vail's tray than the image of Iris Vail.

He sat at the table, overpowered. To root down into that middens of old sketches, generations deep, churn them up, rend, group, relink, to touch off another alchemy groping toward a cloudier design:

THERE IS NO CONTAINMENT BUT THE FACT…

The manifold infoldings of the fact: so many to raise up, dead and half dead, let them drink of the blood, moisten the secrets from their tongues. Aeneas' penetration of the rock-hemmed lake where later Romans lolled among rose blooms in Sybaritic ennui, the bloat flesh of imperial rule—nothing; not the ghost of a single father, but hundreds of world-witnesses to question.

The phone rang. It was the Baltimore wife Daphne, Even the disturbed rat learns some avenues are blind.

Under the cliff, ringed and islanded in mist, the pool of the Patapsco, these fall evenings, hardly stirred by the current, so reflected its trees—no lack of golden boughs, tulip, elm and sassafras—it seemed the Lake of Avernus indeed. The problem as always was to find the Sibyl's cave, the deeper than hell opening bayed round by the trivial, daily hounds.

PART IV
Spring

1. Avalon

Investigation might have been expected to cut a man off from the world; but for Daren, isolated before, it went the other way. *The Hostile Witness,* kicked from him like a fart out of a dead donkey, thrust him back into life, the renewal of ties. It was Hank Brown now, who after years of separation, neither knowing where the other was, took up the correspondence:

Avalon, Ga., Feb. 20, 1959

Dear Daren

I have a book club in Atlanta that would like to have you bear Witness, Hostile though you be. They will subsidize your flight and add fifty bucks as honorarium—the honor, of course, to be theirs.

If you think this is a device for getting you into range, you won't be off the trail. If you ask then why so fast after so long delay, what can I do but offer to explain *(mea culpa)* in this mead hall I have built with my own hands?

When I came back from the war, being a rubber-stamp editor in New York seemed an idle trade. Bleak House put me in charge of southern sales. I had bought this land from a friend before I knew what to do with it. It has been my Roman farm.

The whole of America is geared to pump the ephemeral, get trash on the shelves and reviewed and fools to buy it and forget last year's numbers. Keep the crap rolling fast enough and people will not only eat it, they will call it good. With my left hand I serve that, but with my right Avalon, *The Atlanta Messenger,* reform. Have you anything I can print on my hand-press and distribute while I'm pushing the trades?

I have plowed all my black hair into the land and got back gray, but the game is worth the candle.

There'll be some newspaper friends to meet you, Berg of Savannah, & Waring of Atlanta, besides a guest from Reading, Alabama, who knows you of old.

Yours,

Hank Brown

The only person Daren remembered in Reading was Bella Wynne. If, in the face of that, be decided to go, it was a measure of how much he wanted to see Hank Brown.

The explanation Hank had promised for the mead hall got revved up with the car at the airport for the thirty-minute drive. Shades of halcyon summer.

"There were problems. Even before pacifism and pentameter prose."

"Problems?" It was in such moments that Daren gauged his own monadic oblivion. His library was sprinkled with books Hank Brown, poor as he was, had picked up for him at Oxford sales. And what had Daren done in return? Made Hank a caricature in the Diary of a Rhodes Scholar. "What problems?"

"Anna. I was drawn to her. We liked movies. And you were glad to get her off your hands."

(She had complained of those films, and how long it took Hank to get change by his *fuppence, fippence* rule.)

"I proposed to her once. I never thought you were right for her."

(Russian dolls opening up all the time.) "And there was Clyster. Remember?" "Medic from Oregon. It's in the Diary."

"I mean the time he came back from Paris. It was like Renoir that summer, parks and children, a Punch and Judy show, Duke Ellington at night, floating you under lights and colored balloons—a city so alive, and on the verge of war. We lived in a little hotel on the Ile de la Cité——'*Pas de bains ici* we called it. 'Ah, m'sieur,' the manager used to say, as if you'd asked for a whore, *'Il n'y a pas de bains ici.'*—'It's an enchanted garden,' Clyster told me. For him that was a reach of pure imagination. He brought back some pictures, remember?"

Daren remembered. Wishy-washy boulevard junk.

"That was his great venture into art. He had cash enough for four more days of that idyllic vacation, when he saw these watercolors in a window in the Avenue de l'Opera. He kept coming back to look at them, and finally he went in. The lady told him how the artist, a drunken genius, would arrive after a binge and paint for a week in a frenzy, a dozen of these little masterpieces, get his money and go back on the town. Clyster sorted through a stack of fifty and came up with five. They were a hundred and fifty francs each, and he couldn't choose the one he liked best. Two for two hundred and fifty, the lady said. He threw out Chartres and the Bois de Boulogne and there he stuck. 'You choose,' he told her. But she said better three for three hundred. She wrapped up his three beauties, the Opera, Notre Dame, la Place de la Concorde, and he left, blissfully broke, got his bag and caught the Channel train.

"Those were the pictures he showed you in his room, and you called them hackwork imitations of the gay nineties, which had been a mess in the first place. He didn't say a word, but he looked like somebody who had flunked out. I wanted to get you off and pound it home: 'Can't you see anything, feel anything outside your own skull?'"

"OK, so what am I supposed to do?"

"Nothing. You're the Hostile Witness. I'm explaining my own problems.

"And the time you came to my room and I wasn't there, and you thought you'd arrange my books, because you were all for chronology and they were alphabetical. I never understood how you did it so fast, but when I came back every book was somewhere else. 'I'll never find anything,' I said. You thought you'd done me a favor.

'Nonsense. It's all by date. You'll find everything much better.'

"So I knew you were a self-enclosed demon who shaped the universe in your own image. And when I saw that stilted Diary and those pentameter meditations, I didn't think you'd bring it off."

"Don't tell me the O'Malley deal has changed your mind. Better the Meditations or the Journals than that."

Hank didn't argue the point. "Then I went in the Army. I wrote to Prairie College once, but I guess you'd moved on."

They had sailed on the freighter and spent three years together, in Oxford and traveling on vacations, but this was another Hank Brown. Behind the clowning and Negro dialect and corruption of language, this man had waited concealed.

The Hank who had turned his very belch into a vociferous "OGGS-ford"; who at concerts, standing with the rest for "God Save the King," would bawl at the top of his lungs "My Country 'tis of Thee"; who leered at Cyril once at tea, when that baroque worthy, waving aside the cake, announced he had lost a stone—"You too young, fella, to be passing stones at yo age"—that Hank had vanished like the patois of his Oxford protest, and what the subsidence had bared proved the inadequacy of the counter-attack. He had dropped the original hillbilly drawl. What he spoke, after years in the North, war service in Italy, a spell of occupation in Frankftirt, was a southern variant of the international stage-diction Roosevelt and others used on the radio. And the form he stood in, as he grabbed Daren's bag and let him out at Avalon, was a similar universal achievement of free Western man: *Homo Libera Occidentalis.*

It was almost evening. As they approached the house from the carport under an arch of beech trees, a song came from a corner window, far away—more like a memory than a song.

The beech roots gripped into the ground, knuckled, warted, gray fingered. The shadowed approach, the limestone and cypress house Hank had built around the structure of an old barn—Avalon, island of the dead, where King Arthur waits recovering his powers,

> Waxing well of that deep wound
> In slumber soft, and on the ground
> Sadly sits the Assyrian queen…

—the voice came from there, windblown, singing of all words those most calculated to lift the moment beyond the actual:

> And we'll all go together
> Where the wild mountain thyme
> Grows round the bloomin heather.
> Will ye go, Lassie, go?

All those years Jeffrey had waited far back, as in the recesses of the room, a presence coming forward under sleep. Like every power of the unconscious, she had woven herself a myth of things experienced and heard and imagined, central to which was the time that had fixed that song as a leitmotiv in her awareness, and by her telling of it at the Door, in Daren's—the gathering of the clans at Childe Manor, after the death of her mother.

You would walk out in the mists of evening, or in the morning when the sun contended with the vapors of the Tamar, and strolling through an island of green, far off where oaks spread and the hedgerow elms soared into the light, you would catch the sweet sound. It was the dewy time of the year, and the whole estate was streaked and flowed through by rivers of whiteness, out of which the plaids appeared, marching from shadow into the clear. Or from another pale sea across the way the colors of kilts would flash, break, merge, a company of men practicing for the funeral, tuning up with a gay snatch or a sad ditty, and then it would be the air Jeffrey had sung in Wychwood Forest and over Green Bay, and that came now from the half-opened window of Hank Brown's hand-built Avalon:

> I will build my love a tower
> By yon pure crystal fountain,
> And on it I will build
> All the flowers of the mountain…
> Will ye go, Lassie, go?

A complicity of joy and grief—*Manibus O date lilia plenis.*

"You met her in England, long ago." That was all Hank knew. How could he feel space crumpling under the years' struggle to put down what rose now against the inner cry: "I have shifted the locus of our love to the stars; so it's absurd to expect earthly correlatives."

"She used to be Jeffrey Strange. But she's Jeffrey Lawless now. The woman who's saved Alabama from its own worst. She's the one bit of life in Reading, that red-neck crazy town."

Night. Five of them were sitting around the fire in the mead hall—a flagstone floor thrown with rugs and furs, a raised hearth of cemented fieldstone, above them the raftered space of the original barn. Hank's wife, Tad, who had put the children to bed, was moving between the kitchen and the hall, getting the salad and garlic bread ready, while Hank broiled the steak; Jeffrey sat beside him: Daren focused in guarded amazement on the changeless profile against the flame. It was Mary and Martha in the Gospel, Tad unobtrusively working, Jeffrey pouring the ointment of talk and charm.

("This is Tad," Hank had introduced his wife. "Her father came from Charlotte, Judge Ashman." It had been a famous case, a decision that opened the Democratic primaries to Negroes. The legislature had voted him a one-way ticket out of the state; and in time had their way. "People used to phone," Hank said, "and ask, 'Is this Judge Ashman's daughter? I hear you fuck niggers.' They were living in New York when I met her. Now she's back in the thick of it; except out here in the country and with the guns and dogs, people pretty much leave us alone.")

The slab of steak sputtered, dropping fat; the yellow blaze leapt up, "A sweet smell scaling heaven called the immortal gods."

"And for God's sake, Daren, pour a libation. Not my bourbon. Be Homeric. A little of your Maryland wine."

Daren reached over Jeffrey, and splashed a few drops, hissing, onto the coals. She smiled. *In flagrante delicto.*

"To Dionysus and Aphrodite," Hank intoned like the *pontifex maximus.*

"And Night," Leflore added, "eldest of things."

Jeffrey was telling of the time she and Hank Brown and a reporter come from New York witnessed the Klan's assault on Stone Mountain, that bare granite breast heaving over the Georgia plain, called among countless contenders, the Eighth Wonder of the World—Valhalla now of the Kuklanic gods and sheeted fire worshipers, pressing for a *Götterdämmerung* they had no comprehension of. In Jeffrey's bright voice it became a redneck comic saga of torch lights in the dark: out of Night the petty stir.

Cars from neighboring states had converged, under the backside of the mountain, on a cowplop, anthill pasture, lit up like Nero's festivals by smoky torches—in want of classical material (he favored Christians), oil cans filled with bum-wad and kerosene. They had been arriving and picnicking through the afternoon, hard-jawed Klansmen, raw-boned or big-bellied, barbers, garagemen, storeclerks, farmers; perky Klanettes in rubbery white rayon capes, taking out their compacts' and powdering their noses; security guards striding around in white and green uniforms and high black boots, pistols swagging from their wide belts and their faces under white crash helmets set in the home-grown bigotry of natural and moral wrong: "No drinkin, please. This is a Christian society of law-abidin famlies. And no cussin. We're all friends here." They had been sitting in the cowplops and slapping ants and passing out their newspaper *The Fiery Cross* and talking and steaming themselves up, and now it was time for the speakers.

After a prayer to the Heavenly Father—"Put thy blessin on this group here, and may meetins like ours spring up everywhere to save this nation through thy leadership, amen"—the Infernal Wizard and the Grand Dragon and whatever other high mucky-mucks started the powwow:

"They call us night riders and hooded law breakers. But we're here to uphold the true, God-given laws of the country we were born to. You see sugar advertised one hundred percent pure. Nobody'll buy it if it ain't pure. Now why take the pure blood of the white race and mix it up with the nigger race? In no way, shape or form. Votin's not a right, it's a privilege. It takes brains. No hot-headed irresponsible nigger, none at all, is gonna take this country away from us. These are the facts and figgers..." He screamed into the mike until the speakers went into feedback howl, and you heard nothing but noise, while the giant shadow danced on a backstop of trees. Somebody would fiddle with the amplifiers and the voice would take shape again, roaring through the incoherence: "The nigger does not have the intelligence, he does not have the morality to set forth the program we are faced with." The crowd yelled.

"What's he saying? What does he mean?" Jeffrey had whispered to Hank.

"Who cares? He could say the Lord's Prayer backwards, they'd cheer."

It wasn't the ordinary jamboree. The Klan had come for what they called the tradition of burning their torches on the mountain. For the first time the government had denied them access to a national shrine. The U.S. militia had been called out with guns, tear gas, police dogs, fire trucks and fire hoses, and had formed a line at the foot of the mountain. The palaver slowly worked around to the point. They were going to walk right through that gang of nigger-lovin communist stooges gettin their orders from Russia through the United Nations and Washington. People were milling around, going to their cars, unloading weapons, guns, knives, clubs. Others were getting the crosses ready, tying them with rags and soaking them in oil. Led by the speakers and bullhorns they broke into a chant: "We gonna go up that mountain. We gonna go up that mountain."—"Who's gonna lead?"—"Make way. Make way." The purple-nosed Grand Dragon pushed forward.

Jeffrey and Hank and the reporter had come in farm clothes, like hillbillies, Jeffrey retelling it, her southern stage drawl laid down rather winningly on the melodious British: "Get yerself a billy, gal," a robed figure told her. "They're under the car. And you, big guy, pick up a handful o rocks. We gonna wipe up the earth with them Yankees. But git yerself a billy, gal. There may be some nasty niggers up there."

"If they found out I was that radical Jeffrey Lawless from Reading, I'd need more protection than from the niggers; so I crawled under the car and pulled out a stick. Then I started for the mountain with the crowd. Skinny hicks with big Adam's apples and hefty bruisers and chinless scum with gap mouths were pressing from behind. 'We gonna go up that mountain.' As long as they were in the rear they were full of beans. They shoved and sent everybody stumbling ahead, but the front line had come against the troopers.

"'Draw back,' the guard shouted, 'or we'll shoot.' But nobody could draw back, except the people pushing up on the sides, and they peeled off like majorettes in a drill and slunk back to the rear. But the Wizard and the Dragon were bunched in the middle and the Dragon so potbellied and jammed in, he couldn't do anything but wave his standard like a lance. They pushed him from behind until his purple sausage nose got in the way of a trooper's billy. It burst out in gouts of blood, as if he were under pressure. 'Oh, these communist nigger-lovers. Look what they'v e done to a patriotic American.' 'Draw back, or we'll shoot,' cried the guards, while the flanks peeled off and slipped to the rear.

"'Send up the women and kids.' The cry came back from the Grand Vizier. 'I want to go home,' said a boy by me, hanging to his mother, while the roar went up: 'Send up the women and kids. They won't shoot at the women and kids.'"

"The bastards," said Berg from Savannah, "those chinless bastards, I wish I'd a been there with a gun. Those troopers shoulda shot. They said they'd shoot and they didn't shoot. They let those bastards go up that mountain and light those goddamned crosses, and it was a shame to the nation."

(Berg had started out as a teacher between the wars. But at Southern U. it hadn't taken him long to queer his welcome. "I led a student club," he had told Leflore over his bourbon; "and we invited the distinguished author of *God's Trombones* to give us a reading. When he came we had no place to put him up. I went all over town and found one Negro doctor who would take him. For me, I didn't dare. But after the reading, when the outsiders had drifted away and it was late, we slipped him to my place for a drink. Next day the head of the department called me in. We can't have any nigger-lovers on this faculty,' he said. That's how I turned to journalism. Well, now I've made a name for myself, that same Southern U. is· always asking me to come lecture. And on what else—believe it or not—but Black and White relations."

But it was Jeffrey's voice again, invincibly scaling Stone Mountain. Daren sat a little withdrawn, at loggerheads with this emergence out of the water-spirit Jeffrey of The Door. And yet, what else had he called for at Dan Byrne's, when he caught the first glimpse of his fiction, but such a well-born British Anna as active counterpole? And it couldn't have been more polished, more beautiful, a flawless show…

"What a night," Bob Waring said to Hank, "to go through all that, and in the presence of two of nature's wonders: Stone Mountain and Jeffrey Lawless."

(Let the local chapter of the Jeffrey club be declared closed. It had members enough already.)

"Don't you overdo that steak, Hank Brown. I'm not that British." (She spun the shimmering strand.) "Tom and I took a London reporter out to dinner last week. Said he wanted one of those American steaks he'd heard so much about. We ordered him the thickest hunk of Porterhouse. Well, every time he cut it, it was still red, so he kept sending it back. Finally the waitress caught on. 'I get you,' she said. 'You want it cremated.'"

The fat sputtered and the fire roared up.

"OK, Jeffrey," said Hank. "Call Selma."

A Negro girl came in, but not to serve; she took her place at the table. "This is Selma from Tupelo," Hank said. "She's eighteen and is a bad girl. She's been in jail and reform school for two years. First thing, she sat in the white section of a bus; and she meant to. Then she marched in a protest when one of the CORE workers got shot over there. Some northern newspaperman got a picture of her on her knees praying, and that cooked her goose. They decided she was a juvenile, which meant she didn't need a trial. Just got sent eighty miles to a Negro reform school as they called it, though it had no school at all. I heard about it and saw the judge—Tupelo's my hometown. He put her in my custody, and she helps Tad with the housework." Though when the meal was over, Hank told her: 'Honey, you go back to your room now, and do that homework. We can fix it up in here."

"Yeassuh."

"She's got exams," Hank said. ""We're hoping to send her North next year, to college."

Daren eased his guard, relaxed by the fire, listening to the southern talk, the rhythms he grew up with and had hardly recognized as lovable until they were lost:

"Sure. Doc Stahr, fine doctor, nice old gentleman; had the most beautiful automatic you ever saw, five first-rate dogs, called em all Sport, never would call a dog anything else; he had everything you needed, but he never hit a bird. We were out once and I saw two birds get up and go over, and behind em the whole damned covey. I says: I'll take care of these and let Doc have the rest. So I shot and I got em both. They came floppin down in the swamp. Then I flattened myself out to give Doc room, cause here they came, a dozen of em, right over us. Well Doc bust loose behind me, sound like the Fourth of July: Bang, bang, bang, bang. When the smoke had cleared off, Abe walked over into the swamp. 'Here's your birds, Doc,' he says, and picked up my two. And those were the only birds old Doc Stahr ever bagged in his life."

Tales of local eccentrics, southern ubiquities, as well of Delta Landing as Atlanta. Jot it down: woman hipped on germs, takes money in a bag from the bank and sterilizes it. Brought some nylons back to the store: "No good." Had put them in the oven against bacteria, and they melted. Sleeps with a sheet between herself and her husband, though the washerwoman has spread it around that the sheet has an embroidered buttonhole in it somewhere around the middle. "I took hold of her arm once," Hank said, "when Tad and I were walking her across the street, and she hauled off and whopped me with her pocketbook. But Tad grabbed her and swung on. 'See here,' she said, Hank and I can touch you as much as we want to, cause we're as clean as you are.' I guess she took it for a mighty special claim; 'It's all right for Hank and Tad to touch me,' she told Bob here, 'because they're as clean as I am.'"

The main talk, of course, was about that natural wonder of the world, Jeffrey Lawless. Everybody in the fan cult took a hand in the praise, passing the tales back and forth amongst them, though the original source most of the time could only have been Jeffrey herself. They wanted to actualize her for Daren. And indeed, he found her a phenomenon. All the mystery he had known at The Door seemed to have been taken back to the counter and exchanged for manifest force, though that remained mysterious enough to leave these admirers awed: This Io stung by the gadfly, this lovable Jeffrey, what was driving her on?

How she parked in a loading zone, "No Parking" posted everywhere— the only way to find a place quick; and when she came out of the church bearing a first load of flowers donated for the Negro hospital, a cop was writing her a ticket. "What are you doing, my dear boy?" she asked, with a wag of her finger.

"This here's a no parking zone, lady." He reached her the ticket.

"It's a loading zone, and that's what I'm doing. You tear up that ticket and come right on in this church and help me load."

It wasn't a loading-flowers-from-the-church zone, and he had been instructed not to tear up tickets, but when he came out of the church looking like a resurrected corpse buried under bouquets, garlands and funeral wreaths, Jeffrey was swinging along in front with a mighty gay air. "Just hold them, now, while I lay them in carefully. Oh, you're so kind to help me."

"Please, miss," said the cop, "could we hurry up and get this car out of here before the chief comes along and sees me. I'd never hear the last of it."

That wasn't the only case, and sometimes the ticket didn't get torn up; but after several accusations had been pursued in the courtroom to a *non possumus* ("After all, I'm serving the city," she smiled, "and the city will have to get used to serving me"), Police Commissioner Lusk, though the arch enemy of most of Jeffrey's aims, presented her with a specially engraved black celluloid plate almost as big as a car license and equipped with a brass· chain; it was inscribed with her name in gold: Jeffrey Lawless, with his name down under, so that whenever she parked in a forbidden area, she just had to hang that on the steering wheel, and not a cop in town would bother her.

One had heard of Chief Commissioner Lusk, Snapper Lusk they called him, and it was hard to see him as Jeffrey's (potbellied) *pater seraphicus.*

"Of course," she said, 'he taps my phone and records all the conversations, but personally he's quite decent. I can wrap him around my little finger."

"I've never believed that implausible story about your phone," said Hank.

"Don't be silly," said Jeffrey. "I can hear it."

"What if he got something really juicy?" Berg asked. "What could he do with it?"

"He's curious," Waring winked, "like the rest of us. Wants to know what the enigmatic Jeffrey is up to."

"He'd blackmail her for a bit of sex, old as he is," said Hank. "Our Jeffrey'd get a rise out of Methusalah."

When it was time to go to bed: "Now Jeffrey," Bob Waring said, "do you know where you're going to sleep? If you aren't satisfied, let me know. I'll swap rooms, beds, anything ... You heard what she did to me at Robertshaw's in Charleston, didn't you? She came late for the press conference and wanted a bed. I wasn't going to give her none because I was there first, but I offered to share it with her. No, she was bound to sleep on the sofa. 'But you'll be sorry,' she told me. She's so damned right. Everything she says is just bound to happen. I was plagued all night; maybe they were Bobshaw's cats, but they jumped on the bed like damned spirits and sat on my face, and before morning the ceiling fell in the room and hit the foot of the bed, and almost buried me. I told Bobshaw he ought to strip her, and if she had a great unnatural tit under her left arm she was a witch and should be burned. But he gave her a clean slate, 'How d'ya know?' I said. Well, he wouldn't answer that."

To be the infallible witch had become a part of her mask. Daren went to sleep wondering how far the mask had taken her over; though he couldn't know, until the next morning, when he joined her in a walk through Hank Brown's woods into his limestone valley—Jeffrey's talk rippling along like the brook they followed, that shallow and bright, that much the same for all comers. Until the path steepened and they went down through gray strata, layered blocks overhanging hollow grooves and foldings.

Did Verrocchio, Leonardo and the rest who seated the Madonna among foliations of limestone sense the fitness, that in those smooth concretions of an ocean bed, rock had assumed the mood of water, the mothering element?

She had been relating her civic and comic enterprises: how needing an entertainer lately for some fund-raising banquet, she had remembered a Scot of her mother's clan who at a party in New Orleans had mentioned an act he called his Highland "fling," so in a fit of impulse she phoned him, thinking he would pipe and dance and it might be gay, but when Sir Reginald came, though the kilts were right, all he did was put his left hand to his bosom and recite Bobby Burns in the ultimate singsong. It was the flop of her life in the way of fund raising—

Her voice and eyes sparkling like diamonds on display, as when Mrs. Hardy brought her to Daren's room for tea, and she put on a mime of his hip-shot Apollo stance, or how he would tilt his head back to swallow, like a bird—

"Talent-scout Jeffrey producing her great find, old Sir Reggie, of the Cameron clan."

Nothing that could not equally have been offered among the cult over cocktails, not a glance, not a word to betray the lost intimacy they skirted as in policy or fear. Then he took her hand down the declivity of the weathered stone. Silence. Her face assumed the shadow of the layerings against which she paused.

It was Jeffrey who had engineered The Door meeting, enrolling in the knowledge of Leflore's name; it was this Giorgione hand he now held which had sketched their love in potentiality, and then wiped it off the board. After twelve years, it was Jeffrey who had chosen this renewal. But Daren had no mind to gamble as before.

In the pre-spring hush and waiting where they hung, the laurel on the slopes above glinting through leafless trees, all of that was suspended in the glances that rocked them like waves. Its total expression required only the single word which Daren launched against the spell: "Why?"

"Couldn't you hear me all those nights whispering to you, walking the fall woods along the ledge, you striding ahead? And you know what ran in my mind? I kept asking why the leaves stuck to you so. When other people walked they fell off, but they landed on you and stayed, on your head and shoulders and arms."

"Those were dead leaves from the ground. They stick to anybody, like beggar-lice. Suppose I wasn't the only one always living that night over Green Bay. Suppose that's why you've planned this. Why now?"

"I thought it was high time." Jeffrey's smile shimmered back.

"You know what the brazen head says in the old play?" Daren asked. "Time will be, time is, time has passed."

She settled into the beech leaves in a walled pocket of sun. "When I was rushing from one thing to another, always ready to take on another cause, and people were wondering: 'Is that woman trying to get away from something,' and friends and even strangers would ask me: 'Jeffrey, what are you after? What makes you tick?'—I thought that was our secret, though we couldn't talk about it."

Daren settled down with a mocking croon: "Lawd, Lawd. This kind lady gonna mother this po chile."

He kissed her forehead and then her eyes. The lost yearning of all the romantic sots he had repudiated and despised opened in him like his Civil War grandfather Captain Quincy's old wound... *ghost, come back again.* He studied the bare calligraphy of the boughs.

"The shepherd in Vergil," he said, "found Love to be a native of the rocks."

He had never known what that enigmatic quotation meant; for the first time it took on solemn significance. He leaned against an oak, picked a stem of grass and chewed it thoughtfully. "Jeffrey," he said, "I love you as always. But you are too costly for my love..."

On the inspiration of that word, the scene had melted back to Patapsco, the solitude from which Daren contemplated Avalon, thinking how Jeffrey moved through nature like a stream through limestone, where Anna had gone burning into the night—to follow a woodland road by the starry gap overhead, by the foxfire on either side, to return drenched with dew, fallen leaves, rain—an apocalyptic rapture.

"When you and Hank drove me to the airport," Jeffrey wrote, "it was cold pale sunlight, like a forced smile. I came home to the usual round of meetings: mental health, hospital board, to set tables for the church dinner, to judge in the P.T.A. talent contest, and it was all emptier than ever, all stale. I have had a phone call from an old friend, Micah Glenn, who is passing through town. He cheers me up. 'Jeffrey,' he told me once, 'you use men like pep pills.' 'Well,' I said, 'I never heard any of them complain.' But now I must confess to him that a certain Daren Leflore has, and that I am thrown into the Slough of Despond."

When they had put her on the plane that afternoon, Hank took Daren to the book club, and when that was over, to Avalon for the last night.

Berg had gone back to Savannah. Waring and Hank talked over dinner about the New South. Not a phenomenon Anna would have subscribed to, this projected society of opulence whose salvation from the old bigotries was to be the chamber of commerce cult of the almighty dollar. She would have called it exploitation, as in Puerto Rico or any other sphere of capitalist investment—as if it made much difference when the chick embryo is organizing the egg proteins what's being developed and what exploited. The problem was to keep the whole thing alive and subtly guided toward a living good. Which didn't necessarily mean Waring's chamber of commerce chicken.

"Look," Bob Waring pronounced, "the New South can just be thought of as the business South. There's plenty else there: old plantations and decadent writers and Negroes and rednecks; but the crucial force, the new force is business. And all the other forces have seated themselves inside it—even the universities and the NAACP. It's in business that the Negro is waking up. And that's why people are making room for him—business. Because if the Negro is down and out, he can't buy. Oh, there are stuffy businessmen and business Klanners, but even they begin to catch on that wherever there's race violence business is hurt, like Reading. So even a Klanner who's in business wants law and order. That's your citizens' council—on the surface it's a force for reaction; but underneath, it's headed right where it doesn't want to go, to integration, social justice, equality."

Maybe there was Hegelian truth in that. As Daren had been telling Anna twenty years ago: "The reason we're still here, despite the sensible predictions of Marx, is that everything one might call dark is always hatching a center of light in itself, and vice versa, as in the Taoist sign." Or as Cader Ayres had remarked: "Nineteenth-century capitalism, by the intervention of our Ford, has become socialist sharing, and what was called socialism has turned out in Russia to be worker-exploitation, that is capitalism, under state rule. The trouble with such a dialectic, it was so balanced either way, so recklessly poised, nobody could tell when it might explode or go into feedback howls.

Hank Brown saw the indeterminacy. "There's a boys' school near Reading," he said. "Jeffrey took me out the last time I was over there. Her youngest boy is a senior. It was founded by a racist millionaire to preserve segregation and Aryan purity. Now liberal education has crept in, and the great books, and the headmaster hopes to admit some Negro students. I talked with a picked group that couldn't have been more enlightened. The next night their choir came to Reading and gave a concert in the big Shriners Hall. It was when Snapper Lusk took the benches out of the parks so Negroes and whites couldn't sit down together, and the fountains so they couldn't drink together, and those boys closed that concert with a performance of "The Battle Hymn of the Republic" that brought the house up standing and in cheers. 'That's' it,' I said; 'the Aryan school has changed sides. But when I talked to the boys who'd been singing, I found most of them didn't make the connection with John Brown, and there were some who could have sung the 'Battle Hymn' while they were spraying machine-gun bullets on resisting blacks. I sometimes think nothing short of an army of occupation will do the job down here. And with the Negro ghettos in the North, who's fit to occupy?"

"That's one advantage," Daren said, "of having written off the West thirty years ago. All this continuance of desperate possibilities seems pure gravy."

"Make mine pure beer," said Hank. "Let's go to the Beehive." It was a roadhouse by the fire station, where the locals gathered of an evening. "We call it the Three Marys," said Hank. There's Mary the wife of Abe (she runs the joint), and Mary the sister of John (who farms nearby) and another Mary nobody knows anything about, except whatever you tell her—if she asks, 'Is it rainin?' and you say, 'It was, but it's snowin now.'—'No shit?' she'll say. Or if you should say, 'I got a new car,' or 'My wife's left me'—'No shit?' she'll answer. So there was Mary the wife of Abe, and Mary the sister of John and no-shit Mary. But those days are gone. One night no-shit Mary got to dancin and drinkin and her Irish blood got hot. She lifted up her skirt and put the feather duster between her legs. Mary the sister of John, who was always a religious sort, took off her apron and walked out from behind the bar. 'This ain't any place for a decent lady to work,' she said. And she's never been back since."

The room was jammed. They had hardly found a seat when a waitress caught sight of Hank and came over to give him a hug. "How's the weather?" she asked.

Hank flung her a wink. "They's a lovely moon, Mary." He reverted to the old talk.

"No shit?" she said. Hank could hardly smother his pleasure,

They got a couple of pitchers of beer. The jukebox was going, a big Seabird as they call them in the South. A few couples were dancing. A snag-toothed woman was swinging her hips alone in the middle of the floor, a semaphore of whorish distress, followed by a sodden old man at the next table, She fixed her eyes on Daren and came swaying over like a snake charmer. "Hi, honey," she said, coiling an arm around him. "I'm a single woman. I keep house for that old fellow, see, He pays me five dollars a week. He has to, every week. It's my alimony for livin with him. But I'm a free woman, Free as a bird. Where you stay, honey?"

Plenty of women; but not all up to Jeffrey. Daren gave the hag a hug and said they were just driving through, and she danced on, free as a bird—though followed by the old codger's oyster eye.

Hank took the privacy of the general noise. "Our witch works fast," he said to Daren. "Not that drunk woman, Jeffrey. She likes to call herself a witch, you know, and arch that devil's eyebrow she's so fond of."

"Maybe she works slow. Maybe I loved her when she was a child."

"Child or granny, we all love her. When she's stretched out dead it'll be like Cleopatra: 'To catch another Anthony in her strong toil of grace.'"

"What does your wife think," Daren asked, "when you and all the rest cluster around her so?" For he still saw that Mary-Martha deal, and Tad so simple, plain and hard-working.

"She's used to it. But women will all be jealous of Jeffrey, the same as men will fall for her. She's shameless, really. I met her at a banquet after I got the Pulitzer for my editorials on the bus boycott. She gave me the double whammy. After that she'd send a letter every day, sometimes two, special delivery, right at breakfast, and the envelopes sealed with lipstick kisses. What an imprint. It made Tad wild. Then Jeffrey came for a visit, and Tad began to like her. It's hard not to. 'You can ease off, Tad,' I said, 'Jeffrey collects scalps for a game.' But whenever I've been with her it takes Tad days to get over it, always asking whether I love her, and do I really love her, and would I rather have Jeffrey than her.

"Well, I do love Jeffrey, and don't think anything else; but you have to take her with a grain of salt. She's a fighter from way back; and yet I never saw such a Narcissus, always building up that beautiful, brave Jeffrey-image. I've seen her work for Negro rights with one hand and lead the most pampered social set in Reading with the other. 'You two-faced, self-centered grande dame,' I thought, and loved her the more—like a spoiled, incorruptible child.

"You know how she sees the South? A great big wilderness, with a handful of brave men sprinkled around. And one brave woman. Who loves them all. And they all love her. And she's made it true. There's Gerard in Little Rock, Robertshaw in Charleston, and you've seen Berg from Savannah and Waring and Hank Brown from here—and all on the string. And now the unfortunate Daren Leflore, who tangled with O'Malley."

"How does her husband stand it?" Daren had asked.

"He's not one of the brave men, I guess. But she keeps him happy. She's very proper, though she flirts like all hell."

*

Affabilities, recalled, as Daren, at the perennial Patapsco window, looked out on a cold March mist in which the spring refused to be born.

He had been working six months at his novel, and had only gotten far enough to know that, like Dan Byrne's *Married Land,* it must be another amorphous investigation, another life-pursuit and non-story—to explore

443

the tangle of a constituted identity. And since in this case the foreground love-search for the lost and saving Lucy was not available, what was to get him out of solipsistic enclosure, spinning and fingering the threads of self? He needed Jeffrey in a way he had not been aware of that winter of longing after the temptation at The Door.

But she had got his scalp once, and she could do the war dance (and the hula and the cancan) before she would get the chance again. Better imagine Jeffreys than open the chronicle to the actual one. Did he have to be the sufferer of this fiction in order to write?

He faced the page and got nowhere. While the mist outside the window shrouded a glory unable to be born.

2. Circe's Isle

Leflore had not answered Jeffrey's letter, though he had kept it on his desk and clutched for it sometimes, when he felt himself sinking into a sea of papers.

As the plane, over the rolling Piedmont, had banked north, taking him home from Avalon, his landscape had stretched into projective existence, and in it, clear and essential, Jeffrey, against whose presence he had been fighting.

He knew what he had to do. But for a year almost, and at times under the half-illusion of success, he had tried to believe that he could do it without her—could go it alone.

And Jeffrey too—as if the fruit for which she had waited ever since The Door was not yet quite ripe—had bided her time.

Until another February, when Daren got an invitation, in her most promotional southern style, to come to Reading as featured author in the Festival of the Arts and speaker at the banquet, which under her pastoral care could be expected to feed and fleece a thousand local aspirants to literature. She promised full press coverage, sale of countless signed copies of *The Hostile Witness,* with feasting and fawning from the elite of the city, in particular (was it a gag, or had she so far corrupted her taste?) from one "radish rosette or strawberry blonde, booterful, kultured, charmin" (when Jeffrey put on southern baby talk in orthography, it was a sign perhaps how unnatural the plug), who had breathed the name "Leflore" with such rapture, he could probably enlist her as sugar-mammy in any project he wanted to name. If Daren had not seen Jeffrey lately at Avalon, he would have thought that letter came from the most nerve-shattering culture-hag that even Reading, with all its talent for crassness, could have made of willing material.

He went because (at the end of another winter) he knew how stranded
he was. And he began to prepare her beforehand for the sacrifice she had
to make.

> I enclose proof of a novel called The Married Land. Dan Byrne, also from
> Delta Landing, has sent it for my reactions. Which I have rendered. It will
> initiate you into a Mississippi cult.
>
> For I begin to see my life too as such a paradigmatic fiction, but bigger and
> harder to bring off: Anna as immigrant mining-and-working-class first love
> of southern idealist Leflore—all to be reconstructed from the troublesome
> consequences of some postwar, O'Malley now.
>
> I foresee a use for you in this construction, though if you insist, I will ob-
> scure you past public recognition—you beckoning, after the crack-up of such
> youth and radical involvement, a sort of last tie to liberal life and action; and
> I believe destiny has put me back under your spell at this time, though it is as
> dangerous as any encounter with Circe, and I have not the guidance of a god,
> or even Odysseus' shrewdness.
>
> I have just the residence for your childhood, and of course we will have
> scraped the dirt from each other's shoes when I was a student and you a pixie
> (twelve or thirteen were you?). I see you standing on that dam, your hair (shall
> I change you to fair and make Anna the Shakespearean dark type, or let nature
> have its way?) falling over your shoulders, you waving and the water falling,
> while Leflore goes back to Oxford and the risky toils of Anna.
>
> Of course she has got to be something special too, and the clue to her being,
> no doubt love; but as in Bovary it can't lead always to the right roost.
>
> Gather up your memories and prepare yourself, as the highwaymen say, to
> stand and deliver…

She dreamed rather of the event—of Leflore's triumph, how everyone,
when he began to speak, would know that Jeffrey Lawless had bagged something real this time. She planned the luncheons, dinners, press conferences,
radio. Yes, and to escape all that, their quiet time together. She wrote him of
a limestone valley, her favorite place near Reading.

The rocks, it would turn out, weren't limestone at all, though gray
with lichen, layered, broken off in blocks thrown down among oaks and

dogwood, with wild lilies in the clefts and pockets—not of the slow ocean building, but red sandstone, laid down on mudflats and torrential plains where flesh-eating dinosaurs had chased their prey.

The likelier for her mythology. For she thought of her valley not as eroded by ages of water, but as the old Vulcanists assumed, formed by fire; she pictured the orogeny and pain which had heaved jagged rocks out of the earth, a raw wound to be healed, to be softened by time—the parallel of her own convulsion, which years had made almost tranquil now, rounding toward such a valley. She wanted to walk there with him; for him to draw out, as at The Door and almost at Avalon, the silence under her surface, to mingle it with his; for their two silences to be conjoined.

She drove alone to a parking place on the ridge, climbed down the rocks to the stream; she took off her shoes and dabbled her feet in a cold pool. This nameless clobber of rock seemed richer to her than all the famous prospects, mountains, viewpoints, gorges. She lay back under branches sprinkled, against the sky, with the first brightness of buds. By the time he came, all this would be a green bower. She picked up a bit of moss she had scuffed loose with her toes, and put it in her pocketbook to send him. If he would write her a poem, wrapped in a green leaf and tied with a daffodil, if they could read it there together, among the silences:

> Transcending those and all that's made
> To a green thought in a green shade...

In the prospect, she knew again how she loved him.

Though it didn't turn out like that at all.

Jeffrey met him at the plane in the sports car she had already put at his disposal in her letters:

My husband loves automobiles; I think they're his status symbol. He bought this pale blue convertible, white leather, buttock-seat job, and then decided the four-on-the-floor wasn't quite *man*ual enough (and I do mean *man*), so he gave it to me. After the luncheon, rd as soon skip out of town, before all the dear ladies I've conned into buying tickets by telling them they'd have front row tables wake up to what a great and handsome speaker they've missed by being seated back around the washroom somewhere. So if you want to drive over to that Delta Landing your friend Dan Byrne describes so passionately, my buttock seater is rarin to go.

It went, at colossal speed, across town.

"What do you mean, his status symbol?" said Daren. "Look at you, zooming around in this one."

I'd rather have a little old flivver," she beamed. "But when he bought the Volvo I had to have this. And he'll never give that one to me because of the name. His rival, Stabler, gave his wife one, and she's always asking men at parties if they wouldn't like to go for a ride in her 'Vulva.' 'Volvo, Jane,' Brandt says. It makes him furious."

They stopped at the hotel only long enough to check Daren in and leave his baggage in the big plushy room reserved for him as guest of the city. They went up together rejecting the bellhop, she carrying the battered briefcase and he the bag. It was top floor corner. He looked out over the city which even from that height seemed to send a curse against him.

"You know what I said, Jeffrey, when I first got your gracious invitation? 'Hell no.' I swore twenty-five years ago I'd never come back to this god-awful place. My father was found shot in a house on that ridge over there."

Jeffrey had heard about it from Bella Wynne. Who was of course the "sugar-mammy and charmin radish rosette" provided for Leflore's button-hole. They went immediately to her house for a luncheon and reception by the whole Festival of the Arts constituency.

On the way they passed the deserted parks where Snapper Lusk had not only ripped out the benches and cut off the fountains, but posted signs: "Legally closed," so that any Negro could be arrested if he walked there. Jeffrey talked a little about politics and the coming elections, which might (she knocked on the steering wheel as if it were wood) "get a nice reform stuffed shirt in there." But mainly she wanted to give him the lowdown on Bella Wynne.

He knew more already than he let on; but he had missed the latest installments, about her beautiful daughter, who took up ballet, to Bella's delight, as long as it was the pastime of a southern debutante. Bella had even promoted her as star of the local company Jeffrey was helping form for the Civic Arts, getting her picture taken at just the right moments (if possible with the old dame, and standing in front of a portrait of some assumed ancestor) and published in exactly the right places. But when the girl fell in love with a ballet dancer come from New York to join the company, Bella blew up. She must have wanted to marry her to a French count or British peer or one of the Cabots or Peabodys at least of the cultured East. She tried to intimidate Dido, but it didn't work; so she had the boy, with one or two others, accused of being in a homosexual ring and run out of town. That worked even less; Dido stormed out of the elegant home they were now driving toward, to a cold-water flat in Greenwich Village, married her dancer, worked with him in what roles they could get, until they were invited back to Reading, without the mother's promotion this time, and in fact without the harridan's acknowledging their presence.

Daren hadn't realized that the witches' cauldrons of the South were still bubbling such feuds and poisons. A doggerel rhyme that had run in his head with the clacking of the rails, all the way down from Reading to the Delta, the time he came home from Oxford to his brother's attempt and his sister's breakdown, stole back over the thresholds like the ghost of his father Bella Wynne had raised:

> What can you do with a harridan bitch?
> Tell her you hate her worse than the itch
> Then kick her in the belly and kick her in the britch.
> This you can do to a harridan bitch.

The brick and columned pile they stopped at was the "ancestral mansion" Bella had been telling Daren (back in '37) she was going to build on a wooded ridge out of town whenever, as she put it, "her ship came in." The war boom and expansion of cold-war stocks which had answered the hopes of many a cargo-cult (all those strip-mined Alabama hills, gouged red, eternally spoiled for any use of forest, field or farm) had not only framed the place but stocked it with enough pseudo Louis Quinze and other art forgeries to have kept the antique makers of Europe and the East hopping.

"One of her friends," Jeffrey burbled, "would come back from a trip to Virginia: 'Oh Bella dear, in the little antique shop on Crown Street of old Williamsburg I just happened to see a portrait—the manager pointed it out to me—it has an inscription on it; Bella, I'm sure it's one of your family, Thomas K. Wynen, the governor's wine merchant, who fought so splendidly at the Battle of Bull Run.' What they don't know," Jeffrey went on "is that Bella is so famous for ancestor hunting that a D.A.R. researcher and an art-restorer in New York have a complete file on her, and when they find some grimy old puss in a bin, they add an inscription, so they can plant it on her in Williamsburg. And she pays whatever the dealer wants to pry that painting loose from him—which, as he says, is unfortunately the principal display piece of his collection."

It was a big cold house full of marble mantles and nary a fire, of antiques and bric-a-brac and primitives and nary an artwork, of people on the board of the Arts Festival or the Civic Orchestra who didn't know art from bull-dookey, raving about how fine Leflore's book must be, though they hadn't got a chance to read it yet.

And here came old Bella 'Wynne over to greet him, bloodless but unbowed, that ivory patina of too many trips to Europe barely showing the cracks, a little flaking here and there—why she looked as if she'd just bought herself in Williamsburg for a cleverly faked antique. "Dear Daren," she said, while his eyes groped around the walls, wishing for those pink self-nudes of his father's day instead of these dubiously pretentious ikons and oils. She was as kittenish as ever. "Oh," she cried, "these shoes are killing me," and kicking them off, tripped over deep Persian carpets, com plasters on her beat-up feet showing through sheer stockings—"Follow me"—through a roomful of rich phonies tyked out in their luncheon best, and into the library in the left wing, where she had stabled the artiest of the company.

It was at this point that Daren discovered he was not the only honored guest and speaker for tomorrow's banquet. It was the custom to have four, though the principal drawing card hadn't arrived and (as Jeffrey was privately to confess) had wired from Hollywood that he had no mind to. But three were incontestable, besides a roomful of whatever journalists, illustrators, master builders the city had persuaded, over the years, to use the Reading Festival as a trade mart. They came all the way from Memphis and Atlanta and New Orleans, and a shot of Jeffrey-charm had inveigled a few from New York and Washington.

The clutch in the bay window had been struggling through the Depression and thirties to get established in their fields and all of them seemed to have absorbed the avant-garde and antibourgeois idealism of art, which they still mouthed, though it no longer seemed to apply. "How should art be understood by the world?" one would say. "Creation is its own reward." And to a friend on the left: "Did you see my cover on *The Saturday Evening Post?* Twenty thousand for that one." Another: "Gimme a shack, some corn pone, paper and a pen; that's all it takes." And from across the way: "I say, Smith, whatdja get for that serial?"—"Oh ten thousand, but there are movie rights. Sure." Then a languorous voice from the center: "New design, real design? Who wants it? I keep on anyway… Oh, that set of offices? Thirty thousand I think."

After cocktails and balancing food and drink and a little roll and butter on one's inadequately tabular knees came an interview with the press. Daren followed the other speakers and was so put out by the histories revealed that he emphasized nothing but the serious labor of scratching his head in the windowed cave. "What," said the journalist agape, "no excitement in your life?"

"Well—I did give a Rotary speech which stirred up a tempest in a teapot, and later I was in prison for almost a year, and as my book describes, I have been investigated twice as a member of the communist conspiracy. I have been told by a friend in the FBI that I have a file there as big as *War and Peace,* but that it all culminates in a summary scrawled across the top page in red: 'Harmless Crackpot.'"

Jeffrey was furious that Leflore would give the press a caption for discounting the author; but he insisted that everybody should have just the amount of rope he needed to hang himself—as if the punishment for fools was simply to have lost enlightenment.

The bucket seats received them. The interval from three to five Jeffrey had marked on her schedule as a quiet time. "Now I'll show you *my* rocks," she said. "And you can wash all those people off, like scales." Did she speak advisedly? It was a windy day. The green bower she had pictured was lacy-thin. The better for those sun flashes that spilled through billowing clouds to trickle down—a warmth of which Daren soon found himself in peculiar need.

The witch act—like it or not—had become so much a part of her that not the sway of limestone, or at least of this red sandrock could take off its edge. When they came to the stream and Leflore stood out on a fallen log, touching the rock casually with one hand and with the other carrying her purse, which he had taken as they were climbing down: "You're going to fall off that," she said. (Look out for her," Bob Waring had warned; "she's so damned right.")

"Peddle your oracles in town," Daren told her. "'We walked logs all my life."

"You're going to fall, anyway," she repeated.

She didn't have to say it three times. Like an alligator the log heaved up, came to life, began to roll. He tried to tread it but it went all the way over; he fell on his rump in the pool, splashing in almost to his armpits, only the pocketbook lifted above that drench of cold spring water. If that was the female element, god deliver him.

He came up blowing, his pants and half his coat drowned, his shoes full, and nothing for it but to scramble up the rock, trying to see it as funny, while Jeffrey, throwing back her head, as on that other occasion by the brook under Wychwood, filled the valley with merriment. Then the child-delight yielded to the limestone look of Gea Tellus. "We'd better go back," she said.

"See here," Daren told her, "if I aim to worship nature, I'm not going to give it up because she turns out to be a stepmother in part." Jeffrey followed him to a hollow in the rock where the low sun, under a bare beech tree, bronzed a ground deep in leaves. He began to shed clothes, dumping the water from his shoes, wringing his socks.

"I'll hang them up." He stripped off his pants, heavy with water, twisted rivers from them, handed them to her, the coat, shirt, drawers. She placidly draped them on the gray limbs of the beech. Wrapping his mackintosh around him, he flung himself down. The loamy smell of earth filtered through the dry tang of leaves, the acrid heightened by the base.

She took off her shoes and stockings and laid them by his. Then she sat beside him, stretching her bare toes. Her laughter gurgled again.

"Did you wring your legs out with your trousers? They're like El Greco."

He raised his head. Her feet were short and broad, the peasant feet of a Piero della Francesca angel. His were the opposite, rabbitshaped, call it Botticelli, the toes separate.

"And your foot's a cloven foot—like my devil Marvin. Remind me to show you Marvin. But beware my witch's mark." She touched her brow. "It means I can master devils."

Clouds came over the sun. As in England. He shivered into the wind-rustled leaves. She opened her coat and rolled against him, covering them both. The words *woman* and *viper* said to come from the same root, of *wave*.

They had been apart too long to be sure of anything. As Daren would write, when he sent Jeffrey the sketch describing what he thought had happened in that valley: "Joyce is supposed to have got his insights from his wife and Lawrence from his Frieda; but poor old Leflore will go on floundering in the bog of ignorance. Will Jeffrey enlighten him? When she said, 'Not here, not now,' was it for ideal, or practical reasons? If he assumed the latter, what was left but the Presbyterian art of denial, the no-art of withdrawal, the Tantric art of suspension?"

The sketch was supposed to have made clear which he had chosen:

Water, light, all energy, rushing to its fall. *La Chute d'Icare*. Against which living things (birds into the sunset) bank, wheel, heightening desire. Restrain too far—the death of void; yield too soon—the death of flame: deflect the downward upon itself (willingly)—love in its musical delays.

But where was the point at which a deflection could be made? Not lips, not touch, spilling as into a sea. No barrier reef. Her Wait, wait," like "Take,

take," a sigh. No containment but the rounding of the field. As if April would continue with bloom after bloom.

Until eyes focused on eyes through a blur which incongruously was tears. That was the pedal-point over which bodies relinquished, unsatiated, in their prime, what only thought held, irrevocably.

"Tell me about Aunt Betsy. Is she real?" It was Jeffrey's approach on the return drive to the problem of a fiction.

"Everybody in the damned book is real."

"Why do you call it a damned book? I love it. I love Miss Betsy. I love Dan Byrne. He reminds me of you."

"I'd rather be his opposite. Lucy's the wonder. When I was there we were talking at breakfast about his first wife Sibyl. I told Dan Byrne he ought to change that part; it had too much rancor. 'No wonder poor Sibyl had a break-down,' Lucy teased. 'You know what he tried to read her the time she was in labor and the book says she couldn't fix her mind on the things he was inter-ested in? It was Rabelais, the birth of Gargantua, that stuff about the bum-gut falling out. He read it to me when I was in the hospital waiting for Hester. What a jerk,' she said as she looked at him lovingly. And Dan laughed, as if everything he did was bound to be enjoyable. He's good humored—a sulky Dan Byrne would be a catastrophe—but it depends a little too much on his own godhead."

"Did Aunt Betsy really drive that way?"

"Like a dope fiend. She almost hit us once, with her car full of D.A.R. ladies. Our chauffeur Rooshie had to stop dead. 'Dah she goes' (he was one of the Dark Leflores). 'Look at dat woman. She drive like de town grew up round her. "

"Well, *The Half Gods* will be better. 'We've got to make sure of that."

"We? Are you giving consent?"

"I'm thinking about it."

On an elm-shaded avenue they nosed into the drive of a bungalow Jeffrey had already compared to Aunt Betsy's, it was so cluttered with the souvenirs and papers she had saved. Her husband kept wanting to move to something grand, but she and the boys loved "the old junky place." "See," she giggled, 'he's got no room for all those fancy cars. One tiny garage way back there, and when I park like this he can't get in or out." She unlocked the door. "It's Delta style, so you ought to feel at home."

It wasn't old really, one of those comfortable tile and screen-porchy houses from the twenties and thirties, but it was on the cluttered side, a treasure-trove of junk, Jeffrey opening arms, displayed it with fiction-loving pride.

The first job was to find Daren some dry clothes. Jeffrey tore through the house, catching his hand and taking him along. She grabbed one of Tom's shirts here, a suit there, socks and shoes from somewhere else. She couldn't find any drawers until she pulled back a door she called the skeleton closet and they were almost inundated by washed clothes waiting to be sorted and ironed and put away. "That's how I keep house," she chortled. "It drives Tom wild. But I want you to see how a British-born Betsy does things." She whirled through the clothes on the floor like a dust devil, came up with some shorts, and stuffed the rest back into the closet.

"Now come see my file," she said. She took him into her own room and lifting the bed valance made a clown's face and a motion down. He went down. "Those are the clippings and letters I'm saving to put in scrapbooks." There was a pile under the bed that would have covered a corpse. "But I've got a worse one down here." She lifted a great trap in the floor, as in *Hamlet* when the ghost comes up from the cellarage. Daren peered into a sunken bin of papers. "I had it specially built. But it's a mess." She clapped it to and led him across the room.

"Here's where I keep my treasured letters. That's Marvin. You see how he reaches them out to me?"

It was a carved mahogany devil with real cloven hooves and inlaid agate eyes; he was shaggy, crouched, his horned head and Pan face raised and his arms holding a silver tray, on which Daren saw the letters he had lately sent Jeffrey about his coming.

"He's a gift from Micah Glenn. You've got to meet Micah. He knew your father. No, he told me that last year. He's abroad again, for the Quakers. But I'll bring you together; I bring all my friends together."

When Jeffrey first came to Reading, Micah Glenn was there, trying with his independent newspaper to give the place an honest voice. And maybe Jeffrey's reforms, which had saved her if not the town, had been kindled those nights when her "Daddy-Long-Legs," as she called him, would come to the house, and Tom would yawn off to bed, and the two would sit half the night talking in front of a glowing fire. Or in the day, if she had wanted advice ("a whetstone is no carving instrument"), she would go to the house Glenn's father had designed in 1907 in a style already informed by Sullivan and Wright, and if it was cocktail time, this old Creole devil called Marvin (suppressed Christian name of Snapper Lusk) would be proffering sherry on his tray. And as the *Independent Observer* ate up Micah Glenn's patrimony, there was sure to be talk about the league between Marvin and Mephistopheles and the Boss Commissioner. This was the souvenir Glenn had given Jeffrey when he sold out and went abroad as a field worker for the Friends.

Since they came into the house the phone had rung three times, people wanting to know whether front table seats had been reserved for them at the banquet. "Yes, of course," was Jeffrey's formula.

She pushed Daren into the bathroom without bothering to close the door. "Now you bathe and dress. I'll try to find something I can wear to dinner. Tom's got a board meeting but he'll join us at the club."

"What'll he think when I come in his clothes?"

"He'll love it. Don't worry about that. Or anything else. Mum's the word."

When Daren came out Jeffrey was in the living room. She had built a fire. She waved around the room: "Is it as good as Aunt Betsy's?" As if that were the essential consideration for any fiction. He walked to a long coffee table built as a glass-topped case, the shelf under the glass loaded with souvenirs: a jeweled vanity case from a first English ball, a baby's shoes, a buckeye, a little crystal and gold liqueur glass.

"What's that?" He pointed to a nondescript gray splinter of wood broken across by another half, split from it but still joined, an accidental cross, lying by a string of amber beads. What it evoked (as if in a pasture a bay mare had been glimpsed with its foal, or in the woods a doe with its fawn) was the image of generation—Jeffrey's first son, whose fine hands she had noticed at the breast and wished he would be a musician or an artist, though what he chose now was philosophy—

He had just started school at the time, and was walking there one morning late, when he saw this shape lying in the grass. It was covered with dew, and the sun struck it, diamond, ruby, emerald, sapphire. He snatched it up. He had been told to hurry, but he ran the other way, back home, crying "Mother, oh Mother," opened his palm on two damp little splinters somehow threaded together. "Look, Mother, the beautiful sparkling cross." So she saved it by the pressed rose from her father's Devon garden.

"I haven't seen Miss Betsy's house for years," Daren answered. "But even when I was a boy, it had the feel of death and decay. Your place is whimsical and alive; it's cheerful. As they might phrase it at Patapsco College: The souvenir here becomes a phenomenon of hope, there a phenomenon of despair."

The phone was ringing again. Jeffrey took it and returned. "The old bitch," she blazed, "trying to find out if it was true, as rumored, that Leo Preston has conked out on the banquet."

"What'd you tell her?"

"I told her of course he was coming."

"But he's not."

"What business is it of hers? Gossipy old cat. I won't have her scaring my birds with her claptrap."

She sank back softly into the mood of the sparkling cross. She had borne her sons and reared them and still it seemed life was before her. She sat by the fire on a footstool, like a bride or young mother, sewing. And though it was only a hem on her own silk dinner dress to replace the safety pins from the last outing (she saved that story for another time), it might have been the gleaming robes of generation which the daughters of Vala weave for the souls of this world, to keep them from falling into the abyss of Ulro.

She was such a wife and childbearer as any man who had caught glimpses into the ways of ceremony might have wished to establish at the hearth of his tranquility. So that even Leflore, overcome by the lamplit appearance, saw his life as if beginning over, where he had started with Anna, but with this ageless Jeffrey—like the Edwardian portrait of her mother on the wall, a cloudy tiara of hair, a head held high like the antlered head of a stag…

Still, they were not that ageless. If anything was to be created now, it was not by going back, but forward, not into Jeffrey's matronly womb, but his own brown study—though maybe he needed her even for that, provided the womb image could be reversed.

He stretched out a tentative hand. She looked up with the glad smile of a beauty so brave against change it might almost have stirred to tears. His fingers brushed her hair, rounded her shoulder, just grazing and caressing the wave of the breast, then fell away, while he shut within itself a sweetness forever lost and found.

"Let's go, Jeffrey," he said. "Out there. Reading is all before us. Where is it tonight? Dinner on the mountain? And then the radio? Well, I'm with you."

They were put on the balcony at the club, suspended by the glass wall that looked over the night city, the other way a perfect view of the floor show. Too perfect. A black-head babe who was supposed to have made good on the radio (but how? and why? and how long ago?) had come back to whoop it up for the hometown. She was swinging that arm like cranking up a rusty sex engine, her long gold dress tight as swaddling bands, the squeezed fat bulging at the edges ("You poured yourself into there, gal, but how you gonna get out?"), grinding out number after number of shrill seduction, the voice a bastard progeny of Grace Moore and honky-tonk, scraps of the thirties served over cold. "What kind of old musical vomit will the dogs go back to in the provinces?" And they broke into frenzied cheers—that band of dedicated industrialists, businesswomen, housewives, and art-lovers who formed the elite of Reading and to whom Jeffrey sold her civic concerns: Mr. & Mrs. Stewart Lathrop, reigning royalty of the Festival, he with the pinched complacency of the unfortunately balding big-boss-man, she in a pompadour as stiff as an African mud-job, her face like the cat that stole the art-cream, and her hubs (as they grow onions abroad) quite out of the Décolleté. Why detail from one to the other the differentiated sameness of those tabled rows? Was it the strain of having risen too fast, like forced plants, in a generation or two—that stringy-necked dowdy catching their eye: "Yoo hoo, Jeffrey! Wavy-wave"—or as some Negro author had said, the strain of keeping the blacks down that had bled the southern whites this way? No, it was American, it was worldwide, the strain maybe of keeping truth down, the posed authority; they were all pretending, not even directly but at second and third remove, acting like movie stars who had tried to act like characters authors had fained to imitate thinking they were some-bod-ies. Certified color and flavor.

Tom searched them out and took his place, gracious in his rather trou-bled way. He had rushed home for some reason or other and found his duds rifled and Leflore's wet things cluttering the bathroom. "I took him out in the woods," Jeffrey said, "and threw him in the creek." It was clear Tom thought her capable of crazier things than that.

And pleasure of all pleasures, old Bella Wynne was here too, looking like the whore-queen in Goya's picture of the royal family. The lines on that woman's mouth, a soured hauteur, the dark pride of decayed charm. By now all her palliatives and pastimes must have let her down. She had given up painting when her breasts began to sag. It seemed that even romance had deserted her. 'What was left but antiques and civic functions: opera, the art museum, symphony, drama; to gossip of other people's affairs, mess with other people's lives?

Tonight, as Jeffrey pointed out, a real miracle was being enacted. That thin dark woman at the same table with Bella was her sometime dancing daughter. What a concession to the Festival that the leading spirits of Painting and Ballet should appear at the country club on the mountain, tit to tit, like a Picasso mirror image. Poor Dido, and looking more like her mother every day, but for one distinction: she ill at ease, unsure, a plaything of the other's haughty power. They were practicing, it seems, for their appearance at the formal Wynne reception tomorrow night, the final event of the Fair, which Jeffrey was driving Daren to the Delta to avoid, when the photographer would snap them reunited, as the paper would describe: "Their evening gowns in fabrics gleaming and gossamer, enhancing the French Decor of the fabulous Mansion."

Leflore's look returned to Jeffrey with a kind of wonder. How had she done it, immersed in that falseness where she had maneuvered and schemed, where she had swum like a dolphin, her back hardly showing above the element she moved in; how had she kept the immediacy and joy of what could only be called Nature, while she outdid all the rest in the ruling artifice of charm?

The entertainer gave as come-on a wiggle as a chrysalis breaking into a butterfly, though you knew what came out of that cocoon wasn't going to have wings. The crowd roared, as if each one had a secret ambition to snuggle up to that warbling blubber. Outside, in the moonlit night, a few pines of the mountain stirred; then space, dark, and the bowl of the light-studded city. Negro waiters in immaculate white were bringing bright drinks, steak and lobsters "on unvacillating trays." The performer went into another number, flinging tight hips again and again, as a fisherman keeps casting at a fished-out stream.

When far out and down, almost insignificant from that height, just seen and faintly heard, came a flash and boom, and then in the dusk of Negro town a little area of increasing flame.

3. *Jeffrey Pitches In*

The womb," she wrote, "the womb was my undoing."

Anna had bought Daren the briefcase their first summer in Patapsco when he was working on the Diaries of the Oxford years. Anything he was wrapped up in he wanted to take with him wherever he went, in case he should think of something to jot down. As the project grew, the satchel swelled, and that, with his lugging it about as if it fed on his life's blood, made it so ridiculously like a pregnancy that in time it was bound to be christened the Womb.

And when that book was aborted, having never reached its term, and relegated to the numbered and lettered shelves that turned the back wall of the Patapsco workroom into a two-dimensional array, and the philosophic inquiry took its place, to be lugged and fostered in turn, the womb was already beginning to be stretched and frayed from those Gargantuan child-totings.

Later, when the philosophic lifework yielded under more immediate urgency to the political investigation—having from the first two branches, the specific and even practical handling of what was relevant to Daren's defense, and, like the hidden root of the iceberg, another vast projection, *Ground of the Twin Republics of Self and World,* that bag, in the act of voiding one charge to receive the other, came unsewed, and opened down two of its already weakened seams. So what should one do but speak of the Caesarian birth, though still no progeny had come to light?

Daren bound it around the belly with a couple of cords, found an old belt to go over and under and through the handle, easy to unbuckle for filling and emptying, and it was with this battered sack, from which *The Hostile Witness* had been delivered, that he flew south. When they came down in Reading, a crosswind slewing the tail like the devil's at the last day, and he stepped off the plane, and Jeffrey met him at the gate, eager to help in her efficient English way, it was on this rather than the larger suitcase that she seized. But she had hit on the heavier article. For the Womb not only held an annotated copy of the published product, on which he was supposed to speak, but the chaotic embryo of the symbolic fiction he had conceived at Woodruff Farm, as if in the old contention and tree-climbing rivalry with Daniel Byrne.

"I did not catch hold of it," Jeffrey wrote, "it took hold of me. I wanted to look inside, to see the wonders it was hatching. The cord that bound it has bound your Circe."

That was the womb of their reunion, and as far as its quickening went, the four weeks between Daren's first and second Reading visits constituted the honeymoon; and as imagination telescopes the sequences of reality, that brief time compressed into a single hymen of letters, her consent, their consummation and childbearing.

> You say you have just the residence for my childhood. Do you think you can improve on fate or outrun fortune, or that I would have been given to you for what you call your fiction, if I had not been such as to fulfill it? I will tell you the truth, and it will be better than all your make-believe.

Moss, bluebells, ditches, hawthorne; how she ate the buds on the hawthorne and called it butter and cheese; how she went blackberrying down the lanes with servant children. Daren, struggling to keep afloat in the flood of yellow pages—now the warm weather began, above his own scrubby valley, blackberry runners budding on the Patapsco rock—felt, in knotted complicity, the reward and surfeit of this love-play:

(Margaretta Eugenia Queenie Swan Haywood, sixteen, redhaired, lusty to look on, when her mother brought her to be interviewed for the place of fourth parlormaid and Jeffrey's attendant, and when the name was proudly announced by the parent who had hatched it: "Well," said Jeffrey's mother, "we'll call her Maggie." So they went on, bargaining over the wench, as if she were some kind of barnyard fowl not a party to the negotiations—Jeffrey, though small, already putting herself in Queenie Swan's place and writhing. Afterwards they would slip off, companions, to Maggie's house in the cottage row, where the nasty black and white cur-terrier Gyp would run yapping, but subside for tea. And with what delight Queenie's father had his treat of the day, the boiled egg stirred up with bits of toast and butter; and how they made tea with the water that had boiled the egg, and Gyp begged for the tough floury dropcakes, and Jeffrey longed to eat the smelly oil-dripping kippers they always had, but was afraid the head nurse Bertha Chadd would smell her out, and Maggie and the cottage would be banished forever.)

Daren had what for some reason he had thought he wanted. But how weird in a carrier already stuffed to the guards to welcome so prevalent a stranger, tell everybody to get up and scrunch over to make room for the dominant Jeffrey with all her life-baggage, chattels, souvenirs, portfolios, dolls, clippings, suitcases, trunks, bandboxes, hatboxes—letters fired in volleys, two and sometimes three a day, scrawled in every moment she could snatch, early morning, meals or late nights, from a schedule always full—the loopy drunken red pen racing over the paper, while everything flooded back: people, actions, scenes, poetry even—a love that had lain fallow through a life of hustling. She would wake with fragments in her head, things she had written herself in the lonely years in France, or copied from obscure journals, or read in Aunt Ev's commonplace books, old talismans:

> When fierce the hand of fate
> Is linked with yours across a board,
> And then the struggle till a hand goes down…

Chaos enough to make the maker himself draw back from creation, staggered (as Daren with the Oxford Journals into which so much had been poured) by the hopeless war between fact and design.

And Jeffrey was no ordinary fact. She had a life-force and will to power which instinctively set itself to transform and appropriate whatever context she moved in, She was not trying to take her place in any existing book but to generate a new one—"bright effluence of bright essence increate." Like the first soul spawned and detached from the eternal being, she asserted her own and universal center. Another entire novel was waiting there, though not the one Daren had spread his nets for. He, seeing fiction at such a crossroads as drama must have appeared to Plato, challenged by the hard sphinx of meaning, was no less impatient than Anna with what he called outmoded: those sagas of personal development.

They had lived in the rolling country between the Tavy and the Tamar, under the great dark expanse of Dartmoor. She was the last and favorite child. There had been others, but out of her range: a brother killed before she was born, in the last days of the First World War, a sister married and gone to New Zealand, another brother, off at school through her youth, himself to die as an airman in the second war. She was the fruit of her parents' forties, and she gave a new touch of youth to what had been a celebrated marriage. They used to take her with them on trips, to London, to the sea, on visits and to concerts. Like the child in a portrait by Gainsborough, the six-year-old Jeffrey completed the composition.

That was all suspect in Anna's terms, an elegance raised on colonies and the exploitation of labor. Even if Jeffrey had tried to protest: "But it's not just goods, not material," she would have had to admit that things said it better than words, those used-up faceless coins: *home, family, love*—say rather, *the morning room:* high-ceilinged, windows filled with flowers, daffodils, roses, chrysanthemums, flowers for every season; and through the green and color of the flowers, sunshine flooding the yellow papered walls, chintz chairs, light curtains blown with spring when the casements were opened, drawing one out: something new, a primrose in the woods beyond the tennis courts, a third egg in the nest in the espaliered pear. The same room had its winter face, a circle of leather chairs around the fireplace on the inner wall, the mantel and tables set with family photographs, friends, pictures from the honeymoon in Italy. And there were the other rooms, drawing room, billiard room, library, study, dining room, upstairs bedrooms with huge ancient beds, day nursery and night nursery; the octagonal tower, windowed, with views over paddocks, stables, horses grazing in fields, woods along the bluebell stream, then the rolling patchwork between hedgerows, rising to the shadowed moor.

That was the setting. And with whom did Jeffrey people it?

The spirits of paradise return to their prime. So Laetitia Strange in Jeffrey's memory. Packing up to leave the manor, the twelve-year-old girl had found in her mother's portfolio a page torn out of an art magazine, the rotogravure of a painting, a woman in a diaphanous windblown gown. She was leaning against a tree, her eyes lifted in a soft look, her face lighted by a Pre-Raphaelite ray that struck through the leaves. "The Priestess" it was called (Greek or Druid?), anyway, it was Lassie, and no doubt. Jeffrey took it to her father in the library.

"Look," she said. "Here's a picture of Lassie."

"No;· he answered, "that's not your mother." And tossed it into the fire.

It was on such a mystery of art and love that Jeffrey had thought to model her own highborn appearance.

Her father was more factual. Though there too the account began with painting: "Like someone from an Elizabethan portrait. As if he should be standing by a horse in a brocaded doublet and hose, with a ruff around his neck and a plume on his hat."

The horse, in any case, was sure to be there. In the First World War when Roger Strange was invited by a canny set of friends to invest in a closed group making machine guns for the commissary, an underwritten ticket to success, he turned the option over to his brother Athol; and when those brilliantly caparisoned cavalry units charged with bannered lances and *esprit de guerre* against an enemy they did not see, and were mowed down (Edwardian head thrown back, articulate right hand caught to the chest, the other dropping the reins, reaching out long-fingered, through a mist of blood), it was not for the lads that an equal idealism in Roger Strange took its cue to act (were not men shaping for themselves every day the explosion of shot, gas and mud in which they died?), but for the beasts lashed to it resisting, heads lifted in wild wounded neighs, hooves upside down Railing the air; like St. Francis writing to the Emperor Frederick II, who was wading under anathema through war, advising him (the note delivered perhaps the day he cut off the hands of the papal emissaries) to put out food in the winter all over his kingdom for our little brothers and sisters the birds—Roger Strange put his fortune into a teamwork for the prevention of that cruelty, to get injured animals cared for, the starved and ailing fed, the stranded removed from war areas; there were continual reports and counter-reports going back and forth from the vets and horse leeches in the field to the antivivisectionists and money-leeches in the offices; it would have wrecked a richer man than he—God save the foundation!—though little was accomplished.

Even in peace horses remained his consuming passion. When the fine estate was gone, the stables and grooms and hunters, he couldn't be without a couple of his old favorites turning the paddock behind the Cotswold house into the whinnying fields of Eden.

Jeffrey's account, vested, like the imagined portrait of her father, in all the trimmings of custom, seemed to move between that morning room and those horses.

She wore whipcord breeches with leggings of felt, and the buttons had to be just so down the inside shinbone and over the boot at the ankle; she would stand before her father at the east window, and if any wavering offended his eye, he would hand her the silver and bone buttonhook, saying 'left' or "right"; she would undo the fourteen buttons and set them back in line; then they would go out together for the early morning ride: to canter up the sunrise, like the father and daughter in the Cuyp on the dining room wall, their golden picture, Roger Strange pointing with his riding crop at a new foal, a budding blackthorn, a skylark ("I missed them most of all, in these dry Alabama fields, out of sight, as in Shelley, until the sun would light the mist and you'd make out that little beating speck high up, filling the whole air with trills and warblings"), Jeffrey noting the gesture: to point with a riding crop, yes, with the forefinger, never. Or they would pass one of the thatched cottages and her father would wink at her and assume the squire's role: "Are you raising white Wyandottes or buff this year? Yes, Orpington is a fine fowl..."

Better even than the ride was to come back to the morning room, to read the paper (she had sat there with him, pretending to read it before she knew the words), to have tea and toast together, or in the afternoon, after a hunt, *patum peperium,* brawn, smoked fowl, the strong cheeses men preferred, she relishing the strange smells and tastes—the morning room was the center…

Center also of the oncoming blight—"as killing as the canker to the rose." She was eight when she began to notice those conferences between her father and relatives and then her father and legal men, brokers, talk of debts, mortgage payments, the worried pacings, paintings and rugs beginning to disappear, collateral against the idealism of the past or the horses of tomorrow. The sunny small Corot in the morning room was the first to go. Uncle Athol, who had made his pile out of Roger Strange's option, he of the florid face and walrus blond mustachios, in his Norfolk jacket and knee britches, roaring around the country in a racing sports Lagonda, slipped the improvident brother a hundred quid (Jeffrey observing the paper change hands), tucked the picture under his left arm, waved cheerily with his right and walked out. It was only later that she realized that the money advanced on the grounds of not selling treasures out of the family was less than would have been offered on the open market. And maybe she was still unaware that it was not just her father, but the whole of ideal England, undermined by wars and depressions, riding the old course, against odds, on a flagging mare.

She milked those old ways of all their tenderness: white-bearded Alan with his ruddy cheeks and sparkling blue huntsman's eyes, gamekeeper in his youth, head gardener for the last twenty years. He had nailed pads of felt on the wheel of Jeffrey's little barrow so she could trundle it across the grass without making a track, and they used to walk the lawns, she following, catching up with him when he stooped to pick up anything, twig, leaf, feather, that had no place in the perfection. She paused too, he dropped in the debris, and together they moved on, his long stride heading for the next offender (only the slight limp betraying his rheumatism and ninety years: "A little weak on the left, miss," he would say; "but the right'll hold out a time yet."), she pushing the felt-wheeled barrow, falling a little behind.

Perhaps Jeffrey's mother would come over to ask a question. Old Alan would touch his cap and tell her when the nectarines in the glass houses or raspberries under the nets could be picked; for he was the only one who knew, or could decide which blossoms in the garden must be tied with brown paper sacks to make seed for next year. "No, mum, the currants a'n't ready for pickin yet." Or to Jeffrey's father as he went to the stable: "Sir, the low field's wet; you'll not be able to take the horses on it this week." And whatever he said was accepted like the law of gravity.

When they had done a thorough job on the lawns, Alan would take Jeffrey back to the lodge for a sip of wine. "Meg," he would say, "get Miss Jeffy's glass." And his younger wife, who never joined them, would go to the locked cabinet and bring a little crystal and gold goblet, which had come, Alan said, from the palace of Louis XIV, though how it wound up in his cupboard he never specified. Meg would pour Jeffrey a sip of her mulberry concoction and old Alan a bit more; then the two would go out to the bench by the yew tree. "'Ere's to tomorrow," and Jeffrey's precious glass would clink ever so slightly against the plain one he used for himself.

When the family left Childe Manor for Oxfordshire, of course old Alan stayed. As Jeffrey walked to the lodge to say good-bye, it was her own misery she was absorbed in. Only as he gave the last toast and could not stammer out the word "tomorrow," she realized it was worse for him.

"Good-bye, Alan. Take care of the cemetery for me."

It had been a bond closer than the yardwork or the healths in mulberry wine, that bank of mounds in the wood, at the head of each a small slate recording the dates and names: Timmy Squirrel, Bertram Cat, Roger Robin, Jenny Wren. They had fetched them out in the wheelbarrow, and Alan would stand with his cap off while the casualty was lowered onto grass and flowers in the shingle-lined grave (as on everything he was the authority on how deep it should be dug and which flowers were appropriate to the season)...

She had set down her glass and was about to go. "Here," Alan said, "it's yours." And put it in her hand. She tried to give it back but he shook his head: "For old times." She turned and walked away, pressing the glass against her cheek, telling herself again and again: "Cowards cry! Cowards cry!"

"I have it still," she wrote, "under the glass-topped table. You saw it there. The gold is as bright as ever, though the stem broke when it was shipped to America."

"My God, Jeffrey," he answered, "that blue-eyed old retainer with the buried birds; that's sentimental."

She didn't waste much time justifying it: "Well, that's the way it was." But she responded to his more particular demand: "Not just local color, not ye olde English rapture; show what you are, and how you got that way."

The long envelope sealed down with an orange sticker in bold type (had Micah Glenn sent it and she daubed it on for the splash?): "Help Stamp out Human Beings! Contribute to the War Effort through your Local Tax Collector," jolting him a bit, as if Anna had resumed the correspondence under another name. And inside, page after page scribbled up and down and across, and every page with a different letterhead, and each naming Mrs. Tom Lawless in some official capacity, president, vice-president, secretary, board, a documentation of the drives she served on: Youth Employment Plan and Mental Health and Planned Parenthood and the Reading Zoo, the Museum of Art and Civic Ballet, Friends of the Symphony, Episcopal Aid, Salvation Army, Women's Auxiliary—charities as numerous as her Victorian antecedents had maintained: A Laudable Society for the Relief of Clergymen's Widows, Mission for Propagating Christianity in the Highlands of Scotland, Bridewell Hospital for Dissolute Apprentices, Philanthropic Asylum for the Reception of Penitent Females—Jeffrey Lawless was up to her ears in WORKS, WORKS, WORKS.

In a week the bundle had grown to a file, with photographs, tributes, news clippings. As if one had opened an anniversary issue of *Looksee* or *Livelife,* a national magazine of pictures, some crucial double-stuffed number with a tree trunk of pulp in every copy, a celebration of "Good Times, U.S.A." and all this had come tumbling out: "What one incredible woman can do for a town."

"When I was a child," Jeffrey wrote, "and found a dead bird, I used to wrap it in leaves and tie it with flowers. Then I'd bury it. I thought they were deserted birds that had eaten mistletoe and died. So when I brought you that buckeye you say you still have around, tied the same way in a green leaf and with a dandelion, it must have meant something. There I was, a little girl in kilts and an old regimental sporran; and I might as well have eaten mistletoe.

"That was twenty-five years ago. When half that time had passed, I saw you again; and I came to this town feeling rather the same way. Everything bad that was in me, I began to project out, to blame it on this dried-up stuffy steel town. I can change that, I thought, before it changes me. I always liked the theater, so I started there. Then the Negro college and hospital. Then the museum. I discovered I could get money out of anybody. The tougher they were the sweeter they fell.

("If you want a source for that, note that Childe Manor was lent every year to the benign old rector, whose wife had gone mad, for his church bazaar. The lawn was dotted with stands where donated cakes and wines and hams were to be rallied off, and the paddock beyond the ha-ha was set for bowling and coconut shies, and my mother would open the fete by sweetly assuring the crowd that on these occasions the Lord loveth a cheerful spender. For my contribution I would organize the village kids into work gangs and lead them all over the neighborhood begging odd jobs, until we had exhausted everybody's patience and made a panful of small change.)

"I learned that all I had to do was to watch the man's face and keep talking. When he began to look at me, it was like a nibble on the line. Then that smile would come out, and I knew I had him hooked."

Photos, her witnesses: A big handshake clinching the deal with Tony Jenks, top thug of the Builder's Union, who had lately given an interview on the old labor wars: "They tried to bring some scabs in on the railroad. 'We was hidin behind the embankment like you see commandos in the movies. Man, all of a sudden it starts rainin. But it warn't rainin no rain like in the song. It was rainin bricks. And those scabs divin under the boxcars and everywhere they could to git away. Now we run everything peaceful and have strikes by telephone. Al here's got caulla-flowery ears answerin the phone. I got caulla-flowery ears answerin the phone." Today Tony Jenks had been talked into a mellow mood: "Yes, indeed, Miz Lawless, I guess we'll floor it for you free."

Or she was receiving the check for the Civic Opera deficit from the highly groomed manager of Vulcan Steel: "Vulcan, Mrs. Lawless, is always glad to lend a hand at the forge." Or she bent over dispensing tea and cakes at the fund-raising Party of the Arts, her Renoir breasts almost popping from the antebellum robe; or stripped to more exciting rolled-sleeve denim like one of those irresistible girl workers in an Israeli kibbutz she tossed up a dinner for a hundred businesswomen in the basement of the Episcopal church; or on the sun deck of the Hospital for Crippled Children, she was helping some paralitics fly kites, which for all the March wind they were not likely to keep in the air without her.

("Also note," she wrote, "that the motto of my father's family is *Miseris succurrere disco:* I learn to succor the unfortunate. I try to remember that, as he did. Though when anybody opposes me, I revert to the Cameron war cry, which was my mother's: 'Sons of the hound come and eat flesh.'")

"To see what I am," came the next letter, "you must take time when you come next month for the Negro Festival to go around with me and study your heroine in action. As for how I got that way, here are four stories from my youth which almost explain themselves."

Curious how each had a setting of its own, like scenes of a four-act play, though there was no necessary order among them. One could begin at the center and work out: the library, the kitchen, the stables, the village lane outside the wall.

The library—shelves to the ceiling, fine leather bindings, tattered volumes in paper and boards, newspapers and magazines hung on racks like towels, parchment tomes opening to marbled endpapers, to pages with marginalia written in crabbed old hands, tunnels of bookworms sometimes from cover to cover, the library, its fireplace ringed with red leather seats, a fender box meant for wood, where Roger Strange pitched his bills in unpaid confusion—that library had for Jeffrey the right smell of wisdom. Though she minded other sport there.

"There was an iron letterpress," she wrote, "we used to crank down on walnuts, a dozen at a time to hear them crunch. Or put in an apple and get somebody to squint through the crack, hoping a squirt of juice would catch him in the eye. I had loaded it with gooseberries one day for a secret experiment, when my father came into the room. I ducked behind the revolving bookcase in the corner. The housemaid came after him. 'Urgent and private,' she said. 'Has to speak with you alone, sir. He's got Honeybum.' I didn't move.

"Honeybum was a poacher. But he had never been caught. The game-keeper pushed him in. 'Red-handed, sir. I watched the snares. Two plovers and a rabbit in his coat lining. And out of season, sir. Just wanted to show you before I took him to the constable.'"

(Would Anna have remembered, from her first socialist book, the one the opera singer had given her, Shaw's cry against the game laws: "Men were transported with the worst felons for poaching a few hares or pheasants?")

"Honeybum wheedled, looking at the ground, talking about his little Rosie, and, 'Honest, Guvnor, she's not had a piece of meat for a month.'

"I heard my father's voice: 'Honeybum, this time I'm going to let you off.'

"'But red-handed, sir,' cried Archer. 'Snares, sir.'

"Honeybum started a drivel of thanks.

"'Leave the game on the desk.' When the crestfallen Archer had led him out, my father raised his voice: 'Jeffrey, come here.'

"He pointed to the rabbit and the birds. 'How could I condemn a man for trespassing when my own daughter was trespassing in a worse way? You heard Harriet say *private* and *with me alone.* Now more of these will die in his filthy snares.'

"For the first time I saw him look old. 'Go to the nursery. And no riding and no dining room for a fortnight.'

"I couldn't beg: I had heard Honeybum do that. It wasn't the punishment, to eat alone in the nursery from a tray. It was my father's look: like God's in the Garden.

"When the time was up, he sent for me. He was sitting in the library. I climbed onto his lap; he put his cheek against my hair. Then he looked over the fireplace where there was an inscription in Gothic letters: 'Old wood to burn, old books to read, old wine to drink, old friends to trust.' He read it out loud. 'Jeffrey,' he said, 'it's time for our ride.'

'We rode down the lane past Heathercombe and over the pack horse bridge into Cornwall, little workers' houses, abandoned mine shafts and tin smelts, with grass growing on the crumbled rims of the old stacks. From the beech wood high above Tamar Weir, we looked back to the green patchwork of our paradise.

"Once in Lent the old rector said sin was separation from love. I understood that. My father wouldn't have blamed me for what happened to us at The Door. He wasn't a Puritan, But about the family, I could hear him quoting Wordsworth's poem: 'Duty, Stern Daughter of the Voice of God.'"

The second scene, laid in the kitchen, might have raised the problem of class, Daisy Snead, scullery maid, cutting up old newspapers at the back table and threading them on a piece of string to take home (they had hung that way in Anna's toilet out under the sidewalk), who when Jeffrey asked, "What is that for?" leered at her: "If little girls wouldn't ask questions they wouldn't have to be told lies"—one would have wanted to side with that kind of poverty—except that, in the face of those wavering piggy eyes, Jeffrey could never think of it as a problem of rich and poor, master and servant, but simply of good and evil. She had seen Daisy cutting the stable boys' bread thin, saving the extra ends of the loaves, which she buttered heavily and slipped to the milkman in brown paper bags. What he slipped her in return she had no notion of, even when she saw Blodget with his hand up Daisy's dress; but from the way they jumped she thought it must be something wrong.

For a week there were smiles in the scullery and always a jam tart that just happened to be left over. Jeffrey ate them until it came to her that she was being bought off, and not even with thirty pieces of silver. She stopped Daisy Snead one afternoon taking the pudding cloths out to the copper house to be boiled. "Daisy," she said, her head tilted up to one side, "I haven't told anybody about your giving Blodget the bread and I don't mean to, but I won't have any more tarts, thank you."

"I never give Blodget no bread"—

She would run into that face the rest of her life, mostly in crowds— (those women picketing a school when the marshals brought the little Negro girl with the white bow on her hair and wide brown eyes, the woman with the squint and flat chin shaking her fist at the car window: "Black bastard! Keep away!" And then breaking from the group: "I'm goin in thet school and git my chern. I'm no niggerlover") or in the mob on Stone Mountain— and always the piggy eyes shifting distilled into the pit of the stomach the child-sense of lurking nameless evil...

"I never give Blodget no bread. But if it was said as how I did, I might tell things about the stable boys you're so fond on."

"I scorn to tell. My father doesn't like tattletales, and I don't either. But no more jam tarts."

It was not long before Daisy left. From the way the other servants would snicker about the milkman and then hush when Jeffrey came near, she gathered it bore on that.

"I've never been able to get presents or flattery or even praise since," she wrote, "without hearing a little voice: 'Watch out, Jeffrey. This looks nice enough. But how do you know it's not jam tart?'"

"My favorite stable boy," she began the third account, 'was called Darkie. I've often thought of that down here, where you can't look into a colored boy's eyes without wanting to weep. He had such eyes; they said it was Gypsy blood. He started with the lowest work, mucking-out the boxes and the standing stalls. You would see him looking up . . And he had a way with horses. I told my father; so he was made exercise boy, to keep the horses walking when they came in panting and lathered with sweat. About then I got a colt of my own, and I let Darkie break him for me. We used to talk about turning that horse into the steeplechaser of the century; and he had the form, but a bad mouth, used to take the bit and do what he pleased. Maybe he should have had an older trainer, certainly a curb bit, but when Darkie galloped him in the trials, he preferred to use a light snaffle, and I let him have his way.

"They were out in the fields one morning before the races at Newton Abbot, and I was with my father watching, when Tristan bolted with Darkie as they went behind a little belt of trees. I sat as I had been trained. The most you were allowed, no matter how excited, was to raise yourself a little in the stirrups for a clearer view. But when the other horses came out and no Tristan, I started for the place at a canter, and my father after me, more slowly."

If Darkie had been Jeffrey's prototype for the Negro race, to be brought from deprivation to light, she couldn't say she hadn't been warned. They found Tristan on the ground, Darkie at his head holding him, while he struggled to rise. They took one look and knew it was a cony-burrow, the leg broken. To defend her colt from everything implicit in that lost floundering, Jeffrey ran to Darkie, flung herself on Tristan's neck, joining in the attempt to keep him down.

"It's broken," her father said. "I'll tell Jarvis."

At the imperturbable voice, fatal as falling bodies, Jeffrey began to cry. Her father had dismounted. He looked at her, thrown by her emotion into another which altered his face and bearing—a flush of pride and contempt (tears, and before a stable boy): "Cowards cry," he spat out, and setting his foot in the stirrup, swung up and rode away.

That saying, which Jeffrey had breathed in Daren's arms on another occasion, had been traced to its source. Which pointed the irony of her editorial remark: "You will see from this account and that of the poacher the influence that has formed me. Poor Anna, never to have had a father. How can a woman who has missed that not be crippled somehow?"

The last instance left the walled bounds of the estate, though not the limits of ownership. The village was her father's too, though like everything else it was mortgaged into ruin; so why shouldn't the village kids think her one of the snobs who cut out the cores of shiny apples and, filling them with mustard and pepper and replacing the plug, left them by the road, then jeered from the top of a barn when the victim bit in. There had been battles before now, shied pebbles returned with a rain of conkers ("Ladies and gentlemen never throw stones".) What did the villagers care for Jeffrey's budding sympathies, that she had left a sound apple on top, like a booby lure; or that last Christmas when she saw the poor kids playing with little tractors they'd made out of spools, a matchstick and a rubber band, she went home and hid all her fine toys in the big closet, and spent the rest of the day hunched over hacking at spools? As Anna would have said, you don't live down your class and you've got to pay.

She had been to the woods along the stream. On the way back, as she passed Heathercombe, some boys took after her. She crossed the meadow to the brick wall around the paddock far from the house. She was climbing the toeholds they had hacked out in a corner of the wall there, when the villagers pulled her to the ground. One sat on her chest and another held her arms, while a withered little dark one, like a caricature of her own stable boy stuffed dirt in her mouth. She was too angry to be afraid, but all she could do was squirm, or get in a kick now and then at the one on her chest. When they had taken off her shoes and rubbed mud in her hair and on her pinafore, they let her up, and keeping the shoes, told her to go home.

She went, in a fury of shame that gave way to tears; but she never told. Not just because she had been warned about fighting with villagers. She hadn't fought; she had been grabbed from behind. But she knew there would be a rumpus, and their fathers, who worked in the stables or on the land, would get the sack. So she said she had lost her shoes playing in the bluebell stream.

Years later, as she waited for Maggie (Queenie Swan Haywood) by the fish and chips stand in Tavistock, she met the biggest of those boys. He was eating greasy potatoes. They looked at each other without speaking until his eyes fell and he walked away. What she felt at that time was a troublesome kind of sorrow for the mother-born man-thing to whose lot she was involved.

"What men will never understand," she would tell Daren, "is that for even the sorriest human relic, the woman in us says 'I could have given birth to that.'" (Mater Misericordia, all mortals sheltered in her robe.)

Whatever had planted Anna in Leflore, so that, though she was at the other end of the world, he was marshaling these facts against her, had planted the wretched in Jeffrey.

"Sentimentalism," the dialectic wraith accused. As Marx, though born of the middle class, discounted the reforming peers who read the Bible every night and prayed to forgive their debtors. But Marx had missed seeing the adaptiveness of capitalism.

"It's paradox, the subtlest leaven," Daren answered, opposing Anna's shade with the light-in-shade of Jeffrey, growing up by her bluebell stream, all that ferment working under the mask of training: "Never let anyone know you feel sorry for him." "Betray your feelings and betray yourself." "Never laugh if a smile will suffice." "Common people and cripples hold hands and arms." "Walk straight and look ahead." "Keep your dignity and your mind your own."

Why even William Blake, patron saint of impulse, could be quoted on the other side: Never tell your love; love should not be told… So why shouldn't propriety as well have bred its antithesis?

Not for Anna. The proverbs told the story. She lurked in the shadows, warning.

Now Jeffrey was pitching in, body and soul, bound to make a success of the fiction, how could anybody tell if what she was supplying was fact or fancy? "You can make a lot of the first meeting," she wrote; "as they came through the bluebell wood and out by the brick wall where the roses grew, and they kneel and scrape each other's shoes—such an intimate office, gouging, with a stick under the heel—and he picks her a rose; and she would have it still in the glasstopped table." Rose! In the woods, the darkest time of November, going to the Thanksgiving party Mrs. Hardy had arranged for the Americans.

And it wasn't just material she was cooking up, but all sorts of themes and formal considerations:

Our name was Norman, Lestrange, until a seventeenth century Puritan preferred to clip it down and give it the English look; so you and I are alike in origin; and maybe it would be better reversed, you Strange and Jeffrey the Flower.

Note that Jeffrey is born in April in the sign of Aries, Leflore in October under Scorpio, opposite signs working to a strange identity. For we are too much alike.

Often I've asked myself, is it right I should be younger than your Anna. And

I decided it was. Because if her soul had a birthtime when it was really alive, it must have been long ago, and she swung to it until it dried up around her. But my time is now, to make every moment live.

Daren's got to give his love to somebody who'll re-create him. He thinks he's looking for the old water-mother where he can float passively, return to the dark arms. But he doesn't know what he wants or what his life needs. If it's got to be water, let it be a brook—give him a sparkle with his love. To break that Anna-gray, to flash right through him, all the way back to his Bleary Hole beginnings.

For, of course, on the buttock-seat Delta drive they had made the graveyard and Blue Hole return.

This tide of suggestions was raised to flood when Jeffrey began to receive carbons of what had already been sketched. Her demands for revision bounced back before Daren had half grasped what he was setting down.

This Reading Love among the Rocks is impossible. You have to warm it up. Leflore sounds calculating, a cool customer. If he's a Mississippi fish, English Jeffrey's not. It's got to be like Bronte: "Unuttered harmony... earth lost to me... outward sense gone, inward essence feels... a final bound... intense the agony, when the ear hegins to hear... the brain to think again... soul to feel the flesh, and flesh to feel the chain."

And Daren: "With dispassionate calm. With the readiness of an artist to work endlessly to improve his art. With stubborn fury. With the incapacity of an artist to change his art on any other ground. That scene among the rocks, as I wrote you, is an attempt to describe the mystic art of *prolongatio,* which some Christian heresies have borrowed from the East. As for Bronte, she had no lover; she was writing about death and God. Maybe mortal love can be like that. It can also be the corniest thing possible. And who wants to call a green goose a goddess because divinities are thought to exist? In any case, it would be the night-, death- and water-love you have told me I should avoid."

And she: "Why do you call it a fiction? Aren't you even going to change the names?"

He: "Reality comes to me as abstract enough, presences sliding into focus from shadowy suffusions, shedding glints of themselves everywhere, and subsiding like damped waves in attenuated fringes. Let them keep their names. The problem is not to invent but to reconcile existence to the page. To feel out the convolutions and infoldings as you would a topology of sculptured stone."

And Jeffrey, more cuttingly: "Why are all your voices your own voice? Why not let us talk?"

To which: "Voices? Yours? Mine?—Didactic ventriloquisms of that Author whose identity remains so much in doubt."

Sensing how little control she had, she began to back water:

> All night my judgment has waked me, warning, "Don't get carried away by Daren Leflore; he's your evil genius. It was bad enough years back, but it's worse now. All he wants is to get you in that book, to hang up the soiled wash of your soul where everybody can talk about your underwear!
>
> Why should I be your stepping-stone across your infernal water?
>
> You have set your heart on such a rock there is nothing in earth or heaven that can touch you. But I am exposed. I don't call you vengeful. I am ready to assume it is not in your nature to wish me harm. You will do me harm for all that; and at night my reason wakes me, saying. "Beware!"

To which Daren:

> Anna used to say I could write but lacked material. She wanted me to tell her story. She put her youth and loves and politics into my hands, thinking I would be her voice. But the Oxford sketches let her down. "Why pussyfoot?" I told her. "You thought you could use me and I thought I could use you. That's why we played Common Front. If it was still to do, you'd do it again."
>
> As for you, Jeffrey, love, you are another who's wanted to create a world. And bobcats wouldn't stop you. So don't protest too much.

The envelope that followed was the bulkiest of all, the four life accounts, with this scrawl of unrelated surrender:

> When I pick up one of your letters to remind myself of something, Marvin, with his knobby cheeks and ivory grin, looks up, as he must have looked when

he offered New Orleans debauchees the lotus absinthe: "Help yourself, Jeffrey; help yourself. And I wish you joy of the worm.

I am like the mermaid in the story, who was given legs to dance with the prince, but at the price of walking on pins and needles all the time.

Leflore had known, as soon as he moved into the mead hall at Avalon and down into the valley of rocks, that he was entering a field at least as strong as any he could muster. He had thought of it as Jeffrey's field. Could it be, as mythology assumed, the field of a god, into which she too had been drawn, thinking from her side that it was his?

The second appointment in Reading, which Jeffrey had arranged when Leflore was there for the first, neared. Again he boarded the plane. He had muffed the white Festival of the Arts. Now he was speaker for the dark.

4. Meet the People

Go back: first visit, first night, Leflore driven to the hotel, late: "You're shameless. That's it. Jeffrey Shameless. And on the radio; 'Buy this book tomorrow at the author's banquet. Get it autographed and leave it to your children. Because a time is coming when they'll say: Daren Leflore signed this when he was at the Arts Festival in Reading.'"

"Well, it's true, isn't it?" came from Jeffrey's jaunty innocence.

"How do I know if it's true? And suppose I wanted to pretend it was, it's not for me to advertise it."

"Ah", she smiled. "but it is for me."

They had gone from the club to the broadcasting station, and Jeffrey and her friend the announcer had led Daren into the sound proof studio, and when the clock came straight up and the announcer said, "Here is Jeffrey Lawless, first lady of Reading," you'd have thought she'd been born on the radio and at the salespitch too—that persuasive sweetness going over the air, while Daren blushed before the unseen and (after so starry a presentation) no doubt sniggering audience. "And here is Daren Leflore, author of *The Hostile Witness,* ready to Meet the People."

But he was relieved almost immediately of the burden of saying what his book was about. It was a question and answer program, the questions telephoned in by anybody who wanted to take the trouble, and the first voice Daren heard when the light flashed and he clicked the switch which simultaneously launched it on the air might have come from the dark of the Delta the night Uncle Hazy lay in the hospital after the heart attack, and Daren, home from Patapsco, waked in the timeless hours and groped, bumping walls and tables, for the phone that was ringing, ringing; snatched it off the hook: "Hello. Yes? Hello. This is Daren Leflore. What is it?" To hear through the pregnant silence at the other end the heavy slow voice, not apologizing, but assuring its dull-witted self: "Lefloh? Lefloh? Ah got de wrong numbah."

"Thiz book o youhs. Ah figgah fum what chu say, iss about freedom. Izzat right? Weull. Does zat mean freedom fuh white folks uh fuh colored folks?"

The fire witnessed from the windows of the club having been a Negro church, gasoline bombed and still burning, the discussion, like every other in the South, was usurped by the only subject anybody could fix his attention on—philosophy, poetry, science, life itself yielding to the urgency—as if Shakespeare should be squeezed down to a line or two from *Othello:* "to the sooty bosom of such a thing as thou."

"'Come to the banquet and buy this book!' You tell em! And nobody calls in but Negroes, and they aren't invited."

That was when Jeffrey had apprised him of her plan for another Festival of the Arts. "I want you then as the only author. I'm going to spin my web for the *Times* correspondent tomorrow. You can watch. If I get the Negro festival on the culture page when the white one's never made it, it'll be a *coup.*"

(Anna could have pegged that one: "Coup for segregation?")

Daren slept at the hotel. The interview was the first thing in the morning. They met in the Coffee Room over breakfast. The correspondent had come to Reading to cover the race crisis. Jeffrey gave him some tips on that affair and then sprang her project. She turned her fascination on like throwing the switch of an electric chair. That gray-haired hard-bitten newsman sat riveted, his will sizzled like a fly under a burning glass. It seemed some embracing human love had for the moment been kindled between Jeffrey and this random male object she was going to wangle for the promise and all-clear ("Go ahead. I'll write it up."), which as a matter of fact she extracted before the egg could be downed or the coffee cool.

"Jeffrey Shameless," Daren whispered as she sat down by his side at the banquet. The old babe who had phoned her the day before about the Hollywood hot-shot and whether he was coming had just challenged her on the evidence of the program; so Jeffrey, with her most disarming smile had faced the thousand people jammed around tables through the space and into odd corners of the square-pillared Egyptian maze that turned the hotel's convention floor into a single warehouse:

"I'm sorry to have to announce that Leo Preston phoned last night that he was too ill. It's been unkindly rumored that we must have known before, since his name doesn't appear on the program you have. I wouldn't want you to believe that. He's been recovering from the flu, and we printed two versions· of that page, hoping he might come."

("Why should I fly to Alabama for promises?" he had phoned days ago. "'We got a big deal out here for cash."—"But he'll be sorry," Jeffrey told Daren. "I have friends who'll let him know.")

The notion had been to have a writer on politics (that was Daren), an entertainer (he had fizzled), a novelist hitting as near the best-seller mark as could be talked into coming, and some other writer of nonfiction about whom Jeffrey had been reticent. She had wanted to invite the journalist who had just written the best-selling *Life and Loves of Taft;* but a coalition of forces she couldn't operate without now and then appeasing (the D.A.R., the local legion, the citizens council and the chamber of commerce) had railroaded in their own oracle on education. So after the beloved southern author of that deathless novel *Listen to the Mockingbird* had told stories of her childhood already partly exploited in the fiction, and before Daren Leflore, who had made his one bow to the reading public with a book about how he was investigated as a Left Winger, could say how fruitful the leaven of the Left had been for free society, they had to listen to Professor J. Westbrook Foote, who, as the D.A.R. who introduced him detailed, had been an unknown teacher of English in a small midwestern college only four years ago, but was now the world authority on subversion and Marxist propaganda in American education. Undaunted by opposition from all invested centers of pinko-intellectuals and fellow travelers, he had ferreted out of old newspapers, the *Congressional Record* and other neglected sources the evidence he had so frighteningly hammered home in his epoch-making books: *Walk the Communist Line, Brainwashing Children,* and *Iron Curtain in the Ivy League.* "We owe to him," the lady beamed, "that list of one hundred and seventy objectionable textbooks which Moral America, Enterprise Rearmament and Young Americans for Freedom have stressed the danger of. He has touched off (she buried her head in her notes) "the schoolbook controversies which have cleared the atmosphere in California, Texas, Oklahoma, Georgia, Arkansas, Mississippi and Virginia. He has been called before the House Educational Committee to present the case for a Textbook Censoring Bill; and he has recently been hired by the state of Alabama as an expert in the field of subversion in public schools. "I want to close with one little patriotic touch. I'm told that Professor Foote has a flag in his garden and a tape recorder, controlled by a photocell, so at dawn the flag goes up and the recorder plays 'The Star Spangled Banner.'"

"Yes," Jeffrey leaned to Leflore's ear, "and they say one night there was a thunderstorm and the flag and the anthem went into orgy."

"I present Professor J. Westbrook Foote."

What followed was a synoptic assessment of the danger from liberalism, collectivism and the welfare state (though talking to an Alabama audience, he commendably overlooked mongrelizing), the need for every true American to embark on what he called "a campaign of patriotic hate."

The rather moth-eaten professor sat down, and Jeffrey introduced Leflore.

Daren hadn't wanted to talk about *The Hostile Witness* anyway. His mind was taken up with the fiction. Now old slew-Foote had crapped up the political field, a Leflore couldn't be expected to slog around there. Do something better: give them a sense of the search for form: how a homing pigeon thrown into the air wheels and looks lost, as presentiment gropes through trial and error, until you see him bank and straighten, high up now, and the clean wings cut in for the home flight. For there is always a way home, though to be known it has to be created.

But this particular homing pigeon got off to a bad start, trying to detach himself from the other speakers:

"Writing books—I don't mean anything anybody might happen to call a book—

"And I'm not pretending to any great purity or dedication of purpose.

I'm a man who's been offering himself on the market for years, waiting to be prostituted. But nobody's made an offer. So I remain fairly virginal. I don't say that's a virtue; but I have to speak from the perspective of my virginity—

(Jeffrey thinking: "He could hardly expect an offer, if this is what he calls putting himself on the market.")

"Writing a book isn't a trade, it's a madness. So I ask, why has the public in our time got so taken up with this form of madness?

"I think it's because the artist faces the unformed, knowing (guessing anyway) what he has to do. No laws can guide him, and timidity won't work. Warned back by every consideration, he can only cry with Luther: 'So help me God, I can no other'—and push on. So the average man, maybe without knowing it, looks to the artist, not just for amusement, but for an example of the courage life requires.

"How sadly the artists have let him down…"

He hadn't meant to take that turn. It put him on another track altogether. But his eye had struck the dowdy Mrs. Lathrop at a front table. She had summoned a Negro waiter for more coffee, though they were supposed to lay off during the speeches. Now she had turned and was vapidly smiling at Daren. Entertained. By God. He was going right along with them. Like Jeffrey.

No wonder his father had done himself in, or if he hadn't, let this sepulchral city open its maw and swallow him. But it was not from his father but his mother that the old claustrophobia came over him. His nostrils flared, sniffing the carcass of a world. Courage! As if the eternal Anna had entered from somewhere and caught him by the shoulder and given him her loving angry shake. To wake him up: "Not again, Daren." There was one way to appease that ghost and that was to wipe the smile off Mrs. Lathrop's face.

"For example. When I went on the radio last night to talk about freedom and my book, none of you phoned to ask a question. It was the Negroes, wanting to hear what freedom was about. And the only Negroes at the banquet are waiters. The rest aren't allowed. They can't walk in the parks or drink from the fountains in our earthly city of police and dogs.

'You want artists to come from above and talk to you about art. And here we are, at your call. It doesn't strike you how deeply we've betrayed you. Sold out. You don't complain. Because we're all sold together, and we'd rather stay sold than face the testimony of that courage we thought we wanted but in fact we feared."

*

Jeffrey had loved the idealism in her father. But she didn't like to be reminded how much idealism costs. If one could only pick winners in the world as simply as with horses. "Good we planned a trip," she said. "After that talk, I've more reason than ever to clear out of town."

They cleared out, fast, racing in the low-slung sports job down long empty roads through stands of slash pine on the red gullied hills, Jeffrey warming up for the self-revelation that would break into letters once he was gone:

Telling how she drove Bob Waring to the rocks one night to show him the phosphorescence, and a cop put his spotlight on them, then recognized her: "Oh, Miz Lawless. Are you all right?"—"Yes, officer, perfectly. It's a beautiful night."—"Well, you may be all right, Jeffrey Lawless," Waring said; "but your reputation…"

Then they drove to the club, and Jeffrey ripped the lining of her dress getting out of the car (that was why she had to mend it later by the fire), and the only place to get safety pins was from the Kotex vendor in the ladies' room. She put in both her dimes and still needed a pin, so she beat the box and yanked the handle, until Waring called through the door: "Take it easy, Jeffrey, you'll have the management on us." The machine coughed up, and as Jeffrey came out pinned back into propriety, she ran into Tom, whom Bob Waring had just hailed. As a controversial newspaper man, Waring wasn't Tom's favorite, and he didn't get any more so when Jeffrey joked about the affair of the rocks and the hem.

As they crossed the line into Mississippi and stopped for gas at Skinny's Garage and Motel on the banks of the Tombigbee, and Daren went in the men's room and faced the urinal, he saw where a traveler had inscribed: "Caution, use of this article may prove habit forming." And under the official characterization on the prophylactic vendor ("With a light lubricating jelly designed to prevent premature climax") made out another informal

486

scrawl: "CRASH HELMETS FOR HOT RODS"; and as they drove on, sharing a can of beer, they observed how the Mississippians (who, as Mark Twain said, would vote dry as long as they could stagger to the polls) had swilled case after case of the only inebriant they could get, until the grass shoulders of the road were littered with cans. "Drain it," said Jeffrey. Daren did; he almost made a motion to hurl it out the window, but the Leflore pride crossed his face. "A drink and fling culture," he said, and tucked it in the paper bag.

Zooming down the last slope under the more burning sun and over the Yazoo to the oceanic horizon of black land, cotton, winding bayous and woods, how would it not bring into the throat all the other home-descents of other years, stretching through his childhood and his father's manhood and back of that to Quincy Leflore's first settling at Ararat in the bitter ebbing of the Civil War? Especially now, under the commitment of making this swamp earth come alive for Jeffrey: the brown Yazoo at flood, backing into yards and fields around the weather-warped cabins, the lean hound at the door, the rooster on the ridge pole crowing of rain (Co-co-ri-co), the lazy stir of field hands and bandanaed bright-aproned women (they might almost have come in last year from Haiti or the Congo, but for the work-song indomitable croon they had formed under chains) still, for all the advance of the machine, hoeing around the cabins or taking the mule out to plow—the Negro soul most of all, the deepest vitality of the place, moving now in Daren's life, as in history, to a crescendo.

Bring it alive for Jeffrey, trace it down the years: homecomings always to the Dark Leflores:

The first summer from Oxford: "Where's Elmonia?" And Uncle Hazy: "Gone to Chicago, to visit Lou. I'm helping him through the University. He's a bright boy."

Lou, cleaning out the white boy's allowances when they were young, putting on a show, ten cents admission and five per encore, to see him bite the heads off grass snakes caught in the jimpson fields along the canal. Lou, of whose buck-toothed lankiness the storekeeper mused: "Uncle Caldwell,

I think I could throw my seed against the side of a barn door and make a better boy than that."—"You shouldn't say that, Mister Lowry; that's my own sister's son." Lou, the rights-fightinest black boy ever to come from those parts.

Uncle Hazy never accepted the arguments against sharecropping. "When the slaves were freed," he would explain, "they had no knowledge and they had no land; they had no capital. What could have been fairer than a bargain to help both parties: 'I'll give you land and seed and a house and food, and I'll take all the risks, and if you make a crop, since you don't have any money, I'll pay myself back with a share.'" He focused on the moment of that free contract, which his father, maybe, had been the first to offer, If you tried to put it into the context of time, telling him: "That bargain of yours has perpetuated an inequality never to be justified merely because it exists. How are the children to grow out of the condition of their fathers?"— he returned to the bare legality. Yet this Southerner, so inhibited in theory, stood ready, when they were almost bankrupt and on the point of losing Ararat, to borrow money to send Lucius to the University of Chicago, and foot Elmonia's excursion fare to join him.

As Anna said, it was still *noblesse oblige,* the magnanimous gift of what should have been a social right; but Daren, who had watched Lou decapitate snakes, and felt how easily rights-fighting might assume that character, could almost have closed the argument in Uncle Hazlewood's favor.

Yet how could compliance have survived those returns? The first trip down with Anna after Oxford, when they got off the train in the steam-bath immersion of that air (a liquid you wanted to swim through): "Lord," Daren hailed the stationmaster, "I'd forgotten how hot it could be down here;" to be drawlingly assured, "Iss pretty cool right now; we been havin showers." And there was the race problem like the atmosphere lowering around them: an old Negro with a rickety wagon and a flea-bitten mule lugging trunks, a plump Rotarian just off the train yelling at him: "Hey boy, jump down here and get this trunk of mine up there and take it out to Belmont Avenue, number six-nine-three"—the wheels already creaking and wobbling, the old man shaking his head: "Ah's fraid to put any mo on heah, boss. This heah wagon loaded." The seersucker swelling like a puff adder: "What chu mean, loaded! You're loaded, you drunk scoundrel. Now get down offa there and do what I tell you."—"Yassuh, boss. Ah do it. But she sho is loaded."

Year after year, from the prairie, from Chicago, from Patapsco… 1952: for Uncle Hazy's dying, when Elmonia was full of sorrow also for her youngest son:

"You member de wahtime, honey, when dey had you in jail?" (A feat of the unconscious if he could have forgotten it in eight years.) "Thas wheah mah Styles is. Seem like de bes always git de wus fortune. He mah younges— naw, Nabby de younges, she mah Flood chile" (nature's last great fling, when Uncle Hazlewood offered Elmonia a room in the house and she wouldn't take it, and he got her a place on a barge to Vicksburg and she never showed, took a holiday with somebody, until the water went down, and she came back as always—"If I've been merry, what matter who knows? and nursed Daren through pneumonia, and when he had his tonsils out). "Styles come three yeahs befo, but Ah call him de las cause Ah thought Ah never have another. And now he a poet, like de res o de Leflos—write de stranges stuff; doan know what it mean, but it sho is beautiful."

What she brought from the drawer to the not very expectant Daren set the whole place adrift with fire and ash, as if one of those Vesuvius fountains had gone off in the room:

> I awoke suddenly, no more in calm;
> the sounds of the city… conspicuous.
> Long years ago, to me what happened,
> that I must seek the abyss,
> my body of the rain… dampened.
>
> The land that is mine alone,
> where I let the wind blow
> and I flow as a leaf—
> why should it be mine alone?
>
> I sleep in the darkness and the night
> between the spaces of the stars… [4]

4   For the origin of this and the following poems, see Acknowlegements.

Not even Uncle Hazy could have got Styles free, and Uncle Hazy was on his deathbed. All Daren could do was to detour north by Detroit to piece it together: that runaway jazz-mystic caught up in the Ford assembly line, each night riding the melting-pot tram home tired, black jammed in at first with white, pretending an equal right but sensing the scam, until the ghetto deepened around them and the hostile eyes withdrew, and one who wanted to share not in black culture but in white could only despise himself for the heaved sigh of relief as the last chalk-man left the car, and the blacks, facing only each other, could take a breath, laugh, feel easy; he would climb the sad flights to his room, turn on the radio, hoping for cool jazz, walk out in the evening, trying to be dapper; always looking for love, while love and hate soured on him. He had taken to the needle for a while, not to get high so much as to hold himself together, to walk those border streets facing eyes glaring at his, thinking: "By God, if I can stand you, you ought to be able to stand me."

A gangling man-boy trying to write, and nobody but his folks a thousand miles away to write for.

"Heah one he wrote de Yaller Gal what he stab de no-count white trash over…

"You mean all that happened while I was in Chicago, and I didn't know anything about it?"

"Lawd, chile, we doan know nothin bout one another. We heared you wuz off in jail, now heah, now deah. We live all our life side by side, white and colored, and jus as soon be strangers."

"Not with that poetry. I'm going up there to find him."

But all Daren could encounter was a vaguely familiar youth, who greeted him under guard with the nonchalance of no comment, trying to the last to play it as cool as the jazz he loved. Before the year was up ("Lawd," Elmonia would say, "Ah knew he wuz gonna die; he wrote me a dream about a black-leaf tree"), Styles joined in a prison break, another man fired on a guard; they were searchlighted and mowed down as they ran from the stockade at night.

Next it was Uncle Caldwell. The word came from Daren's sister, June:

Poor Uncle Caldwell has died of prostate. So much pain; and then everything about the funeral so absurd. His half-sister came up from the old Natchez place.

"Jus in time," she told me, with satisfaction.

"You don't mean you got here before he died?"—because Elmonia hadn't wired until the hemorrhaging began.

"No, ma'am. Tha's too ghashly. Ah mean Ah come in time to view the remainders."

Then she went to the station. You remember Sleepy Reynolds, our cadaverous old ticket agent with the two long yellow teeth he uses for paper clips, sticking the ticket or the baggage checks under there when his hands are full? "How much is a round trip for a corpse?" she asked him.

He was staggered. "Boss," she said, "our Elder desisted, and we de fambly, and some live heah and some theah. Now if we have the fun'al heah, all us down theah gotta buy tickets and come up heah; and the other way, all them up heah got to ride down theah. So we lowed it'd be cheaper fuh the remainders to go down fuh the fun'al and come back fuh the buryin. And we want to know how much that round-hip ticket on them remainders gonna be?"

Sleepy Reynolds wasn't going to sell her any such thing at all, and I had to send Orville down there to get it ironed out.

What a trial for a wonderful old man like Uncle Caldwell, to have his remainders trafficking up heah and down theah. He wanted to see you before he died, to talk about his poems; but he left you this bundle and said I must send them to you, so here they are.

The green-tinted cardboard box of twenty-two carefully penned pages gathered with a pink ribbon into a sheaf, the title page flowered and lettered in crayon, *Wild Violets,* by Caldwell Leflore, offered, under the frail surface of sentiment, Victorian rhymes and trite effects, a lost lifetime of plaintive romance. Not Hollywood in all the quaint yearning of its early years had distilled a more nostalgic perfume than Uncle Caldwell in these poems.

Head leaned over the banjo, deep-sunk, face creased with elemental brooding, one of those Egyptian carvings of the god-ape Thoth—though he would have put on, if he knew you were coming, the white shirt with heavy gold and agate cuff links in spotless cuffs, the expanse of whiteness shrinking the powerful figure already shrunk by age—a man of sorrows and acquainted with grief: *emissit spiritum suum*—the crooning voice against picked and syncopated chords, expiring the deepest soul of the Negro South.

> Blues night, and me alone;
> Tried to get you on the phone;
> Called again, nobody home.
> Can this be true?

Daren prompting himself: If you can't who is there among the palefaces who will: to enter the Black Cloud; he was your uncle, he bore your name, Leflore. To make the leap—more than outwardly, not to black the face and ride the bus and suffer and write—but to go down, as sense into flesh, into the conscious stream, to become the infinite close brooding of that love:

> I'll be glad when it's day again;
> I'm so tired of heartaches and pain
> That come in the night with wind and rain,
> Makin me blue.
>
> Blues night, and me alone…

When the young Caldwell used to take cotton on wagons from Ararat to the compress and on to the steamboat landing, and won for himself the title of "Mister," lifting a bale and dropping it neatly into place, he had the run of the town. Until he met his Annabel Lee, who came from New Orleans, pale, fine and sickly, and made her his idol, through all vicissitudes:

> Flowers were blooming along the east highway;
> My dreams and I went to spend the day.
>
> Picking dream flowers and never blue;
> I've spent a lifetime just dreaming of you.

Porcelain-pink mallows yellow with pollen, false buttercups—a dream name for a dream flower. The actual relation (childless) must have been fraught with pitfalls:

> You are a man;
> Hold my hand,
> You understand?
> I'm always afraid of stormy weather

Both Shelleyan love and verse had failed somehow:

> We started out for Lovers' Lane;
> Vacation time had just begun;
> The golden clouds made a sweet refrain,
> And through the spaces came the sun.
>
> We saw wild flowers on ahead:
> We'll pick them later in the day,"
> But failed to find them as we said;
> The road had turned away.
>
> We thought the day would go on bright,
> We strolled along with foolish aims;
> Too late now; it's almost night;
> No shelter from the rains.
>
> The wind blew, the night birds sang,
> The storm was not far off;
> Miles away the church bells rang,
> And the rain set in for life.

She died of consumption, but her death did not release them from a destiny of dark metamorphoses:

> I know that I have lived before—but where?
> That decent home I thought to build, out there.

Old haunted house, wild garden by a shore,
Where with a ghost (like you) I tried to live, before.

The collection closed with the poems he used to sing in old age, "'Four Words," "The Secrets of Life," his strains of gentle philosophy.

Now there was nobody in the old cabin by the railroad track but Elmonia, living on her pension and Social Security and what her boys sent. She was in the front room rocking, half asleep. When Daren rattled the screen door, she got up nursing her rheumatism. Then she recognized him: "Lawd, chile, Ah'm glad to see you. Where you come fum, and how long you gonna stay?"

"Elmonia, I want you to meet Miss Jeffrey; she's a friend of mine from twenty-five years ago, in England."

"Go long. Ah doan hardly believe you. She not dat old. Miss Jeffrey, Ah'm proud to know you. Ah thought my Daren got himself a fine new wife." And then, as a big-pawed, overgrown puppy flopped from the house and climbed on Jeffrey, "Christ, the Blessed Redeemer, dawg! Can't you let Miss Jeffrey alone?"

They had hardly sat down when Elmonia got up reaching for the mantle. "You member that poem, when Ah got so inspiahed in my busted down fliv-ver, an you always atter me fuh a copy? Well, Ah foun it tuck away in a ole magazine." She held out a clipping, a schoolgirl hoping for praise.

As if coming back with Buckeye Jeffrey had turned his luck at last, he took it, hearing Elmonia's laughter from long ago: "Ah jack it up and spin roun de lef hin wheel." He groped the faded print and found stiff doggerel, stale rhymes. Could anybody bring it to life? "Read it," he told her. She stumbled on her own words. He took over, dropped some letters, tried to put it at ease:

You see me struttin along lookin so fine,
Look in my pocket, sometime you can't find a dime,
Ah'm jus as happy as a bird in a tree;
Talkin about a raggedy millionaire,
Tha's me.

Seems we are livin in a progressive age;
To be modern you must keep up the pace.
Drivin an ol Ford, scufflin to pay the fee,
Talkin about a raggedy millionaire,
                              Tha's me.

You got to learn to live in this ole worl
Where everything is in a twirl.
Greet eveybody with a smile and see
If you won't feel like a raggedy millionaire,
                              Jus like me.

An Aunt Jemima of a poet. But it was too ridiculous for Jeffrey to hear nothing but this as the product of the Dark Leflores.

"Show Miss Jeffrey Styles' poems, Elmonia." She went to the bureau and brought out the already brittle pages. "And have you got that typed copy I made of Uncle Caldwell's *Violets?* Let's show her that, too. And then I'll copy yours. Because I want them all. Where is that one Uncle Caldwell wrote about segregation?"

"Das's call 'Nabby.' He wrote dat fuh mah Flood chile."

Come here, little brown gal,
Nobody knows how sweet you are but me.
Why cling so tight to my hand, little pal,
And gaze so weird into eternity?

Here you are, just learnin to walk,
In a world cram-full of doubt;
You keep raisin your head, tryin to talk;
Not able to tell what it's all about.

Brown eyes that sparkle like the dew,
A shyness that invites romance,
We'll make a Queen of a girl like you;
If fate gives us any kind of a chance.

Handicapped girls have to take every dare

If they hope to be considered nice;
In humiliation they pay so dear
For the little things they get out of life.

Be proud of your virtues if you live alone,
It's divine to know they are true;
If no one helps to sing the Sweet song,
Then, take it to Heaven with you.

Because segregation cuts your chances,
Don't think for once that nothin matters.
Strive each day to make advances;
Turn on the light; remove the shadows.

Daren had saved Styles for the last—to enact the sequence by which the Negro had entered Hegel's world of the half gods. Slowly, as if he himself had written it for Jeffrey, he read the poem to the Yaller Gal, while the words fell around them in showers of spark and ash:

You are shamelessly seductive
and a young girl:

0 my lovely Autumn
leave me not
in the willow
to rot.

But let me lie
in your arms and sleep
while the moon
and white stars
clear my mind of the dark and deep.
Lest you be laid too soon.

Poor I,
every time you leave me
I die.
The room
goes black and cold

signifying my doom;
the body
no more a thing of joy,
I become once more
the overall
lost boy.

Undress not the tree,
Cheat not the day,
give the rose
no cause to hate you;
she, like all,
dreads decay.

Elmonia, shaking her head and talking about that poor dead boy, came to her other two, Lyjah and Lucius.

("What I know," Uncle Caldwell had said, "I mostly got on my own, with the kind help of Miss Willi Mari. But these children got to get all the schoolin they can. You hardly can walk down the road today without a high school education; and they got to walk as far as they can, and as fast as the law allows.")

"Ah got two mo boys in trouble now—thass what the white folks say—but the colored folks say they the Moses an Aaron gonna lead the lost tribes out of captivity; so Ah doan know whether Ah'm mo proud or worried. Ah try not to talk with white folks about it. Jus make em mad. But they in Alabama now, preachin an astirrin up the marches."

*

"Elmonia was only one station of the Delta pilgrimage. There was the Leflore town house where June lived and where they spent the night, Jeffrey in the bedroom that opened front left off the balcony of the skylighted hall (Daren and Anna had waked there long ago to the declaration of war, and there Aunt Willi had died): "Shall I make it a brick house with columns?" he asked Jeffrey. And she, "Columns have had it."—"Good," he invoked Conrad: "I could never invent a convincing fiction."

There was the river and the cemetery and the Blue Hole and the shell of Ararat. Yes, and B. J. Farnham, the only brave southern editor Jeffrey had still to wrap up in her toils. June had prepared them for him: "And B.J.'s got a beard. 'Why are you growing that awful thing,' I asked him. 'Doctor's orders,' he said. 'All that hair inside, Doc says it's got to come out.'" He was eager to join in the talk about Dan Byrne's *The Married Land,* seeing as he was in it: he gave them a tour of the fictional town.

Miss Betsy's had been torn down for a filling station, so they couldn't inspect that; but they stopped to visit Dan Byrne's beautiful old mother in her front apartment of the brick and columned house. She had lost her memory almost entirely and had a lot of pain and trouble, but was weathering it with a funny kind of humor. She had had an accident on her way to the bathroom and the maid had cleaned it up. "It's kinda woresome," grim Savannah said, "When Ah got raht smaht to do, how she make a sturbment." While she opened the windows. "Ah'm jus airin it out a little, ma'am"—"More air coming in than going out," said Mrs. Byrne, wrapping her shawl around her. "Seems like a right cool morning to me."

B.J. had brought his little dog, and Mrs. Byrne petted it and somehow got mixed up and thought it was hers, so when the hound ran back to B.J. and stood up wagging it's tail: "That dog's right glad to have you with us," she said. "We generally don't have any other dogs for him to play with."

While they were there the next-door neighbor came in to see how Mrs. Byrne was, and they got the local slant on the race battle. There had been a riot at the university about a Negro student, and all Mrs. Wells could see was the outrage of those federal troops upsetting her daughter. "Poor Milly! It just gives you the creeps. We were up half the night trying to get a call through; couldn't reach her until two-thirty in the morning. The tear gas had seeped into the dorm, and she was in a state. I started right out to get her. They wouldn't let me on the campus of our own university, can you imagine? But I sent a message and she met me on the highway. I've always been for Nigra rights, but all that for one Nigra who could have gone to school somewhere else isn't worth it. If the U.S. is going to keep up a civil war down here, I've got to sell out like you, Daren, and move to the North."

Last thing, B. J. took them to the bootlegger for a liter of Chianti.

Then they headed for Ararat and Alabama. They were supposed to have dinner with Tom's parents that night, and Daren thought the wine might make a handy offering, though Jeffrey warned him old Lawless wasn't strong for drink. But as they climbed over the barbed-wire fence and sat on top of the levee where Daren chewed the second weed Jeffrey was to designate as moly, and contemplated his ancestral scene, he warmed to the comfort of a swig, and went back to the car for the flask. But they had nothing to open it with. Jeffrey reverted to *The Married Land.* "Knock it on a tree, like Dan Byrne," she cried.

"That bottle broke," said Daren, "and this is blown thin; that's why they wrap it in wicker."

"Dan Byrne would have opened it. Bump it on the tire." "What about that rifle in the back seat?" Daren remembered.

Jeffrey's son Roger used it for turtles when she drove him to school. Daren set the bottle on the levee and paced off to a sporting distance. "You're too far," said Jeffrey. "You'll never hit it."

"Tell it to Dan Byrne." He hadn't shot since he went to Oxford. But it was the old hunting ground.

Crack.

The cork and the round of glass that encased it scampered off like a rabbit and left the broached flask impaired only at the drinking end with a ragged snag. Jeffrey melted. "I told you our book would be better than *The Married Land.*"

She brought a silver cup from the car. When they had drunk to the spirits of the place, Daren set the cork deeper in the broken neck. Then they started down the levee for the house and the Blue Hole…

They stayed too long. Jeffrey was bound to make that dinner appointment. Daren had never seen anybody handle a car with calmer recklessness. She would ease off to fifty or sixty through the dried-up tin-awning towns, then boost it back to eighty or ninety as they came into the clear. They barely stopped at Skinny's Motel to snatch a pickled egg and another can of beer. She drove with the man-conquering smile of power.

Your well-beloved's hair has threads of gray,
And little shadows come about her eyes.

"You're corrupted, Jeffrey," he said. "False values. You'd better have run off with me long ago."

She depressed the accelerator a notch more toward the floor and hurtled into Alabama, flinging him one glance of the beautiful British lady-matron-child, so sad, fragile, gay and brave, the word "corrupted" was consumed in its art…

The old Lawless house, even when Tom was a boy, had been endangered by Negro shacks pressing in from both sides. There were tauntings and rock fights with Negro boys. During the war Lawless senior sold out. Some white realtors ran the place a while as expensive apartments, to see if they could hold the neighborhood. But it wouldn't rent. Nobody ever knew whether the Negroes set fire to it or the realtors touched it off for the insurance. "Yo house burn down," an old Negro told Tom when he came back from the Air Force; "gone back to de woods." So the Lawless invitation was to another modest bungalow.

"Don't talk about Negroes with them," Jeffrey said. "It won't do any good." But there were shocks enough without that.

Her legs were scratched from the barbed wire fences of Ararat. "What happened to you?" Tom asked.

"Daren Leflore did it to me." She pulled her skirts above the dimpled knees and displayed the injured items.

But the climax came when Daren brought the wine and set it on the table—the old folks politely unapproving ("This really is a boogeois town"), Tom enough staggered to exclaim: "And what happened to that bottle?"

"Leflore shot it off. But it's good. Pour it round."

*

Patapsco followed, letters, childhood memories—soon, impatient inquiries, as if a fiction were the work of a weekend. Which Daren answered:

"How far in the novel am I? Like Tom and Becky in the cave, so far that down any of the branching tunnels I can't see light anywhere."

—That book he had read over as a boy until the scene grew in him, the place of the water-drip where the candle died, from which he probed with the twine how many radial arms, each to be explored, each to pin hopes on? A fingered five? Why else when he dug the orchard caves had there been the central room, five radial passages, down one of which only was light, and down another the innermost hideaway and secret den?

And now, from the seasonal rooms of the life-search, groping down corridors, he found no outlet anywhere. Dante redone: the pilgrimage of a mole.

Jeffrey's response was further detail: the daily rat race, meetings, a civic dinner—her maid cautioning ("I don't have a regular maid," Jeffrey insisted, "but Delia moonlights for me"), "Miz Lawless, you too tired. You ought to take more time and make yourself happy, like when that nice Misser Leflore was here."

With the letters came packages, little souvenirs:

A handkerchief printed with kisses, with one in lipstick, that was real.

A miniature beer can with a collapsible opener, a souvenir of Mississippi, DRINK AND FLING.

A gilded key to the city of Reading, conjured, before the election that threw him out of power, from arch-enemy Snapper Lusk, for the guest-author who had baited the town.

Pebbles from Avalon, which an old woman put in a shuffie machine and took weeks to polish into jewels…

When I saw you chewing the weed from the Delta pasture, I knew it was moly and that you had less to fear than I. Who saved the moss from the rocks, the pebble from the valley, the cedar sprig from the cemetery, the acorn from the oak of Ararat? Who watched you eat a pickled egg and drink and neatly stow the can, almost wishing you would DRINK AND FLING? Who climbed the barbed-wire fence and turned "surprised by joy, impatient as the wind"?

Doubt as you choose, but never doubt my love.

That love was now to be tested by the crisis of the second Reading haul.

5. Black Arts

Now that Leflore had come for Jeffrey's own and specially arranged Festival of the Arts (Black), she took the opportunity of getting herself into focus on the fictional screen. He was to have the spare rooms in the dormer for as long as he pleased, to write his book in contact with the material; though, as it turned out, she left little time for writing.

The first morning it was the Ladies' Investment Club.

Tom Lawless thought of himself as a sharp investor, but according to Jeffrey, he was too cautious to do more than plod. When she first put a thousand dollars Uncle Athol had left her into Standard Oil, it had been with his lukewarm approval; and as it slowly doubled and divided until in ten years it had increased almost to five, he had heaped himself with credit. But when she sold and, with the advice of a *Fortune* editor friend, bought into a Texas company he had never heard of, making something called transistors, he was staggered that anybody would sacrifice a gilt-edged security for an unknown risk; though in three years, when it had multiplied her five by ten, even the lists of stocks approved by his trust department began to rub it in how wrong he had been. At that moment, when he was almost ready to admit she had done a good thing—for her to sell again (at what turned out to have been peak) and put all that multiplied cash into a more experimental process going under the outrageous name of Xerography—at least, he thought, the financial loss would bear the compensation of his being able to say, "I told you so." But already Xerox had multiplied over tenfold, and Jeffrey was independent, might even have a million before she was done.

Daren was almost as shocked as Anna would have been to hear how casually the old money pump on Wall Street had pumped sheckels out of somebody's pockets into the lap of one whose fitness consisted mainly in having the right friend.

"But those are great companies," Jeffrey said. "I believed in them and helped them grow. As my friend on *Fortune* says, the market regulates production, and maybe it does it better than bureaucrats and cheaper too."

Elevated thoughts. Though the danger Shaw had pinpointed for Anna (capitalism builds what is profitable, luxury flats, not what society needs, low-cost housing) reared its horned head as soon as the chittering ladies had piped down for Jeffrey's speaker of the day. Being secretary of the club, she had to dig up a stock booster for every meeting. A cosmetics man rose today with the real moneymaker's grin. The future, he said, was bright. They had built up such a reputation that (though he hated to put it that way) women would smear anything on their faces if only it was sold under the name Sweet Swan. They were "putting over" all kinds of new products: a host of makeup lotions with (a novel idea) rollers for rolling them onto the skin. That they were way out in front in that fast-growing market of beauty creams for men. They had just made two educational films which were being shown in schools, one on cosmetics, how to choose and use lipstick and the rest, another on perfumes, under the ingenious title "Sweets for the Sweet." These were now being seen on television at little cost to the company by millions of Americans. Though educational rather than promotional, he wanted his listeners to know those little films were doing a great job of selling for the old firm, besides strengthening Sweet Swan's Corporate Image. That all this meant Good Business for investors, and Prosperity, Progress and Freedom for America.

He revived the grin which had flagged somewhat under presentation, swiveled it left and right—a cosmic assurance. Jeffrey, who could sum up a company instantly by the audacity of its representative, called her broker to buy a hundred shares, which in six months were sure to treble her money.

For lunch Jeffrey had invited a few friends—nice people; but it was strange to fly to Reading for a banquet and talk at a Negro college, and sit down the day before for crab salad on the sun porch of the patroness and organizer of the scheme, and hear the same old talk and nigger tales that had afforded the South minstrel amusement, like Step-and-fetch-it in the movies, for generations—if that was what coming into the relative meant, then face it:

"They'll always be like children. You know what my cook said to me?

"'Misser Warden,' she said, 'I want you to give my boy a good name.'

"'What's he need a good name for, Sally?'

"'Well, suh, that child in trouble; but you give him a good name, he be awright.'

"'I don't know your child, Sally.' (She's only been with us two years.) 'How old is he?'

"'Well, suh, he not as young as he used to be.'

"'That's not what I'm askin you, Sally; I say how old is he?'

"'He gettin long in years, sub, he sholy is.'

"'For God's sake, how far along, Sally? Is he grown? Is he seventeen, or eighteen? Is he twenty?'

"'I reckon he bout thirty-five, suh.'

"'That's a mighty big man to call a child, Sally. What's his name?'

"'I name that child Vermount, after the state.'

"'Well what's this Vermount been up to?'

"'They got him for bootleggin, suh.'

"'I wouldn't worry about that, Sally. They won't do much to him for bootleggin, not the first time.'

"'This heah the fifth time he up, suh. They got him in jail now, cepn on weekends, and they say they goan send him to Parchman.'

" 'What do you mean, got him in jail except on weekends?'

"'Why, the gentman what run the jail, he like to go home weekends, so he let eveybody out, tell em to port back Monday mawnin. He say they jus a nuisance on the weekend anyway. But all you got to do is talk to the judge, and my child be awright.'

"'Sally, I'm a lawyer. I'm sworn to uphold the law. I never saw this man you call a child, and how'm I going to give him a good character when he's been bootleggin five times? He should a thought of his character before he did so much bootleggin.'

"'All you got to do, suh, is say he good as gold, and he go free. He will, he sholy will…'"

The devil of it was that story had the ring of truth, however outmoded it ought to have been. But when Tom Lawless took the ball, it was with a smaller commitment to fact. But for the contemporary allusion, Daren could almost have closed his eyes and thought it was Uncle Teddy thirty years before:

"'Ah tell you dat Suupreeme Couht really is a couht; dat's de bes couht evuh wuz.'

"'It sholy is. It sholy is.'

"'Man, what a couht. Don't you jus bet de white folks wish dey had one lahk it?'"—

To be succeeded by someone a shade more benighted, approaching red-necked Cousin George: "You know what happens to a nigger when he dies?—He dis-integrates."

And would there be some Anna who would crash the gate, flamingly rebuking the whole performance: "Maybe decent people in the South don't know what's going on. The Nazis said the same thing. That's no excuse. They're on the wrong side, and they'd better start shifting over, even in their funny stories."

The mention of the Court, anyway, would turn them to the reality of its latest decision and Snapper Lusk's muddled rejoinder. (Lusk, as shallow-shrewd and deep-dumb as pasty Bull Slaughter, but florid as Satan, and vicious where maybe old Bull had thought he meant well.) "Any city is bound to suffer for putting fools in office," Leflore oracled.

"Snapper's no fool," Jeffrey cooed; "he's a smart man." (Imagine! With the watermelon belly, the britches belted tight under, to hold it up, but it sags over, as unashamedly as the jowls and flabby wits sag.) "Read the decision," said Daren. "The Court avoided saying anything about what a private owner could do with his property, whether, if he wanted to run a store for nobody but short men or fat women or Holy Rollers or blue babies, he could or he couldn't. They left that undecided. All they said was the state couldn't legislate segregation or require segregation of an owner."

(Because where the town might have come around a bit like other places, Snapper had blocked it, sending his stooge cops to the restaurants in the bus depot and Woolworths, ordering them: "Put those signs back up or lose your licenses.")

"The Court couldn't have been clearer; and what was Snapper's comment? 'A turrible thing when the U.S. guvment won't let a man run his own store. That's communist tyranny and no mistake.'"

Jeffrey laughed. "Snapper Lusk knows just as well as anybody what the Supreme Court said."

"Then he's a greater fool than ever to abuse his understanding such a shortsighted way. If that's what you call intelligence, no wonder the town's in a mess."

But another conversation was taking over: "Shocking that people who can't read and write are invited to go to the polls and promised federal marshals to make sure they get their way."

Should one butt in everywhere with the generalizations that come so easy, like the platitudes Anna used to acclaim?—"And why weren't they taught to read? If that's white management, isn't it time they went to the polls?"

The exhibition for the afternoon was Jeffrey guiding the fortunes of Planned Parenthood. She had written entertainingly about it: the Negro bride who exclaimed: "Twixt de dishes and de douches, Ah'm in hot water all de time"; the woman fitted with the diaphragm who came for so much contraceptive jelly the case worker pinned her down: "Have you gone professional on us?"—"No'm, Ah'm a decent woman. But Ah rents it to de nabbers in de daytime when Ah doan need it nohow."—"But it won't work unless it's fitted."—"Well, ma'am, dey satisfied. Dey had a very good success wid it." As for success, the owner had practically paid for the icebox.

But the drive now was banking on the ring and the loop, with side emphasis on the pill. The field workers met first to give their reports, to be cheered on to nab those breeders in the month or two sometimes available between the birth of one child and the getting of another:

"I saw Martha Washington today." ("Good old Martha," Jeffrey whispered, "and how is George?") "She is twenty-eight years old. She bore the first child when she was eleven and has had nineteen in the seventeen years following. I am trying to get her interested in child spacing. Martha is a single woman, never been married, no means of support."

An open session followed in the auditorium of the hospital. It was for general question and answer; but there was a lecture which seemed designed to suppress inquiry. A representative from the national league droned on about the population explosion and the new but inadequate techniques, until Jeffrey didn't have the courage to look at Daren, but fixed her eyes on a thread of light by the drawn curtain of a window (there had been slides of a graph or two); outside was the cinder court of the hospital, beyond it, the other wing, brick, with air-conditioners poking from favored rooms, nothing natural but a space of blue and cloud. She had meant to burn for Daren with a bright flame, "the happiest social Jeffrey." But the pensiveness she sank into moved him more:

> ...such a woe, believe me, as wins more hearts
> Than Mirth could do with her enticing parts...

Questions came at last: the side effects of "de piuhll," whether "de piuhll fuh de mayul" had been perfected, and how you could get the "mayul" to take it, until one raw recruit bared her basic confusion: "Ah hear a lot o talk bout de ring an de loop. What Ah want to know, whah do dis ring go, and who goan put it deah? An dis loop, what do it loop ovah? Cause a woman Ah talk to say her man doan want no loop loopin ovah him."

"I swear to God," Tom would say, when Jeffrey aired these matters at cocktail parties for visiting bankers, "I don't know why you have to get mixed up in such an unseemly business." And it didn't help when letters would come from big-name doctors rubbing the salt of Jeffrey-praise into the wounds. "Why can't she spend a little time cleaning up the house for a change?"

That night, after a life class at the art museum, it was Jeffrey's theater club. Daren remembered Mattie Crump running the Presbyterian Auxiliary back in Delta Landing: "I'll be president, of course. Now if there are no nominations for other offices, I'll appoint Willi Mari Freeman secretary, and Patricia Towne Dudley treasurer." But where everybody hated warhorse Mattie's guts (she, sprawled in the love seat of her own parlor, the other women facing her on the stiff chairs), they seemed to love Jeffrey whatever she did.

"The nominations we are about to make," said her dapper secretary, "require you to waive the constitutional restriction that officers can serve only two consecutive years."

"Do we have to vote on that?" somebody asked.

"You can't vote down the constitution," said high-handed Jeffrey.

The nomination, of course, was for Jeffrey as continuing president. "I would suggest we make it unanimous by acclamation. All in favor…" There was a roar. "Are there further nominations from the floor?"

"That's impossible," Jeffrey beamed.

"Why?"

"Because it's against the constitution we just waived: Article twelve: Nominations shall be by the guiding committee."

So by the constitution just waived Jeffrey was simultaneously nominated and elected to an office she had held since the inception of the club. Who else would do the work and make things go, or with rocking her famous figure back on its heels, and clasping hands in chestnut hair, spread laughter around like a waterfall, so businessmen looked forward to serving under Jeffrey's gavel as much as to a movie or a dance?

"If this is what you call writing a novel," Daren said as they walked to the car—Jeffrey illustrating her character as a woman of action with an account of how she had parked a year ago just about here, and when she came back near midnight, found a man trying to start the motor. "What are you up to?" she demanded. And when he got out and ran, she took after him yelling "Thief, thief!" until it came to her how much better off she was letting him escape—"If this is what you call writing a novel, at least it's a full-time job."

She caught his hand. "What can you expect? You're my property now; and you have to do what I say."

—Anna in one of her old diatribes on the corruption of capitalist literature: "American writers are valued as 'properties.' That's the phrase. If your work sells they call you a 'good property' and you get rich. They're going to have to pay for depraving standards. They can't blame the Russians for that."

—So much from the sound-grooves of memory; then the astral voice superseding: "In the war you tried to climb the mountain of belief and sacrifice; and now, like America, you are sliding down, into the flashy and trivial, fleshpots—Jeffrey's 'property'; and what's Jeffrey? The British upper-crust transplanted to the slaveholding South."

*

Though that South, like the Marquis de Condorcet's aristocracy or Ruskin's middle class, seemed leavened against its own predominance.

When Daren had raced from Delta Landing back to Reading the month before, it was with an intention of looking up his dark kinsmen Lyjas and Lou—though for him they were Leflores, and Elmonia had not mentioned their family names. But someone had phoned in his absence and left a number, which Daren called: "Wood? Lucius Wood?"

"I grew up with you. Elmonia's son."

"But you're a Dark Leflore. You're Lou."

The educated Negro drawl did not lose its friendliness by taking on an ironic edge: "My father was named Wood. It's a custom to use the father's name."

Roxie, Rooshie, Lyjas, Tabby, Lucius, Easter, Styles and Nabby—that sequence going in the mind like Mother Goose, admitted no patronymics from the drift of transients through Elmonia's sky—no Lucius Wood, no Reverend Elijah Lee. So Daren didn't dodge by protesting: "It's not just with Negroes I forget names."

"I heard you on the radio," Lucius offered. "I liked what you said about the races. I wish I could have come to the banquet."

"Apart from the principle, Lou, you don't know how lucky you were."

That was the night Daren poured Chianti from a shot-up bottle into the bosom of the Lawless clan, where, as Jeffrey said, it did no good to talk about the Negro. Next morning, a little heavy in the head from trying to finish the flask, he had met Lou at Rex's Motel. It was to be distinguished from any other vulgar swimming pool and TV motel by the complexion of the shrewd new-rich promoter who ran it, by its being on the edge of colored town, and sporting more black Cads than such white joints. There was also a conspicuous patchwork where the office had been bombed and rebricked. For, as everybody knew, Rex's Motel had become the officers' headquarters in the racial campaign.

"If I had known you were leading the marches, Lou, I'd have been in touch."

"I guess I've lost the habit of activity. I'll cancel my flight and march with you today."

"We don't march today. Last night, the strategy committee met with some white liberals, so-called. They think they can get Snapper Lusk out of there, if we hold off until the election. Then we can see if the new bunch are stringing us along. Like all the rest."

In the intervening month of letters and novel-sketching, the political campaign had been waged. Lusk had lost; but he was still in office and contesting the legality. So now, on Daren's second visit, the freedom marches had been resumed.

The Arts Festival (Black) was one thing. It was staged at Union College, and like everything Jeffrey shared in was meant to be civilized. While radicals were stirring up the waters, she wanted to have a rallying point for the conservative Negro establishment, the professional men and especially teachers, who couldn't afford open defiance, though as their young people and students marched and were arrested, they secretly applauded. Daren started the day with a chapel-talk on "Art and Action." There was a tour of the campus with the college president. Then interviews with sample students: the heavy bosomed girl who had worked as a servant since high school and now, ambitious, had enrolled in college. "Why did you decide on further education?" asked the president. She gave her slow rain-river smile. "Mah feet hurt" she confided.

Lunch was a banquet as conventional as any Kiwanis or Rotarian dinner. Fifty distinguished whites of Reading had been invited—an opportunity, if they wanted peace, to back the more settled Negroes. Except for Jeffrey and Leflore, two came, and one of them was too old to count. Speeches followed;

the opening of the Negro art show; cash prizes, financed, judged and awarded by "that beloved college benefactress, Mrs. Tom Lawless," In the afternoon Daren led a panel of students in a seminar supposed to demonstrate the Patapsco methods of Cader Ayres. That night there was an operatic musical, Broadway stuff, put on by Negro students, a pure white imitation, nothing signifcant, original, or even appropriate, though one had to applaud, on the theory of encouraging Negro culture. The *Times* correspondent made a brief appearance, got the dope from Jeffrey and gave her the promised coverage. She had brought off her little coup.

Around this conservative Arts Festival, the great Kermess of the Black Arts was another thing. Here the Dark Leflores led their volunteers against last-ditch Lusk and all his summoned powers—a climax Daren was as bound to join in as Jeffrey was to oppose.

"I don't like it, that's all. The very police, who hate what I stand for, will do anything for me—even Snapper Lusk, because I flirt with him and make him feel like a big man. I kid him about tapping my phone and he loves it and helps me along, provided I use charm and don't go too far. If I got mixed up in these marches that would all be over; I'd have to sacrifice everything that's Jeffrey Lawless, get arrested and beat, hate the police and make them hate me, and for a revolution I can't conb:ol, and at a cost nobody knows. I'm in sympathy, but it's not my way; and I don't see why it should be your way. That's not what I invited you down here for. But if you're bound to make a fool of yourself, go ahead!"

To drown perspective, to march (as sometimes with Anna), to sing crappy songs:

> This whole wide world around…
> It's O in my heart I do believe,
> Black and White together now—

what did joining a cause mean but self-surrender, that salutary stooping? Still a sop, too little ever to pay for a lifetime of nigger tales, silent sharing in the old injustice.

He had waked from a dream that night: herded at gunpoint to a sheeted rally, where a Klansman, seated, with two children on his knees, gave a bigoted long harangue. From which Daren stole away, and heading for home, passed a Negro boy by a cabin, a bloody bandage on his head. The boy glanced, and saw what Daren held and had forgotten, a scrap of flag handed them at the rally. The boy turned away, mumbling broken blame. Daren woke, trying to crumple the flag, to throw it out of sight in the weeds.

To dump it in raw, like sewage in *the streams:*
Turnbow, Negro farmer on the Yazoo, having studied two weeks not just the Constitution but the trumped-up disqualifying questions, walked into town with the others, keeping ten feet apart not to be called demonstrators, was stopped by the sheriff at the courthouse, one hand on the blackjack and the other on the gun, himself fidgeting a bit, under scrutiny of the national law, his deputies blocking the entrance behind him: "All right," clutching the pistol, "who's going to be first?" Turnbow, looking back at his friends, shrugged: "That's what I'm here for," was let in, and after a three-hour wait, a federal marshal happening into the courthouse, was in fact registered. Turnbow, whose house a week later was bombed and set on fire by men who fled in a car so fast he didn't get a shot at them, Turnbow, charged with arson, cried to the sheriff: "You think I'd set my own house on fire and not have insurance?" to be silenced: "Suspected of arson; bail two thousand dollars. Take him away." was hustled off to jail.

I am a Unitarian minister. I rode the freedom bus into Alabama. At Anniston we were attacked by a mob. There were no police in the station, though we had phoned ahead for protection. Windows were cracked and the tire casings slashed. A police car finally opened a way through the crowd and we drove on. Some miles south one of the slashed tires blew. A mob, following in automobiles, attacked us on all sides with pipes, clubs and chains. In about fifteen minutes the safety glass of the bus was all sagging. A state trooper drove up and watched while the bus was fired. So we had to get out, some through the back window and some through the door. We were knocked down and clubbed as we came. I waked up in the hospital with concussion and fifty-three stitches in my head.

I, Olton Scott, Negro, was walking home from the voter registration school along Highway 61 with Lewes Washington and Philip Gill, when I saw a

1960 Chevrolet Impala, green and white, coming along the road toward us. A man seated in the back on the right hand side leaned out, pointing a pistol in our direction. He had on a white shirt. I believe I could recognize him. I was closest to the highway. I jumped back and pushed Philip aside. The man fired three shots as he approached and drove by. The car did not slacken its speed but kept going south.

When I came from the meeting in the motel there was a queer smell in my car. Police standing by said nobody had messed with it. Told me to get in and get driving. Soon I felt a stinging in the seat. Before I got home I was doubled up with pain. For two days I have been in the hospital under sedation, being treated against homemade mustard gas. The police refuse to be interested, say my friends played a trick on me. Strange friends.

The worst terror is from the police. That distinguishes the fascist state from a state of crime. I am a Negro CORE worker. I am stopped by the highway patrol. "Are you one of those educated niggers or one of those uneducated niggers?"—"Neither," I say, The patrolman takes an ice pick from the glove compartment and a jackknife from his pocket. "Nigger, you need a shave." Holding the pick against my throat he hacks off my beard. Then he rips the Kennedy button from my lapel. "He's a white nigger. We'll kill the bastard." I have to lie face down by the roadside for 45 minutes while he searches the car. All he can find wrong is my driver's license which I have forgotten to sign. He takes me to jail.

Outgoing Commissioner Lusk had staked everything on the old desperate po-white radio appeal:

"Now is the time for every red-blooded white American to get behind his loyal city government, which is pledged to fight to the end, not to negotiate and not to yield. Don't trust any so-called businessmen making a biracial committee to sell out our old traditions and loyal statesmen the way nigger-lover Brown and the rest have sold out Atlanta. They're a bunch of quisling liberals and pinko-reds mixing in here amongst the whites and blacks—bubbleheads sucked in by ruthless nigger agitators, Yankee aliens, hoodlums and commies come South as always to make trouble and boost their power. But we have the fire trucks and the policemen and the guns and the dogs, and we're going to hold the line against all the devils of hell."

And behind him states' righters, Klanners, Birchers, dumb mouths a generation of "smart leaders" had pampered and given voices, joined in chorus: "We stand for Jesus Christ, America first, no world government, abolish the U.N., no more foreign give-aways, a free white, constitutional America, deportation of all commies and leftists to Madagascar, freedom of speech, a loyal press, only white Christian immigration, free enterprise, high wages, racial segregation, and give all Africans' in America a rich country of their own in Africa. Join today and save the Great White Race,"

Brandt Stabler at the business leaders' luncheon club introduced a resolution that they place themselves squarely behind the biracial committee and its compromise settlement. Tom Lawless had to qualify anything Stabler proposed: "How can we afford to integrate at the point of a gun?"

"How can we afford not to, Tom?" (He couldn't leave it that way, it had the look of weakness.) "Of course we could bring those agitators to their knees by refusing to deal with them. But how many are you prepared to sacrifice?" (Magnanimity.)

"As many as show their heads," Snapper had threatened, "will be mowed down."

In the face of that Tom could only throw up his hands: "But they want all those arrested rioters let out of jail."

The measure passed, business interest outweighing desperate remedies.

History—a great live incubator hatching innumerable eggs, each with its appointed time: this Negro liberation coming to life over hundreds of years. "You claim your bill of purchase proves this man is your slave. But you must show me a contract going back to Adam and signed by God the Father to establish your right of ownership over a fellow creature." It had slowly gathered strength through the Civil War and the rights amendments; had not one heard it in those passive-resistance agitations at the Ashram during the forties, pecking at the shell? And was it to step forth now into its perfect summer at last?

When the direct action campaign had begun in Reading months before, only a handful had been prepared to join Lucius Wood in the sit-ins and freedom marches intended to flood the jails. Then his brother Elijah Lee came with his preaching, and the Klan and Commissioner Lusk stepped up the brutality, until the climax of that blazing church Daren and Jeffrey had seen one night from the club over the city. Jeffrey must have done what they said she had done at the rally on Stone Mountain, But as she drifted down the chrome stair in the silk dress Daren had watched her hemming (her only concern to get him to the broadcasting station for his author promotion), she had seemed more a creature of fabric than of fire. The truce had followed, the hope of election. Now, after its seeming betrayal, the marches had been resumed; and the handful of Negroes ready to stake their lives and rather inadequate fortunes had increased to a population.

On Monday 900 students, carrying signs of protest and singing, went out from Sion Baptist Church in groups of ten to fifty. Some got as far as the white business section, a few reached the city hall. Seven hundred were arrested. The jails overflowed into patched up cattle stockades. On Tuesday the march was met with the hoses and the dogs; it was turned back and bottled up in the church. Only two hundred slipped through to be arrested. That was the day Leflore fulfilled his obligation as visiting author at Union Negro College. Wednesday the crowd at the church had swelled to a thousand; Daren was among them, and Elmonia's Elijah was speaker.

It was ages ago, a different style and custom, when the dark folk of Delta Landing first witnessed the promise of that young Elijah. The preacher of the Gospel Church, one of those foaming epileptics who slowly brought himself to a frenzy where words and language melted—repeating "An de Powah, and de Glory," in more and more panting heaves until it became "An de Pow-wow": 'An de Pow-wow an de Glory… An de Holy Ghost in heah… Ooooh!", trailing off in a throaty moan, as if that white-sheeted ghost of God had just walked in the door and was coming down the aisle—Elder Davis had to be out of town, and Uncle Caldwell had suggested that Lyjas address the congregation.

"Did you hear Lyjas las Sunday preach at the Gospel Church, chile as he is?"

The yard man would have entered the kitchen drowned in sweat, asking for a glass of cold water, and Elmonia, to attach an ear, would have given him lemonade. He sits in pious gratitude, sipping from the tall glass beaded with dew, while Elmonia's voice floats on the lazy air: "Did you see how he jump high as the back o that cheer?

"'Christ is the Lawdl' he sung out.

"Oh there is a preacher like the Bible saints of old. And me his own bawn mammy, bless the Lawd.

"He foam at the mouf an jump high as the cheer, an sing out, 'Up thoo tribulation to the stars!'"

He had come a long way on that road, but he had never lost the passion which had stirred Elmonia's tears

*

"They claim peace, peace. And to throw down rebellion like starry angels defending bright citadels. But we know heaven from hell, my people. We have seen the hell-hounds unleashed under the banners of boasted right— this Right of States to do Wrong…"

And the unheard chorus from the clouded sea of faces: protests, testaments, narrations, filling the sighed "amens" with a grave burden:

("When I was in uniform and headin for overseas, I walked into a restaurant. 'Get out o here, nigger,' the man yelled. He pushed me out the door and spat after me. That was the country I was sent to fight for. But I told myself, it can't be that way forever.")

Lyjas' voice resounding in all the hollows of their wrong: 'We also were born in these states, where the police race at night with sirens through our streets and when we are bombed and mauled by gangs, can never be found to give us aid…"

("When the dynamite hit the ground in our front yard I fired and they drove off in their car. Then they came back real fast and shot twice into the house. My husband slept through it all. I had to wake him up. He grabbed his gun and ran outside. Next time they came around the block he let em have it. The dynamite blew him off the ground still shootin. From then till now I don't sleep good at night.")

"Is this our government which throws tear bombs in our churches on the pretense of keeping the peace? Whose peace? Is it the peace of Caesar or the peace of Christ?"

And the echo of days and weeks and seasons over the land, not just from Reading, but from Louisiana, Mississippi, Georgia went sighing up through all he said, filling the responsive "Amens" and "Lord God Almightys" and "Holy, Holy, Hallelujahs" with quiet testimony:

("Today our elder told us, 'We're too close to the promised land to go back now.' So we walked uptown about a hundred yards until they hit us with everything they had, the billies and the cattle prods and the hoses and the dogs. Those they didn't take in the wagons went back to the church, and the hoses broke in the windows and the tear-gas shells come amongst us and the crowd was tromplin and yellin, because they had barred the door. And when they opened it, here they come, in helmets and gas masks and with the billies and the guns. And I saw them knockin people down and beatin the children. Then I went to the office to call Judge Weems, but one of em grabbed the phone. 'Get back in there, nigger woman,' he said, 'before you find yourself shot.'")

"This Alabama peace, Brethren and Sistern, is only the peace of Rome. We have set our faith higher. Higher than the Supreme Court; higher than Washington. We believe in the Justice of the Lord. But we can't sit and wait for it to come. We got to work together to cause it to be."

("When I was little I hated myself because I was black. I knew I was just a nigger. It was like original sin, always being pushed around for somethin you didn't do. Now I want to be like a white man. I want the white man to know I'm as human as he is. And maybe a little bit mo human.")

"For the first time in history we have filled and overflowed the jails of a great city. And without a single act of wrong. Hallelujah!"

("I am not afraid anymore. I've gone down to register three times. They haven't passed me yet; but I'm gain to keep on every month until they do. Let's all do the same. And everybody talk loud. The Uncle Toms will tell the white folks anyhow. It's too late to start playin children again. Let them know we have woke up.")

"W e have paid their water bills long enough, so they can turn the hoses on us now. But we thirst for another water, in which he who bathes is free."

("Amen. We need you, Jesus, old Marster. We can't go against the dawgs without you.")

"It's a long road before us. It's not just Alabama. When we walked all the highways and filled all the jails of this state, Mississippi's still to conquer; and I know about Mississippi, brethren, because it's the state where I was born. Let us leave the church together."

The congregation thronged into the yellow brick semi-cloister of the side yard, a space like the courtyard of a brewery. Elijah's voice boomed: "I want to sec the hands of all who are ready to march."

The sea of dusky arms snaked up, open hands, clenched fists, pointed fingers, signs of blessings, signs of defiance, of ecstasy, a waving grove of arms over devout faces, as a chorus of voiced "Yeas" and the unvoiced (*"We will not go back. We have done woke up. We are not afraid. We will overcome."*) shook the yellow brick court and the air.

To which Elijah's voice replied: "Not in hate, but in love. An army of the Lord."

Faces out of Michelangelo, ellipsoids of energy: here a black Moses, Dark Ezekiel strides forward arms raised; dark Joel carries a sign: "We uphold your rights, will you deny us ours?" They move slowly along the wide street toward the city hall.

Two motorcycle cops roar up in white uniforms to present the legal pretext why this church-attired company of housewives, students, servants, responsible laborers, professional men should remain as they are, law-abiding, go back, give up the march for today. Even as Lucius and Elijah confer, trying to dignify the parley, a wave of laughter gleams over the jungle of faces, and the hands, by hypnotic signal, dance up, the forefingers mocking and warning, a gay, derisive waggle: ("We know a trick worth three of that.") The first officer wrinkling the red of his neck, glares in baffled chagrin over that impudent collusion of mirth. He picks up his walkie-talkie and calls for the dogs.

Under that attack the march broke into knots of encounter. No technique was at hand to practice nonviolence against beasts. A Negro had hunched up from the pavement where he had been thrown, at the same time scuttling backward on his heels, hands and seat, like a crab upside down, while a dog that had torn the shirt off his belly and the flesh in a puckered wound, curvetted against the leash, snarling for the meat he had bared. Another man turned, a big black dog set heavy like an Aberdeen Angus bull tearing out his britches, handkerchief, pocket, a chunk of flesh, as he wheeled toward a third dog, gray, that reared in front of him like an heraldic lion; a group of Negroes look on, beset but not panicked, waiting their turns, harried souls in hell, while Snapper Lusk, directing in person from a jeep, yells to the patrol holding back the white spectators: "Let em come on in. I want em to see the dogs work. Let em watch these niggers run."

The white gang surged forward throwing chunks of brick. A two-by-four hurtled through the air and caught a young Negro on the arm. What all those classes at King's Motel and the Y had been teaching for days: nonviolence, how to yield without yielding, go limp, play it up for the press, to fall covering the vital parts—that passive resistance melted in blood. The hand went to the pocket for a knife. "Grab him," said Lucius, "hold him. Don't let him get away."

And now Elijah's voice came over the captain's bullhorn (Lusk's thin, not inhuman deputy, refined, against the barrel-chested dogmen, a spark of intelligence in the face, despite a troublesome resemblance to Himmler in the old days): "Listen to your preacher. We have done enough for today. We are not a mob. We are a just and united people. We have made a testament. Go home now. Pray to Christ, our Redeemer. And meet at the Church tomorrow." (The microphone cupped in the great hand, the eyes deep-sunk, imploring, the prophetic round of mouth—while cops at the verge of the crowd were dragging limp non-resisters to the paddy wagon—a college girl caught by stockinged ankles, turned upside down, her frilled pants showing, dragged off by a hulking sergeant, her head bumping the asphalt.)

Peace almost had settled in, when Snapper gave an order, and the fire hoses were turned on...

Against the flare of what would occur that night, the disturbances of the day were to seem small. For Commissioner Lusk had already given the Klan authority to hold an interstate rally at Legion Park outside the city. And when they had palavered and bullhorned and stewed each other up, burned their torches and driven away, half an hour later, from two racing cars, concerted, almost at the same time, one at Sion Church and the other at the Negro Y, bombs were thrown, dynamite from each front window, a naptha incendiary from the rear, killing two boys, injuring bystanders, opening walls and setting them ablaze, beacons larger than Daren and Jeffrey had glimpsed a month before from the mountain.

A riot began in which passive resistance with all techniques of nonviolence blew off like the cap of a volcano. Cabs and police cars were overturned, set burning. Fire trucks coming to put out the blaze seemed, after days of hosing, agents of another cause. The firemen, met by a hail of bricks, bottles, stones, dropped the high pressure hoses and ran, pursued by a screaming mob. The dogs, sent in as if they were Platonic guardians, only heightened the frenzy. The police called them off, stopped threatening, and began to plead. An armored car with a loudspeaker rumbled along the streets booming: "We are your friends. Help us put out the fire."

As the quarter was subsiding into a many-throated growl, Snapper Lusk roared in with what he had been waiting for, a motorized detachment of troopers sent by the governor at his appeal. The slim deputy, who had begun to catch on as peacemaker, begged them to leave: "Commissioner Lusk, we've about got it under control. If you would call off the troopers. Those guns aren't needed. Somebody's going to get killed."

"You're damned right they're going to get killed. I'm in charge here, get that straight."

They started down the street, clubbing spectators, swatting with gun butts at Negroes who had been helping to make peace: "Clear out of here, goddammit! Git!" The riot flared into its final and worst phase; three policemen were stabbed, and five Negroes killed. A violence for which the governor and Commissioner Lusk next morning publicly blamed the communists:

"I have experience enough with radical subversion to know that communists and northern agitators have thoroughly infiltrated the Negro movement; they have set off these unhappy events to discredit southern leaders who oppose them. I hope the House Un-American Activities

Committee will carefully investigate what has happened in Reading during the past weeks."

It was almost Snapper Lusk's last pronouncement. His attempt to contest the election was thrown out of court. The compromise businessmen he had called pinko-red (though they were only flesh color, a kind of pinko-grey) came in. Maybe Snapper's Black Arts had almost taught somebody something.

Leflore, in any case, could not roam the Brockenberg that Walpurgis Night. The last event of the afternoon had taken care of him:

The great white jet of high-pressure water, almost as unbending against gravity as a beam of light, shot from the helmeted cluster of five firemen handling the hose; it struck the forms gone down on the pavement interlaced, backs against telephone poles, curbs, any support, not to be hurled, battered like leaves. The street, between brick and stone prison-faced walls of the inhuman city, hisses, swims under rivers, rainbows in spray. The jet fingers them out: four standing pinned to a wall, faces covered. Clothes go slick like rubber,wrinkled, taut over breasts, shoulders, buttocks. It touches a lank young man in the small of the back, curls the belly forward, loin socketed, something wild from the twist, the frug: leaves him. He stands, shirt to the muscled torso, veins bulging the arms, water beading the skin, close-cropped hair, ridged forehead, stern cheek, parted lips, a Roman portrait bronze from the late Republic, Julius Caesar, when power erupted on the world—gods coming to birth on the streets of Reading; and beyond the cordoned space, white fools gawking in, to see how the niggers like the water, spit, drawl, blind to the glory.

And now, from a hosed cluster, a woman panics, the man trying to get her down: "Don't run, honey, keep low," but she runs: the jet clips her knees and she goes rolling, screaming, he wringing his hands: "Oh Lord, Oh Lord"; then the jet hits him and he follows her down; as the whole sheet in gouts of spray bursts in writhing forms, an impassioned dance raised by the rhythm of terror and rage to a new Black Kermess, the baptism of defiance.

Lucius had flattened out against the curb, pliant, one of Dante's irrefrangible rushes; Daren, untrained, stood and waited, stiff, until the jet struck and sent him reeling, his back crashed on a mailbox, stopped, the head whiplashing, unsupported, his neck, like peanuts, crackling, with a deep stab of pain.

6. *The Hanged Man*

LEFLORE sat in harness stretching his neck like a goddamned fly. But where the fly pops it out and in and rubs his hands with pleasure, Daren swung at his table and could not ease his pain. That link so crucial between the me and me.

"Easy on the treatment," he had told the doctor, "I got no salary to pay for it. I've waited a month, but it's worse instead of better. Every time I swallow it goes like an ice pick down my spine."

A "little picture" was unavoidable, but they gave him the student rate. The crack could be called negligible, but above and below it, the crushed disks were giving the trouble. The doc fetched out an old metal collar some patient had rejected. "It's the worst I ever saw, but if you can stand it, it's yours."

Daren stood it three weeks. Then he went to the office and was jammed into the waiting room. It wasn't the pain but the impossibility of wasting so much time that drove him to the kind of arrogation he deplored. "I can't stay; I've got things on my mind," he told the nurse. "When the doctor's ready to see me, you call, I'll get here in a minute and a half."

"But we don't do that. Everybody waits."

"That's their business. I work for posterity." This from the slim, rather anguished face poised like an Elizabethan portrait on the flaring chin-pad produced no answer.

It was the doctor who strolled over, knocked, walked in, found Daren stretched on the divan, flat, a book on his belly (for a month he'd had to raise it above his head) and on his eyes the right-angle prism glasses the other

Anne, that Sister of Charity, had brought from Baltimore.

"What's the trouble now?"

"Same old trouble," Daren said. "I can't sit up to work. I don't want to look a gift brace in the mouth, but it can't ease my neck without wrecking my shoulders. I'd rather get an osteopath to pull it out" (that image of the fly still with him), "and pop it back into the socket."

A trick to catch the old one. "Look! You got a injury. You can't get it fixed by poppin it. You got to wait." (The essence of pain, as in Dante's Hell, its everlastingness.) "Or else I can take you down and operate. But that might work and it might not."

"'Well, we're never going to find out. I'd rather ease it in that river."

"Of course, you can fix up some traction right here at your table. Is this where you work? You screw pulleys in the ceiling and put a halter through them. And you can rig up another on the bed to stretch you while you sleep."

They folded a cloth, cut a slit for the head, safety-pinned the back band shorter to catch the base of the skull, left the other long to fit under the chin, tied the ends up and to a cord. "Now you put that cord through your pulleys and on the other end whatever weight you need to lift your head."

Daren clapped on the iron maiden and made for the hardware. When the pulleys were in and the cord threaded through them, he grabbed a half gallon of wine for a counterweight. Ready. He stuck his head in the noose and sat down. The counterweight rose. For the first time since the waterspout struck him, he floated in a kind of lightness, the grim weight of gray matter raised off the neck and shoulders. In an ecstasy he sprang up to get his notebook. The wine jug hit the flagging, shivered; poured blood of the grape. When he had cleaned up, he got an empty gallon, half filled it with tap water (not that spring water it cost him so much now to lug from below), tied it nearer the floor, put a bath mat under it, in case he should forget, sat down and went to work.

That was where the healing motion began. The body still had its desperate days, wet weather setbacks when the least unguarded twist would pop something and pains would shoot down the spine and out the arms to the fingers, or through the chest as if it were the heart that had been smeared; there were mornings (after so much time, so cureless) when he would look over the cliff to the eddy under the rock, deep enough to do a man's business… But what bathtub, what teacup wasn't? Like the world before the bomb, always in its power to wreck itself, only not with such a splash.

No. It wasn't easeful death he was after, however much a token dying seemed to have been required.

"Just what you need," Jeffrey had told him when she got him out of jail, "for that fiction you can't invent without living it—to make an ass of yourself in a race tangle and get knocked out of commission. But why in Reading and on my invitation?"

How right she was. Until that moment the fiction had been a bog of personal exhibition. It had to be the inside Leflore projected out; but how to get it cleaned up and crystallized into the vectors of an energy array? A turning point in the death motion, to be broken from the self and in that estrangement find the rebirth of art. "Except a grain of wheat fall into the earth and die…"

Richard Ramon Richards had died (one might say), of the first stroke; except he came back, where nobody thought he could, got a bonus of seven years he hadn't asked for, while successive strokes closed in, his poetry more gleaming in the void of loss.

Cracked up and thrown out of the race, in harness, Daren turned out to be where he should have been all along, through fragmentation of body beginning to draw his soul's weight.

Life was always committed to a kind of dying to inherit its glory from itself. That was not just post-romantic, not Tristan and Isolde, not Faulkner with his wild palms rattling in the night; it was deep in all mysticism, the search for quiet as for a woman—the most beautiful love songs in Bach always of the soul for death: *"Schlage doch"* and *"Schlummert ein"*.

But even when flu added to the other trial and he would wake from a fever-nightmare where sickness is the total war fought between being and nonbeing; as he would sink back to a dream of Anna recounting some hardship of her childhood, catching crawdads for meat, with her toes, and she would break the narration, taunting him: "One of those crawdads; how can they love anybody, shut up each one in his own hole?" (for he had never before been so alone as now)—the issue of life against death would read itself over into the battle of the book: to charm irreconcilable elements of a world flying apart; the lion and the lamb to lie down together, and a little child to lead them; against her storied indictment of the trivial capitalist arts dancing their dance to please the moneyed powers, to advance the magnitude of the project as a vindication of the Western Soul:

"My grandfather died in the earth, holed up; and the last word my mother spoke was of smothering in that cave; and maybe the same disaster ('Long years ago to me what happened') has set me here in what you call this closure; but I call it a mine,

"The change from Rome to the West was when the cave-tomb became a place of birth, when everything private and brooding flicked over into the life-giving plus.

"You want to cancel the whole commitment: from Descartes egoizing in the room with a stove to Joyce forging the unconscious of his race; you think you can take refuge in outwardness. But there's no way for me but the infinite expansion of the subjective, which I call the Transformation of the Cave."

As he stared out through that summer and fall, or as mists gathered and drizzling rain grew feathered with flakes of snow, what he fixed on was not the Patapsco pool (or if that, with a look as actionless as the Lute Player in Titian gives the naked Venus—subliming into music), not the church beyond the river (though the cross had a relevance to his condition), not even the life-tie of the gray horizon of woods—his life-tie at a third remove, between that world of prime being and himself; in distress of carcass the other compensation dawned: imagination, the comforter: visions playing against that ground:

Those rides over the Delta before his parents' death, to visit a family friend, in one of the old plantation houses, a woman stricken with crippling arthritis, racked but smiling, she and her affliction confessing no point of contact. How the images rose now (we agonists, at sickbeds and wakes gathering costly examples against the unforeseen—reluctant: the boy released from the sickroom fleeing out to build levees under the crepe myrtle tree; even Prentiss Leflore, drawing breath as he handed Iris into the shiny Pierce Arrow and took his place with a sigh: "Incredible the power of the spirit. She's a saint, that woman, a saint"), how she materialized in the misty life reaches of the woods. It was all before him, father, mother, the invalid with the El Greco eyes, the boy squirming on the straight-backed chair. He had passed through death and saw his own body as from outside, the slime of self washed off - one of the configurations in the other Self, which was eternal. Oh death, where is thy sting? Oh grave...

Luminous.

His pen flew over the paper. He waked early and went to bed late. Going like the engine without the governor, like the broody hen. Good. Such a continent before him he could shake his flivver to pieces and only half arrive.

Why not the central mystery, once and for all—as the devil showed Faust, to reach for the motherly? The key. The tripod. Stamp!

Ins Unbetretene... wirst du die Mütter sehn...

Earlier in his life than might have seemed possible she had read him the myth of the cave, leafing the Plato her mining-bard father had given her not long before the disaster which tied the painful ascent from underground not only to love and beauty but to dying. By that catastrophe, liberation and entombment built to such an ambivalence in her, one could not tell if the claustrophobia she more and more suffered under was a divine or demoniac possession—"one of those madnesses which are also gifts of God."

"Your mother, Iris Vail," Tilman Page had mused that day at Woodruff Farm, "was a mystery, a beautiful mystery to us all" And he told a story, like something out of a Celtic fairy tale:

When she was teaching in Baltimore, overworked, in the run-down dregs of winter, she had been invited to a musicale at one of the brownstone apartments near the Monument, She opened the heavy outer door, expecting to find a directory of names in the vestibule. As she entered, that door swung behind her with a sighing force of its own, shut like a portcullis to a subdued metal clang. She was closed in a narrow space, bare walls rising to a high ceiling, rectangular, an Egyptian tomb. She still did not see any mailboxes, doorbells, names; coming from outside into that fastness, the light not on or burned out, the outer door closed, the door in front of her also closed, it was hard to see anything; only a yellow dusk filtered down from a transom far above that inner door.

She turned. Did she try the outer door and find it too heavy for her, or had her fear divined from the finality of its closing that it was beyond her power? Like a bird caught in a room, dashing itself against walls and windows, she beat against the outer door and then at the inner, imprisoned, until her friends in the apartment above heard—not words (Tilman said), not English words—strange musical cries, as in an opera, from a princess changed by spell into a swallow, a dove, or swan. They went down and found her lying beneath the transom by the inner door. She had fainted. That door, like the outer, was unlocked. "See," her hostess said when Iris had revived, "it's open." She pushed, and it yielded to the hand.

The recurrent wild urge to break with enclosure altogether, to peel off the skin like a glove, turn fingers, arms, feet, legs inside out, like pulling off knitted tights, to throw back the face, nostrils too narrow, tethering the soul over like bark, to open the body to the air—if these attacks were almost self-destroying, they came under color of a kind of blessing, of escape from the cave. Her sickness had a character of mystical ecstasy—a Platonic claustrophobia. ("Now that we are imprisoned in the body, like an oyster in his shell, let me linger over the memory of scenes which have passed away.")

So how could one know if the words she spoke before the car left the bridge—and he dimly remembered—were of holy welcome to the liberating seizure ("Medically certifiable, son; she did not drown"), or expressed the longing which chose the death that followed?

There had been a time when that question seemed as crucial as any he could ask. And now, swung in a harness which like a Buddhist monk he had almost elected, and which might, with a little greater weight of water, have been death itself, he found the distinction had lost all meaning. Perhaps every ultimate wrestling between soul and adversary must occur in a night so dark that nothing could give a clue whether the contender's wings were of the bat or the dove.

Poor Iris, sacred Iris, what matter? Iris. How could you strip the rainbow from the rain?

Jeffrey had sent Daren off to the march as a Shakespearean parent might banish a rebel child. For her own property to stand out against her. He had been dumped into the paddy wagon with other disturbers of the peace and had spent the night in the segregated jail, the twelve beast cages barred off a single barred runway, a tap of cold water in an iron basin and a built-in flushing head with a cover for a chair, a wooden bunk with a ratty shuck mattress and soiled quilt both for sheet and blanket. To lie there in pain over the cement floor and the southern earth fuming with dreams, thankful for the bars between him and the other prisoners, who had been told he was a nigger-lover and might make the most of it. Remembering what he had read lately in a circular from CORE, he wondered when the fingerprinting would begin:

> When they came for the fingerprints I didn't cooperate. They hauled me out with the metal wrist clamp. When they put my hand on the ink pad I wouldn't move my finger the half inch to print it. I was beaten with blackjacks and hoses. The wrist clamp was tightened like a torture instrument and my fingers bent back until I passed out. My pants were torn off and an electric shock probe brought me back to consciousness. I still refused, They hoisted me into the air by my private parts and then gave up, cursing. The next day I was tied down, they clamped the hand and pulled the fingers forward with pliers. They got the prints they were after.

For years now Daren had held with the proprieties of office, house, college, sometimes teaching, other times writing, listening to music, talking with friends, skating a Jeffrey-surface as if ignorant of what was under it;

and yet all one had to do at any moment was to push the social question harder, or pursue justice a little more fiercely than those Platonic guardians ("A dog's obeyed in office") were used to having it pursued, and the ground would give way and one would wake up in this mob- and police-state of violence, sadism, eternal brutality. Since he had climbed up from there at the end of the war, that hell had been lurking out of sight, swelling, increasing, festering, slowly preparing for the moment when it aimed to take over all our daylight values.

But this time Daren's confinement had been only for a night. Jeffrey was on hand in the morning to spirit him away. He was interested in how she had sprung him; what about those impossible two-, three-, five-thousand dollar bonds famous in these cases?

"I told Snapper Lusk you had the key to the city, so you ought to have the key to the jail. Snapper is a gentleman, as I've said before. 'All right, Miz Lawless,' he said, 'you can have him. But get him away from here. And get him away fast.'

"You might have been killed, and where would our novel be? I tried to argue with you. But you were bound to go ahead. The only man," she blazed, "who ever set himself against my will."

"Tough titty, girl," he winked, his neck so grim he could hardly wiggle his jaw. "You're not fit to deal with men, anyway."

"What do you mean? Waring and Berg and Hank Brown are the best men in the South."

"OK. But with you they're little boys. It's taming the Centaur. I see it all now: Why you even look like Botticelli's Pallas. But I can't afford to be tamed."

She grappled with the scrutiny of his Gallic crow foot. "It wouldn't have worked anyway. We're too much alike. Each wanting to be the boss."

"John Knox wrote a book," he offered: *A Blast of the Trumpet against the Monstrous Regiment of Women*. There were two women who inspired it, that's all: Bloody Mary and Mary of Guise. Shall I sound a blast of the trumpet against the regiment of Anna and Jeffrey under whom most of my life has been swayed?"

"You can sound what you please, but that regiment of women (and I imagine it's more than two) has loved you."

The calling of the plane flung them together, a gravitating destiny; wave-moments: Green Bay, the Blue Hole. "You said we're alike. Not entirely. You're woman. And that's an opening. But it's out of my hands. I've already written it, remember? *It must be Jeffrey this time who takes the lead, pushing her invasion to the fortress on the rock.'* For me, I've rambled until the butcher has cut me down."

Swinging in his web, the perpetual hanged man of the flesh, he did not even send her the carbons. If they were getting better, it was by throwing off her lead. Soliloquy.

He was like the melodramatic villain hatching a plot, how the many-layered strand of simultaneity could be betrayed into sequence. And as any small juxtaposition declared itself, slipping into relationship, he would cry with Iago: "I have it! Hell and night must bring this monstrous birth to the world's light."

Slowly the project began to sway, to tug at the guys. That's what it was, a great big hot-air balloon, almost ready to lift itself up and become a making. Through all that struggle he swung in the halter, detached, ready to cheer if ever the billowing huge mass should leave the ground.

But in one form or another, fictional or real, Jeffrey was bound to recur. And for Daren the two realms were not yet so merged that he wouldn't have preferred one to the other. If the three motions of the room—out the window to the actualities of sense, back into the labyrinth of mind, down to the shuffleboard where the outward internalized and the subjective-made-material aped the half gods—it was with a grudging predilection for the window that he sought the face of Jeffrey.

And then one day they appeared, punctuating the year's suspension between spring and spring, not one face but three: Jeffrey smiling in the center, on the left Hank Brown, his nose pressed against the glass, a lovable reversion to the Oxford clowning, and on the right, standing back a little, a noble white-maned man, a face as old as Egypt, weathered, creased and lined, but as supple with life as if he had come into being yesterday, and sprung, like one of Deucalion's earth-children, to such maturity. "I bring all my friends together," Jeffrey had said. It was Micah Glenn.

So here was another lifeline to trace through the fabric, how it went over and under, looping with already established threads:

Point of origin: Call it the big house in Reading (though that was built after 1900, so Glenn must have started in another); there Jeffrey would go for comfort when she had hurled herself down from the aerie at The Door, the house her devil Marvin came from, with his ivory grin and inlaid eyes, Marvin, still proffering the fruits of Daren and Jeffrey's epistolary honeymoon; that house to be plotted parallel with the Art Nouveau one where Willi Mari watched Teddy Freeman swill himself under and Bella Wynne wrestled with her Princely ghost, or with the other of the same vintage old Lawless had built, now burned and gone back to the woods.

Early Manhood: How he rebelled from his opulence and worked in the steel mills until World War I, when he wound up in the Air Force, flying a two-seater with Daren's father, a history to be explored.

In the twenties and thirties, pacifism. Patch it together out of books and journals read in the CO camp at Prairie College and in the Chicago Ashram—for Micah Glenn had always been waiting in the purlieus of Daren's cognizance.

He had told, in *The Sword of Peace,* of a conference at Antietam on the waste of war (Cader Ayres, it happened, had been there too), Antietam, where the brook at sunset still seemed to flow with blood and the sunken road in the shadow to mound with corpses. Soldiers there, Union and Southern, had plunged bayonets into bowels, pulled the trigger to blow it clear, spurned the body and stabbed another; there the makeshift hospitals had been so overcharged that ambulance drivers were given knives and told to finish off the wounded. Glenn had surveyed that bloodiest of American fields from an observation tower: eastward a blasted oak in whose branches a Confederate sniper had been found riddled by forty-two bullets after killing advancing Feds all morning. Westward was the gold cross of a steeple. "Ye have heard… an eye for an eye, and a tooth for a tooth… but I say resist not evil." On that tower and in the face of that history, Micah Glenn resolved to give nonviolence a try.

How he did it in the Second World War, after studying and writing his books in India, made one of the livelier bits of reading from a dark time: *The Peaceful Objector,* May, 1942, when the 45-65 age group was called to register, and he refused, covered his car with pacifist posters and a big sign on top: "The driver of this car has refused to register for conscripted war service." So he started from Philadelphia, where he'd been free-lancing, to present himself to the district attorney in Alabama as refusing to cooperate with the law. On the way he picked up some boys, and while they were spelling him on the driving, he went to sleep. They got on the wrong road and kept it up a good part of the night, and by the time he straightened them out they had used most of his gas. He'd been given just what he needed by friends, since earlier he had refused to have a ration card. So he stopped at the police station in Atlanta and asked for enough gas to get him to Reading for his trial and probable imprisonment. They went out to look at the car, and there it was plastered with seditious signs and that great big one on top boasting of not having registered. So they called the FBI...

When the war was over, some queer southern loyalty took him back to Reading. He had worked on the newspaper before, when he first came home from India. It had been during that brief deceptive hint of a Golden Age in the city. A few people who believed in progress had got the notion that the coal and steel giant of the South was the natural place for a rebirth. There was an interracial conference on human welfare—though it was discouraging when the police came through the municipal auditorium swinging clubs, forcibly segregating the colors. Even in the Golden Age the citizens of better will were fighting a red-necked gangsterdom which already called itself The Law. So when the chancellor of the university gave lectures on better race relations, and was entertained by prominent citizens, the police got the tip-off, and after a cocktail party at which he had a few drinks, they waited until he stepped in his car and nabbed him for drunken driving.

The chief need was for a newspaper. Glenn had tried to build one under the old management. He had managed a bold article or two and then he was blocked: "You ain't worth your salary. If you wuz worth that much, what the hell would you be workin on this old yellow rag for?" When he came back after the war, he bought the paper out, poured what he had into it, but ran out of capital. "Your father's death in Reading," he said, "was a turning point. And the failure of my newspaper. And then they shot that one liberal priest in the back. Nobody was left but Jeffrey, who was too pretty to shoot."

They had come into the house and Jeffrey had gone to work in her irrepressible way, fixing lunch, humming, talking. She went down to the spring with Hank for water: "But it's wonderful. You've got a spring too where we can lean and look, like Lucy and Daniel in *The Married Land.*" Now they were sitting around Daren's gibbet while Jeffrey cut and stitched him a better fitting halter, trimming it with the feather-stitches she had been taught when she was a girl.

"I went to a finishing school, of course. It was run by two old ladies who were quite finished. Every time I did something wrong I was punished by having to sew. I got a lot of practice. Once I had to hem a duster with a fine seam, and in the corner I put an S. D. in chain stitch, which I told one sister was for 'Silly Duffer' and the other, for 'Special Duster,' but in my heart I knew it was for 'Shit' and 'Damn,' my treasured dirty words."

After what Daren had told her in Reading about her narcissism and compromise with the slave south, her coming at all was an act of humility. But she was bound to push on with the mockery she was given to: "It's all ready," she said, "let's try it." She put the halter over his head and stepped back giggling. She had adorned it with cut-out long ass' ears, on which she had lavished the principal flourishes of her needle.

Why had they come? Like Hamlet of Rosencrantz and Guildenstern, Daren wanted to know to what he owed the honor. Jeffrey, it seemed, had talked of coming for some time. And now she had a meeting in Washington. But as a matter of fact, the urgency was supplied by one Daren had scarcely thought to be indebted to, and Jeffrey was not long in blurting it out, the blithe mask a little shaken by concern:

"Is it true that you found the gun in Delta Landing that your father used, and your brother, and that you have brought it back here?"

Old Bella Wynne had been refurbishing her tales. "That's what she told me about my brother twenty-five years ago. Only he was supposed to have bought the gun in Reading."

Micah Glenn had guessed as much. He stretched out in the chair, crossing his long legs. "'I've known the old bitch from the beginning," he said, "when she looked like that painting she used to have over the sofa—the lustiest thing in Reading. I've watched the menopause turn her sour. Oh, I've seen what few have seen." Micah put himself across like a whole cluster of men, under the social protest and prophetic fervor, this tale-loving life and humor of the South.

"She asked me to speak once to the Tea Party Chapter of the D.A.R. It was the time of those ridiculous short skirts, and she sat in the front row with her legs cocked up—until my talk shocked her so she put both feet on the floor. I could hardly think what I was about to say. Those dusky gorges were rowed with glittering spots of metal. Gold in them thar hills. And then she crossed her legs the other way and I saw it was medical. A treatment I had read of for varicose veins. Poor change-of-life Bella had gold clips and skewers clamped all up those lovesome thighs. Ever since, she's been the Gold Dust Wynne for me. And now she's dying of cancer. And still dishing up those lies."

When you came right down to it, Daren had never believed that woman; but he hadn't known how to disbelieve her either. And here was Micah Glenn teaching him: "Where'd she get that stuff about the barefoot man in the attic pulling the trigger with his toe? Same place she got all her other notions about pistols carrying the curse and her son-in-law being a homosexual. If you think she was prime in the thirties, you ought to hear her now she's had the practice of all those people she's invited to her house all those years to listen to her. She told me in sacred confidence that same story of her Prince and said Professor Rhine had come from Duke to get a documentary on a real ghost, but she had refused: 'How could I turn the place into a laboratory waiting for Leflore to walk?' As for any ghost chasing her out of the house, it would more likely be the other way round. She bought it for a song and made a big profit and never talked about any ghost until it was sold and she was out of there. Then the yarns got better all the time.

"Shotgun in the attic! Even the papers said Prentiss was found on the library floor with his pistol beside him."

"Maybe that takes care of Bella. But it doesn't tell me how my father died."

Daren hadn't let so many years pass without inquiring. Thrown back long ago from Uncle Hazlewood's deathbed (where anything concealed, he had thought, might come to light; but there was nothing to be concealed: "A blank, my lord"), he had gone to old Bull Slaughter, dying at the same time in the adjacent hospital room, and still so touchingly fond of his "war-friend Hazlewood" that he used to be wheeled in to visit and talk about old times.

This was the man Daren had spurned like the antagonist Apollyon, forgetting the signs of regard. How the old coot must have suffered from Daren's radical defections; and maybe that report to the FBI was an act of tragic loyalty à la Corneille; and surely the clippings sent through the jail and wartime, on his own hero son, and (belatedly) on the hero-death of Vail, were well-intended; not to mention the instructions to be found a few years later in Aunt Willi's files, copied in Bull's sprawling hand, what she should do for the arthritis that was troubling her:

DON'T DON'T DON'T: Don't use sweets; Don't use anything sour. Don't use vegetable fats; don't use animal fats. Don't drink water during meals; water and food won't mix. Don't drink cold milk; cold milk turns to calcium.

DO DO DO: Eat rare lean beef and liver. Eat butter. Eat green salad. Drink warm milk. Take cod-liver oil until skin and hair get oily, fingernails get soft, and liquid wax begins to run out of the ears—

Bull was pitifully glad to welcome Daren, though his visitor, less affable, had gone right to the point:

"What did you know of my father's death?"

"Nothing."

"What did you think?"

("Think, my lord?"): "I was opposed to violence. You might not believe that. Your father and I disagreed, and later I disagreed with you; but I honored your family. Your uncle was good to me when I was down. That fellow who came to your house and tried to get your father out to his car was from Alabama. When I heard that, I laid down the law.

"What did I think? I thought your father killed himself. That's what the papers said; and you know yourself it was in the family. I asked old Colonel Stump once, and that's what he claimed. But one thing I know for sure. If Prentiss was framed, it couldn't have happened here. It had to be in Reading."

Daren had inquired; but it was to Uncle Hazlewood's dictum that he necessarily returned: "I knew nothing; I had no way to learn. Years ago I put it out of my head. It was the only way."

"First," Micah Glenn said, as Jeffrey served them broiled chicken and wine that evening, 'I'll tell you how I knew your father. It's like going back to another life, when I felt the heroism of war. There were Owens and Sassoon and all the doughboys and footsoldiers dying by millions of gas and shells in fields the rain and bombardment had turned to a mud-jelly laced with barbed wire; they caught moments of sleep stacked up on sandbagged wet shelves, gnawed by rats, and waked to face it again, the blinding and mutilation and death—the most degrading trial in the history of war; and there we were in the sky above, and never since the Homeric age, or anyway since the jousts of chivalry, had war had such a splendor (Why should I deny it?), what Yeats wrote in the poem on the Irish Airman: 'A lonely impulse of delight/Drove to this tumult in the clouds...'

"Our first squadron leader could hardly read a map, and our Commander Daugpuss (Dogpuss we called him) had no judgment. Only man I ever knew could turn a car over on the least curve. Drove it off the cliff once, the car lit in a tree and he tumbled in the brook. But he could stunt the wings off a plane. 'It's easier than a car,' he said, 'there's no road to stay on.' He could say that again. He led half the squadron against a head wind when your father refused to lead, got them out of gas and landed them in Germany. The Bosch sent us a message: 'Happy to report the visit of your third squadron. Any instructions?' And our command wired back: 'Send the planes and keep the commander.' But that was after your father was leader.

"We were flying the two-seated DR-4's. The pilot had to fly the plane, and the navigator sat behind with his bombs and machine guns and a folding linen map of the country blowing in the wind and tried to figure out where they were and give the pilot directions with a pair of reins. Our first leader was always getting us lost; but your father had been cycling through France with your mother on their honeymoon, and he got a reputation for finding his way.

"One of those early raids, we came to a cloud bank. Our leader gestured to Dogpuss in the plane behind his: "Up or under?" Because we didn't like to go into a cloud and break the V formation. They got mixed up, and one went up and one went down and some of us coming after plowed right through.

"When we came out on the other side the squadron was separated and the sky was full of fighters. Purple, yellow, checkerboard, all colors came tumbling off the cloud like beetles. Three of ours went down in flames, and the rest never made any destination, shot a fighter or two, dropped their bombs wherever they could and dodged back hugging the clouds. I was with another navigator and he kept looking down and pawing the map and couldn't make out anything. Then Prentiss took the lead and we followed him home. The leader had been shot down, so your father got the job. He could choose any pilot he wanted, and he chose me.

"From then until the Armistice was two months, and we crashed out just before; but when I look back on it, it seems we fought together through the ten years of Troy. I got the feel of knowing what your father was.

"We were shot down twice. The first time was a morning raid. We started out with twelve planes, though with engine trouble and such, we had dropped to eight before we got to Grandpre. The trick was to fly high, and in formation so the fighters couldn't come at you from the tail; but clouds drove us down, and as we came over the target the antiaircraft was banging away. One burst tipped the plane up like a loop-de-loop. I swung to the stick and swerved off, almost out of control. Prentiss didn't fiddle with the bomb sight at all, just loosed both ninety-six pounders. They blackballed down and by a fluke hit right on the railroad tracks—best hit we ever made. We started back a little tattered here and there, and right away ran into a pack of fighters. They kept out of range at first, your father popping away for the hell of it. You understand, the navigator had two water-cooled Lewis machine guns mounted on a swivel so he could aim anywhere but underneath him; and there were two Browning guns in front that the pilot could fire through the propellers, but nobody got in front and the synchronization wasn't reliable (you heard of people blowing their own propellers off); so we didn't use those.

"Your father stopped to put in a new drum. One of them saw that and dove in at an angle, tracer bullets streaking all around. Prentiss slipped that drum in, swung the gun and let fire; and the plane rolled over and spun down. Another one came from the other side and he got that one too; we were in luck that day. Then he nudged me into a cloud as a couple of others came from below cracking away. Funny, when the mist closed around us, we were sitting there, everything still. That last burst had knocked out the engine.

"We settled for the longest glide we could hold to. Your father had taken his bearings before he went in, and it was a huge cloud. By the time we trailed out under the stratus the fighters were gone and we were over our own sector; but woods, nothing but woods. One of our planes had landed in the woods the day before, gone through like a scythe, sheered off both wings, hit in an oak and bashed the flyers' heads in; so we weren't keen for that. Then we saw a quarry, steep rock, and above it, between the cliff and the woods, a little space of pasture. We cleared the quarry by a wonder and panned down hard between two white rocks in the field, with nothing but a broken landing gear and a cracked wing. We were safe, though I don't think they ever got the plane out of there.

"After that, every time we took off I would look back at Prentiss and he would raise his hand, like drinking a toast to our luck. Now the rains set in; for days we couldn't fly. Somebody had a newspaper clipping how 'on rainy days the aviators are straining at the leash.' Your father would pull the blanket around his ears and say: 'Boy, I am really going to be straining at this leash today.'

"So we went on until almost the end, and one day, after an easy raid, the dogfighters kept on our trail ten or fifteen miles popping out of range. We were down low following the Meuse, when one of them dove in and hit the gas tank. It was pressurized and always spewed out in the exhaust, so they called those planes Flaming Coffins. I plowed down into the swamp along the shore, just as we began to burn, a total wreck. Broke my arm and a shinbone, and Prentiss cracked some ribs and fractured his skull, though we didn't know that until later. I don't know how he got me out of there, but he did; and he couldn't remember anything, because after we got to the base he went into convulsions and for three months didn't know who he was or where he came from, or recognize anybody.

"It was after the Armistice when I was visiting him in the grounds of the hospital, that a French plane came over, stunting, and did a power dive right above us. Prentiss heard that roar and looked up and saw those wings, and all at once the whole thing flooded back, down to crashing in the swamp under a diving Bosch plane. He waved to the pilot like the shepherds waved to the angels. And then he got out of there and went home. Where you had been born in his absence.

"In Reading your father was under attack. If he got shot, it was fighting. It wasn't brooding in an attic or a library, or anywhere else, however moody a spirit Bella Wynne, who wanted a lap-dog for that upholstered crotch of hers, may have found him.

"I know; I lived through it. I was in the lobby of a Memphis hotel (my father had had a stroke and I was traveling around for him) when the papers came out with that stuff about your father betraying the South: 'A paid hireling of the Chicago Socialist League, a Jewish organization bent on Integration.' I heard the talk all around me: 'They've caught him with the goods on him, this time.' 'There's a statesman-aristocrat for you.' And, 'No wonder he hates the Klan.'

"I walked out on the street to get one of the papers. No trouble finding it. A boy under every lamp post yelling about 'Secret Telegram. Read all about it.' No trouble reading it, either. It was in black type over the whole front page with the telegram quoted in full, how the Socialist League was happy Leflore would be working with them, and that they and the Young Communists and some Jewish organization were pooling their resources to retain his services in the fight against states rights, white supremacy and the Klan.

"If I hadn't heard a whole lobby of excited fools taking the thing seriously, I'd have laughed on the spot. Who would send such a telegram, and how would the *Courier Times* which was a Ku Klux paper get ahold of it?

"I was on my way to New Orleans so I stopped in Delta Landing. That was when I heard about that man who had come to your house in the night, saying his wife was took bad out in the car and would your father come help him; and when Major Shields came from the billiard room and said he'd help too, the fellow stole away, just disappeared. It was the time of the Klan murders over at Mer Rouge, so Shields, who was sheriff, went to Slaughter and said if anything happened to Prentiss he'd hold Slaughter responsible and shoot him on sight."

"No wonder Bull 'laid down the law' as he told me on his deathbed."

"I tried to see your father, but he had already gone to Reading. So I asked Marion in the office if she knew anything about any such telegram. She said yes, the telegram had come yesterday, but your father had thrown it in the wastebasket. 'Crackpots,' he had said. 'Never heard of them.'

"Whoever sent that telegram gave it to the paper. And they could plot more than that. In New Orleans I read about the death—headlines again: 'Suicide.'

"I got to Reading as soon as I could. And what was the evidence? His own pistol. Were there fingerprints on it? Did the slugs match? Nobody asked. We had a Klan sheriff, a Klan mayor, a Klan head of police, a Klan coroner; you couldn't even be dog catcher or work on the garbage truck unless you were in the Klan. I had no proof, of course, none but the looks I got when I tried to investigate. Those looks told me by God I was taking my life in my hands to ask a question. I guess that was the first time I thought I ought to settle in Reading and start a newspaper."

Hank Brown had been eating and listening. "If there was a plot," he put in, "somebody must have known."

"Snapper Lusk," said Micah Glenn, "was the man who could have told you."

"Lusk? I thought it was Stump in those days?"

"Stump was the windbag. He and that old Governor Connor who said the Pope was building a fleet to sail up the Potomac and capture Washington. But Snapper was already in control of the police."

"For God's sake, send Jeffrey. He's her gentleman. He'll tell her anything. Put her to bed with him."

"Don't you read the papers?" Glenn asked. "Snapper's dead. They say he died of a broken heart after he got thrown out of office. Though others say the liver was involved."

"The pure white virgin snow about his heart did not abate the ardor of his liver."

"And not even Jeffrey could have wheedled it out of him. He followed the Bible in that: 'Let not thy right hand know what thy left hand doeth.'"

Next morning Hank Brown went out for a paper and came back with headlines of one of those outrages by which the South so often shocks the nation: a young northern minister shot in a march on the highways of Mississippi. Micah Glenn's reaction was to be expressed by letter, a week after he had gone:

> Everything in time has been opened out and held by sacrificial daring. I am taking up a placard, as I did in the war, but on foot this time (and for once with the backing of the national law), and I will walk through Mississippi aiming at Jackson and an audience with the governor. If I do not see him, there are times when a man speaks louder dead than alive.
>
> I am old, have no dependents, and have not gone without warning of troubles that will hardly lessen with time. Remind Jeffrey of that, if it becomes appropriate. I am not telling her, of course. She would argue against any crazy scheme she did not invent herself. But because the death of Mavors, falling as it were on the renewed death of your father, determined me, I wanted to let you know, and to wish you well.

Three days later the nation was shocked again. The result this time was a pilgrimage of unprecedented dimension, by which the whole legislation of civil rights began to be changed.

The death of Prentiss Leflore, of course, was no more settled by Glenn's example than by his testimony. As with all the fields of faith in which the living worlds are spun, there was no way to silence doubt but to stare it down. And now, when Daren, for the first time, had the purchase for such an act, he found, as with his mother's death, that he had lost the urgency.

Whether his father had taken, as the world would say, a coward's way out (whatever courage that might imply), or had gone down fighting like a hero (however desperate heroism may appear), meant less than to have displayed the antinomies of the field, where the suicidal drift skirted and feared became the inverse of a precious coin—the readiness to step out, at the drop of a hat, against total odds. Given that radical mutant of self-murder in the genes, by what decoy could integrity be brought down? Money? What those devils crap into the mouths of pursy usurers in the San Gimignano hell? Fame? Even Hank Brown announced of his publishing venture: "I'm not interested in anybody's judgment but my own." Power? What was that but to live and die for a cause? Love? "When the half-gods go, the Gods arrive."

"The soul," he had written Jeffrey when she asked for action, motivations, real involvements, "leans in solitude on an impalpable certain rest, and all that happens around and in it are vicissitudes." To which, at the Reading jail, she had responded: "For a man who doesn't believe in action, you put yourself through some pretty crazy vicissitudes."

The Gordian knots dissolved without the sword. As in the Promethean tableau, always his model, the notion of a vindicating action quietly dropped off, leaving the science of what is and the poetry of its celebration.

Or if a symbolic action was required, he and Jeffrey had already performed it on that Delta trip of theirs, which was still holding its ground under the cadences of their lives. After the night in the old house (his sister's now), they had gone to the graveyard where all Delta writers seemed to come home (Antaeus to that soil).

Jeffrey had been arguing about the fiction as they went in, objecting to what she called melodramatic names: "Bull Slaughter," she said. "You out-Dickens Dickens. Some day you've got to invent names for all of us, and, if you invent them like that…"

"Invent?"

He led her from the Confederate monument twenty paces down one of the side arcs that made up the circular design, and paused at a heavy upright marble, like a Mithraic altar, carved with an ox, the head thrown back and the throat laid wide—Slaughtered. "It was his own idea. He even punned on the nickname, Bull." At the base was inscribed: "William Slaughter, 1882-1952. Patriot."

A political joke that Anna used to tell came into Daren's head: about the three Italian leaders—the Christian Democrat, De Gasperi, the communist, Togliati, the socialist, Nenni: how De· Gasperi died and tried to pass St. Peter, but got whirled down into hell and lit up to his chin in boiling oiL He looked around and there was Togliati beside him, and he was in only up to the middle. "How is this, you antichrist? I was always for Church and Pope."—"What do you want?" said Togliati. "Under me" (with an Italian gesture down) "is Nenni."

"There's Bull Slaughter," said Daren; "and under him are many."

Then he pointed beneath the great oaks, where his own father's bronze knight stood against its limestone slab. From far off, in the dim light, it had a strange bowed look. They walked toward it—the face always pensive, looking down in sorrow, but more than ever now, bent to the yoke with the patience of an ox drawing the weight of the world. Was it some admirer as chuckleheaded as Bella Wynne, who out of sick concern had burdened Prentiss' memory and Daren's thoughts so long, or some old Klansman slipped at night from his own grave maybe, to make a mockery of virtue still—who had picked up from some-where that huge funeral wreath of dark yew and cedar, and thrust it over the head and neck and down onto the armored shoulders?

There had been times when Daren had wished that statue less flat-foot-edly on the side of the angels, leaner and wilder, more pathetic, tattered, in a word, whackier; and there was something touching about a Red Cross

Knight bowed this way under a funeral yoke—a grief attuned to every heart. Always easier, as from the windowed Patapsco room, to let the world have its Way and the memorial go on haltered like a beast. *Why should the One overflow?*

But it must. He stretched out his hand for the passion of changing what might as well have been left alone. "Jeffrey," he said, "Uncle Hazlewood thought of this statue as an image of my father. With your kind help I am going to take this wreath off and lay it on the ground where it belongs." As he caught one side Jeffrey reached for the other. They lifted it together and placed it at the foot of Iris Vail's tomb of slate bordered with wrought lead flowers. Then they went to see Elmonia and afterward to Ararat.

7. The Second Coming

THE IRON MAIDEN had been returned to the doctor. When Daren went out for groceries or to the joint for a meal or for a walk in the woods, he held his own head up, though he turned from the shoulders and carried his upper story like a sack of eggs. When he came back to the typewriter, he would still put on the donkey-halter for a blessed stretch.

Trees had purpled through the Febuary haze; the onset of March had almost brushed them with green. One of those wet snows came, the kind that falls when the magnolia is about to bloom and your thoughts are set on warm days. You wake and curse it; then you go out into the backyard over the cliff, snow big on every twig, the whole place gone white and gray; you stand in the slush that melts and seeps into your shoes; you step through the honeysuckle and winter brambles, ignoring the heaped damp around your ankles; you mount the one bit of bare rock at the last verge, as the wind brings a powder of flakes over the workers' houses and the river and far-off woods; and your curse veers into praise—God knows why—that the snow begins to melt oon the daffodils in the Quakers' tiny yard, and kick the snow down to the soggy leaves under the horse chestnut tree. The leaves scruff up; and there are last year's buckeyes raising traps in the brown shells, and white rattails reaching out to tap some soil.

Jeffrey, of course, was back on the mailing list.

As Micah Glenn had said of her on the second day of Patapsco, when she withdrew to Washington for her conference on Birth Control and Human Welfare and Micah and Hank and Daren went to Buzzy's for lunch, to be served by the blonde run off from her family in Tennessee, who knew all about Daren and his books and that he came from Mississippi, and laid her arm around him with the affection of a fellow exile (though her winking assurance when he introduced the others that she was from the South too and wanted them to know she agreed with them on lots of things must have been a miscalculation of how they felt about the issues of the day):

"I've doubted Jeffrey as much as anybody," Micah said. "When she first came to Reading I thought: 'How can one town stand it? Another Bella Wynne. And more beautiful.' It was at a reception her in-laws gave, aand you'd have thought she was under fairy wager to have the whole male population eating out of her hand by midnight. But when she came to my place later, I saw, for all the sprightly act, that she was sad, and maybe frightened. Then I noticed she was really interested in my newspaper and in the fight I was making. Well, old Bella hand never been interested in anything but her own bust measure. 'Jeffrey,' I used to tell her when she'd get so headstrong you couldn't talk against her, 'you're like Cleopatra: the very priests bless you when you're riggish.'"

"Age cannot wither her," Hank intoned, as if he would admit nothing but loyalty; though he tempered it a bit: "You don't expect gods in life, you put up with what there is. And Jeffrey's what there is.

Her existence had never been in doubt, and now her correspondence confirmed it: she was collaborating again. But this time she and Daren were working, push-me-pull-you in complementary phases.

He, in successive despairs and elations, went on searching for the whole form, something Jeffrey was long past caring about. His letters reached her vestiges, like regressions to some creative infancy:

> The form of Byrne's *Married Land* is, as you once said, natural. It is the gift of the vector, of that love-search which fires the Beulahland of Generation. But the childless Half Gods have no such tectonic drive. Their being circles and returns on itself. How is such a wheel of infolding to be brought into line?

> Of all the recurrences which have worked themselves into our mythology, the cycle of the year is most central; and it yields immediately an ultimate geometry of stasis, the square of four seasons. Into this, everything can be poured. Even the Oxford Journals, a three-times fallen dough, are being swallowed, and with pains and gas, digested by this voracious fiction.

In such a cycle, it would go hard if two seasons could not slide a little together, superimposing three on four, Innocence, Experience, Regeneration—the involucre of growth.

While Jeffrey gave herself to specific problems:

I don't know what your letters are talking about. But we've got to figure a way of getting Leflore and Jeffrey together. You can talk about circles of return and squares of stasis, but if they don't live happily ever after, you've missed the boat.

I've avoided writing about Tom, or Jeffrey's relations with him; but you've got to build up the basis of a rift between Jeffrey and old Lawless; and since all you seem to deal with are what they call high-order abstractions, I'm going to send you the stuff, though you may sit there in that fool's cap with the drooping feather-stitched ears (how is your neck getting along, my love?) and make no use of it.

In the first place old Tom can have an inferiority complex because what made him get out of the Air Force and into the bank was wrecking a plane. It was one of the first of those beautiful little Viscount Turboprops, and he forgot how the automatic pitch control threw the propeller into drag when the landing gear touched. He brought it down too fast and it bounced; the drag went on and dropped it so hard it broke the landing gear and nosed the plane over. Didn't kill any of them, but almost. After that he was washed-up as a pilot, like a beat cur.

In the second place, Jeffrey's activities would get on his nerves. Not just the politics, or that whenever Time or the Post comes out with a sockdolager on Reading, it turns out the reporter has talked with her. It's that he can't tell one moment to the next what I might do.

Like the sketch you made that evening in the life class at "my art museum." Remember, I asked for it, and you inscribed it: "For the beautiful Jeffrey by her loving admirer, Fiore Fapresto." I took it home and pinned it up, and when Tom saw it: "My God, Jeffrey," he said, "you haven't been modeling naked?" Of course I wouldn't tell him. If he can't see that's a Negro woman and not me, he's underprivileged, that's all.

(Victorian Jeffrey holding her dream of a Last Judgment of Love when the body would rise from its cerements and stand nude in sun and air, but with the husband going veiled, as eighteenth-century women tossed up their petticoats, covering their face, hiding one shame as the other appeared.)

He's sensitive about my figure anyway, because once I went to a masquerade ball here as a devil in red tights with a face like Marvin and a long tail curling behind.

That's a good chance to bring in the childhood, a fancy dress ball in Tavistock where Jeffrey went as a flower basket, and of course was a wallflower, because who was going to waltz with anything as hard to get hold of as that? Small consolation when the country gentlemen would lean under the handle to kiss my corolla and say what a lovely child. But I took it out on Red Mortlock, a stubby Scott in his kilts, with his scrunched up face and bug collection in his sporran. He tied a beetle to my handle—I never liked bugs—but it discouraged the old gentleman. Then I teased Mortlock into dancing a polka by himself: one-two-three HOP. I wanted to see if he wore anything under his kilts. "Higher, Mortlock, higher; kick higher, Mortlock!" Until our dancing teacher made him leave the floor.

I guess I was still breaking out of that wallflower basket when I dressed up here as a red fallen angel. For years after, Tom thought every man in the city was lusting after me. They'd stop him on the street: "My God, Tom, what a wife you've got. I'd sure like to dance with her in those red tights again."

"Your morals," Daren had told her on his second trip down, "are your own affair. But if I'm going to write about you, maybe I ought to know what you're up to with these ardent admirers of yours."

"Aren't you an author? What do you imagine?"

"That you're not a prude."

"Quote me on this," Jeffrey smiled: "The moral decay of our time is mostly a decay of privacy."

You've seen my house. Apart from birth control and red tights and nude models, you can guess how the clobber I keep would upset an orderly banker like Tom...

What I do to a tube of toothpaste is a crime. He tries to keep one of his own. But when I go to bed late I grab for anything. And I can't help laughing the next morning when he picks up that gummy mass.

And the bills. The English way is to leave them a long time. And they get mixed up in my papers and thrown in the cellarage. One night I put a dun notice marked URGENT, OVERDUE, and FOR GOD'S SAKE PAY, in a novel for a bookmark. Well, the book was one Tom had borrowed from his rival banker, and when it went back, Stabler began to tease Tom at the bankers convention about going to debtor's prison. "Look here, Jeffrey," Tom said, "we can't wash our dirty linen in front of the whole town."

When I pay the bills I do it by check to the nearest dollar. Then they send more bills and credit slips for those pennies I won't pay attention to. It drives Tom wild. Once I got so sick of one of those little machine-perforated bills coming, I punched a lot of new holes in and sent it back. That was when the machine sent me five dollars refund.

Here's a scene:

Old Tom gets up early and wants his breakfast. Sunday, Jeffery's been up most of the night packaging what she calls Italian Chestnuts, (buckeyes from the Reading Park) to mail in an appeal for the restoration of Italy. (She raised $10,000 and was awarded the first class "Star of Solidarity" by the Italian government.)

Tom wasn't going to wake her, but he slammed in the pantry against the wall of the bedroom grumbling about not finding anything but old stale cereal. (Geoffrey rips a new box open whenever she wants some Post-Toasties, stuffs it on the shelf and forgets it.)

Jeffrey jumps out of a good dream and comes in like a banshee (he can never tell how much she's playing): "You're mean and selfish and a big noisy brute to make all this fuss every morning."

"Well why don't you clean the shelf?"

"I'm going to clean the shelf," says Jeffrey; and she jumps on the chair and begins flinging canned goods, jars, cereals, everything onto the floor, tin cans bending and the glass jar shivering.

Old Tom goes white. "No, no! Calm down, Jeffrey. Take it easy. I'm sorry, honey. I'm sorry."

"You want it clean and you're going to have it clean," Jeffrey giggles her gayest way, crashes the last box off and turns around calm and sweet: "You see, lovey; if you wake people so early wanting action, you're going to get action."

Old Tom pipes down. Next morning he creeps around, not wanting Jeffrey to go berserk again.

That one was years ago. Here's another, from last week:

"Corne on, Mom," the boys say. "We want to go yard rollin," That's when you throw toilet paper all over somebody's yard. I get some of my special comic rolls out of the messy closet, and we pile in the car. (Because when the boys are home from school I take them on crazy junkets.) And when we've done Bella Wynne's mansion and the Lathrop's Tudor Job, we start for Brandt Stabler's French Château…

A dim view Anna, always sensitive about toilets and two-ply tail-plush, would take of that conspicuous consumption—the boys throwing the usual Soft as Silk like long confetti, while Jeffrey tossed the first of the live precious rolls stored up for such an occasion—the only bum-wad fit for a rival banker's lawn: perforated ribbons of greenbacks (like Broome's story of the live pound note) each stamped with Old Bigshot (shot?) chewing his cigar, and below: "One Hundred Filthy Lukers," and to the left: "This note is not Legal, but it sure is Tender." Yes, Brandt Stabler had his whole place rolled with nothing but money, yards and yards of money; and when he heard the giggling and rushed out, he would have been furious, but the sight of Jeffrey caught him up in the fun; he threw one roll himself, clear over the house, and gave her a hug and a kiss in the bargain.

Still, it got back to Tom, whose reaction was less joyful. "I swear to God, Jeffrey, I don't know why you have to do such weird things. There's Brandt Stabler telling everybody in town you threw toilet paper all over his house and up into the trees. We can't keep friends that way."

"Nonsense. He loved it. He helped us roll."

"Maybe he'd love anything you'd do over there. But he won't love me. And I'm the one's got to do business in this town. You shouldn't put such a burden on your charm. You've got a natural talent; but you overwork it."

There are problems in all this. You've got to show the rift between Tom and Jeffrey. But don't make Jeffrey seem too much to blame. Or Tom either— because then she might look cast-off. They just drift apart. None of that unhappy stuff. She's had a good life. All those years until her boys are grown (that's why she's ready to leave now) she's given them a good time. And old Tom too.

Maybe you can use one of their summer trips—driving to Maine—make it gay: the boys always looking for a swank motel, "Television and Swimming Pool."

One day we passed one that didn't look up to par. But the farther we drove the worse they got. Tom went back, ten miles, though the boys grumbled. Had to pay in advance. Then it turned out the pool was drained. And the television in the room was on the blink.

"If Pops wasn't so timid, we'd get back our money and go on. I can't sleep in this dump."

Then they saw a vibrator on the bed. They'd never run into one before. "We'll put on our pajamas and vibrate ourelves to sleep," said Jeff.

They dropped a quarter in the box, but the vibrator didn't vibrate. They beat it and kicked it and shook the bed, but it wouldn't go. So they went to sleep growling about Pops and what a crummy motel.

In the middle of the night the vibrator came on, and the bed began to rock and shimmy and creak. It waked everybody up, and there was no way to shut it off. They got up and jumped on the bed, until it fell to pieces. They had to finish the night on a mattress on the floor.

That place really was a shambles when the Lawless family left at dawn.

Anna had cut off too soon. All those novels of the New Order she had read and discussed—how she would have longed to be here, pulling an oar against Jeffrey, trying to get this construction headed the way it ought to go.

But the Anna who lurked in the manifold at the back of the room could come forward as well as the absent Jeffrey. She was there, hanging over Daren's shoulder as in the old days when she thought to appropriate his utterance: "Mind you get it right now. The human relationships. That's where your weakness lies. I won't say more… For fear of hurting… Would bite my own tongue before I would wound you… or anybody. But if you have made Anna what you should, and Leflore is going for Jeffrey, that makes him a certain kind of man… Weak. Watch out there.

"That most sensitive part of you, don't smother it with conformity. This book had got to be right. I want it so much. There are too many already that aren't. But if Anna is the political woman, she will have to be the heroine, stronger than Jeffrey, the capitalist family woman. And already, halfway through the book, in the chapter you call "The Door," Anna has gone. That's a danger.

"Mind now. You must get it right. Must. MUST."

While opportunist Jeffrey schemed ways of getting to Patapsco, for the finish.

I've worked it all out for you:

For years Tom has wanted to get out of that dinky little bungalow—no place for his cars, mine in the drive blocking the garage, his hanging around the street; no prestige; can't entertain his bankers; the whole place littered with Jeffrey's junk. But Jeffrey won't hear of it; and the boys have always liked it, feel easy there:

"Honest, Mom, Guy Lathrop took us to his place for milk and cookies last night. Mrs. Lathrop was on the edge of her chair, watchin to see where every crumb fell. No kiddin. I couldn't live in a stuffy museum like that with all those carpets and polished floors. I like this junky house."

Once I bought a lot (that's your Jeffrey speaking), on a ridge near the rocks where I loved to walk, until people began to build it up. Tom talked so much about putting a house there, I sold it in the end. He had advised me not to buy, and I got four times my money, so he couldn't object; but it left him with no land to put his house on.

And now he's president elect of the State Banking Association (and dreaming of the national league). "These are the times that try men's souls," he says. "And how'm I going to show Southern Hospitality in this cluttered up dollhouse when the bankers come? We've stalled too long. It's almost too late to build."

But Bella Wynne has died of cancer. Her son is in California and her daughter hates the place; all she wants are those fake portraits (I don't know why she doesn't hate them). It's ready-made for Tom: all those carved-up Renaissance tables and French chairs and Chippendale bureaus and glass cabinets of art works and candelabras; that den with the tarpon and antlers and a built-in bar and the king-size bed in the master bedroom, and the court with all the gravel space and the big garage; the biggest barbecue pit anywhere around; and a garden that's been on the pilgrimage since the first year (though the cement walks were a mistake)—just the house old Tom's been dreaming of, and ready for the reception of converging bankers.

"Merle," I told our real estate friend long ago, "get this straight: if you sell Tom a house while I'm out of town somewhere, I'll ruin you."

Now it's happened without my even being away; and what I tried to avoid is what I've been looking for.

"Jeffrey," Tom says, "get ready to move. I've bought the Wynne place, furniture and all—and at such a bargain you wouldn't believe it."

"Are you kidding?" I say. "That house is a phony, and everything in it."

He goes red. "You can come or you can stay. But I've bought it. And it's the showpiece of the town."

Now Jeffrey, as you can imagine, isn't going to shift over to the showpiece of the town. And Tom will be afraid to leave it empty once he's bought it. Let him move over and camp in the circular bed in the great master bedroom. While Jeffrey waits for the next holiday to talk with her boys.

Or maybe Jeffrey will leave town. Who's going to help Tom entertain his bankers? Let Jeffrey fix it up. She can suggest their friend Sadie Maude Lyell, the sweet young widow of Tom"s boyhood chum. She can be hostess for the convention—Oh a perfect one, with gardenias in her long fair hair. And Tom has been sentimental about her for years. She can bring in a family of "good country niggers" from her plantation, to live on the place. And won't they be ready then for whatever Jeffrey and her boys decide?

Of course there'll be problems in time—but they're not our concern. Small regrets: changing Jeffrey's French herb cooking for Negro southern. And Sadie Maude will be awfully particular about the boys' parties and crumbs in the house. And she'll take a dim view of Tom's washing his cars and tinkering with the motors until he's covered with grease. And maybe she'll be a little jealous and open his mail.

Sooner or later there's bound to be that famous bankers' luncheon in New Orleans or Atlanta, when Sadie Maude, as wife of the Association President will be asked to give a talk. Tom will write it out for her and they'll go over it again and again. She'll be full of confidence, until the master of ceremonies introduces her, and it's plain as day, he's thinking about the former Mrs. Lawless: "One of the most remarkable women in the country, has done so and so, and so and so, an accomplished speaker and charmer: Mrs. Tom Lawless."

What can Sadie Maude do but push on: "After such a glowing introduction, I hardly know what to say," bury herself in Tom's MS, and drone through—to get it over with and get out of there…

Jeffrey had breezed along, letter after letter, hatching such corny contingencies of turnabout as a would-be serious author must blush to read. "It creaks, Jeffrey," he wrote her, "it creaks. *Ladies' Home Companion* stuff. You think I could use that? Sadie Maude and the rest?"

"Why are you so sure it's not true?" she answered. "He *has* bought the house. If it's not Sadie Maude Lyell it will be somebody else. Anyway, she *will* help him entertain. *The witch knows.*"

And the next day:

Picture your Jeffrey by the dormer window at the desk where you sat, looking out through a spring fog, listening for the cardinal. On the way to Mississippi, once, you called me "Honey-hunk" That's what the cardinal will sing: "Honey-hunk, honey-hunk," and the sun will burn off the mist, and every tree, even the fig (my father grew a fig in a corner of the brick wall of the garden) will be in bud.

To run, as in childhood, to leap into the wind, catch at a branch and swing into a tree, take a peek in a bird's nest; or, lying in the grass, wonder at an acorn, the patience of desire; to shake a bough of lamb tails so the pollen blows yellow in the sun.

Last night I dreamed clouds and waters swirling, grain blowing in the wind, sands melting and mounding, liquid motions, but deep in me; it was a dream also of you. So I wait for the cardinal to sing, believing it is time to answer and to go.

Daren turned out the gooseneck lamp and sat at the window, waiting for the dark to grow luminous. From the Patapsco the night mist was rising. It crept up among the trees and took into its foldings the rays of the moon. He was still reaching out in the romantic manner of the science he had pursued as a boy: if the blending of particle and wave lies under every mingling of vapor and light, why should that not stand as a central metaphor of the world—the marriage of what Descartes had separated (and by separating made all process, all becoming, all love incomprehensible), the specter of matter and the emanation of soul?

And if Jeffrey should come to him now like that light to those wandering masses, nothing would be realized which had not been hinted at on their one Delta Landing trip, crammed like a fig or pomegranate with its fullness of seed:

After the graveyard, they had taken the other pilgrimage. It led north of town along the shore of Lotus Lake, which was slowly filling up, the cypress wood on the far side creeping across, at either end the great lotus leaves expanding a green sward. But as they came toward the head of the lake where Panther Burn once joined it with the Blue Hole and the trestle had crossed to Ararat and the old landing, the scene was changed. A great new levee had been built, angling out from the swamps behind Lotus Lake right across the gardens and groves of Ararat, filling in and cutting off Panther Burn and circling out wide of the Blue Hole, leaving all that to go back and be spilled into by the river, to which it seemed not even the Lord himself could say "so far and no further."

They climbed the fifty-foot hogsback of a levee and looked down where cows were grazing around the ruins of Ararat. When Uncle Hazlewood had thrown in the sponge and divested himself of the place, the house was already too threatened to add much to the value. The shyster Forbes, who had made his pile and wanted like any Delta aspirant to play at planter and educate his sons at the University of Virginia (if they couldn't get into Harvard), had bought it for the debt, with a mind to salvaging what he could toward a new house on the lake shore nearer town.

But as always in an age of ephemerae, conditioned to build and junk, build and junk, it hadn't proved practical to use much of the old. The shell of Ararat stood, stripped of roofbeams and floors, waiting for the water, which so far the old levee had held.

Leflore crossed the formal gardens, pastures now, picking his way among the cow-pies; Jeffrey followed, silently. They climbed the mound and stood by the front door where Quincy had heard the voice of Gracia Hazlewood singing "When this cruel war is over." They looked into the gutted hall, then walked around the house. The windows of Daren's mother's room had been removed.

From the old levee they could look before and after. East, the rusty trestle bridge still crossed the half-filled neck of Panther Burn. West, the long struggle against the river had come to a brief stalemate. Out of the swirling brown water banks of clay and sand snagged up, matted and aproned with old cable-tied revetments of willow and cement, which had been undermined, tossed and tousled, until they hung in shreds like torn spider webs. Each year they had been forced back. Now the sector had been surrendered and the new defenses reared. Nothing but the crest of the old levee, already undermined by a huge gaping, opposed the thrust that would take Old Bleary, Panther Burn, trestle, Ararat, memories and all, under.

The midday sun burned like summer. Daren straightened in a kind of defiance: "For God's sake, Jeffrey, let's have a swim."

They hung their clothes on the branch of a sweetgum. Twelve years had not much changed the form he had seen in the moonlight by Green Bay. He caught her a moment as they stood, their bodies settling curve in curve.

"It was in the cards," Daren said, "that I should get you only when you were old, beautiful and past childbearing."

"Nonsense. I'm not half as old as Sarah. But we aren't after a child."

The witch always so right. "It's the high-order abstractions," he said, "that have to reproduce themselves."

They turned and waded out on the hard sand where a fallen willow shelved down. It was as clear as alluvial water ever is, the bodies half-visible, but changed to fish-color, snake-color, gray-green, yellow-brown. Already a warmed layer of summer floated over the cold. Jeffrey lounged in the barkless crotch of the tree, kicking the water foamy. Daren slithered between her legs.

"Crazy," she said as they drove back, "to get so flooded with lake water."

But for the moment it had gone beyond sense, beyond sensation.

As if the spring pond, full of green plants and algae, frogs' eggs and fishes' slime, had opened to inwardness, mythical sexuality.

To merge there, and then for safety draw away, the white jets in the mothering water. To look back and see the dark between pale limbs, languid, floating and rippling through the amber green.

Daren felt a residual twinge run from his neck into his shoulders. His hands went up in the darkness, caught the old noose and brought it down:

> Turning and turning in the widening gyre…

That poem, written at the end of the First World War, when Daren's father shed his amnesia and came back to try to make silk purses out of sows' ears in the political Delta—before Daren could remember anything (except maybe his first experience of gyres, leaning one night over a toilet almost as high as he was, staring down into the great white whirling bowl)—

> The falcon cannot hear the falconer;
> Things fall apart…

A poem which had already foreseen and expressed what Uncle Hazlewood was to learn painfully from life, Cader Ayres from life and Spengler, what Daren, taking it from Cader Ayres, would brood over in the Second World War, searching through cracks in a symbolic wall for glimpses of the winter stars.

> And what rough beast, its hour come round at last,
> Slouches towards Bethlehem to be born?

He had not discovered the poem in those years. Yet he had looked for a Second Coming, had asked: would it be Christ or Antichrist? Or were both always one: "Christ the tiger," the concentration camp cross Heloise Frank had envied so many nameless saviors? Could it be what Yeats called antithetical, a pagan rebirth and water-mating, some Leda and the swan? Whatever it was, abstract cycles could never predict it; in a time of automation, the electronic brain, atomic energy, space-flight, other worlds, there could be no foreseeable Great Year's return, no mere "changing of the tinctures," however drastically sex, art and law were bound to change. It was the building up under paradisical hopes of a new volcano in the mass psyche, the widening of world-antithesis toward a breaking-point of appalling potentiality—what Anna thought she had gone East to prepare for.

And all Daren could do was sit and face the small task of mind, the hopeful synthesis with which Western consciousness had saddled him.

"All right. Suppose you weaken. Suppose you give up. Who is to do it? To gather the strands history has brought to focus in this room, stretching time with imperative possibility: MAKE THIS VISION REAL."

To bare and put in order the fourfold universe of powers. Against that demand, the terminus of the fiction, as he neared it, began like Faust's Helen to go to pieces in his arms. Not what he was after, incommensurate with the prompting urge. Mere subjectivity, not real, not alive.

It was in such crises that the phantom Anna would glide from the shadows: "To create life, the essential thing is love. Have you got it?"

Wide-eyed, the angel of our exigence, her yearning soul a reflection of his in an altering mirror…

"And yet you have chosen Jeffrey."

Even with the ghostly voice he was doomed to fruitless wrangling. "History has chosen. Jeffrey is our fate; as Hank Brown says, what's actual."

"If she's your fate, you've had it, She's what's wrong with America, the façade of liberal causes. She says she's a witch. Remember Spenser: I'm Una, she's Duessa. Strip her; you'll find a fox's tail matted with dung—a social horror. But you won't. Ever since you took that bait of diamonds from imperialist Rhodes, you've been a spoil to Jeffrey."

"You begin to understand. But don't think it's only Rhodes scholars who make the compromise. You liked honesty. Be honest."

"Very well. Because you complete your regression by loving a child image of old-world refinement lying in the whited sepulcher of the South, don't try to justify it with history and metaphysics. Call it by its name."

"What is its name?"

"Opportunism."

"I never denied that. I have no other way to operate in time."

To tie the center to the periphery: the spirit room, ghost Anna, the other ghostly inhabitants, to the wheel of everything that kept probable recurrence outside the window.

The steeple was of the lighted foreground, part of the inhabited complex passed down from whatever centuries a new country had known – the whole heirloom town lately condemned, declared a fit slum for anybody's clearance. And maybe it was in response to the wanglings afoot, to substitute for all this characterful old city of diorite the usual jerry-built rows of modernity, that the church had come out these last weeks with a showy new sign (where the old 0 VOS OMNES had burned out so many lights it was snaggle toothed) in neon tubing and plain English (though it might have come from the *Tao te Ching*): I AM THE WAY.

Beyond that foreground the park woods still stretched under the moon, print of an archetypal being, the metabolic leafwork, which now the infolding of consciousness, nature by inwardness working on itself, had convulsively transformed. What was this pulsating power-field of world-psyche up to? What was it bent on?

What Teilhard de Chardin, Faust ignoring Satan, blandly optimized?:

> It is thus entirely by its tangential envelope that the world goes on dissipating itself in a chance way into matter. By its radial nucleus it finds its shape and its natural consistency in gravitating against the tide of probability towards a divine focus of mind which draws it onward.
>
> Thus something in the cosmos escapes from entropy, and does so more and more.

Or had evolution, like a Nietzschean will-to-power, gone wrong, painfully elaborating in the genes of time the lethal factor to destroy it all?

> Nature's polluted.
> There's man in every secret corner of her
> Doing damned wicked deeds...

The world so launched on the gyre of its imbecility.

In a time when mushroom clouds had taught everybody the impossibility of war—for strategists, instead of banking on that, to scheme how limited engagements could be fought without escalation under nuclear umbrellas (everybody wants to play mumbleypegs got to get his umbrella), as if the madness of wars were what we always wanted provided only they didn't get too big…

No strategy at all, but the eruption of a secret malice, not just to kill off man, but to let him in his death throes make the globe uninhabitable, to poison the springs of life.

If we didn't know how suicidal nature was it was only because we hadn't grasped the whole. Maybe she eliminated things only in a context where she could afford the loss. But if the starry universe should turn out to be everywhere sowed with life, it wouldn't be inconceivable if now and then a world like ours might be a prey to folly.

While spirit heightened as never before the charge of creativity, crying—like a man summoned from thought by mere defect of body, malfunction of the pump, stopped plumbing, cancer—demanding the human synthesis which the rebel political body, from a bungling president down, threatened to deny.

That fall, to save heating the house, when what he needed was the chill off the one room, Daren had the old fireplace in his study opened and relined; so now with the spring he could turn the central heating down (English style) and keep a live warmth at his back. It didn't fit the myth, unless one took up the Paracelsian *fire of life,* the fluttering *stranger* Coleridge watched at Nether Stowey, Thoreau's *health,* with its *smoke,* for which one asked pardon of the gods.

But it was cheerful, and chopping the dead wood and thinning on his own steep slope gave him the exercise he needed after sitting all day at the pen and clatterbox. A real economy, letting every stick of fuel warm him twice before it was done.

The fire had burned low. He slipped out of harness and put on a log. As flames leapt in the dry bark, he saw a spider come from a crevice and dart over the upper side, driven back everywhere. What for Daren was the contained antithesis had become for that small creature what it intrinsically was, the Heraclitean devourer of the worlds.

As in youth, the first instinct was that of Schweitzer—at Virginia, when Daren would interrupt his reading, of a spring night, to catch every moth that flew in the open window and heedfully hurl it outside.

But what did he want with another spider in the house, and who could tell if that was a house spider anyway? Man everywhere hollowing his living space out of other life, virus, bactelia, plants, insects, fish, quadrupeds, birds; he came down with the flat end of the poker. Euthanasia. But the small intelligence dodged, rushing to the end of the log. Safe. Then lost hold, and fell, through the blaze into the hot ashes, writhed, shrunk up, still. Outwardness everywhere hinting at the same throes: black ants from holes under the Delta oaks, boiling up scalded, gnawing their viscera; victims in Cologne screaming from airless shelters, their hair and clothes frenzied into flame.

No wonder Heloise Frank, at the core of her cosmos, had set that lightning-bolt of the cross, God racked from rock to sky for the song of men and angels.

If the universe hung there, its breathing the systole and diastole of plant and fire, rearing up and tearing down, who was going to change it? Not Anna. Not Jeffrey. Not Daren Leflore. The will that drove them to try had come up out of the same whirl. That was one of nature's subtleties in working on itself.

"I never could believe in a God," Uncle Hazlewood had pronounced on his deathbed, "who tortures his creatures."

"Believe?" asked Daren. "It's loyalty—to the universe of process and pain, or to that shrunken little hope of moral man."

Uncle Hazy wanly smiled: "You're lost either way."

"Then affirm them both."

Two things were required, though contradictory: to hold the course as if everything depended on the will; to yield to the ocean as if it could be trusted to look after its own. As in walking: an active foot thrust forward, a passive receiving the fall—not alternately but the two at once, the crest and backwash of a wave.

Next morning he began to make notes on the advance of spring:

The last of March too warm. In the Quaker yard the foreign plants were gulled, quick believers. April Fool. The weeping cherry dripping in a cold fog… New moon… The Japanese magnolia dropped its petals, frost-nipped, unsightly brown. Mid April: Confirmed. The quince, the plum, and already the pear… Now the native trees: shadblow fading as the dogwood stars. Willows green as mold, babyshit green. Swamp maples red, oaks tawny-tasseled, birth like death, coming in the colors of fall… Today the Gothic moment, the sassafras pointed with pure leaf-gold… Acme: the unlikely blend of brightness German romantics gave spring scenes. Where is Böcklin's Flora, the nymphy look on her face, her hand held to her ear to catch the pipes of Pan or the trill of a bird?

May Day. If Anna were here she would be yeasty with her own human spring: workers, marches, slogans, songs: "The answer my friend is blowin in the wind," Watching a bird hop in the grass, she would be making it an image of glad life breaking out over the world: Burma, Haiti, Cuba, Mexico, China, the Negro South. Her hair blowing across her willful sweet mouth, she would murmur: "Oh Jesus. Oh Jesus. A good May Day!"

Wherever she was, to what bigger and better May Days giving her soul…

That afternoon it clouded up and poured rain. Slow clearing. Water roaring to the sea. Stars through the cloud-veil.

He sat for hours watching, as if half god Soul had projected the show from its unknown and inexplicable turbulence; as if the long tragedy of Christendom, the self-mutilations of the Marxist dream had sprung from the collective brain; as if he himself had given birth to it all: Anna bursting from him like Athena from the head of Jove, even Jeffrey, so vibrantly, so laughingly alive, his own emanation; and all that generation of global waste and overreaching never to be grasped or imagined by any historian or poet-sage, the fire-stormed cities and invasion beaches, the cognate and affiliate mortals swept up, heroized and thrown down in its thunderous passage had been the vicarious issue and venturings of his own aging heart.

Of whose laws he was ignorant.

Like Dante's Old Man of Crete, a symbolic world-man, deeply cloven, by some grace hardly understood still pieced together, shedding the purgative rivers of this book, his hell. As Montaigne had said of his: *"livre consubstantiel à son autheur."*

From that Author Leflore too had issued, like Anna, arguing, answering, one as partial as the other. Who was that Author? It had already been declared:

> When the romantic ego, caught and participating in the energy of its source, should make itself indistinguishable from the universe of power it was always trying to comprehend and utter—then it would be cleaned up, proper; one could say it had arrived...

There was a sound at his back, the creak of a door. What was coming to him? Maybe not Christ or Antichrist either, but only the humorous small continuance of the earthly, the exasperating timid politician and lovable charmer, Jeffrey.

It wouldn't have been so surprising if she had walked around as before and waved out there at the window, bobbing and smiling, beckoning him toward the open. But for everything that spoke her active self, the British turn of talk and whimsical gaiety of doing, for all that to appear in the recess which had become the space of his own consciousness, that was extraordinary. But a door closed; there were steps; and now he heard her laugh in the labyrinthine dark behind him.

(The struggle would begin again—Anna gone, the solitude of the rock to be defended against Jeffrey, last tie to time, so necessary, so treacherous to hold.)

He sat there, body like mind fixed in single brooding, while her arm slid round his shoulders.

It was not what he had been in search of, but he would delay the search, even if what he was seeking was of the night and night was falling; even if she was of the day and day had almost passed. She did not come like the all-mother of womb and grave; even at these years, she came like a girl. Delay. Compromise. Be eased.

(Eternity not always shaped by half gods rejecting time.)
He stood up and turned.

"Jeffrey," he said. "It's time. And how's Sadie Maude?"

565

EPILOGUE

When

Indian summer had held its own with colored leaves all fall. December had passed with hardly a winter freeze. The sunny extravagance of Christmas brought the Gulf of Mexico up the Chesapeake Bay. By noon it was seventy in the shade. Spring buds. loosed from their moorings, were sending up first green. Four seasons met in one, out of time's conformity.

Jeffrey had picked up her boys from Brown and Princeton and driven them to Patapsco for the opening of the holidays—a night of heady talk about philosophy, politics and art. One would have thought the ghost of Cader Ayres had slipped among them, to steer them into what Jeffrey had wished for, a Symposium of the kind she had heard about. Though the only relic of Ayres' faculty to join them was the scrawny impulsive artist A. B. C.

He had been doing a portrait of Jeffrey lately (he had painted them all in the past, Cader, Daren, Anna, set them up and torn them down), so the involvement in his art had come to the fore again.

"I should have stolen it from him the first day; but who can stand up against him when he gets a notion in that skull: 'Oh no, I won't touch the face. The face is good, though it's only a sketch. But just a few things in this corner, to bring up the background.'"

That was the way he always began to "fight it out to the finish," peripherally messing around, until Mars Orange or Cadmium Red entered like a clarion.

"Say what you like, that head has almost got a little existence. *Cuerpo,* that's what it needs. *Cuerpo!"*

The whole canvas by this time stuck up with scraps of paper painted every experimental color and attached with spit, on the pretext of not painting, to hold back from painting so he could think awhile.

For he had learned that much, not to be hasty. It took him weeks now to really mess up a picture. But inevitably, after a certain Veridian Green or fierce Alizarine had been tried again and again in spit-paper, down it went in oil, transforming the harmonies of the first day's intuition, triggering scores of changes all over the fabric. Out came the knife and solvent. Areas of paint had to be scratched off, washed and rubbed, while the new lot crept in, hope breaking out like a fever. "This motion just here, across the face and background, is possible for the first time."

"My God!" Daren cried. "It didn't need any of those color shifts and changes to stiffen it up and give it *cuerpo*. It was fragile and lovely; it had all the life of Jeffrey, everything fresh in your art; you've set out willfully to destroy it; and if you don't know that after slxty years, don't see it's a vice, and all that talk about it's getting better is the smoke screen your death-urge operates under—then you're like the drunkard who says one more glass won't hurt and it might help this cold, and winds up every damned time passed out under the sofa."

A. B. C., humorously impenetrable, the astonishing master he obviously and essentially was, brushed it aside: "Tsh, tsh; you're chattering, *amigo*. The head may not be there; but that stretch of sweater over the right shoulder has arrived. And I haven't touched it. It's the green under the chin that puts it into relationship."

Daren took a breath. "A simple proof: when you get forced into giving a little show, which is about once a year, you fetch out a few portraits. Now every one that you let anybody see was done fast and by some accident left that way. But all the ones you worked over and gave relationship and *cuerpo* are rolled away in the attic. You can't abide to look at them. And you're so damned right."

A. B. C. squinnying through his fist clear across the room at the picture began to hum one of his burlesque songs:

> "It isn't my affair; it isn't your affair;
> It's old Tanta Cuba, so we needn't care…"

"Well, is it true, or not?"

"Suppose it were? The picture's nothing. It's a question of what I learn."

He grinned, and daubing his finger in Cobalt Blue rushed forward and struck, as with surgical force, a murderous slash across the hairline, that tightened the face like an Egyptian mummy. "Don't chatter. That's what it needs. We're on the road now."

Until Daren walked out of the room, bowing his head with the gesture of one who renounces all earthly goods. While the master, his voice rising in another wild hum: "Ma is rich, pa is rich; so what do we care?" gathered a brushload of Manganese Violet, and danced for the canvas, the helpless body and face, sparring, feinting, lunging.

Now Jeffrey and her boys had flown to Reading for Christmas. The Byrnes had driven up from the Susquehanna for a Quaker gathering next door, a dinner to which Daren was invited; so once more he was drawn into the life of generation: the Byrne girls almost grown, Hester impulsive as her father, Mardie with the quiet of Lucy, even the cousin, little Shasta daisy, as Daren knew from waving to her across the fence, a nymphette now—telling about a party she bad been to:

"They tried to dance and that stuff. Hush-hush."

Cousin Barbara, troubled: "What do you mean, hush-hush?"

"You know. That sex stuff."

"Sex stuff?"

"A magazine. Jimmy holding it out and the boys snickering." "Well! What was in it, Debbie?"

"Photographs." A bosoming gesture. "Who cares? I don't want big things like that. You fall down on em and hurt yourself."

Whatever is begotten, born and dies.

The brindled son of a bitch Brawn was getting weak in the hams and hardly staggered out of the yard; so you couldn't come up the sidewalk without stepping in one of his great sultry dogturds.

In the afternoon Daren and Dan Byrne had climbed down to the Patapsco pool (the rug factory left it clean on holidays), had thrown themselves in and swum across the eddy a time or two—not that it wasn't cold enough to turn them blue; but just to prove it was possible, that you could swim on Christmas Day right here in Maryland—Dan Byrne telling about the time he tried to swim across the whirlpool under Niagara and got picked up by the Maid of the Mist. A wonder they didn't challenge each other to ape leaps in the trees.

That night a cold front moved down from the Appalachians into the Gulf air and spawned tornadoes all the way up the Piedmont from Alabama into Maryland. *Solvet saeclum in fa villa.* "You see," Anna would have said; "everything in life you have to pay for."

When Daren went to bed it was still close and warm.

Anna was the first to tune in, like television, the voice before the image, round and round, the hurdy-gurdy of the old harangue:

"And suppose there are working-class creeps; and suppose some get in the Party; and suppose he's one..."

(Who's one? Think way back, 1942, that prairie hick Joe Jones, the time he sided with the administration on the grading scandal.)

"Does that deny my vision and my youth and all I loved and saw? You want me to turn around and be as fake and dead as the people who have sold us out? Go to grabbing instead of sharing, profits instead of peace? Like the America that failed me and put me in the slums to rot?"

(America's failure always.) "But what about yours? In a melting pot or chances, to sour and go for a bigotry?"

Bigotry? It's the future of the world.

Her voice or his?

(As he told O'Malley: "Why should I discuss it with you, Senator? I'd rather teach where there's a chance of being understood."

"You are ordered to answer: Do you think the communist system is better than our system?"

"If by our system you mean what lurks in your cloudy head, I would prefer almost anything…"

"I am trying to be patient with you, Mr. Leflore. I have never tried so hard to be patient with any witness. You are insulting, you are out of order, you are in contempt. But I repeat the question: Do you prefer the communist system to ours?"

"Then I'll be patient with you, Senator. If I stood out like this in Russia, I guess I would be eliminated. So I have no hankering after that government. But whether communism or free enterprise has more to offer the masses of the world, neither you nor I can decide…")

If Mozart would not write out a score until the whole time-fabric came to him in an instant of total hearing, like the God of Genesis, creating the foreknown, Beethoven had gone down into the muddle, a man stepping from tuft to tuft in a swamp—no, there were no tufts even, but as if the foot, trustingly advanced, had the power to consolidate a small portion of the flux on which to stand and move.

And now the face of Anna materialized out of the voice, bending over him in searching motherly care:

"Since Oxford you've been brooding. Writing poems, plays, philosophy. And nothing comes of it. Tell me: do you still think you're going to do something great?"

A question so habitual under sleep it could only be parried, as by moving the horse on a chessboard: "Did Quixote think he could right the world?"

She was beckoning him up a slope of goldenrod, her hair and skirt blown. "Something is operating up there…" She pointed to the sky like the Truth of Apelles.

Now the dry cliff gorge of the Pisan Allegory of Death closed around them in Gothic clarity, a fox dragging a pheasant into a cleft of the rock. She led him, mounting, until they came out on a peak high as Petrarch's Mont Ventoux, from which the lands of the earth spread before him.

"There," she said, and pointed east, where the snow-drifted forests of Siberia opened to a city of science, the kind of plan she had always been talking about, a research institute, a university, a prep school, merit pupils drawn from a nation stretching half around the globe. "Industry," she said, "promise, devotion. A new greatness of aim."

She waved to the west. He saw the continent he had loved and believed in unfold in space and time from the quiet mansions and lawns of the East, over the Appalachians to the corn and wheat of the central bowl, the grasslands rising into mountains, Buffalo valleys, wooded ranges, the peaked Sierras, down into the sun-bowl of California, and out where the Coast Range sheered in crags under the Pacific's heavy swell. He saw that power spend itself, go soft, quiver and shine like a beached jellyfish, a drowned swimmer, the phosphorescence of gangrene, the rivers foaming with detergents, the air infected with radio waves, TV pitching for the short-sell, everybody debauching everything in a gobbledygook of lies, pushing deodorants, sex, stupidity, the comic-book masses rising from ignorance into hate, self-hate, nigger-hate, commie-hate, spewing the napalm of hate wherever in the world it suited the interest of the Makers Making America—a thunderhead spreading over the world, until it should veer back where it came from.

> My God, my God, look not so fierce on me;
> Adders and serpents, let me breathe a while...

Anna stood, as in the wistful joy of their English years, smiling: "And this is what you have chosen, in place of me."

And still he shook the fabric of the dream, crying against her: "The imposition of your philosophy. You have left out saxifrage, Cader Ayres, love, this room, you have left out me."

But as the thrust of defense became almost the waking voice, it was washed over and drowned by the rustle of a continent gone to worms. Not the smiling Anna but the old woman rambling the house, her memory lost—Sally Stoval, Anna's Mom, his own mother under a protean change?— caught him in her arms and bore him under: "East or West, no matter; all roads lead to void." He half waked, struggling against water...

Rippling sands...

England, an island of almost escape, calm in the lingering of the privileged past; they would go there, he and Jeffrey, hunting scenes of childhood.

They would stand in the heather-rattling wind on the great gray rock over Haytor Vale, looking past moors and tors and grazing ponies south where the garden valleys fall to Teignmouth and the wooded Dart, and Torquay in an inlet of the sea.

In a little open car they whirl through the miraculous landscape of a generation ago, skirting new towns and row-house spreads; then taking the plunge, they wind into cathedral cities, Exeter, Wells, Gloucester, each with its festival of music or drama performed with the finesse of the Third Program; they hear concerts in old houses owned by the National Trust, see Shakespeare in the castle ruins where Milton mounted the *Masque of Comus.* They visit families in Queen Anne houses, Jeffrey's Uncle Leslie, Daren's tutor once, now retired to Boar's Hill; they talk with decent people about the ventures of American diplomacy and high taxes under socialism; on the radio they listen to impartial lectures on the pros and cons of the world—until intelligence seems so near the threshold of actual command, one almost supposes this residual island (with some small divine push never to be supplied) might startle the world with a state planned and organized for the general good.

Talk. Talk. While labor loafs on the job and bureaucracy expands, the economy bogging down, youth as everywhere wild, crime and dope on the rise, Shaw's *Heartbreak House* still current, the great problems evaded, Hushaby and Utterwood bored, strolling tasteful gardens, waiting for somebody else's bombs…

And there would be the old vacation routes of Europe, by fall now and in that lively open car, along the straight roads of France, up the Alps from Lake Geneva, the glacial scoured heights, until the Pass of Moloya cuts down to the south, sheer drops amber with larch under lifted snow, falling to the grape slopes of Italy, sun, the purple and gold clusters powdery with bloom, Como winding through olives, cypress, gardens. They mount the autostrada and sweep over the Po, up the bare Apennines and along the Mugnone through the Tuscan hills to Florence. Florence will be the mecca, and Pippa to greet them in the pensione.

Telling about the war, shells over the Arno, the danger which gave life briefly a tragic gleam—how when the bridge was made-to-leap, the explosion shook the palace, and down came all the little partitions that made their rented modern spaces, and they found themselves in dust and plaster in the great old Renaissance rooms. And then of the time before, when they had looked together from the window and seen Hitler and Mussolini in that silly parade…

She leads them at sunset to the roof garden over the city—the same, but for the suburbs dwarfing the center, factories sending up smoke, tall apartments; the same, but for the roar of traffic world prosperity flushes through the incommensurate alleys painted by Masaccio.

And for Pippa even the terrace will be endangered. The Contessa, who has always owned the house and rented them the upper floors, has emerged from the poverty of the thirties. Under showers of graft from Marshall money that should have helped the poor, but has left them begging in the streets where they were, left the workers as hard-pressed and revolutionary, and refurbished the old aristocrats and ruling families, that spoiled dame is rich now. So nothing will please her but to break the old lease and snatch the terrace, put in an elevator from below, block off the pensione stair, and appropriate the view over Florence.

Pippa, thrown back from life at every turn: that same Contessa whose son had fallen in love with her and recovered in England, and long since been lucratively married in Rome; this very Daren, whose sighing and bungling had deepened the harm, making a cult of impossibility; that singer, who had also come to nothing (if anything had been designed), hurrying back to Australia when war set the capstone on a generation of romantic folly. It was the family that had taken over, an ailing father, a forceful mother, a married brother, the brother's children (Pippa shaped by nature to serve and yield), most of all the pensione, the tourists who crowded to Florence for their souls' good, and to Pippa for the directions, schedules, insights of her trade. She was running a boarding school for aspirants to culture. One would wait like a youthful lover for a brief word: could she possibly get off for a drive and a meal in Fiesole? And what about that long-promised boat ride on the river, the two of them canoeing, as in youth, among dangerous looking rocks? To be interrupted by the American schoolteacher or the conscientious Cockney requiring information, which Pippa in gentle tones and with sweet patience purveys: "In the cloister of Santissima Annunciata is a Baldovinetti, one of the loveliest things in Florence. And you must take a number nine bus in the morning to the Belvedere. There is a mostra of the frescoes discovered during the war and brought from the churches and villas where they were cracking off the wall."

As she looks over Val d'Arno, her dark hair brushed with silver, her face with the beauty of all who have given their lives for others and for dreams; as the sun sinks and the autumn wind sighs from the mountains, and she wraps her cloak around her—she stands for an instant in her eternal aspect: In the Gothic clarity of a painted city, balconies, carved loggias, each appears in her own spun robes of spirit. Hers is the lacework of the tallest tower. And what should one of those gross donors praying for intercession, earthy as Daren, do (though it will not secure the terrace) but kneel and kiss the last fold of her star-hemmed gown?

Was anybody above her? Is that Heloise Frank windowed in an aureole of light somewhere over cotton pillows of cloud? But of the fire that goes out from her, kindling, consuming ("Let the void within fall to the greater void!"), nobody can tell if it is of heaven or hell—the Cyclopean hammer pounding the nail of torment into the soul.

The Gothic bubble, Pippa, Jeffrey, Florence, bursts in fragments; the West goes down in the world: Apartheid Boers (Pourpus of Oxford, spouting Protestant morality) lash black Africans from the river they have to cross to be born. Is this a race of children—lifeforce deflected on itself, springing like dragon's teeth into fire and blood?

Selma. Greenwood. Placquemine. A Negro preacher jerking like a mannequin twisted on a string; the mounted deputy poking him with the electric prod: "Git along, nigger; git along." He opens a pale mouth; it is Moses St. John; his voice sounds:

"They stood at the barricade and watched while the gang beat us with clubs and chains. When we were on the ground they came up with the dogs and warned the others back. They arrested us for distubing the peace and took us to jail, and when the jail was full, to the stockades out of town in the fields." He goes under in a wave of looting and flame.

"O *vos omnes, qui transitis per viam, attendite, et videte...*" Is that Anna's voice lifted in penitential Latin: "Look and behold ...?"

"My hand over my mouth to keep back panic and sadness for this city, I searched among thousands cheering and waving for what is. Where are the few with the solitude to stand for what should be? And now I find them, a cluster of proud young men, raising flags of the Viet Cong and singing of brotherhood. Crowds press in against them, booing, advancing placards: 'Kill Professors! Free Kerosene: Burn Yourselves! Kill a Commie for Christ's Sake!'

"Watch the red-faced black-shirt pulling down the flag. The other with kerosene. The flag is burning. The brave youth lifts it up, more glorious—the flaming banner of love."

The panorama unrolls from the voice, but changed in temper, picketers chanting not as Anna had described in the pat praise of Sholokhov, but with abstract frenzy, seized by brute powers, the eyes of hawks, a clamor of wings:

> "Hey! Hey! L. B. J.
> How many kids didja kill today?"

Counterpickets driving in en masse, distinguishable mainly by the hundred dollar bills as big as table napkins and great political dinner plates they wave, their shouts merging with the others:

> "All the way with L. B. J.!"

Maybe what the world needed was somebody strong enough to go into those backward parts, boost them up and stay on the job—education, Peace Corps, land reform—the old white man's burden, but better than the British had done it, with a new morality and will to sacrifice; but to use all that as a blind for imperialist grubbing for tin and oil, for every outrage and face-saving blunder—how many wrecked nations was our face to be saved by? And how could we keep it up and not be brutalized?

When the Sunday school was dynamited in Reading (after Daren hurt his neck, at the end of that smoldering summer) and the news fanned out over the nation, the mother holding a shoe, the father telling his wife, "She's dead, baby; she's dead," touching even the South almost to Biblical strains (oratory easier than reform): "We created the day; we bear the judgment. In bitter ruins we stand with a Negro mother, weeping, holding a shoe"—at that outrage horror had gripped America.

And now, for reasons not much clearer, we were inundating a people 6000 miles away, who had not attacked us and on whom we had never declared war, with more explosive and fire than the Nazis had poured over the whole of Europe, destroying and mutilating enough children, mothers, fathers, to stock the Sunday schools of the South, and the papers were writing it up as an operation to be condoned, one might almost think, applauded.

In the resolve, even in dream, not to go callous, not to be shrugged down, to preserve at all costs the one poor assurance of humanity, the power to be appalled, Daren tore at the veils of distance; and it was there, inescapable as Dürer's nude study of himself, the archetypal Son of Man, an Asian peasant, standing in a Delta of rice paddies across a little pool. His image in the water was Daren's naked form.

"To us in the past, America meant Beautiful. But now…" The voice trailed off. The body decomposed in the shaking of the water. A deafening noise of planes…

Unbelievable, the blinding flash, the thunder crack and deep offgoing roar.

Leflore had loved storms since he was a boy. But living in a country where commerce has fastened on the fact of fear, so many people, journalists, manufacturers, politicians, psychiatrists, cashing in on mass hysteria, until every fire siren in the night goes through the unconscious like the last trumpet—the jolt and unseasonable surprise, on Christmas night, of so much lightning and explosive sound, had Daren up and standing at the window while he was still half wrapped in dream.

The dark came to focus in another flash, an instant, ear-splitting roar. It was brighter than summer lightning, incredibly, weirdly bright. His eyes widened.

On the cold front that had brought the storm, the rain was changing through hail into snow, great driving flakes of snow, which suddenly whitened the whole earth and air; and at the heart of that winter-white cold, the summer-fierce lightning seared again, a blinding consummation of ice and fire.

At dead center, the inversion and intersection of cones where the moment opens to a timeless and spaceless sphere, the blaze of opposites. *Reinentsprungenes.* All time gaping, panting for that seizure.

When would it be? The mystical year 2000? At the turning of a hair? Everywhere and always?

Was it Now?

Had He made this, or was this the fury where He was being made?

The Third Kingdom

Some Author Notes Concerning
The Incomplete Fragment Of The Third Kingdom

Now the work most crucial for me to complete is the third novel of my trilogy. It is not in narrative that the three novels are sequential, but in idea. The first, the Married Land, rests its stabilities on ancestors and traditions; it corresponds to Joaquim de Floris' Kingdom of the Father. The second, The Half Gods, focuses on the search, especially through institutions, of my own generation; it becomes Joachim's Kingdom of the Son. In the third, Joaquim's Kingdom of the Spirit, my alter-ego observer must break away to share, with his five daughters, in the psychic frenzy of the young—with the fire on their foreheads and talking in tongues.

From this work, *The Third Kingdom*, [find here] an unpublished episode concerning one daughter (later a Jesus freak). Large parts of the novel are sketched, but it will take at least a year or two to through-write and pull it together. (1978)

*

Why shouldn't an account as factual as this not be written in the first person? It is not enough to stress the monotony of "I" against all of the father variants used here: Second Kingdom Seeker, Old Bard, paternal dignity, other prodigal, Sugar Daddy, cloudy seer, the Old Guy. That very range points to something more, which is not simply how to clean up a mess by the impersonal; but that there is no way, in whatever person, to write of the self without fictionally precipitating it, and this story, however based on certain days I spent with one of my daughters on the Street in Berkeley, is condensed from an unfinished novel, *The Third Kingdom*, as equivocally related to me as *The Married Land*, which Carla here blames for having prophesied her fate, or

The Half Gods, from whose autobiographic make-believe some have assumed Charley Bell, like Daren Leflore, actually worked on the atomic bomb, went to prison, tangled with Senator McCarthy, called there O'Malley. You may read "I" if you like; I suspect it of misplaced concreteness.

(the above before, the following at the end of the story:)

If *The Married Land* had foretold Carla-Charlotte's disaster, the close of this story too would become a foretelling. A year and a half after it was written, when the street tortures had climaxed in near-death from methadone and (for haughtiness in the clinic) being thrown off methadone, Carla found Christ, or like a broken Roman, was herself found. Since then she has been freaked on nothing but the Bible and Jesus. And while she preaches the end of time and expected Coming, her own time has been renewed – another husband, children foretold by dream to one presumably burnt out that way. Gathered, as by love, her joy, even her beauty have impossibly returned. The derogate body of the earth I thought her an image of, has not been so gathered. Or is tragedy its gathering, always?

*

The Third Kingdom, June 1985 morning insight:
Tell it pretty straight, in a series of extended episodes more or less chronologically ordered. But have a preface at 70, pass all tests of routine medical check like a 21-year old – but it's time to finish the Trilogy. Tell the story of the trilogy; of inner & outer worlds; how first conceived and how transformed: Originally a progress from pre-war paranoia & destruction, Inferno, through a crest & turning point, where the disruptive turns on itself, Purgatorio, to a regenerative construction, Paradiso. But the last was first written etc. Kingdom of the Father. The original first became a Kingdom of the Son.

What remains is the middle one, the original post-war turning point, but viewed from a generation after, it seemed in the hippie time to have become a kingdom of the Holy Ghost. But that thrust too has ebbed, gone to reaction.

584

At the moment, at the hale age of 70, the Now as always is indeterminate, to be felt out in the light of the conscious past. To be realized in the search of the fiction itself.

Sooner or later we have to think of committing to live on the world or our posthumous heritage – Why don't the trogloditic idiots pipe down?

Prodigal Father — from THE THIRD KINGDOM

She was sitting on a pad on the sidewalk, scrunched up in a doorway, with a pale sick-looking boy. Her father walked up and stood smiling, Carla, most impulsive and rapturous, once perhaps most beautiful of his five — reminiscent, with his other namesake Cheryl, of his nature-mystic mother— Carla had the look of Huck's nap, pasty and undernourished, a belly bloated by hunger or enlarged liver, her feet bare, the rest of her draped in loud-colored gypsy rags.

For the world-traveler, he looked more or less as he had for the last ten years, since his hair at forty-five turned silver-gray. But the youthful form was deceptive. His eyes, for all the exercises of **Sight Without Glasses**, grew more and more blurred. His memory too was blurring, as his mother's progressively had done. He was losing the mastery of the ordered realms. If the imperative on which he had built his life, to manifest through himself and his the reach of spirit, was to be realized, it must be now. Yet he had left his job, his house, the shelves and files of his college study on quixotic pilgrimage, the day-tor day features of which he could hardly recall. He had traveled in his life too much, too long.

His daughter looked up with a blankness that might have been his seeing a ghost —though she was the ghost to be recognized. Then light broke; she sprang up and fell on his shoulder, hugging him, laughing and weeping, while she said to the pale companion: "I told you about my Daddy? Well this is my Daddy, ray real Daddy."

The boy made it to his feet. "Far out." he murmured: and then something about having to see somebody about a deal. Carla waved him on, as she caught at the prodigal again: "My real Daddy."

Had he overplayed the self-interest of her response? She had never been much at letters, and it was often need that had got her over the hump, most of all after she threw herself from marriage into Fillmore and drugs, though by that time the pleas from jail or lawyer's office for bail or fees used to come by phone, collect. But there had been greetings not so aimed, scrawls on yellow or blue torn notepaper postmarked from crash-pads of her wandering:

Just to tell you how good' everything is. Hug all the people for me, and yellow dog, Ribby, and if I go eastward I'll see you,; but I love it here,

X X X Her Fondness, Carla

Or the gay call from Boston bubbling with love, until it came out she was using a credit card, and he knew what that meant (the phone company after him a long time about who would pay); so he stiffened to father-upright, until she put it to him: "I love you. Daddy, more than anybody; and why do you hate me so?" He protesting: didn't hate her in the least, but mighty upset by her ways; though he knew too well you'd as soon cleave soul and body as part a person from their ways.

Right now anyway she expected nothing of him, support, salvation or a fix; and what was he on pilgrimage for but to get off his proprietary perch and, sitting on her spitty pavement, a3k her about Berkeley and the Street?

"You should've been here last night. I was on that corner when about two hundred people in Halloween costumes came running, with a blow-torch and wire cutters, yelling about the People's Park, We all stormed up and they cut the fence and the police came with helmets and gas masks. They came down the street real slow; but the people had brought their children."

"Children?" —

"So they didn't <u>gas</u> them this time, Because last year they <u>gassed</u>" (like gagging) "everybody."

"Did some get arrested?"

A sleep-dancing powerful Black leaned in: "If you see anybody wants anything, let me know."

"Sure will, honey. Meet my Daddy."

What had seemed, far off, plots of the murderous Mafia, felt different here among the fallen. "That's my true love, Zulu, Only man ever got me to a climax, and he never could do it but once."

She was the granddaughter of a Delta judge, an old Southern liberal who had taken a Black share cropper's usury case to the Supreme Court and won a precedential settlement, "Independent as a hog on ice," as Time vexed him by reporting; but what his liberalism meant was impartial justice, no "judge not that ye be not judged" (though he taught a Bible Class), but the self-righteous resolve of all establishment, that morals can be upheld by force, and must.

The protagonist's point of departure. So it was no accident (the psyche they say admits of none) that a rebel daughter would pick a husband of the father's name, then spurn both for what the grandfather would have called immeasurably a fate worse than death. Withess his own hand:

When son Charles, then at college, had inveighed against a publicized lynching, the Judge, from the second story study of the brick and columned house over the leaky cabins of what the well-bred called Colored Town, wrote;

Agreed. But do not let living in what is called the effete East prevent your seeing that justice is the end and is sometimes summary.

When the levees were built by Negro workers, driving muledrawn scrapers — the best mules, they used to say, and the worst Negroes — each levee camp was an isolated unit with commissary and stores, living tents and eating quarters, in charge of a single white man.

At such a camp in the wilderness south of Delta Landing, a shanty boat moored from up river, a white man, his wife and baby, with a stock of candy and gaudy goods aimed at the Negro trade. They had also a horn phonograph, a novelty at the time, which the workers liked to listen to.

One night, past two o' clock, a glare lit the sky: the camp poured out to find the boat in flames. There was a smell of kerosene. When the blaze was put out with water from the river, they found the body of the man, his head split: open from behind; the baby, it:s skull crushed, was flung in a corner; the woman lay on the bed.

Two days later a Negro laundry woman attached to the camp told the white foreman that one of the men had brought her clothes that were blood-stained. Confronted, he broke down, admitted his complicity, but said another black worker had done the killing. That man too, when called in, confessed, but claimed they were both guilty.

They had gone to the shanty boat late, bought some trifle, and asked the man to play the phonograph, As he bent over the machine, one of them smashed his head with an axe.. The woman was gagged; the baby, whose crying annoyed them, had its brains dashed out against the wall.

What that woman went through between then and two o'clock when the boat was fired only her tortured soul and God can know,

"Boss," the second Negro said to the foreman, I got to die, and that's all right; but befo I do I sho would like a chance to kill that nigger give me away." — "You can try," said the foreman.

Taking some rope and his pistol and mounting his horse, he drove the two men before him to a place on the river bank away from the camp. "I'll give you thirty minutes," he said. They fought under his eyes, but the second one's strength was not equal to the task. Panting and exhausted, he said, "I can't kill him, much as I want to."

The foreman tossed them each a piece of rope; each put a noose around the neck of the other; each climbed a neighboring tree, tied the other end of the rope to a limb and jumped off, their bodies twisting and squirming in the air.

The genius of law is to quell the dark passions.

Our Negroes are unreasoning animals in many ways, and when crazed by cocaine, whiskey or lust, can be as dangerous as any mad dog. This foreman, away from all courts, and confronted with arson, murder and worse, dealt out justice in the spirit that enabled his Saxon forbears to establish the greatest system of common law the world has ever known.

The Judge had written that from the Kingdom of the Father, which he never abandoned. Even on his deathbed, the darkest time of the Nazi spread and engulfment of Europe, his own possessions deeded to his wife and children against possible bankruptcy, the bitterness of private and world failure could only add urgency to the voice —

Saying that the task of mind is to preserve the civilized order. That in the South of Black and White this has crucial reference: to save the sanctities of morality, law and culture, the inherited best from savage incursion, from those abandonments which under Harlem masks of jazz, jungle-dance, sex and drugs, were already sweeping out, worse than Hitler's Panzers, to unstring the world...

And here the Second Kingdom searching child of that generation come on pilgrimage to the holy ghost children of the Third, the smoky flame burning on their foreheads and gabbling in tongues, hell's angels of impulse, gone beyond good and evil — his daughter to her black hustler, fixer, screwer: "OK Honey," and "Meet my Daddy" — that troubled Daddy, nodding, smiled.

He had forgotten the question Carla was answering; "They arrest somebody every night. They come in a squad car and get a few, or in a paddy wagon and load on a gang."

His response had the ancestral ring: "How many people you got down here need to be arrested?"

She took it up: "What do you mean? Nobody needs to be arrested."

"I mean people they think need to be arrested." He pointed to a fat-jowled, snake-eyed minion of the law the old Judge himself (or most of all the old Judge maybe) would have had a hard time siding with.

"Shit," Carla said. Then like a naughty girl. "'Scuse me. They think everybody needs to be arrested."

A pair of beauty-parlored housewives were high-heeling past as gingerly as through a bog. "They wouldn't arrest those ladies."

Carla spat across them into the street. "No, but they'd <u>gas</u> them if they got in the way."

"I doubt if they'd even arrest me."

"Of course they would." (A curious loyalty.) "They arrested a priest. Have you seen the pictures? They're beautiful. They had one of me bathing in the University Fountain, and another playing guitar in the Park; but they're in the museum now."

She led him to the bulletin board by the old bookstore, sad little notes tacked to the frame:

If you know Laurie Gilpin, 15, who disappeared Sept. 20, please tell her we're sorry, come back to us, we love you. Mom and .Dad

Under glass were the apocalyptic pictures of the seizure of People's Park. Carla's ex-husband, Carlos Sastre, radical student socialist, had been writing about that for the underground press:

There is a growing movement to put an end to the poverty, racism, war and violence, which is all this society has to offer.

Against stirrings of black rebellion, student unrest, labor-insurgency and third world liberation, an eroded capitalism defends its profits and prerogatives only by repression.

More and more of our ever-soaring taxes provide the armies, police, missies, gas, guns, by which popular hopes are put down.

Even the smallest movement of reform, as it threatens the status quo rule from the top is met by a fantastic overkill from all the agencies of class power. That is the meaning of the Berkeley gassing and firing at student crowds.

Those who have hoped for liberal reforms may learn from People's Park that nothing remains but revolution.

Governor Reagan has pointed out that the nark was "a phony issue, seized upon for the purpose of promoting a riot." He has not revealed that it was he who schemed that seizure.

The mood also of the pictures. But the traveler was compromised. It was the University which had triggered the guards, bulldozed the flowers, turned the place to asphalt, a parking lot, though the hog-wire barricade had kept anyone from parking there. It was the University of California in Berkeley, and not only was his trip out, this portion of what he called his pilgrimage, financed by a lecture there; he had been giving his life and zeal to hardly more enlightened institutions for forty years— ever since he learned at college to do as he was told, and the staggering percentile success won him what Sastre would have called "that bait of diamonds from Imperialist Rhodes." Let Sastre then, who had not only written but spent a visit east talking of these things, tell the story of People's Park:

Last summer there was a block of old brown-shingle houses in Berkeley that the University bought up to force the Left Bank people out of there, just as the University of Chicago buys up property to force out Blacks. They were going to wreck the houses, so a couple of us went down to see what we could salvage.

At one house we found a man already there, trying to remove some bevelled glass. That had to be the moment a couple of University realtors 'who handle these big deals would show up, the worst kind of Chamber of Commerce types in slick summer suits with big cigars, along with campus cops. They told us to clear out, it was their property and they were going to knock it down. They'd rather smash the glass than have anyone take it, that was their mentality. Well, a couple of nights later there was a street riot, cops chasing and clubbing people, and that house got burnt down. I don't know who did it, but it seemed funny to me.

Anyway, they got the houses knocked down and left it that way, foundations, rubble, broken glass, people trying to park and churning up the mud — hideous. I had moved to L.A. but I came back for visits, and 1 heard Savio talk about a plan to bring the good out of the Flower Poeple, plant flowers on that lot. "Those people could get arrested," I said. "Yes," he said, "but can you think of a better thing to get arrested for than a people's park?

He and Shahn and some others sent out a call for help, that was all, and I guess it was mentioned in the underground press. That Sunday hundreds of people showed up, university people, street people, old ladies from the run-down pensioner hotels; the park was for them too, it was for everybody.

Of course the mayor of Berkeley got on television and said: "There are twenty-one parks in Berkeley, so why do they need this?" Well, I used to live in the flats right across from one of those parks, a whole block of blacktop, every inch, except for a sandbox for kids. That's their notion of a park, see?

Anyway, these volunteers were doing a beautiful job, rolling on turf they took a collection for and putting in trees and flowers. They had one guy who ran a bulldozer and dug out a fish pond — fish pond or wading pool, they weren't sure, because they didn't get to finish it. People brought in sculpture, someone had brought an enormous wood sculpture painted orange, in the shape of four letters.'K N O W for kids to play in, and somebody else brought a nude sculpture. I kept hearing about it down in L.A. and drove all the way up with the boys several times, just for that experience of unalienated labor. There were no bosses and no directors. In a true revolutionary community things happen from the group, without orders. Like when the pigs went in there, suddenly ambulances sprang up from nowhere, VW buses with mattresses thrown in the back and red crosses on the sides and student medics to help with the wounded...

Strange how he told it without a word of Carla, though she had been there, at the pagan pig-roasting, orgiastic dancing and chanting, drinking wine .and smoking pot —- mad Frankie, as the street

people called her, in that last paradise garden of the natural good —
she would sing and play guitar all day, then curl up with the others,
peaceful as in Yosemite, and go to sleep. He never mentioned her;
she had cost him too much by then.

Now it was she and the pilgrim father who looked at the pictures
— that occupied city, the bayonet men, gas-spraying airplanes, the
slugged priest, guards firing buckshot into the watching crowd —
while around them spread the same depicted Berkeley, spit and
image of the old Our Town-America: wide streets, houses haphaz-
ardly turned to shops and stores, among telephone poles webbed
with crossing wires and leftover residential trees, signs in the yards,
"Realtor" or painted on the walls, "25 Wet and 10 Dry" — already
on aesthetic grounds the mess of free enterprise gone wrong; but
it had retained, through the long agony of Depression and Second
World War, some early-century feel of College town, football, Our
Gang, informal, free, slap-happy America.

Now soldiers had lined the streets in invader masks, the smoke
of guns and teargas blowing; the photographed Alameda posse man
who had brought down James Rector, observer, fatally wounded on
a roof; those moments had seared their way into the presence of
the street. Whoever had called out the forces and let it come to that
— not a question of blame but the pitifulness of the fact that men
pretending to power, sitting in elected offices, could be fool enough
to think the smoke would blow away, the movie reel run backward,
the smiling old America peep out —fools not to know, once that trigger was pulled, the whole street and air, cops and kids, patchwork
stores and ugly signs, would be changed, gone forever the last vestige of hometown U.S.A., that from that moment on, private failure
was public oppression, what had seemed Leftist propaganda indeli-
bly stamped as true,

Carla was laughing about a guy she knew, so tough he stood and
watched when the armored cars sprayed gas on the crowd, and they
came to a bunch of cops without masks and went right on spraying every last one of them, police gassing police. While she guided
him down a cross street to the galvanized barrier around the new

blacktop with the window-dressing basketball goal — the communal hopes gone underground -- "So that's the People's Park."

"And it was so beautiful. All flowers and sandboxes, and over here a huge deep pit with an ever-burning giant fire in it and a cauldron with soups boiling. 1 slept there every night. The cops would come and ask everybody how old they were. But I've been here so long they know me. They wave and say 'Hi, Frankie, how are you today?' And I say, 'Fine. I'm fine. How are you?' I canlt help liking them. Behind their masks and guns they're just people."

She had a harder time humanizing the National Guard. "They weren't friendly, like the police. I used to dress up in this real skimpy costume and go dancing down the middle of the street, and I'd wave to the soldiers and ask if they wanted to make love or buy some dope. But they'd only jab their bayonets at your guts; and they shot people too, and clubbed people with their guns." If she was hunting for a human trait, what she found made her spit: "Because they were getting <u>paid</u> for it."

A big black dog wagged over, Park exile too. "Hi Bucky!" She gave him a pat. A police car sirened past.

"And there was our rock-and-roll band, and a huge hole, man, with big fish; and there we had dug the underground palace and the caves, all kinds of groovy things for children, nothing like it anywhere in the world. And they came and destroyed it." Her voice a Gospel whisper: <u>The blasphemy against the</u> Holy <u>Ghost</u> <u>shall not be</u> <u>forgiven</u> <u>unto men</u>.

"What's that up there?" He was looking at the top of one of the eight foot steel fenceposts. "There's an old rag up there. Above you. Somebody's thrown a quilt on top of the fencepost."

She raised her eyes from the ground. "That's mine," she cried.

"Yours? Is that your bedding?"

She was climbing the forbidden fence, her toes in the two inch lattice. Another police car gave it the gas and the siren. "Hey, let me go up. It'll rip if you pull it that way. You aren't high enough. Come down. I'll climb."

He sprang up beside her. (Faustian fathers vaulting since childhood into forbidden places,) "Jump down. I can do it faster. The cops'll think you're climbing in there."

But she had got the tousled comfort off the pole. It was ripped and charred from some Halloween prank of the night before.

He dropped off the fence. She flung it to him in a cloud of dust, all in his face, eyes, hair. "Wooh! It's dirty, I say that bedding1s in bad shape."

A louder siren. "Here they come. Get on down."

She lowered her toes slowly, unconcerned -- musing "Somebody burnt it. I wonder who did that?"

"How'd they get it? Where do you keep it?" The siren was on them, fierce. He wheeled. An ambulance. "Well, that one's on a mercy call, anyway."

She was turning the rag over: "That's really weird.,. Who would want to burn my quilt?" (His mutter unnoticed: "Quilt:?") "At least I have a blanket now. Because I was sleeping over in those bushes."

She pointed across the street to some fir trees in the yard of a white gingerbread house, proper Victorian establishment of ancient widow or maiden aunt. "Right over there, where those bushes are, there's a little cubby hole. I used this for my pillow and mattress, it was so torn up. And I had a sleeping bag, They were gone last night. But it's amazing I'd find the quilt flung over the fence of the People's Park."

No time to debate who had found it, or (if that was a gain) the advantage of keeping your eyes heavenward: "You mean you live behind those bushes? Wouldn't it be better up in the hills?" He waved at the green amphitheater above the town.

Only to recall what her friend Chuck Abrams had told him not an hour ago in the crowded cheap restaurant of the Street's most broken block: us protest professors, student hippies, long hair, beards, spilled coffee —' that other namesake Chuck who had traced him as Frankie's father, phoned, and initiated this travel. They had met over brunch, Chuck talking of Carla, while he groped for what in a father could have shaped such a fate for the child.

The big-nosed, kind Jewish face dropped over the plate, then

lifted in baffled concern. He had been through the wringer too, graduate school mathematician who had missed out in the university
job-shuffle, had taken an underpaid, servile place in the bookstore,
was harboring melancholia, an ulcer, and worst of all maybe, a
selfless love for Carla —

Telling how he watched her go down, learned she was on heroin
(he would have assumed pot, even LSD, but to hear the worst, and
be cut off: "I don't want to talk about it"); of her begging for food
("Once right here I saw her reach for a piece of meat somebody had
left on a plate; but the waiter cracked her knuckles with a knife
and flung the meat in the garbage. It made me want to rage; but
what can you do?"); how he began to take her out to lunch at the
sandwich shop and tempt her to talk with a bottle of port ("Port!
So sweet! She's got diabetes on both sides of the family." — "Well,
it's what she likes."); told among the rest how he had seen her lying
on the pavement, her eyes black and blue, and found she had been
robbed and beaten in the hills by goons she had led there.

The voice of Cinderella longing betrayed none of that. "Oh, it's
beautiful. Real big trees and woods and everything. In the summer
I used to meet people on the Street and they'd say 'You know any
place I can stay? 1 can't sleep here on the street, I'd get arrested.'
I'd say, 'Don't you worry; I got a sleeping bag and five blankets —
'cause that's what I had, and now all I've got is just one blanket — so
I'd take everybody up and show them the woods and say, 'Whenever
you need to sleep, you come up here." She waved. "It's right at the
top of this street, and you can see the whole Bay area."

She was bundling up her quilt. "I'm going to put this hack in the
cubby hole."

"Leave it," he said. "It's too burnt."

She was already dodging over the street in front of the cars. He
yelled as to a child in his care: "Watch your step on the road."

She disappeared through the hedge and. into the bushes, her
walk a writ of ownership. He had read them <u>Tom</u> Sawyer and <u>Huck</u>
<u>Finn</u> almost from infancy, beginning with Octavia, while Carla, as
she came along, used to protest, 'Too deep a 'tory," but listened. And

now she was Huck Finn herself — though how everything had hardened, Jim, the raft, the river.

The day which had started out clear was getting pale. The old bard squinnied at the sun, weatherwise. Carla ran back through a traffic thickening all the time. "Why don't we go up there," he said, "before it gets too foggy." But they had not gone half a block when she turned, the Street tugging her.

They were standing in front of a huge-timbered meeting hall, like a Wright transformation of Gothic. "What an extraordinary place," he said. Her response almost broke the other gravity "Maybeck, Only architect to build anything beautiful in Berkeley, And he built houses up there" — she looked again toward the dilettoso monte — "like mushrooms sprouting out of the woods."

— Art, the one chance, maybe, for anybody liberated from the frame: "I'd hoped she might record or do some entertaining, just enough to get her off the street," he had told Chuck in the restaurant — those blues she had made up in the pain of adolescence and sung to the guitar still poignant in him, an offering of the heart. But Chuck had found the fly in that ointment, which the scribe might have inferred from his own case :"What do I care who'll read me? I'm writing for the gods."

"Her approach to music is strange. If you're paid at all, she calls it prostitution. She won't mess with entertainment or any sell-out of what she calls soul." (Holding that sanctum in a life that seemed nothing if not sold; the tragic flaw always opening under the stretched ideal.) "Besides," Chuck added, "I haven't heard her play since People's Park." —

So now, looking at Maybeck's hall: "Have you got a guitar? I want to hear you play while I'm here."

Living with the loss of everything, even her regret was less bitterness than a kind of dreaming joy; "I had a guitar. I had a beautiful guitar. Until they closed the Park and I went back on junk," "Well, could you borrow one? You must know people who have guitars. He wasn't trying to show up the poverty of her relationships.

"There was one man I could have borrowed a guitar from, but

last night I went to his place and he wasn't there, so I took his radio to the campus to listen to, and later he came running and snatched it away: 'You're not going to steal my radio;' so I've made him mad, and that was dumb, because I don't care that much about a radio anyway."

Her backward gaze reminded him of Chuck waiting in the restaurant. They had talked of taking Carla to lunch. "Maybe we ought to go back and eat with Chuck, like I told him, and then go' up the hill."

The loophole she was after: "Maybe I better go back myself and make some money."

"How you gonna make money?"

Silence. ("I shouldn't have done it," Chuck had said, "but I told her once if she wouldn't go on her own, you would come and commit her.") Then the sober sound: "Sell some dope."

"How much money you need?"

Longer, deeper silence.

He had to guess: "It's not true, you know, what Chuck said about my coming, I can't work against a person's will; it's my weakness. Most of all, I have no truck with the police."

She shook her head. Traffic building up. Cars full of boisterous people going by, sports cars, open roadsters, flags, banners, the rock and sales pitch of their radios rising to a peak, then failing. Where was middle class America headed on this Berkeley back street?

Her voice low: "Twelve dollars,"

"How often do you have to take it?"

"Not too often."

Sirens again, somewhere to the left, down the road-sterred cross-road.

He glanced at the misty hills. What a plucky walker she had been when she could hardly toddle up the rocky hill past Princeton, when he would cycle them out, Octavia in the basket and Carla behind, and the day he swerved and caught her foot in the spokes and chewed it up, and she seeing his face, responding more to his shock than hers (for at a glance you would have despaired of her walking again), stifled her sobs. Such hopelessness took him now, "Then you can't climb up there," he waved; 'you'd pass out with the shudders before you ever got to the top."

The challenge, always, what reached her. "No, I wouldn't at all...I'm strong,"

"If you need your dope, you'd go nuts,"

"I haven't had it all day. Chuck has seen me. when I haven't had it for three days and I'm perfectly all right. It's only a desire."

A desire. Well, he had desires too — as to climb those hills, "Is it possible, from where we are, just to walk up there?"

"Uh huh."

"Then let's go, right now, and let Chuck and lunch wait until we get. back."

They crossed to the crowded back road, worming through jammed cars.

What were they all there for? he could think only of a catastrophe, that ambulance a while back, sirens, some wreck. He asked a guy and a girl in a red M.G. "Where are you going?" Like bug-eyed fish they stared at anybody who didn't know that — and indeed they were tricked out in blazers and pennants like cheerleaders — "To the football game!"

Crowd-happy boosters. As in the 'thirties at Virginia, when it was the style of Our Town, but he had turned his back, heading for the trails of the Ragged Mountains — so now they started in earnest up the sloping street, he, after New Mexico, with his blood and lungs set for 7000 feet, pushing the pace, hardly gulping the oxygen-dense air, looking at her —- a medical examination.

Since Chuck had evidenced a Black doctor in the city who thought she might have T.B,, he and Abe Shalin had taken her to the man, said to be good with addicts, promising to drive her back if she didn't dig the scene. When they had eaten supper with the family in the kitchen, Carla decided to spend the night and go to the hospital next day. So they left her. But by morning she had chickened out and they had to go fetch her again. Which was when Chuck had summoned the paternal power, "The doctor said she coughed all night, and I've noticed before how much she spits."

(Ratified: money wired three months before to bail her out for spitting in a restaurant, though more from temper than bad health.)

He kept his eye on her as they hit the hill. Whatever her cough meant, she was certainly undernourished, her liver half-shot, some likelihood of diabetes; yet she never lagged or complained, pegged on, panting and chattering, staunch as her Mississippi Great Aunt Bess those last vacation rides by Greyhound bus night and day over a country all the then forty-eight states of which she was determined to see; gritty as the old Judge beat down with his fatal four disorders, diabetes, arteriosclerosis, enlarged heart, pneumonia, coming back from a collection trip over the Delta, staggering to the office to file the briefs and answer letters, then to the hospital in fever, to be seized and bedded down for the crisis that never passed.

It was warm for November, climbing the south-facing slope in the milky sun. "If you're going to camp and bum," he said, "you've chosen the right climate."

"Yeah," she mused; "but man, how I miss the snow."

"Go to the High Sierras; you'd get plenty of snow,"

"Well, I've been there. But it's not the same as when a Christmas snow is failing over a town of white houses with lights and fires inside." Invoking what was lost to her, lost maybe to the world.

He had written them a Christmas story in Princeton their last year together, how their gray cat, Mr, Bigtail, learned to operate in a world of tooth and claw; and he had filled it with all the married blessing he. would ditch them to find: a big clapboard house like theirs — but where he and Sibyl squabbled as they wallpapered and slaved at repairs and rented rooms to meet the mortgage, he with his teaching and wanting to write — that was changed in the story to the happy couple, a little inheritance to keep them going, five children even (his own generative tally, though it would take the second marriage to bring it to that), the old colonial town, the farms, the woods on the western ridge, and that great snow falling over all, windows, snug rooms, Christmas lights, love — the, vision he had summoned and missing, had withdrawn still in search of.

A glance at her opened both ways, hyperboloid in time. She had always been strange and bright, over-loveable, smiling, caressing, kissing, pouting, sobbing: the time she came crying: "O Momma, Momma, Tavia hurt myself." — "Tell her you're sorry, Tavia," and she ran to Octavia, blubbering, hugging, apologizing: "I'm sorry, Tavia; I'm sorry." And the other way — pasty, bloated, rambling on as she toiled up the hill — he saw his mother in the bad time, out the long west-leading streets under the smog of the Eastern city, praying, smiling and dying in the old folks home for strangers. He reached out and caught her hand, and there was another link; he should have brought the clippers, as he used to when he went to the nursing home. "Don't you ever cut your nails? I'd think they'd break and bother you."

"They never bother me. Only when I play guitar I have to cut them."

A measure how long — "But it's not good for you to be hooked and have to trap other people to make your fix..."

• She could always find a bright side: "It was worse the first time, when I was really hooked bad and prostituting myself."

(When she had gone to the emergency clinic for help and been scorned and scolded for a street whore and kept waiting without treatment, until she had left between rage and despair, and by the time Octavia located her and got her to a doctor, the clap had fulfilled the curse of Lear: _Dry_ up _in_ her _the_ orga_ns_ of _increase_.

"It was horrible. But I won't do those things now."

(Beauty expendable: say can't.) "If you want to beg and bum like God's folk in old Russia, OK — I've had enough pretensions — but not in this slavery."

"I know. It's so dumb, when I'd stayed off so many years."

— My God. And his worst encounters with her had been in these rosy years, when he brought her from California to escape the psychiatrist who had got her unhooked, but by using amphetamines, and she flung off the plane In her rags with her tousled old sleeping bog and into his arms, desperately needing a father's rescue, but too far gone for him to know how to give it — off heroin, but onto anything psychedelic that would suppress the real world or the accommodations it required -- convinced reality was nothing but a congeries of subjective trips good and bad, those endlessly narrated visions he found so boring — or was the exclusion moral? — to brush off duty, study, discipline, the long labor of humanism and democracy, great models and forbears from Milton to the Old Judge, from Jefferson to Adlai: "You people havin a bad trip with jobs and police and Korea and Vietnam, a bad trip; but I get on acid and have a good trip" (though the chorus of mystics in his head from Laotse to Blake took her side: "And what is ultimately real but the visionary?")

She lived for him in a solitude no actual voice could penetrate, from which she emerged only to the extent of going to the dentist to have her teeth pulled, the front pair neglect and the drugs had rotted, and a little bridge made, of which he, crass materialist insisted: "That bridge is not imaginary; it belongs to the world in which the bill will come and I will pay, the world you countenance by wearing it."

It was then, when he had told her — as teacher and as father of the younger two — that drugs were out either at the College or at home, that she went straight to the former and returned to the latter tanked on marijuana; and in protective rage he almost called the cops, but grabbed her instead and shook her (as his grandmother and father used to say) until her teeth rattled (those costly new pearls); then phoned friends in Baltimore and gave her a chance at therapy for herself and work with handicapped kids at John's Hopkins hospital; but she opted for New York, wandering on her own, and as he had promised not to hold her if she came, he put her on the bus and paid her fare.

And then the phone call, remember, the loving child-rapture of that voice: "O Daddy] I've run into a friend named Merrie from Reed College and I'm staying at her aunt's beautiful penthouse high over Greenwich Village, and they're so nice to me and let me do whatever I please. And thanks, Daddy, for the teeth; I'm all pretty again."

He growling at so much easy transport and that she hadn't buckled down for the cure, could hardly keep from telling her, "Wait and see. You're going to bust it. I give you three days in that lovely penthouse doing what you please before you get thrown out."

And sure enough, next thing he heard she was on the streets, and he phoned his writer friend Hanrahan, who agreed to lend her his studio. That was when Carla appeared at Hanrahan's (an apparition celebrated in verse) late at night and with a high Spade, frightening the pregnant wife and maybe even Hanrahan, though he was hard to scare; seized a guitar that was lying on the sofa ("Maybe you can tune it," said Hanrahan, for his wife had been taking lessons and he had been messing around, but neither one could get the thing in pitch); she gave it a shake and rammed a few pegs and put a tune on it like it never had before, sang a couple of folk songs as well as they'd ever heard them, but broke off, saying: "But I'm tired of that; here's what I'm doing now." Gave the pegs another slap that threw it into some twelve--tone scale and began the weirdest bongo hair-raiser Hanrahan had ever encountered, though he wasn't ignorant of the popular avant-garde.

So he gave her the key to his downtown studio and she moved in; but it wasn't many days before the landlady called the police; Carla must have run an open house for the bums of the Village; so when the cops came the place was a shambles. The rest had vamoosed, but not Car]a; she was on hand, and she tangled with the sergeant as if he were the offender against law and order -- would have mauled him too, if they hadn't ganged up and toted her off to Bellevue.

Which was where the paternal dignity saw her next — a horrible mad house, and she more frenzied than ever, though he took her an old guitar and talked with a young doctor, assistant there, deeply moved by her case, who wanted to take her home for special care; in fact, it might have been arranged, but the next day she climbed out somehow and split.

So if that was when she was off heroin, God help her now she was on. (Though she seemed to have grown more sane — or was it the other prodigal?)

"And what might save me is my music. Because when I take heroin I don't feel music. I don't feel anything but Arrgh!" She hawked up one of those doctor-troubling lungers. "I'll have to go to the hospital, but on my own..."

She stooped for an orange someone had dropped in the gutter. As she stuffed it into a pocket of the jacket she was carrying, there was a jingle on the road. "Hey," he said, "you're dropping your money." He squatted to pick it up, feeling a twinge of his mother's arthritis.

She stood brooding. "I'll be threatened, of course, all my life. But I hate to talk about it. I hate even to think about it." She took the quarters, nickels, pennies as carelessly as she had thrown her college money into junk.

For the first time her being, alien to him before, was clearing and opening, a sad human light shed on what had seemed dark and sinister.

"What about that time you used to phone from New York in the middle of the night — weren't you on something then? Not Bellevue, but later. You sounded so high, and those big parties roaring and banging. I thought you were with the Mafia or lord knows what."

"No. No. It wasn't a very big party, and I hate the Mafia with all my heart." It came back over her, and her voice sang, as when she had phoned and he thought she was stoned: "It was a juke box, in our very house. I tried to tell you on the telephone: 'And we have a juke box in our own house.' But you wouldn't listen. The reason I called was because I was scared. I had run into some heroin dealers..."

"Ah."

"And I had heard about Cheryl, that she was living with some hippies and a pusher in Washington, and that they were taking dope. You remember, the first thing I said was 'I had a dream about Cheryl —' I called it a dream — "how is she?" And you wouldn't talk; said 'O she's fine; don't worry about her."

They had written Carla off by then. But that her sway might draw Cheryl, so much like her, into the death-love vortex our civilization whirls in, most of all the youth, the sensitive, the free — had been their dread all that time. So that any hint of a contact, even in dreams, not to mention long distance inquiries to the ground-noise of New York revelry, had frozen his protective blood.

"I knew I might go to those dope peddlers, and I was frightened."

"For yourself or for Cheryl?"

"Both. So I ended up going to Cambridge, where there's no dope — well, almost none."

(Yet she had got sent to Mass General on some ground, from which, by the time they managed to notify him, she had, as usual, escaped.)

"To get off, you have to go where you can't find it, and that's always harder, because there's more junk everywhere."

(To see it so clearly, yet settle like a dog-flea on Telegraph Avenue in the drug-block of the nation --- to settle and not wont to move on.)

He had been so sure the New York tie was criminal, "But what about the telephone? You said they had a private line the company didn't know anything about — not a credit card, you said — and I thought, that must be the gangster ring to end all rings."

She laughed until she coughed. "They were Yippies, college Yippies (I told you they were going to the Convention), who knew about telephones, and they plugged into the main line — I don't knew how — and we didn't have to pay."

"But what about that sailor who phoned afterward, said he'd found you beat up on a roof, and now his ship had to sail, and would I help send you west? There it is —- I thought — that phone-plugging gang has dumped her; and it's a wonder she's not dead."

"But that didn't have anything to do with it. That was after I came back from Boston, and I met this black guy, a Biker, on the street when I was high, 'Hey, you're awful handsome,' I told him. So 1 went off and fornicated with him, and I must have made him mad, because he said something and I hit him and he hit me; and that was how I lost those teeth you paid for. But the Yippies were kind and gentle."

"Well, it's a pity you didn't stay with the Yippies, instead of taking up with the Biker,"

"I only met him one evening," (as if that explained everything) "and I was lousy drunk on wine and cough syrup, which'll kill you a lot faster than heroin."

When I <u>had stayed</u> off so many years — it must have hit them together, that was the time when she had talked of being free.

"I don't know what's wrong with me, I don't like the way I feel naturally, so I want to drink something or take something to feel better. Dumb, I guess."

"The whole world's drunk on wishing too much. And you had a bad youth —- unhappy, and those allergies."

"Unhappy? I don't remember that. But you can be very unhappy in your youth, and grow up to be happy."

They were panting now, the steepest part of the hill, her bare feet padding the road, the hiss of his corduroys.

"If you don't get too hooked on cough syrups and God knows what. Some people think the laws of nature are habits matter fell into. What a defeat gravity must have been. It's like history; if it takes a wrong turn it may never recover."

Her face full cycle — the mask of gloom.

"You got a steep hill here," he said.

She raised her eyes to the green crown, nearer-now. "A little more and you see the whole Bay Area."

"You won't see it today; it's too misty,"

She looked back for the first time, "Aw, that's a pity."

But you could see plenty: the smoky bowl, the Bay an industrial cesspool, surrounding hills slashed with highways, powerlines; and everywhere through old forested slopes bulldozed bare earth for new apartment towns, shopping centers. The derogate body of the landscape as a nude. And Carla in her rags, with her lost teeth and fish-belly skin: I bruised myself...<u>calcined</u> myself...no <u>reason</u>... <u>the</u> way of my <u>love</u>.

"Where's the ocean?" he said.

"Ocean? You don't see any ocean. It's behind that big range across the Bay."

"And that's where the redwoods are, is it? Let's get a bus tomorrow and go out there, I've always wanted to see that."

Her voice a lark again, reentering paradise: "All right. The ocean's there and Muir woods, and it's beautiful." Tones too dreamy for it ever to be real. She felt it too: "I was telling my girl friend Dona about my Daddy, and I said it would really make him sad if he knew. Or maybe it's me that should be sad. Well, I'll show you the woods anyway."

The paved road ended among lanes and private estates. She led him down a path to the left which plunged into a little valley dense with sweet smelling myrtle large and dark as live oaks. The steep earth gave, she slipped; they caught each other, leaning on the sheer slope. "We're sliding."

Down to the little stream tumbling clear over sedimental black dirt, where a rope hung from an arching limb. "I made that for some children. They had the rope, so I climbed up and tied it where they could swing over the stream."

He looked at the dark foliage. "Must be live oaks."

"Oaks?"

He broke a leaf and crushed it, "No, you're right. Myrtle, I guess. Smell." Their voices in the grove had become hushed and low.

Hers: "Like some sort of menthol, only super"good. Put Where are the Eucalyptus?"

He saw them up the other bank, soaring over the myrtle, mottled green and pale. "There."

But she was searching the ground. "No. No. Here." She pressed through a tangle of briars, her feet and legs bare.

"Look out for the thorns," he said.

She never noticed. Bending she scooped up a handful of scented balls. "These are what really smell good." She poured a bunch in his pocket. "Take some to Cheryl."

Then she drew him around the briars up the other slope to the foot of a peely-barked Eucalyptus and pointed to a burrow under the roots — as in German fairy tale, Melusinda in the hollow tree. "I dug it out," she said, "with a board and stone. It's my Hobbit Hole, It was good to sleep here; but some boys found it; so I went up higher and started another one, under a rock. But this was the best. A real Hobbit Hole."

It would have served a rabbit or a fox, but a person couldn't have squeezed in out of the rain. "You need a roof on it though."

"The roots of the tree would be the roof'," she said, "But I'd have to dig it way down. A gigantic cave," The throaty ecstasy he had heard when she was tiny and would make up tales of elves for her sisters. "But those kids were sure to tell."

He was groping all the time for an opening for her, any way of life besides impossible commitment. He searched her face, the black eyes under the tow-headed mop of hair: "You like living like that? You like it better than trying to go back? To get in the deal?"

She was mounted on Pegasus, "Ugh! I wouldn't want to get in the deal."

He pulled the noose. "Well, you're in the deal anyway, like, it or not."

It brought her down. "That's what's creepy about it, I'm right in the deal. It's what everybody tells me. And six months ago they couldn't have said it, because I wasn't. I was a new child. And now I'm right there working for them again, police and junkies and capitalists."

"You pay them off?".

"I don't. But it's what a friend of mine, a beautiful yellow guy told me. He said he watched them a long time and he knows what they're at."

"One thing: if there are revolutionary groups around the University, they'd rather get them on drugs, because nobody's a revolutionary on drugs."

"Right, right."

"If you want to fight a power, you've got to keep clean of it."

She had sat down, her feet in the Hobbit Hole. "That's so strange. Because the only thing that caused me to get strung out again was the power.

"You mean when they broke up the Park?"

"Yeah. I didn't want to see anybody everjf again. When I saw the majority of people in the world are completely messed up, just robots, and that they run things, and can send armies with guns and gas to destroy what's beautiful,, it'freaked me out. And Dona kept coming to my basement (1 had a basement some people had left so X didn't have to pay for it) and shooting up and asking me if I didn't want some (because when you're clean, just the scraping of a wet spoon makes you more lo . ‗d than they are), and I thought I'll forget about those soldiers. And I did it and I didn't care anymore, and since then I've never stopped. And it's really sad. But if I could have stayed off three years, after being hcoited the way I was, it can't be that hard; it's just a matter of going and doing it."

"Why don't we go to Mendocino right now, while I'm here? It's not like Cheryl in Washington, You're no child."

Her voice barely reached the outer world: "I don't know. Maybe it's easier for a child. At least a child thinks there's something to live for."

"What about that Black doctor Chuck and Abe took you to? Why didn't you go ahead with him?"

Her volume came up to par: "You know what happened with that man? I don't care what color man he was; but that man, late at night — I was sick and rolling all over the floor — and I felt this man kissing my cheek and feeling on me. It was creepy. And next morning he looked at me like weird, like 'Don't be mad at me, I'm sick too,' I never told Chuck, because the man was a friend of his and I don't like to tell bad things on people; but that's why I blew the whole thing. If that man had been a fine person, I would have gone to the hospital."

And her mother in the breakdown after the first birth had thought the sanatorium doctors were practicing on her: sodomy, onanism. Put it to the test — "Maybe he was sorry for you, rolling and coughing. Maybe he meant it lovingly."

Not like paranoia to think it over in silence. And then: "Maybe you're right. He may have. That's why I never want to pass judgment." Another pause. "But I didn't think so." She seemed to canvas it in her mind, "No, I don't think so."

"Anyway, he was only going to get you into the hospital; he wouldn't have been the one to treat you."

"No," she said. "But that blew my mind. That really blew my mind."

She brought out the orange. "Want some?"

"Better you."

"Well, I'm thirsty when I sweat so much." She peeled it into the Hobbit Hole.

He felt the resistance that met every thrust, but the pauses left no choice. "One way or another, you've got to go through with it. And then clear out. You said your own girlfriend helped hook you. So you can't stay with these street people and not fall back."

"The Street People," she pronounced with conviction, and a mouth full of orange, "are very pure and very beautiful. They smoke grass and they take a little acid and they play lots of music. Those are my people. The Junkies," she spat seeds, "are another thing. They live in apartments and have money; they come on motor bikes and hustle all the time."

A hopeful separation for pilgrims of the Third Kingdom. But it seemed to leave no place for her. "Then who hustles the acid the street people use? Don't you hustle?"

Had she jumped a cog? "It's not real. You think what I'm selling when I make my money...? I don't sell no dope. I sell you a vitamin tablet and get your money, I'm a burn artist."

He stared. "'Well, no wonder the police protect you." (Chuck puzzling about why they would cruise around watching her deal, and come back again, and not nab her.) "All you're doing is embezzling from the poor to pay the Mafia to pay them."

Her beautiful yellow guy had told her as much, but she rejected it: "No. It's not that complicated."

Why argue? All he knew about it came from Lincoln Steffens, "Well, I didn't come west to muckrake California." Better to ease off, like going to the woods, in careless love. But he took up the old boomerang.

"You know you need help. You had Floyd before, though for me he's the jerk who gave you Speed."

"The Speed helped enormously," she said, "with the heroin. But I didn't go to Dr. Floyd until I'd been off more than a month, and it's the first month that's so hard."

The unkindest cut of all — that so much money and methadrine risk, skin damage, tooth damage, brain damage (the 19th century curing opium with heroin, Freud's pushing cocaine for a panacea), not to mention Floyd's cult of power over matter, body — his voice on the phone (for his only letters were bills) proving at the other's cost the outmoded subjectivity of pain, as if whatever happened -- injury, seizure, loss, betrayal, had only to be accepted as information for all pangs to vanish: "Just yesterday, at the hospital, woman hit by a car, threw her into the air, lit on her head on the road, no bones broken, but bruised, could hardly breathe, ache in her throat when she swallowed, lump on her head, nauseated, crying for sleeping pills, pain-killer; rejection had closed her veins, trapped pain chemicals, produced swelling...Well, by getting her to be very geographical about where it hurt (in the pit of her stomach, yes, and what was it like?), by making her describe and visualize, I got her to accept that information: circulation opens, chemicals dissipate, congestion, nausea quiet down; I go for the chest, ease that off; work up, make the ball go in the throat, the headache: it took me about twenty minutes to get her hack in shape..." "Yes, Dr. Floyd, but how is Carla?" "That's what I'm telling you; if she'll just learn that it's subjective, that suffering is unnecessary...I think she is learning. By the way, I haven't received payment on that last bill." And only after he had hung up would he think to ask: "It's not that you're suffering over it, Dr. Floyd?"

The unkindest cut of all, that all that had been superfluous, post-dating the cure, and that ordinary love and care might have brought her round. Or was the whole thing, then and now, a morass of time in which the judgment would always flounder? "You mean you'd been off on your own before you started with Floyd at Zion Hospital?"

"Ask Octavia, Ask Monique,"

He had. He would. But it was too tangled, too many hopes, tries, failures. What she came up with left him groping:

"I only said I was a junkie for Carlos, The draft was after him, and if I went to the hospital they'd never bother him again, because of the boys. So I said 'I'm a junkie, help me,' and they did. They sent me to Napa for ninety days, a horrible place; they penned me up with the nuts, and the old ladies shit on the floor, and they made me clean it up all the time."

"But what about Floyd and Zion?" She didn't pause.

"But I escaped. I went out the front gate with a fellow who had weekend passes, a big black fellow..."

(Yes. There had been that letter:

Good you've calmed down a bit and begun to accept that your loving daughter is a fugitive from justice, though she still loves music and the beauty of this world (a miracle I'm not witnessing the beauty of the next.) Your worries don't help; send money. And get it out of your head I'm a flighty little girl before I decide you're a silly old man. You haven't known me since I was fifteen and cried to the guitar from my sentimental and evil soul...)

"and the guy who kept the gate was a little old patient. 'This is my wife,' the black man said, 'and if you want to make anything of it...' The little white patient got so up-tight he waved us on. That was when I went back to Carlos and tried to make it at home."

"And got in a fight and the police came." He couldn't stop; it ravelled out: "and you had marijuana on you and I sent bond and you skipped, which would have cost me plenty, but they caught you on another charge?" Though surely if was the wrong thread, years later, while she pulled the other from the sump of dark reminders:

"It wasn't marijuana; it was stolen property. Gold rings, diamonds and stuff. Some old lady had it in her drawer, I saw it there, so I took it. I always liked jewelry. I'd do it now..."

The toils of bungling and misfortune going back like a genetic helix in her childhood and blood, so ensnared him that he heaved a hopeless sigh which she took wrong: "I'm sure it must be very boring."

"How could it?" he answered. "Only I'm baffled. I can't stay long, and I don't know what to do, I'd hoped to get you to Mendocino. Though of course, it's good just to have seen you," She had got up, her coat trailing again; the money fell out, this time into the hole. Hardly worth picking up, by what she had lost; but he bent down.

She knelt too, and he saw a patch of scab and blood on her scalp, "What's that? You've knocked a hole in your head somehow."

She fingered it: "Oh! A huge hole." Shaken — though she knew: "When I shoot smack I claw my head. I'm such a fool. Oh! What a horrible hole."

(Have you really given up on me, are you bankrupt, indifferent, or what? I've gone this far and to stop at this point only leaves me in a state of confusion not relating to myself as a drug addict or a person, trying to find out what happened and why I've been trying to kill myself for about ten years. The state of mind I'm in is too frightening. I have never faced reality and now I am facing it. With help 1 could learn to love myself, then maybe I could stop punishing myself and others for things that were never even done, I found it necessary to move away from San Francisco. I'm in Portland, Oregon...

(Letters over the years mislaid, sent late, addresses obsolete, his answers, worthless anyway, returned to sender.)

The sky was overcast. As they came to the road they looked out again on the ruin of one of the world's beautiful places.. She swooped down on a dirty cigarette butt, then groped in her pocket for a match. "Aren't they bad that way?"

"Better," she insisted. "The fresh ones are weak. These are funky and strong. I like old funky things,"

And then: "Tell me about Cheryl," Like asking of her own life before it got funky and old.

So he told her of the child marriage (Carla had had hers), the search in eastern communes and now in New Mexico on their own land to reconstitute the Arcadia of pioneer and subsistence forming, away from town and the money mill. He did not dwell on the handicaps against it, the draft, inflation, taxes, or how unlikely at this phase of America it might prove.

They were swinging down the hill. "And what I heard about her in Washington? What scared me so?"

Though they had been the scared ones, "It's past. And she's got the right husband. One of those mystical fierce hippies."

"If he satisfies her, she'll be all right. So many men don't satisfy a woman. And it's all she's looked forward to from childhood, growing up to have a satisfying sexual partner. I know because I'm pretty messed up. Men make me angry. They take their pleasure and can't satisfy me. I satisfy myself."

They were nearing the People's Park, motorcycles, cars, sirens building up around them again. "When I get a sexual urge, I just lie there and rub myself in the morning and Ahh! (a joyful sad little sigh) "I'm satisfied. It's nice. I don't need no man. I like to satisfy them, but they're no use to me. I'll probably turn into an old Lesbian. I haven't yet, but I know my girl friend — she's very attractive to me, and she's always hugging me, and she doesn't get satisfied either, and I say 'Quit hugging me, you don't like girls.'"

The child-simple laugh. "I don't know why I started that subject. I spent thirteen hours once trying to figure it out and didn't get anywhere. They had come opposite the Victorian house with the bay window, stained glass over the stair and the dense fir trees surrounded by hedges in the yard. "I'll just put this old jacket over with my blanket."

"If you do, they'll steal it all."

"I'll wedge it in the tree. Nobody'll see it."

She ducked in. Glancing through the hedge, he surveyed the hideout. She wadded the quilted bundle into a limb crotch and squatting down made her waters. He walked out to the sidewalk looking back at the prissy gingerbread, the greenhouse shrubs, a convenience for street-Carla's bedding and pissing. One was always getting symbolic glints off her.

They had only a block to go, "Then you really weren't happy with Carlos?"

"I was happy; I loved him; but look what was building up. I didn't know anything about sex, that a woman needs to be satisfied, and he didn't either."

"How could you grow up not knowing that?" Though the carnal traveler, a student of sex since boyhood, had not talked with her about it before.

'Mother never told us shit. And the older she gets the worse. I tell you she's sick."

He had thought the final explosion at Bellevue, when he had said "Use your reason; you're acting like your mother," and she, shouting, "I love my mother and I won't have you speak against her," stalked into the "No Visitors" ward and slammed the door, had been literally the protest it seemed; but maybe, like everything else in the world, it was deeper,

"I got to hustle," she said,

"I'll see you, then." He went to his room to work at his lecture.

Though all he could think of was Carla, and that his schedule allowed three days, of which one was almost gone...

Two days on that street, sinkhole of free desire settling to its own negation — flower-children pumping pills and powders of all colors fake and real bought from police-protected rings as the media pump trash and lies (beware of the leaven of the Pharisees), no more effectively in revolt against Behemoth-Leviathan than the birds that wait on the rhinoceros or the little fish that clean the shark's teeth — two days, with nights brooding the futility of love's collaboration.

He had given his lecture now, in that other world of disciplined students, old professors, faculty club, that University, its gate, or gateless mouth interflowingly flared into those blocks where the hate and curse of the West, the backlash of Vietnam, the fall of Resurrection City, armed guards on the campuses, had oozed and gathered like brown dreck.

The next day was his last. For all his urging and counseling with her friends, Chuck, Abe Shaim — bearded lion, of Judah -- and the rest (talk of hospitals, talk of commitment — memory like a dark Piranese. opening to the dirty huge bedlam of Bellevue, night-clad neurotics, schizophrenics, addicts, defectives thronging up and down, staring with wounded animal pleading at any visitor, Carla more pent-up and scornfully destructive then he had ever known her), they were no nearer a solution than before.

And now, louring dusk, having hustled and got her fix, a

"cotton" of somebody's leavings, she, robed in a voluminous blue evening dress of cast-off sateen, led him through the fierce street, Hell's Angels gunning motors, Krishnas dancing in eternal drugless hypnotic joy, a pack of acid kids, Red Rockets, howling, beating a mailbox like a tom-tom — led to her usual packing-case, where they settled back in shadowed quiet, withdrawn to contemplation from the lights and noise — to contemplation in a blue gown.

If she had ever been part of the neurotic street-hippy show, she had burned through into a terrible and costly solitude. It was not the solitude housewives complain of behind their sheltering walls. She had made herself a thoroughfare for the traffic of broken flesh; yet she loomed, alone, impassive through the passing, a queen beyond tragedy. She had been cheated, one could say, of many things, father, early family, love, husband, children; but she didn't much blame herself, others, or the world.

In youth she had boasted, bitterly, that she didn't believe In God or man; now she lived her plight as if it were God-given.

He remembered what her older sister Octavia had written after taking her several times to Synanon: "She's too proud for Synanon, They have to come to that place broken in body and soul. She's not defeated, and she never has been."

Hard to praise a demonic strength. But had the little virtuous people ever got themselves so snared in an Ulro of lies, naptha and world poison?

In Spenglerian youth he had given up the West for lost; then in the glow after the Second War he had got on the bandwagon, reaffirmed democracy (SONGS FOR A NEW AMERICA), worked for Adlai, and the New Frontier, watching it harden, as the Marxists had warned, into the exploitations of a world- Vietnam. The romance of Lucy (after Sibyl) was a phase of the liberal turn to light; he had even written a novel which saw our time as capable of such regeneration, "a house where all is ceremonious," And now in the life of his children it was fake and sold, the-soap-opera of THE MARRIED LAND (two couples billowing past in the Mercedes, headed for cocktails", discreet amours à l'ancien Régime). A comedown, in the climax of history we had tried to serve and celebrate, to confess to these young: "A pity our Periclean age went so hollow, allowed so few tolerable or even honest alternatives.

While Crazy Jane Carla talked on: something about her worst years and a friend she had lived with, "a beautiful old Spade man" — back in that Black slum time, when he had wondered if his duty was to come out with his father's pistol, and track her down.

Gentle tall Dona, of the brown hair and brown eyes, swayed in, unstrung in every joint, a carton of orange juice loosely held: "I bought a big bottle cause I thought you'd like some, and you weren't even here, you bum." She had been Carla's excuse lately for stalling on the cure: "I'll go as soon as I can persuade my girl friend; she's worse strung out than I am."

That anyway seemed a statement of fact. They squeezed in on the box like roosting chickens, "And what about you, Dona, where do you come from?" She spilled out in a fuzzy drawl, her lids half-sagged over soft eyes:

"Connecticut. My father...one of these...start poor...get rich quick...went to his head...you know, real estate. Power, power...big guy. Wanted me to marry money, do this, do that. Wouldn't send me to art school. I had talent, lots. 'You can't leave until you're twenty-one.' Following me around the house, glaring, shoving, trying to get me to shove back. Then he'd swat me and say 'You learn who's boss around here,'

He wanted to kill me...really...Once he went WHAM with his fist in my face, like I was a man, cause I wouldn't tell him who'd bought me a can of beer. And I was nineteen and had a job. So I blew it. Ran off with this Arkansas hillbilly my father told me not to see. Ignorant as the day he was born, ignorant and prejudiced...thought women had to walk ten paces behind and were there to cock and clean and serve a man's physical needs..."

Strange for an account of such passion to slur on in the bleared and listless voice of entropy, especially against the airy salience of Carla's asides, as defiantly young as if all those years of beggary and dope, jails and beating had been a cheerful game — not interrupting

Dona and not listening to her, just greeting people as they walked by and if they responded at all: Hey cool cat, got a cigarette?" in the tones of a Krishna celebrant: "A stick of incense, brother divine?" Until somebody w) would hold out a pack for Carla and Dona to pull from and for the Ancient of Days, doubtful of sotweed as marijuana, to decline: "Thanks, I'm only addicted to piñon nuts." Or as some college types would approach, Carla would flash a plasic bag of powder or a vial of pills, intoning quietly and gaily, almost to herself: "Buy some acid? Buy some speed? Thrilling. Exciting." And in her father's ear: "After all, it's better for them than something real."

If it was for more than curiosity he had come, of if, say, for love, and that love was to bear fruit, there was only tomorrow. "Why don't we get a meal and you come to my place?" he said. "There's an extra room and a mattress. You get a good sleep and in the morning Abe Shahn can drive us to Mendocino. Dona can come along tonight or meet us in the morning, whichever she prefers."

Well — they had promises to keep. But Carla noted the address, hugged him, said she would come later on, spend the night and get ready for the ride.

He went back to the upstairs apartment lent him by friends of friends, their goods and furniture not yet unpacked, a mattress on the floor, crates and boxes for a table and chair. Here he had tossed, after the days' appeasement, in the debate of remorse and "Why Remorse? You tried protective righteousness, to seal off the predestined sinner. Time you found another way, some mystery of touch that would put love above morality," Dozing, he would wake far in the night, not even a clock to tell time, to the scream of sirens, squad cars, fire trucks, ambulances (Berkeley since People's Park a beleaguered city under police power); would lie listening, reliving the impotence of the day.

He went there now, wrote what would otherwise slip out of his head, sunk without trace. The town noises died; he guessed it must be one or two; and still no Carla. He lay down; though every sound heard or imagined brought him to the stair. By dawn he gave her up, dozed into the day, waked, ranged the still empty street, finding no clue. At ten Abe and Chuck met him in the restaurant. The car was available, but not the rider. At two she appeared, hung over as the other days, but in proud pace beside the sagging Dona.

At least they were together. And Dona, for a wonder, had decided it was time for a cure. She had been nagging Carla all morning to get her started. Now the others pitched in, though the more they urged the more she shied: "I don't want to be taken; I want to go on my own."

"You mean your own feet? We're only offering you a ride."

Over and over, the afternoon passing, Dona desperate to start before her shot wore off. No. Zulu had mentioned an underground movie about the People's Park showing at six. A write-up in Outcry had named Carla the star in fact "Super-star Frankie, mad toothless Frankie, pregnant ragamuffin of the streets, infant of a civilization which murders its own children because they dare to dance and sing, because they dare to plant a flower in a muddy parking lot." Carla had undertaken to get Zulu in free, and nothing was going to shake her.

"You said you couldn't go without your girlfriend; now she's packed her clothes and is ready, the car's ready, everybody's ready; and you say you've promised Zulu to go to the movie. Well, I say you've promised Dona more, and she needs you more."

"I've got to see that movie, anyway. We can go afterwards. There's plenty of time."

Abe, warned by the other time he coaxed her to the doctor's and she backed out: "I don't care, whether she goes or not" (he didn't even j.ook

at her); "but if it's the movie that's bothering her, I know the man that made it, and I'll bring him up and we'll show it in Mendocino,"

"I want to see it tonight. I promised Zulu."

Dona turned on the klaxon of her street-whine. "I don't care. I've got to get up there. I'm going out of my fuckin mind, see. If I wait around here I'll get the fuckin creeps." Over the bleat of passing horns, the roar of Black bikers relaying in from San Francisco with the drug supply (that peanut head, that face, reptile core of

the new movement, older than Tyrannosaurus); everybody arguing, time slipping by, clouds closing in, colder, darker.

Dona had snivelled off writhing, Carla calling after her, calm as
a church and as crazy: "It'll be over by seven, and we'll go then," she
had plunged out of sight and even sound; Carla strode after, only to
find her squealing to a policeman, the whole affair, how Carla was a
junkie and wouldn't go to Mendocino, and they ought to arrest her
and send her anyway.

When the bucket-brigade next caught sight of the daughter, she
was blazing at all portals: "I won't make up with her. Let her cry.
She did a terrible thing: snitched on me to the police, almost got me
arrested. So I'll never go to the hospital, not at all,"

Not even a groping father was blind enough to argue, he caught
her hand, stroked her arm, asking what difference it could make;
besides, if she wanted to see that movie she'd been talking about, it
was almost time; and where was Zulu supposed to meet her, here or
there?

Zulu never showed, Carla would have staked everything on that
appointment, but his breaking it didn't trouble her. She was only
upset, when they walked to the place, at the ticket girl's refusing to
let her in. Sugar Daddy was about to pay, but Carla would have none
of it: "Pay for yourself. I'm the star." She pushed past the booth,
strode into the dark theatre, flung herself into a seat. He took his
place beside her.

They sat as the Park blossomed around them. And she blossomed from her sulks, leaning against him to comment and admire.
The daughter he had come to help yielded to the other on the screen,
in her fanciful robes, singing, playing with the children, swinging upside down from the cross bar, sleeping with the rest by the
ever-burning fire. "The joy and anguish of being human at any cost."
Her moody guitar yields to the closing voice: "On this flowering
square block of sanity in civilization's asphalt madness, the bitter,
the disgusted, the sick and wretched still huddle together; and if
the National Guard of fear should peek through the bushes, they
will still find us smiling, still saying:'Let a thousand parks bloom!'"

They left arm in arm, her scarred and shell-pitted landscape wrapped in a softening shower of tears. And there stood the great-bearded Abe in front of his car; Dona hove into sight through the crowd, swinging an almost finished bottle of the grim white port. "Afraid of the, creeps," she murmured; "no fix since morning." Chuck hurried from the bookstore to wave goodbye, looking in at Carla with a deserted sad smile. Even speed-blasted black-genius Zulu floated up from somewhere: "Don't worry about Mendocino, honey; It's a good trip."

"You better come too," said Carla, But the little M.G. was full, and Zulu was already drifting away. And now they had slipped north past rowed flashes of mercury and neon; the city fell behind; they were headed for redwood country under moonlight — a long night drive.

Nestled in the back, under the hum of the car and road, the two could talk together, hearing only from the front a murmur of indistinct words. To make this ride, like the climb to the Hobbit Hole, smiling. Begin with the magic word, remember.

The summer at Long Beach Island, a circle of kids crouched around a wave-stranded jellyfish as big as your head, incited by whom but three-year old Carla, crying: "Poker-man, poker-man, poker all the way" — jabbing it with their fingers until it melts into a muck of foam. Or night in the little cottage, the scribe with a lamp in the low garret wording his Earth Epic, troubled by Carla's suggestive chant below, and the smothered laughs of the others: "And Besa Borsa Plunger-man took Enema Pedema down the stroilet strool to get a drink ('I'm sick, go get the doctor') and scritcha-scratcha hole in all the little places. And a big wave rode Barga Pelarga, and she said 'Rock-a-by baby, it's going to take me all the way out.' (All the little Dotties have to go up to the light to cook.) And Besa Borsa Stick-her-in-the-rorsa squatty on the potty and it all broke. (I'm sick, go get the doctor.') And Betty Baby and John Staby,,,"

To skirt bogs and precipices: Sibyl and the children lodged in the third floor Princeton attic, the rest of the house rented to keep solvent while he searched abroad; then the torture of divorce, squabbling through lawyers over non-existent funds — vault over all that and settle on happy vacations, white Christmases, summers in New Hampshire, Door County, the Isle of Shoals — no! her passions developing with her breasts, already had everyone in a dither there.

It was not worth the censorship, What was needed were the dark secrets of her life: the year she slashed her wrists and was sent back to him — that letter her mother had written, "Read and destroy", but he had filed it, like everything else:

Her date took her to a cabin in the woods where about twelve boys were drinking. He forced her into a room. She beat him off and climbed out of the window into the woods, but he followed and attacked her. She got away and wandered all night in the cold and rain. The boys found her in the morning, brought her torn and battered to her girl friend's house, where she was supposed to have spent the night. We knew nothing.

She had her 'worst attacks of skin allergy after that, with terrible staph infection. She was too sick to go to school and slept much of the time. Not even the doctor who was treating her knew she was pregnant.

When it was over she told me the story. In March she delivered on the floor of her room at three in the morning a dead five-month old girl. She went through torture and never cried out, When the afterbirth came she thought her insides were coming out and tried to stuff them back in. I know you will weep for her.

She cut the cord and tried to shake life into the baby (she says she loves babies), but it was dead, and so small. She gathered up everything in a towel, climbed down the big bluff behind the house, placed it between two boulders and rolled another huge rock against it to keep it from the dogs. When she went back later she could not move that rock.

When the trees bloomed in April her skin began to clear. But when we sent her back to school this fall, a boy said something which made her think he knew. She came home, broke the garage window and slashed her wrists on the jagged glass.

All this is to help you understand; but it is secret.

Never mention it to her. She generally wears long sleeves to hide the scars, and says she was cut in an accident.

Of course he should have ignored the injunction, but probity had taken silence for a shield.

"Before you came to us that year, your mother wrote — I wasn't supposed to tell, but we're past that now — about a child, embryo, you bore and buried. Right?"

Her voice a duck's back that sheds the water of tears, a musical uplilting: "Yeah."

"Were you a virgin before?"

"No. I'd had a boy I loved. That was the worst of it, that he was in on it, took me out there for the others, three guys, to do that horrible thing. The one I had really loved. Told me there was a party; then they pulled me into the loft.

"I didn't want the child. As it grew I kept hitting myself in the stomach. I killed the baby. I still feel bad about it. And only after it came I realized how much I wanted it. I'd been; in labor for about a week and never told anybody. And that night — I must have been in shock — I climbed down the cliff and ran all the way to the stream and rolled that huge stone — when they wanted to check later it took two men to move it — and I ran all the way back up, I think I stayed in shock a long time after."

"Why didn't you tell your mother?"

"I never could tell her anything. As if she lived in a dream — both of us, in different dreams. 'If only you'd told me,' she said later, in a cold voice, 'we could have done something,' I'd rather have done it myself."

And now her other children were gone, and her capability for more. Too much life in the world. "And after that you came to Maryland?

"Right."

"Tell me about…" But he broke off.

"You wrote that already," she said, "in that novel. 'The seed you sowed in Sibyl's darkness.' I knew it by heart once and knew it was me, though you called her Octavia. I was married then and had a child, thought I was happy; but that street woman in Chicago you compared me with hit me like a fate: 'whatever career of passion and divorce she was slated for.' I thought of it often when I was hooked: Is this what you wanted, what you prophesied?"

(As if to write probabilities were to spring the trap — fear, as in Dante, turning to desire. He had treated art as a trans-moral realm, lives to be probed without effect, though even in physics there was the feedback of all measurement. He was doing it still.)

"You remember the night in the hall when the Marine I ran off with the next day brought me home late, and you scolded and said if I kept on you'd have to send me back to Mother — when it was Mother who'd sent me to you? And I said..."

(Blurred almost beyond recall: his eyes adjusting to the pale moonlight by the door, until her face shows dim around the Maya cenote eyes he had seen in her mother and been divorced from — had the offence of that ideal state he called, from Isiah, The Married Land, been the distance he thought he could rear between himself and those depths he should have loved? — the eyes of Eve in the garden, serpent haunted, wild for every forbidden fruit?)

"You remember what I told you? That since I was a child I felt I had never been loved. Since you went off and left me with mother, and now she had sent me to you, and you were threatening to send me back to her — as if I didn't have a home."

"You didn't make it easy. Lucy's mother dying in the next room — and to run off with a Marine you didn't even know, and be picked up hitchhiking and have the police phoning in the night."

Was it a weakness in Freud to knuckle under to the reality principle? Her dreaming voice:

"Funny. 1 had met him at a dance. Hating the navy and knowing it was wrong. My being went out to him. He wanted to run away and go AWOL..and I was a nuisance at home and guilty about Granny -- children feel guilty about everything, and I was a child; I'd been sweet and loving, the only one of the kids to help Mother around the house, and she was proud of that — until this demon broke out in me.

"But what happened with that marine was so innocent. He was a virgin and didn't know anything and I didn't either, though I'd had that trouble. And when you brought us back and left us in the car a minute to say goodbye, we had a short little intercourse, because I felt so sorry for him,"

(Abusing Nobodaddy's chivalric trust.) "So we sent you back to your mother, and the allergy got worse?"

"I was clawing myself all the time, raw, itching, burning. And nothing I could do."

(Yet how her music had grown, as if anguish only could pluck those strings.) "So you wanted to try the desert, and we found that ranch school..."

Abe had stopped at a park-in; they rode on now washing down clamburgers, Dona with white port, Carla with red, Hollow-daddy with a tenth of Zinfandel — though Abe, his inextricable tangle of hair and beard a come-on to the law, shied at passing cars -- nothing the cops would like better than to nab the inventor of the underground press on an open-liquor charge.

Carla lowered the bottle, wiped her mouth with the back of her hand and let fly at the Arizona school: "A terrible place. Coldest man I've ever seen. No more feeling than a snake. All he wanted was money.

"1 had this housemother, about ninety years old, I guess, seventy anyway. How she could still have passions I don't know, but I noticed that the little girls were getting upset. She would take them into her room with her to spend the night, have them sleep in her bed with her so they wouldn't be frightened. People sent a lot of sick children there, retarded, arthritics, asthma kids with artificial pipes; the girl she took in most was an idiot girl, 'No,' I said, 'this really isn't right.'

"Then one night I was out on the ground and I was crying. After that horrible trouble at home I used to cry a lot and get in fits. I'd gasp and get paralyzed so I couldn't move."

"Hyper-ventilation."

"Right. But I didn't know that then, and it frightened me, Well, once this housemother came out and I was completely stiff. She touched me on my back and said, 'There, there, dear, don't worry.' I felt her hand slip around and she grabbed me on the tit. It brought me to, anyway, I flung her off, got up and went into the schoolhouse.

"After that she knew I had something on her, and she probably knew I wouldn't tell, because I've never been that kind. Well about two weeks later I was playing my guitar in the hall during break, when I wasn't supposed to, and she snatched it away from me and banged it on the corner of the table until she smashed a hole in it.

"My music was all I had. I took the guitar and looked at it. Then I flung it down and walked fifteen miles through the desert. I was ready to drop, thirsty, my fingers swelling. I went to a ranch and a pack of dogs rushed me. But a beautiful woman came out, a red-haired Western woman with sons about my age. 'What's the matter; what's the matter?' she said. I told her about the guitar and the school...

"And the old woman grabbing your tits?"

"Not that, but the rest. She took me in for the night, was going to let me stay. But her husband said no, they'd be in trouble. He called the school. 'You bring her back,' they said. 'She's underage. We'll look after her until time to send her home.[1] So they locked   me in a little room and only let me out once a day under guard. Then they sent me back to my mother."

(Pocketing the remaining fees. Pay your money and take your lot.)

"Then I met Carlos, and we were in love, I came to   you for the summer, remember, to be near his boot-camp. You were on our* side then, wrote his parents."

(Marriage her only hope, and besides, nobody could have reasoned with her.)

"So we got married, and my skin cleared up. Even now it's clear —except when I shoot smack I claw my hair, freaky."

(He had seen. Like lifting the bloody skull on a maggoty brain.)

Then the miracle of housekeeping Carla, that happy little ranch house marriage, the two squeaking to each other like lovey mice, writing notes to those imaginary friends the Duckenbergs, with answers back to themselves: the Duckenbergs couldn't make it to dinner, but the Sastres must guard the Duckenberg treasures — three student years, concealing under child fantasy some unknown lack, then the plunge into the Berkeley ferment of free speech, free action, free four-letter words, Carla like an oversensitive receiver, vibrating such frequencies; it was then that she had begun to slip off nights, weekends, then longer, went out of sight at last altogether, her husband hunting her in whatever drab locales rumor guided him to, sometimes with a loaded gun, whether for her or the locale unclear; until her older sister Octavia, married to another rebel, Saul Gurion, and come west, joined in the search (unarmed), and they found her in Filmore with what Octavia called a horrible old Black Man, her contact, Carla burnt out on heroin, with the whoring and stealing to earn two-hundred bucks a day (besides gonorrhea), lucid only a few hours after her shot, then down again in a sickness from which she surfaced next day not remembering what had occurred — days blotting into weeks, months, a year, under the chronic agony of trying to get her off — state hospitals, Synanon, which she tried twice and left, calling it a fake scene.

(A parent's backward looking blurred with self-blame; yet even now, after the event, how to have answered love-needs which took the form of rejection, flip, as from the Napa stay she called horrible:

I'm not a poor miserable child and have no intention of going to anybody's analyst; I'm having a nice quiet vacation at Napa with no desire to be anywhere else till 1 do my three months. Don't, extend the embarrassment my well-meaning sister perturbs me with any further, I have apologized to the doctor here and told him laughingly (though with bitter tears in my heart) "My whole family is crazy."

Please stop trying to help me before I collapse entirely under the burden of your love, and thank your gods I humbly refuse the kind but untimely invitation to live with you in your home.

Forgive the hurt (if any I've caused...)

About that time, between incarcerations, the friend of Gurion's fell in love with her, as who didn't, and thinking to help, took her with another man to a cabin back in the mountains to break her cold-turkey, but gave up after four days, afraid she'd die in the convulsions which had already wrecked the cabin. So she was dumped on Octavia and Saul, who took shifts all night holding her down sitting on her, her mouth gagged to smother the screams — three more nights, and she surfaced, took a bath, her sister sitting by the tub while she talked, for the first time a human being again. Though in that down, it was reason itself that began to hedge: "Ridiculous" and "I don't care" and "If life means nothing anyway, why struggle? I was happier on junk."

That night she left, got a shot and came back: "I'm feeling great; I'm sorry; I want to try again." Months like that -- when she was loaded planning to break and when she was sick, too fed up to try.

And now her other sister Monique flew in from mystical pursuits in India, fresh to the conquest of soul over matter, took Carla to the house of a Zen friend, seemed to be succeeding, until, not to be tearing up the house (that was the claim) Carla swallowed the overdose of sleeping pills, and Monique, finding no' pulse, panicked. So it was the emergency hospital, Carla coming to, sobbing "I'm a junkie; I'm a junkie. Help me!"

Help me? Surely that was another time. Get it straight. Focus on the Maryland table under the willow tree, three years later, Octavia and Saul over from Washington, looking back to revive scenes better forgotten:

"You had offered to pay, and we wondered how to get her to a hospital; so when Monique called, we rushed to the emergency room, phoned Zion Sanatorium and Dr. Floyd had it all lined up, when in walked the cops, strapped her to a stretcher and carried her off, Monique running after them wailing. Same old thing — Oakland General for observation. We tried to visit, but missed her somehow."

Firebrand Saul supplying the reminder in his quiet tone, one taking the clue from the other as memory warmed -- Aristotle's delight in recognition, even at so grim a recall; or was it the

Chaplinesque perfection of the scene — "Because just as we reached the parking lot she was coming out the door handcuffed to that enormous matron."

Octavia, as it flooded back, with a sigh suspended between regret, wonder, and recovery's strange joy: "O God, yes, yes, right. Being carted away, To Napa, And we yelling that we'd have her in Zion in a week.

"But it took longer, going and haggling, with the red tape and crap you have to go through to get somebody out of their hideous public holes to where they might get some care — as if you insulted the state. 'Yes, and if you can afford a private hospital,' they say, 'why aren't you paying for the last two weeks she's been here; and besides, we did her the favor of incarceration to clean floors six months last year, and you owe us ten thousand dollars for that. Disgusting system. And we weren't getting anywhere until (most disgusting of all, because it depended on chance) the regular man was sick and a Black doctor was so taken up with us just as two white chicks that he filled out the forms like snapping your fingers. So there she was in the private hospital, with a man said to be good in such cases."

In Octavia's face the dream of human possibility blossomed again, as in a world after war. "That you would pour in all that money; and to have her so near, and in a progressive ward, where she could visit home as soon as she was off drugs — and Carlos still wanted her then — and how beautiful she was: she had never been more beautiful. So much pain had left her mysterious, shadowed. In the hospital gown and negligee she looked like an angel in some faded old picture, A different person, wasn't she Saul?"

Saul didn't answer. He lowered his head. Silence, Because she had been the same. And the doctor, a Third Kingdom medicine man who, when his faith-healing failed, tried psychedelics, LSD and Speed, huge doses of Speed to shake up and enlarge her mind. And the beauty and promise of the moment, that wistful hope, was floating, as for the human kind, on a current which had flowed down from the dark past and was borne irreversibly toward a promise no sooner dreamed than lost...

The cloudy seer wrapped bar in his arms, as if the body's hold might resist the downward power, "Like a nightmare it must be, that time, that horrible Black man Octavia begged and threatened and got nowhere with."

Instinct should have told him that horrible Block man would be the one she had spoken of before: "A beautiful old Spade man." — "Octavia didn't know anything about him."

Had she none of the antibodies of blame? "But surely he was the one you were giving two hundred a day for dope, and prostituting yourself?"

"Uh-huh. But he helped me get off, when he knew I really wanted to. He'd let me come to his house and he'd shoot up in front of me, but he wouldn't give me any; and I got to where I could watch him without going crazy for it. He used to say: 'You look beautiful now, and your soul is beautiful; but when you're strung out you're mean and ugly."

The front seat talk had died down. The car-noise privacy of the back yielded to Dona's chime-in: "It's true, you change completely." (She, who had offered the ruinous cottons.)

The terrible thought hammering itself home, that for Carla, as for society, maybe, the only safety would be in righteous and repressive rage: to shun the past like leprosy, all touch of it; never go back, even in mind, to that-old Spade connection, never call him beautiful, shooting up heroin in his underworld house; but hound him, indict him, hang him; be moral, vindictive, bourgeois, forewarned. Though as he thought it, he knew such salutary hypocrisy of law was not in her soul's range. And would he have wished it to be?

Brooding. While she and Dona hatched a gay trip together, as soon as they were unhooked, to visit friends along the wooded stretch of mountain beach past Big Sur. It would have been easy to preach that another bumming might not be the approach to reality required; but the hour was too sacred for anything but the gospel of love. He offered sleeping bags and bus fare once they were cured.

All the ride up (and with the bottle of port) she had grown more amenable, hopeful, human. She who had been so stubborn against leaving the Street, now nestled up to him like a child, her tousled head on his cheek, saying how happy she was, how glad he'd taken her away, that back there she had seen no future but dope and hustling, and already it seemed a nightmare from which she might awaken.

"That's why you've got to find a new life," he said, "get away from that Street, not just heroin, but all those cough syrups and acids…"

Her voice had never been more open, more sure: "O, I love acid. I'll always take acid. It saved my life. That's why I kicked the first time. I took some acid when I was strung out and everything came clear."

The car threading the moonlit valley of giant redwoods north, he wondered why love and nature should fail to be enough. Though he sipped the Zinfandel as he listened…

(And those parties at Chicago with Borgese, Thomas Mann, Hutchins, Adlai and the rest, the talk, the insights as great as he had known, after cocktails and wine with dinner and brandy and beer; and he went home and wrote for the first time sentences of reckless abandoned beauty hardly able to hold the pen in his hand -- all vision riding a chemistry of body maintained and fired by dangerous addtives…)

"1 have to take acid to play really good music. At People's Park, before I messed up again, my music was so beautiful, my own kind of Mississippi blues…"

(He had taken her when she was tiny on his farewell trip to Delta landing before he left for Rome, and to hear the pentecostal spirituals that Sunday in Lethe's chuch, and afterward to B.J.'s where old Caldwell Leflore had played his own improvisatore guitar blues, and she had abandoned herself to the music, as he, in a poem begun that day, had seen our world doing: "Through all the aseptic channels of the modern/ This wild release is pouring,")

"It flows out of me in rivers, like an ocean, hardly me at all; I feel guilty after I've played. People crowd up and ask for more:

'That's great, great.' They think it's me playing, but it's not.

When I'm alone and nobody plays through me, what I play is simple. But then I'm a medium; the soul of somebody seizes me, How do you call it when you play one note after another in a complicated pattern, make a beautiful set, and then put them together. A tone row. That's what comes out of me when I'm on acid or on grass. And if I take some acid and go down to Dick Bends and cut a record, like they asked me and I wouldn't, it'll go over big, with the far-out people; because it's really good. But when I shoot smack, I have no music. My music is sexual, pounding, longing, but sweet. And heroin kills your sex. Like money. So there's no love, and no music. You don't know how horrible it is."

Standing, she thought, on the hopeful verge of cure, she looked back to the shell-pocked landscape of pain, of which she had said before "I don't even like to think about it."

"If I don't get dope enough, I wake up in cramps, doubled over, coughing, vomiting, with diarrhea and sick sweat; and every morning there are chills, and the blankets wringing wet."

He groaning: "But what a price — my Gcd — and for not much satisfaction. Because I've never seen anybody high in so much better state than the spirit and spring water will give you."

"Right, For two years I'd wake up rejoicing, because I didn't have to run out and get a shot. And the third year I forgot, can you imagine? I could still wake up rejoicing — and I never did when I was young. So there's some gain, if I could just keep it."

(The landscape of peace so easy — the death-wish buried deep under.)

"The hardest thing to understand," he said, "is how you could leave Carlos and your boys and fall to that Spade in the first place."

(His life work a study in that field: to buttress gravity against itself, what satanic pacts to make, what inoculations by a partial taint -- Carla and Sibyl his holocausts.)

"It was jealousy, wasn't it?"

"Yeah, it broke me up."

"But you had run around yourself?"

"Only when he did. It's true I didn't know. But I felt it: a horrible fear, like a snake coiled around my throat."

(Her soul divining what it chose ---- now could it be anything but fear unto death?)

"Everything between us died. He was tightened too. He saw he was going to lose me. That was when I had an affair with another man. And then I found out what I had already known, that he had done it before." She shrugged. "Though I wouldn't feel that way now."

(He and Sibyl tussling in that Aceldama before Carla was born. Easy to cry with Blake: "Love, love, free as the mountain wind;" but a labor of sainthood to make it real.)

"But I was so young. I didn't know jealousy is a cruel thing."

"'As cruel as the grave' it says in <u>The Song</u> of Songs . Your mother and I should have taught you. But we had hardly learned it ourselves,"

"If only I had married him later. Such a trivial thing he did as he told me, it meant nothing at all; yet to me it was doomsday. The only man I ever loved, with a true, devoted love. And it was beautiful, how we were happy and played."

(But the summer in Vermont, charging the black horse at her own child, until they screamed and she swerved — brinkmanship?)

"That's my great sadness. It's what ruined my life. And there's nothing I'd love more than to go back with him, but he's scored; and doesn't want me anymore."

(His letters, after trying and hoping, getting her back from Napa or Zion, to watch her slide out again, come home high, at her worst shoot up in front of the boys, in the dark-love violation of needle sex:

I can't go down every day as I did wandering the streets looking for her. And such letters as yours of wishes and might-bes destroy the strength I have to build. I don't plan to marry and would welcome Carla as a wife and mother if ever she could return; but I can't go on dreaming, always dreaming of the impossible.

To which the father assumed the voice of the Old Judge:

I don't know what choice means, or how it is compatible with sickness; and one does not like to abandon the sick; but at times the myth of morality revives again, and we cut off from offenders as if by choosing it was they had canceled obligation.)

"Though I will love him always," Carla said, "and deep down he still loves me."

(And when there is nothing but ash — the Frankenstein mill of grinding wheels we built and are setting the torch to, calcined — would that ghost of love remain, a luminous lost inwardness?)

"Didn't he tell me, when he brought the kids, they saw you dancing in People's Park?" (Carlos had avoided the subject, though cross-questioning had elicited the image of her dancing in colorful drapes, then coming up and bowing to her boys.)

"Only for a minute. He said he'd bring them back. I sat on that corner three months waiting, and he never did. I guess that's another reason I broke down." The voice not of blame: she must have known, as party of the first part, what made him stay away,

They turned off the highway into the hospital drive: like a college, a campus of trees and lawn under the moon. Dona's siren whine filled the car — all the hospital fears they cultivated on the Street, of being penned up without methadone in vomiting convulsions: how she couldn't stand it, she would go crazy; while Carla said nonsense, they had come on their own; they knew what the program was; everybody said it was a good trip.

Dona'a alarm lapsed back into talk. She had been telling Abe of her mother, bullied by the father into repeated breakdowns: "I hated her at first. She used to cry and cry. But that changed over the years to an infinite pity that a human being could be so pathetic. When I was fifteen she said I was the coldest, hardest person she'd known," (Carla astrologizing: "You're Taurus, man; that makes you bitter,") "'But you'll suffer,' she told me; 'because insanity runs in our family.' She brought me up to think I'd go insane and kill myself, the way her people had all done. And I believed it until I was eighteen, and one day it hit me: There's nothing wrong with me but being around these people. And it's not hereditary; I don't care what they say. I refuse to believe it. Environmental, yes, but not hereditary." Though her veins proclaimed against her.

They stopped at the office, Abe went in. They watched him through the window. From the way he gestured at the receptionist, something must be wrong, and one could guess what: they had come without referral papers, banking on appeal. In the dread — after the buildup to hope and tenderness — of having nothing to offer but return to the street, the Old Guy went in too, leaving the girls in the car.

Abe's doctor friend had been sent for; he appeared, one of the blessed Blacks this time; he broke through the red tape: let the blame light on him, they would take them tonight as guests and worry about legality tomorrow

In the car the girls had almost lost heart. They were brought in now; but there was a long wait while the secretary filled out forms. Ox-eyed Dona sat in a blue funk, no fix since morning, the wine wearing off, the red barbiturate she had gulped while they waited outside not taking effect, the horror of prison cold-turkey come on her; she reached a trembling hand in a blue-lipped mouth, caught one of her snaggly, loose, carious teeth, pulled half of it out and dropped it into the metal waste-basket.

The doctor called her to the examining room — a routine needle-scar check to confirm junky status. She had worried about that too: he might not believe her, since, she was using her fingers now where the marks didn't show. Though as he told them afterwards, one had only to pull up her sleeves to see why she was shooting under the fingernails: every vein blown with scar tissue

Carla, meanwhile, was waiting alone, her father and Abe phoning Berkeley for a line on the neglected referrals. And now she, who had ridden the euphoria of love and release, who had seemed so strong, heard a cry somewhere far off down the hospital corridors, and everything came flooding back, as from before birth, the soul's claustrophobic fear of bolts, chains, cave-walls, the archetypal hell-dread enforced by years of bad jails and barred asylums — to have usurped a word of refuge (doles _asylo_) for those thronging snake-pits she had hardened in and escaped from.

The secret sharer entered to see her being change with her face. She was leveling, as at an enemy, and the Black doctor, her friend. "Then I won't stay, I ask you a straight question and you don't answer straight." A defiance he knew instinctively from his own youth, against father, law, police, all canons of coercion and restraint, most of all the army's absurd claim to brutalize his acts. But in her case, wide of the mark.

Though the doctor's smile was vaguely equivocal: "Frankie, I don't know how you listen. I said it's hard enough to get you in anyway, that you're a guest here and you choose your own program. But it's a hospital and I'm the doctor, and I can't say you're free to do whatever you please."

"Then It's a creepy bad place — a jail — and I won't be locked in like a crook when I came on my own."

The wanderer's hand went out, groping. He could no more tell than the blind what It would reach: the nestling daughter of the car, the chemical body of rabbia. He touched her cheek. She shied — his hand leagued with tyranny, rape, perversion. He tried again, caressing. "Carla, love. Listen. Don't act crazy. You can see he's a fine man. He's on your side. You know I love you. You think I would leave you in a jail? But it's what you came for. A new start."

She moved toward the door, repeating under the Medusa stare: "I put a straight question and he won't give a straight answer." But softer. As in Gluck's taming of the infernal spirits.

So once again the Orphic lyre: "Carla. Remember: the hustling, always hustling, and sweats and sickness. You're no child. Stay on and work with them, I'll get you a guitar. Think of your music. Sad, to back out now."

She bowed her head and sank into the chair with a gesture of profound defeat. Bending over, he kissed the. red, chapped, scaly dirtiness of her street-sleeping harried face. In the cloudy vault of her prison she did not stir. He walked out tormented, as through all the years, with the fact of that world-betrayal: above the dream garden the ever-threatening sword. He put his hands to his father-aged face under a tumbling whiteness of hair,..

And in four or five days or a week, when the methadone was tapered o f f, and she fled (redemption so rare, however dewed and rainbowed with tears) and hit the Street bleak under November rain, she wilder than ever; when Chuck would shelter her in the bookstore, the drug scene spilling in around her, and as had been threatened before he would get the sack, and the sleeping bag and guitar bought as promised had gone the way of all Carla's possessions; when even poor Dona would be back shooting heroin into the veins under her tongue —

It would be easy to say "I told you so" and to look back almost blushing for hopeful sentiments, almost swayed by the law-and-order gang with their police state hardening willy-nilly toward purgative euthanasia. Though all it would have proved in the end was that a little love might go a little way.

So if a total love should offer itself in total sacrifice, it might once more be written: 'Come out of the man, thou unclean spirit.' And they were amazed and said, 'What is this? With authority he commands the unclean spirits, and they obey him.

Even for Carla. Even for the world she is child of.

Fomite

Writing a review on social media sites for readers will help the progress of independent publishing. To submit a review, go to the book page on any of the sites and follow the links for reviews. Books from independent presses rely on reader-to-reader communications.

For more information or to order any of our books, visit:
http://www.fomitepress.com/our-books.html

More novels and novellas from Fomite...

Joshua Amses — *During This, Our Nadir*
Joshua Amses — *Ghats*
Joshua Amses — *Raven or Crow*
Joshua Amses — *The Moment Before an Injury*
Raymond Barfield — *Dreams of a Spirit Seer*
Charles Bell — *The Married Land*
Charles Bell — *The Half Gods*
Jaysinh Birjepatel — *Nothing Beside Remains*
Jaysinh Birjepatel — *The Good Muslim of Jackson Heights*
David Borofka — *The End of Good Intnetions*
David Brizer — *Cacademonomania*
David Brizer — *The Secret Doctrine of V. H. Rand*
David Brizer — *Victor Rand*
L. M Brown — *Hinterland*
Paula Closson Buck — *Summer on the Cold War Planet*
L.enny Cavallaro — *Paganini Agitato*
Dan Chodorkoff — *Loisaida*
Dan Chodorkoff — *Sugaring Down*
David Adams Cleveland — *Time's Betrayal*
Paul Cody— *Sphyxia*
Jaimee Wriston Colbert — *Vanishing Acts*
Roger Coleman — *Skywreck Afternoons*
Stephen Downes — *The Hands of Pianists*
Marc Estrin — *Et Resurrexit*
Marc Estrin — *Hyde*
Marc Estrin — *Kafka's Roach*
Marc Estrin — *Proceedings of the Hebrew Free Burial Society*
Marc Estrin — *Speckled Vanities*
Marc Estrin — *The Annotated Nose*
Marc Estrin — *The Penseés of Alan Krieger*
Zdravka Evtimova — *Asylum for Men and Dogs*
Zdravka Evtimova — *In the Town of Joy and Peace*
Zdravka Evtimova — *Sinfonia Bulgarica*
Zdravka Evtimova — *You Can Smile on Wednesdays*

Fomite

Daniel Forbes — *Derail This Train Wreck*
Peter Fortunato — *Carnevale*
Greg Guma — *Dons of Time*
Ramsey Hanhan – *Fugitive Dreams*
Richard Hawley — *The Three Lives of Jonathan Force*
Lamar Herrin — *Father Figure*
Michael Horner — *Damage Control*
Ron Jacobs — *All the Sinners Saints*
Ron Jacobs — *Short Order Frame Up*
Ron Jacobs — *The Co-conspirator's Tale*
Scott Archer Jones — *A Rising Tide of People Swept Away*
Scott Archer Jones — *And Throw Away the Skins*
Julie Justicz — *Conch Pearl*
Julie Justicz — *Degrees of Difficulty*
Maggie Kast — *A Free Unsullied Land*
Darrell Kastin — *Shadowboxing with Bukowski*
Coleen Kearon — *#triggerwarning*
Coleen Kearon — *Feminist on Fire*
Jan English Leary — *Thicker Than Blood*
Jan English Leary — *Town and Gown*
Diane Lefer — *Confessions of a Carnivore*
Diane Lefer — *Out of Place*
Rob Lenihan — *Born Speaking Lies*
Cynthia Newberry Martin — *The Art of Her Life*
Colin McGinnis — *Roadman*
Douglas W. Milliken — *Our Shadows' Voice*
Ilan Mochari — *Zinsky the Obscure*
Peter Nash — *In the Place Where We Thought We Stood*
Peter Nash — *Parsimony*
Peter Nash — *The Least of It*
Peter Nash — *The Perfection of Things*
Michael Okulitch — *Toward Him Still*
George Ovitt — *Stillpoint*
George Ovitt — *Tribunal*
Gregory Papadoyiannis — *The Baby Jazz*
Pelham — *The Walking Poor*
Christopher Peterson — *Madman*
Andy Potok — *My Father's Keeper*
Frederick Ramey — *Comes A Time*
Howard Rappaport — *Arnold and Igor*
Joseph Rathgeber — *Mixedbloods*
Kathryn Roberts — *Companion Plants*
Robert Rosenberg — *Isles of the Blind*
Fred Russell — *Rafi's World*
Ron Savage — *Voyeur in Tangier*
David Schein — *The Adoption*

Fomite

Charles Simpson — *Uncertain Harvest*
Lynn Sloan — *Midstream*
Rana Shubair — *And No Net Ensnares Me*
Lynn Sloan — *Principles of Navigation*
L.E. Smith — *The Consequence of Gesture*
L.E. Smith — *Travers' Inferno*
L.E. Smith — *Untimely RIPped*
Robert Sommer — *A Great Fullness*
Caitlin Hamilton Summie — *Geographies of the Heart*
Tom Walker — *A Day in the Life*
Susan V. Weiss —*My God, What Have We Done?*
Peter M. Wheelwright — *As It Is on Earth*
Peter M. Wheelwright — *The Door-Man*
Suzie Wizowaty — *The Return of Jason Green*